THAT WAS NOW, THIS IS THEN

BAEN BOOKS by MICHAEL Z. WILLIAMSON

THAT WAS NOW, THIS IS THEN

MICHAEL Z. WILLIAMSON

THAT WAS NOW, THIS IS THEN

This is a work of fiction. All the characters and events portrayed in this book are fictional, and any resemblance to real people or incidents is purely coincidental.

A Baen Books Original

Baen Publishing Enterprises
P.O. Box 1403
Riverdale, NY 10471
www.baen.com

ISBN: 978-1-9821-2576-9

Cover art by Kurt Miller

First printing, December 2021

Distributed by Simon & Schuster
1230 Avenue of the Americas
New York, NY 10020

Library of Congress Cataloging-in-Publication Data

Names: Williamson, Michael Z., author.
Title: That was now, this is then / Michael Z. Williamson.
Description: Riverdale, NY : Baen ; New York, NY : Distributed by Simon & Schuster, [2021] | "A Baen Books original."
Identifiers: LCCN 2021044262 | ISBN 9781982125769 (hardcover)
Subjects: LCGFT: Time-travel fiction. | Novels.
Classification: LCC PS3623.I573 T48 2021 | DDC 813/.6—dc23
LC record available at https://lccn.loc.gov/2021044262

Pages by Joy Freeman (www.pagesbyjoy.com)
Printed in the United States of America
10 9 8 7 6 5 4 3 2 1

To the veterans of Afghanistan,
since time immemorial.

THAT WAS NOW, THIS IS THEN

CHAPTER 1

Shug, Stalker of Hare, was enjoying a warm day on the Ridge. A day north of him, the village nestled against the Great River. He was here to meditate, and hopefully hunt something more impressive than hare. He had a deerskin spread over the brush as a shelter, another to sleep on, his spirit bag, knife, spear, and some dried meat.

It was the nicest day so far this year, and one of the nicest he recalled in his motions of seasons. The sun was lowering toward the ground. For now, he had good shelter, a good view, and two more days to find a sign and game. He was alone and could think. It was as perfect as life could get. He dozed off.

The thunder woke him, and he jerked awake. He'd slept long enough for a storm to move in. From where? He hadn't felt it in the weather.

Then he realized the sky was still blue. It was earlier in the afternoon. Had he slept that long? It was warmer, too. Hot, in fact.

The moon was in the wrong place.

He was in a gouged hollow.

Grunting noises caught his attention, and he looked down the ridge.

There was a game path, a huge one, where one had never been before. Huge beasts, much bigger than bison, moved along it in a single file. They were fast, too.

Another noise startled him, and he looked to see a huge,

strange-looking bird roaring as it lowered toward the ground. He could swear it had smoke coming from its backside.

He clutched at his spear with one hand and his spirit bag with the other. Was he in the spirit world? But he felt alive, and didn't have any signs of injury.

The spirits must have gouged out the land he was on. That's how he was here. He called to them silently, arms against his breast, for guidance.

That done, he scanned the horizon.

It might be best to wait for dusk to look around. The beasts should be settled by then.

He sought shelter. There wasn't much here, but he did see some scrubby brush. He ambled over, pulled out his digging stick and scraped a slight hollow, and lay down. Covering his feet in dirt, with the tip of his spear out beyond his head, and brush above, he had some shelter and protection. He lay back and breathed deeply.

The air was scented and awful. It smelled like burned resin and dust. He could hear the beasts growling steadily as they charged endlessly along that path.

All he could do was wait.

His sleep was intermittent, and he was thirsty and hungry. The sun dropped behind the hills, tired and red and needing to sleep itself. He wished it a good rest and cautiously scrambled out of his hide.

Down below was strange. It must be the home of the spirits. Many lights showed, but they weren't fires. They were more like small moons hanging from tall trees, or on the backs of beasts. The beasts' eyes shone the same way as they moved.

People moved among the beasts and huts. The huts were very nice, very straight and even. Around it all was a strange net of woven vines tied to stakes, and a trench wall. The entrance was marked and that's where all the beasts entered and left.

Up in the sky, another bird came in from the west, with more trapped moonlight, and a loud roar.

It must be the spirit world.

Shug braced himself and gathered his possessions. If this was where he was, he would go to meet the spirits bravely. Perhaps that thunder had killed him. Or perhaps this was a vision.

With his spear, gourd, and bag, he clutched at his totems and started down the hill.

The terrain was irregular, and he let his weight pull him forward, bouncing on his legs as he went. There were more beasts on the path, and he didn't want to get too close. They might spook. He was at least two spear throws back when one of the moonlights suddenly shone at him. He held up a hand over his face.

There were shouts, but he didn't recognize the speech. There were men running toward him, and surrounding him. There were six, then more.

He held his spear across as a block. They carried...things. They acted as if they were armed, but he didn't see spears, though some had what could be knives on belts. They were all massively built, wearing tight-fitting leggings and tunics that were splotch colors. The clothes must be dyed, braided fiber. The men were obviously hunter-warriors.

One of them was close and grabbed his spear. He didn't know how to react. He could fight, but there were so many. They hadn't actually attacked, though. They just seemed to think he was too close to their territory. Was he not allowed in the spirit world?

The spear came out of his grasp, and he saw one of the men pointing at the ground while shouting. He assumed they wanted him to sit. But he already wasn't a threat. What more did they need?

One of them spoke slowly, but it wasn't speech, just noises.

He lowered down and sat.

The gesturing man walked around behind him and grabbed his arms. He started to struggle, and was rewarded with a knee in his back while his hands were bound.

This was not good.

They raised him to his feet, patted him all over, and took his pouch and spirit bag. How was he supposed to reach his spirit guides now?

He walked with them, one on each side, until they came up to one of the beasts. It was rumbling and noisy, but holding still. What wizards were they?

Its ass was wide open. The men started walking up inside the ass of the beast. He had no idea what this was about, and it was very, very disturbing. He struggled again, and they just picked him up and dragged him, then put him down on the ground inside, if it could be called ground. It was hard, flat, and rough, like coarse rock.

After that, he couldn't follow what happened. The beast's ass closed, there was dim light inside, and the animal seemed to move, bouncing them along. Shortly, it stopped. He was lifted up and they walked back out to the ground. It was night overhead, but brightly lit here, with moonlights shining in his face from all over.

They took him inside one of the lodges, and it was sunlight bright inside, with strange chairs for sitting, and shelves in front of some of the chairs. Spirit objects were everywhere—the walls, floor, ceiling. There were the spirit suns shining brightly. All the men and some women wore heavy clothing that had to be too hot in this weather.

Then he realized it was cool, almost too cool inside. He wore leggings, a breech, and a light shoulder cover.

One of the men spoke to him, and he noticed the man was very pale, but most of the others were even paler.

He had no idea what the man was saying. It wasn't speech of his people, or any people. The sounds made no sense at all. They all spoke in noises.

He hunched in on himself. He knew he should be brave, but he had no idea what the rules of the spirit world were. It seemed he wasn't supposed to be here, and perhaps they would send him back to the people world?

He spoke back. "I am Shug of River Bend. I am a learning hunter."

They chattered back and forth in weird noises, and tried to speak to him again. He didn't understand a sound they made.

They led him past the chairs and down a cavelike passage. They weren't mean, but they weren't gentle. They led and pushed, he went as they told. It seemed safest for now.

Shortly they came to a wall made of perfectly flat rocks. It must be a magic place, to have so much attention paid to fitting stones. There was an inset that opened, like a flap, but sideways.

They unfastened his hands and directed him in. He went.

It was the most unusual lodge Shug had ever been in. The sides were flat as stretched hide, but made of rock.

They closed the cover behind him, and it made a strange noise, almost like that a large rock makes splashing into deep water.

He assumed that thing was a raised bed, and it was. It was very soft, as was the woven bedskin with it. In fact, there were very thin, very soft bedskins, and thicker, slightly coarser ones. At least he would be comfortable. Possibly he'd have to learn spirit speech, though he always thought they heard him. Whoever these people or beings were, they didn't know people language.

Martin Spencer and his best friend, Bob Barker, were working. Their business, started the previous year, was a survival school, teaching everything from shelter and firemaking to improvised water filters, cooking, and even metalworking. They taught backward from a reasonably well-equipped car to wild materials only. They were only a couple of hours from St. Louis, but this area was nearly complete wilderness. They did spray for mosquitoes. Otherwise, it was a very wild September, cool in the mornings, warm later. He was used to extremes after eighteen years in the Army, a chunk of it in Iraq and A-stan.

Currently, Bob was teaching a fire-by-bow drill, first with a bootlace, and then with peeled bark. The man could get a fire going in two minutes even in the damp. It was impressive.

The class was attentive as he demonstrated finding a piece of wood for base, a spindle stick, a socket, and tinder. They formed a circle and watched.

Barker said, "The thing to remember is this is a technology. You need a coarse, fibrous wood for the drill and base, a smooth hardwood for the cap, and a stringy bark for the bowstring. You're just sawing to get black oxidized tinder at first. Then a wisp of smoke..."

Along for the class was a well-known TV personality. Martin liked the show, but the guy was always a bit of an ass, even out here. While grinning smugly, the dude pulled out a cigarette and made a flamboyant gesture with his lighter.

Yes, lighters are more efficient, Martin thought. *When you have one.*

A couple of students were distracted by the act, and looked around.

Time to make a point.

"Hey, could I get a smoke?" he asked.

"Uh? Sure." Still grinning, the big man waved the pack so one cigarette came loose, and offered the lighter.

"Thanks," he said, taking the cancer stick and fumbling the lighter. It slipped from his hand into a muddy spot on the ground.

"Whoops!" he said, while turning and stepping on it.

He looked around and said, "Oh, here it is."

He bent down and retrieved it.

He clicked it. It was a piezo at least, but even those had issues with mud. Click. Click.

He said, "The mud's going to have to dry out before it works. Hey, Bob, help a guy out here?"

Barker said, "Sure thing," and bore down on the drill. With a dozen brisk strokes he got a smoldering, smoking ember, which he tapped into the black carbon dust, into the bark strip tinder underneath it. He picked it up, blew on it, produced a flame. Stepping forward, he waved that under the cigarette until it lit, then folded the bark and grass over it, bent down, and stuck it under the fire lay he'd built.

Ten seconds later, the fire was flaming, Martin handed Bob the cigarette because he'd quit, while the smart-ass looked irritated. There were even a couple of chuckles.

Martin said, "You should definitely use the best technology you can, but always have a default. Anyone remember that family that almost froze to death in their car in the Cascades a few years ago?"

There were a couple of nods.

"They had a car with a battery, gasoline, oil, flammable seats, and they were in a forest full of trees, and they couldn't get a fire started. Our Stone Age ancestors could strike or rub up a fire in a few seconds. With all the technology those people had, they couldn't."

"We'll practice this after lunch. First with premade kits, then we'll show you what to look for. For lunch, Emily is going to show you how almost every plant you're stepping on right now is edible. Emily?"

Emily, dark, quirky, and energetic as always, said, "Hi! Did anyone else see the wild garlic at the edge of the trees? Mixed in with the dandelions?"

The day went well. He should be happy. At the end, he locked the trailer, shouldered his pack, and climbed into the Suburban. Emily was already off in her old ambulance. Bob waved as he got into his F150.

The drive home was dirt road to secondary to state highway, to another winding secondary, then dirt again.

The house was great. He'd found a hunting lodge, log and plank with a wraparound porch, roomy enough and with some shop and garage space, at a very good price. Part of that was there weren't major jobs out here, so other than retirees and wealthy retreats, it was vacant. The land was cheap.

Andrew was supposed to be in from Georgia Tech this weekend. The boy needed to work harder on his classes, too. Beverly was doing well in her first year at U Ark in Fayetteville. It was just him and Allison most of the time.

He'd been looking forward to that, and it should be wedded bliss.

He sighed as he parked, then got out and walked into the house proper. Wooden door, wooden paneling, wooden floor. Good thing there was a fire suppression system, but it looked and felt like home.

"Hey," he announced.

"Hi," she muttered back from the kitchen.

He approached and waited until she turned from the stove.

"How's the class?" she asked.

"Full, paid, and in progress." He said that first because money was important, but it was about the only part of it she cared about.

"Good."

"How are you doing?" he asked. It shouldn't be this awkward to talk to his wife.

"Fine. I leave for work in an hour."

"Yeah." She was inpatient administration at the nearby hospital, though not earning as much as she had near Fort Bliss. At least this was a permanent position, not subject to him getting orders. She should be grateful for that. And night shift paid an extra $2/hour. He couldn't quite help but wonder if she'd chosen that shift to avoid him.

He inhaled something savory with chicken. "Smells great. What do you want me to have ready for breakfast?"

"Ham and eggs, the usual."

"Okay." He stepped slightly closer, arms relaxed.

"I need to shower and get ready," she said, and left.

Not even a "welcome home," he thought, sadly.

He let her leave with barely any pleasantries. It didn't seem worth it.

He dropped into his chair, put the pack in the cubby next to his left leg. At his computer, he reviewed notes for the next day of class, checked the news, cleared a hundred pointless emails out, and unsubscribed from three news sites he had no idea he'd been on.

He was still stiff and awkward online, after two years in the Paleolithic. He'd never been much for surfing the web, anyway. He didn't game, didn't do much of anything with social media. He used a computer as a tool.

He did have messenger programs, and right then he got a ping.

GINA: HEY.

Sigh. She was a friend, he shouldn't avoid her.

MARTIN: HEY.

GINA: HOW GOES?

MARTIN: THE SAME.

GINA :(SORRY TO HEAR THAT. MY WEIGHT IS UP SLIGHTLY AGAIN. AND MY LETHARGY IS BACK.

MARTIN: GAH. THAT SUCKS.

GINA: IT WAS GREAT HAVING MY METABOLISM BACK WHILE IT WORKED. I'LL SURVIVE. THEY'RE TWEAKING MY CORTISOL LEVELS AGAIN.

MARTIN: GOOD LUCK.

GINA: THANKS. MY MEMORY IS TAKING HITS, TOO. I COULDN'T FIND OUR DEPARTURE POINT ON THE MAP.

MARTIN: OH, LET ME FIND IT...

He went to Google Maps, scrolled, zoomed, shifted, zoomed again, tagged the point, and copy-pasted the link.

MARTIN: HERE IT IS.

GINA: YEAH, HOW COULD I MISS THAT?

MARTIN: METABOLIC ISSUES CAN SCREW EVERYTHING UP.

GINA: BLAKE IS GREAT AT HELPING ME STAY ON TRACK. BUT HE DOESN'T KNOW THINGS LIKE THAT.

MARTIN: RIGHT.

GINA: SO, NOTHING NEW ON YOUR MARRIAGE?

MARTIN: I DON'T KNOW WHAT ELSE I CAN DO.

GINA: WHAT DOES THE THERAPIST SAY? YOU WORK WITH FAIRLEY, RIGHT?

MARTIN: YEAH, SHE'S GIVEN US SOME EXERCISES. ALLY ISN'T DOING THEM.

GINA: MY PARENTS WENT THROUGH THAT. YOU NEED TO.

MARTIN: _I_ AM.

GINA: COLLECTIVE "YOU." SORRY. SHE NEEDS TO.

MARTIN: WELL, SHE'S NOT.

MARTIN: JULIE SAYS I SHOULD DIVORCE HER. SO DOES BRANDY. AND ED. BRUCE SAYS TO STICK IN THERE. HE'S SEEN THIS BEFORE post-deployment. SO HAVE I.

GINA: IF YOU CAN, YOU SHOULD, BUT IF YOU CAN'T, YOU'RE NOT HELPING YOURSELF OR THE KIDS BY PUSHING THROUGH.

MARTIN: IF THE MARRIAGE FAILS, IT WON'T BE BECAUSE OF ME.

GINA: IT SEEMS IT ALREADY HAS. ALL THAT'S LEFT IS THE PAPERWORK. LIKE A DEPLOYMENT.

MARTIN: I HAD AN OFFER FROM JANIE. I'M DOING A THING ON TV IN COLORADO ANYWAY. SHE SAID I COULD STAY WITH HER. SHE ONLY HAS ONE BED. IT WAS PRETTY CLEAR.

GINA: ARE YOU GOING TO? YOU KNEW HER BEFORE YOU WERE MARRIED, RIGHT?

MARTIN: I DID. SHE'S BEEN DIVORCED TEN YEARS NOW. NO. I'M NOT GOING TO. I'LL ONLY SEE HER IN PUBLIC.

GINA: YOU SOUND VERY FRUSTRATED.

MARTIN: VERY. I'M TENSE, TAUT, AND TWITCHY.

GINA: I THOUGHT SHE SAID YOU COULD DO WHAT YOU WANTED? AS LONG AS IT WAS PRIVATE.

MARTIN: SHE APPARENTLY FORGOT SHE SAID THAT. INSISTS SHE NEVER DID, EVEN IF I WOULD. OR MAYBE I'M FORGETTING.

GINA: SHE'S TAUNTING AND GASLIGHTING YOU. THAT'S REALLY A BAD SIGN.

MARTIN: SHE'S STRESSED OUT FROM THE SEPARATION.

GINA: SO ARE YOU. YOU'RE NOT ACTING LIKE SHE IS. NEXT SHE'LL CUT YOU OFF ENTIRELY.

MARTIN: SHE HASN'T SLEPT WITH ME, OR HAD SEX WITH ME, FOR FOUR MONTHS NOW.

GINA: :(SORRY. I HATE BEING RIGHT.

MARTIN: I NEED TO GO. SOME KIND OF RELEASE, OR SHOWER, OR SOMETHING, AND THEN SLEEP. WE'RE DOING EARLY CLASS ON WATER FROM DEW AND SOME GAME SPOTTING.

GINA: I WISH I COULD HELP. EVEN IF IT WAS JUST KEEPING YOU COMPANY WHILE YOU GET OFF.

MARTIN: I WISH YOU COULD, TOO. UNLESS AND UNTIL SHE LEAVES OR THROWS ME OUT, I'M MARRIED.

GINA: I KNOW. YOU DESERVE BETTER.

He was about to get defensive when she added:

GINA: SORRY, I MEAN A BETTER LIFE. NOT HER PERSONALLY.

MARTIN: THANKS. GO HAVE SOME SEX FOR ME?

GINA: WELL, IF YOU INSIST. ;)

At least one of them was getting laid. Shame about her metabolism, though. What had the Cogi missed when they fixed that?

Jenny Caswell liked dance music. She liked finding people to dance with. She didn't like drunk assholes. Especially in a dark club where they felt the need to be louder and more obvious.

The guy trying to hit on her was decent looking, but drunk, and the personality under the drunk was eyerollingly bad and offensive at the same time. He'd paused at the table, deliberately not-stared at her while talking loudly to his buddies, then turned his attention down on her from his standing position.

"You should smile," he said. "At least you're not in Afghanistan. They don't have anything like this."

"I know, I've been there," she said.

He tried to latch onto that for commonality, and said, "Oh, doing what?"

"Female engagement team for Security Police."

"Ah. Shame you weren't able to go with the Army."

"I was attached to an Army unit, actually."

"What was that like? Culture shock, right? I'm Brant, by the way."

"Not really. Decent guys. We had a sailor as well."

She didn't mind talking, but it wasn't going to go anywhere, and he was condescending.

Then Brant's buddy came over. He swigged from a pitcher of beer, shoulder-nudged the guy, and looked down.

"Woo-hoo, redhead!"

Brant said, "She's AF security. Was in A-stan."

His buddy was a clown, and went straight for the macho card.

"Oh, Air Force. How cute. Ever see any combat?"

"Yes, actually, I did." She wanted to disengage from this, because he was going to be slinging testosterone-laden bullshit. She also wished she could shut him up.

"Oh, I'm sure," he said. "Lots of it on AFN, right?"

She avoided eye contact.

"Cool story, bro," she said. "I spent months outside the wire."

"Yeah, right. 'Chair Force' 'females' are only outside to ride around in trucks."

She shrugged and tried to ignore him until he went away.

"I'll bet it was fun, having tea with the local women while the men cleared the area. Or was it more fun to pat them down?"

"Yes, yes, we're all lesbians," she said. "That must be the only reason we don't like men."

"Or you just can't find any on a Chair Force base."

He continued, "The only reason for females in the military is as comfort women for the men doing the real work."

A red haze clouded her, and she realized she'd just slammed the base of the plastic beer pitcher with the heel of her hand. It cracked, so did his teeth, blood streaked through the rivulets of beer streaming down his face, and the rim left a mark on his forehead, too.

She knew she was going to jail for this, and because of that, she was damned well going to have a reason. While he still looked confused, she punched him in the guts. He slumped and bent, she grabbed his head, and *smashed* it into the table. She latched onto his ears for a second swing, as hands grabbed her and pulled her back.

He came up a bloody mess with a flat face, and two big guys grabbed him, too.

"Woah, woah, woah!" Brant said. "Shit, get him to the clinic, he's a mess...no, seriously, dude, you got fucked up; sit down and hold this." Brant shoved a napkin at the man and guided his hand to his nose.

Then another man was in front of her. Obvious older NCO. "Let me see your ID."

Someone let her right hand go, and she fished it out of her pocket. She held it out. She was still breathing hard and her pulse hammered. Goddammit, that had felt good, shutting that dickless little bastard's face.

"Well, Staff Sergeant Jennifer A. Caswell, I'm Sergeant First Class Ronald Fulmer. I am an MP. You are under arrest..."

CHAPTER 2

Shug was very unsure of the clothes they'd provided him with. The leggings met and covered his lower parts, and hung around his waist, all as one piece, not tied together. The tunic was shaped and covered his arms, too, but it wasn't really cold enough to need anything long. Still, if that's what they wore here, he'd do as they said. The fastener for the leggings was like a flat, round toggle. Clever.

He was thirsty, but there was no water. He looked around the hut. It had walls of perfectly cut stone, a floor of one solid piece of very flat stone. It looked like limestone, but was completely plain and unlayered. The bed rose on sticks, but they were fastened into the stone with pegs he couldn't dislodge. The mattress had a finely woven cover that was soft and warm enough. There was a depression that from the smell was used for waste. He used it, and urine ran down. He wasn't sure if he was supposed to scoop out turds later, or if they'd bring some basket for that. There was a shelf with a depression that could hold water, or animals for sacrifice, or a small fire, but nothing like those was about.

There was a sound at the cover. Shug turned as it moved aside, and one of the men brought in a tray. He placed it down and left.

Shug went over. That seemed to be food, though he didn't recognize most of it. That was rice, though it was pale and short, but tasted okay. There were large seeds of some kind in it, rather bland. Then he realized it was spicy, like garlic but sharper. He grabbed the tall bowl that had water in it and gulped it down. That helped.

There was a scoop made of some pure white, very thin bone that he could use for picking up the rest. That was good, too.

The vegetables were okay. They weren't quite roasted, but were cooked and still warm. The other things...they were fluffy, and sweet. Very sweet. They didn't taste like honey or berries, but very sweet.

He really wanted more water, though.

Tentatively, he slapped on the cover. A few minutes later, the man came to the opening.

His tone made it obvious he was asking what Shug wanted. Shug raised the water bowl and pointed at it. The man pointed behind Shug, toward the shelf. There was no water there. He pointed at the bowl again. The man pointed behind him again.

Sighing, Shug spread his hands and shook his head. "I don't see any water," he said, though no one so far understood speech.

The man sighed back, shouted at someone who shouted back, then rattled something and the cover moved open again.

The man reached out his hand, and Shug assumed he wanted the water bowl. He let the man take it.

Taking two steps, the man grabbed a protrusion above the bowl-shelf, and pulled. Water started flowing from a stem beneath it.

"Ohh!" Shug exclaimed, nodded, and said, "Thank you!"

The man nodded back, apparently at least somewhat pleased at helping resolve the problem.

After two more bowls of water, Shug felt a lot better. They were keeping him here, but offered food, water, and shelter. He assumed there were reasons not to go about, either taboos or danger. So he'd wait patiently for their Elders to discuss things and decide what to do.

Daniel Oglesby had a lot of time to think aboard the planes.

He wasn't on the military rotator, or a transport, or even a civilian charter. This was a military executive jet. From Pittsburgh to Andrews Air Force Base near DC, onto this. The three other passengers were officers, a general, and two colonels. They nodded briefly if they passed him on the way to the lavatory, and otherwise ignored him and he them. He was in civvies, per the orders emailed to him. His rank wasn't apparent.

The seats were spacious, at least, and reclined a good amount. The E-6 flight attendant kept him fed and watered, and he had a shot of rum to help him sleep for part of it.

"Let me know if you need anything else, Sergeant," she said. She was cute enough, but they were on duty and no porn fantasy of the Mile High Club was possible. Food and drink was enough. It was a painful flight. He watched some bits of movie and TV, skipping from feed to feed. The whining roar of the jets changed tone. They were descending.

They stopped in Germany to refuel and change crew, and the officers debarked. No one else boarded. The new flight attendant was male, as efficient, less interesting.

From there they flew to Kuwait, and he managed some sleep across the seats. In between zoneouts and unconsciousness, he had moments of lucid thought to think about the destination.

What had been said was that they had to follow up on his deployment and needed his linguistic skills. What was unsaid was that the only linguistic skill he had that wasn't readily available in country was the language of the Urushu. If they were flying him fast and secretly to A-stan it implied they had one of the Urushu. How had that happened? Another time displacement? That seemed to be the only rational answer.

He didn't like that answer. If another error in time had occurred, others might. Had those damned Cogi screwed up again? Or someone else?

From Kuwait City they flew to Bagram. He staggered from the plane, grabbed his duffel and ruck, and they had a godawful Chinook ready for him. He hoped it wasn't just the one bird making the trip, was relieved to see several others and various troops and civvie crew.

"Welcome, Mr. Oglesby," the flight engineer said.

He nodded back. "Hi, thanks. You know where we're going?"

"Yes. Mazar-i-Sharif."

"Good. This is the first I knew, actually."

"Now *that's* classified." The man grinned. "There's sandwiches and soda in the cooler, and water. Help yourself."

"Thanks." A regular sandwich would be a nice change. Ham and cheese on wheat with tomato, lettuce, and mustard. He thought about a Ripit, and stuck with water.

The crew was grubby, bearded, and looked well experienced.

The engineer said, "If anything hits the fan, there's a spare weapon." He pointed at an M4 on a rack.

"Roger that. How's the route?"

"Quiet for months. Shouldn't be a problem."

"Good. I'm going to try to zone until we get there."

"Sounds good."

That also meant he wouldn't have to talk. He grabbed ear protection, stuck the plugs in, and leaned back on the webbing.

He slept harder than he intended. He felt some pokes and corners and shakes, but that was just how these craft were. Then the shaking picked up.

"You okay, sir?" one of them asked.

"Yeah. Thanks. We there?"

"Yup. Enjoy your stay." That was tinged with sarcasm.

An MP met him at the ramp, shook hands, said, "Welcome, Sergeant Oglesby. I'm Sergeant John Gilead. Follow me."

They certainly were keeping good track of him, from home all the way here.

Most of the base was German Bundeswehr. The US presence was increasingly diminishing. They didn't talk to anyone not American.

The building was a typical semi-secure facility. They were manually let in, ID checked, signed in, and then Gilead led him down a hall.

Ahead he saw a familiar face.

"General McClare," he said. "Good to see you again, sir." Actually, it wasn't at all good to see the man, but he had no personal issue with him and he wanted to be courteous.

"And you, Sergeant Oglesby. Do you prefer Dan or Daniel?"

"Either is fine, sir."

"Well, Dan, do you have a guess why you're here?"

"I can only think of one reason, sir."

"You're probably correct."

"More time issues?"

"A boy, we think from the past. No one can find any language he speaks. This is his gear."

A stone-tipped spear, a stone knife, a pouch with several colorful stones, and a couple of bits of bone. That was probably a breech-cloth. He wasn't going to touch that. That was a shoulder drape.

"I'll try, but the language I learned only fits one very small area and time."

"You're all we've got. This way."

He followed to a locked door. Inside was a standard interrogation room.

Daniel stepped into the room and saw a very wary-looking boy in a standard set of pajamas. The boy was skinny, dark, had straight hair with a few tangles, and prominent cheeks. He was against the back wall, facing an MP, ready to fight but not starting anything. As Dan entered, the kid shifted to face them both. Then he saw the general and his escort and retreated into the corner. Likely, he'd been dragged where they needed him and he was worried about more manhandling.

He couldn't blame the troops for not having any idea how to handle this. Hell, the locals were different enough. This kid was an alien, and there was no guessing if Dan had any way to communicate.

McClare said, "I can watch on video. Jeffords, Sergeant Wylie, out." He indicated the door, his escort nodded and opened it, the SP joined them, and they left.

That might help.

Dan reached into his bag and pulled a beef stick out. He held it up.

"*Vest'k?*" he said carefully in Urushu.

"*Wes'k?*" the boy queried back.

Dan nodded. "Food." He proffered the stick again.

The boy walked over, took it with a grunt, and stepped back against the wall. He started chewing, widened his eyes, and mumbled "*Soge*" around a mouthful. Similar to Urushu "*'xok*," for "tasty."

He spoke a related language or dialect, or possibly one changed with time, but was it earlier or later?

Very slowly and with gestures, Dan tried his best to phrase the language.

"Our hunters not know-see your people. Confused." Finger to head. "You they bring here." He pointed. "I am Dan Who Speaks."

The boy looked at him, looked down, finished chewing the beef stick, and said, "I name Shug."

"Shug. Sit?" Dan asked, pointing at the other chair. He sat in the one marked for him.

The boy came over and carefully sat, legs pulled up, like a lonely school student.

Jesus, the poor kid was here alone, in an entire world of things he couldn't even recognize. How to even approach that?

Well, being friendly was the first step.

"How are you?"

"Confused. Spirit world very different."

"Not spirit world," Dan said. "Far away. Different people. Still day world."

"Not spirit world?"

"You fine. We're people, too."

"Go home?"

"I don't know, Shug. We don't know how people move magically."

"Home by river."

"I think I've been to river. It's not river near here."

Overhead, the general spoke over the PA. "Find out where he's from."

"I'll get there, sir."

And, of course, that spooked the kid and he had to reassure him it was just an echo through a hole.

Two hours later, Dan and Shug were doing better. Shug explained some problems with his cell, and Dan told him how to hose down the toilet. He made the boy a chart with pictures of a drumstick, a drop of water, and a star to indicate he wanted to talk to someone. He could point to them for the MPs.

He knew quite a bit about the boy's culture, which wasn't terribly dissimilar from the Urushu's, but Shug had never heard of that group. Shug knew how to use a bow and spear, and quite a bit about his spirits, who traveled between worlds.

Dan kept at it, with his own fatigue eating him, being reassuring. He got a plastic cup and poured water into it, in lieu of a bottle.

The kid relaxed as the discussion went on. Dan found out about game, the village size, their neighbors. He made copious notes, and Shug seemed aware the markings were some kind of record keeping. When the boy pointed curiously, Dan grabbed another notepad, and showed him how to hold a pencil. On the boy went, scribbling happily, making rough figures and possible tribal marks.

After another hour, Dan was passing out where he sat. He let the boy finish talking about his cousin's spear technique, and got a word in.

"Shug, I need go. I see tomorrow you."

"I see tomorrow Dan. Thank you helping."

"You debt."

Dan rose, walked to the door, and waited to be let out.

In the anteroom, the general was waiting.

"How did it go, Dan? I gather you were able to communicate with him."

"Somewhat. He's got a different dialect, changed by time or distance or both."

The general looked relieved. "Still, it's progress. So where is he from?"

He shouldn't be surprised at that question, but he was.

Dan burst out, "How the hell would he know? Sir? He mentions a river, the mountains, and a stream. That's the limits of his world."

The general nodded in comprehension.

"Do you have any idea when? From talking to him?"

"He speaks a vaguely similar language. I was able to puzzle it out. So I'd say he's from within a few hundred years and miles of where we were. I get the impression he's later. He mentioned spirit visitors and great beasts, which could be our vehicles, but he wasn't sure where or when or what exactly, just that it had happened a long time ago. And of course, that might be some other myth entirely. He could be talking about mammoths."

"Does he know anything?" The general sounded exasperated.

"He was doing a rite of passage as a solo hunter, a few miles from his village. He knows how to hunt and track. He can make some tools, cook some food, find or make shelter. That's about as much as he needs to know. He knows lots of basic stuff we largely don't know. Nothing about modern tech. Not even agriculture, though they do worship certain plants and keep the demon weeds away from them."

The general sighed. "I agree that's important for scientists to know. It doesn't give me any clues on disposition. He's going to have to stay here for now."

Dan said, "Yes, sir. I would like to keep meeting with him."

"Yes, you will. Is he going to be okay in those quarters?"

"He'd like more time outside, but he's fine with the bed, water, a toilet now that he knows what one is; you won't have that problem anymore. He has some food choices, and I think you need to limit his starches."

"What does he eat?"

"Meat, mostly. Organ meats as well. A little salt, roasted meat, that's all. Seasonal fruit, but keep the quantities small. Wild rice cakes and acorn pancakes work. From what I recall, and discussions we had, rice might be okay. Wheat and corn are completely out. He won't like beans. Avoid modern hot peppers. The food for Hajjis is not going to work for him."

General McClare turned to his aide. "Did you get that?"

The aide nodded.

"Okay, Oglesby. Do please meet with him daily and see what you can find out. I really wish I could assign an interrogator to assist, but we've got to keep this close. There are specific things, though. I'll get a list."

"Sir, I spent a couple of years back then. I know what to ask. If there's any way to have SFC Spencer come along, he had a really good background on the era and could help."

"I'll have him contacted. Thank you."

Just then, someone shouted, "Shit, General! This way. We have another...anomaly."

McClare strode off and moved to a jog. Dan followed along, figuring they'd send him away if they had a reason to. Anyway, he hadn't been assigned a billet yet.

Across the packed sand and concrete, into a large K-span, and there was a familiar bare depression in the ground.

Next to it, in a dull gray uniform, was a man he recognized.

"Hello, Cryder," he greeted.

It was the Cogi officer from the far future.

CHAPTER 3

Martin Spencer slept badly, woke up groggy, overcooked the eggs and ham until they were dry.

Allison walked in, and didn't even attempt to offer a courtesy.

"Ah, ruined my breakfast again, did you?" She took the loaded plate and utensils he offered.

He admitted, "And mine. It was an accident."

"Yes, always conveniently when I get home." Her tone was accusatory.

He didn't want to go there. He wanted out of the conversation to avoid a fight.

"I'm running late. I'm sorry."

She heaved her shoulders. "It's fine. It's not as if I spent all night dealing with intake documents for a car accident."

She seemed to really want an argument, prodding like that. He said, "I'm sorry. I'm sorry. How many times do I have to say it?"

"You've said it. I'd rather you got it right. Go play in the woods."

Sigh. She still didn't grasp it was a job. "It's work. We teach people."

"That's fine." She turned away with her plate.

He grabbed his backpack and stormed out. He had snacks at the office. He'd eat those instead.

He did relax a bit while driving. The old Suburban was a reassurance. Though he'd probably need to replace it, soon. They'd done Allison's last. Actually, she'd gone through two cars while he was still on this one.

That part wasn't her fault. He was just being pissy.

He pulled up at the office, grabbed coffee and a pack of jerky, and got to work. The students were up and waiting.

"Okay, your tarps are covered in dew. And the ones we set on the frame have filled the bottles. Go ahead and taste them."

The water would be cool, fresh, and as long as the tarps weren't too dirty, very tasty.

The students agreed. "Mmmm." "Nice!" "That's refreshing."

"We'll work on river water filtering shortly. Notice how you can roll the tarp to make puddles. You want to conserve as much as possible. Drink what you can't store, so you're hydrated."

Bob was on his way with a couple of shovels. They'd use shovels for their sand filters. The students got E-tools.

His phone rang. He pulled it, glanced at the number, and his pulse hammered.

"Go ahead and work on that. I have a business matter to attend to, but will be back ASAP. Emily, can you keep an eye out?"

"Sure!" she agreed.

"Thanks." He took a last glance around and headed for his cabin office, so he could call back in private.

He knew what the call meant. It was a military number through Washington.

The voice mail just said, "This is David McClare. Please call me back ASAP."

David McClare. Not *General* McClare. If the man was being that circumspect . . .

He stepped into the trailer, closed the door, kept an eye on things out the window.

He pressed call back. It was answered on the first half ring. "McClare."

"Hello, David. Are you still using your rank otherwise?"

"Martin Spencer, thanks for calling back. Yes, this is official, just discreet. Are you in private?"

"Yes, sir. In my office. No one in hearing."

"We'd like to recall you to duty."

"Where and why?"

"It has to do with your last assignment and is not for public discussion."

"Ah, that." He nodded. Maybe. More likely not. If they wanted more questions and were paying, sure. He didn't want to be a lab subject again, though.

"Your contacts from last time assure your safety."

Contacts? The Cogi?

"That's interesting," he said. "Are you in contact with them?"

"They are here, and yes."

"What about Barker?"

"We assumed one of you would stay to cover your business. That's better for us, too."

"Right. Do we get a choice?"

"Yes."

"Let me think about it."

"Please get back to us by tomorrow, close of business."

"Understood."

The Cogi, the future soldiers, were here. That was either a coincidental problem, or it meant they had reliable time travel. It sounded like the latter. That suggested others were also doing it.

He'd have to discuss this with family.

Who was he kidding? Allison wouldn't stop him for a second.

Going away wouldn't fix anything, but he wasn't running away, just getting distance. Anyway, he didn't know what was up yet.

It bugged him all day at class. He drove home wondering how to discuss it.

Really, there was no good way.

He walked in across the wooden slat porch, opened the door, and said, "Allison, the Army needs me for another project."

She had no expression as she said, "Well, good. That's reliable income."

Charming. Thanks, wife.

"They may need me in A-stan."

And suddenly she actually did look compassionate.

"You came back a wreck. Your POW time hurt you badly. You retired early. You never let your bug-out bag get more than a foot from you, even in bed." She pointed at the pack, which he'd put next to his boot. "Do you really think you're in a good mental state to go back over?"

He actually wasn't sure. "They've given reliable assurances. We'll have heavy allied support."

"Then there's my feelings to consider."

"There are." That was a legitimate matter.

Then she threw out, "So what's the deal with you and this Gina woman on Facebook?"

Oh, hell, this could be bad. His pulse hammered and he tried not to blush.

"We were very close. Personally close. We were both married and never did anything physical."

"And what did you do that wasn't physical?"

"We know...a hell of a lot about each other."

"I know how the military can be. And stressful situations. And emergencies."

"Only talk, dear. We were both afraid we weren't coming home, and we had lots of time to talk. We couldn't possibly touch each other."

"It still feels bad to me."

"Yeah, it felt bad to us."

"I saw your Messenger chat."

He wished she hadn't done that. Why had she done that?

She said, "I didn't get who most of these people or groups were. I guess local tribes. But it looked like you weren't exactly prisoners, and were doing something intel-wise."

And this is why he should never have mentioned anything on Messenger to anyone, ever.

"We can't say. Allison, we both talked about our relationships, and we did not cheat."

"No, but you did talk about it. In detail. And about me."

"All I can say is, this time we won't be left hanging. If it looks like that, I'm turning around, because I can't handle that again."

"This means extra retirement points, doesn't it?"

"Yeah. And pay on top of my share of the school. And maybe other perks."

"I am very unhappy agreeing to this."

"Do you want to say no?"

"I want you to consider the kids."

The kids were adults.

"I'll make it work," he said.

He really didn't feel at home here anyway.

Captain Sean Elliott had just taken command of an engineer company when he got called to go back to sunny Ass-stan. His "allies from the last deployment" meant only one thing, and he wasn't thrilled. He'd thought that had all been sorted out.

Whether this was the Army's screwup, the Cogi's, or something else remained to be seen.

There was no "wait" on this leg, only "hurry up." He was off the plane, into a waiting HMMWV that was even hotter than outside, and across the dusty flight line at once. It was filled with mostly German aircraft, and German cadre. The US contingent was reducing steadily. He did text Mariel that he arrived and would be out of contact for some time. Sucky way to treat a girlfriend who was willing to tolerate Army schedules, but then, that's what it was.

In the US section of the base, General McClare was waiting.

He saluted, the general returned it, and extended a hand.

"Good to see you again, sir," he said as a formality.

"And you, Captain. You're looking fit."

"I got that way and decided I liked the look," he said. He did like the physique, and so did Mariel, who had a pretty good build herself.

"Excellent. Come right on in to my office."

They entered the steel fire door, down the hall past some admin offices, and to the small suite that the general needed mostly for appearances' sake. There was no receptionist in the outer office, though there was a desk for one. He led the way into the office proper. Sean followed.

Three men stood as they entered, and Sean pulled up short.

The first was Specialist—no, apparently now Sergeant Oglesby, who he knew easily. Well, hell.

"Hello, Dan. Congrats on the stripe." He pointed at the sergeant's insignia.

"Thank you, sir."

Next was Cryder, the Cogi soldier from the future, who they'd met in the distant past.

Sean said, "Cryder. Greetings. I'm not sure I can say it's good to see you."

Cryder stood to his 6'6" height and imposing physique. "Greetings, Captn. I've been workin' on my language. Can guess why'm here." He shook hands firmly, though Sean knew the man could crush his hand if he leaned into it.

Sean could guess. "You want us to do something in the past?" he asked.

"And future."

He turned to the other and offered his hand again.

The young man declared, "I am Shug,"

Shug was young, about eighteen, very skinny, and looked not quite Afghan. Wait...

"He's from the past."

Oglesby said, "Yes, sir. Probably not far from the Urushu. I haven't been able to determine much beyond that yet, but Mr. Cryder says he's a couple of thousand years later."

Sean shrugged mentally and said, "It is good to meet you, Shug."

"Tank you."

To the general, he said, "So Shug arrived here and Cryder came to help take him back?"

"To start with, yes." McClare elaborated. "The Cogi have identified some more of our MIAs as displaced in time. It's much easier to recover them if we have US forces along, and we don't want to open up the group to anyone not already cleared."

Cryder resumed his seat, leaned back a bit, and said, "Nor do we. There are technic reasons you guys work easier than others." After he sat, the others followed his lead.

"I see. I'm guessing your presence at this exact location and time means your people got better resolution on the time warps or whatever?"

He kept an eye on Shug. The kid paid attention, but didn't seem to grasp much if any of the conversation.

Cryder noted, "Within days now, yes. Each jump refines it more, but each one creates sort of like ripples, and those make it a bit harder."

He asked, "How many jumps have you made?"

"This is my first delibrate one."

"Overall by your people, I mean."

Cryder shook his head. "I dunno, and that's restricted. They sent me to help localize you people for pickup and return."

"That's good, I guess."

Cryder said, "We'd like at least five of you. Unnerstand you're not all available. General wants to send two life scientists to research. I recommend against. Whole point is the techs have your data on file to make it accurate."

McClure said, "I argued that first so we have some sort of idea what effect this had on you and your troops, and on the ones we hope to bring back. Then, there's pure scientific interest."

Sean nodded. "So this is a planned mission."

McClure said, "Sort of. It's planned in detail, and three officers have the details. You'd be number four. All other documentation describes a completely different civil affairs mission, and cites your people as having developed useful contacts, et cetera."

"I'm surprised we've kept it quiet this long."

"There are rumors and conspiracy site posts. Usually about ten percent facts and the rest out there with aliens."

"Time travel, not aliens," Sean joked.

"Exactly."

It was nerve-wracking, but Cryder was here, so it seemed there was actual control of the process.

"So what about those ripples you mentioned?" he asked.

Cryder said, "More jumps means more interference. We can deal with it, but it takes more zero baseline, which means more travel, which means more interference."

"How many jumps have been made?" he asked, then realized he'd just asked that same thing.

"We don't know. How many rockets have been made?"

Sean replied, "That depends on your definition of 'rocket.' Thousands to billions."

"Exactly that."

"You mean short jumps? Seconds?"

The tall man shrugged. "Lots of people making their own and fucking up everything possible." He looked at Shug, and the young man looked a bit tense.

Oglesby reassured the paleo with something in the native language, then explained, "I told him he was fine. He knows he's part of this, but not how."

"Oh . . . how bad is that? Risk of things getting screwed up in the past?"

"No, but it's like having a hundred imagers running around in the middle of a play."

"Okay." He imagined kids with cell phones running through a formation or patrol. That would suck.

Cryder continued, "There's no way to stop them. Most dis-placements are not people, or only a few moments and don't cause any real effect. Some are significant. They act like waves. Lots of little ones can suddenly cause a big one."

"Got it. So you can work around it. It's just a very variable thing."

"Bingo, gringo."

That was just a hilarious comment, and Sean laughed.

"So why us? You can go back and find them. You speak English."

"I could, probably. Same with Arnet." His counterpart from the previous event. "Tried sending someone else, couldn't get within a century on the first approx. Existing personnel work a lot better, and we need more'n two for safety and support. They say they can get us a lot closer."

"Human auras or something?"

The man nodded. "Guess that term works. Thousands of factors, those on file are easier."

"And how hard is recovery?" He didn't want to be stuck for another two years or longer.

"Recovery is simple. Or is as far as the user. Deployment is the hard part."

Sean grasped it, but not entirely. "It just seems odd to come here to get us to go there."

The man almost smirked. "How much production do you send to China and India?"

That took a moment.

"I can't see that being a relevant comparison, but I guess I see the point."

He asked, "Okay, so, General, do I contact the element or will others?"

McClare replied, "You do. It minimizes risks and they'll trust you."

"I don't know about that last, sir."

"Do what you can."

Cryder added, "The longer they're displaced, the more chances for things wrong. Got to get them back, Shug home, and they said there may be a couple they're still sweeping for."

"Damn. Nice mess."

Lieutenant Colonel Kevin Rosten hated when his phone rang during the middle of the night. He squinted blearily at the clock. 0346. That probably meant...

"Yeah, Rosten, go ahead."

"Sir, this is Sergeant Dormund at the desk. We have one of our troops here for a barfight."

"Ah, hell. Do I need to come over? Who is it?"

"Sergeant Caswell."

"What, Jennifer Caswell? Female, about five five?"

"Yes, sir."

"What happened?"

"Apparently she smashed some infantryman's face. He's at the hospital now."

"Is she okay?"

"Other than bruised hands, she seems fine."

"What the hell happened? She's not exactly large."

Dormund said, "We're still taking statements."

He blinked again. "Roger. I'll be there ASAP."

Why did it have to be Caswell? She was smarter than hell, and just had completely the wrong chip on her shoulder.

Still, she was a bona fide combat vet and former POW from that mixup in A-stan. He'd find out what the issue was before making any decisions.

Twenty minutes later he was at his office, with coffee in hand.

He glanced over the statements. Caswell's friend, and the other guy's buddy, both agreed the victim had been mouthy and inappropriate. "Comfort women." Yeah, he understood why she'd take that personally. Not only female and very feminist, but the few documents of her experience said she'd acted as escort and grief counselor for native women in theater. Smashing the guy was probably a bit much, but it depended on delivery. His injuries were minor, mostly bruises and splits. He had a couple of sutures and a tooth with some reinforcement while it reset.

The resolution was obvious to him.

"I think it's best if we just make it go away."

The man's commander, a twenty-six-year-old captain, politely argued, "No, sir. I respectfully disagree. I've got a good soldier who's going to be on quarters for at least a couple of weeks, and isn't going to deploy on time."

"Yeah, well maybe your 'good soldier' shouldn't have been making sexually harassing comments to a decorated combat vet, impugning her service, and implying she should sexually service him. It's not only unprofessional, it was stupid, since he had no idea about her background. I offer instead we call it even, he takes his ass whuppin' like a man and goes about his business."

He understood why an officer would stand up for his troops. He was doing the same. He understood why an infantry officer would care more about his combat soldier than someone he regarded as a mere REMF. At the same time, the soldier had been wrong, and it was actually quite amusing to know a female SP had worn him out in a puddle of blood and beer.

"That's your final word?"

"I'm afraid it is, Captain."

"I'll give it some thought. I'll see how he looks in the morning. On the one hand, it's a problem for my manning doc. On the other, I really don't want to escalate, either. That just makes work for everyone. I understand that, Colonel. But she took it from words to violence."

Very calmly, because presence mattered, he said, "I can be reached at my office. It may be Monday before the relevant offices have their comments available. Do please let me know how you'd like to proceed."

"Yes, sir, thank you."

The captain sounded put upon, but he probably knew how this would play out, and someone was going to have to explain to the mouthy grunt about target selection, and, well, courtesy in public.

Caswell was released, with a cautionary letter to remain available pursuant to possible disciplinary procedures.

She looked exhausted, angry, and rather embarrassed, but challenging.

She took a deep breath and said, "Sorry, sir. I didn't want it to escalate like that."

"I'm sure you didn't. I've advised them that pressing charges will complicate things for everyone. He was absolutely wrong to talk to you like that. That doesn't justify hitting him."

"I'm aware of the regulations, sir."

Nice phrasing.

"You are. That's also not any kind of admission or apology, is it?"

She gazed in restrained antagonism. "It isn't, no, sir."

"We'll discuss this Monday. You will please remain on base and away from any of the establishments serving alcohol until then."

She replied, "I understand, sir. I'd like to note for the record that I wasn't drinking."

"I saw. But he was."

"I . . . Yes, sir."

That was as much admission as he was going to allow that he was on her side. She seemed to grasp the hint and the discretion that went with it.

"Your friends are still here. Can they take you to the dorm?"

"Yes, sir."

God, it was early. He might as well be up for the day.

It wasn't five minutes later, just as he got in his car, that his phone rang again.

"Lieutenant Colonel Rosten, Security Forces Squadron."

"Colonel Rosten, I don't think we've met. I'm Captain Elliott. I'm in Mazar-i-Sharif."

"What can I do for you, Captain?"

"You have a Staff Sergeant Caswell, Jennifer, in your unit."

Goddamn. What was it with her?

"I do. She was over there about a year ago, I believe."

"Well, we need her back."

What? "Uh, that's unusual. What for?"

"I'm afraid I'm not at liberty to say, sir. She has specific information regarding the events that took place while she was here with my element, and we need her in person to assist with them."

"I assume you're sending orders over?"

"AFCENT is. I just figured it was polite to give you a heads-up so you can relay it through chain."

"Yeah, I'm not sure how she'll react. There was an issue here last night. Tonight, actually."

Elliott sounded concerned. "Is she okay?"

"She's fine. Apparently, someone made comments about her deployment and they were not well received. A bar fight."

"Ah. Well, if you need any backup from here, we'll do our best to get it cleared and get her en route."

"Thanks. I'll let you know."

Really, Caswell was competent, but annoying, and this might be good for her. She might be one of those troops who missed the war.

This also resolved the matter of the bar fight. Orders from higher up, she's gone. Deal with it.

It also meant he wouldn't be dealing with her for the duration.

⇒ CHAPTER 4 ⇐

Armand Devereaux sighed and tried to keep positive. It wasn't that he had trouble with the work. Making rounds in post-op was easy enough. He could handle the odd hours; the Army had taught him that. The pay was decent.

What he hated was the snide condescension from civilian medical personnel, that he was somehow inexperienced as a mere resident. He'd saved sixty-three lives in combat, and saved several butchered limbs on top of that. He'd done some of it with duct tape, and some of it with sticks, rags, sinew, and leather thong, in a time and place he couldn't even mention to these people.

But he was the new guy, so obviously he needed help.

And a couple of them seemed to think it was impossible for a black man to grasp science.

The current attending, Dr. Berilley, was quizzing him yet again on a relatively routine procedure they'd done four times in the last two months.

"What would you do about sudden bleeding from the porta hepatis?"

It was almost rote as he rattled off, "I'd immediately apply direct pressure to allow adequate exposure. If needed I'd call for assistance. If bleeding persists, a Pringle maneuver might be necessary. Suture ligation of bleeding porta hepatis structures should be careful and precise using five-oh polydioxanone horizontal mattress sutures."

"Very good."

Berilley at least assumed he was competent and was just drilling him for practice. Olmsted, on the other hand, tried to explain everything to him, without giving him a chance to either perform the task or explain it from his end. If they wanted to make him wish to be back in the field under fire, they were doing a damned fine job. No one explained to him while he was sealing bullet holes and chest wounds.

Sean wasn't looking forward to the rest of these calls. Half the element was already accounted for. The others...

He punched the number. The phone rang, a woman answered, and he recognized her voice.

"Hello?"

"Gina, it's Sean Elliott. Your former commander."

"Oh...hello, sir."

"Hello. How's your health these days?"

"Not as good. It's slipping again. Though I'm still better than before, but that's a low bar."

"Well, that's mixed. Good on the latter, sorry about the first."

"What's up?"

"I can't discuss much, but there's one of those consulting gigs we talked about. They need us overseas, going back where we were for a short stint. I'm trying to reach everyone and let them know."

"I see...hold on."

"Sure."

There were mumbles and sharper comment he couldn't hear, that had urgency in it.

A male voice came back on the phone.

"Captain Elliott?"

"I am. Is this Blake Alexander?"

"It is."

"Is Gina okay?"

The man spoke very bluntly. "Let me give this to you straight, sir. I'm an investigator. I puzzled out exactly where you guys went, and I know about these Cogi. She spends every night clinging to me. Despite their medical care, her metabolism is slipping again. By military standards—hell, anyone's—she's old, broken, and fragile. She held up admirably, but you used up her durability. She's not going back."

That was direct and fair, but he needed to know. "Is that from you or from her?"

"It's from me, for her, by way of my power of attorney. She told me you called, she asked me to talk. She's in the bedroom crying."

Really, it wasn't unexpected. Gina was older, damaged, sick, and had put out a lot of effort. She was closing in on fifty. There were limits to human endurance.

"I understand, sir. Please give her my very best wishes, thank her for considering the offer, and let her know she will not be pressured in any fashion. She can contact us if she likes. We won't call back about this matter again."

The man's voice softened slightly. "I'll let her know. Thank you for understanding, Captain."

That was two. Caswell facing charges for fighting, Alexander old and broken. Oglesby seemed fit enough. Between Barker and Spencer he'd rather have Spencer, and did, but he was old by Army standards, too, retired, and probably wasn't going to be super enthused.

As for Armand Devereaux, he was working his residency.

He took a drink of water to keep hydrated, and checked the file.

He tapped the number, and it was answered almost at once. "Dr. Devereaux."

"Doc, this is Captain Sean Elliott."

At least the medic sounded cheerful. "Hey! How are you doing, sir?"

"Excellent. I heard you're pending a commission?"

"I am. The paperwork should be done next week. Just have to wait for drill."

"Good luck. How's your residency?"

"It is what it is. Ball busting, but medical work. Easier than the field, which seems to confuse some people."

Oh? Civilian-military divide?

Sean said, "Ah, well, that's part of why I called. Our allies from the last rotation are here, now."

He could hear Devereaux's attention prickle. "As in . . . the tall blond guys?"

"One of them. They're asking for help. They have much better navigation and transport this time."

"I see."

"There's another group lost."

"They can't get them?"

"They need us to work out the details. Imagine you trying to deal with Chaucer. Totally different cultures."

"Got it. For how long?"

"The trip itself should only be a few days, as far as anyone here is concerned."

"Oh. That's doable. I'll be glad to take a short break, actually."

That was interesting.

"Okay. You're getting orders emailed ASAP, with travel itinerary and allowance."

"Thank you, sir. It'll be good to see you again."

"Consider your commission approved, Lieutenant. They can have a ceremony later." He was sure General McClare would agree.

"That's a nice gesture, sir. Thank you very much."

That was two.

Okay, down in South Texas, literally on the border, Ramon Ortiz had finished his service and gone back to work on the ranch.

"Hello."

Sean asked, "Is Ramon Ortiz available, please?" It sounded like Ortiz, but he wanted to be sure.

"This is Ramon."

"Ramon, it's Captain Sean Elliott."

"Ah, yes, sir."

"We have one of those consulting gigs we talked about."

"Ah. Where?"

"Back in A-stan."

"Impossible."

"They're offering a bonus."

"No, sir. I've got four hundred head to move pasture as the weather changes. Then God knows how many chickens to keep up with. We've just started rabbits for a local restaurant. They want fifty a week. I can consult by phone if I can juggle things a bit."

Impressive. Well, he was a skilled vet tech, raised on a ranch. It made sense he'd expand into that.

"It's more of an on-site thing."

"Then I've got to decline, sir. Sorry."

"I understand. Good luck with the rabbits."

"Thanks, sir. They're very tender. If you get down here, we'll beer-braise one for you."

"Sounds good." Sean actually wasn't a huge fan of rabbit. He'd eaten enough in the Paleolithic. But if Ramon cooked it, he'd eat it as a courtesy at least.

He wasn't having much luck here.

It was probably a good time to catch Dalton.

Then-Corporal Richard Dalton had been promoted to sergeant, and then to civilian. It was interesting how almost everyone had gotten out after that. Not surprising, but interesting.

Dalton answered his phone. "Richard Dalton. I'm at work, this better be important."

"Rich, it's Captain Elliott."

"Oh, hello, sir! What's up?" Dalton sounded cheerful.

"That depends on how important your work is. We could use you for a consult back here in A-stan, and then on-site at our previous location."

"Wait, go back? How?"

He phrased it as "Our allies have improved the method."

"So why go back?"

"To recover another element."

"I'm in," the man said at once.

"I haven't given you the details yet."

Dalton said, "Sir, if other troops need us, I'm in. Email the details?"

"We'll email orders. Details when you get here."

"Hooah, sir."

Dalton had been an exemplary troop. A tad too religious for everyone else, but his faith got him through it. It sounded as if he still was very religious, and very charitable.

Later that night he called Felix Trinidad in the Philippines.

Trinidad replied, "Sir, I've got a family here. You realize this isn't the safest place in the world, right?"

"I know."

"I'm trying to get a visa for my wife, so we can both be in the US, and then work on her citizenship. I can't leave her alone."

"It should only be a few days."

"Without a guarantee, and backup in the area, I dare not."

"I understand. It's tough enough with a girlfriend. A wife is a bigger deal. Good woman?"

"Spectacular. She can take a chicken from the yard to hanging in about ten minutes. Very pretty. Always cheerful."

"Sounds as if you lucked out."

"I really did."

"Good luck with it."

"Thanks, Captain."

Well, he had about half, which was probably better than he should have expected. Though most of the older, steadier troops were out. Still, he had Spencer as a solid NCO. Doc certainly held up his end. Oglesby seemed to have matured. Dalton was very reliable if a bit annoying at times. And Caswell...she did have a lot of relevant skills. He didn't want to judge the fight without details, but part of him suspected she'd gotten sensitive to some comment and gone to town.

Shug wasn't sure what to make of all the happenings. Dan Speaker said these were just people, only a long way from his own. There was some sort of magic involved that no one really understood, but the tall pale man, Cry-der, was a traveler for those shamans. The two women who just arrived were...not quite shamans, but wise women of some kind. They were very learned and carried special names.

He was still fastened into the room every night, but during the day Dan took him around several places. They had an exercise place that let you do exercise for any single limb, or all. It had ropes and sticks attached to perfectly cut stones you could pull and push and lift. People ran around outside, wearing clothing that was perfectly fitted and only for exercise.

They kept the indoors very comfortable, though outside was quite hot, and they all insisted on wearing two layers of dress from neck to foot, and these heavy boots that were so hard to feel the ground through. Nothing like footskins. The food, though... the food was that of the spirit world, no matter what Dan said. Salt, fat, sweet, savory, with tasty spices and leaves. The fruits and plants were cool, fresh, and completely clean. The meat was tender. The sweets were very rich and so varied. The water was always cold and perfectly clear. There were juices and odd bubbly things to drink, and a hot infusion that was black and bitter and had magic energy, not unlike the sacred black drink at home, but less harsh, and could also be sweetened.

He got used to the dress, with one tunic inside and another outside, in the mottled colors they wore. He asked, and Dan said it was to blend in and hide. That didn't make sense. One hid through careful movement, shadow, and proper thoughts of emptiness and oneness with the earth.

He was dressed and ready when the cover opened, and Dan was there for him.

"Shug, we will try to start our journey in two days."

"Back to home go?" he asked.

"It will take time, but we will start in two days, yes."

He cheered politely, which seemed to amuse the hunter-warrior standing in the tunnel.

Dan continued, "We have prepare to do. Come."

Martin Spencer was tall enough to hate long flights, and goddamn, this one was torture every time. He couldn't sleep well aboard a plane and would get almost nauseous. He actually preferred the C-130 leg, since he could stretch out and lean on his ruck.

They knew who he was on arrival. A USAF E-6, cute and professional and clean, had him sign in, and stand by.

"Right over there, Sergeant, at the bench. Your transport should be here momentarily."

In fact, it was less than five minutes when a van pulled up. He climbed in with his bags, and the driver rolled at once.

They pulled up at an operations building that looked like most of the others, but there was a staff car outside, and two guards at the door. A specialist and a private first class.

He had his ID ready in his neck wallet, pulled it out as he approached, and offered it.

"Thank you very much, Sergeant." The specialist nodded. "They're expecting you." He opened the door for Spencer and stepped aside, to let him drag his bags in.

Inside was a classroom of sorts, with a desk beyond it.

There was Caswell. She turned, saw him, and came forward. She was sprinting. She leapt into the air and tackle-hugged him.

"Sergeant Spencer!" she said. "I missed you."

He wasn't sure how to take that. Their interactions had been generally very distant, formal, and not very friendly, though she had lightened up a bit at the end.

"How are you, Caswell?" he asked, as he gently put her back on the ground.

She actually smiled. "Much better than when we were there, thank you. How's your family?"

"Um ... my kids are good."

"That's a very careful choice of phrasing," she replied, and yes, she guessed. "So let's discuss something else. What do you know?"

She was definitely doing better. That had actually been diplomatic.

"About what's going on?"

"Yes."

"Nothing, other than they want us to consult, and possibly meet with our former hosts."

"Yeah, they didn't say here or there."

"That bothers me, too," he said.

Rich Dalton walked in from the hallway, came over and offered a firm handshake. He looked a little different, but it was mostly just being slightly older and less stressed.

"How are you doing, Sergeant Spencer?"

"Work is very good, kids are grown up and making their way."

"Excellent. And your wife?"

"Not coming to the Stone Age," he joked to try to divert the question.

"Hah. Yeah."

There was Captain Elliott.

"Sergeant Spencer," he greeted, also extending a hand. "Sorry I wasn't here to meet you. Nothing but conferences here, to improve efficiency."

Martin chuckled. "It's the Army way, sir."

Elliott said, "Welcome. We're all sort of accumulating, and we'll be briefed shortly."

"Looking forward to it." He was. At least as far as finding out what the hell was going on.

Oglesby showed up with ... a native boy. The uniform with CONTRACTOR tapes didn't hide what he was.

He said, "Soldiers, this is Shug. We're trying to take him home, and recover our missing unit."

Martin said, "Hello, Shug."

"Hel-lo."

Fair enough. The boy was about sixteen to eighteen, maybe, and very out of his depth.

His eyes widened at something, and Martin looked behind him.

He followed everyone else's gaze. Colonel Findlay had apparently flown in, too. Martin remembered him from their last recovery. He was arriving with two women.

"Soldiers, these are biologists Amalie Raven and Katherine Sheridan."

Two fat chicks. That was his first thought.

They presented well. Minimal makeup, functional clothes, tailored enough to fit and slim their figures, but it was going to take more than that to actually slim them.

Raven looked serious but in a good way. She shook hands firmly. "Captain, Sergeant." She was short, stocky, and muscular under the fat, with a massive rib cage behind her breasts. She had high cheeks, dark bronze skin and dark hair tied back. Hispanic with some Native American, maybe?

Sheridan was more cheerful, but had a gentler handshake. She had a warmer smile and looked typically Euro-American, with a bobbed haircut. She was just fat. She didn't look weak, but she didn't come across as able to handle a ruck march.

"So you'll be researching...?"

Sheridan said, "Genetic lines and potential disease contamination. The Cogi agreed that's acceptable and won't cause temporal trouble. He doesn't like it, though."

Findlay said, "With the holes in your element, it was possible to add others. Mr. Cryder agreed that could be done, said it would help balance mass, but everything else would be off due to auras, or biometrics, something."

Sheridan said, "It's entirely possible they have readings for bioelectricity, mass balance, and other fine points we're aware of, and others we don't. But if he's agreeable to sending us, we'll go."

The captain said, "Glad to have you aboard, then. I hope it's been covered, but I need to ask for my own confidence. You're aware this will involve field conditions with an Army unit and there may be little or no privacy?"

Raven said, "Yup. I'm more concerned about my data than me. I grew up on an Indian reservation and a ranch. I've done field exhumations and excavations. It's not like anyone wants to see me naked."

Martin didn't want to agree with her, but it was not inaccurate from his point of view.

So he said, "I'll remind the troops about the data, then."

Sheridan said, "I've also worked in the field, and I'm an Army brat. Don't sweat it."

Elliott said, "Okay. I'll trust you've got everything you need off the checklist, and all your stuff. We can't run back for it."

"Obviously." Raven looked irritated.

Okay, he'd assume they got it, and it was their own problem if they didn't.

"We may be hiking several miles a day."

"I'm good," Sheridan said. "I walk daily."

Raven said, "I try to, but I blew an ankle out years ago. It slows me down."

"Noted," Elliott said. At least she was honest up front.

Findlay said, "And you deploy in about eleven hours. You need to gear up fast."

Wow, they really weren't kidding.

Elliott said, "Sir, I'd like them all to get some rest in there. We'll be hard at it as soon as we move."

"Yes, that should be first. We've got empty offices down this hall, with cots and air mattresses. Not first class, but better than the ground."

"Much appreciated, Colonel."

Martin wondered how this was going to turn out. Women often had trouble keeping up, simply due to stature and muscle mass. How were these women going to manage?

CHAPTER 5

Eight hours later, Sean Elliott had arranged for food to be delivered to the building, and everyone had eaten and gathered back in the conference room.

Lieutenant Armand "Doc" Devereaux had arrived, and was actually a doctor now. He looked wired and sipped a Red Bull. He was still tall, lanky, and seemed very aware of goings-on.

The OCP uniforms the two scientists wore were civilian purchase. He didn't think the regular sizes went quite that high. The women weren't huge by civilian norms, but they were definitely fat by Army standards. Sheridan tugged at her sleeves uncomfortably, but they both seemed okay otherwise. Their uniforms had branch tapes reading CONTRACTOR rather than US ARMY.

Spencer seemed to have gotten some sleep and food. He looked a lot better now. Good. He'd been worried at the man's initial presentation.

Oglesby showed up with Shug.

"Greeting, Shug," Sean said, hoping he remembered properly.

Apparently it was close enough. Shug smiled and chattered something. He didn't look at all comfortable in a uniform with boots. He also wore a CONTRACTOR tape.

Oglesby interceded, likely telling him no one else knew more than a word or two, and even those would be barely the same language.

Cryder arrived in a tan uniform that could be that of a dozen elements. It probably wasn't his native uniform, but that might arouse curiosity. In sand-colored tactical, he was just some dude on base, and could easily pass as Scandinavian. No one would question that.

Though he did have an MP following him around, probably to keep tabs on him.

Other than Sean and Oglesby, the others hadn't been reintroduced yet.

Dalton immediately spoke up.

"Cryder! Good to see you. How have things been?"

"Good to see you, Rich. Apart from our current issue, things have been well." The tall man shook hands all around. Caswell was friendly enough. Doc straightforward. Spencer seemed a bit reserved. Apparently the scientists had met Cryder, and they just nodded to each other.

Colonel Findlay arrived with a dolly of coffee. It was amusingly cool to be served by a colonel, but the only reason was to maximize OPSEC. They'd spoken to almost no one outside this building. The American contingent was decreasing by the day. The German support element hadn't been told at all.

"We have a breakfast buffet down the hall, and then a bus to take you to the K-span we're using as a transfer point."

The food aromas were present as soon as they turned the corner in the hall. Once through the door, Sean could see scrambled eggs that were actually cooked properly, sausage, biscuits and gravy, bacon, ham, hash browns, several types of bread, pancakes, waffles, cereal, and fruit. There were coffee, juices, milk. It was decent quality, and plentiful. No servers, of course.

He sipped coffee while the enlisted piled food. He waited for Spencer, nudged Doc to go next to last. Then he filled his own plate with eggs with ham and hash browns with a side of biscuits and gravy. He poured some tomato juice and sat down. Since it was to be the last American food for a while, he enjoyed it as much as circumstances allowed. It did require pepper.

Shug took a bit of each, seemed to adore bacon and rye bread, and went back for more.

Findlay spoke.

"Please keep eating. We'll bus you over in about an hour. The gear the scientists asked for is ready. Mr. Cryder says his people will provide all the field gear you need."

Cryder stood and took over.

"We have better gear, and fit to the mission. The less we transit here, the easier and safer it will be. You know our era is safe. We'll load up before we go back."

Fair enough.

Raven said, "Some of our equipment is specifically...tuned, you could say, to our needs. I don't know if yours will be as effective for us."

"If you can bring schematics, we can produce a clone or possibly an upgrade."

Sean heard her mutter something that started with "Obnoxious asshole" as she zipped open her backpack, grabbed a laptop, and apparently started looking for files. She nudged her counterpart, Sheridan, who also grabbed a tablet and started getting data.

Everyone else seemed fine for now. Not necessarily trusting, of course, but accepting. The Cogi did have good kit.

Everyone got their fill of breakfast and a lot of coffee. They mostly gathered their leftovers and plates back up, and Dalton took it upon himself to lead a cleaning detail.

Then the MP said, "Transport inbound," and everyone grabbed gear and walked briskly to the door. Sean left last, making sure everything was accounted for.

Out in the warm, dusty morning, the bus was a standard small coach as used all over the theater. Sean idly wondered who contracted them. Probably some local company. It would be ridiculous to fly them in, but hey, it was the military, maybe they did. It wasn't important, and they needed to minimize discussions with outsiders, so he sat quietly as they drove a quarter mile or so.

The K-span structure was well secured, sort of. The same MP unlocked the door. There was another NCO inside. She was an SFC who checked everyone's IDs carefully against their picture, and against an access list.

They had come in the only door. That is, the side and rear doors had heavy timbers over them, bolted to the structure.

Other than the small entryway and office, the building was a shell. Several ECUs blew cold air in one side. The floor was locked runway matting. Sean knew the Air Force was trying to reclaim all that, and it was going to be a bitch to remove it from under the walls, but that wasn't his problem.

There was a painted area that apparently was for transfer. Cryder led them over, unslung his ruck, and sat on it.

As he approached, Sean saw the marking was—

"A pentagram," Dalton said.

Raven and Sheridan giggled. Spencer snorted. Caswell rolled her eyes.

Dalton continued, "I really, really don't like that."

Cryder said, "One o' your technal people painted it. Shape has no significance for transfer, only central marking point here." He indicated it. "We found this building on a map and it was a good test. I transitioned approx twelve cemeters high, no scouring or other damage to the ground. Did damage two vehicles in here, and greatly surprised your mechanics."

That explained the flooring. He'd arrived in vehicle maintenance. Sean wondered how that was kept quiet.

Dalton seemed nervous, but walked over and sat with his gear.

Sheridan said, "Technically, it's a pentacle, not a pentagram. Christians used both symbols, even for Sir Gawain, and in Amiens Cathedral, among others."

That did seem to help. Sean wasn't very religious, and this obviously was a joke, but it was really uncool to make a presentation that was going to offend or concern people to no point.

Shug made an odd gesture, but waited patiently, then moved where Cryder pointed.

"Make yourselves ready," Cryder said.

"Go ahead," Sean replied. He looked around at his people and the two technicians. Given the previous experience, he was nervous. The first trip had displaced them 13,000 years or so. The return trip got them within six months. This time the Cogi had been spot on coming back, and both trips forward had been correct.

Cryder said, "It is time ticked for three minutes and nine seconds from now."

They waited. They were reasonably comfortable, but everyone looked nervous. Doc and Spencer gripped their bags. Caswell jittered slightly. The two scientists looked excited—Raven nibbled a knuckle, Sheridan rubbed her hands. Dalton seemed to be praying. Shug kept looking around, with Oglesby keeping a grip on the boy's field harness.

Sean was nervous. Last time hadn't been planned, and the return had been less than precise. This time—

BANG!

They were in the Cogi hangar they'd arrived in last time,

on a flat white painted surface with markings that looked like a landing pad.

This time they fell about three inches to the floor, just like stepping off a curb. He wobbled slightly and regained his footing.

"Welcome, soldiers," he heard.

It was Researcher Alexian Twine from their last visit. She was as tall and elegant as he remembered, wearing what was almost a lab coat over a turtleneck that fit her very well. And she was holding an animal on a harness.

Caswell said, "It's Cal!"

It was the caracal they'd rescued from an injured foot and almost tamed to hang around the camp. He'd followed them to their departure point from the past, and been kept here in the Cogi future.

Cal slunk down out of Twine's arms, came over, and put his paws against Caswell's waist.

"Come here, big fella!" she said, and picked him up to her shoulder.

Sean said, "Hello, Dr. Twine. I didn't expect to see you again."

"Nor I you," she said. "Welcome back. We have your same quarters ready, though you will have slightly more access to things here. You understand we must limit the information you get."

She was certainly courteous.

"Yes, but this seems like a more secure trip."

"We hope it will be. I see your element has changed."

"Yes, ma'am. Sergeant Alexander does not feel up to it. Sergeant Ortiz is running his family's ranch. Petty Officer Trinidad is occupied with family matters. Sergeant Barker is running the joint business he owns with Sergeant Spencer."

"Obviously, there are other obligations besides us. I fully understand. And you have new people."

"Yes, these are doctors Raven and Sheridan. They are biologists, along to study..." He realized he wasn't entirely sure what they did.

Dr. Sheridan said, "We're here to study genotypes of edible flora and the local human population, and potentially of domesticable species. Our other concern is the study of communicable disease vectors, both for historical data expansion and for potential medical development."

"I see," Twine replied. Her expression was carefully neutral. Sean gathered she wasn't thrilled with professional scientists along.

She continued, "And I note you did recover the displacee we identified. A single one?"

He said, "Only one that we know of. This is Shug of River Bend, as best we can translate."

"Shug," she said with a nod.

The boy extended his hand to shake, and she did so. He managed to say, "I am please to meet you."

Introductions apparently done, she said, "Then let's proceed to the lodging." She gestured for them to follow her.

As she led, she said, "Can you tell me more about Trinidad, Alexander, Ortiz, or Barker?"

Spencer said, "Bob and I opened a survival training school. He stayed back to run things. I guess as much as it freaked me out, I really wanted to see this again. Gina is really not emotionally up to the trip. She declined, but sends her wishes."

That was a polite lie, Sean noted. Gina Alexander hadn't said anything. Her husband had made it clear it was "Hell, no." Though she'd be unhappy at missing the cat. Eh. Minor matter.

He added, "Felix is recently married and didn't want to disrupt his family, given the situations in the Philippines. He's trying to move Stateside, but his wife's family has concerns. As far as Ortiz, he's the senior adult on his family's ranch. He's handling livestock."

Raven was wincing, acting like a severe headache, as she said, "Ma'am, to expand more, I'm a forensic paleobiologist. We're concerned about potential contamination, but also how earlier diet and environmental factors affected the human metabolism. Dr. Sheridan covers the other end—the evolution of cultivated preagricultural plants, and feral animal nutritional factors."

"Very well," Twine said with a nod. She didn't seem pleased, but not outright bothered. "I think we can work something out with that. I believe I understand the details of your friends. Please relay my well wishes when you talk to them again. Shuff Cryder, I'll need your input with my council, and I can assist with your leadership."

"Got n thank," he said, reverting to their dialect.

"Here we are," Twine said. "You remember how things work, and the patron will help you."

The dwelling was a large dome, creamy white, with indistinct borders that became distinct as one approached or interacted with them.

"Thank you very much," Sean said. "We hope to get to things soon."

Sean tested. "Good morning, House."

The local AI or whatever replied, "Good afternoon, Captain Elliott. May I call you Sean again?"

"Of course you may. We have two new members."

"Cryder informed me of doctors Raven and Sheridan. May I call you Amalie and Katherine?"

"Please."

"Sure. Or Kate."

He said, "House can provide food, entertainment, privacy screens, help sleeping or waking. Basically a sci-fi butler. Anything at all that you want, he can provide."

This needed to be tested.

Amalie Raven said, "I would like a coffee, medium roast, a quarter liter, with thirty grams of goat butter, please. Also, anything you have equivalent to ibuprofen. I have a headache from the transfer." Gods, did she have a headache. There must have been a pressure change, and the demon with the pitchfork was stabbing her right temple.

The butler replied, "I will provide the coffee at once. I have what you would call a Turkish blend that is full-bodied and less bitter when not sweetened. I can provide ibuprofen in ten minutes, or I have a vasodilator that will work faster."

Well, the . . . entity hadn't stuttered at the request.

"I'm leery," she said. "I have a complicated metabolism and a lot of allergies. That's why I went into biology."

"Please wait a moment," House said.

Twenty seconds later, she heard, "Ma'am?" and turned.

"Yes?" There was a young man in lab coat and pants holding a small kit.

"Greetings. I am a physician. If you will let me scan you, I can determine which limits to impose on the patron."

"Please," she said. That was quick.

The doctor placed a clamp on her hand. It was firm, but not painful, and apparently read the dermis or through it.

"Interesting," the doctor said. "Yes, you do have a complicated set of limitations, but I think we can work around them." He tapped, swiped, and waved at his device. "I have instructed the patron, and the recommended vasodilator should work for you. We also may have a long-term treatment to reduce your headaches, if you're interested."

Oh, did they? "Very. Thank you."

She'd wanted Mars. Her physical condition made being an astronaut impossible. She decided this was a close second.

The coffee arrived on the table next to her, almost as if teleported. She picked it up and took a sip.

Oh, damn, that was good. Definitely full body, creamy, strong, but not sharp, just the right bitterness to offset the butter.

"Very nice," she said to House. She leaned back against her chair and closed her eyes. The room darkened slightly, and she squinted. It was a local effect, a shadow over her.

"You are welcome," he replied. "The medication is in the coffee, and the caffeine will assist in delivery. Interpreting your need, I pushed the caffeine up about thirty percent."

"I can feel it already," she said. It was a rush of cool clarity into the throbbing mass of her brain. "Can I move here?" she joked.

"I am not able to discuss that matter."

"I was joking. But thank you. I'm better faster than I ever have been."

The soldiers seemed to know what they wanted, and were digging in. The younger ones ate in a way that made her jealous. Pie would be great, but her wheat and sugar-sensitive Natchez metabolism didn't allow it. And, she realized, even if they had a workaround, she didn't dare let herself get hooked on sweets. She had to go back to the land of starch and sugar.

However...

"House, I would like a strip steak, seasoned with salt, pepper, and garlic, grilled medium rare, with steamed and buttered broccoli and lots of sauteed mushrooms."

"I will deliver that in ten minutes," the House replied.

"Thank you very much."

"You are welcome, Dr. Raven."

This wasn't Mars. But it might suffice.

Dan took it upon himself to show Shug around. He went first to the bathroom, and said, "House, show us the opaque walls and facilities."

"Certainly, Dan. Here is your wall." The air thickened and

turned translucent, then solid. Shug reached out and touched it. His expression said he understood. It wasn't air, wasn't solid, but worked as a screen.

"This is for waste. This is for washing. This is for hand washing. These people have our same manner, to wash every time after waste, and before eating. The spirits here demand it."

"I will, Dan."

"Please use your words for each, so the...servant can know them." He pointed at shower, sink, toilet, as Shug said the words. "*Vuweh, lowey, kloa.*"

"Now we are here you can undo the clothes you don't want."

"Thank you," he replied in English. Then he switched to his own speech. "I will not boot." It was obviously far more inflected and nuanced, but those were the key words Dan could grasp.

"I know how you feel." He helped the kid unlace the boots and pull them off. Shug sighed and wiggled his toes. And damn, those were impressive callouses.

That done, he led the boy back out.

"These are for sitting. You can lie down on them, and ask for it to be dark to sleep. House, can you demonstrate?"

The chair reclined, the air thickened, and light dimmed. After a few moments it lightened again.

Shug nodded.

"Tell him your word."

"*Zesamay.*"

Then it was to the central table.

"Food comes from here. We will help you, but you can always ask for pictures and point. *Shoreyga?*"

"*Shrega,*" Shug agreed.

"Do you have that, House?" Dan asked.

"I do. I can hear similarities to the language of the Urushu. I do not hear similarities to the Gadorth. I can't speculate further."

"Good. Please help him when we're not available."

"Of course. I deduce his diet will also be high fat and protein, limited starch."

"Correct."

Martin Spencer noted Oglesby helping the poor kid, who was metaphorically a speech-challenged toddler. Shug couldn't have any comprehension of most of the technology around him. Even a wheel wasn't really a normal part of his environment. He was holding up with dignity and courage, though.

Martin forced himself to stop after the one slice of apple pie. He could eat this stuff all day. It was crisp, tartly sweet, very flaky, and would command a high price in a twenty-first-century restaurant. He weighed enough as it was, even not being accountable to Army standards anymore.

He sat down to relax, since the captain hadn't given any specific orders yet, and everyone was in the same space. He did keep an eye out, though.

Caswell was cautiously talking to the two scientists. Doc and Dalton were sort of hanging out. Elliott, like he, was watching everyone. Cal strutted around checking on the humans' doings, and waiting for snacks, probably.

Twine returned a few minutes later.

"I have good news," she announced, as she walked into the central meeting area, between the couches and chairs.

"Yes?" Elliott prompted.

"Our leadership has agreed to you having limited access to the rest of this facility."

"Other parts of the building?"

"Sorry, my English is inexact. This facility has multiple buildings and over ten thousand people. Perhaps 'research village' is closer."

Raven looked interested at once, as did Sheridan.

"This entire community is a research center?" Sheridan asked.

"Yes. I can try to elaborate more. We don't have nations as you think of them. Nor do we have corporations. We have . . . interest groups, who trade their product to others in a network."

"So there's no money?" Dalton asked.

"Oh, there's money, but not in the cash tokens you were already phasing out. Each patron, and the network, keeps track of a person's exchange. The cic—common interest community—has its own net worth, which it distributes to members based on their productivity and interest."

Martin said, "So, citizens are also employees and stockholders? Kuwait was doing that."

"Let me see . . ." She appeared to consult a reference in air, and probably was. "Yes, that's a simplified variation that is adequate to explain the concept."

Caswell asked, "What if you don't like the cic you're in?"

"You can apply and negotiate to join another. Just as you would change jobs or which state or nation you lived in."

"But they are specialized?"

"To a degree. Bykostan and Bykop, the operating leadership, is primarily a technology research operation, in physics, chemistry, astronomy, medicine and now temporality. We do produce engineering output, but also trade the raw knowledge for productivity. But we produce food, art, material goods of our own as well."

"Ah."

"Anyway, of necessity, this temporal research facility is remote, for both security and safety. You are welcome outside, but you must remain within twenty kilometers for now. If you are allowed access your patron will know. If not, you will be informed. The personnel have been informed of your status, and there are subjects you won't be allowed to hear or see."

"Fair enough."

She made a gesture that commanded attention, hand across with a finger wave. "I must caution you that anyone might be studying you. There are designated researchers, as you have met before. There will also be any number of people interested in everything you do. You are not required to interact with anyone you don't feel comfortable with, and the patron can tell you a person's status and relevance. Authorized researchers will identify themselves to you."

Sheridan asked, "How can they observe our natural behavior if we're aware of them?"

She gave a single shake of her head. "Oh, there's enough of that information. If they're studying you, it's your reactions to other things around you, and your learning and interaction process, which wouldn't be significantly affected. I'm socsci, but not that area. At this juncture, I'm acting as host, not case worker."

Martin asked, "What is there to see?"

She turned back to him. "Only a small amount of our culture, not as much as you'd find in the capital or one of the ports. But there are restaurants, some art and music, gardening and architecture. I expect you'll get invites to parties. Those are likely to be taxing or overwhelming. I would suggest a personal escort as well as the patron."

He asked, "Is the patron going to follow all of us?"

House interjected, "My personality can matricise to follow each of you, and share information between each of my parts.

I am not truly a single personality, nor multiple, but more of a gestaltic sensory interface with a personality behind it."

"Well, we must check that out," Martin agreed.

"For science!" Raven added.

"For science, indeed."

Twine said, "The rest of the day is free. Tomorrow, Shuff Cryder and Gajin Arnot will familiarize you with equipment."

House said, "Dr. Raven, your steak is ready. I also have one for Shug, and the BLT for Sergeant Dalton."

Martin said, "And even the quarters aren't bad, as far as hotels go."

Raven already had steak in her mouth, and was cutting the rest up fast. Damn, could she work a knife. Probably a useful skill in a bio lab. The cat was already demanding a piece, and she scratched his ears and fed him a sliver that he snapped down.

She looked very happy. Shug, though, picked his up in his fingers and took a bite, and his expression suggested he really was in the spirit world. His eyes lit up, he made a universal "Mmmm" sound, and proceeded to chew and swallow, and go straight for the next bite.

Dalton's response was only, "They do make a damned good BLT here."

Researcher Twine had left with a polite nod that was not quite a bow. They were alone except for the...patron, which monitored everything. Martin wanted to warn people of that, and realized it should have been brought up ahead of time.

So he said it.

"House hears literally every whisper. If you invoke him, he'll respond. Otherwise, he won't, but everything is still archived for later reference if needed, and I'm going to assume their scientists watch it like we would a zoo."

Sheridan added, "Or like an anthropological study."

That was a nicer term for the same thing, he thought. "Exactly. It's polite not to invoke by name unless you need something, and much more comfortable to just relax and get on with things. Though I still find some discussions to be sensitive and personal around recording devices."

He hoped he'd done that right. He'd phrased it as concern about personal privacy, without actually stating it was a massive COMSEC and OPSEC risk to say anything here.

CHAPTER 6

Shug wasn't sure what all this was. It was even more clever than the things he'd seen so far. All the women were so shapely and lush. They should be having healthy babies. The food thing was delightful. He tried several other foods, though the Voice didn't speak well. He just asked for different meat and was rewarded with a bird, an ox, some sort of something else, another bird, a fish. He then asked for sweetened acorn cake and there was stumbling before it understood. That was good, too. Then a rice cake. An apple, which it understood at once.

He stopped. He wasn't sure what the rules were and he didn't want them angry.

He looked at the flat bench the *solzhes* sat at. There was all kinds of food there, much of it stuff he didn't recognize. Their cooking was very elaborate. He understood aged meat was better, cooked with fire was tastier than boiling, salt made things better, so did a lot of herbs cut from plants. He knew how rice was grown, and fruit. What they had was far beyond his understanding.

He moved close to Dan Speaker, and pointed at his meat then at himself.

Dan said, "Yes, later," but grabbed one of the flat food holders and Shug put his food on it. Dan must have meant, "Yes, here."

He said, "Tank you," their way, and went to sit, but another seat came over for him. Char? A char. He sat on the char, and the eating flat was just the right height. He understood the one implement was for stabbing the meat, and the other thing was a knife, very long, thin, and cunningly made.

The meat was so tender, and cut easily. He lifted up the thing with the meat on it...

Spirits around! That was the tastiest ox he'd ever had. It ran with juice, had salt and other flavorings, and chewed as easily as cooked rice.

Those were mushrooms, also salty and tasty.

He had to find out if it was possible to bring his whole clan here, where the food was free and the lodges were too tall to reach the roof.

This place was even more magical than Dan's place. The shaman speaking from overhead wasn't a total shock. Dan's people had done that. This food was even more wonderful, and the seat that became a bed with perfect darkness but fresh air was truly spiritual.

He missed fire, though. He tried asking the shaman. "Can we have fire?"

The voice replied, "Please, that term not known, speak with Dan."

"Dan?" he asked.

"Yes?"

"Can we have fire?"

"Let me ask." Dan said something in his language, and there was a reply. A spot near the wall cleared, things moved and took shape, and there was a rock-covered hearth that suddenly grew a fire.

"Is that good?"

"Good, Dan, tank you."

If this wasn't the spirit world, how amazing must that be?

Sean Elliott made sure his people, including the civilians and Shug, had food. Oglesby had taken the boy around already.

"Sergeant Caswell?" he called.

She came over at once.

"Yes, sir?"

He asked, "Can you make sure the two civilian women know about the facilities?"

She nodded and agreed, "Certainly. I've shown them everything except how to activate sleep quarters. I don't think that will be tough. Dr. Raven is already testing the limits of House's capabilities."

"Yeah, on the one hand, I'm glad they're smart. On the other hand, they might be too smart, and not used to taking orders."

On the one hand, he liked knowing they might find useful information from the past, or even hypothetically from the future. On the other, he didn't want to irritate the Bykos, and he didn't like having civilians treading over his military operation.

Caswell said, "I've considered that, too. I'll try to bring it up in conversation."

"Thanks, please do. Enjoy dinner."

She half smiled. "I already was, but thanks."

It was nice to have a fire, in what looked like a stone fireplace. He decided to go with steak himself. Though tomorrow he might have pizza. It was a very nice perk to be getting per diem based on rations not available, and to have the best restaurant he'd ever eaten at ready to serve anything at all.

His steak arrived, and he ate at the table with Dr. Sheridan, Doc, and Spencer.

"How is everyone acclimating or reacclimating so far?" he asked.

Doc said, "Awesome, sir. I feel a lot more confident this time."

Spencer finished a bite of chicken and said, "Yeah, I'm not terrified of being left behind yet. The food is good. We're better prepared."

Sheridan looked around. "For what's basically a holding cell, this is amazing. I'll have to watch what I eat. I'm heavy enough as is. Hopefully we'll be doing some walking."

"What do you think of the people?"

She admitted, "They're all really tall and disgustingly attractive. I feel like a dwarf."

He agreed, "Yeah, we never got used to the height."

Sheridan started talking. "It's got to be partly diet and development. I'd need to know time frame to determine if any evolutionary strains have had time to effect. Then of course there's the possibility of genetic manipulation, or in vivo or even in vitro chromosomal..." She looked at the soldiers. "Okay, there's all kinds of possible factors and I could talk all day."

Sean laughed. "That's fine. I'm glad you're enthused about the project."

"Very," she agreed.

Sean was glad of Spencer's reminder on being overheard. There was literally no way to have a conversation private from their hosts, and if the Byko or whatever were along on this recovery mission, then everything for the duration was intel for a foreign government. It might be a somewhat friendly, somewhat allied government, but it had its own agenda, and the US had to keep as much separation as possible. He was only a captain. The Byko might know everything they needed from history. Or he might have intel that would work against their or his nation's interests. No one must slip a word, and he couldn't really say that, though it would be better to do so than risk leaks. He'd do so if he felt it necessary, and the hell with risking offense to the hosts. After all, they had plenty of their secrets.

In fact...

"Listen up. Reiterating what Sergeant Spencer said, our hosts have certain information they can't share with us for their own reasons. We also have information we will not share. If in doubt, keep silent." There.

"Sergeant Spencer, Doctors, please come here for a meeting."

Devereaux asked, "Including me, sir?"

"You are a doctor and an officer. Please." He very much wanted the man to be comfortable acting as an officer.

"Thank you, sir."

He nodded back, and waved the couches over. House could even respond to certain nonverbal cues.

His leadership staff—which was most of the group.

He raised his voice and added, "In fact, we're small enough we'll just go with all personnel for these. Everyone grab a drink and get comfortable. We've got some updates to discuss."

In short order, the troops had beverages and were sitting in a group, except for Raven.

"I don't sit well," she said. "I need to pace, if you can allow it."

"I guess," he said. He didn't like people lurking around, but she was a civilian scientist and they had some quirks. He'd deal with it.

"Okay, we're going to have some local access here. I want everyone to keep under control, even though I know our hosts will help with that. We shouldn't need them. Then, we already have a training schedule before hopping back. If we're learning their equipment, that shows a level of trust."

Sheridan said, "It does, but I also assume we won't be able to figure out the technical specs behind their operation. So they're not risking much."

"That reassures me," Sean said. "I don't want them deciding they need to detain us, erase memories, whatever."

He moved on with, "Okay, going around, thoughts?"

From the back, Raven said, "So if I had to guess, 'Shuff' is something akin to 'Chief.' The inflection on 'gajin' suggests it's 'guardian.' A leader and an enlisted."

"That's plausible," Oglesby agreed. "Why not just ask?"

"This way I have a hypothesis to test. I like learning languages."

"Hmm. True. So do I."

Sean had just ended the meeting when the door chimed and Cryder entered with Arnet, his subordinate from the previous time travel. They were in what might be an official uniform in bright orange and red. The cut was flattering. The colors were absolutely to draw attention. He figured that was on purpose.

"Hello, Captain, troops," he greeted.

"Hey, Cryder, and Arnet," Doc replied.

"Torand is fine, or Tor. We're two elments and don't have one line of command."

Arnet said, "Rusen or Rus is fine." He still looked odd to Sean's eye. He was definitely male. They'd all seen him naked in camp. But he looked strange for some reason. His entire stature and bearing weren't quite right. He didn't look feminine either, so that wasn't it. The shorter of the two, he was only 6'3". He shook hands all around with a firm grip.

Sean said, "We remember, but we'll probably be a little formal by default."

Cryder said, "You will all need to be trained on our field vehicle and on tools, in case of emergency."

"Good idea." He was pleased they were going to share that sort of information.

"We have a training range nearby outside."

"Outside?"

The man explained, "In a wilderness area, not far from the facility."

"Oh, cool."

"Can we start tomorrow morning? On your clock, it would be oh nine hundred."

"That is perfectly doable. Do you wish to depart here at that time, or be training at that time?"

The man said, "Depart from right here at that time."

"We can do so."

"Excellent. We'll leave you to settle in."

It was later in the day here than it had been back home, but they were all still a bit off from time zone changes, so what was one more?

"We'll sleep until oh seven hundred local, which gives everyone two hours for hygiene and breakfast. Until then, let's show the new folks what amenities there are—video, games, everything."

"And pet the cat," Caswell said. Cal was enjoying something from the server that looked like it might be liver.

"And pet the cat. We found Cal injured, managed to treat his paw, tossed him some scraps, and he domesticated himself enough to bring us food—rabbits, birds, decent-sized stuff. Of course, he also sprayed urine on every vehicle and hooch."

"As cats do," Raven said. She went over to look at him.

"As cats do."

"He's very handsome," she agreed. "Definitely a caracal, and definitely different from modern breeds. His ears have more tuft, and the hair seems thicker, though with a single specimen I can't make a solid call."

Sheridan said, "We could check DNA from his fur."

"Sure, good practice. He's from that era, so he's within our scope."

Sheridan already had a few hairs and took them to be tagged.

They were an odd pair. Nerdy as all get out, but they obviously liked the cat as a cat, too. Sean thought he understood. The entire world was a puzzle for them to solve.

Sheridan said, "This plus the hide you guys brought back gives us two single specimens to compare against change rates. Which of itself doesn't tell us much, but if we can find others, even different species, the delta R might give some hints as to climate-induced variance."

He almost understood that.

He realized his brain was foggy for other reasons.

"Doc, Sergeant Spencer, I'm going to lie down early. I may be up early. Can you take charge until mandatory lights out at 2300, and wake me if needed?"

Doc nodded soberly and said, "I can, sir. And mandatory means no one wandering around after that. Sleeping quarters only, and make a solid effort to sleep. House can assist you."

Spencer added, "I'll back him up as needed."

"Great, thanks." Sean hit the latrine, walked to his couch. "Private, please," he said. The walls turned opaque, he stripped to underwear, and said, "Dark," as he crawled onto the couch and felt it soften into half bed, half recliner. It was utterly black.

"Can I get a soft lightshow, please?" he asked.

"Will a view of the evening stars please you?"

"That's perfect, House, thank you."

"You are welcome. Sleep well, Sean."

Overhead, the sky turned to twinkling points of stars and deep washes of more distant ones. He tried to pick out any he recognized and fell asleep.

Rich Dalton liked the late morning. He was fresh and alert at 0700, House having tweaked the light and sound so he just woke up on his own. There was no PT scheduled, so he hit the latrine, changed into clean clothes, and went for breakfast.

"Hey, House, can I get steak and over-easy eggs with onion?"

"Certainly."

"Thanks a bunch."

He found a spot next to Dr. Sheridan, who was eating fruit and a single pancake. Next to her, Dr. Raven had scrambled eggs, a slab of ham, and very black coffee. Most of the troops had variations on pancakes and bacon or sausage, Sergeant Spencer had biscuits and gravy. That looked pretty good. Shug seemed thrilled with fresh strawberries and thick-cut bacon. The cat patrolled around, paws on laps, demanding tribute. He shrugged and gave the creature a bite.

Spencer took charge and said, "Soldiers—and we're going to use that generic for our contractors, guest, and USAF element as well—we've got an hour. We're familiarizing with Cogi equipment and some of us will be involved in planning the transition to find our lost element. Feel free to enjoy the hospitality, but unlike last time of reacculturating, we're here for a mission, no matter how awesome the field conditions are at present. Do any cleanup you need. We should be ready fifteen minutes early."

That was simple enough. He repacked some of his gear that

got loose. Then he asked, "House, can I get these clothes cleaned?" He may as well have everything as neat as possible.

"Yes, please place them on the servace."

"Servace. Serving surface?"

"That is correct."

"Will do. Thank you very much."

He hung out on a couch and did nothing while people took care of similar details. The clothes were back, clean and dry, in under five minutes.

Cryder arrived at exactly 0900, per the clock readout on the wall. He was in a gray field uniform that seemed to be separate blouse and pants, but melded together.

The man said, "If you're ready, this way, please."

He added, "Shug," and the young man tensed. "Please stay here, the patron will help you."

The captain led the way, Spencer brought up the rear after Rich. The contractor chicks were ahead. They followed a blinking light down the walkway, into a corridor, and outside into a clear day, sun rising. He got the impression it was early summer here.

He realized it was the first time he'd been outside in their world.

Shug wondered what he should do, with the Amercans away with the others. He had the entire large hut to himself.

"Do I what?" he asked.

The shaman said, "I can show pictures. Mountains? Trees?"

"Paintings of trees?"

"Better than paintings. Watch."

The wall flickered as with sunlight, and Shug saw a mountain and forest. He said, "Ohh!" and ran over, only to bump into the wall.

It really was just a painting, but it was the most real painting he'd ever seen. It was nothing like a lodge or cave painting. It seemed completely real.

"River!" he said.

"Please explain."

"Water moving on ground and rocks." He waved his hands to demonstrate.

"I understand."

At once, Shug saw a river so real he had to reach out and reassure himself this was still a painting on a wall.

How wonderful must the spirit world be, if this wasn't it?

The fire was still burning, with the smoke all going away, no puffs to sting the eyes. He could bathe under hot rain any time he wished. Now was a good time. The strange clothes took some struggle. The flat toggles were awkward, and the zippar was a wonderful but strange thing.

He asked for more food, and the shaman said, "You should stop with sweets and eat meat and plants." That was good advice. He almost felt ill from all the sweets.

Then he went back to the pictures, of anything he liked, any season, any weather. He could watch a beautiful bangstorm from here and stay dry. Snow-covered hills were even prettier when you didn't have to stand in the cold.

It was a good day.

CHAPTER 7

Sean was very pleased with how smoothly this was going with a hand-selected element of professionals. No layabouts, no one rushing up with fast food, no one hungover or half out of uniform. God, it was great.

The floating egg that approached on the ground was obviously a bus. It settled, the side opened, and Sean saw there actually was a seam for the door, it was just very fine. It made sense that their engineering was better and allowed tighter tolerances.

He stepped in and up, and the seats were almost couches. The control console had no driver, but it did have a seat for one. He took the seat behind that, sat down, and sank into it.

"Wow," he said. He'd been in expensive recliners that weren't as comfortable. It wasn't overly large, though. A lot larger than commercial airliner or bus, as far as the seat went, but the footprint wasn't excessive.

The troops came in, followed by the scientists. Everyone had the same pleased response he did.

Arnet and Cryder came up last. Arnet flopped into the driver's seat and said, "Port," and the vehicle started moving, while rising slightly off the ground. It did feel like an air cushion.

After that, though, Arnet turned to face the rest.

"We're going to a separate site for training. It's in the wilderness about fifty kilometers from here. It's a range spefically for weapons and wilderness training."

"Do we need the latter?" Doc asked.

Arnet actually laughed. "No, course not. But we'll look at some stuff and try the weapons."

"Sweet!" Caswell let out. "I do want to try yours."

They quickly reached what was apparently a heliport, and those looked like sci-fi helicopters.

The bus slowed and stopped. Arnet stood, the door opened, and Cryder went straight out to the aircraft.

Sean tried to stand up and thought he was trapped. He tensed for a moment before he realized the seat was just that soft and encompassing. He changed posture, pushed, and came right out.

As he debarked, he realized the bus had been about as silent as the Cogi military vehicle.

The aircraft wasn't quite as appointed as the bus. It obviously was meant for efficiency and mass savings. Still, it was far better than a C-130. He sat in a seat facing forward, with a port next to him.

This craft made some noise as they lifted. It moved on ducted fans, but he had no idea of the power source. If it was anything like the vehicle the Cogi had in the Paleolithic, they'd spoken of several years of onboard power, which implied nuclear or something even more sophisticated.

They lifted on a short roll, rose fast enough he could feel the G, and leveled out. Everyone was glued to the ports, watching the liftoff.

Once in the air, he had a glimpse of the tech village, which was on a broad plain with islands of forest, and some sort of lake to the west. A large one. They were heading south, and he could see a river off to the southeast.

About as fast as they reached cruise, they started the descent. Really, at any kind of aircraft speed, it wasn't a long flight. He timed it at under six minutes on his watch.

The terrain below was now all forest, with occasional clearings. The one they were landing in was a rise in the terrain, not really a hill.

The forward velocity shed and turned into a downward vector, then slowed and they settled to the ground. Within seconds, the two Cogi had the hatch open and were around back, where they opened that part of the shell and started pulling out crates. Behind that was a big cargo hatch that would almost split the craft in two.

Arnet pointed as he pulled gear. "We'll take an armament each, and two vehicles with support equipment. We can plan on supplemental food, premade food, and plenty of power this time. We'll have what we call field conditions, not what the Romans call."

"Sounds good." Damn, it was clean out here. Beautiful sky, air fresher than the mountains of Montana. Not a sound or sight of another human being.

Cryder said, "For now, this is a good starting point. We'll run a target down the range."

He dropped a device that quite literally ran down the range, planted wires in the ground, and erected itself into a target.

He held up the amorphous object with a grip that they knew was a weapon.

"This is the Arm-9. It sets as single projo, adjusts from prox thirteen to eight thou newtmers."

Spencer said, "Wait, let me see if I've got that. One projectile. Muzzle energy anywhere between thirteen and eight thousand newton meters. Which . . . hold on . . . nine to six thousand foot-pounds."

"I guess," Cryder said. "Your first part was correct. Dunno your measurements."

Dr. Raven said, "Yeah, that's correct for conversion. Damn. So it can go from pellet rifle to elephant gun. Nice."

Cryder nodded and resumed. "Point at target, grip, press here, focus, and weapon adjusts." It flowed into a more linear shape.

"Squeeze."

There was a crack of a supersonic bullet, but no muzzle blast. The target registered a hit by changing color from white to red and rolling over. Then it stood back up.

"There're other settings, we'll just use this. Try."

He thrust it at Sean.

Sean grabbed it reflexively, tried not to look intimidated, and did as he'd been shown. He raised the weapon, gripped and pressed, and it shifted. He kept hold of it as it writhed, trying to avoid dropping it. He didn't like his guns to squirm.

It settled out, but didn't look quite right.

"No, not that. Press a bit higher."

He did so, and it lengthened more.

"That's it."

He pointed at the target, found a sight channel, aimed and squeezed.

It banged like a blank, thumped mildly against his shoulder, and the target reacted.

"Again?" he asked.

"Certainly."

He fired again, then one more.

Arnet said, "We'll do more later. Next."

Dalton stepped up, and after a few seconds' familiarization very smoothly raised and shot. The target reacted, bounced, and reset. Really, it seemed like a very instinctive, intuitive weapon.

Caswell stepped up and placed four shots, as fast as the target could reset. She'd always been very effective with a rifle.

Oglesby took it next. He hefted it, raised it, gripped, squeezed, and it morphed. That wasn't it. He started over. He got it the second time, and shot, though not quite as centered as the rest. Arnet and Cryder nodded. Arnet said, "Good enough."

Sean asked, "Do you ladies want to try?"

"Duh," Raven said. She stepped forward.

Oglesby handed her the weapon.

Raven hefted the device, looked very professionally scientific, shifted her stance, and it melted into gun form.

Crack, crack, crack.

The target tumbled and reset between each. The color splash indicated solid hits.

"Oh, I like it," she said and giggled cheerfully. "This would go great next to my Krieghoff .375 double."

Jesus. Sean had an idea what a Krieghoff double rifle cost. She certainly was well paid.

Sheridan took over, and the weapon flowed instantly into shape. Her shooting was so-so, but she had no trouble at all with the mechanism.

Doc was as effective. It looked like the younger and techy types had better instincts for it.

Spencer stepped up last, took the device from Doc. It flowed back to neutral again. He got into a good stance, raised the weapon, and shifted his grip.

It stretched and formed into something thick barreled and vicious looking.

"HALT! Not that!" Cryder snapped.

"Roger," Spencer agreed. He lowered it, raised it, gripped again.

This time it half flowed into shape, then stopped.

Sighing, he lowered it, shifted his grip, raised it again. This time it shaped into something squarer and boxier.

Arnet said, "I don't think that's anything. It's sort of halfway."

Spencer nodded with some frustration, shook his hands, raised the weapon again.

Nothing happened at all.

No one laughed. They'd all felt the interface and knew it was based on specific touch.

"Is there a button or something I can press instead?"

Arnet took the weapon, said, "Right there." He pressed and it shifted into form.

Spencer nodded and sighed again, took it in hand, pressed, and got the first shape again.

"Argh," he muttered.

Again, and once more.

Martin Spencer picked up the device again, and thought hard about a rifle. He tried to grip it the right way, and it shifted slightly, then stopped, solid.

"Still not working," he said. It was really fucking aggravating. It was like gaming. The kids just grabbed it and went. He shoved and pulled and twisted and nothing happened.

Cryder said, "You should put yourself in the mindset of shooting."

"I'm *doing* that!"

He sighed, relaxed, tried to clear his mind. He saw the target, estimated range, raised the device, shouldered and cheeked and thought about the shot, and the trigger squeeze . . .

It shifted, morphed, and turned into a . . . something. But not a weapon.

Giving up, he said, "Look, this isn't working. Can you print me some guns based on developments in my era? We'll take them along for backup if space allows. Otherwise, I guess I make do without."

Cryder said, "We can produce them. I assume you meant using whatever tech is appropriate, not printing specifically."

"Yes. I want these. Hold on." He got his phone out and struggled through that. Gadgets were really not his thing. He liked simple devices. He plugged in a memory stick. He copied technical data packages for an AR-10, and a DRD Kivaari in .338 Lapua Magnum to the memory stick, then added a .45-caliber Glock Model 30. He brought the AR-10 up on screen.

"Can you do that?" he asked.

"Easily," Cryder assured him. "You should keep working on the proj, though."

"I will. I just want things I know will work if I'm in a hurry and tense."

The man nodded and didn't criticize. "Reasonable," he agreed.

Elliott asked, "So how does the stun setting work?"

"It causes unconsciousness for a range of time."

The commander followed with, "Right, but what does it feel like?"

"Oh, like this." Cryder raised the weapon, and it morphed.

Elliott said, "Wai—"

Martin didn't like the grin on the man's face, and turned. He was two steps into a sprint when . . .

Shaking his head, he woke up from a nap. Oh, right. Stunned. Felt like a nap. Awake. His boots were tangled across each other and in the weeds, and his face was in a clump of grass. His wrist ached slightly.

"Motherfucker. Was that a joke?" He pushed himself to a sitting position.

"Your commander asked what it was like. Now you all know."

"How long?"

"About four minutes."

He was moderately pissed. That wasn't cool at all. Elliott looked both embarrassed and angry. The rest all looked angry.

Raven looked as if she was devising some neurotoxin to slip to Cryder and cause him to collapse into convulsions.

"Don't you test nonlethal weapons for effect, for understanding?"

"We do a test with tear gas. I guess some police test their electrical weapons."

"As I deduced. You're all unharmed and recovered quickly."

Yeah. This was a different culture, and the test was logical, but he didn't like that approach at all.

He stood up carefully, and felt okay. The side effects weren't terrible, but the ground seemed to sway a bit.

He followed the Cogi back to the aircraft for the vehicles, and swapped a glance with Elliott, and then with Raven. Yeah, they were all thinking it.

The vehicles by contrast were not only easy to drive, they had a typically military illustrated manual. One was accessible on the vehicle's computer system. The other was printed on untearable pages.

"Who does the vehicle respond to?" Dalton asked.

Arnet said, "All of us are authorized users. It will not respond to any locals or other Americans."

"Good."

"Let me show you the basic operation." He leaned in through the door and pointed. "This is the start button. I think you are familiar with the manual controls of steering, brake, and throttle control."

Martin said, "Those are mostly familiar. Though we use a wheel, not a tiller."

"A wheel is available for road, and you can adjust the steering ratio here or by voice command, so as to prevent over- or understeer."

"I like it."

"This is the camouflige and color control for the skin."

Martin corrected with, "Camouflage, or just camo."

"Thank you. It's unlikely anything we encounter can damage the vehicle."

"How unlikely?"

"One of those charging rhinos or a mammoth might damage the suspension. A large enough rock will damage the shell. None of your group's weapons will affect it, though the launched grenades might degrade the wheels."

"Okay."

So it was stronger than a WWII tank, the size of a HMMWV, and looked like a futuristic SUV.

They each took a turn driving around the clearing, then across and back, with Arnet in the second seat as instructor.

Martin had no issues this time and felt reassured. The vehicle was simpler and more familiar. He steered, gassed, braked. The details of how it worked could wait.

Once they all had a vehicle run, Arnet gave a quick lecture on the accessories.

"Roller One has the shower, sink, and commode setup. This is slightly more elaborate than what we had last time. It also has the onboard manufactory for producing materials. Roller Two has more elaborate fabrication facilities and a portable kitchen. Both can sleep four in the seats and two in the bed, but we will also have individual shelters for the field."

"Will we still need to hunt?"

The man said, "If you wish fresh meat, you can hunt. It's capable of furnishing basic nutrient biscuits, cookpiling some basic meals, and we'll take reconstituted rations as well."

Well. He said, "This certainly sounds much more comfortable than last time."

Arnet assured him, "You did impressively well last time, even without our equipment."

Doc asked, "This can produce medicine and chemicals like last time?"

The man nodded. "Yes, that is a standard feature."

"Good."

It was a hell of a feature, too. Toss mineral-rich rocks in the back, along with organic material, and it could produce basic medications, liquor, medical alcohol, certain food, fuel. Every field maintenance unit should have that.

Cryder took over for the next class.

Rich Dalton was enjoying the show so far. No formation BS, no slackers late for formation, no mandatory fun. Just professionals gathering for a class. The gear was top notch, too. He was still annoyed at being stunned, though. That was crap.

Cryder reached into the vehicle and pulled out another item. "These are individual shelters. Pull here, twist like this, and shake."

It turned into a bivvy bag with overhead cover. It even had ties that looked like they turned it into a hammock.

Arnet pointed at the fittings. "Fasten down or tie to a tree. It will insulate to minus forty-five degrees, and can cool effectively up to forty degrees. The capacitor will need to be charged after five days. Shade can lengthen that to seven."

Rich blurted, "Damn, that's impressive. And padded?"

"Not as well as a bed, but it should be plenty for you."

He knew how comfortable a bed here was. That should be fine.

"Also, it adds additional barrier factor. It will stop your personal arms while expanded. When compressed, it is worn on the front of the harness and will stop your lighter support weapons."

"Holy crap!" he exclaimed.

He suddenly understood the harnesses the Cogi wore. All their gear attached to it, all served at least two purposes, and minimized weight. They'd solved the power issue as well. He remembered these two guys had survived for nine months, apparently comfortably, with the gear in their vehicle, before they'd come looking for the Americans.

Cryder explained the harness, which was different from MOLLE gear, but analogous. All the fabric offered some level of ballistic protection. They had insertable plates for both pockets in the uniform, and the load harness.

Captain Elliott said, "If I get these numbers right, these will stop a fifty cal. You'll probably be knocked sprawling, but it won't penetrate, and will disperse the impact all over."

That was impressive, too. "Damn."

Next were night-vision devices that were also daytime magnifiers, like the AN/PVS the snipers used. They went over the eyes basically like shades, though were a bit thicker. Far less bulky than US-issue NODS, however.

"This enhances automatically for low light. You can press here to switch to thermal imagery, or combine both with the onboard process to provide best mix."

There were knives and machetes available, or they could bring their own. Cryder handed each of them an analog to a modern cell phone, with similar controls, to use as in-unit communication in the field.

"I guess we don't have to worry about anyone cracking our signal back then."

Cryder agreed, "Right. Though these are encrypted."

He continued, "As last time, we will have tethered recon. We will also have deployable drones. I plan to take extra, within our mass capacity, to ensure adequate resources."

"Definitely those."

The man pointed at his fingers. "Yes, but they must be balanced with rations, supplies for the recuperees, onboard water capacity, fuel and ammunition, and other support gear."

"Well, I'll work with whatever you can bring and be happy." He would. They already had better equipment than he'd ever had in the field.

"We will return to the facility and end for the day. Can you assist in stowing gear?" He looked directly at Rich.

"Absolutely."

They were wearing headsets that wrapped very lightly around the ears, weighed no more than earrings, and apparently included a directional mic.

"Comms, Arnet, broad, test to element."

His voice was perfectly clear in Rich's ears, starting with "Arnet."

The captain said, "Comms, Elliott, responding, audio is perfect. How do you receive?"

"Also perfect. Just talk when you need it, and preface with 'Comms' as you did. It is reasonably good at determining intent. Identify yourself, then address whom you wish. It correctly interpreted 'responding' to me. Did anyone else hear it?"

Dalton shook his head. "Negative." The rest concurred.

"It works that directly from your end. The explanation is more complex."

Amalie Raven was tired when they returned to the village and their dorm. Shug sat in front of a screen showing a documentary of lions stalking gazelles. He turned, smiled, waved, and said something that House loosely translated as "I have watched pictures. It is interesting."

"I bet." It was good he had something to do. She'd been worried for him. There was no reason to train him in anything technical, and good reasons to not let him see anything outside his era.

She was actually surprised at how much *she'd* been allowed to see so far. It was a good thing they apparently hadn't checked her history and seen her other PhD. Nor all her secondary training in aerospace engineering. She was absolutely the last person they wanted to see their gadgets up close. Which was, of course, why she was here. She found the biology at least as interesting, but the US's interests were far more in the tech.

That also left her a moral quandary on what she should actually pass on if she found anything of interest. Though first she'd have to theorize the functions she'd seen. That was going to take time, and had to be entirely mental. She dare not put any notes on paper or device. Numbers, possibly. Text, not at all.

The soldiers thought their mission was important, and it was. However, their secondary mission was to support her while she dug into future tech and the biology of both past and future. They couldn't be informed, either.

She wished she drank, and was glad she couldn't.

━ CHAPTER 8 ━

The next morning, Armand Devereaux went with Arnet to get a primer on the future medical gear. He was in awe.

They'd perfected the autodoc. Well, maybe not perfected, but they had autodocs.

They were in another part of the hangar/dorm/transfer point, at what was apparently a support gear warehouse with learning aids. Everything had a slot, but it was wide open generally. On the other hand, he knew a frame or visual block could be asked for and appear in seconds.

With a training dummy for demonstration, Arnet explained, "Immediately control any bleeding. Apply the mask to the victim's face like so. Attach these sensors to any pulse point or, if none are reachable, the center of the bare chest." He ripped open the clothes on the dummy.

"The system will treat for shock, ensure breathing. If in doubt as to cardiac function, apply these to the chest here and here. You are familiar with defibrillation?"

"Yes, that part is familiar."

"Then apply this module over any vein. Attach using these straps. If necessary, it will provide IV medications, fluids, plasma, or simulated corpuscles. Then proceed to seal any damaged vessels. This is the linear knitter, this is the cross knitter for amputations or deep lacerations."

One carefully moved the probe through the flesh, a bit like

cutting soft cake so as not to break it, and the tool sealed the flesh as it went. He practiced several times on the dummy that seemed to be actual flesh, and possibly was. It had no head, so he assumed it wasn't actually a person, but it certainly seemed as if it was lab raised for practice. That was a bit creepy.

"The readings are pulse, respiration, blood pressure, ECG, EEG, and NCC."

"NCC?"

"Neural continuity check, from the remote probes to the central nervous system."

He thought he got it.

He said, "If I understand correctly, that advises if there's any significant trauma to the spinal cord."

Arnet nodded. "Correct. There are limited nano restructuring measures in the unit. Beyond that, stabilize and evacuate to the best available facility, which will be here at the end of the duration."

"Better than permanent paralysis. I assume any damage is repairable here?"

The man replied, "Neural disconnections? Trivially. The important thing is to ensure circulatory integrity for the CNS, integrity of the CNS, and function or support of the cardiovascular organs. All else can be managed."

Wow. Impressive. "Awesome. You've automated half my job. The important part."

"There are plenty of other field medical tasks."

He agreed, "I wasn't complaining, my man. I'm thrilled."

Here, at least, everyone including the Cogi was aware of his field credentials in medicine, and wouldn't denigrate him. Better tools just meant more lives saved, if it came to using them.

Which always brought him back to the dichotomy of wishing everyone well, and hoping to do his job.

Kate Sheridan felt strain. She knew she was too gregarious, and really couldn't be here. She was tasked with finding real data for the contemporary science community, and its source would have to be disguised and carefully presented. The data was critical for disease vector study, though, and for potential spectrum cures. That was easy enough.

The second part was finding out everything they could about

the Cogi, to try to pin down where and when they were, and what might have happened genetically between her time and theirs. Raven was critical to that, more discreet, and would be trying to acquire that data, also. Which meant Kate's duties included being gregarious and harmless appearing for their hosts, without actually letting anything slip, and without contrasting too much with the younger woman and her functions.

Growing up she'd always loved stories about spies, and that drove her into investigations. She adored finding and sequencing data, and felt accomplished when it helped with either criminal apprehension or scientific discovery. Being an actual spy, though, even at this low level, was mentally challenging and hard on her sense of humor and self-control.

She was also sure Raven had yet another purpose, based on her background. She couldn't ask. Even if there wasn't complete surveillance in progress.

Sitting in the common area of the dorm, getting familiar with the Cogi phone and her laptop, she tried to make a point about their official bio research.

She asked Raven, "You have their pre-deployment charts, yes?"

The woman looked up from her own screen. "Pre-deployment, in theater, and now post-arrival. I'm logging all of it. I've also already got their previous event's data, and their baselines before that."

"I know, I just get antsy and like reassurance."

"That's fine. But that's all confirmed and we don't need to rehash it."

Raven was telling her not to keep bringing it up. Fair enough.

"Got it. We'll track what you find here, about everyone."

"Obviously, and we don't need to discuss that, either."

She sighed. This was utterly fascinating, and she couldn't breathe a word until they were home, then only in their study group.

"I may ask, just for clarification and to refresh at each stage. You know I can be forgetful."

Raven gave her a glance, interpreted the message correctly and said, "Sure. That's fine."

Kate didn't forget anything technical. Regular attention on their safe data, though, might help keep the clandestine research unmentioned and out of sight.

Remembering to think about people as people, she asked, "How are your headaches?"

Her associate smiled. "Fantastic. Whatever they dope the coffee with shuts them right down. That, and I think they have at least some weather control. Smoothing out the pressure drops reduces the triggers tremendously. I'm aware of changes, but not hindered by them."

"Good to hear. If that's something usable, think you can get on the list for Mars?"

Raven half frowned with a twisted lip.

"Not with my leg. Even if that's fixed, not with my metabolism. I am good at what I do, we both are. But they're only taking top physical specimens first."

"Hopefully they can get to us soon enough."

"Hopefully. I'm probably eligible, past those issues, for another fifteen years. You?"

She shrugged. "Maybe ten. I have no expectation of making it."

"Neither do I, but goddammit, we have to try."

"We do."

At least they could agree on that, and work well enough professionally. Though the woman's default arrogance and apparent hatred of people generally made her hard to deal with.

The end result was lots of good data, and they both knew it. Then, possibly a paper that would get them more recognition.

They were interrupted by Devereaux returning.

"Ladies!" he greeted.

"Hi, Armand," she replied.

"How were things here?"

"More science administration."

"Ah, the fun part of your mission."

She smirked. "Yeah. Not."

Interested as he was, he was a potential risk since he would understand a lot of the data. He should be solidly on their side, but her orders were to trust no one. It wasn't the catchphrase it had been on TV. It was a real thing.

She wondered what it was going to be like when they were actually in the Paleolithic.

Shug had no idea what these other people were up to, nor what Dan and the Amercans were doing here. He knew none of their language, and didn't recognize any of their magic tools. This was inside, but the most huge lodge he could imagine, even bigger than the great one the Amercans had. Even without fire the temperature was perfect. It also wasn't hot from the sun. The food was cooked somewhere and brought here magically.

The others were all off doing magic things and he was alone. He had pictures to watch and he could ask about them.

He sighed. He knew there was everything to learn, but they knew more than the wisest elders in the village. There was nothing they needed. They had shelter, water, food, sweets, clothes, more clothes, fancy clothes, shoes that would stop any rock, moving huts that could travel anywhere very quickly. The beds were more comfortable than he ever dreamed of, softer than twenty well-tanned elk hides. There were no predators. No one was sick. Everyone had all their teeth. It was a paradise, but they were so urgent about taking him back home, and about other things he didn't grasp.

Kate and Amalie had a title that he interpreted as meaning they were shamans. They both looked around as he did, but seemed to know what they were looking at in this strange land. They had to be exceedingly wise. Armand had the same title, and obviously knew a lot of things. He was from somewhere else, with that dark skin. No one Shug ever met looked like that.

He was bored. There was nothing for him to do until they took him back. The shaman with the magic voice provided him samples of every food and drink he could try, and he was too full for more. There was nothing else to do here. He tired of looking at paintings of outside, without being outside. He joined the Amercans when they exercised, though it was very little exercise, really. Then he had answered two questions and off they went. He sat on one of the chairs and let his mind rest, just like when hunting. If something happened, he'd alert. Until then, he'd wait. He did find the tame smallcat to be interesting. It didn't seem as useful as a dog, but it was friendly.

CHAPTER 9

The third day took care of final issue of gear for the redeployment to the past.

In their lodging, Arnet showed up leading a powered dolly with a box. It held US Army MultiCam uniforms.

The man said, "These uniforms are made of our textile, modified to appear as yours. Again, these will stop small arms and any native impact weapons. You have three each, patterned from your own. That helps minimize mass while allowing plenty of wear. They can be washed in water, air dried, and reused. The boots are also sturdier than your own."

Sean Elliott said, "Sounds good. We'll want to try everything on to see how it fits and feels."

"Please do. The patron can assist if anything needs adjusted."

"When do we head back in time?"

Arnet said, "In a little over two days."

"Is there more training we can do?"

Headshake. "None is necessary. You can do whatever you feel you need to. There is recreation time." His presentation was relaxed, but so different from their own that it took a moment to process that.

Dalton piped up enthusiastically. "That sounds good. Predeparture pass. What do you think, sir?"

Sean said, "I will consider it carefully, discuss it with Sergeant Spencer, and let you all know. Sergeant Spencer, with me, please."

"Right away, sir." The NCO hurried over.

Then he said, "House, private for us, please."

"At once," the system replied, and the air shimmered as everything got quiet.

"I plan to say 'yes.'" Sean grinned. "I just want to double-check with you."

Spencer noted, "They've done good work this week, sir, both home and here. We're ready to go. I also think as much as we can see, especially in a relaxed state, is good for...social connectivity."

Sean decided Spencer meant it was good intel gathering, and wasn't going to say that where it could be heard, which was anywhere.

"Very good. We'll set a curfew?"

"Yes, how about a late formation of ten hundred tomorrow morning, and a return time of oh three hundred local?"

"That works. If anyone needs to be out longer they can let me know. House, we're done."

The air shimmered and he relayed the orders.

Doc said, "To confirm, we're free until oh three hundred, formation at ten hundred, variations can be approved by you."

"Correct. This also applies to civilians under my control."

"As expected," Sheridan agreed. Raven just nodded.

Doc replied, "Right. Then my standard safety briefing is going to be nonstandard."

"Go ahead."

"Be careful what you eat or drink, make sure to ask about any intoxicants. I gather they have a lot. Don't overeat. Ask House for advice. If you plan to hook up with any locals, double-check with House and one of our advisors first."

Dalton smiled and said, "That's certainly the loosest pass restrictions I've ever encountered."

Sean chuckled. "Don't make me regret it."

The man was dead serious but still smiling as he replied, "Absolutely not, sir."

Right then, Researchers Twine and Larilee Zep arrived through the door.

"Hello!" Twine called as a courtesy. She wore something like a pantsuit, but it flared at ankles, wrists, and throat into not-quite ruffles. Zep wore the almost-lab-coat and slacks that were pretty much standard daywear here.

"Hi, Doc," Spencer replied.

"I understand you have a schedule gap before you depart," she said.

"We do."

Twine was very tall by twenty-first-century standards. She looked down almost imperiously as she said, "Excellent. There is a party this evening you are welcome to attend. A friend of mine is hosting it, and the patron can guide you there and act as a social interpreter."

Sean said, "That certainly sounds interesting. Does House know where?"

"I do now," the intelligence replied.

Spencer asked, "Who is hosting the party and why? What theme?"

Twine said, "Hamota Fedori. She's one of the regional personalities."

"Personalities? Like TV, movies, media?"

She nodded. "All of that."

"What does she primarily do?"

"Host parties and promote herself."

Sean wrinkled his brow and asked, "So this person is just famous for being famous?"

Zep replied, "Yes. Why else would someone be famous?"

"For their accomplishments."

With a friendly grin, Zep said, "That's what fame is."

It seemed to be a cultural incongruency. Had social media had that much effect on society? Entirely possible.

Twine raised her voice a fraction and said, "You are all invited. The party will open about nineteen hundred hours your time."

"When do you suggest we arrive?"

Twine said, "I suggest about twenty-one hundred. By twenty-three hundred it will be crowded and near max. Earlier and it will be quiet, but those present will be discussing business."

Caswell asked, "So it's a business first, play later event?"

Her eyes twinkled and she almost sighed as she said, "No, it's just that those who arrive early always want to discuss business."

"Ah, that."

Larilee Zep said, "Doctors Raven and Sheridan, if you have some time, can we discuss the nature of your research?"

"If we're free for now, yes," Sheridan agreed.

"Go right ahead," Sean said.

The soldiers messed about discussing what to do and if they could get civilian clothes. Zep came closer and a forcewall solidified around them.

Kate watched the soldiers chatter about. She turned back to Larilee Zep.

"What can we tell you?" she asked.

Zep said, "I must apologize for being a hindrance."

"Not at all. Go ahead."

The woman still looked flustered as she said, "We weren't expecting your presence. While your curiosity and purpose are understandable, there are limits on the information it is... safe for you to have."

Raven glared suspiciously and asked, "Safe for whom?"

"For your future, our past. We still don't fully understand how the Temporality works, so the less interference, the better. This specifically and unfortunately includes knowledge."

Kate replied, "What we seek is to help our understanding of the past, and of how various diseases evolved, with particular attention to certain genotypes and ethnotypes."

Zep nodded. "Yes, that should be safe. We will need to examine your documentation to be sure and, of course, we will also find that of interest. We will even furnish sensors you can use for the purpose."

Kate understood that readily enough.

She noted, "That will allow you to dictate only the info you want us to keep."

Zep nodded. She seemed very uncomfortable bearing this bad news, but she pushed through.

"Unfortunately yes. I was able to get even that approved only by pointing out the advantage to us of the data. I had to be persuasive that scientists from your time would have the capabilities and training for it."

Raven sounded insulted as she said, "Obtaining and documenting samples is absolutely within our capabilities, or even that of several of the regular soldiers."

"I know," Zep agreed, looking embarrassed and a bit flushed. "Keep in mind I've made some study of your era. Many of the council responsible for this have not, and had only vague notions of your actual scientific methods."

Kate replied, "I guess that's not unreasonable, given that much of our process was only developed in the last couple of hundred years. Given the gap between then and now..."

Zep moved into that opening. "That, but more of a cultural... I think you would say provincial attitude that preceding cultures couldn't approach our sophistication."

"We've had that in our own time and with earlier," Kate agreed.

Zep hadn't taken the bait, nor given a single hint of when this was. Damn. Hopefully Raven's surveys would yield something, if they were allowed to keep the data. And it was obvious that was an issue.

The woman noted, "Also understand that we can't validate anything on a first examination."

Kate didn't get the meaning of that. "I don't follow."

Zep elaborated, "Meaning there are minor irregularities and inconsistencies through temporality. We're not positive of what side effects happen from these transitions, on anything around you. There is also inevitably to be some bacterial and other con-tamination from it. Both together make it very important not to be tempted to examine more than the minimum. Anything you encounter as part of the operation is a valid subject. Deliberate investigations beyond that should be limited."

Raven replied, "On the one hand, we understand that. On the other hand, thirst for knowledge. You as a scientist should know that." She was trying to be persuasive, but it was obvious she was angry.

"I understand that, but you must avoid certain lines of research. That isn't from me, but from the council." She bit her lip, and continued. "There are ways to adjust your memory. They are repugnant to us, but to protect our society and information... It's unfortunate we find ourselves in a position we would have advised against."

Kate took that in. If the Cogi found certain of the data she was seeking a potential hazard, they'd wipe her memory. There was an implication that it couldn't be done perfectly and would cause some other amnesia.

Suddenly, spying wasn't sexy anymore.

Raven replied, "You'll understand if we don't thank you for this discussion, and I for one will not be socializing with you."

Zep sighed. "I do, and I'm very sorry we find ourselves

in this position. I'd greatly enjoy a lengthy discussion of your background."

Amalie's voice was sharp glass as she said, "Ordinarily I'd be sorry to disappoint you."

"Yes. Thank you for your understanding, as disappointing as circumstances are."

Kate said, "You are professionally welcome."

She wasn't feeling very friendly, either.

Zep resumed. "There's another factor that hasn't been covered. You're new to the algorithms, as far as transition."

"Meaning?" she asked.

"Meaning you're a new variable. The others' characteristics are on file from our previous interaction, and this arrival. Yours are a single panel of data. We'll need to do a full scan of you before transition."

Kate thought she got it. "So you think it will affect the transition to have us along."

Zep spread her hands. "We don't know. This is new territory. But the temporalists say you both created a complication."

Raven's voice was soft, but sarcastic. "Then they better fix it quickly."

Zep left awkwardly. As the door solidified, Raven looked over, her dark eyes burning.

"Their open society is rather insular, I find."

Kate said, "Yeah. I don't want to blame them because I don't know the context. But I'm certainly pissed about them dictating our research. Especially as they plan to keep whatever they feel like, but only let us keep what they decide."

Armand was definitely interested in the party. He wanted to try what local culture he could—the food, drink, music. Here he was in a foreign country, a foreign time, and he knew nothing about them other than that they were tall, white, spoke some variation of English with a dusky accent, and had better technology, but not how much better. He wanted to meet people.

He was about to head for the shower when he heard Twine call from the seating area.

"Armand, can we talk a bit more?"

He really wanted to look around the facility, but if a smoking hot science babe wanted to talk...

"Sure, about what?" he asked.

"Nothing in particular. We are both off duty."

"Okay," he agreed, walked over and took a seat. She was educated and beautiful, and he had nothing pressing. Her ruffled blouse was cut very low between those large, well-mounted breasts.

"How was your return?" she asked.

"To our time? Well, we obviously managed to make them believe us. Eventually. The transmogrifying tool helped, as did the ancient hides."

Twine did look relieved. "Good. As a social scientist, one of my concerns was how you'd be received."

"Yeah, eventually they accepted it, made it secret, and brought in scientists." He indicated the fuzzy shadows of the two women talking to Zep inside a force field. "I don't know how long it can remain secret."

"We have very few secrets here," Twine said. "Privacy is a cultural construct we maintain, and simply not talking about a subject makes it less present for people to even ask about."

"Yeah, obscurity. In our case, few would believe it anyway." He paused to give a thumbs-up to Spencer and Dalton as they walked out of the dorm.

She replied, "That seems logical. We maintain a semblance of privacy because the patrons aren't supposed to assist in violating personal privacy without cause, though some have been manipulated."

"What is the nature of their intelligence?" he asked.

She shook her head a fraction. "I still can't discuss that. They are legally human, with rights. Think of it as a job, not a state."

"It makes me think there's someone with their brain wired into a network of data and microphones."

She did meet his eyes as she said, "That's a reasonably passable definition of the concept."

He sighed. "I wish I could learn more."

She smiled. "You will, just not from us. But you'll see more than you did before."

It didn't seem condescending, but it still had a feel of *Wait until you're older.*

"Yeah, looking forward to it."

"Do you drink beer?" she asked.

"Yes," he replied at once.

She nodded and called, "Serve, tu ambeweet."

Two amber wheat. That hadn't changed much, but those were

very simple syllables that wouldn't shift much with time. Not the way "American" had morphed into "Merghan."

The beer popped up at his elbow in a glass that felt like glass, but he was sure was plastic. It was almost bottle shaped, enough to minimize spilling.

She raised hers in a salute, not a toast, he did the same. He took a cautious sip...not bad at all. It was richer and heavier than he expected, but tasted like beer, and was nicely chilled.

He realized the scientists had finished talking to Zep and were over by the fire with Shug. Everyone else had left.

Twine finished a swallow of her beer and asked, "How has everyone dealt with it? I understand Regina did not want to return."

She said she was off duty? This certainly sounded professional. On the other hand, it could just be human interest since she'd worked with them for weeks.

"Uh, how long has it been here since we left?" he asked.

"About a year," she replied.

"Huh, same for us."

She explained, "We wanted a time frame that gave you the opportunity to de-stress, while still having your familiarity fresh. Our research into the discontinuity took about the same time."

"That makes sense. Yeah, Gina apparently didn't like it after the fact. She's retired, resting. Her metabolism is having some issues. I gather she made a strong bond with Sergeant Spencer, even though nothing happened between them that I know of. Both families are really stressed."

"Unfortunate but not unexpected," she said. "How was it all overall for you?"

He was pretty sure they'd covered this. "Overall? Well, it was terrifying to be lost, then to know where we were lost, since I had enough astronomy training to date it. Then there was the fascination of all of it, the frustration of not having the gear I needed to save people I know I could save. It was a privilege to save several people I could, and make their lives better. Then we gradually adapted. Then when the Cogi showed up, it got fascinating all over again."

"'Cogi'?" she asked, looking puzzled.

"Is that your demonym? Or is it specific to their group?"

"Cryder referred to themselves as 'Cogi'?" she asked with more intensity.

"Yes."

"I see," she said, looking rather serious and a bit annoyed.

"Is there a problem?" he asked.

She almost blushed, and did frown.

She said, "The word is not exactly correct. But it's very apparent he was twisting another word into a reverse epithet."

"Oh?"

Very flatly, she said, "The actual word is 'cogni.'"

"From . . . cognizant?" he asked.

"Yes. It's a colloquialism that means the person is very aware of goings-on. Events. Activities. Cause and effect."

"So he was calling them the smart people."

Now she did blush. "Yes. I apologize that he did that." That came out quickly. She looked distressed and uncomfortable.

He shrugged and took a sip of beer. "Well, it's not your place to apologize for him, but thank you." He considered for a moment.

Then he said, "And I guess that's fair return, because we had troops who'd do the same with local villagers and workers."

"Refer to yourselves as the smart ones?"

"Not exactly."

It was his turn to be embarrassed.

"I remember two incidents. The first was a bunch of local kids shouting, 'Give me candy, please.' But someone had thought it was clever to tell them the English phrase was 'Please give me cock.'"

She looked appalled.

"Why would you do that?"

He blurted, "I didn't, and I warned people not to, and we had regular briefings that it wasn't clever or helpful."

"I would say so," she replied with a shake of her head, hair flowing as she did.

"There's always one troop who's got to try to be clever."

She sighed. "Some things never change."

"Very true. Do you want to hear the other example?"

Her headshake was vigorous. "No, I comprehend enough. I appreciate that you don't support it. So what happened after you debriefed?" she asked, changing the subject quickly.

He was grateful to get back to that. "I went back to school, graduated, and am doing residency work. That's frustrating, because I keep being treated like a regular civilian who doesn't know anything other than books. I've performed lifesaving surgery in the Stone Age, dammit."

"I imagine that's frustrating," she said.

"Very," he agreed.

She stood.

"Well, it's good to see you again. Do you mind if I meet you at the party this evening?"

"I'd like that," he said carefully, trying to sound interested without gushing. *Are you kidding?* he thought. *Any time you want to spend with me is good.* She was smart, educated, expressive, and smoking hot. He'd hang out all she wanted.

"I'll be there about...twenty-one hundred," she said. "I'll change out of work clothes."

These were her work clothes...She'd worn some striking outfits last time.

"I look forward to it," he said.

Amalie Raven was very unhappy with the local restrictions. "Livid" would be a better term. Certainly she expected oversight from the Cogi, Bykos, whatever they were called. Absolutely she expected to share data. As far as what that data would show, it would reveal the number of generations in question, which she knew, the divergence from the root population, which she had a very good estimate of, and the presence of any significant vectors and viral populations. That wouldn't affect anything as far as the "temporality" went. It might assist in developing treatments for various diseases. So unless there was a major plague pending, nothing about it should be a problem.

What she could not even hint at was the other data she hoped to acquire. While it wasn't impossible the future twits had anticipated that, this could be a blanket protection against any such findings, inadvertent or covert.

Right then, Sheridan said, "I'm very eager to compare genetic lines between the three time frames, and—"

Raven cut in with, "Of course, we can't do that, but it will be fascinating to learn what we can about any potential microbes and viruses."

She gave the other woman a careful look and thought, *Shut up*, very clearly.

Sheridan took the hint. "Yes. Whatever we can learn will be useful and fascinating, but I'd love to spend a year here."

That was hopefully an effective cover for the slip.

She replied, "We've got a few weeks. But it will all be useful for our health and history. We need to check over some of the gear, make sure it's still calibrated."

"Oh, yes. We should," Sheridan agreed, hardly hiding the fact that they were hiding things.

Amalie sighed. She could have handled this just fine with a lab assistant, possibly Marisa or Elna. Sheridan was a terrible choice for anything regarding discretion.

She needed a drink. Possibly some of the other people here were less intrusive. Or she could just ignore them. She was stuck in that state of needing to be alone, but really wanting to look around.

Sigh.

"Jenny," she called to Caswell, who hadn't quite left yet. The younger woman turned.

"Yes, Doctor?"

"'Amalie' is fine. Are you heading for that party? May I join you?"

"Yes, and sure. I told the guys I'd catch up there."

"Okay. House, can you ensure Shug is kept entertained? Pictures, interaction, any staff on call if necessary?"

"All that is possible. I will do so."

"Great." She hated leaving the poor kid alone. He was older than her own, but she recognized the loneliness. A futuristic rave would probably freak him out, certainly confuse him, and lead to more stories they wanted him to avoid spreading.

At least he'd be home soon, hopefully.

Sheridan said, "I'll check this over, see what I can do for Shug, and come later."

"Okay."

She caught up with Caswell at the door and they headed out.

They'd already seen from the air how small and isolated the facility was. There was one long, lonely, narrow road entering from the east. The airfield was in regular use. It was possible there was an underground train or other entrance. Possibly they got regular heavy air supply and support flights in between. It really was a remote site in the woods.

The architecture, though, was stunning. For a remote "village," it resembled Disneyworld.

The raised walkways and slideways led in long arcs, though there were also others that were direct between buildings. The ground had marked roads, in addition to walkways for pedestrians and bikelike conveyances. Flowers, bushes, and trees exploded from islands in the pavement, and filled marked gardens in a more orderly fashion. Those other things...those were buildings, with plants growing in and through them, like cybernetic treehouses.

The building they walked toward had no definable shape. It was oblong, oblate, and asymmetric, with multicolored crystal polygons on the surface.

Caswell said, "Damn. I don't even know what I'm looking at."

Raven said, "It's gorgeous, though."

"Oh, yeah."

Then they were striding downward and into it, across a threshold of colored mists.

Inside was like something out of sci-fi, which made sense. The stairway swooped and curved, with arches and buttresses.

"God, that's amazing," Caswell muttered, sounding awed.

It was. It was pure style. It didn't present as an attempt to be anything or show anything, just "this is pretty." And it was.

"There's the guide," she commented, watching the blue beacon process along the ground.

There were some more stares here, though the variety of people were enough that the Americans didn't stand out particularly.

Though, she thought, they wouldn't move like the locals, and most of them likely knew most others on sight at least. Nor did her body type blend in at all. Short, broad, differently colored. Everyone had to know by word of mouth who she was.

Martin Spencer suddenly realized they were on an escalator. Or, more accurately, a sliding walkway, except they seemed to stand vertically, and it appeared to slope upward in front of them. He took a quick glance to the side and realized it was snaking under them to maintain a flat surface as it rose. Then he looked back quickly, because that was disorienting.

There was a sign, and he could just puzzle out their letters. It said PRIVT REZS. Private Residences. These were apartments, then.

Every door was personalized—size, shape, color. The guide led them down and around to the right, back toward the side they'd came in.

"I'm glad of that dot, because I'm completely turned around right now," he admitted.

"Tell me about it," Elliott replied.

Martin pointed at the lighted arch ahead. "That appears to be our party." There was a sign in several languages, including the sort-of English alphabet, naming it the MAD LABORATORY.

The door opened as the guide approached it, and light and sound emanated from inside.

Elliott stepped in front and led his people in.

Martin followed him, and his senses were almost immediately overwhelmed.

It was like every other party, and yet not.

There was music, and he could feel the tempo, but damn, it was complicated, and few of the instruments were recognizable, even as synths. The sounds were entirely different.

Lights flashed. The colors were in broad shades. It was hard to distinguish purple from pink from red until suddenly they overlapped. Some seemed to be in time with the music, some doing their own thing in multiple sequences that interacted, sometimes in phase, sometimes cancelling each other out.

The music had phase cancellations, too.

Two of the musicians were completely nude, a man and a woman, and they danced and writhed through what seemed to be triggers for some sort of theremin, because the music shifted constantly with their movements. It was a form of performance art he'd never be able to properly appreciate, though they were both buff and the chick was definitely hot. She wore an enthusiastic smile of someone enjoying her work and the feedback, which from the crowd seemed to be a mix of artistic appreciation, lust, and interest in the beat.

He'd go insane if he tried to figure out any kind of pattern.

That was a bar. He'd go there and hope they had something recognizable.

On the way, he smelled perfumes, inhalants, vapor.

Those were a couple, apparently male. And another. That was a male/female couple, and several more. Good. Gays didn't bother him, but he wasn't sure how he'd feel in an entire party full.

The bartender was stripped to the waist, male, very fit, and had cuffs and a collar, almost like a stripper. He was wearing pants, though. His hair was darker than most, with high cheeks.

"You are one of the American guests!" he said in carefully enunciated English. "It's excellent to meet you."

"Thank you very much. I'm Martin Spencer. My rank is Sergeant First Class." They liked titles here.

"I am Rec Chem Conard Medyva, in your sequence."

Got it. His first name was Conard.

Martin greeted back, "Good to meet you, too. Is there a specialty beverage or all to order?"

Conard waved across the bar that contained bottles, decanters, tubes, garnishes... "Anything you like, we can mix or fabricate. The human touch is always better than a machine. But if you'll allow me a moment."

"Okay," Martin agreed and waited while Conard stared at him.

In a few seconds the man said, "Yes. I have something you may like." He turned, reached, grabbed three bottles in quick succession, splashed from each into a small glass, and waved it over a lighted, rippling surface. Then he turned back.

He presented the glass in a move that was almost formal, almost a dance.

Martin accepted it, said, "Thank you," and nosed it. He had no idea what was in it, and wanted to ask, but figured he could trust the patron to warn him of anything.

It was smoky sweet and slightly pungent in scent, but not sharp like liquor.

It seemed safe enough. He took a sip.

The flavor was rich, and very, very smoky. It wasn't Scotch, nor bourbon, and not quite rum. If he had to guess, it was made from sweetened grain, or made to fake it, since it had come from three bottles. It was smooth, tingly on his tongue, with fruit notes in the finish.

And it packed a kick.

"Wow. What is that?" he asked.

"The active ingredient is ethanol, high proof, with a buffer. The rest are added flavorings."

"It's like a combination of three of our drinks, which I'd never think would work together, but damn, do they, at least the way you did it."

With a bow that was almost a nod, Conard replied, "Thank you. I'm glad you liked it."

Martin looked around, but didn't see any sign of a tip jar or of tipping. And he had no way to pay or tip anyway.

"How do I compensate you?"

Conard smiled cordially.

"The host is paying for the service, but you have credit on file as a contractor from another natcor."

"Oh. Good. I'll ask the patron, thanks."

House spoke in his ears. "You can choose to offer a small gratuity from your account. As all your functional needs are taken care of professionally, you have plenty of allowable credit against Bykop."

"House, can I be screened for a moment?"

"Certainly. Can you move toward the wall?"

"Yes." He didn't want to block traffic. There were fuzzy outlines against the wall and near the window that might be other people. Or even couples.

He stepped over to a corner of the bar that was against the window, in an acute angle that shouldn't be in anyone's way. The air shimmered and everything got quieter.

"Thanks," he said. "I'd like to offer him a standard tip plus a little for the thoughtful attention."

"Done."

"Thank you. Can you tell me our geographic location? Or the origin of Bykop?"

"I am not authorized to discuss that, sorry."

"Because I have a theory based on our displacement in the past, our latitude now, and certain terminology."

"I am not authorized to discuss that. I'm sorry. You may speak as you wish, but I cannot respond further in that line."

"Understood. Well, we'll see how it plays out."

"Thank you for accepting that. In the meantime, it appears Armand may need some minor assistance."

"Oh?" he asked, as the air cleared.

He turned and scanned the room, then stepped out of the corner to view the rest. Over there. It was still odd to think of a 6'1" man as short, but in this culture, they all were.

He saw the problem. The women positively flowed toward Devereaux, like moths to a light. His expression was a combination of thrilled and terrified.

"House," he said, "I do think Devereaux could use a bit of breathing room. Maybe two people at a time?"

"I see and will assist," the voice responded.

Some of the women paused in stride, listened to their avatars, and changed course. The three closest to him took turns introducing themselves and offering hands. Doc seemed cheerful and pleased, and Martin figured three was manageable, but nine would probably have scared the young man.

He stepped to the bar, asked Conard for another of the smoke shots, and took it with him. His head already had a smooth rush to it, a pre-buzz. That was from one shot of the stuff. Even if it was pure grain alcohol it shouldn't hit like that.

The song playing was vaguely familiar. He listened and wondered, as it taunted him. He knew this song. Something.

"Beat It." Michael Jackson, 1980s. Only, it was played in some orchestral synth-metal jazz combination that was utterly weird.

He stood in that protective corner watching people, trying to gauge activity. He liked watching people. He liked interacting with people. He wanted to know how, first. Being a displacee with no commonality didn't make it easy to just jump into a conversation of strangers.

It seemed basically familiar. People greeted one another, gathered in groups and around tables, drank, chatted, joked. The music was present without being overwhelming, and there were certainly acoustic effects in place to keep the volume over the dance floor. It was fairly quiet here. In fact, he was sure the conversations were also muted for comfort and discretion. They might not have much real privacy, but their social contract was organized around it.

"Greetings," he heard a woman say.

He turned to his right. She wasn't overly close, but he hadn't heard her approach, and the arc of the window meant she'd been slightly past his field of view.

Damn. She was amazing. Mid-thirties to look at her. She obviously wasn't wearing a bra under that gown and didn't need to. She had a rock-muscled chest. He took in the rest of her figure with a glance. Oval hips, long legs, supple skin where it showed. Looking back up almost immediately, her face was high-cheeked, with very faint epicanthic eyes. She was far northern Caucasian or Eurasian in ancestry. Her skin had a gorgeous light olive tone. Her eyes were walnut brown pools. Her lips had a faint bit of pout outside of perfect teeth, and her hair was a unique coil of brown with a bare red tinge, almost like streaked rosewood, that flowed over her right temple, down her shoulder, and between her breasts. He saw another wave of it down her back.

"Greetings," he replied.

"You are one of the Merghans?" she asked, stepping fractionally closer.

"Americans, yes." He remembered they liked titles, and gave his. "I am Sergeant First Class Martin Spencer."

That seemed to be consent for her to step even closer. The music dulled slightly as the air thickened, though it remained transparent.

"I am Temporal Archivist Oktabro Maralina. Maralina is my personal styling."

That was a good opening. That meant he could ask questions and keep looking at her. "What do you do as a temporal archivist?"

She explained, "I log any and all data we acquire from the past, and scale it to known or documented information. I weight reliability of source, and then it is forwarded to Data Comparators who attempt to correct our knowledge to the best quality and source."

"Fascinating. I could have used you when we were lost."

She cocked an eyebrow. "Oh? How so?"

"I know a bit of prehistory and our early history. Much of what I thought I had right was off by years or even centuries."

"Ah, but without my files, I wouldn't be able to help."

"Yes, but I had no references at all. Just what was in here." He tapped his temple.

She looked quizzical. "I understood you had credible density for information storage."

"We do," he agreed, and pulled the necklace with the memory stick out. "I didn't have it with me, and our ability to read these was largely improvised from devices on hand. It wasn't issued equipment."

"That's . . . impressive," she said, eyes flaring slightly. "Did you study that time frame in school?"

"No, it was just a hobby. My knowledge is mostly theoretical. My business partner knows how to knap flint and work hides. I was able to make an iron reduction furnace and forge, though."

"I saw reference to that. You made it from memory of secondary sources only?" Her eyes widened and she sounded impressed.

Well, honestly, he had done admirable work, given it was all theoretical, from memory. He now knew several important additions to the process that would have made it work better. But he'd made iron from ore, and worked it.

"Yes," he said.

An amazingly gorgeous Eurasian history buff, obviously interested, and I'm married . . . and I shouldn't be regretting it, dammit.

"Is something wrong?" she asked gently. Damn, did he want a hug, and he was pretty sure she'd agree, and then . . . no.

"No, just a memory."

"I gather the experience was traumatic, with no knowledge of the cause."

That was a good cover. "Very. I kept being afraid everything would reset, and I'd be separate from the rest and lost forever."

She shivered very slightly in sympathy, and even that looked sexy.

She said, "I'm glad we were able to recover you. The process was entirely misunderstood at first, and not even—"

"THIS CONVERSATION IS RESTRICTED." Right in the middle, House had blocked the words.

House continued, "I apologize to both of you, but that reference is outside the permitted scope."

"I understand and I am very sorry," Maralina replied.

Martin said, "No problem. I'm sure there will be more. I know my knowledge of history is incomplete. You have more of it to deal with."

"Can I offer you a drink, Sergeant Spencer? And may I ask about your family relationship?"

"You can call me Martin. I would like a drink, thank you. I'm not sure what details you want." Yeah, another drink would be a good idea, but he should probably stop after that.

The woman rapid-fired something to her patron, who apparently informed Conard, who responded by walking down the bar, reaching over, and delivering a glass with a different flourish.

"This is a sweet wine," she offered. "I hold the design on the flavor profile."

"Oh, well, thank you," he replied, accepting the glass.

He raised it and took a sip.

It was warm and chill in ripples. Certainly sweet, but without being cloying. There was a musty bite under that, and an explosion of dark fruit. Plums? Blackberries? Both?

"That's delicious," he agreed.

"Thank you. I was inspired by tales of northern fruit wines of the higher latitude barbarians."

"Vikings and similar?"

"Yes."

"It certainly reminds me of that with the heaviness and cool texture, but I don't think they had anything as sweet."

"I would think not," she agreed. "This is my modern interpretation."

"I would say you captured the spirit, and it has a rich, almost dense profile."

"I'm glad you like it," she said with a smile that melted his brain. He noticed she wore earrings, complicated pieces that looked like futuristic tribal designs. Were they possibly Siberian in origin? Maybe. He didn't know much about that area other than the Andronovans.

Damn, her poise and posture was sexy.

To distract himself, he asked, "Are these beverages available to my patron?"

House suddenly said, "Yes, they are. I can reproduce them on demand, and Ms. Oktabro receives a small royalty each time."

What was that like? Where you could treat your friends and the machines made sure you got your cut as well, at effectively no cost to them?

This was even more fascinating than the Paleolithic, and a lot friendlier.

"I will do that. Thank you, Ms. Oktabro."

"Please do call me Maralina."

"Certainly. I go by Martin."

"Martin, then." She smiled and continued. "What is your current relationship?"

"Ah. Married once, for twenty years now. Two children, both adults starting to leave the nest."

"I deduce that is a monogamous commitment."

"It is." He had to be honest, problems or not. Hell, obvious failure or not. He just wanted to look at her.

She said, "I applaud your determination and durability. I understand a lot of marriages in your era did not last so well?"

Yeah, he wanted out of this line of discussion at once.

"Many don't, many do. It entirely depends on the people."

"Certainly," she agreed. "I am paired, prime to another researcher, though he is not at this facility at present. I have no second at present. I wouldn't try to involve with a third."

"I'm afraid to wonder how complicated that is," he admitted honestly. "I know a couple it works for. A trio, I guess. I know others who tried it and had it fail dismally."

She smiled. "It has become more common and workable with anthropological study of relationships."

He blurted out, "I expect so. Maralina?"

"Yes?"

"My relationship is...an awkward subject in public. Can we talk about something else?"

She tossed her head a fraction. "Certainly. Shall we sit over there?"

She indicated a couch that looked as futuristic and comfortable as everything else, even more so than the ones in their lodge.

"Lead the way," he agreed.

She did, and he had a perfect view of her from behind. Those hips rolled like a dancer's, her shoulders were square, taut, and shifted gracefully. She turned and sat and her dress flowed for just a moment.

No underwear. He didn't think that was a deliberate come-on. From their last trip and some other attendees, he gathered a lot of them were casual about nudity, using clothing only for decoration.

He might be making a lot of use of that accessorized shower.

Keeping his eyes on her face, not that phenomenal chest, he asked, "How did you get into this work? I assume it's new since time travel seems to be for your culture."

Her eyes looked fascinated, and fascinating, as she replied, "It is. When I got my first professional credentials, twenty-three years ago..."

He about choked.

"Wait, how old are you?" he asked.

"Fifty-three."

Holy shit.

"You don't look a day over thirty. Seriously. I wouldn't even assume that old."

She smiled very warmly. "I look fairly typical for our culture. Do I recall there were significant strides in diet and exercise in your era?"

"Yes, and still ongoing."

"Then you are almost there."

"That's all? Lifestyle, not medicine?"

"Both are the same," she said with a quizzical furrow of her brow.

"Good," he replied. "I may be lucky then. Uh, what credentials?"

"History, specializing in the Industrial Era, including yours."

"Okay. Then?"

She discreetly said, "Other eras, some I can't mention. I love technology, then music. I never really cared for sports or most visual arts."

"Fair enough," he said.

"What about your training?" she asked.

"Me? I enlisted in the Army at eighteen. I started out as a helicopter flight engineer and door gunner."

"'Door gunner.' Shooting from the craft in flight? Without automated systems?" She looked fascinating again, but a bit put off.

"Yes. I never did any in combat. Some craft have computerized weapons."

"How did that work out? Considering all the conflicts?"

He shrugged, and tried to be reassuring. "Oh, most of them are low-scale conflicts. We haven't involved the whole Army in anything since World War Two. That would be 1941 to 1945, our dates and involvement. We have lots of little conflicts, but units rotate through."

"I see."

"After age caught up with me a bit I switched to being a vehicle mechanic."

"Those are what you called trades."

"Yes. Hands on, not theoretical."

"Your knowledge exceeds that."

That was valid. "Certainly. I like studying. Our element had a huge spread of skills. Better than average, and it served us well."

"I learned about a lot of the development of trades," she said. "Starting with the medieval guilds. Do you know the . . . fourteenth century?"

He thought back about what he'd read. "Not well, but passingly. That's when the guilds started defining the skills and training."

"Yes," she said. "You did iron reduction. I've always wanted to see that in historical scale. We use electrical consolidation . . . Hey, the protocols let me say that. You must know of it, then."

"If you mean electrical melting and stratification, I can guess," he said. "My way was much messier and cruder."

"That's what makes it fascinating," she nodded. "Starting with raw ore and a heat source, it was early in that era that puddled iron came into being, and eventually the blast furnace."

The conversation drifted from there to mechanical shaping, paint schemes. She knew about hot rods, though not in detail. He had a few pictures on his phone, including a supercharged Dodge called the "Blow Dart."

She was fascinated more by his phone. Then they got on to clothing, and talked about textiles.

"Gina in our group set up spinning and then crochet and knitting, eventually weaving. Bob knew how to tan hides. We made it workable."

She said, "I would be very excited to see demonstrations. We all would."

"I can ask our commander about it," he said. Sure. Whatever she wanted to see, and it would be less stressful here.

"Oh, please, do," she said, with a flash of perfect teeth behind dark lips, and heave of her chest.

He would do his best.

They talked about history, and she was absolutely rapt. So was he, but less for the history, he admitted.

He needed to get out of here. He was overloaded on people, except for her, and with the booze thrown in, he needed to leave.

Sighing inside, he said, "Maralina, it's been wonderful talking, and I hope to again, but we have tasks in the morning and I have to go. I'm sorry."

"I have work also," she said.

She offered her hand, and he offered his in return. She clasped it in hers, raised it to her cheek, and pressed warmly against it.

"Thank you for talking to me, Martin. I hope to see you again. I can always be paged through the patrons." She lowered his hand but kept light hold.

If you drag me off I can say I didn't ask.

"I would enjoy that. The conversation is fascinating and . . . I must say you look spectacular." He buzzed with endorphins.

She glowed and grinned, with sparkling eyes. "Thank you very much. Have a good evening, and safe travels. I'll enjoy documenting anything you bring back."

He wanted to document every inch of her body.

✧　　✧　　✧

Jenny Caswell understood the tribal origins of the dancers, and the artistic relevance of being nude. It was suggestive, but not sexual per se. It certainly said this culture wasn't very inhibited.

Next to her, Dr. Raven muttered, "Flanging... frequency oscillation. That's a round wave with gated release. Am I hearing a phase inversion on a rising attack?"

The woman was analyzing the technicalities of the music. *Nerd*, she thought, in a friendly fashion. The two scientists seemed very, very competent.

Katherine Sheridan had just arrived, had a glass of wine, was all eyes on the nude male, but responded to Raven with, "I think it's all controlled from that corner. The sensor field seems to be a flux that feeds back on itself, but roughly x horizontal, y vertical, and z depth. Its own envelope adjusts the level of sensitivity."

Still watching, Raven replied, "It's just too damned cool, and I bet they have to be naked for cleanest signal. You could mess with it by wearing lace or chiffon or some sort of mesh and it would fuzz the edges, but probably not quite distortion."

Sheridan said, "No, probably a comb-filter effect. That would be neat."

Sure enough, the woman waved a scarf through the matrix, the texture changed, and again as she wrapped it around her leg and ground into it.

Jenny didn't grasp most of the discussion, but apparently the scientists understood electronics, or optics, or something. But after hearing that, it did seem that one corner was the focus.

The dance wasn't quite ballet, not quite bossa nova, not quite tango. It also seemed likely the two were a pair. They moved very well, limbs sliding past each other, ducking and twisting, and walking over each other forward and back, feet, hands, arch, and back upright.

She said, "I'm going to sit by the bar."

Raven replied, "Sure."

As she sat on an open chair, House said, "Jenny, there are two different men asking if they can introduce themselves."

That was interesting. And courteous. She replied, "I'd like to say yes, but we're about to travel, and I haven't actually seen anything yet. Can you thank them for the courtesy and interest and tell them I'm really too busy to socialize that much—I mean, in person?"

"I will relay that."

"Thanks."

The bartender was named Conard, who looked every bit a stripper, but friendly and polite. He got her a golden ale, and she decided the one would be enough, but it was tasty.

Doc was surrounded by women, which was partly amusing, and partly informative. He was literally the only black person anywhere here. They'd asked about that last time and no one wanted to answer. But the attention was positive.

Way in the corner, Dalton was talking to some guy with a beard, and it was a serious conversation.

Sergeant Spencer was sitting with a striking-looking woman.

The captain was watching it all. Good. He really was a competent officer, and she liked serving with him. He'd kept them all in order in their own displacement.

Sean Elliott leaned back on one of several couches in a conversation area, where he could watch the exits and his own people while sipping a beer. In between he watched the crowd.

The soldiers seemed to be doing okay. Doc was sitting between one woman who was tall, lithe, and willowy, and one with a body solidly packed with muscle. They were *focused* on him. He seemed distracted by both.

Spencer was talking to a woman who was stunning even for here. She looked Siberian.

Caswell and both scientists were watching the dancers. Well, that was certainly an anthropological thing. The female dancer was seriously smoking hot, but the music just sounded wrong to him and he couldn't be nearby. Though he could probably get House to mute or change it.

Oglesby was sort of dancing with a woman. Dalton was talking to some guy at a table near the wall, very animated and intense. Probably religion. Good luck to him with that here.

Dr. Twine appeared near the door, waved and smiled, and approached. She was in a gown so black light seemed to disappear into it, with openings at midriff, shoulders, all down her back, and up the thighs. Wow. He stood up.

Her manners were perfect as she offered her hand, shook, stepped back a foot, and said, "Captain Sean Elliott, allow me to introduce my friend and tonight's host. This is Hamota Fedori."

The woman was slim for her height, and slightly shorter than average, only about six foot. Hamota was older, apparently late sixties. Here she might be a lot older than that. She could certainly be a mix of Japanese and Russian. That was perfectly reasonable geographically, and while not local to the area, certainly made sense in Asia. She bent her head just fractionally.

"Thank you for hosting us," he said as he made the same token bow back to her.

Hamota stood back. Her gown was half dress, half robe, in layers of black, blue, and purple that flowed in beautiful waves as she moved. It was tasteful and striking.

"You're welcome," she replied. "I'm pleased to bring you here. I always have the most interesting guests and travelers, and you've traveled more than any."

That was completely true. They'd travelled entire millennia.

"I hadn't even considered that. Do you want us to talk about it?"

She shook her head and smiled. "No need as a group. You can talk as you wish with other guests. Just having you here enhances my own aura. Whatever refreshments you all wish are complimentary, of course."

"That's gracious, thank you, ma'am."

Her smile was amazing, even as an elder. It put him perfectly at ease. If he guessed correctly, that was part of her function.

She assured him, "Just 'Fedori' is fine. I have my own lengthy titles, but this is a social function."

"Are you a researcher yourself?"

A bigger smile. "I was. I'm now an interlocutor between them and the genpop."

That sounded like... "Public affairs?"

The woman nodded. "That is probably accurate enough. I explain things, elaborate, promote, promulgate, and present for benefit and investment."

"I'm told you're famous for it."

She smiled. "I have a lot of experience and a trained mind. I am well received in many places."

There was a moment's pause, and she added, "I would like to ask a couple of questions when time permits, but I must greet some others. Please excuse me. A pleasure to meet you, Captain."

She'd even managed to prevent an awkward silence. Well done.

"Good evening to you, Fedori."

❖   ❖   ❖

Rich Dalton sat at a tall bar table near the wall. He definitely liked the scenery. The women ranged from pretty to smoky and mysterious, to blatantly stunning like peacocks, to sheer exotic beauties unlike any he'd seen.

As much as he liked female company, he didn't like hookups. He found them unsatisfying, frustrating, and demeaning. One had control of one's baser instincts. That was the point of a healthy relationship with God. The three extended relationships he'd been in were all based on finding a suitable wife. That wasn't going to happen here, so he'd enjoy the view and philosophize, while learning what he could about their culture.

The dancer was interesting, but strippers never did anything for him. He thought she could do just as well clothed, and he didn't really care to have the naked guy dancing around.

Much like people anywhere, this was a gathering to meet, greet, socialize, network, swap contacts, and seek relationships. The similarities were obvious, but the differences were fascinating. He thought he could see five classes of people, including political types, ranking researchers, technical workers, support staff, and artsy types.

As they passed him, quite a few clearly recognized him as an outsider, and some as to which group he was with. Several gave slow nods, almost bows, which he returned politely.

Their dress and demeanor told who they were. The men's dress was more elaborate than he was used to. There were pants, shorts, kilts, and garments he'd call skirts and dresses, but the cut made them obviously male. They still made him a bit uncomfortable. The women also went for pants quite a bit, mostly very shapely over their asses, and flared lower down in some current style. Those who wore dresses...well, those were more like gowns and very elaborate, even when made of what looked like a single wrapped piece, like the Greek chiton or Roman toga. Actually, some looked quite a bit like that.

Most of them were European or Eurasian, with some definitely more Asian. A handful appeared to be Pacific. No Africans. There were certainly demographic distinctions here.

One gentleman who looked quite a bit Middle Eastern approached, made eye contact, and raised a hand.

"Hello," Rich greeted.

"Hello. I believe I recognize you. Do you mind talking?"

"Not at all. I'm Rich Dalton."

He nodded. "Yes, you are one of the American solders."

"Soldiers, yes."

The man said, in introduction, "I am Alakri Mommed. I am a medical doctor."

"Pleased to meet you. I presume Mommed is from our time's Mohammed."

Alakri grinned. "Yes, there are still many variations."

"Have a seat."

"Thank you." The man sat across the table from him, on a chair that moved into place for him. "I recognize you from your presentation on Christianity."

Rich felt a frisson of appreciation. "Oh, you saw that?"

"I did. Your presentation was inspiring."

He smiled as he said, "Well, that's good to hear. The active audience didn't seem to get much from it."

Mommed shrugged slightly. "Religion has changed. It is more philosophical now."

Rich nodded. "That's exactly what I noticed. To me, it's very real."

"It showed, and it carried, and it was exciting to see," the man assured him.

Rich remembered the Parable of the Sower. This one seed had at least made it to ground.

"Thank you. That's always what I hope for."

"I am also religious more than philosophical. I did some reading from your time. Radical changes taking place, that I probably shouldn't discuss in modern context."

He agreed, "Yeah, that's frustrating. We'd love to know more about your era."

"Will you share a drink, Rich?"

"Depending on what it is, certainly."

Mommed spoke to the server. "Two sekanjabin, please."

"That's fine," Rich agreed. He'd had that here and there, though it was more Persian than Arabian.

Tall glasses with iced liquid were presented momentarily, garnished with beautifully cut mint leaves. He raised it in toast and took a sip.

"This is alcoholic!" It wasn't supposed to be. What was in it, vodka?

Alakri raised his eyebrows and looked concerned. "Yes. I'm sorry, would you prefer it without?"

"No, this is . . . tasty." It was. Very. "I wasn't expecting that. I presumed you were Muslim. They generally don't drink."

Mommed nodded. "Ah, yes. I know a very few who still follow that stricture. Though technically, the liquor is made with neither grape nor grain. But now it's not something most worry about."

Rich wasn't sure how to feel about that. In a perfect world, everyone would convert to the salvation of Christ. He did respect many of the Muslims he'd known, but for them to lose their discipline in this matter disappointed him slightly. Were all beliefs in God fading?

"I do feel a bit . . . out of my depth in a world where faith is declined."

"I can see that perspective," Mommed replied, "though rather, you may want to consider that faith has served its purpose and receded to the background. We still have political strife and unrest, but less than you did. We feed poor you tried very hard to. Our civilization generally is very happy. Sectarian violence has largely disappeared."

It did sound almost too idyllic. "All good. And I've noted people clutch at faith when they most need it, but it's something that should be maintained, so it doesn't have to rediscovered."

It was a truly enlightening discussion, and he thanked God for the encounter. His words had been seen and received, had touched others, and in return, he was learning new things about himself and the world.

With a delicious drink, a fascinating point of view, and gorgeous women in the background, it was a good evening.

Amalie and Sheridan came back early, before 2300 local. They had equipment to check, and she wanted to confirm her portable sensors were working. Besides, she'd had too much people overload, and her counterpart looked pretty wired, too. Neither of them handled crowds or long contact well. Another strike against getting to Mars.

Shug was napping by the fire, but woke up as they approached.

"Hello," he said, and grinned.

"What did you and Shug do, House?"

"I offered him several exotic fruits, some carbonated water, a single beer, and he watched a variety of animals hunting and rushing, from a close point of view."

"Excellent. Glad he's occupied." She had been looking at the ceiling even though there was no reason to. She looked down. "Shug, we're going to work on our tools. Can you help by holding things?"

House helped translate into pidgin, and the boy said, "Yes!" and clapped his hands once.

"Over here," she indicated.

Their gear was in crates near the bathroom area. Once the first rolling box had its doors open, she had Shug hold a meter stick out from one side. They made a point of bringing things by so they could measure them. She wanted him to feel useful, and Sheridan followed her lead. Then she had him apply voltmeter probes to various batteries to check levels, which actually was important. She showed him where the terminals were, he'd place them and wait for the readout, she'd confirm and say, "Okay."

He seemed absolutely giddy to be helping the shamans, as he called the two of them and Doc.

They did check the equipment over, puttering around, taking longer than necessary. That was cover for the real research she was doing. The longer she could justify on the schedule, the more time she had for the actual work she was here for.

"You know I don't socialize," she said to Sheridan.

Sheridan agreed, "Yeah, me neither. I don't know how to act."

"I just don't like people," Amalie said. That was understating it. Though this group of soldiers wasn't bad. Bright enough overall that they didn't bore her to death.

She continued, "But I think tomorrow we should see what we can show Shug, just so he's not left alone so much."

The boy twitched hopefully at his name, then sighed and resumed his huddle on the couch. He'd learned to pet Cal, but it was apparent he wasn't from a culture that did much with cats.

"We could go back out after this," Sheridan suggested.

"This is going to take at least another hour, remember?" she chided.

Sheridan smoothly said, "Yeah, but . . . oh, I see. The time."

Good. She was learning.

Amalie raised her voice slightly. "House, are you listening?"

House said, "I am always listening, but I do not always pay heed. Should I review your recent conversation for content?"

"No need," she replied. It was good to know the snoop was a recorder, but not necessarily an observer. "I'd like to find out what rules there are for showing Shug around tomorrow."

"I will inquire with project leadership."

"Thank you. In the meantime, is there a ball or something he can play with? He's been shut out of everything, and I can't create more makework."

"That is within parameters."

"And a wall surface over here."

"At once."

The wall slid up first, and damn, that was a useful resource.

Momentarily, the delivery surface provided a geometrically dyed ball, much like any back home. Really, it wasn't as if the technology of inflatable rubber would have changed.

Amalie grabbed it, said, "Shug, watch."

He looked up, she threw the ball to Sheridan. The other woman fumbled slightly but got hold of it, threw it back. Amalie caught it, showed him how it bounced against the wall, and then bounced it to him. He caught it, squeezed it, bounced it, and chased it as it went awry.

Once he recovered it, he looked much more enthused, smiled and said, "Tank u."

"You're welcome."

He started bouncing it and chasing and laughing. The caracal suddenly appeared from the furniture, and disappeared behind something else.

Amalie sighed. It was the right thing to do, but that bouncing noise was going to . . . wait.

"House, can you quiet the bounce so I don't hear it?"

"Of course. I take that is a request?"

"Yes, thank you."

Damn, this place wasn't bad at all.

She was aware that Caswell had just returned, and the woman immediately grasped the issue and went to help Shug bounce the ball around. She made a good big sister.

Good. As a female in STEM, multiply so, she found Caswell tolerable, but the woman was awfully opinionated for someone young and definitely not in STEM. Her social ideas were half correct, half sheer liberal idiocy. Which, she noted, was better than average for that generation.

A bit after midnight, they concluded. Her tests and models seemed sound, and more important, neither House nor any of the locals had intruded.

It was about then that Devereaux came back.

"How are you doing, Doc?" she asked.

"Daaamn," the man said with a huge grin. He looked slightly buzzed and very distracted.

"Oh?"

He detailed, "All the chicks wanted to dance, but I wound up talking to Alexian Twine."

"Ah, yes. She's one I don't despise. Sorry, that's not a good way to phrase it," she realized, as she saw his expression. "I'm very asocial, but she's okay. Interesting conversation?"

"Almost too interesting."

"Then why are you back here?" she bantered.

"I have to set an example, and I prefer privacy." The poor man was blushing purple under his dark skin.

"I can see that," she said. "Well, hopefully you can meet up again. We're prepping gear and entertaining Shug."

"Oh, I can throw some ball. Do we have a hoop, or a goal, or something?"

Sheridan offered, "How about the Aztec style, just without the traditional executions?"

"Funny," he replied. "But I can spare a few minutes."

CHAPTER 10

The next morning, Sean called a class so they could go over in more detail their recovery response. They had equipment, transportation, a timeline. They needed to talk about specifics.

Cryder and Arnot arrived as requested, exactly on time, along with Researcher Zep and another he didn't recognize. Male, looked early middle age, so here, maybe seventy? He waved them to seats and took the head of the table himself.

Zep announced, "This is Senior Researcher Barzer. He is from our management council."

Barzer was slightly shorter than the local average, slightly darker, and not nearly as handsome. He was still fitter and better looking than half of Hollywood's elite, though. He had almost a Spock hairdo, and didn't seem unfriendly, but didn't smile.

"Greetings. My predominant purpose here is to be informed. I will comment if I see a need or have questions. Please proceed in your regular fashion."

Sean thought, *Fair enough*, and started the discussion.

"We need to discuss our response to this missing element, assuming we find them."

Spencer said, "Likely, they didn't handle it as well as we did. We lucked out on skill set. These guys don't seem to have that kind of background. The terp might actually help them a bit, he's used to a less technological society. There's the two females."

"I'm worried about them," Caswell said.

Of course you are. On the other hand, there were legitimate concerns.

She said, "I want to take some makeup and manicure stuff. Do we know their sizes?"

That was on file. "Yes. Or, what their sizes were."

Spencer asked, "Girly stuff to make them feel more modern?"

Caswell nodded. "Exactly. Just like you got a haircut as soon as you could. And you should take shaving gear and stuff for the guys."

"Right, I wasn't criticizing. Good idea. Then we need to worry about food so they don't get sick the way I did. Doc?"

Devereaux said, "Yeah. So, we literally want to start them on a bite a day of modern stuff—bread, candy, beans, sweet fruit, probably dairy. But we should give them one of something at each meal. Let their guts get used to it again. This assumes we can take enough to do so."

Cryder said, "No problemo. We'll have vehicle capacity. Also, we can adapt clothing on site with the vehicle tool set."

Sean sighed. "I keep forgetting to ask about those amazing capabilities. Please remind me as needed."

The man grinned. "Of course. I just did."

Dalton spoke. "Uniforms. We get them dressed immediately. What's the ranking officer again?"

Sean replied, "A lieutenant, and his date of rank is after mine."

"Good, so even if they did field-promote him, you rank him."

He nodded. "Yes, the general said they'd have breveted me if necessary."

Continuing, he ticked off on his fingers. "So we recover the people, if possible. We account for remains, if necessary. We recover all the equipment it is possible to recover. We tell the locals they didn't see anything."

Dr. Sheridan blurted, "Wait, how does that work?"

They all laughed.

"Last time we told them we had specific rules from our spirits on how we conducted ourselves. Everything was explained as being 'far away,' but still in the same world."

"Ah, yes," she agreed. "I read about it. Got it."

Sean made notes as he went. Command would want a heavy AAR, and he was going to write FRAGORDERS and OPORDs for everything, just to have them on file. He'd even be able to retroactively fix any errors before they were submitted, with SFC Spencer to verify. That would make the wrapup on this mission a whole hell of a lot quicker and easier.

They covered a few specifics, including potential remains recovery and isolation/preservation of same.

Cryder said, "We can store in a state of inert atmosphere and suppression of cellular activity. Your sciencists can take samples and analyze and we'll secure them. If there are memorial services you need, we can assist."

Dalton nodded. "I guess that's me as the closest to a chaplain, unless you want to do it, sir? You're in command."

Sean shook his head. "You are far better at it than I could be, and have a talent and the inspiration for it. Please take charge of such duties and inform me if you need to. That reminds me of something. Chaplains have privileged communication. You don't and I don't. However, I want us all to have the same verbal understanding as last time. There are things that our people back home do not need to know about. If our own laws and regs run up against necessities in this environment, we do what we need to do, and never mention it."

There was a chorus of "hooah," as he remembered taking charge of four badly injured Neolithics, gutshot or worse, who couldn't possibly survive and would have died horribly. He'd sliced their throats as a mercy, which wouldn't have raised an eyebrow in most historical eras, but would have resulted in a war crimes charge from the Army. He still felt cold and empty about it over a year later.

Dalton replied, "Roger that, sir. Do I need to inform you on matters of personal counsel?"

"If you think it is necessary, or if you are unsure, yes. I'll trust your judgment otherwise, but bear in mind it's my ass in a sling if it slips past you."

Spencer leaned forward and said, "It's entirely possible they'll blab everything. So everyone needs to be prepared to shrug and insist we have no idea what they're talking about. At the same time, if it happens too often or if their stories are consistent, we're going to blow it."

Doc whooshed out air. "This is a hell of a juggling act."

"It is. Scientists, do you follow all this?"

"Yes, sir," Sheridan agreed.

"We will comply and assist as best we can," Raven said firmly.

Sean looked around. "Okay, then. Anything we haven't at least touched on?" There were shakes. "Researchers Zep and Barzer, any comments?"

Barzer looked around and replied, "I'm impressed. I have no present comments. Your element operates in a very cohesive fashion."

"Thank you, sir."

The man asked, "Do you have any questions for me to respond to or forward to our leadership? Understanding my responses may be limited."

Sheridan said, "What I don't understand is why you need these troops personally. We could have provided data, even recordings, to show your bona fides, and it's not as if they'd refuse a ride home. Glad as I am to be here with them, it's hard to grasp."

Barzer explained, "The nature of our displacement technology is that the more factors are on file, the easier it is to transition. We had all of your biometric, neural, and other data charted from last time. We wanted all of you. We had no idea there'd be substitutions and hadn't accounted for it. That was our false assumption. Sending Cryder back was actually more complicated than bringing you here, though you two scientists and Shug complicated things in counter to some degree. We will need another scan of you before we proceed."

"So you have us here, why send us back again, then?"

Zep said, "We sent a pair. A different pair. They couldn't get within the time frame and struggled with location. We didn't get as good a read on them. You're familiar with the element, experienced in the past, and by zeroing on your tempus, we were able to refine the technique further. Beyond that there are several factors. The mission ideally requires more than two people, the system can easily handle more than two people. You will more readily be able to interact compassionately. You will recognize any incongruities—behavior, other inconsistencies—that we'll need to deal with. There's the issue of potentially misplaced equipment and other anachronisms that must be dealt with. From our research, it appears there are both loci and people who are easier to transition."

Sean asked, "Is that due to us being there, or due to it being near us? Or both?"

"Unknown."

"But every time you do it adds to the inconsistency, right?"

Zep almost shrugged and replied, "It's more complex than that. Every jump creates incongruities, misalignments, and the possibility of further inaccuracy. Are you familiar with the Heisenberg Uncertainty Principle?"

Sheridan replied, "Certainly in concept. The observer becomes part of the process."

Zep nodded. "Good enough. However, as we refine it, we can be more precise, create fewer incongruities, and eventually we should be able to minimize it, though we'll still need neutral monitoring to ensure we don't overlook anything or damage the Temporality."

He wanted to clarify. "So it's literally easiest to use the same people, and that's more important than the time frame."

She said, "Yes. Random persons mean randomized jumps. It's going to be awkward enough with your replacements along."

"That makes sense. So it's becoming less of an issue?"

"It's becoming less of an issue for Bykostan and Suhrny, the two major actors in the process. Shain and Brazil are catching up fast. Hundreds of smaller entities and private operations are experimenting and making messes. Fortunately, small ones usually make smaller displacements."

Sheridan nodded. "But each one causes a problem when they interact with the past," she said.

"Some of the time. The Temporality is fairly elastic."

"To what extent?"

She raised her arms. "There are too many factors, some of which we don't know yet, to give an answer."

Sean said, "So avoid killing anyone we don't have to."

She looked quizzical. "Don't you always?"

"Yes. Humor. Okay, back to it. We have weapons, shelter, transport, food and water. Those are covered by Bykop. We need uniforms for the recoverees, familiar food, whatever we can get in medical and dental care for them. Toiletries and cosmetics, and I assume feminine products." It was logical and he tried to sound matter of fact.

Caswell said, "I'll cover all the female gear. Don't forget underwear for everyone, and bras."

"Well, don't you forget them. Thanks for mentioning it."

Spencer said, "Recreational stuff. A handful of movies and books, and something resembling phones they can use for connecting and viewing. We may be waiting some time."

Zep noted, "You will be."

"We can load any video or games onto the vehicle systems," Arnet assured him.

Doc said, "PT clothes, we want to get them exercising."

Sean thought he had it all worked out, though there was a lot of data there. It was a good thing they hadn't tried to explain the mechanics of time travel to him. He had more than enough to juggle already.

"You ladies have been quiet. Any science section input?" he asked.

Sheridan said, "We've already talked to Researcher Zep at length. I'm mostly concerned with the human end. I'll need to get samples from them—cheek swabs, skin swabs, urine, feces, possibly even hair samples and ear wax. I'll preserve most of it. We'll study it when we have full lab facilities."

Raven said, "I'll be doing the same, and whatever I can get from any plants we recognize, anything edible they're eating, some of the fauna, and especially any parasites. So, more feces samples. We have containers to store them, and the Cogi have offered to hard-freeze the specimens at forty-five Kelvin."

"Oh, damn," Doc said. "That's impressive."

"It is. I gather they have better nuclear batteries than we do, which makes sense. They're also obviously not afraid of it to put them in ground vehicles."

Doc put in, "By the way, the correct name for them is Guardians, more or less. 'Cogi' is not accurate." He stared at Cryder as he said it. The man stared back and did appear a bit awkward.

Sean asked, "Oh?"

"You know those stupid pranks troops play by mistranslating for the locals?"

"Yeah? Oh."

"Yeah. It comes from 'cogni.'"

"That sounds like—"

"It is. I guess I can't entirely blame them not wanting to give more information than they had to, but it's certainly derogatory, given how much of our resources they used. Even when they shared, they made us do the work."

"I remember," Spencer agreed. "Still, we need to get along. Guardians and soldiers it is."

Cryder said, "I apologize for the slight."

Barzer's expression was half annoyance, half amusement.

"I will discreetly mention that where it will be received," he commented.

Rich Dalton raised his hand. "I'd like to take at least three Bibles, New American, I guess. I have mine, if it can be cloned." He even had it with him, and held it up. It was well maintained but worn from their last trip. He'd taken especially good care of it. Whenever he felt frustrated or overwhelmed, it was comforting.

Zep said, "It can."

"Please be careful. It's very important to me."

She smiled and took it very gently. "I'm aware how special it is to you. It won't be harmed. We can have that done within the hour."

They all dove in for lunch, and Rich decided on a ham steak and duck eggs, because why not? Duck eggs had more yolk and an almost meaty flavor. He'd missed them. There was miscellaneous chatter, and Shug was still very much an outsider hanging on. The scientists were incorporating well enough. He really wasn't sure how to deal with them. Everyone else was in good morale and getting along.

Zep returned after lunch with four Bibles. Dalton accepted them, turned them around and over, looked inside.

"Um . . . which is mine?" he asked. "Ah, the one with the liner notes. The others are clean."

"Correct," she said. "I understood that was what you wanted, your personal notes kept personal."

"It is. These are perfect. I can't tell them apart."

"I also made a copy for our archives of your incident, if that is acceptable. It does have your notes."

That was very cool. "Certainly. I hope it will be read and enjoyed."

She said, "It will most definitely be studied in context of you and your beliefs."

"Thank you."

Perhaps their intellectual interest would turn spiritual. If not, his documentation persisted, and he had spare copies of his most valuable possession.

✧   ✧   ✧

Sean Elliott, with Doc, Spencer, and Sheridan, was in conference with the...Byko leadership council, of whatever description it was. Cryder accompanied them, but was representing his own element. Senior Researcher Barzer was seated among several others. They sat in a ring, with the subjects—meaning him and his troops—in the middle, swiveling as needed and called. It made one feel like a bug on a plate.

The council might only be local in reach, but they had effective life, death, or lifetime detention authority over he and his troops. So far, they'd ultimately been fair in all decisions. He'd learned the year before, however, that there was nothing like having your safety be bandied about in debate to focus your attention.

This time, though, their English was better, and the discussion was on the transfer.

The current Speaker of the council was Yral Luvaik, a blond woman who actually looked older, to the point of gray hair. Based on their encounters, he guessed she was probably in her eighties or better.

"Captain Elliott, you of course understand, and we record for clarity, that interference with other groups is to be minimal, nonlethal weapons used where possible, assuming peaceful solutions are not of order. Our window is fixed at forty-seven days, and you must be at the recovery point at that time, regardless of mission achievement. The observations of your group, including your scientists, will be shared with our academics, who will assess the value and risk of said data, whereupon you may keep as much as we can safely allow. Your primary priority is the rescue of your fellow American soldiers, and as much of their equipment as is feasible to recover. Secondary is the return of the displacee Shug to his people or a group with whom he is comfortable. Third is the gathering of data. Is this agreeable and understood?"

He didn't have much choice, but that did fit his orders as well.

"It is, and I understand and agree."

"Excellent. Your chain of command will be parallel to Shuff Cryder. Please make every effort to cooperate with his command of equipment and process. He will extend the same courtesy to you relevant to your operations."

"Absolutely."

"Feel free to ask any questions you would like clarification of."

Good. They still hadn't said, so he asked, "How close can you get us?"

One of the other councilors answered, "Within a few months and a few kilometers. Shug should be able to find his own people."

"Well, that's good."

The man warned, "Keep in mind he must be after their time. I don't know how to stress that to him."

Sean said, "That could be an issue. So we want as close as possible for our people, but we absolutely need to be past that time for him."

"And for them. You have a limited window to find his people, and to find your displacees."

"Yes."

The man reiterated, "As stated, we've been able to allot just over forty-seven days for the mission."

"And we have to remain for the duration?"

"Correct. We have no way to monitor a displacement at this time. There are discussions of launching reconnaissance satellites into that era, but there are many issues to work out."

Sheridan put in, "I'll say. People seeing bright lights in the sky. Potential wreckage. Sheer overload of data."

"All that and more, yes."

She reiterated, "Your scientific rules have been explained to us, and we will abide by them. We remain uncomfortable with restrictions on data."

Luvaik replied, "I personally understand your concern, but I am aware you operate with similar restrictions in your time."

Sheridan almost chuckled. "I do. I disapprove of it there, too. I'd hoped here would be more open. But there is no reason to argue. You have made rules, we will comply."

Sean was glad that was at rest. He was afraid she was going for a lengthy argument.

He confirmed again, "So, we have forty-seven days to find, relocate to extraction point, and be done. If we find them, that doesn't seem to be a problem. If not, what then?"

"We will have to discuss a further response."

"Okay. Find them, secure the personnel, equipment, and site. Sanitize whatever we can. Move to extraction point. Be ready for extraction."

"That is the outline, yes."

"Doc, Sergeant Spencer, any input?"

Spencer asked, "Do your troops have any specialized equipment to help locate lost, abandoned, or displaced gear? I know we have reasonable odds of finding the people, but if they panicked and dumped rucks on the way, what then?"

"Yes, our sensors have significant reach on chemical signals. It will take some time of that schedule to conduct searches, but there will be sweeps made. This will also provide other data on environment, entropic markers, and life-forms."

"Good."

Doc asked, "Are there quarantine procedures to follow?"

"Whatever you and Arnet deem necessary and appropriate on location is acceptable. Quarantine on return will be as last time, taken care of here, largely without intrusion into your lives."

"Got it."

CHAPTER 11

The next morning, Rich Dalton rose, offered a quick prayer of thanks, and hurried for breakfast. This was the day.

They all dressed in their updated uniforms, checked off the gear, loaded it onto a broad, rolling dolly, and prepared for departure. Shug came along in his linen and leather, and it was fascinating that linen dated that far back. Though the Bible certainly referenced fabrics early on. Another myth of primitive savages failed in the face of evidence.

Cal the cat seemed to grasp the humans were leaving, and came by for skritches. He was happy to see his people again, and he seemed to have a comfortable life here, as mascot for the temporal group.

They had cloned Bibles and AR-10s, future weapons, rucks, personal effects, electronics and paper for documenting everything, a bale of material to fabricate uniforms for the displaced element—assuming they found them—defenses for the perimeter, cold climate clothing, tools. Whatever they'd need for a wartime deployment was on hand, though at a fraction the weight of their own era's equipment.

The walk to the processing center in the dome was becoming familiar. They arrived at the platform with their dolly, and the two vehicles were already present. Cryder and Arnet indicated for them to bring the gear, and showed where to stow it, depending on how quickly it might be needed. They even helped this time.

Rich made another quick prayer, for their safety, and that of the unit they were trying to recover. With faith in God, this could be done. And if any of them needed ministering, he'd do his best.

Dr. Twine was there to see them off, in a long purple robe tied in at the waist. Another woman was with her. She was tall as they all were, dark and exotic looking with a slight slant to her eyes. Modern Siberian, possibly? Then Larilee Zep arrived, along with Ed Ruj. The gang was all here.

"Good luck to you all," Twine offered. "If this works as it should, I'm told we'll be standing right here when you return. May your recovery efforts be effective."

"Thanks, ma'am," he replied. It was nice to be supported.

"Good luck to you all," the other said.

Spencer replied, "Thank you, Maralina."

So he knew who she was. Interesting. She was strikingly beautiful even by the raised baseline of this time. He remembered her from the other night.

They stood waiting on the platform. Rich looked around and tried not to be tense. Caswell appeared to be praying. Shug seemed to grasp they were about to move, and was nervous. Spencer was breathing steadily. The two science chicks were each looking in a different direction, Raven toward the control panel, Sheridan at the people. Oglesby and the captain were agitated but he couldn't tell which way. Arnet and Cryder were completely casual.

There was the familiar *BANG*, not overly loud, and longer in duration than an explosion. Now that he had a chance to hear it while relatively unstressed, Rich realized it was more of a displacement shock, sort of like lightning. Which made sense.

He looked around and saw landscape, but no immediate threats. He looked down. They had less of a chewed-up area under them this time. He looked again in detail and saw it was a prairie-looking slope with wildflowers and brush. In the distance, trees were just barely starting to show some color. So it was early fall. Late September, perhaps? Off to the east was a herd of something, and the juveniles were a good size. Definitely reaching autumn.

Shug suddenly looked much brighter. He recognized this as his home environment.

Cryder said, "Wer through, nd everthn seems to've ccompnied us. I's slightly worrd bou that, but they calced the mass crecly n here we are."

His native accent returned when he wasn't paying attention. That was something to note and mention. It could matter in an emergency.

Sean Elliott said, "I understood you but that was slightly uneven."

"What? Ah. Okay," the man acknowledged.

Cryder followed with, "Think that clearing a good place for camp. We're visible enough, have decent fire fields, and are on the southeast of the crest. Minimizes weather and maximizes sun. Thoughts?"

Arnet said, "I concur."

Cryder nodded, and looked at Sean.

Well, it was nice to be consulted. It did mean he was part of the team leadership.

"Yes, that's fine for now. I'm not opposed to moving if we find something better as we search."

"Probably'll have to," Cryder said. "May not be that close. Sar'int Spencer, your comments?"

Spencer said, "I see nothing to disagree with. I'm confident in you and the captain. If I see a reason to raise any comments, trust me, I will."

"Very good," the man agreed with a nod, then pointed. "That's camp. If I may: Spencer, Arnet, move Rollers, drone will mark the positions. Everyone walk, then pleece the area for obstacles and positions."

That was clear enough. Sean said, "Spread out, two-meter intervals. Obstacles are boulders, stumps, holes, anything we might have trouble with on foot. Positions I assume are useful points for a defensive hasty. We'll prep those."

Sheridan said, "So this is a lot like the Romans. Move in, secure, then either fill or mark for later use when we leave."

"Exactly that," he agreed. "Some things, once developed, never change."

He turned, hefted his ruck and shrugged into it, and started walking.

The local animal noises started to resume. Apparently the transition had startled them.

It wasn't more than couple of hundred meters, but it was upslope on broken terrain. It felt a good five times that, but he was in decent enough shape. It wouldn't hurt to find a way to keep working out, though.

He gave the women this, they didn't protest about the hike. That had been partly his doing. The rucks could have gone on the vehicles, but since they were already carrying them, there was no reason not to continue doing so. He wanted to see how they handled it.

They didn't complain. They were a bit unsteady at first on rough terrain, but they trudged along, keeping pace with the rest. For two hundred meters. It was a good first test, though.

The chosen area was fairly clear. A half dozen bushes were visible enough. There were two sizeable boulders near the surface but not high enough for cover. The terrain had just enough slope for drainage, and they'd want to put their heads uphill to sleep.

Cryder and Arnet handed out gear and directed. He took it on himself to post Dalton near the crest and Caswell toward the woodline on sentry.

Arnet floated up a drone. Sean recalled the model from their last trip.

"That thing is solar powered?" he asked.

Arnet said, "Yes. Is very light, with a durable capacitor, and solar recharging. It droops at night and climbs in day. It has IR spectrum sensors and also acts as a commo relay."

"Line of sight, I recall."

"Yes. Don't go more than forty kilometers from here." He grinned in irony. Although, given the vehicles, he might be serious.

Arnet popped up a shelter and pointed inside. "This is the light switch. I recommend five lumens for reading or personal matters. Brighter, your vision will be affected, and above forty lumens will start to show. It has monochrome six none zero nanometers for best nighttime vision protection. Limited capacity enviro unit. If you need it, it will last all night for several nights in this climate."

Cryder and Spencer had spent this time setting out posts, about ten meters apart.

Cryder said, "Wards are now set. Don't exit except between vehicles. I have them set for a heavy stun, assuming predators."

Sean sighed. The work his element had done with logs, bark, hand tools, and backbreaking labor over weeks was duplicated in an hour with futuristic tools.

He asked, "What about the latrine?"

"Behind Roller One. It will drain into a ditch we'll fill tomorrow."

Arnet was pulling the curtain around right then. Field primitive, but with privacy. Good enough.

Sheridan hurried that way and said, "I need to test that right now."

Arnet then said, "If you want fire, it's acceptable. I recommend that hollow there." He pointed at a depression. "You can take a wagon out for a load of wood. I'll start warming food at Roller Two. There'll also be a small alcohol ration. We'll eat in one hour."

Dalton and Oglesby took the collapsible wagon for wood. The conveyance had tall, grippy off-road tires and a decent capacity. It had its own power supply, like a powered dolly. With one of the flex tools, that Sean knew could be turned into a silent chain saw, they were off and back in twenty minutes with enough cut wood for the night.

Dinner was ready right on time, and it was great not to have to use field spacing for rations. Sean urged everyone else ahead.

"Commander eats last," he said. "By rank from the lowest."

Raven seemed amused. "I'm pretty sure my contract rate is well above captain, but I appreciate it, Sean." She and Sheridan lined up after Spencer. Doc was next to last.

"Rank is also a position," he agreed. "I want to make sure everyone is fed."

Oglesby asked, "Where do we put Shug?"

Sean replied at once with, "That's a good question," while he thought quickly. "Put him with you so you can help him, and explain that his status is that of an advisor and subordinate leader."

"I think he'll like that, sir."

The young man's eyes widened as Oglesby translated, and he did seem very flattered.

Oglesby helped Shug choose foods suited to him. The boy had grasped how to use knife, spoon, and fork efficiently if not neatly enough for formal events. He looked much more comfortable in breechcloth, leggings, and tunic than he had in the ersatz native Afghan clothes or US uniform.

The Guardians' field kitchen setup was very efficient, and included dishes. Dinner was close enough to pot roast to be called so, with minimal gravy and crisp carrots and onions he'd swear had not been preserved in any way. There were baked potatoes stuffed with some sort of cheese, ham, and onions with a sprinkle spice on the side that seemed reminiscent of Hungarian. He tasted it and decided to skip that, but added a shaking of very flavorful pepper to the beef.

They sat on rolls of something that were good enough for a hasty setup. Spencer and Doc just stood over the hood of Roller One and ate off it.

Dessert was a frozen fruit ice that was quite light on the stomach. It was very refreshing after a couple of hours in the field, even laid back as it had been so far.

He was still hungry, so he wandered over to the kitchen awning and looked at what else was there. Some sort of bread rolls, and stuff to spread on them. Cheese? Yes.

There were eleven cups, each with liquor. It smelled like rum.

Arnet came up and said, "Mix that," and pointed at a small tube of flavoring, "with the liquor."

It was suddenly spiced rum with a nutty finish.

Arnet took a small tub, poured powder and water into it, stirred it, then drew a hose from the kitchen apparatus, much like a drink dispenser. He gripped it, and a blast of vapor rose from the tub.

Oglesby asked, "What's that?"

"Liquid nitrogen. Field-expedient ice cream."

The man exclaimed, "Holy shit! How do I enlist?"

Arnet grinned and noted, "You have this technology."

"Yes, I've heard of engineer and medical units doing similar stuff, but it wasn't built into the truck."

Dalton called, "Did someone say 'ice cream'?" and arrived at a brisk walk.

The ice cream was also a base with flavor. One took the mixed liquid, added the contents of a packet—the strawberry included freeze-dried strawberries that puffed back to full volume quickly—set the container in the kitchen cubby, and pressed a surface switch. The nitrogen fumed and hissed, and five seconds later, the bowl had ice cream in it.

"That's amazing."

"It's not bad," Arnet agreed. "I understand you had much better rations than the generation before."

Spencer said, "Or the ones before that. The military went from gruel and scavenging, to crackers and beans, to bland packages, finally to something almost good. It looks like you've taken it another level."

Sean and Spencer took strawberry. Doc had butterscotch, as did Oglesby. Dalton had chocolate. Caswell went for vanilla and gave a couple of spoonfuls to Shug. Raven frowned and took one bite herself, thanking Caswell for it. Sheridan dug into the chocolate all out, and Arnet and Cryder both had pear, which Sean was willing to try next time.

After dinner, Oglesby and Arnet wiped the nonstick dishes, which were then UV sterilized in their compartment. That was it. The onboard cistern was full of water for drinking and limited washing, would be refilled by rain or when they crossed a watercourse.

"You certainly make field conditions easy," Sean commented. "As much as I like movies and expect you have some, I think I want to check out the stars."

"They're very vivid in this time," Cryder agreed.

Everyone gathered to watch the sun set, the sky clear, bright, with orange blazing to light blue to violet then black. Stars appeared, more luminous and plentiful than could be seen in either future era, though Sean seemed to recall the future sky was clearer and less obscured than the twenty-first century. It was refreshingly cool with a gentle breeze, cooling steadily as the night progressed.

"Wowww," he heard Raven say softly. Doc had an app up on his phone and was checking the ephemeris, probably, to compare actual versus predicted.

Sheridan said, "I recognize constellation patterns, but they look battered."

Doc looked ecstatic to have a way to place himself. Shug seemed very pleased to recognize stars, and be able to see them clearly. That was probably something he was keenly aware of. Everyone else just stared. There were animal noises, insects, wind sighs.

"You know," Sean said, "if I have to bivouac, or even just camp, this is the way to do it. You could set up tours and make a fortune."

Cryder replied, "That's a thing we're afraid of. Too much presence will eventually affect the Temporality."

Sean asked, "Yeah. How much?"

He shook his head. "I don't know the figures, but I know

Bycop and Suhrny are concerned about it and greatly restrict travel. My reward, and Arnet's, for being displaced is to be two of the very few trusted as escorts and recon."

"I hope it's enjoyable, not a chore."

The man sounded calm, but said, "It's very enjoyable. I also find myself tense with concern."

"I hear that."

They resumed watching the sky, completely black where the stars weren't. Then more, faint stars appeared behind those, and the Milky Way, spilling across the sky to the south. Was that the faint trail of a meteor?

After a while, Cryder said, "We have sensors on the perimeter. Arnet and I are armed for response. You're welcome to post watch but need not."

Sean said, "We'll trust the equipment. Anyone who wants to stay up is welcome. What time are we waking up, Cryder?"

"Oh eight hundred your time is good."

That late? This definitely wasn't the US Army.

"Fair enough. We're likely to wake up around sunrise."

"Keep noise moderate, please. We'll eat as soon as we're up, recon, then hopefully strike biv and move to contact."

"You heard him," he said to make it official on his end.

He went to his shelter to get his toothbrush, and headed for the latrine behind the first vehicle.

Shug found the knowledge of the others frustrating. They had these moving huts. Veeculs. They could shake a piece of fabric into a portable lodge. They could have hot food without a fire, and with no time taken.

The lodge was just enough for him, very comfortable, and magic. He would have slept under grass or a hide if he had one. They just waved hands and a rolled piece of weave magically became a tiny lodge to sleep in.

He had no idea what to do, so he climbed in and thought about sleeping.

He actually felt alone and unsure with everything closed, even though he knew Dan and the others were only a few steps away. He left the end open. It wasn't that cold of an evening. Also, the sleeping hide he was wrapped in was quite warm. He was very comfortable and, once he could see the fire and the others, relaxed and calm.

The sky held lots of stars and they looked right. There was the Cup, and the Mountain, and the Raindrops. That made him feel a lot better.

The fire by the veeculs was a good size. Just large enough to be seen and provide warmth to those around it, with some smoke to warn animals that people were here. Fuel didn't seem to be a problem. Besides wood, they had those small bundles that burned for a long time.

He really felt unsure without his spear, but Zhenny and Martin were up with their magic weapons. He understood they could stop a lion with one. Then they had their magic seeing thing. Fedeo, it was called. This was a strange camp, but it should be completely safe. He did have his knife, and he put that next to his headroll.

All that done, he curled up in the hide and went to sleep.

CHAPTER 12

Armand Devereaux found it hard to sleep late in the field. The fully darkened shelters helped. His alarm woke him at 0600, and he stretched. That was later than the usual Army roll out, earlier than planned. He wanted to shower, clean up, and keep tabs on things as people got ready.

He felt well rested and far more comfortable, knowing he wasn't trapped and lost this time. He actually had enjoyed the previous day. Work had been light, the environment pleasant.

It was a cool morning, probably in the mid-fifties. He wanted to stay in the bag and be warm, but there were things to do. He dragged on pants and flip-flops, and crawled out of the tent with his kit. It was misty and dewy, but that was better than rain or scorching heat.

He was first for the shower. The onboard tank meant they each got a short, sanitary wash. At least the water was hot, and the curtained area worked as a good windbreak, keeping the steam in. He stepped from the shower to the vestibule and chilled at once, his skin prickling into goose bumps, until a waft of warm air took the chill off. Each section was just big enough to stand in, much like any field shower, which made efficient use of water, and apparently heating air. He dressed in a fresh uniform. The Byko-provided outfits really were comfortable, and looked correct. The ballistic resistance was a nice plus. The camp and gear were certainly above average for a field function.

Dalton was waiting a short distance away.

"Remind everyone to combat shower," he said.

Dalton acknowledged, "Will do, Doc. Wet, soap, rinse."

That was all they had for now, but it was certainly adequate. When they got next to a water source, however, they could have long, hot showers and even fill a tub, as long as no one was waiting.

Arnet came out shortly, even though it wasn't 0800. The man got to work with some sort of container in the kitchen area, and grabbed some package from storage.

"Anything I can do to help?" he asked.

Arnet pointed and said, "Can you get the plates? Also, that package is condiments."

"Got it."

Cryder also came out, waved, and went to do something else.

Armand gathered the preparation was a combination of defrosting, rehydrating, microwave, and convection heat. It was minutes only before he smelled pancakes of some sort, fruit cocktail, and what looked like sausage links. Not bad. The pictorial directions on the balloon-like package he picked up indicated it was a beverage and he should fill the container with water and shake. He did so, and they had some sort of juice. Pineapple, mango, and guava, maybe? It smelled like good stuff.

With the plates out, Arnet started dishing out food.

Armand called, "Hurry up, we won't bring it to you."

SFC Spencer came over and said, "Well done, Doc. I'll take two plates to the scientists. They're apparently already digging in the dirt for clues." He pointed where the two women had sample kits out. They had a table and an awning.

"That's dedication," Armand agreed, and handed over a plate of food. Then he grabbed another and left the pancakes off—he remembered Dr. Raven was on a no starch diet.

Dalton came up with Oglesby and Shug. Shug looked thrilled at having food ready without a hunt or fire, thanked him, and moved aside to start shoveling it in. He made lots of "mmmm" noises.

He certainly seemed happy to be back in familiar surroundings.

The captain was last, said, "Thanks, this looks good," and walked off to eat while patrolling the perimeter and checking the ground.

Everyone ate fast. The science chicks munched between samples, and weren't at all bothered with ladylike manners. Sheridan wrapped all hers in the pancake and chomped it, then slurped down the fruit and juice. Raven just stuffed a whole sausage in her mouth between each process, in a fashion probably not meant to be suggestive, but damn. She was overweight, but stacked. She was wearing a civilian outfit at present. That khaki field shirt stretched over her rack. The T-shirt was being tortured. She'd declined the fruit and juice, too. All she ate was meat.

She might be a bit heavy, but she had good muscle tone, and bent over, he suddenly heard Sir Mix-A-Lot. Rubens would probably have sculpted her.

She stood up and caught his glance at her breasts.

She grinned at him and said, "Yes, they're large. It's okay if you look. Men can't help it."

He felt a blush and, "Uh, ma'am . . ."

"It's fine." She smiled. "I know how big they are, and I know how biology works. Just no comments where I can hear them."

That was fair enough. "Yes, ma'am."

Next to her, Sheridan giggled. She was more round, less stacked, but obviously not offended, either. Well, good.

The scientists scooped, tubed, and labeled samples of several plants and the dirt. He wasn't sure what their criteria were, but they apparently knew their job. They finished their specimens about the same time everyone finished eating.

Cryder had eaten while prepping what was obviously another drone. It was similar to the one from the night before. It was a small balloon with ducted fans, powered by both capacitor and solar array.

He did something to it, gave it a loft, and up it went, trailing that fine monofilament behind it. The wind caught it, it weathercocked and corrected, and rose quickly.

Armand noted Shug was staring in rapt fascination. He looked very confused as the drone's surface blended to match the sky above and disappeared from view. He stared at Oglesby, who shrugged and told Shug what Armand interpreted was "That's what it does."

The wire seemed to be both tether and cable. Cryder had a tiny console out that was mostly screen, but took touch and voice input.

He didn't seem to be worried about secrecy, so Armand watched without getting too close. The onboard camera had good resolution. Cryder panned and swept. The orientation shifted and turned. Then he zoomed in. Zoomed out. Repeated.

"Arnet, launch the PD."

Arnet replied, "Willdo, Shuff." He turned and spoke to Armand. "Can one of your element stack the dishes back in the box?"

The box section would clean the dishes and have them ready for the next meal.

That was easy. "Absolutely. Dalton, can you do that?"

"Glad to." The man sounded happy to have a task.

Armand replied, "Thank you. I'm interested in watching, but let me take care of business." He turned to the camp and raised his voice a bit.

"Sick call! Anyone need sick call? I'm here and available for any complaints or issues."

There were a couple of noes and an "I'm good." No issues. He hadn't expected any. That was good, though he did enjoy his work. Especially without pompous surgeons harassing him.

The drone Arnet prepped was a lifting body, appeared to be as light as Styrofoam—and perhaps was—and snapped together.

While Armand watched, Captain Elliott came over.

"Thanks, Doc. What's going on?"

"Watching the drone prep, sir," he replied. "How's the perimeter?"

Elliott said, "Per the cameras, lots of small animals came by. A couple of larger deerlike things may have. No predators I can tell. There seems to be that herd down there." He pointed down the slope to a distant group of antelope. "Otherwise, complete wilderness."

"Sounds good. Any housekeeping that needs done?"

"No, and that bothers me a bit. If we get bored we'll get slack. There's nothing that needs done at present, though. We're fed, secure, bivouacked, and awaiting mission."

"Any training we can cover?"

The captain shook his head. "I wish. We should probably start PT up again, though, once we decide where we're going to be. We need to stay in shape, and anyone we rescue is probably going to need Army discipline."

"We managed okay, but we got lucky. You did a great job of keeping order." He wanted to make sure the man understood he'd been a very effective leader.

"Thanks. That was a team effort. Everyone deserved medals we can't get."

Armand shrugged. "That's the Army way, sir."

The captain agreed. "Sometimes. I still want you all to know you have my respect."

This was much better leadership than the hospital. "That does mean a lot, sir."

"How is your real career going?"

He shrugged and muttered, then said, "The medicine is going great. The administrative stuff can be some ballbusting bullshit. And I wish certain doctors wouldn't assume I'm pig ignorant."

Elliott said, "Yeah, you've done impressive battlefield work on the ones we could save."

Then there's the ones we couldn't, so let's change subjects, he thought.

"I didn't want to interrupt the scientists, but now I'm curious."

"Me too," Elliott agreed. "Let's ask. Ladies?"

From thirty feet away, Sheridan heard him, glanced up, and asked, "What's up?"

They walked over together as the captain asked, "We're curious about what data you're gathering."

She held up the packet in her hand and said, "Hands-on is a soil sample for comparison—bacteria, fungi, potentially viruses, and any microbial evolutionary change. We know of some, but fresh material for comparison is loads easier than decayed matter. We'll be sampling the troops as we recover them, very important for infection control. Then, we're both wearing weather monitors that are sampling CO_2, methane, O_2, particulate, ozone, and trace levels for climate research."

Elliott said, "I'm still a bit surprised they allowed that."

"Us too," she said.

Raven added, "We'll need periodic urine and fecal samples from everyone to compare to baseline. That's for environmental study on metabolic contaminants and their effects. Don't worry, we can take them discreetly enough from the latrine, and we only need a little. The same with anyone we recover, and possibly with the locals." She looked carefully around as if counting people, then whispered, "And some from our hosts so we can determine as much about them as possible."

Armand nodded and said, "As a physician, I offer any services you might need."

"Thank you," Raven replied with a nod. "We were not going to discuss that anywhere they might hear, and I'm leery even here. Some of their drones are tiny, and could even be in the clothes. You'll notice I'm wearing what I brought."

He'd wondered about that. It made sense in that context.

She raised her voice slightly. "Kate, let's get the samples stowed. Captain, can we help do any cleanup or chores?"

Elliott said, "Cleanup is welcome, anything of ours needs to get recovered and trashed. Teardown depends on the Guardians." He turned and raised his voice. "Cryder?"

Cryder looked over his shoulder, raised a finger for "wait," and adjusted something. That done, he stood.

The captain asked, "What about teardown or movement?"

The tall man replied, "Teardown is simple. Looks like we're about twenty kays from the river, and there are seval settlements. We'll need to drive closer, then unass and walk."

Sean Elliott laughed. "Did you say 'unassed'?"

Cryder replied, "Yes. It's a slang word for getting out."

"I know the word. Where did you get it?"

"Used it long as I've been on duty, why?"

"Because we use the exact same word."

Cryder laughed hard as well. "That's very amusing," he agreed.

He continued, "I find no evidence of electronics, nothing resembling vehicles, no chem traces of explosives. I didn't expect any. Just a precautionary check."

"Understood. When do we leave?"

"Soon as possible. If we drive in shifts, we can make it tonight and set camp in the morning, then have all day for meeting."

"Okay, let's do it."

Striking camp took less than an hour. The bivy tents shook down and into their bags as fast as they went up. With no predators or other threats in sight, the wards came down in minutes. The vehicle assemblies folded into themselves. Once the fire was out and the latrine sump covered, the Byko wound down the drones and saddled up.

Cryder said, "We'll rotate on driving, but Arnet and I'll start to maximize speed. You should observe."

"Sounds good," Sean agreed.

The vehicles were built for four each, crowded with eleven split between them. Cryder and Sean were up front. The two scientists seemed a bit squashed in back, but neither complained. Doc stretched along the deck behind them, in front of the cargo box. The second vehicle had Arnet, Spencer, Caswell, Dalton, Oglesby, and Shug. Shug snuggled into a gap between seats and seemed comfortable enough, and he was finally used to the idea of vehicle movement.

When the US troops had done this before, they'd had three people walking as ground guides against the possibility of tumbling the overbalanced MRAPs. The Byko vehicles moved smoothly on their not-quite-track-sort-of-wheel locomotion, smoothing out all the terrain bumps and dips into rolling waves. Occasionally the dash would beep to indicate some sort of obstacle ahead, and Cryder just guided around. The display showed terrain features, and had shading and color coding for depth and texture. Sean felt he'd be able to use it given time. It was like a really good game interface.

He understood they'd only had a very rough intro in the future, but this could be important. On the other hand, so many tasks and equipment.

"Cryder, how is your military training organized?"

"In what context?"

"Selection, qualification, initial training. A rough outline."

"Volunteers are tested for endurance and determination through an increasingly difficult series of problems. Lessons are given at each point. Then we select a specialty and study that in detail."

"What is your specialty?"

"Crowd and scene control for major disruptive events."

"Good choice, as it happened. And Arnet?"

"Arnet is a technical operator and maintainer. I deployed a drone for practice. Ordinarily that's his task. He supported our vehicle through some damage last time."

"...What does it take to damage this?"

"A stampede by *!ketchethanu* as the Gadorth said. Woolly rhino, as you call it."

He nodded. "Yeah, that seems pretty rough. How is your initial entry reception?"

"Please elaborate."

"Do you do PT, uniform issue, lots of hurry up and wait, shouting, ordering?"

The man looked confused. "Why would we shout?"

"Our instructors shout to motivate people."

"If we weren't motivated, we wouldn't volunteer."

"Right, but being motivated isn't just enough. It has to be fast, reactive response."

"That's why we have tasks of increasing difficulty. Each one is a challenge."

"How do you handle people who fail?"

"They can try until they succeed, or decide it's not where they are suited. Many don't like heights, even with airborne transportation in our society. Taking the vehicle and all its safety mechanisms away makes it much less comfortable."

"It does. So, just tougher activities all the time?"

"Yes. Running, lifting, hiking, equipment, medicine, terrain orienting and crossing, building access and scaling, weapons usage and unarmed fighting. Then specialties in equipment and management."

"Can you compare our ranks to yours?"

"Not really. Yours are harder codified. Ours are a sliding scale, I think you say."

"I see."

The man explained, "Arnet is in charge if we must perform maintenance. You'll be in charge during interactions with your displacees. I'm in charge of our movement otherwise and our transitions. We have the cooperative leadership for bivwac location and schedule. Does this suit you?"

"It seems to work well. Do you know any good jokes?"

"Possibly." Cryder said nothing for some time, concentrating on terrain, but also seemed to be in thought. He cautiously maneuvered around the edge of a herd of goats. The animals drew back, leaving space, but since the vehicle didn't smell like a predator or make any move toward them, they didn't flee.

Cryder maneuvered generally downward, over lips and contours, around boulders and copses of trees. The man gave his attention to steering, and Sean stayed quiet.

It was about five minutes before Cryder said, "I don't know if this joke is appropriate in your group with mixed sexes."

From the back, Raven said, "Go for it."

Cryder shrugged. "What do you call a woman who can start an impeller engine with her mouth?"

The answer, obviously, was "Darling." Sean had his mouth open when Raven cut in.

"If he can call me anything at that moment, I'm not doing it right."

Cryder laughed. Sean followed, then the others.

Good answer.

"I've rarely seen you smile," Sean said. "I've seen cheerful people in your time, but few jokes."

"We joke, but not generally in public."

"Why is that?"

"A joke's funny because of shock factor, but everyone's limit is different."

"True. Some of our culture have taken that to an extreme."

Sheridan leaned forward and said, "We call those 'assholes.'"

Cryder chuckled.

Sean was glad. It was an unintentional test of the contractors, but they weren't spoiled snowflakes who'd whine about soldier slang.

"By the way, rations are in the middle box," Cryder pointed at a console. "Choose what you like."

Sean acknowledged, "Great, as soon as I puzzle out your lettering."

"Not that different."

"Different enough to slow me slightly. I'll see what I can find."

Raven said, "I need mine starch free, or at least wheat free."

"Cryder, can you advise?"

"It's all wheat free. On the other, give me a sec," he said, and turned, letting the vehicle drive itself. Well, it was probably equipped for that and the terrain was smooth enough. He leaned over the seats, stretched back, and dug in the box.

"Beef sticks with spice sauce, Siber chicken roll, chicken chowder has corn but no wheat."

She looked relieved. "Thanks. I'll make sure to plan ahead for tomorrow."

In the other vehicle, Arnet followed the lead. Martin Spencer sat next to him, wondering about details. The terrain was less lush here than when they'd been in similar geography. This was a different era.

"What time frame is this?"

"Younger Dryas, as you called it."

"Ah. Later than we were?"

"Quite some, yes."

"When were we?" he asked, trying to sound as casual as possible.

"Thirteen thousand, two hundred ninety-one years before your calendar dating."

Holy shit. He'd said it. Doc had been close with his guess. And damn, that was precise, but then, once they had a point established, each one should be easier, right?

"Do more points make it easier to coordinate these things?"

"Of course."

"I didn't want to assume."

Arnet shrugged. "This is about as much as I know."

Martin said, "Civilization started a few centuries before this, near as we can tell, then this cooling period stopped it dead. They seem to have had to start over again."

Arnet almost smiled as he said, "I can't comment even if I know about it."

"I understand. It would be fascinating to look around, though."

Nodding agreement, the man said, "It would. Time and energy costs don't permit that, and there're numerous uncertainties regarding how safe that is for the Temporality."

Martin understood that. "Yes. Any observer might affect outcomes, to any number of degrees. Which might snowball into a disaster."

"Correct. I don't know at all, but our scientists are being very cautious, which I think is wise."

That was valid. "Yeah. If you don't know, don't mess with it."

"I hope they'll be able to eventually send observers and drones back to get accurate data of all these events and natural processes."

"Very much. That would tempt me to move to your society, if I didn't have ties back home." He didn't want to continue that train of thought, either.

Arnet saved him by saying, "Anyway, let's have lunch."

They ate and talked while proceeding at a slow, methodical rate.

✧   ✧   ✧

Pitching camp that afternoon was as easy. They halted on an even area next to a tiny trickle of stream, with scattered trees and rocks. Rich Dalton helped set the wards, pressing them into the ground with a heel, just like on a shovel. It was that simple. They'd sense anything approaching, sound a warning, create a shock barricade that would at least slow most fauna, and could provide illumination. Neat stuff. It didn't seem it was that much more advanced than modern technology, though an Army unit would need a generator to power them. These fed off a large battery, and could recharge slowly from the sun, quickly from the nuke plants on the vehicles. Another package unfolded as a scaffolding with a sensor atop the second vehicle. That was the guard tower. One hose went upstream for water intake, the other downstream for discharge.

Rich asked, "How processed is the wastewater?"

Cryder assured him, "It's sterile on discharge. Though there's some chemical sediment. The manufactory takes minerals from it."

Arnet followed along with Oglesby, erecting lightweight screens, struggling slightly against the gusty breeze.

Rich asked, "What are those?"

Arnet said, "One-way panels. We'll be near invisible from the sides. In the field, we can erect them overhead."

"Cool. That makes sense. No reason to freak out anyone finding us."

Arnet noted, "We are leaving the downstream arc open." He pointed to that side of the bivouac.

"Got it. Arnet, who do you guys fight?" The question had been bugging him.

The man looked up and replied, "At home? Few."

"Okay. Riot control?" What did they do, then?

Arnet put down the sheet he held and nodded. "We train for that. We're a cross between your military, police, and rescue contingents. There are occasional disputes over border territory, product and process control, or material resources." He raised the sheet back up and snapped it against the wards.

That sounded familiar. "Those get violent?"

"Less often if we're present, but yes, it has happened. The last was ten years ago."

He was still curious. "For which nations?" He raised the next panel for Arnet to attach.

Arnet shrugged fractionally. "You wouldn't recanize them, but in Central Europe. If you're asking who we are fighting presently, there's no notable conflict. We hope that continues, we've made responses twice in the last year to contentious events. I also participated in an Arctic rescue of some adventurers."

"What were they doing, hiking to the pole?"

"Cycle racing."

Rich whistled. "Yeah, that doesn't sound like the safest thing in that environment." He shoved a panel upright and Arnet pinned it to its neighbor.

Arnet said, "They all survived. Two needed stabilized, stasised, transported and significant recovery time."

Rich asked, "Was that a onetime thing?" And idiots still liked to risk their lives, apparently.

"It's a regular event. As is the Chomolungma Power Climb."

"Chomo...?"

"The tallest mountain, northeast of here."

"Everest? Mount Everest?" He rested the next panel on his knee, adjusted grip, and hefted.

"That sounds like the name I heard, yes. The native name is what we use."

"Cool. Our National Guard does a lot of disaster response. Forest fires and such." At least they had something in common.

Arnet agreed, "Those exist, rarely affect our habitations."

He noted, "You have much better environmental control than we do."

"Not completely, but yes. Earthquakes remain poorly predictable."

"Volcanoes?"

The tall man barely sounded strained as he raised another screen and snapped it into position. "We avoid living on them generally, though houses built on them can resist lava, and most owners have air vehicles for evac. We did lose several patrons in one last year. They lost connection and were cut off, so the personalities failed."

"They're legally people, aren't they?"

"They're people," Arnet assured him. "Just not entirely biological. I can't discuss further."

Rich had no idea how that worked. "Understood. Sorry to hear about the loss." Were they people uploaded to the network?

Or purely AI? Did they have souls with their personalities? He hoped so, but only God could say.

Arnet replied, "Thank you. We have few lethal disasters. It's always a shock."

There were all these things the future people were quite willing to share, and a handful that were utterly taboo.

The last tool was basically a rotary trimmer with a rolling ball to keep it at height. Arnet demonstrated with a cut around the vehicles, and a clearing for formation. He passed it off to Rich.

"Switch there, tilt to shift. Can you clear to each tent, the fire, and the obtower?"

"Sure can," he agreed. It was larger than a weedwhacker but handled as easily. In minutes he'd cleared the areas in question, and figured they could clear more later if they remained.

With camp set, food followed quickly. Cryder had worked on that meantime, with Dr. Raven helping. There was a chicken stew, quite tasty, with carrots, onions, peas, and some other root as well as potatoes. Fresh bread was available. There was something like focaccia with chopped meat and cheese filling, some interesting herbs, and a lot of garlic. Fresh fruit. Drinks included cold water, fruit juice of several types, the alcohol ration, and something sweet like a mango soda, but not carbonated.

"Cryder, what is this juice?" Rich asked. He'd chosen a deep purple one that wasn't grape, but was tasty.

"It's...a cluster-type berry. Dark."

"Blackberry? Raspberry?"

"Something like that. I don't know which is which. It's similar to something you had but bred and engineered to be more robust."

"It's good. Thanks."

There was an informal formation around the kitchen area. They had a mix of chairs, rolled seats, and the vehicles at present. Cryder sat leaning out of Roller Two.

He said, "The drones are dark capable, I prefer to fly them by day only. I'll start them in the morning and attempt to find habitations, then your contingent."

The captain put in, "Thanks. I was going to ask how the timeline went. On the one hand, forty-seven days seems like plenty. On the other hand, it can get away from you quickly." They were already through Day 2.

"We'll start at once now we're emplaced," Cryder agreed.

Dr. Sheridan waved for attention and said, "We'll need to take further samples here and as we go, of dirt, flora, fauna, and each of you, to track contamination."

Oglesby asked, "How detailed of samples?"

"Nothing overt," she replied. "Skin wipes will take care of most of it. Arnet has the toilet facilities programmed to test urine and feces and tag it."

"Well, that's a fun dinner conversation."

She blushed faintly. "Sorry. Bugs and dirt are what we do."

Doc snickered. "I've heard much, much worse at the hospital," he offered. "There was this guy with a circular saw on his lap—"

Spencer interrupted with, "Stop now, please." He was grinning as he said it, though.

Doc grinned back. "I was going to stop. The setup was all it took. Besides, everyone knows about plastic kneecaps. Plastic testicles, however . . ."

Rich cringed. Damn.

Dr. Raven said, "Serves the dumbass right. Some people shouldn't breed."

"Drugs may have been involved," Doc admitted.

"Shocking. Shocked, I say."

Cryder spoke up, "As a note, network is operational, so you have access to music and film libraries of your era, your encyclopedia courtesy of Sergeant Spencer, and some games and other stuff. Anything off limits won't respond."

Spencer said, "Porn and private tents. The ultimate field condition luxury."

Rich noted a couple of people laughed a bit too loud. He didn't try to figure out who. One was female.

Captain Elliott said, "We can sit by the fire, you can hit the sack whenever. We're up at oh five hundred, Army style."

Spencer groused. "I hate getting up early. So what do I do? Join the Army. Then I retire and take a job that requires me to get up early, by choice. Then back in the Army. One day I'll learn. But today is not that day, apparently."

CHAPTER 13

Sean Elliott was woken by his alarm sharp at 0500, crawled out, dragging a jacket because it was damned chilly in this clean, crisp, clear air, with fog wafting down the hill, and cleaned up. Leak, wash hands, shave, brush teeth, skip shower for now. It was too cold to bother unless necessary, and he'd be fine for today.

A herd of antelope surrounded them, moving slowly west. Mixed in were bactrians, some horses, and a family group of the hairy goats. The animals didn't seem really aware of them, and just moved around the wards.

Caswell and Spencer were getting breakfast ready at the vehicle kitchen, heating sausage, bacon, and what smelled like eggs and pancakes. Meanwhile, Cryder and Arnet worked on the foam plane drone again. Shortly, Cryder held it up and tossed it, and it flew off. That was it.

They finished breakfast and stowed the dishes in the washer as the sun rose and burned off the fog and the dew. The troops were in good morale.

The science chicks were already testing something. He guessed it was like taking photos. You could always toss what you didn't need. On the other hand, if they had room, they'd take everything they could to analyze the environment.

It was a nice day, relatively. It was still jacket weather. Few civilians worked outside enough to grasp that 70° F could be cold, after hours standing around in a breeze. It wasn't more than 55°

out here. However, the breeze was low, the sky was clear, and the sun bright and unhindered.

The continuing problem was there was literally almost nothing to do as far as chores with the Byko vehicles handling it all. He directed Caswell and Oglesby to assist in erecting an awning, almost a tent, that acted as a weather shield for some of the equipment and the dining area. After that they set chairs of thin wire that was as strong as a steel bar. With a vehicle on each side, an outcropping uphill to the south, and fabric sides, it was quite good shelter. It even had a small climate unit if they needed it, and the sides could be polarized in sections for all clear, windows, or blacked out.

The Guardians had a table set up with chairs and two tablets that looked almost like current tech, only he knew they had generations more processing power and ability. Frankly, they scared him. There was nothing he could enter into his phone they couldn't read if they chose, and he knew their tech base was capable of tiny mics and recorders that might even be cast into the buttons in his uniform, to listen in. Their civil society worked similar to the Japanese, in that one politely didn't notice the private matters of others. This, though, was a military deployment, with civil government support. Their leadership had every reason to monitor literally every breath of the participants.

He wanted to keep some things private, and he knew the scientists would want as much discretion as possible for any data they might bring back.

This was probably what it would have felt like operating alongside Eastern Bloc observers during the Cold War.

At one of the terminals, Cryder viewed the drone's cameras. He didn't even swipe the screen, but just pointed his finger in the air and the image shimmered and changed. He touch-wrote notes in a window on one side.

Sean watched the process. The drone was quick, and had impressive resolution. Periodically, it zoomed in on features. That did look like a footpath along the river.

"Are those fish traps?" he asked, seeing a familiar pattern of stakes.

"Appear so," Cryder agreed. He moved the drone and Sean saw what were definite habitations.

A few minutes later he said, "I have more detail now. We're

about six kilometers from the village. It seems to be about one hundred fifty inhabitants. I have an aerial view of habitations, working areas including leather, meat processing, and what may be primitive cord making."

"Okay. Is it the village we need?"

"Unclear, but it's a local contact, may have further information."

"Right. Shall we see about a patrol?"

Just then, Sergeant Spencer came sprinting up, boots thumping. He stuck his head between the awning sides, drew a quick breath, and spoke.

"Sir, we have a contact." He pointed.

Sean looked where the NCO indicated, as Cryder handed him binoculars. He raised them, and found they had tremendous magnification. It took him a moment to dial them down and get them aligned.

There was the subject, outside the wards, downslope, near a thicket. The movement resolved as a human figure. The subject was a male, tan, wiry muscle and scars, a thick beard and chopped hair with dreads in back. He wore bits of a uniform—MultiCam Gore-Tex over a leather breechcloth, above ratty-looking US-issue boots.

"Let's go. Carefully. Cryder?"

"Coming."

As they strode, Sean pointed and said, "Doc, you are in charge."

"Hooah, sir."

Sean, Spencer, and Cryder slung weapons over their armored jackets and started down the hill. Spencer had his rifle, which might be primitive but was certainly reliable. Sean watched the ripple as they exited the screen, and led slightly, the others spreading out behind him.

"Ho!" Spencer called down, and the man turned, spear ready. He didn't seem spooked, just cautious.

Sean waved high overhead as they passed brush and rose over a lip in the terrain.

"Ho!" he called.

The man stared, eyes wide and confused.

"Do you speak English?" Sean called down.

The response was a slow nod.

They stopped about thirty feet away.

Elliott said, "Sir, I'm Captain Sean Elliott, US Army. We're here to help."

The guy kept staring at him in complete shock. Finally he spoke up. His words sounded like a second language speaker, chosen carefully.

"You have a way home?" the man asked.

"We do, soldier. It's not direct, and there's a lot of debriefing, but we're here to take you all home."

The man's lip trembled and he burst into tears. He planted his spear like a staff and sagged against it, sinking slowly to the ground.

Martin eyed the captain, got a nod, and approached slowly.

"Can you tell us who you are?"

The man kept crying.

"That's fine, take your time." He squatted down and took a load off.

Finally, the guy said, "You're US Army really? This isn't some nash dream?"

"I'm real," Martin said. "SFC Martin Spencer. Want to shake hands?"

He extended his right hand, and the man slowly reached forward, took it and shook it. Then he leapt up and Martin did, too, and then the guy threw himself against Martin's shoulder, still gripping his hand. Goddamn, did he stink. Breath, sweat, musty clothes, natural tanned leather. Ugh.

"Thank you. Oh, thank you. Goddamn, it's been five years. Five fucking years. Thank you."

Martin understood the feeling. He'd spent two years dreading being away from anyone, in case they went home and he got left behind. This guy had adapted, now saw rescue, and wasn't going to get away from that rescue until it happened. But, five years? Shit, they'd planned to be a lot quicker on the uptake. It had only been two last time.

Had changing the personnel done that? That was something the Bykos had mentioned.

The captain's expression said he was just as bothered by that. But he asked, "How many are you?"

The man adjusted his spear and counted off his fingers. "Ten. There are ten. Of us. Brycol, Lieutenant Brian Cole. Anburum, um… Andrew Burnham. Staff Sergeant. Crizano. Sergeant Christopher Lozano. Jaziara…I don't know what his name is back home."

Behind him, Elliott asked, "Jachike Uhiara?"

"Yeah. Corporal. Hosemando. Jose Maldono—"

"Maldonado?"

"I guess. Moldy Nachos. Yeah, that's right sounds. For'd obsevr. Frenchy. Denise Noirot? And Tisho. Tish Oyo. Two females. Florimose. Florian Munoz. PFC. And KKsuke. Kevin Keisuke. PFC."

"That's all of them," Sean said as he read them from his phone. "Wait, where's Akhtar Malik? What happened to him?"

The man shrugged and said, "He died. Here. Three years ago. Hunting."

Martin offered, "Damn, sorry to hear that."

The man shrugged it off again, almost casually.

Elliott said, "Well, we're here to take the rest of you home."

The man nodded vigorously and grinned, while dancing lightly.

"Can we come to your village? Will we be welcome?"

He nodded vigorously. "Yeah! Should be. Argarak likes us."

"Is that the chief?"

"The *umma*, yes."

"We haven't yet asked who you are." Spencer knew, but it was procedure to make them identify themselves.

"Oh, sorry. Tavsto. That is, Travis. Travis Steven Hamilton. Specialist."

Elliott said, "Okay, Specialist, we'll have you lead the way. Hold on." He turned and spoke to Cryder. "I think we should go dismounted."

"Yes. Packs on, weapons for predators." He spoke silently into his mic, updating Arnet in camp.

Hamilton said, "There shouldn't be none predators over this way. I was along a hunting party. Let a shit, catch up need."

Martin parsed that, and how the man's English had slipped in five years.

"Thanks. We'll bring them in case. Show us the way."

Hamilton nodded, and headed off at a brisk walk, then stopped and looked behind. His expression suggested he didn't want the hallucination to go away.

Elliott said, "Wait just a moment, we'll bring our element." Already, most of the team was coming over the lip. Hamilton might not actually see the barricade from his location, which was good. One less thing to explain.

Taking charge for point, Martin called, "Dalton, you and me up front."

Dalton replied, "Hooah, Sergeant Spencer," and jogged forward. He had the Guardian weapon. Martin had the big AR variant in .338. That should be plenty for anything.

Elliott asked Arnet, "Do you have the rear?"

"Yup, got it."

Cryder was just coming back, carrying a large ruck.

"Diplomatic and trade goods," he commented. "Including fabs and wine."

"Great. Caswell, please watch left. Oglesby, we'll watch right."

The scientists took the middle, and didn't fuss about the ruck weight, though it was only a light patrol load.

With Martin and Dalton along, Hamilton moved briskly, looking side to side and talking about something. Dalton seemed engaged with him, and Martin kept an eye on the route.

The terrain undulated, with a projection from the woods along some damp drainage hollow, then drier, hummocky grass, then another finger of woods. It was only a few meters across, the low area slightly damp but not muddy. As they cleared that, the village became visible, down a slight bluff, near the river.

Closer inspection showed it was on a raised flood plain, below the terrace they were on now. It was likely safe enough most years.

"I expect they flood out from time to time," he commented to no one in particular.

Raven said, "That's—" as Caswell cut in with, "That's not uncommon, and they'll just shrug and rebuild in the same spot."

Raven sounded barely annoyed as she said, "It's a fatalistic acceptance. The river floods when the gods say, so there's no reason to worry. If they were higher, it would be harder to get to water, and that doesn't please the gods, either."

Martin chuckled. "Yeah, sounds like a lot of people in our era, too."

They worked their way down a worn path on the bluff, which could only charitably be called such. It had been worn by years of foot traffic, the bare ground eroded by runoff, and had exposed roots, rocks, and slippery slopes.

The dogs detected them first. So these people had domesticated dogs. He recalled the Neolithic element during their displacement had those. No one knew the exact start date, but evidence showed up sporadically for a long time, and yes, was well established by now. Good to have confirmation.

Right then, Dr. Sheridan said, "Confirmed domestication of canines. Useful."

"Yes," Raven agreed. "Definitely not wolves, but much closer than modern breeds."

The animals looked a lot like huskies or malamutes and seemed a bit less domestic. One man slapped them down and they complied.

Martin commented, "Finally a breed I'd consider."

"Are they for hunting?" Dalton asked.

"Sometimes," Hamilton agreed, nodding. "Alert to predors also. And scares them off."

The locals saw the party coming and started to gather. Martin remembered their displacement, and how they'd been swarmed when they first arrived at a local village.

As they reached the flat terrace, the crowd got excited and rushed toward them. The first half dozen seemed to be the rest of the hunting party, armed with spears. They'd been carrying two young goats. They wore breechcloths with leggings, tunics, and wrapped moccasins. Their hair was styled as Hamilton's—cropped with dreads.

Oglesby shouted, "*Moqe teh!*" Shug called, "*Muqa!*" and they stayed at a reasonable distance, but still formed a ring.

It was actually hard to pick the soldiers out. They wore what was left of their uniforms, but they acted a lot like the Paleos. Most were paler-skinned, but they'd tanned and weathered.

That was one of the females, and a girl about three peeked around from behind her leg. Cute kid. And shit, that was a fucked-up complication they didn't need.

The village wasn't dissimilar from that of the Urushu village Martin's element had visited when displaced. The huts had similar form, but were in a neater, more semicircular arrangement around what was apparently an important hut—for the leader or shaman or meetings, he assumed—near the river.

The locals were Central Asian dark, with faintly epicanthic eyes and thick black hair, some of it in dreads, some in braids and wraps, especially on the females, and some cut short with shaven styles. They had coarse fabric and leather clothing and a few wore moccasins.

There was the other female. She looked a bit better. Tall, black, fit, and carrying a spear.

Then they were crushing in, chattering in fractured English.

They smelled, they had shaggy beards, and they were excited beyond anything he'd seen before.

"Are you real?"

"God, MultiCam. Clean, too."

"This can't happen."

"Did you get lost, too?"

Dalton replied, "Yes." Then as the man's face sunk, he added, "But we got home. Now we're here for you."

The man's beard split around a grin of disbelief. "You came for us?"

Spencer spoke clearly, "We're here to take you home."

"You're really real."

Dalton nodded and assured him, "We are. Mixed element—Army, Air Force, Contractor, allies. We're here to recover you."

They started shouting and whooping, though a couple shied back, probably unsure.

Sean Elliott caught up to Spencer, and confirmed Cryder was still alongside. He whispered, "I'm assuming that's a lodge for single hunters nearest the river. It means they can be defensive, and are separated from that lodge over there, for females."

Further inspection showed the huts to be mostly thatched and only partially hide. They were lower and, while more sophisticated than the previous encounters, looked less weatherproof.

Caswell said, "Oh! I see some signs of agriculture. Notice over in the woods, you can just make out a clearing. I bet those are tended berry bushes. Those stalks in the water are definitely rice, and it looks like they dug a shallow bay on purpose."

Raven said, "I'm loving the chairs."

He looked where she pointed, near the community fire, and there they were. Tripods lashed together, with leather seats hung from them and strapped to the back pole. You sat down between two and they were almost hammock chairs. Nice!

The displaced soldiers were very excited, and forced their way in to tug at the uniforms. Sean kept an eye out. Caswell looked very, very wary, but not ready to kill anyone yet. Raven wore a scowl. Sheridan seemed cheerful. The male troops seemed mostly concerned about weapon safety. Cryder and Arnet were tall and built enough that no one got too close, and they weren't in US uniform. Their neutral tan-gray was surprisingly indistinct.

As before, the locals crowded in to be friendly. He watched until Caswell twitched, with Raven right behind her.

"That's close enough, please," he announced firmly, pushing his hands away and indicating a circle. "Back off. Oglesby?"

Oglesby looked at Hamilton and said, "Can you tell them we need space?"

Hamilton said, "Oh, yeah...um...Sergeant?" while staring at Oglesby's chest insignia. It was half covered by gear.

"I am, that's not important. Get them to back off, please."

"Ooah." Hamilton raised his voice and rapid fired something with a gesture like the arms in jumping jacks. There was hesitation, but the crowd did retreat slightly, leaving breathing room at least.

Shouts from farther away indicated a party approaching. It appeared to be the chief with two retainers flanking him. He had a headdress of feathers and antlers, a cape woven of fibers in geometric patterns, and a necklace of stone beads. He had dreadlocks above shaven sides.

Hamilton stepped forward, and started talking. The chief spoke back, pointing and gesturing.

Hamilton faced them and said, "Argarak is umma, chief of this village and...relative of others where else. 'Relative' isn't the right word. People who went from here to there, he still is of them."

"I am Captain Sean Elliott, US Army, commanding this element and, by instruction, commanding our lost soldiers."

Hamilton translated for Argarak, who looked very suspicious, then enthused.

Facing Elliott again, Hamilton said, "I unthink he got it. He thinks you've come to join the village like we did."

"Ah, well, we need to explain that we're visiting only, and will leave soon, but have some gifts for him and his village for their hospitality."

"You should really first trade and be nice."

Caswell, Raven, and Spencer all simultaneously said, "Yes." They looked back and forth, shrugged, and Caswell elaborated.

"We definitely want to make him happy before we make off with people he regards as his."

Sean realized everyone local was quiet. They were waiting for their chief to judge.

"Come here and we'll discuss that. Sergeant Spencer, invoke the gods for cover, please."

"As you wish," Spencer agreed, folded his arms, and high-stepped as he'd done when they'd met locals before. He pointed at the sun, then the river.

"The Sun Lemur wishes we talk with Argarak and offer gifts. It is a goodness thing. It beats a ham sandwich. Speaking of which, that would be good for dinner. Along with..."

As Spencer made a loud, visible presence, Caswell got close to Sean.

"Sir," she said, "they're going to be pissed when we make off with the troops. We need to offer gifts fast, then try to get out fast. The longer it takes, the more trade and interaction they're going to want. And they may get pushy."

Raven said, "I concur. It's a tribal band society with proto-agriculture, meaning they need all the hands on they can get. They'll have adapted to this group and not want to lose population."

Sean nodded. "Got it." Crap, that was going to make it awkward. "Cryder, can you help if we need to be pushy back?"

"Certainly. I'll follow your lead. Nonlethal means are available."

"Excellent."

He looked up to see Spencer making one more pass and intoning, "...it is a sign from his most excellency!"

"Spencer, we're good, come here."

Spencer strutted over, and Sean made a show of nodding to him.

"Right, now they think we're religious nuts. Hamilton, please tell Argarak we have many gifts to share, by instruction from our spirits."

The man nodded vigorously. "Yeah, okay, sir." He still seemed nervous, tense, excited, but agreeable to helping.

The man gestured to the chief, pointed at Elliott, and back. He rattled off something, with a couple of pauses for words.

Argarak grinned and made a "come here" or "welcome" gesture with both hands.

Oglesby tugged at Sean's sleeve and said, "Sir, Shug says he thinks he recognizes some of these people, but they've gotten older."

"That they have. Five years. It's good to know we're in the right place, though."

Indeed, Shug was bouncy and cheerful. He was no longer the only one of his people in the universe.

Cryder unlashed the rolled package he carried. He handed it to Sean, Sean made a show of bowing with it, then handed it to Spencer, who likewise acted reverently, and carried it forward. He motioned for Argarak to squat down with him.

Spencer put down the bundle carefully, then unrolled it. Once open, he started lifting items and presenting them. Sean generally knew what they had, but only from a summary. The Byko had done very well with this haul.

The four dozen arrow and spear points he produced were beautifully finished, ground to a polish like the late Neolithic. Argarak held his hand out for each one in turn, examined their symmetry and color from all angles, and handed them around to others to appreciate. They really were nice, having been made to look like polished agate, with stripes and layers winding through them. Within a year, all of them were programmed to crack and become useless, then decay and disappear entirely. It was dishonest on one level, but they would serve well in that time, being more resilient than actual stone, so it wasn't a complete cheat.

Next was a bag of bone beads. Those were real, made from bleached bird bone, and if not quite accurate for this culture—though they weren't sure—not inappropriate as trade goods. If any survived, they shouldn't be too remarkable.

Then there was a ceramic jug full of a very sweet and potent Byko wine. Spencer popped the stopper, which made an appropriately musical *thunk*. He poured some into a broad wooden cup, took a sip, and handed it to Argarak.

Argarak nodded his thanks, raised and likewise drank. He looked puzzled, drank again, then licked his lips.

A few moments later the alcohol made its first incursions into his bloodstream.

Grinning broadly, he exclaimed something to all, who cheered in response.

Hamilton translated. "He says it's very sweet and making him high."

Sean replied, "Oh, excellent." That was, in fact, the intended purpose of bringing booze.

There was a vividly decorated poncho, of woven, dyed grass and bone and quill tubes. That was followed with a pair of leather leggings, also beaded. They didn't look American, probably based on some European find.

Since pot was pretty well established as being common in Central Asia, both from archeological finds and their own trip, they had a package of what was supposed to be very high-quality stuff, or as it was technically known, "good shit." Argarak looked at the buds, sniffed the aroma with wide eyes, tested the texture by touch, and seemed very satisfied with the quality.

Then Spencer produced a long-stemmed pipe.

That was unknown to them. Sean understood they probably burned or roasted pot in a small tent and inhaled while communing with their spirits, or else just rolled it up loose.

Spencer demonstrated by loading some into the pipe's bowl, lighting it with a lighter, which again impressed them, and taking a careful puff. He handed the pipe over with a gesture so it seemed ritualistic, coaxed the chief into repeating the gesture, and then to take a huge hit.

That did it. Argarak inhaled until his chest swelled, coughed, wheezed, coughed again, grinned a yard wide, and said something that absolutely translated as "This is some gooooood shit!"

There was some more back-and-forth, then Hamilton asked, "What to him I say, Captain?"

"Tell him we're from your tribe and want to share words with all of you."

There was some back-and-forth while Argarak took a few more hits and seemed really mellow. After some proper prostrations, he agreed, nodding.

Hamilton excused himself by stepping politely back. Spencer followed, leaving the hide roll of goodies.

Finally, they were able to gather around a hearth with the lost contingent.

"Greetings, soldiers. I'm Captain Sean Elliott. My element was also lost. We were recovered by Guardians Cryder and Arnet"—he indicated them—"who were lost from their future time. Once it was determined where you were, we were sent to find you. We're here."

"You can take us home?" the black woman asked. Letitia Oyo, Specialist, Military Police, he knew from the list.

"We can and are," he said.

The chattering rose and there were actual cheers. They'd

obviously hoped for that, but just as with his displacement, or any deployment, until you actually were feet-dry on US soil, you didn't assume so.

He held up a hand for quiet.

"First we have to go to Cryder's time. They have the time travel equipment. They need to debrief everyone, do health checks, all that kind of stuff. Then we go back to our time, as accurately as we can. Then the Army will need to debrief everyone all over again. This is complicated, and officially secret."

"It won't be secret." That was Florian Munoz.

"Probably not, but we have to try."

"Why? I plan to sue the government for putting me in this mess."

Sean tried to defer that. "Soldier, now is really not the time or place for those discussions. You need to save that for later. There will be legal counsel for you to talk to, as well as technical specialists. We even have two with us for some of that." He indicated Sheridan and Raven.

He made a note. He wasn't sure what could be done, but that soldier was going to need counseling and possibly legal advice, and possibly very stern orders amounting to threats to keep his mouth shut.

But hell, he was surprised it hadn't leaked out already from their encounter.

One of them asked, "So, how long?"

"Our pickup here is another forty-four days. The jumps are scheduled, and there's no way to communicate early. We have a location to move to before that."

The news was obviously mixed. They wanted to go home, they were afraid to go home, they wanted to go home now, they were afraid it might not be real. It was just like getting your end of rotation DEROS date.

He continued, "The good news is we can start some of the debriefing and reacclimating now. We even have American food."

Sergeant Noirot said, "Oh, God, don't tell me you have chocolate."

He nodded and smiled. "And coffee, and other stuff. Take it from personal experience, you want to move into it slowly or you'll be in a lot of pain. We'll start this evening."

It was fascinating to see those guarded expressions from the other side. They were absolutely thrilled, but not convinced it was real.

"You have it here?"

"No. We're bivouacked a few kilometers away. We should move there ASAP, as soon as you can grab your gear."

There was shuffling and shifting.

"It's not as simple as that," one said. "Sorry, I'm Lieutenant Cole."

"Good to meet you, Lieutenant. Shuff Cryder and I are in command. What can you tell me?"

Cole hesitated fractionally. "Well, we're established members of the *klup*—the tribe. Then, most of them have family here now."

Sean said, "As to the second, we'll relocate you, but we're not leaving at once, and there's time to address the family issues. They won't need debriefing, or any kind of processing at this time."

"They should come along, though."

"It's best they don't. Make appropriate farewells for the time being, and we'll get things done much faster and more efficiently."

Sergeant Spencer put in, "You have to remember, they'd be familiar with nothing we have—"

Cole interjected, "Actually, they know what some of our—"

Spencer raised his voice just slightly and continued, "—and certainly nothing the Bykos brought from the future. You'll have enough trouble acclimating to that. We really shouldn't have anyone else. It will slow things down, and there are processes that must be done here before we can transit."

Sean took up again and noted, "And that time frame is not subject to change." The man's attitude was really pissing him off.

"What exactly needs done that takes that long? Sir?"

Obviously Cole felt he was being stalled, but did he want to go home or not? Upon further reflection, once acclimated, they might have reservations about either the time jump or going back.

Cryder saved him by stating, "That's our scheduled and locked departure. B'fore then, must have very spific measurements of body and metabolics for the transfer. Even with our gear, takes time. Also, various possible medical issues must clear quarantine."

"Ah."

Doc put in, "I'll be handling medical exams. There's admin debrief. You remember how it works."

Sean said, "Army first, family later. It sucks, but it's always like that."

He became aware a couple of the element had wandered off. He saw one of them loading gear in a hide roll. Good.

He kept going to keep command presence. "As far as the umma, we'll clear that. We're quite serious that we don't have a lot of spare time in the schedule. You need to pack and get ready at once."

Cole nodded. "The Army way it is. We do need to get home, as long as it's been. And thank you. A lot." The man seemed haggard beyond his years.

"We're glad we could find you, and sorry it was so long."

Cole turned and quietly but firmly ordered, "Grab your rost and we ready to walk. Kiss the families, and tell them we'll see them in a few days. It's a hunting wander with our people."

Spencer muttered, "This is going to be a massive Mongolian clusterfuck."

Cryder, next to him, replied, "Not quite in Mongolia, but I interpret your idiom."

Argarak came over with his escort and appeared very agitated and put upon. With all the displaced soldiers busy, it fell to Oglesby and Shug to sort it out. Shug seemed very reluctant to argue with a chief, and acted as intermediary when Oglesby got caught up in language difficulties, which was often.

Argarak was very firm in whatever he was saying, pointing, stating, demanding something. Shug made occasional comments. Oglesby referred to his notes, cocked his head for his earbuds, and spoke slowly. Eventually, he held up a placating hand and turned.

He said, "The chief isn't happy. Basically, he says our spirits sent them here, they've joined his tribe, he wants to know what we're doing here."

"Do the troops have a say in it?"

"Maybe."

"Why aren't they translating for us?"

A couple stood nearby, and shuffled awkwardly.

Hamilton said, "Sir, Sergeant Oglesby is right. But if we ask Argarak, he's going to want us to stay. We'll seem ungrateful, since he took us in and gave us food, lodging, mates."

"Okay. Then we can deal with that as a separate issue. You do want to leave, right?"

There were vigorous nods from three, less vigorous from two, and noncommittal shrugs from four.

Staff Sergeant Lozano said, "I mean, we've settled in here. The first few weeks were terrifying, and then it was depressing and nasty, but we've learned to adapt, and we have families, most of us."

"You have a family back home."

He shrugged. "It wasn't great—with my then wife, I mean. I expect she's moved on after five years."

Spencer made an angry sound in his throat. Yeah, he was trying to save his marriage, and this guy wanted to throw his own away.

"It's only been four months for her."

The man looked confused. "Uh...how? Is time running differently?"

"Time spent here doesn't affect time there. As far as she knows, you're MIA in remote A-stan. Also, the Army really doesn't want MIAs unaccounted for."

That got a blurt of "Oh, fuck the Army."

PFC Keisuke muttered, "I want to go back. I...want to go back."

Sergeant Spencer told them, "Either way, have some chocolate and hot coffee." He held up a broken chocolate bar and walked around, handing each of them a piece. A couple hesitated, but all except Lozano took one. Then from his ruck he pulled a thermos and a cup.

"Oh my God. And coffee. I missed coffee."

Hamilton said, "I'd kill for a cigarette."

"Sorry, we didn't bring any."

"Dip?"

Spencer shook his head and said, "No, no tobacco. Sorry. I quit while I was lost. No one else here smoked."

The man sighed. "I can wait until we get home."

Cryder offered, "I may be able to duplicate some."

"What, like an e-Cig?"

"I don't know that term. I can probably make tobacco in a smokeable form."

"No shit!"

Sean never understood smokers who quit during training or deployment from necessity, were long out of the habit, insisting on restarting. Still, that was their problem, and if it gave them a reason to come home, good.

"Either way, we need to get you all to our camp to be photographed and IDed. We're not leaving for six weeks, but you know how the Army is. There's a lot of paperwork."

It was believable, not inaccurate, and he wanted to get them under control, all at once, not have to chase them all over creation.

"Should we finish packing stuff, then?"

He advised, "All your issue gear, at least. Anything you can't live without for a few days. Definitely bring your daughter, Sergeant Noirot. Does anyone else have offspring?"

"I have a wife," Munoz said. A couple of others offered the same.

Even if it would have been only six months, that could be a problem. They really should have planned for it.

"Say goodbye for the time being. We're limited to Army only at present."

"But Frenchy brings her kid?"

Sean said, "Offspring are different from local spouses." This was getting awkward fast.

Keisuke pleaded, "Look, let's not argue, I want to get going."

Cole suddenly asked, "Where's Lozano?"

Keikuke indicated with a toss of his head. "In his lodge."

Sean muttered, "Crap. Spencer, take over here, and Cryder. Troops, Shuff Cryder is my counterpart from our future. He's co-lead of this operation and will get us home. Arnet, can you come with me to persuade Lozano?"

The tall man nodded. "I can."

"Thanks. Dalton, come help?"

"Hooah, sir."

"Doc?"

"Yes, sir."

Why did I assume they'd all beg to come home and just follow us? It made sense that they'd acclimated, and that the locals liked new members. Now he was going to be the bad guy who broke it all up.

The three of them walked to the hut in question. Lozano was actually sitting outside on a roll of hide, looking comfortable, inhaling pot smoke from a censer. A very young girl sat next to him, working on scraping a hide.

"Hey, Sergeant Lozano," Sean started, trying to sound casual. "You probably didn't hear the discussion. We're moving up to our camp. We've got uniforms, boots, and can get you kitted back up."

The man already looked defiant, even through the mellowing of pot. "I'm pretty comfortable, actually."

Sean tried again. "Good, but you really need to be back in uniform."

"I'm fine, really." He didn't sound challenging specifically. More like dismissive.

That couldn't stand.

He suggested, "We need you. Your teammates need you."

"They'll be fine."

It was obvious the man understood and was just being resistant. Diplomacy wasn't going to work. When diplomacy fails . . .

Sean changed his tone fractionally, and said, "Soldier, it's not a request."

Behind him, Dalton mumbled, "Darn right it's not."

With a smug grin, Lozano asked, "Do you know what date it is, Captain? Because I do believe it's long before my enlistment date and doesn't apply."

"To come home, we have a process," he reminded. The man had to know all this.

Arching back, hands behind his head, Lozano said, "Well, I have decided to sit this one out."

He offered one last chance. "Really? Here? No coffee? No sugar? No spices? No well-cut steaks on the grill? No movies?"

Lozano shrugged.

"Honestly, I'm healthier than I've ever been. I have a woman. I was willing to be persuaded, but I don't see a need, actually. Mark me as dead or MIA and move on."

"I will have to consider that," Sean said carefully. "You can remain for now. We'll discuss it again."

"There's nothing to discuss. Have a good day, Captain." The man feigned closing his eyes, but Sean could see them slitted. Lozano didn't trust them.

This was a turning point. If he let this slide, there was question as to his command ability. If he forced it, he was going to have to have the man restrained even in camp.

He figured he'd try his attempt at the Byko dialect.

"Poss rstrain biv til part?"

Arnet replied, "Ya, can." He'd grasped well enough, apparently. Sean nodded fractionally.

"Arnet, Dalton, Doc, bring him. Minimum force but as needed."

Arnet fairly bounded into movement. Lozano had just grasped the discussion and stood when the Guardian reached him in a tackle, threw him as they rolled, and came up with the man bent into a shape that didn't look comfortable and definitely looked painful. He picked Lozano up as if he was a bundle of gear, shouldered him, and started walking, as if he carried 175-pound men around every day.

Hell, in training, maybe he did.

Lozano was lying over Arnet's shoulder bent on his back, head to the rear, in a position that made struggling nearly impossible. He started with something in the local language, then switched to, "Motherfucker, put me down or—"

Dalton cut in firmly. "Sergeant Lozano, Arnet outranks you, is a lot stronger than you, is a friendly allied troop, and you've got orders from the captain. You're already under restraint. It can get worse if you don't wise up."

There were shouts and stern voices behind them, as the locals realized it was a forced relocation. This wasn't going to go easily. That young one... she couldn't be his daughter, but wasn't old enough to be his wife. Orphan he'd picked up with his mate?

Not turning back, trusting his unit to cover him, Sean led the way through the gathered soldiers and toward the trail. He made to leave, Shug quickly falling in between Oglesby and Dalton, obviously not wanting to be left behind.

Shouts resolved as Argarak's voice, with a couple of his henchmen. A glance revealed them to be armed, and moving fast, but they were carrying, not preparing to throw.

The chief and his flankers sprinted past and got in front of the group.

Argarak made it quite clear he opposed the departure. He even waved his spear.

Sean sighed. "I really don't want a fight, but we've got to establish the position of our own people."

Right then, Cryder raised his sidearm device, which melted, stopped, zapped a blue flash. Argarak fell down and twitched.

Looking over, Cryder said, "He'll be awake in under a minute. Let's walk."

Caswell muttered, "Couldn't happen to a nicer guy."

"Yeah," Spencer agreed. "Much as we'd like to avoid trouble, there comes a point where you make your case and get on with the mission."

Suddenly there were dogs, teeth bared, slobbering and growling. Cryder pointed his weapon, zapped, zapped, zapped, and most of the dogs were napping, but bent in positions he'd only seen cats get into. Two retreated, still barking, but obviously intimidated.

Sean spoke with the best command voice he could. "Soldiers, that way. Move."

The locals shouted and milled about. Several ran to Argarak. Five others ran forward with spears. Cryder zapped two of them cold, and the rest stood back at once, though a single warrior took it upon himself to heave his spear.

Dalton calmly stepped into the line. The spear hit his Byko-issued clothing and bounced off. The soldier twitched at the impact dispersed across the chest, as if he'd been hit by a ball. He retrieved the spear from the ground, made a half salute with it, and resumed walking. He had a souvenir.

Damn, that was impressive gear. It was also courageous. The man had taken the Byko at their word about the armor value. It was good to know it was proof.

The locals shrieked and shouted, made gestures and jumped around, but didn't follow further.

The troops moved at a route march, some of them cautiously excited, a couple obviously pissed, and Noirot had her daughter along. Sean knew she'd have to go to the future. He expected she couldn't go back to their own time. Or possibly she could. It depended on what the Bykostani thought. Though the Army cover story would have to be hellacious.

He realized that was going to be his decision. There was no way to ask up the chain.

And why didn't we anticipate kids, or at least pregnancies, even if it was only a few months? he wondered.

Obviously, because the Army rarely addressed such things and tried to pretend they didn't happen.

Lozano shouted a few more unimaginative profanities.

Spencer caught up and barked, "Son, 'fuck' loses any power after the fifth iteration. You will be at ease."

"Or what? As soon as I'm down I'll—"

Cryder applied his sidearm directly and *ZAP.*

The man hung limp.

Noirot's daughter hurried along, short legs pumping quickly, quiet but obviously nervous. She chattered something, and Noirot replied. Then they were both silent.

Most of the others marched along without any real comment or expression. They'd spent five years walking everywhere. This was just more of it.

CHAPTER 14

Shug was bothered. There were things one did to take people away from a village. Using magic weapons wasn't one of those. It called for discussion between the Elders and Shaman, for spiritual drinks and feasting, and vows. It took time, and had to be managed carefully, even if it was to return a traveler home. The spirits wouldn't like this.

Though he wondered if the Byko could fight the spirits, or ignore them. None of them seemed to care much about the spirits, except for Rich.

He would need to find a way to explain it to Dan, that if they did find his village, which should be down the river a few days, that they would have to be gentler and kinder. His own status and home would be in danger like this.

For now he walked along, alert for any stalking. He assumed the village's hunters would be chasing them. He was sure his people would if something like this happened to them.

He didn't understand why Captin Sean didn't just start back and forth between the villages, if he had many days. Even a double hand of days would make it an easier exchange, let everyone get used to the idea.

Sean was impressed. Arnet carried Lozano the entire way, without a pause or a swap. The unconscious man didn't balance like a ruck, it was like carrying a dead body, or a huge sack, but Arnet held a good pace and didn't seem any more strained than the others.

Both scientists seemed to be in some discomfort and fatigue, but they plodded along. He thought about offering help, but remembered he'd inquired if they'd keep up and they'd said yes. If they asked for assistance he'd do so, but they'd agreed to the terms and he was going to let them abide by that.

As soon as they entered the perimeter, Caswell took Noirot and Oyo each by the arm. "Come on. We're going to the female shower."

Raven dropped her pack and hurried forward, favoring her right leg. Her expression cleared up as she took the other side of Noirot. "I have this olive oil and mint soap. Very refreshing."

Sheridan squatted down next to the girl. "Hey! Check this out!" She put down a toy with blinky lights and buttons, and the child was wide-eyed fascinated.

Rich Dalton felt much better when they got to the camp. He was still buzzing from intercepting that spear. Knowing the clothing was proof against hurled projectiles wasn't the same as experiencing it, but it had worked as demonstrated, and the stiffening fabric had even prevented it from hurting, really. There'd been an all-over *thump*, then it fell.

He put the spear on the hood of Roller One, and turned to see what he could do to help.

Arnet rucked Lozano, awake and again cursing, behind the second vehicle. Cryder pressed something, and it popped up the camperlike shell tent they'd seen last time. They reached in and pulled out another shelter, shook it into a rough pyramid, which swelled up and took shape once on the ground.

Arnet bent and dropped Lozano to his feet; he immediately tried to duck under the taller man's arm and run. Arnet reached out with a hand, grabbed with what looked for all the world like the Vulcan Neck Pinch, and the man collapsed. Arnet hefted, shoved, and Lozano was in the tent. The Guardian zipped the seam closed and thumbed the bottom.

"Sealed," he announced.

"Wooz," Cryder nodded.

The captain asked, "Holding cell?"

"Yup. He can't get out. I'll program a collar."

"'Collar'?"

"Zizzes him if he gets to the wards."

"Like an invisible fence for dogs?"

"From context, yes, I think so."

"Sorry. Okay, then. Dalton . . . actually, everyone. Be prepared for him to try to get violent. We'll use further restraint if we must, but I'd prefer we coax him into agreeing to go back."

Staff Sergeant Burnham said, "No worries here, Captain. I'm ready to go home now." Even shaggy, the man looked like an NCO. Though he looked a lot older than thirty.

"Good. Though it's going to be forty-four days of being a fobbit, with a rough terrain convoy near the end. Then to the far future."

"What's the future like, sir?"

Elliott grinned. "It's fucking amazing, but we don't belong there and they won't tell us much."

"Well, shit. Flying cars and space babes, though, I hope?"

He nodded agreement. "It has both. They're not as cool as you might wish."

"Hopefully I find out."

"You may. We'll have formation shortly."

"I got the hint, sir. I'll wait, you work."

The women were at the shower station for a long time, but with easy replenishment of water, it shouldn't be a problem. There were audible mutters and occasional louder voices, and once an enthusiastic "Woo!" It sounded as if they were glad enough. The little girl went in, too, and giggled, her feet barely visible at one angle, dancing around in the spray. Cute kid. Reminded him of his sister at that age.

Martin Spencer chose a different approach. "Dalton, want to get some beverage?"

"At once, Sergeant!" Rich replied. He picked up on using liquor to both release any inhibitions these guys had and make them homesick, and having the best military bearing possible as an example for them.

He went to the kitchen and grabbed the rum mix and a stack of cups.

Spencer nodded, took the cups, and said, "Pour, single shots."

"Hooah." It was easy enough to estimate, and he squeezed the bottle to dispense.

Spencer turned to the new troops and said, "You can have one shot each for now. I advise sipping. It's going to be extra strong."

"We have beer here," Cole said. "Not very good, made from rice and old fruit and some spit, but beer."

"Well, this is really good rum." Or vodka flavored like rum.

He handed them each a cup.

"Gentlemen, to your recovery."

Rich followed suit. He raised his glass, then brought it to his mouth and sipped. Damn, that was respectable.

Maldonado, a burly Hispanic, slammed his. He coughed at once, got it under control. *Dumbass.*

They settled down and seemed a bit calmer.

Doc came over and made a "gimme" gesture. Rich poured him one, too.

Spencer said, "You weren't forgotten. We had no way to look for you. Our element was gone two years in an older time frame than this—hunter-gatherers only. It wasn't until our future friends arrived from where they'd gotten tossed were we able to combine resources. Their people came looking for them, found us, and the Romans, and the Gadorth—a Neolithic group from what's now near the UK—and some East Indians we barely talked to. They got us all home by way of their place. Then they came for us, to look for you."

Lieutenant Cole asked, "Why couldn't you pick us up the week after it happened?"

"Cryder?" Rich asked. He'd wondered that himself.

"I can't explain it. I'm not that kind of scientist. All they can do is target anything they find. This is what they found."

"I mean, why can't you go back, now that you know where we are? Just avoid it?"

"I'm told it doesn't work that way. Once contact is made it's a locked line. I don't know the math."

Sergeant Burnham put in, "We're grateful, most of us. Just pissed off that it took so long, and that someone else's fuckup caused it."

Rich understood. There was no one to blame, really.

There was an interruption then. Noirot came back in uniform, clean, scrubbed, hair brushed, with a light touch of makeup and unauthorized ear studs. Emotionally, though, she looked a lot more relaxed and secure.

Caswell looked at Elliott and said, "Sir, we applied the Byko soap."

"Great, thanks." That stuff was supposed to flush lice, fleas, ticks, and similar pests right off and gone.

Oyo seemed less bothered, more relieved. Raven bade her sit on a chair, moved behind her, and started running braids back along her scalp. At that, the woman smiled for the first time he'd seen.

Doc walked over. "We have a little more rum. I'll authorize it after I check your pupils." He went around with his flashlight, watching their dilation response.

"Yeah, no more than one more."

Noirot said, "All I need now is a Coke." She had her first shot and looked much less stressed. Her hair was still damp, and a bit shorter where tangles had been cut.

"You're in luck," Spencer replied, as Dalton ran to the vehicle. He returned with a can.

"Only a third," he warned.

Keisuke said, "Oh, damn." He started weeping, eyes damp, and struggled to get it under control.

Rich understood. The sheer emotional shock of being found was going to be overwhelming. He'd wait a bit, and let anyone in Christ know he was there if they needed him.

"It's cool, son," Spencer said. "We've got six weeks to get back into the right mindset."

"Thank you, Sergeant First Class."

"No problem. We'll work on dinner in a bit. Now," he instructed, "it's time to shower. You can have ten minutes each, more or less. I'm not going to clock you, but get thoroughly clean and don't waste more time than that. Lose the hair, you look like hippies."

Cole pointed and said, "Hamilton, you're first. By rank. I'm last."

Hamilton replied, "Okay, Bri..." caught himself, and continued with, "Lieutenant."

Rich was glad to see the officer still retained his proper protocols.

Noirot's daughter came running up in a basic dress that looked like bright pink linen, with a matching hood, no doubt to help keep her located. She stared around confused, until she identified her mother's face. She lit up in a grin, ran over and hugged Noirot's legs; Mom scooped her up for a cuddle.

The two women seemed quite glad to be back in civilization.

❖   ❖   ❖

An hour later, shaved, shorn, showered, and in uniform, the element looked a lot more like soldiers. Martin Spencer used a trimmer to get their hair to spec—tapered and clean around the edges, and a bit shorter on top. It was within regs, mostly. They looked significantly different and aware of it. He had a bit of trouble. Sergeant Jachike Uhiara had grown a pretty respectable Afro, and he had no idea how to trim it.

"Hey, Doc! A hand?"

Devereaux came running over. "What do you need?"

"I have no idea how to shape black hair, sir."

"Uh, well neither do I, but I'll try." The man addressed Uhiara. "Is buzzed okay if we can't get it right?"

"Sure thing, sir. Honestly as long as there's no lice and it's not too sweaty, I'm good."

"Okay."

Martin watched as Doc pruned the mass down to about a half inch and tapered it. The man had a deft touch, definitely a surgeon. Economy of movement, fast and precise.

"That's better than most barbers, sir."

Doc smiled acknowledgment. "Well, good. There you go."

Standing up from the chair, Uhiara flexed his feet and noted, "The boots fit. That never happens."

"And the field rations are good," Spencer told them. "Our head cook isn't here, but Caswell was second, and we've got better than native supplies this time."

"What are we having?"

Caswell was a few feet away and said, "Sirloin tips with mushrooms, broccoli with cheese sauce, and baked potatoes. With orange juice."

Keisuke exclaimed, "Oh my God!"

Uhiara said, "I'm in. What can I do to help?"

"Wash dishes afterward. We have the rest."

The man nodded and grinned hugely. "Done."

Arnet said, "However, first, you must drink this." He had ten small vials that looked a lot like medicine cups with lids.

"Is what?"

"It is a broad-spectrum anti-parasite medication. Anything you have internally or that the soap didn't remove will be gone within a day."

"God, no more scratching! And inside what I have no idea."

They didn't argue. They took the vials and chugged. Cryder took one over to Lozano and, after seeing the others drink, the man complied.

Rich noticed they spoke half in English, half in the native language, but moved more and more to English as it went on.

At dinner, they lined up as instructed, and seemed thrilled at the novelty of actual plates. Then there was eating ware—the oddly shaped but comfortable Byko knives, three-pronged forks, spoons, and tongs that were almost salad tongs, almost chopsticks. They were served actual meat and trimmings. There was a slightly sweet orange juice, dialed down to about one-half normal mix strength. SSG Burnham took a tray over to the tent for Lozano.

Kita, Noirot's daughter, wore an outfit that Cryder had cranked out on his fabricator. It could be Viking, or Russian peasant, or possibly it was Byko. She had an undertunic in white, the dress covered her torso, had a waistline and skirt. It was bright pink, with a matching scarf to keep her hair back. The girl positively bounced at her gift, regularly pausing to examine the fabric and fit. Canvaslike pink sandals confused her, and she shook her feet from time to time.

They gathered at the logs and chairs around the fire, and said almost nothing. They fairly devoured the food, making murmurs of pleasure and the occasional exclamation.

"What do we do with our dishes, Sergeant?"

Rich said, "Wipe them off at the vehicle and line up for dessert."

"Dessert? We get dessert?"

Doc said, "Yup. Two bites of PB and J."

"Are our guts that sensitive?"

"Ours were."

They all responded enthusiastically to bread with sweetened spread. It was good quality peanut butter, and the grape jam was excellent. Kita took the bite her mother offered her, and was giddy. She grinned and bounced and danced and cheerfully took a second one, making "MMmmmmm!" noises.

Meanwhile, Sheridan, Oglesby, and Arnet rolled out more sleeping shelters.

Martin took charge and said, "Okay, gentlemen and ladies, here's the accommodations. The bed is a twin model, very soft, with indirect lighting and overhead controls. Clothing storage is to your left, weapon rack to the right."

Staff Sergeant Burnham seemed giddy as he bent to peer inside. "Holy shit. Clean sleeping bags. Air mattresses, even. And a light."

Oglesby said, "And AC."

Uhiara blurted, "You're fucking with me."

"Nope, AC controls right there." He pointed. "Warm to cold, choose what you like. There is no turndown service, however."

It was for certain these two were glad to be recovered. The debriefing would be the only tricky part.

Spencer said, "You can each pick, but we alternated rank, high to low, for dispersal, even though we don't really need it here. Reveille is oh six hundred. We'll do PT, breakfast, and get to work on paperwork and updates. You'll get a phone with limited access that plugs in here for movies and such."

Maldonado said, "Sounds good." He seemed relaxed, but interested in being back to normal.

Letitia Oyo looked very pleased. "Thank you so much."

Burnham muttered, "*Vristak*, that looks comfortable."

"Yup. Latrine is around there, we have water, and if you need anything, someone will be on CQ near the trucks or the fire."

"Hooah, Sergeant."

Sean Elliott sat back from the report on the screen of his laptop, checked his clock, and it was cooler than hell to have it built into the uniform sleeve.

Crap. It was after 2300. They were getting up early to act like soldiers again. Dalton and Oglesby were still up, talking. He said, "Gentlemen, we'll resume in the morning after the usual festivities."

"Hooah, sir."

He closed his laptop screen, then turned for his tent. It was rather chill, with heavy dew, but the Byko fabric worked very well against it. He felt fine, other than ears and fingertips.

So far so good, he thought. They'd recovered the element with minor squabbles, most were all in favor; the one, Lozano, would probably come around. Now they had to do craptons of administrative crap, then probably more for the Bykos, then definitely more for the Army. They also had to stay busy here before they returned.

Halfway across the field he heard "Captain Elliott?"

He turned. "Sergeant Noirot, what can I do for you?"

"It's rather the other way, sir." Her smile was . . . odd.

"What do you mean?"

"Can we go to your tent?"

"Uh . . . we can talk right here." There were too many problems with her going to his. Assumptions would be made.

"I was thinking of more than talking."

Oh, shit.

"That's totally fine. We came to recover all of you, and we're being paid by both governments. You don't owe us anything." *Christ, how do I get out of this conversation, fast?*

"We all owe you, and it's what we do here. Any good deal is sealed with touch." She was already fingering the buttons on her shirt.

"I see. Well, this is a US Army outpost. So I must graciously decline, with thanks. You do look much healthier and . . . good, since cleaning up. If you want to talk to someone, Sergeant Caswell is certainly the person you should look up. If you need any spiritual counseling, Sergeant Dalton is our stand-in for a chaplain, and very good at what he does. And I'm afraid I've got duty to attend to at present."

"Okay," she said to his back as he walked away quickly. He wasn't sure that was enough.

In fact, Caswell and Spencer were sitting at the fire, talking. It was interesting that they'd gotten onto friendly terms, given the sheer panic Caswell had the entire time they'd been displaced. Spencer didn't seem as constantly on edge, either. Apparently, both were quite different than they'd been under those circumstances.

He detoured over that way, as casually as he could manage.

"Sergeants, I could use your help." He kept his voice soft and as calm as he could manage.

"Yes, sir?" Caswell said at once. Spencer was already standing up from his stool.

"Sergeant Noirot just attempted to sleep with me."

"Uh?"

"She says any good deal has to be sealed with touch. That's how they do things here. I advised her we most certainly don't do it that way on an Army post, no matter how remote."

Spencer said, "Not to cut in, sir, but she's heading for your tent now."

Caswell leapt up, said, "Shit, I've got this," and took off at a sprint, slowing to a run, a brisk walk, a stroll, that took her around to the outside of the tents and then in past Sean's bivvy.

He distantly heard her say, "Denise! Hey, how are you doing?"

Jenny knew exactly what had happened. It probably did work just fine in a society where people grew up with those expectations, and a culture made to handle it. Noirot wasn't from that culture, and was trying hard to make both conflicting societies fit together. On top of that, her mission was the same as Jenny's—search female detainees in A-stan, and accompany them as chaperone for the personal safety and comfort. That job was irrelevant here. Jenny was a skilled food harvester and cook, and could and had fought as needed. Noirot... apparently didn't have a relevant primitive skill, and had been tossed in with other frightened troops seeking any way to make their hosts happy.

Noirot did smile and reply, "I'm doing good!"

"Cool. You should come over by the fire." It was a chilly evening, fog moving in, and that was a good reason to get her over there, away from Elliott.

Noirot replied, "Oh, okay."

Jenny had spoken loud enough for Spencer to hear. He had, and understood the hint. He rose and shuffled off toward the latrine. The captain had already disappeared, probably for the HQ awning.

As she and Noirot walked, Jenny interspersed conversation with a text to Dr. Raven. MEET ME AT THE FIRE. URGENT.

Noirot noticed the device and blurted, "Oh my God, you mentioned phones. They work here?"

"Yeah, but only with the Bykos and ourselves, of course. Not through time."

"When do we get ours?"

Jenny wasn't sure, but offered, "Probably a day or so, but you're limited to talking to us as is."

Her phone buzzed with a text.

Raven: ON MY WAY?

She swiped back, GIRL STUFF, HITTING ON CAPTAIN.

"Oh. Still, a game or two would be cool."

"I'll talk to Cryder. Their vehicles are pretty sophisticated. They have video and games, and we have movies on our phones and in the tents at least."

Raven replied, YOU'RE WHAT???

NOT ME. NOIROT. DISTRACTING HER WITH GAMING TALK.

"That would be something. God, going home is going to be a shock."

"Yeah, it was for us, too. We'll lead you into it so it's less of one."

Raven came jogging to the fire, her weight and bad ankle obvious.

"Oh, hey, Amalie! Denise, you sit here with Dr. Raven and I'll see about a little more rum."

A very little. Loosening inhibitions was probably not ideal, but they needed to distract the poor woman.

As she ran for the liquor, she heard Raven ask, "What games do you play?"

"I'd just got into the new *Doom*, big time. Is it still around?"

"Yeah, that's still around. It's only been a couple of months for us, remember."

Walking by, Spencer asked, "Shit, I remember the original."

Raven giggled and said, "See? Not an issue even for old people."

"I'm barely four years older than you, dirt-sifter." He continued to his tent and away.

Raven giggled again.

Jenny was glad. Spencer was bright enough to have picked up the risk and was going to make sure Noirot knew there was late-night activity so she couldn't skulk around. With a bottle of booze, flavored as a fruity sweet, she returned to the fire.

"Here, try a sip of this."

She handed it over. Noirot took a bit more than a sip.

The woman shook her head and exclaimed, "Oh, that's *good*! Did they bring a whole bar?"

"They mix it as they go. And it's even better in their world."

"Damn."

"Hey, where's your daughter? Kita?"

Noirot pointed. "She's asleep in my tent. She adores the sleeping bag. Hell, I do, too."

Jenny said, "Yes, it's even better than a military bag, which would be pretty damned cool here. We wore ours out."

Noirot sighed. "Yeah, ours are long gone. Zippers failed. Some got torn. Bugs got into them. Eventually we fireburned what was left."

Raven asked, "You didn't keep any for quilting or such?"

"Bugs. Couldn't get rid of them."

"But there's ways to . . . oh."

"Yeah, we didn't know of any. Not that worked."

The scientist replied sadly, "Damn. Some are easy."

Jenny picked back up, "Well, these are awesome, and that won't happen. Hey, Amalie, didn't you say you wanted to check something before bed?"

Taking the hint, Raven glanced at her watch and said, "Yeah, in . . . twelve minutes. Close enough. I'll go do that."

"Okay. See you in the morning."

"Yup. Night."

"Night."

Noirot said, "Good night, Doc."

After Raven was out of the circle of light, Noirot asked, "So, she's a technical contractor?"

Jenny explained, "She's some sort of uber-biologist, geneticist, paleo-infection expert. Checking on things here that could infect us back home. They assigned her to us after we got back."

"Ah, you've known her a while."

"No, we only met when this round started. Everything is secret. Our therapist doesn't know them, they don't know her, everything is sanitized documents. No one would believe us, and we did get some calls from kooks."

"Kooks?"

"Alien abduction types who wanted 'the real story.'"

"Oh." The woman looked concerned.

"Yeah. It's really very serious that you never mention any of this back home to anyone. Sergeant Spencer's wife doesn't even know. Nor do the spouses of a couple of others. We can talk to each other very carefully, but not where it can be overheard or interpreted.

"So, anyway, Arnet probably has some sort of game system that can generate something you want to play if you give it ideas. Just ask the system in your tent, by voice. It can focus video and sound. And a couple of us will be happy to play with Kita so you can have some downtime."

"Cool! I'll give that a try."

Good. Now, how to present this?

"Yeah, just be careful how you describe it. I accidentally got erotica."

"Oh? Erotic game?"

"No. Erotic movie-like thing, with sensory touches and 3D audio and video."

"Damn. And they don't like that?"

"It wasn't a problem at all. They have it for a reason. I just wasn't expecting it. I was in their truck. And I gather he enjoyed my reaction when it hit."

"Hah. Perv." And damn it, the woman looked over that way. To be fair, the Bykos were built.

"Nice enough. He never mentioned it, and the shell is opaque and silenced, so it didn't embarrass me. Just ask the system directly for what you want."

Jenny had. Being able to be alone, mostly, away from her element, made it possible to forget the strain for a short period of time. And if this woman was stressed, recovering, hormone-laden and lonely, it was much safer to have her there than hitting on the commander, or anyone else. She'd warn the Guardians, but expected they'd be prepared and have no interest.

Noirot said, "Got it. I wonder if it has porn games." She snickered, but underneath she sounded interested. Well, good.

"I would assume it does." They absolutely did. "They're pretty uninhibited. Wait until you see what they wear, or don't."

"Oh?"

"Hmm...I think...yes, I can access some on my phone. Hold on." She pulled it out and spoke. "System. Show me images of Byko women in evening wear like at the Mad Lab. Scroll." She moved closer to Noirot and shared the screen.

Her phone began a slow overlay of women in dresses, skin treatments, paint, and flowing outfits.

"Oh, damn," Noirot muttered. "They're fucking gorgeous."

"Well, they all have access to cosmetics, treatments, surgery, and a lot more advanced medicine than we do."

"Still. Oh, that gown is hot."

She liked that one? It was the closest Jenny had seen the Byko get to a stripper outfit.

"Yeah, they have a huge array of styles."

She discreetly asked, "Are you married here? Or whatever equivalent they have?"

"Sort of," Noirot agreed. "But only the last couple of years. I was helping smooth things over between groups, when we arrived."

"Oh?" Jenny didn't want to hear this because she knew where it was going.

"They like to share partners with traveling groups, and Oyo wasn't their type. They really don't go for black girls."

"They either like the exotic," Jenny explained, running a hand through her red hair, "or they don't. Little in between."

Noirot said, "Yeah, most of us are mated, that's going to be one of the complications, and why Argarak was pissed at us leaving."

Jenny said, "That's definitely something I'll bring up with the captain and Cryder. Anyway, I need to go to bed. You probably should, too. Cuddle that baby for me."

"I will. Thanks, Sergeant."

"For this you can call me Jenny. I'm sort of a unit social counselor, since we're basically a fire team trying to do everything. 'Sergeant Caswell' when we actually go out."

"Got it. Thanks, Jenny."

"'Night, Denise."

Hopefully, that had stalled any issues until Noirot could get proper therapy, or at least until they could arrange schedules so she couldn't reach the captain after dark.

Shug jarred out of sleep. It was early, barely dawn, and that sound was a hunter's shriek, with a crackling buzz like a very big beetle.

Why?

He slid the bed fastener and rolled out, pulled the cover on the tent, and sprang into the dewy grass.

It was a hunting party from the flat river village. Three spears stuck in the ground, and one of their party was cocking back for another throw. One of them was down at the magic fence line, not moving.

The one throwing stepped too far forward, reached the fence line, and that crackling noise sounded, with a blue flash. He stumbled back and fell flat.

Cryder and Arnet were running about, along with Rich and Sean, with their magic weapons. Those made their odd thumping sounds, and four more of the attackers were on the ground.

Shug wanted to help, but there was nothing he could do, so he sat back near his tent. It was frustrating and scary to have only a knife. He was a hunter, he could fight, but the weapons the other people used made his useless. Even their magic shiny knife was nothing against the invisible things thrown by the shoulder weapons.

It was all over in heartbeats. The remaining hunters ran off, though they did pick up the body of one of the throwers.

Dan ran his way, and spoke. "It is all right. Are you all right?"

"Yes."

"Good. Be calm."

"I is. *Thanks.*" He said the latter in their speech.

"You're welcome."

There was an immediate council with Arnet, Cryder, Sean, and Martin. Then Steven was called over, and he motioned to Shug.

Shug walked over, hoping he wasn't in trouble for anything and that they needed his help.

Steven asked, "Shug, I think they are scared, angry at our going, and think we rude. Is that correct?"

"That feels correct," he said. "They adopted you, and you have left without asking or trade. There is always trade when someone leaves a village for another."

Steven turned back to the others, talked, then turned back.

"Would more gifts in trade make them happy with it?"

"I don't know. Females are supposed to mate, as you know, and be traded. None of the females here remained. Then, workers and hunters were taken, but not enough food or large things were traded, only shinies. Shinies don't feed the village."

There was more discussion. Shug waited patiently, catching occasional words. "Veecul" he recognized. "March." "Weapon." One of the words for food.

Steven finally turned and said, "Okay, thank you for helping. We like your words."

"Thank you, please tell them," Shug replied.

His words were useful to them. Good. He wondered what would happen next.

It appeared the hunters were waking up. The magic weapons had made them sleep. They shook and rose, looking very confused and tired, then slunk down and slipped away silently, but he watched them.

CHAPTER 15

Sean Elliott relaxed now that things were explained and under control.

"Well, that's over for now. Since everyone's up, let's work on PT and breakfast. I want two people on inside perimeter patrol."

Cryder said, "No need, I deployed a viewer." He pointed directly up.

"Oh? I didn't see them last night."

The man looked sheepish. "They were peaceful on meeting and didn't pursue immediately. I assumed peaceful enough, or intelligent enough to accept facts."

"Well, they were intelligent enough to hold off and plan for what would have been a very effective attack without the wards."

"My error, I won't repeat it. Drones are set to charge, deploy, and rotate through automatically. I've my interface set to monitor, and'll actively check periodically, and track their operation."

He agreed diplomatically. "Very good. I'm still going to have two people walking. It's how I operate. Spencer, can you and Caswell do it?"

Dr. Raven sounded off. "Captain, I can handle an M4 or their weapon, and I'm not able to run much, but I can walk. It's my preferred exercise. I'll do it if you're agreeable."

"Spencer and Raven, then. Caswell, organize the females, Doc, organize the males. PT."

He wondered how the drones fared in the gusty winds that

were up this morning. It was hazy, but chill even with the sun. Definitely fall. The distant trees were starting to turn color.

In formation in the shorn grass, it was classic Army. Up front, Doc called, "Attention! At ease. The first exercise is the push-up."

"THE PUSH-UP!"

On the one hand it was familiar routine. On another, it was the same old crap. But they had to stay busy for six weeks, and get the recoverees back into Army mindset.

Cryder and Arnet watched in minor amusement. After the push-ups, Arnet came over, fell into the back of the formation, and joined in. Sit-ups in buddy pairs. Leg lifts. Jumping jacks.

Sean went along with it, light exercise to keep the body moving, while watching the returnees. Most of them had no trouble, though boots were obviously something they'd gotten out of the habit of. Four of them were barefoot. Fine for now. He'd advise them to work proactively on getting used to footwear again.

As they wrapped up, he sought out Sheridan, down at the end sweating but trying to keep up.

"Dr. Sheridan, I understand there are tests and specimens you need from the returnees."

"Yes, sir."

"Can you keep them busy with that for a couple of hours? Or even until lunch?"

"I don't need that long on the first round," she said. Then she seemed to catch on to his hint and said, "But if we take our time, we can be thorough."

"Sounds good. Hold on."

He called over his shoulder, "Breakfast and showers at your own pace, both are ready now."

Turning back to Sheridan he said, "I'll let them enjoy breakfast. My people have some admin stuff to deal with."

"Understood, sir."

Breakfast thrilled the recoverees all over again. They could be heard enthusiastically endorsing it.

"Bacon!!"

"Sausage! And ohmygod, eggs, from chicken, without anything in them growing."

"Pancakes. Syrup. Milk. Orange juice!"

Sean looked over to make sure Doc was rationing them to about a bite of each. He didn't want them getting sick. Yes, he and Arnet were splitting one serving of each between all ten.

The rest of the regulars munched around the fire. Oglesby had wrapped everything in a pancake for convenience. Raven ate just bacon and sausage. The others had plates with various contents.

He opened with, "Okay, we've made contact, recovered the element. Very good, even if it was partly luck. So we must continue to acclimate them, and some of them are resistant or difficult, and we have a child we didn't expect."

"You should have," Raven chided.

He agreed, "Yeah, I guess I hoped we'd find them within weeks or months, and that they'd hold up half as well as we did. I should have planned for it. In my defense, no one above me did, either."

She said, "If they'd consulted us, we'd have advised them. But it's a null issue now. And had they told us in the beginning about the process irregularities..." She looked pretty angry.

"Correct. And thanks for understanding, and your help."

He continued, "So, we must get them prepared and moved to departure point. We must get Shug back to his people. They're apparently within a few days' walk from here. He's seen this local group at what's basically a clan gathering and fair."

Spencer said, "If I may, sir."

"Go ahead."

"We've got six weeks, which sounds like a lot, but isn't. We need a week of that to move, and we have to relocate Shug. That probably eats three weeks. That assumes everything goes perfectly and we leave now."

Dalton said, "It's the Army. It's never perfect or on time."

"Right."

Sean said, "So I want them kept within the perimeter, occupied with debrief, chores even if we have to make them up, PT, starting to write their AARs. We also need that for any potential cross-contamination."

Doc said, "Arnet and I need to check them over, treat for parasites they had and may still have, and their teeth."

"Right. Do that ASAP."

Caswell asked, "And my first question is where's the rest of their gear? I see no weapons, little equipment or personal stuff, and only scraps of uniform. We had to repair ours, but after two years they were still largely intact, not gone."

"I noticed, but not to that level of detail. We'll start debriefing right after breakfast."

He took a deep breath.

"Next item: Fraternization. There's been an attempt already."

Spencer said, "We'll help cover that, sir. I'm proposing to move your shelter up by the Guardians."

"I wasn't naming names, but apparently everyone knows?" There were nods. "Damn. Okay. Well, that's one possibility."

Jenny stepped in.

"Sir, I suggest staying where you are, we'll adjust the schedule slightly. I can put her on some details, and the docs have agreed to help keep her occupied and an eye on her. I'd not get near the Guardian vehicles. They may be able to keep her occupied there."

Oglesby asked, "Oh? Doing what?"

"They have stuff to keep her busy."

"'Stuff'?"

"Stuff, Sergeant. That's enough for you to know." Goddamn, did women have no agency for privacy?

Elliott said, "Yeah, well, this is going to apply to all of them, since they've been out of Army discipline for some time—and all of us, of course. I'll be talking to Lieutenant Cole and getting him involved."

There were nods.

"That's it for now. Short break and police call while I deal with some other stuff. Two of ours, one of theirs. Firewood and other tasks."

"Hooah."

She put in quickly, "Sir, you, me, and Sergeant Spencer need to have a talk about this, too."

"Okay." He looked tired, but it was just that—fatigue. He wasn't dismissing her out of hand.

Once the three of them were alone, she took a deep breath.

She made eye contact with both. "Sir, Sergeant Spencer, we're going to have to be very gentle with that girl. She's probably not even aware of her own mental state."

"Oh? Something you noticed?"

"Something she hasn't, yet. She's spent five years as a repeated rape victim."

Spencer said, "Huh? I understood it was all entirely consensual."

"No, she was pushed into it by her commander."

He looked disturbed. "Oh. That does make a difference."

"Yeah. It was a quid pro quo with their hosts. And then it went on. We'll need to find out about Oyo, too, though apparently she was less to their taste."

Elliott asked, "Can you ask?"

Jenny shook her head. "No. No one should ask. We wait to see what they offer. Then ease them into it."

"Into what?"

"Into understanding they were raped."

"Why do that?" Spencer asked.

"So they can recover."

It was frustrating trying to explain this without better skills. She thought about calling Dr. Raven over, who seemed to have a background for it.

Spencer said, "I'm not saying it's not horrible. I'm saying if she doesn't think of it as rape, why bring it up and make her think of it that way? That's almost worse."

Jenny understood that argument. Fair enough. She took a deep breath.

"You mean well, and that's logical, but it's not how it works."

"Okay?"

"She may not think of it as rape, but she'll know she was taken advantage of, and demeaned. The only way to heal is to accept what happened, and then move on. Without doing that, it'll just fester."

"Like PTSD or mental illness."

"Exactly that."

"Okay," he agreed. "God, this is revolting all around. Why did they think that was a good idea?"

She hated that she understood it.

"They wanted good relations, and safety, and comfort. Do you understand now why I was so twitchy around you guys for two years?"

Spencer said, "Yeah. But there was no way we'd ever do that."

She reminded them, "I got lucky. You guys were honorable, professional, and willing to deal with it to maintain cohesiveness.

These guys defaulted to women as property, and it was almost their first thought."

Elliott said, "I want to argue that it's not all men, but it's enough of them."

"It only takes one. Once it sounds like a good idea, it's game on. Just like mobs or bar fights."

He said, "Well, I have no idea how to approach it, I'm obviously not the right person for it. It's on you, I guess."

"Or when we get forward again," she said.

It wasn't just the woman. All these poor people were going to need massive therapy, probably for years.

Elliott said, "I have the docs keeping them busy for some tests. Then there's the firewood and some other campkeeping. Then we need to start the debrief. Me, Spencer, you with the females, Doc if needed, one of the Guardians, and one of the scientists. It's going to take most of the time we have."

Spencer agreed, "Let's get to it."

Armand was ready to do full physicals on everyone. He had his gear, Arnet and his equipment, and ten troops and a child to check. He felt useful again, within his specialty. The field clinic was the CQ, with awnings down and seats set. It was typical for deployment and had been for centuries. The tech changed, the layout didn't.

"Arnet, can you think of anything specific we're likely to face? I'm guessing old injuries, scars, bad teeth, torn nails, calluses and wear, joint issues."

"That's probly a good summary."

"Okay. You scan, but I should do most of the talking."

The man concurred. "Yes, they're your people."

Hamilton came in first.

Armand welcomed him with, "Specialist Hamilton. You're looking well."

"I feel better, thank you, sir." Shaved, shorn, dressed in a uniform, he was a completely different person from the ragged caricature they'd first encountered.

"Most of this exam is automated. Have a seat on the recliner," he indicated. It really was a folding recliner, like a beach chair but gossamer light.

Hamilton did, and he reached forward. "Place your wrist in this sleeve."

"Hooah."

Arnet had set the machine to read in English. Armand read the screen and informed the patient.

"This will give us all your vitals. They look good. You should be parasite free. It seems some of your nutrition is a little off. You need more iodine, a bit of calcium, and some zinc. Overall you're in very good health. How do you feel?"

"Fucking awesome, sir. Ready for home to go."

"We'll get there and there will be more exams. Get used to them."

"Small price."

"Tell us about any injuries you've had. Literally everything above a scraped finger."

"God, stubbed toes. Cut feet. Cut hands. My wrist." He pointed at a small, jagged scar. "A couple of head bangs."

"What's that?" Armand pointed at an angular mark on the man's left chest, under the collar bone.

"Oh, that's the tribal mark. We all have that."

Interesting that the left breast was a significant location even in this culture.

"Tattoo?" he asked.

"I think so. Cut skin and ash rubbed in."

Arnet said, "I can make that go away with a salve and some frequencies."

Armand nodded. "Okay, good. Let me see your feet." Hamilton unlaced his boots with some awkwardness from unfamiliarity. He kicked them off, pulled at his socks. His feet still showed heavy calluses. None of the scars were critical, and the bones seemed to be aligned. Nails were ugly and coarse, but intact.

"You'll need to cut those again after you shower tonight."

"Hooah, sir. And my fingernails."

"Yes. Get them soft first."

Arnet said, "We have a lotion. Apply it now, it will feel greasy in the socks, but will dry within an hour or so. After that, the nails will be pliable for the next day."

Armand said, "I need to do a quick visual down below. No probing unless you're having issues."

"No, the tribal elders know how to treat internal parasites with one of the spicy plants." The man slipped his pants down, raised his legs and spread.

Armand nodded. No obvious damage, but damn, that skin was like leather. Probably from thighs rubbing, sweat, and hair. No obvious lesions or damage.

"Good. I need to look at your teeth."

Hamilton pulled his pants up, leaned back and opened his mouth. The monitor's light moved to best illuminate.

Dentistry wasn't one of Armand's prime skills. He could look at general condition and obvious cavities. That was about it.

Hamilton's mouth looked pretty good. The gums were bit inflamed, but tartar buildup was light. Lack of sugar and starch would do that. He had one swollen spot with a shred of meat stuck, which Armand flicked out with a probe. That might be a cavity in back.

Arnet asked, "Were your third molars removed?"

"No, I've never had teeth out."

Armand clarified. "Wisdom teeth."

"Oh, I still had them. They weren't in the way."

Arnet said, "They are now. We can fix that when we get home."

Armand asked, "Is that a cavity?"

Arnet looked at the tooth and his monitor and replied, "Fissure, minor. We'll fix that now."

Hamilton tensed slightly, until Armand said, "We fix it with a gel. First you're getting a mouthwash to clear some of that gunk out generally. Swish this in your mouth for at least sixty seconds." He handed over the cup Arnet had ready.

Then he sat back and did nothing. It was easy to distract someone doing something like this, and have them swallow or spill. It was amusing once, and unprofessional.

He kept a count at fifteen-second intervals, and concluded with, "You're done. Just spit it on the ground. Then open back up for some gel."

He put the syringe where Arnet pointed, and squeezed.

Arnet said, "That has to sit for an hour without any eating."

"Hooah...Sergeant?" The man wasn't sure what Arnet actually was. Armand felt sympathy. He still wasn't sure.

Arnet said, "There's no equivalent rank. Sir or Sergeant are both acceptable. 'Gajin Op Prime' is too wordy."

"And you're good to go," Armand said. "Send in Maldonado next."

✧　　✧　　✧

Sean Elliott hated to start the line of questioning he was about to start, but it had to be covered. The firepit wasn't the most private place, but he'd given orders for them to be left alone. He had Spencer and Caswell sitting a few feet away. He wanted their input later, but the questions were his.

It was too nice a morning for this, but he breathed the clean, hazy air and started.

"Lieutenant Cole, we need to ask some baseline questions. This is official, but not everything here will wind up back home. For example, do not *ever* admit to killing any aurochs or other fauna."

The lieutenant wrinkled his brow. "Why not? Food hunting is a problem?"

"It is when the EPA is asking the questions and it's an extinct animal," Sean told him.

He looked confused. "What the hell? They're gone long in our time."

Sean explained, "And our rep admitted that was the case and it was stupid, but US Government regs are US Government regs. We'll make sure we tell everyone. The question is, are your people able to handle that and not talk too much?"

The man winced. "Probably not all of them. Lozano seems to want trouble. Hamilton has always been too friendly. So has Noirot."

"Well, we have six weeks here and time when in the future. They'll help."

Cole looked and said, "I hope so. I don't want trouble back home."

"It's going to be a long haul, Brian. We're still recovering ourselves, and still subject to interviews."

"Yeah, I bet."

"First of all, what happened to your interpreter? Akhtar Malik?"

Cole paused for only a moment and said, "He married a local woman. They had a son who was stillborn. He died shortly after that in a hunting accident. I think he was trying to get killed. He was very unhappy."

"How was he buried?"

"In a hole, with some beads and stuff. We put his Quran in with him. He'd have wanted that."

Unfortunate the man was dead, but the closure was good. "Very decent of you. Do you know where?"

"Yeah, there's an area we use."

"Okay, we'll need to document that. You can show us from memory? Or on an aerial photo?"

"Yes, if we go. Maybe on a map."

"Excellent."

So far so good, but they had to get to the other issue fast.

"So, as to Noirot, and you're not being charged or otherwise, but we need to know. How did she wind up swapping sexual favors to people?"

He blushed, hard.

"It wasn't like that," he said quickly, sounding tense. "We got here, hacked around, managed to kill a few things and get a fire going, made some lean-tos. We were pretty fucking shocked."

"We understand exactly. Go on."

"We got meat every day. We knew dandelions were edible and found a few. That was pretty much all we had. The meat was tough, tasteless, I'm sure you know."

"You found water?"

"Yeah, we walked downhill to a stream and followed it. We drank the water and got screaming shits. We all lost weight, had trouble keeping clean, had relapses. It was two weeks of sheer fucking hell. I think it was two weeks. We all lost track. We had a couple of lean-tos and a fire, and small stuff we could knock over with M4s. We got harassed by a lion, and then by a bear. We ran through a bit of ammo in the process."

"I bet."

The memory seemed to make the man shrink back and shiver. "We kept going downstream, hoping to find something. We didn't see any villages, no radio, of course, no aircraft, nothing. We thought we'd wound up in an abandoned world."

"We were able to figure it out pretty quickly. Doc knows astronomy and could read the stars. We got lucky. But yes, it's utterly terrifying when it happens."

"It was beyond terrifying. We...broke down. All of us. I tried to keep discipline and order but...there was no way. We all knew to keep moving, so we managed that much."

"How did you make contact?"

"So, we finally got found by a hunting party, and goddamn was that a mindfuck. They were obviously Stone Age. We'd just figured we were lost in Africa when we saw the lion, and maybe some weird world without people when we found the bear as well. We met them, and I knew there were a couple of remote tribes, but all tropical. This wasn't tropical."

"What time of year when you arrived?"

"Fall, like this. It was fucking cold. We had trouble staying warm, basically wore everything we had. No frostbite, but lots of cold injuries otherwise. We finally figured out how to build beds every time we stopped. Not bed-beds, but layers of stuff to insulate us off the ground."

Spencer said, "Yeah, that's standard advice."

"I know, but we didn't remember it, and we were panicky and stressed and not sleeping." The man picked at grass from the ground, looking nervous and tense.

Sean urged him, "That's fine. Go on. You met a hunting party."

"We went with them. One of our guys, Uhiara, figured to kill something with rifle fire to impress them. They ran off in a panic and we damned near started beating him before they came back."

"Things were okay after that?"

"They were still scared, but we had another small deer for them. They gutted it right there and brought it along."

"Okay."

"So, we wound up back to their village. They were glad to see us."

"Glad?"

"They smiled, offered food, wanted to check our stuff out."

Spencer offered, "We had that, too."

"Well, we didn't speak a word of the language, but I made it clear I was umma for our group."

"Go on."

"They fed us. We gave them the meat we had left. They swapped some spearpoints and a couple of decorated blankets. We gave them some bits of MREs and pogey bait. They really liked it. They found a couple of huts for us and it was obvious we were welcome to stay."

"Okay."

"I was given my own place, and two women who made it very clear they expected me to . . . perform."

Spencer shook his head and grimaced. "Fuck, I see where this is going."

"Next morning, Argarak declared that he wanted the blond

woman, and that he wasn't interested in more cloth or other items. Well, he wanted those, too, but she had to be part of the deal."

"Exogamy," Caswell said. "Typical in this type of culture. It can be worked around with language."

"We didn't have any language, as I said." He sounded very defensive.

Sean wanted him on track. "That's fine. Go on."

"So I asked if she was agreeable, for purposes of keeping good relations. We were all still in complete shock. But she agreed."

Caswell sounded very tense as she asked, "And it didn't occur to you that was a very bad idea, and a line you should never cross?"

"We had no other way to stay alive."

She stopped talking and just stared. A moment later she shivered.

Goddamn. She'd been afraid of that the entire time. He'd thought she was crazy. But it had happened right here.

"So how did it work out with other men?"

"As far as?"

"Noirot's actions."

He still looked ashamed. "Oh, that. Well, they have a caste system. Argarak fucks any woman he wants, and has four who are exclusively his. The senior hunters all have a couple each, and dibs on any traveling parties with women, if Argarak doesn't take first cut. Below that, most of the skilled hunters have a mate each. So does the knapper, the boat maker, the weaver. Then the unproven guys have their hands. That was pretty fucking creepy the first time one of them did it in view. Open hut, whacking away. They even have parties to do it."

He didn't need detail about that. "Okay. The experts will want more on that, but that's enough summary for us. So, how many men has Noirot been involved with?"

"Four or five of the hunters. Argarak. Me, though I tried to get her to fake it."

"What?"

"Look, I'm a chief. I'm expected to have a woman. I said we didn't have to, but the next morning, they were joking about how quiet it had been and how she seemed unfulfilled. Did she want another round with the hunters? It...well..."

"Right. So, we'll deal with this in the future, then when we get back to our time, a lot of this absolutely can't be mentioned, and a lot more can only be mentioned to the specific research group. Your people are going to have to keep their mouths shut."

"Acknowledged. Thanks for understanding."

Sean replied carefully. "I didn't say we understood. We'll accept the facts and they'll be addressed by experts."

Cole was damp-eyed and almost blubbering. "Captain, I did the best I could, believe me."

"I believe you. We had two vehicles with a good cross-section of content, and three people with specifically useful knowledge, even if it was theoretical to start with. And I'm an engineer. Building stuff is my job."

Then he remembered. "Oh, who's the father of her child?"

"We're not sure. Not me, though. We did fake it after the first time. They insisted on watching."

Sean must have looked amazed, because Caswell said, "That's also common in early societies. They don't have much entertainment, and they want to make sure the relationship is secure."

"I'm amazed you could get it up like that."

"It really wasn't easy. I had to just shut my brain down and focus on . . . her."

"Has she been with any of your guys?"

"Yeah. They felt left out and got irritated. I suggested it was a good diplomatic measure, just occasionally, to make sure they didn't feel anyone was getting special treatment."

Caswell stood and walked off. He didn't blame her, and ignored it.

Spencer asked, "What about Oyo?"

"Argarak didn't want her. I get the impression dark skin was a problem for him. Sorry."

"Not your fault. And it's actually good for the circumstances. So not him, but what about others?"

"Yeah, two of the hunters from time to time, just as diplomacy. And the flint knapper. We needed spears. Then she settled down with Breotah."

Sex as trade goods. What a fucked-up situation. He now understood why Caswell had been so flipped out. He wouldn't consider anything like this, but obviously, these guys did.

"Does Oyo have any kids?"

"No."

"Okay. That's a positive."

Sean asked, "Where's the rest of your military gear? You said it was hidden."

"We stowed it in a cave."

"After you came to the village, right? Do they know where it is?"

"Yes, but it's a mystical cave. No one is allowed there. They had to ask other villages for permission first."

"Why did you do that? Hide your gear?"

"We did some more hunting. They really didn't like the noise, and said it was unmanly to use magic. Well, first they thought it was fucking awesome. But when we refused to share the magic rifles, they got nasty."

"I can see that."

"I sort of hoped they'd be found in that cave in the future, and someone would figure out what happened."

"We didn't. That cave probably is long eroded by our time, in a valley like this. Or, it collapsed."

"Yeah. It was just a hope. And it seemed best to blend in. We kept most of our clothes, and boots. We got rid of everything tech oriented. Some of it we burned—phones, most of the armor carriers. The plates are hidden in the cave. We kept the rucks for use while hunting, and gifted half of them to the village."

"We'll need those back, too."

Right then, Cryder's voice came from his phone, even without it ringing.

"Armed element approaching. Larger than before."

"Understood." He rose and called, "Incoming hostiles, arm up and form up. New troops, stay near the fire and await instructions. Nonlethal response again."

Dalton shouted, "Sir, should we send out a flanking or contact element?"

"Negative, but we may pursue afterward."

"Roger that, sir."

An arrow appeared in the ground, accompanied by a whisper and faint thud. It was crudely fletched, but effective enough.

Everyone scattered for weapons and position.

Cryder announced, "I count two seven, twenty-seven hostiles. Several appear to have bows, all have spears, some have supplemental short stabbing spears with shields atar dried hide."

Elliott said, "We'd prefer not to kill them if we don't have to."

Cryder said, "That fits my instructions."

He didn't say it suited his preferences, Sean noted.

Everyone was up, weapons in hand, morphing them into stun setting. Spencer stood back and grabbed his AR-10, but didn't shoulder it.

Lozano shouted something in their language. Three seconds in, he went silent in mid-syllable. The Guardians had either zapped him or soundproofed the tent. Either way was fine.

One of the hunters threw himself toward the wards at a full sprint. He obviously planned to get inside them even if he was knocked cold.

Apparently, the wards were programmed for that. They zapped him far enough out he sprawled for a dirt nap.

Another tried for a leap from a buddy's back, for height. That didn't work either. He hit the field, flopped down hard, possibly injuring neck and shoulder.

The arrows, though, and larger atlatl darts—those had been hard to ID until they were in use—and the occasional spear came over the top readily.

Arnet said, "These are proof against most direct fire. We'd need a heavier kit for indirect fire. Those also typically include interdiction and counterfire."

"Yeah, this is serious harassing fire. I wonder how long they can keep it up." He skipped sideways as he saw something dropping near him.

He called over to Hamilton.

"What did Lozano say?"

"He said, 'The tall pale hairs are the wizards, get them first.'"

"Ah. He's just not learning."

"He's been very popular with the local women, and is an effective hunter. He really was enjoying it here."

"Well, sucks to be him. And he's making it suck for the rest of us."

Elliott called, "Dalton, Spencer, Arnet if you're free, we are forming a flying squad and flanking them."

"Hooah." "Hooah." "Will do, Captain."

Spencer called, "Sir, I only have actual firearms."

He remembered. "Crap. Oglesby, you're in."

"Hooah."

That left Cryder, Caswell, Doc, Spencer and Shug inside with the scientists and the recoverees.

"Spencer, arm up, you are in charge, keep things under our control."

"Yes, sir," Martin Spencer replied. He already had his AR-10 loaded and ready. He also understood the implication that the recoverees might still have mixed allegiance. He didn't want to shoot anyone, but his options were limited. A .30 caliber bullet would stop any of them. Especially as this wasn't a war zone and he had soft points.

Elliott's patrol went out on left flank, uphill and past the vehicles, moving fast and low behind terrain features. Spencer kept an eye on the lost troops, wiggling the rifle to keep them near the firepit. It was a good, central location, far enough back from the fence to have warning of incoming shafts. Caswell and Doc zapped hostiles cold. Cryder was atop a vehicle where he could enfilade the troops by the fire or get clear shots at the attackers.

A swarm of zaps indicated Elliott making contact with the attackers, who quickly melted back into the woods and away.

As everyone returned and reset, he pondered just how completely international relations had been screwed up here. There was little possible to make things worse.

But if there was, they'd probably run into it.

Amalie forced herself calm. The Byko tech was good, and the forcefield did its job. She knew what the weapons could do. It was over quickly, and they were still secure. Good. She really did wish she had her Ruger or her XD. The Byko weapons were better, but not handy. She wanted something on her person. She'd ask. It might be something they'd agree to.

The immediate issue was poor little Kita. The kid was hysterical, having seen tribal warfare between one group her mother and she belonged to, and the ones they were with now. She alternated blubbers and screams.

Oglesby was nearby and said, "Fuck."

"What specifically?" she asked.

"She's saying, 'I want to go home,' near as I can tell."

This just got worse all the time. The Army really hadn't

planned ahead for anything. These troops had experience with Paleos, and even they were struggling.

"I need to talk to the captain before we do anything further," she commented. "Meantime, get the little girl some candy, and bring a poncho liner."

"Hooah, ma'am," Oglesby replied, and bounded off. He seemed glad to be away from the domestic issue for the moment.

Noirot was cuddling the girl, or trying to, and making murmurs of reassurance.

Oglesby came back, handed over the poncho liner. He also had a lollipop from the kitchen. Perfect. Amalie took it and carefully squatted down next to the girl and her mother.

"Kita," she said softly. "Here." Slowly and gently, she put the slick, soft fabric against the girl's face and hands.

The girl rubbed her cheek against it, then clutched the thin blanket to herself. That helped.

Then Amalie held out the bright blue sucker, probably berry flavored. She drew it back, took a lick to demonstrate, and then handed it over.

The girl took a cautious lick. Her eyes opened, then she stopped crying as she stuffed the candy in her mouth. Her shrieks and wails calmed to periodic sobs.

"You wrap up in that and get all cuddly, okay?" she suggested. The girl wouldn't understand a word, so she added signs and pantomime, pointing at a spot under the CQ awning that had a floor, corner, and desk. It was a little cave that should be less restrictive than a tent but provide shelter and reassurance.

"Thank you," Noirot said. She sounded grateful.

She replied, "It's fine. This is going to be difficult for her. Does she know any English?"

"No, we weren't bothering. I figured when she was older I'd teach her some as a code."

Understandable. "Okay. Well, switch to English now. She's young enough to pick it up."

"Will she remember our language?"

"The one you've been speaking? I doubt it. I don't remember any of my childhood language. Unless you make a point to use it."

"Okay. Thanks, Dr. Raven." The woman seemed relieved and less stressed.

"You're welcome. I can't babysit with my duties, but if she's occupied with something I can watch her briefly while you manage a task, or shower, or whatever."

"Oh, yes, please."

Sean Elliott breathed deeply to recover. He had a bruise from diving behind a rock, grass burns, and some aches. Otherwise, he felt good. They'd responded, zapped a bunch of hostiles, ended the engagement textbook fashion, and with non-lethal weapons, he had no moral quandaries about the guys he'd hit. The Byko weapons were awesome, once you learned how to control them.

He stowed the . . . ray gun, he decided. They'd never named them. It went on a rack, Cryder secured them with some gadget or other, and he trod back to the firepit. A few points and orders, and it was again clear for debriefing.

"Okay, Lieutenant Cole, we're looking for how many rucks exactly?"

The man replied "Five." He sounded sure of the number. Good.

"Who has them?"

"The senior hunters. I don't know if they're all in camp right now."

Sean nodded. "Understood. What else might be there we need to recover? Absolutely anything of ours. And I do mean anything."

"Uh . . . Munoz had a porn mag in his gear. We offered that as trade, and they basically split it up."

Spencer said, "We can probably not worry about that. It won't last twelve thousand years." He was still slinging the AR-10.

Cole suddenly looked interested. "Oh, is that where we are?"

Spencer said, "Yeah, just after a cold snap called the Younger Dryas event."

"They—the tribe—talk about how it's getting warmer."

Spencer agreed. "It is."

Sean asked, "Okay. Anything else?"

Cole seemed to suddenly remember. "Ah, Argarak has a modern knife. I showed him how to sharpen it against a rock."

"That we absolutely have to get."

"Burnham made paracord bracelets until he ran out. Four of them."

"Do you know who has them?"

"Yes, Argarak, Magliku—"

Those probably weren't an issue. Nylon would decay in time, even if buried. "That's fine. We'll follow up. Anything else?"

"No, sir. We didn't have much to share. Oh, some empty brass as jewelry."

"How many?"

"I, uh, didn't keep track."

That made sense, but it was unfortunately a totally unacceptable answer.

"Lieutenant, I know it's going to be inexact, but it is absolutely essential that we have that information."

The man looked very serious and worried. What was a rescue could easily turn into disciplinary action up to a court-martial.

He said, "Captain, if I had it, I'd tell you. There was a handful from hunting. Maybe ten or so."

"We'll need to debrief each individually until we know. Make that the first question, Sergeant Spencer."

"Will do, sir. I wish we had Trinidad here. He was the intel type."

"Yeah, we'll have to fake it."

After the small raid, regular duties resumed. The captain was doing his debrief, others handling chores. The recoverees were giddy at getting phones, even if they could only call one another and run movies and music from the limited database. Even Lozano grudgingly accepted one.

Armand did like being useful, and damn, these people needed care. He could write a paper on the contrast between an element with an actual medic and one with only combat lifesavers. They'd all been taught things they needed, but hadn't done them. Then, of course, his element had contained experienced reenactors and maintained discipline. As much as it sucked, they'd come out okay. This element had fallen apart and they were lucky they were still alive.

Oyo was next.

"I need one of the females to help with questions."

Arnet tapped his phone, and in a few moments, Dr. Sheridan arrived.

"Hello, Doctor," he said. "I need a female for support while we examine Sergeant Oyo."

"I can do that," she said. "Where should I sit?"

"Right there is fine, minimizing gawkers, unless she wants you somewhere else. It's her call."

She replied, "Perfect, Armand. I'm already impressed."

"By?"

"How you're handling this, and the medical process."

"Thanks, though Arnet is responsible for a lot of it."

"Yes, but he's from the future."

Armand wasn't entirely sure what that had to do with patient support, but it seemed she meant well, and he didn't want to get her blabbing at length the way she did. He decided to move on.

"Thank you," he said, and left it at that.

Oyo arrived. They went through the same procedure. Plug in the monitor, questions, check general fitness.

"Okay, I need you to strip so I can make a visual, but no probing unless there's an issue. Any issues?"

"No, I feel great. That was the first night I wasn't itching from flies and fleas. God."

"Excellent."

She unbuttoned and removed her blouse, pulled her support tee off, slid her pants down. He took a quick glance. She'd apparently already made use of a razor. Her thighs and groin were less worn than the others, but did have some scars, possibly from bites, possibly abrasion. Healed, not critical.

Her feet were about the same as he'd seen so far, but one toe looked broken.

"Yes," she agreed. "A while back. I kicked a rock late at night. It hurt for a few days, but hasn't been bad since."

Arnet said, "That's an easy fix for us."

Her nails and calluses were impressive. Arnet had more lotion.

Armand noted, "You have a couple of minor scars. Any problems? Or you can deal with that with docs back home."

"Fine for now, thanks, Sergeant."

She redressed. He noticed her scalp was in good shape, no dandruff. That might be due to her hair oil, or possibly diet and hormones. He made a note.

"How's your cycle been?"

"Uh, very irregular, and long, and painful."

"How long?"

"Five weeks and a bit at the longest. Four weeks is about normal, and that was some of the time."

"Cramps or otherwise?"

"Cramps and heavy bleeding."

"Arnet, does your equipment show anything?"

"There's a potential hormone imbalance. I'm letting the system adjust slightly. We can do more later if we need to."

Armand said, "Also, we have hygiene supplies. Help yourself as needed."

"Oh, fantastic. Leather and moss is not comfortable."

"Yeah, our females had to improvise." Well, one had. Alexander had been ablated and didn't have any periods. Still.

"And we're going to check your teeth."

Hers were in fine shape, well spaced, cleaner than Hamilton's, and no sign of cavities. Arnet handed him the general rinse that took care of tartar and bacteria. She swilled, spit.

"You're good to go. Call any time it's an emergency, and we hold sick call at oh nine hundred every day."

"Hooah, Doc, thanks." She seemed very relieved.

"You're welcome. Send Uhiara up, please."

As she strode away, Sheridan said, "Did you catch that?"

"Catch what?"

The scientist turned and asked, "Arnet, can I see your metabolic info on her? In English?"

"I think so, stand by."

He made some adjustments and handed a tablet over.

Sheridan swore.

"Yeah, that makes sense."

"What?"

"Painful, irregular, messy periods. Miscarriages. She's been pregnant several times and never caught. Something incompatible, instant flush."

"That sucks, but it's good there aren't more kids."

"Yeah. Arnet, when you said imbalance..."

"Yes, she may be pregnant now. Under ten days. I impaired it. It's not supportable under the circumstances."

"On the one hand, she really should have a choice. On the other, the same thing is almost certainly going to happen. And on the gripping hand, a child would be a massive complication."

"Gripping hand." Armand understood that reference.

"Incompatible how?"

"At a guess, blood group or chromosome errors, or similar.

She's from a different time frame with background on a different continent. We don't know how old our blood types are, though probably older than this by a good margin, but for example, modern native South Americans are all O type. The settlers of the Americas split off from proto-Eurasians, mostly A. Rh factor matters significantly. There are others less important to us, but could be critical back here. Or, she may just have trouble conceiving. Endometrial issues or some other matter."

Arnet said, "I can easily check, but it's not important at this time."

"Right. She's conceived, lost them, been in pain, and had no way to avoid it. Poor girl."

No wonder a lot of officers wanted nothing but fit young men for the Army. Far fewer issues like this.

Armand said, "Well, she's healthy at present."

Uhiara arrived, and Armand told Sheridan, "Okay, Doctor, I'll let you know if I have more questions."

It went smoothly enough. Four had dental caries, though not as badly as he expected. They all had tartar buildup, and stuck shreds of meat and vegetable matter, which were worse. Several had significant foot calluses even by these standards, Burnham a bunion that would take some therapy in Bykostan. Under his cut hair, his scalp was an oozing mess.

"I didn't like the dreadlocks," he said. "But this itches and burns and stings. It's nasty."

Arnet noted something with his fingers on the air keyboard, pulled a vial from his unit, and said, "Apply this."

Burnham took it, squeezed it out, rubbed it in, and said, "Fuck, that burns. But the itching and stinging has stopped."

"It'll be fine tomorrow," Arnet assured him.

The Bykos didn't consider scars an issue in the field, but he catalogued a bunch to be treated in the future. Parasites were already dealt with. There were skin lesions from abrasion, rash, bites, minor chemical issues. Some severe dandruff. Hamilton and Keisuke had torn off fingernails, and regeneration was in process. They'd start growing replacements within the week.

Arnet said, "They all have a local, low-grade genital infection, very likely sexually transmitted. Its easily fixed, and I administered an antibiotic. It presents as a very mild form of syphilis."

He called Sheridan back over about that matter.

The scientist nodded and replied, "That makes sense. There are related infections that are far less virulent, and some speculation that societies with more clothing caused it to evolve to be more aggressive."

"Interesting," Arnet said.

"You don't have information on that?" she asked.

"I'm interested in what you know," he replied.

She said, "That's more Dr. Raven's field. I'll see if she can get you a summary. Or even a detailed account. I'm sure she can cover it for hours."

Arnet smiled. "A brief will be fine, it's personal curiosity only. I'm not a scientist, only an operator."

He continued, "There was some bacteria and a virus they're immune to, but will need additional Byko clearance."

Armand wasn't quite clear on what he meant by "clearance." He asked, "You mean they're carrying a virus and it will have to be taken care of in your time?"

"Yes."

"Okay. Clearance can also refer to approval."

The man nodded. "I understand. It will need treatment."

"Got it."

Sheridan said, "I would like whatever data you can share, and any bio samples I can get from them. This is very relevant to my interests." She looked pleased, by a disease. "And I'll have some blood grouping data, too."

Lunchtime had everyone gathered around the fire. It was slightly cool, but within the capabilities of the clothing, and they were all used to outside activity. Still, Arnet had thoughtfully come up with a thick beef soup with crusty bread.

"God, bread," Maldonado said. "I could eat a loaf."

Armand reminded him, "Better not. You're not used to it. Work up slowly."

"Yes, sir. But it's so good."

"It really is." Especially since it was made in the field.

CHAPTER 16

After lunch, Martin Spencer sought out his counterpart.

"Sergeant Burnham," he addressed, "I need to talk to you. Would you like a drink while we do?"

Burnham looked a bit tense and replied, "Uh, probably, yes, thanks, please."

Martin held up the plastic containers he already had. "Pineapple rum punch."

"Oh, damn, thank you, Sergeant."

"No worries. For this talk, let's be Martin and Andrew."

"Drew is fine. Marty?"

Oh, God, no. He shook his head. "No, just Martin, thank you."

"Hooah. What are we talking about?"

"You can guess. Let's find a quiet spot past the scientists, away from people. We'll go through CQ and grab some folding chairs."

"Thanks."

With drinks in hand, chairs oriented to view the goings-on and ensure they were private, Martin led into the discussion diplomatically.

"So, the LT gave us a rundown on your displacement, justifiable freakout, meeting with the natives, diplomacy and adoption, including loss of Army property and the 'female diplomacy.'"

"Ah, Serg . . . Martin, I specifically did not advise any of that."

He put on an office smile. "That's fine. There's no proceedings here. This is professional, but it's not necessarily official. As we told Lieutenant Cole, there are things that our present-day Army does not need to know, and must not find out about. But we need to know, understand?"

"Yeah. Got it." The man seemed quite a bit relieved.

"Okay, so I need a no-shit rundown from you on several things, most important is who wants to go home and who might want to stay, other than Lozano, who's made it pretty obvious."

"Can do." Burnham nodded, and tried to stroke his now shaven beard.

"But first of all, tell me how you got Dobie."

"My German shepherd? I was eight, he was hanging around and I started feeding him, and then he sort of followed me into the house. We checked with the local vet and animal control, no one could trace or ID him. After about six weeks, my father decided we should adopt him and get him shots and such. That's pretty much what I wrote for my ISOPREP file."

"Yup, that's why I asked. So you are you, which we assumed, but by the letter of the reg we have to make sure."

"Okay. So I'm me. And you want to know about—"

Martin smiled and pointed. "We'll get to that in a bit. How's the drink?"

"Oh," the man replied, looked at his hand, and took a swig. "Fucking delicious," he admitted. "Cold, sweet, alcoholic. It's been almost six years since I had one."

"You're welcome. We managed mead and wine and the Cog... Bykos can make liquor, once we met up."

Burnham nodded. "Yeah, there's that fermented thing here, but nothing like this." He held up the container, then took another drink.

"Good. So, what did you say to the LT about his plan?"

The man sighed heavily. "I said we should keep our distance and maybe be trading partners or such. Try to impress them with some technology, and gradually move in as equals."

Good. "Makes sense. What did you have in mind?"

The man shrugged and sounded awkward. "Yeah, that was the problem. Other than hunting with rifles, or things like lighters and flashlights that weren't going to last long, there wasn't much to offer. But he just wanted to get straight into being part of the group in case of predators, or hostile natives, and to have some sort of lodgings."

"Understood. And when he wanted to trade women for this?"

"I said it was a really bad idea. And I triple-checked with Noirot that she was willing. She was. Insisted the guy had to brush his teeth, and he did, things like that. She helped plan it."

Probably felt she had no choice other than terms.

"Okay. So, that is the first thing that no one discusses back home, at all, except with specifically designated therapists who they'll assign. But do not mention it to *any* US Army personnel. There are several reasons for this."

"I understand."

And Martin felt a fuck of a lot better the senior NCO hadn't endorsed the idea. It should have been stopped somehow, but he wasn't going to judge that. He had no idea who'd said what, or the context. And God help him for thinking there was a context to this. But there was, and even Caswell had said so.

"So which of your people are reliable for going home, and who's going to flake out? Other than Lozano."

Burnham winced. "Yeah, he bothers me. I've never seen him with a native girl over age sixteen. The main one he's with now was twelve when they got together."

"Christ."

"Yeah. I mean, they are more mature younger than we are, but still, under sixteen is under sixteen."

"Okay, this is another subject that does not ever get mentioned to the Army."

Burnham raised his eyebrows. "Oh, I know that. Honestly, I'd rather not talk about any of it. It's all half nightmare, half POW."

"Exactly. And we thought *we* had it bad."

"How were the women and locals for you guys?"

Martin summarized. "We built a stockade and held sick call and trading parties. One of our people got blown by a native chick once, and I think two others had brief dalliances."

"Really? You didn't shack up?"

"We were discussing the idea of them coming to us, and us giving them requirements, and making us overlords of status. And that's when the Bykos met up, so it all got put on hold. Then we got a recovery notice."

"I don't know if I'm jealous or . . . if you should be. We've been getting laid."

"Yeah, we maintained discipline with the locals. I guess it depends on your command and outlook."

Burnham nodded. "Fair enough. We're in shit shape. Other than getting laid, we've got nothing."

"So who wants to go home?"

"Oh . . ." The man considered a moment, then spoke. "Keisuke. Me. The LT. Both women almost definitely."

"Good."

"Maldonado probably does. Lozano doesn't. Uhiara does. Munoz I'm not sure about. Hamilton does."

Martin agreed, "Definitely. He was ecstatic when he met us."

Next question.

"What were you doing for the tribe?"

Burnham explained, "Some hunting, but I'm not as good as others. Though better than Munoz. He sucks and paid for it."

"How?"

"How, what? Oh, well, he rarely gets any pussy. Usually stuck with the single, unproven hunters. It's a pretty serious penalty. Do badly enough times, and off you go to the barracks. Keisuke, Maldonado, Hamilton. They were finally letting Hamilton join back into hunting parties after additional training. Lozano has a knack for it, so does Uhiara."

"I see. And you?"

"I showed them how to use hash marks to track things, including inventory of hides and such. I guess I'm an early bard? It got me my own hut and a serving girl, but she wasn't a wife until last year."

"Scribe. A good position for an NCO. And others?"

"The women help cook, prepare hides, straighten spear shafts, herd kids, trap fish, gather food. They're decent at it, too."

"And the LT?"

"Ah, he's a *gu-umma*. Sort of a chief of our group under their chief. He gave pretty good advice on irrigation."

"Oh?"

"Yeah, they're starting to develop crops. I don't think we know anything about the plants, but they dug shallows and he showed how to trench."

Martin decided to conclude for now. "Alright," he said. "That's all good to know. We'll talk again. Good to have you back."

Burnham said, very seriously, "Thanks. We're more grateful than you can know."

"We have a pretty good idea. That's why we're here. And you're welcome."

Armand decided Jachike Uhiara was a good choice for debrief. The man seemed pretty chill, though certainly eager to get home. He found the sergeant by the fire, splitting wood.

"Sergeant Uhiara, would you like to take a break? I have some questions."

"Sure, Doc," the man agreed. He put the axe down and wiped his brow. "Is this Doc or LT stuff?"

"It's 'I'd like to know how you're doing' stuff, so some of each, and some of Armand."

The man grinned agreeably. "Yes, sir. And I go by 'Jake.' What can I tell you?"

"Grab a drink and let's sit over there." He pointed at a pair of field chairs.

"Sounds good. The juices are great."

"Yeah, even better than back home. They have amazing produce."

"I thought these were faked for the field?"

"They fake the amazing stuff amazingly well, too," he said with a chuckle.

Once the man had a large tumbler of strawberry juice, he asked, "Eager to get home?"

Uhiara nodded vigorously. "Yeah. This was even worse than Nigeria. I mean, we left there when I was five, but I remember enough. I guess there's fewer AKs, but just as many diseases, parasites, less electricity..."

"We had an intel squid from the PI. Remote area. He made similar comments. So, you settled down here?"

Uhiara shrugged. "I've got a wife on...well, not paper. No kids. She had one stillborn. That was pretty rough." He tensed a bit.

"Sorry to hear that. How do you feel about her?"

"She's nice enough. Warm in winter. But not what I wanted in a permanent relationship, you know? She can scrape hides, roast meat, find lots of stuff that's edible if need be. But there's just no way to have a conversation, and I have a wife back home. Did, at least."

"You still should, and yeah, I treated a lot of people in our time. Displaced time. It was hard to even get basic notions across."

"Exactly. I wish her well, and hope she finds someone else soon."

"I wish it had been better for you."

The man gave a very fatalistic shrug. "So do I. But honestly, this place isn't Houston. It isn't Nebraska. It isn't even fucking Uyo. I confirmed last night I much prefer my steak from a store and well-aged, not fresh off a flint spear. I want to get home."

He wasn't quite sobbing, but looked very vulnerable.

Armand said, "Yeah. We know exactly how you feel. I spent two years with minimal field kit, watching people die, who I knew I could save with better gear and evac. And then there's the excessively chewy goat..."

"We tenderize it by aging it, but we all got the shits a few times until we developed some gut flora, I guess."

"Right. That will adapt back quickly."

"Good. We leave in forty days? Like Christ in the wilderness?"

Ironic coincidence, he thought. "They have a fixed departure, yes. Forty-seven from our arrival. We'll be moving and doing more processing. Then the Byko have to do theirs, which takes a couple of weeks, but their world is amazing, even if you only see the inside of their holding area. Then home and a couple more weeks before you get to see family."

"And Angela, my real wife, is waiting?"

Armand reassured him, "As far as I know, yes. It's been a few months only, and they came up with cover stories as best they could, once they understood this."

The man closed his eyes and seemed to pray.

"Now I have to decide what to tell her."

"Your best bet is nothing. It was a mission that went bad, but you were fine and unharmed and recovered, and can't talk about it. OPSEC and COMSEC all in one."

"Yes, but LT...I have cheated on her." The man seemed distraught now.

That was a moral issue.

"I don't see it that way. You had no expectation of going home. Now that you do, you've stopped. Certainly you should talk to Sergeant Dalton, who is very, very inspiring on matters of faith. And despite some...biased positions, Sergeant Caswell is also a good voice."

The man nodded. "Thanks, LT. Anything else I can tell you?"

"Probably, but later is fine. We'll have a list of specifics."

"Thank you, sir. I'll get back to chores, then."

"Sure."

The man actually saluted, which Armand still struggled with. He'd been an NCO so long, being an officer would be new for a while. He returned the gesture and watched the man leave.

Daniel Oglesby had mid-shift CQ duty. Mostly, that was keeping the fire smoldering. Every few minutes he checked the dumbed-down Byko video screens under the awning for anything moving outside the perimeter. The system was trained to recognize most animals, and humans.

It had startled him the first time it spoke. It was an abbreviated AI, not holding human status like the patrons in the future. But it could handle several issues in a conversational fashion.

As he stuck his head under, it greeted him.

"Good evening, Sergeant Oglesby."

"Evening. Any activity?"

"There are typical animal movements, not of concern, and no human presence outside the perimeter. Rain is possible at forty percent before dawn. Low will be approximately thirty-nine Fahrenheit."

"Great. I'll take a quick look."

"If you wish to, but it's not necessary."

"That's fine. I'm bored and watching animals can be interesting."

"Do you like their movement patterns, or their individual poise?"

"Some of each. There are differences and similarities to human movement and activity."

"Yes, that's how I identify them, of course."

"There's a lot more wildlife here than in our time."

"It is somewhat more than ours, but we do have extensive preserves."

"We have some, and quite a bit of wilderness, but it stays that way by not visiting it."

"That makes sense. Soldier Munoz appears to be awake and moving."

"Thanks. I'll check on him."

The screen even helpfully tagged his tent on an aerial image.

Dan walked in that direction, saw the soldier in question, and asked, "Hey, Munoz. How are you doing?"

"Wired," the man said. "I got to drinking coffee again. Now I can't sleep. But I do have to piss."

"Understood." He stepped aside while the private quick-staggered to the latrine.

In three minutes, Munoz was back, still a little unsteady, groggy, and with deep, saggy eyes.

"God, that's good coffee," he said. "And strong. And I'm out of practice. I'm almost hallucinating."

"Want me to wake Doc?"

Munoz shook his head. "Nah, I'm good. You busy?"

Dan replied, "I can talk. I have to check monitors from time to time. The fire's good, and it's home. Have a seat."

Munoz shook his head again. "I'm to pace. Twitchy if I'm still."

"Hooah."

Munoz was wiry skinny, in good health it seemed, and rambled around the fire ring, poking at the coals, squatting to pick up tiny sticks and toss them in, stretching his arms, and leaning in almost calisthenics.

When he spoke again, he asked, "Any of you guys get a settlement from the Army over this shit?"

"Sort of," Dan nodded. "We've got lifetime top-notch medical. Extra points for being officially POWs. Bumped in rank for those who stayed in. I think everyone who got out was near pension age anyway, but got a chunk of bonus pay as well as back pay disguised as a special-duty assignment. That will be five years for you, with all the benefits. We've got free transport to meet up with each other periodically. We have our own specially cleared support staff. The general pulled some sort of string and we get hired as 'consultants' to talk about it to the science experts. We get a thousand a day for that, and first-class airfare and hotels."

"Yeah, that's not what I was thinking. Any of you get a lawyer?"

"No, why?"

He remembered this was the guy threatening to sue.

Munoz said, "Sounds like I should. I figure five years of fuckup is worth five hundred K. I'll ask for a mil and settle."

"Florian...is that your first name?"

"Flor."

"Okay, Flor. How are you going to sue for something that never happened?"

"Never happened, bullshit. I'll subpoena everyone."

"You may want to run the idea past the captain or Sergeant Spencer, but—"

"Fuck them."

"Okay, past Lieutenant Cole, then. But based on what I know of how much cover-up there's been, that would probably just get you put straight into a loony bin. A very nice one, of course. But you're not going to have a case."

"I'll find a way to have some sort of proof."

"The Cog . . . Byko won't let you take anything home. They'll fabricate fresh uniforms"—he tugged at his own shirt—"and go through everything."

Of course, Gina had smuggled some pictures home on a memory stick, and they'd had some fur and other material that proved their displacement. But that wasn't needed this time and he wasn't going to suggest it.

"So we get a 'thank you, here's a steak dinner,' and that's it?"

"It's quite a bit more than that, but there's nothing you're going to be able to prove or claim."

"Unless I get them to all go in."

"Yeah, I don't think I'd mention that. It would probably get the Byko to lock you in their time if you were lucky. A very pretty prison, but their site is remote, and you'd never get away. Retirement watching movies and jerking off to high-class porn. And maybe some future chick wants to slum with a primitive."

Actually, the Byko would make it reasonably comfortable, but he wanted to play that down. But Munoz was looking pissed.

Actually . . .

He tried another tack.

"You know, you may have a point, but the Army didn't fuck this up. You need to talk to the Byko leadership."

"Yeah? They have lawyers?"

"They must have something, and it was their screwup. They did make us comfortable and do what they could to get us back, instead of leaving us there. But maybe if you address it right, you could get something out of them. I'm sure they have gold or something else you can cash back home."

Actually, did he want to consider suggesting they all ask for some benefits? On the other hand, he was happy enough with how things were. But . . .

"Yeah. Should I talk to their captain here? Cryder?"

"I'd wait until we get to their location, and talk to people there. These two guys are basically a cross between a fireteam and a rescue squad. They can't make any political decisions on things like that."

"Okay, cool. Thanks, Sergeant."

"No problem."

He checked the time.

"I'll be swapping off with Dr. Sheridan in a bit. Are you going to keep pacing?"

The man squinted a bit.

"Yeah, I sort of lay down for three hours. I think that's it for me. Hopefully I'll get back on track in a few days."

"We'll have a few days."

He saw Dr. Sheridan walking their way.

"Let me check in with her and I'll see you in the morning."

"Hooah."

Then Dan would go to his tent and text a lengthy AAR to the captain. This group was all fucked up, and it was understandable, but it was stuff that had to be dealt with.

CHAPTER 17

Sean Elliott watched the recoverees adapt back to twenty-first-century Army life. Some aspects moved quickly, others would take a long time, and some would be lifetime scars. For now, they were fit, healthy, in uniform, and enjoying the fine luxuries most people took for granted, like toilet paper, predictable food, and sweet things. Also not being infested with parasites, and comfortable beds to sleep in.

He had one troop detained, who had gone native in a bad way. One who was going to have to be dissuaded from trying to talk to lawyers and newspapers. One with an admittedly very cute kid who was going to complicate things, and a stack of other issues.

The kid *was* cute, and he was glad they could take her back. No doubt she would have fit in here, but if she had the facilities the future offered, she should take it.

He wished he had more downtime, but everything here kept throwing more duties at him. They had to recover those abandoned artifacts, and the ones at the village, account for the interpreter's remains, and deal with two troops who were very reluctant to reintegrate, and who would be pains in the ass the entire way back and then some. On a personal level, the risk of them shrieking to the press back home and looking like deranged fools also led to the possibility that some investigator or other would determine some elements of the truth, and that could fuck up society and, more vitally, Sean Elliott.

Still, he had to take them back and let others deal with that.

The first thing was probably the stuff in the village. The locals were angry enough already. If they got over that and then got raided, it would be worse. If they were hit hard enough now, and became convinced this element of future people were magic or demons or just impossible to mess with, it might help. It certainly wouldn't be as bad as a second round of betrayal later.

He'd write up a FRAGORDER, even though it would be destroyed later, because the formula was how he was trained, and it was good to stay in practice and not get out of the Army's habits.

An hour later he had what he needed, and called formation. He included all his element, Arnet, Shug, and Specialist Hamilton.

Once everyone was in the HQ, he asked, "Arnet, can you secure us against observation or listeners?"

The man nodded. "Yes, done."

"Thank you. I've drawn up a plan, subject to revision, on recovering the known artifacts in the village. We will conduct a raid, secure them, ID them as best we can, and then decide if a further action is needed.

"If the Guardians can assist with reconnaissance, I want to locate what items we can on the approach, to make it fast."

"Sir, why not wait until we have as many items as possible in camp to minimize that?"

He shook his head. "We don't have time. Between troublesome troops, a child, another stash to deal with, and we still need to find Shug's village, we have to get it done fast. If we're clear in a week and my only problem after that is keeping you guys busy, that's optimal. I can't assume that, though."

"Hooah."

"The raid will be Arnet, myself, Sergeant Dalton, Sergeant Caswell to deal with females. Dr. Raven for analysis, tracking, photos, intel and science stuff, and remember she's a bit slow."

"Not just a little slow. I have a gimp leg." She pointed at the ankle.

"Right. Sergeant Oglesby to translate if we must. Shug because he can hopefully guide us on cultural stuff. Hamilton is here to advise on the village, and sorry, soldier, you'll need to be monitored and kept secure until after we return."

The man slumped his shoulders. He understood his status.

He muttered, "I'll do what I can."

"Please note you're the one we trust most."

"I appreciate that," he replied, his tone making it clear he didn't appreciate it much.

"We're not taking Doc or any of the recoverees?"

"No. I'd like Doc, but I need two people here, and one scientist here. Cryder is holding their element's end. They'll be ready to stun anyone they need to for compliance."

Raven said, "I'm a biologist, I know my way around anatomy, and I've done vet surgery on my family's ranch. If anything gets through or past the fabric, I should be able to keep you alive until Doc can help."

"Right. And we'll have drone escort the whole way, with instant commo linkage."

"Good."

"So, Specialist Hamilton, in your opinion, what is the best way to get them to relinquish that property?"

"I really don't know, sir. They'd want a lot of valuables in trade. Much stuff. Probably women, too. Argarak would probably like Dr. Raven. He likes fat women."

She snapped, "The answer is no, and thanks, I'm aware of my weight."

"I'm sorry, Doctor," he said at once. "I didn't mean...I meant, he likes..."

Her response was viper-like. "I'm versed in the culture of this type of society, I know what you meant underneath what you said. But I will burn the village to the fucking ground before one of them lays a hand on me."

Sean rephrased, "Let me simplify the question, Hamilton. Can we do this peacefully, or do we need to stun the whole village, search for what we need, recover it, and then possibly go back for a second round when hunters return?"

"That's probably the only way to do it, sir. I forgot you can just stun them."

"Okay. Attack in force it is. Looking at the terrain, if we detour around there, we can walk down the riverbank. That's stealthier. Arnet, how long can you set the stun for?"

"Reliably, about an hour. Beyond that risks death."

He asked, "Roger. Can you summarize how these work so I understand the mechanism?"

"The discharge creates an ionic path, and then electricy flows through it."

Raven said, "Oh, an Air Taser. Those exist now. Our now."

"I expect ours have more range." Arnet grinned.

"I hope so." She grinned back.

Hamilton said, "I need to learn how to use that. Familiarization at least."

"You will not be armed, Specialist. Sorry."

"Oh. I understand, sir." He seemed embarrassed, again made aware of his status.

"Recovered POWs, which you effectively are, have a status in limbo until properly debriefed. We are not equipped for that. Though if it does come to life or death, you will have access to some spears and we may have a spare firearm."

"Hooah, sir." That seemed to mollify him a little.

Shug's demeanor made it clear he knew he was involved, but not to what extent until Hamilton translated with Oglesby helping with concepts and making sure Hamilton was honest. He had been all along, but Sean was taking no chances.

Hamilton reported, "He says he can help describe things and look, but he wants to make sure they won't be hurt. He's very nervous, since these are distant cousins."

"They will be made to sleep only, and will wake up. Our gods insist we have to take our items home, even if they were given as gifts in good faith. We'll make sure they are given other items of value in exchange."

"Hooah, sir. I'll tell him."

Shug was agreeable to helping, but not thrilled. His presentation was that if his hosts insisted, he'd come along. Sean made a note to find a way to make it up to the kid.

With a small, organized group it took about an hour to get everyone geared up and ready. By then, Cryder had aerial photos and an interactive 3D map that let them plan an approach.

It was a damp, cold day, and he had everyone in what looked like Gore-Tex and was a lot warmer. The Byko field gear was amazing.

Cryder pointed on the map. "You can take a vehicle to here, then walk down to the river path here. From there it's about a kilometer to the village, downstream."

Arnet noted, "I don't need to worry about any power-plant signature. Long as we're slow and shrouded, we should be invisible to observers."

Dalton said, "Yeah, within a klick starts risking random hunters, love couples, whatever." He pointed at marks that indicated wear from walking. "That bank sees notable traffic."

"Zap as needed."

"Hooah."

Arnet hefted his weapon. "The stun is set for about an hour. It will vary several minutes either side."

Raven asked, "Is there any danger to small children or the elderly from the shot?"

"Not significant," Arnet replied. "It's a neural effect, not energy release. Nothing is one hundred percent, but there's no noted risk."

"Fair enough," she agreed.

Arnet spoke to all. "I will tune the commo now."

"Comms, Arnet, broad, test, all receive?"

They nodded and concurred.

Sean responded, "Comms, Elliott, Arnet, confirm."

"I confirm," Arnet replied with a nod. "Note the system is aware it's in use and didn't require a prompt."

The Byko tech was just there. You needed it, you asked or reached for it. It was amazingly convenient. It also hadn't had any functional issues so far, unlike so many US military-issue items, or foreign ones that were frequently worse.

Sean ordered, "Everyone have a bite and some water. We'll take five minutes for latrine. I want everyone fresh for what's going to be a combat mission, even if we don't anticipate any casualties either way."

Five minutes later they were saddled up. Arnet started handling and waving controls. Even with Sean knowing how it was done, Arnet's familiarity and casualness were striking. He fluttered hands, they started moving smoothly downslope and through the wards. It took very little time to reach their advance point.

It took little enough that Sean considered they should move their bivouac farther away.

When they stopped, he gave instructions. "Weapons, water, navigation gear, and we'll get humping."

There was acknowledgement.

"Arnet, I will take point with you. Oglesby, Hamilton, and Shug five meters back. Caswell, you and Dr. Raven next. Dalton, rear."

"Roger."

"Hooah, sir."

"I intend to stun everyone on first contact. As we discussed, it is probable many will run away. If they respond en masse, I will order 'Close up.' We'll keep a tight group. Specialist Hamilton will advise where to search. Caswell and Oglesby will assist. Shug is on call as needed. The rest of us will provide muscle around the perimeter. We need to search fast, then unass the area. Walk quietly, we're in their area. Does everyone know basic patrol hand signs?"

Raven said, "No."

Caswell told her, "I've got it. I'll make sure you learn them."

"Thanks."

Sean led off with Arnet. Behind him he heard each element start in turn, though they were quiet enough it shouldn't be audible more than a few meters. Anyway, humans wouldn't be surprised to hear other humans, but might note the difference in footsteps or voices.

Rich was very alert at the rear. He didn't have a buddy, so he was it. He also had to watch in case the females needed backup, because as good as Caswell was, she couldn't handle both herself and Raven in an emergency. Then, Hamilton was an unknown, and Shug couldn't do much. He might also just unass and leave, since he apparently had an idea where he was.

This hadn't been covered in training at all.

Ahead, hand signs indicated observation contact. They'd seen something. He sank slowly to a squat and waited, ears open for anything human sounding.

Yes, there was a young male, not that far ahead.

Elliott muttered barely audibly. Rich couldn't make it out.

Right then, the man turned. Had he heard even a whisper as being out of place? Or was it something else?

He turned away again and wandered about. He was just flinging rocks and being alone.

There was a boy with him. Younger brother?

Duckwalking closer to the front, Rich heard the captain and Arnet discussing.

"Well, that's fine for us, but we can't get closer until they head back, or we lose a few minutes on him."

Arnet whispered, "That might be a fair trade."

"It might be. We'll give them ten minutes."

The man did wander in that general direction, tossing rocks as he went. The boy followed idly along, picking up whichever rock seemed coolest at the moment, then swapping out for better ones.

As the men moved, Elliott slowly followed, letting them increase the gap. There was no rush.

Rich hadn't considered that he'd be stunning women and children. Better than shooting them, at least. There'd been that one kid in A-stan, big enough to know better, with an AK. Someone else had hit him. Then the two men he'd shot in their last time trip, for whose souls he prayed from time to time.

At least these would just be unconscious, but it was still going to be a horrible experience for them.

"We're within sight," he heard the captain whisper in his earbuds. "We'll start with these two, then pick up the pace and swarm in."

"Hooah," he replied quietly. It was really neat having the captain see all this on that visor he wore.

Two zaps sounded, softened by growth and breeze. The man and boy slumped to the dirt and flopped.

"Go!" he heard.

He rose and started running, automatically shifting laterally and taking cover behind trees as he moved. He realized it wasn't necessary, and continued anyway, because it wasn't going to hurt anything and he didn't want a bad habit. Besides, there was a slim chance of a spear in the face. He paused, sprinted, ducked behind a tree, came out the other side, sprinted in two zigs, behind the next tree.

There was the clearing along the beach. A man and a woman were relieving themselves. Two were gathering water in skins. Kids were playing. Ahead, he heard the zapping sounds and watched people fall.

The woman and one kid fell into the water. He muttered, "Crap," and angled that way.

And the dogs started barking.

"Shit!"

He grabbed the woman's arm and pulled so she was half on the bank, then jumped over to the kid and pulled him far enough back he wasn't going to fall in and drown.

Shouts, screams, and angry voices sounded among the weapon zaps. This wasn't going to be quick. There were four just jumping out of somewhere, one man, two boys, and a girl. He raised the weapon and squeezed. They were just looking his way as they dropped in a heap.

A dog came at him, teeth bared, spittle frothing, and he pointed and shot. It went limp, landed, and tumbled into a flop.

On the other hand, it didn't take that long, as quite a few just dropped what they were doing and ran into the woods. It took about two minutes, but then they had complete control and no dispute.

It was eerie, the village being totally devoid of human noises. He'd forgotten about the large number of kids, too. They stunned easily, but he felt like crap even though he knew they'd wake up. They'd be scared. Some were definitely just past the trees, hiding and watching. It was a real dick move.

He thanked God again he'd had the element he'd had, with their skills and determination. This could have sucked badly.

Hamilton pointed at what Rich recalled was Argarak's hut. Oglesby and Caswell entered first, sweeping with weapons. They weren't bad, considering. Raven jogged in, there was obvious movement in the shadows. In about a minute, she came out with a pack and two items clutched in her hand. She stuffed them in the ruck and tossed it toward the middle of the village.

They moved to the next one, which belonged to the subchief, Argarak's son. The rummaging took a bit longer, but she emerged with a small item. One of the empty brass, possibly? She put that in the ruck.

She moved from hut to hut, into the longhouse, then through the other family lodges. By the time she was done, she had four rucks with some small stuff. She looped them all up over an arm, shifted it across her shoulder, and started walking.

Elliott signaled for everyone to follow, and they trooped back into the trees and upstream.

They traveled in closer proximity now, less concerned about human interaction.

The captain asked, "How did it go?"

Pointing, she indicated, "That's four rucks, three cartridge cases, the knife, two of the bracelets."

Elliott said, "A good start. Do we know who we need to find?"

"Well, I don't know their names," she said, "but I do have their DNA samples, several items off the list, and a way to collate other occupants against the items recovered. Will that let you trace things better, Arnet?" She held up sample bags, marked with some sort of nomenclature she obviously understood.

"Yes," he agreed. "We can mark off negatives and reduce the search."

They hiked fast back to the vehicle, loaded, and rolled back.

They drove into camp without issue. At the HQ tent, she laid out the findings.

Dan Oglesby watched as Cryder logged everything for their records, with photos from a tiny drone and his wrist gadget. When Raven showed him the DNA samples, he replied, "Excellent. If readable, we can use to find them by drone. Also, I sent two drones to look for chemical traces of expended cartridges. Nothing so far, though."

Spencer said, "Boy, I can't imagine they would after months or years."

"Likely won't, but the attempt must be made. Positively, no such items were discovered prior to your time, and after that, they'll be assigned to your time. Nonetheless, I must be thorough."

"Makes sense."

Dan said, "So we need to find this guy Rasatuk's ruck, and up to seven casings—"

Spencer interrupted, "Cases, please." He looked sheepish and said, "Sorry."

Elliott asked before Dan did. "Is there a difference?"

"The case contains the propellant, primer, and projectile. A casing contains sausage."

Elliott sighed, smiled, then said, "Okay, we will use proper nomenclature. Up to seven cartridge cases."

"Hamilton, which lodges would those be? Here's the image."

"Uh, that one, that one, and possibly that one."

Raven rummaged. "Here they are."

Cryder took the bags.

She asked, "Do you know how to properly ID the DNA for tracing?"

"I don't," he said, and grinned. "But the system does."

"Fair enough. Either of us can help if you need it."

"I'll note that." He did seem to mean it.

Elliott said, "I don't want to go again immediately, but we'll need to do so, soon. Or else we get them alone. I suspect they'll stash their precious gifts as soon as they realize the others are gone, though."

Dalton put in, "Or, they may decide to keep them on their person, which helps us in recovering the rest."

"Good point. They might. We'll have to see."

Sean wondered if forty-seven days were going to be enough. They'd already used eight.

Amalie rubbed her eyes and leaned back from the screen. The Byko did have really comfortable reclining camp chairs, complete with headrests. They folded down to the size of a bucket lid.

There were some fascinating leads of the Q1a and Q1b sequences that certainly supported the Dene-Yeniseian hypothesis. It would be interesting to see if any of the present traces carried through to ancient American haplogroups. That would offer a very good cross-check and calendar.

The Army wasn't doing badly, but they were sociologically unprepared for this type of event, or even many cultural events. Though it was unlikely they could get sufficient training for enlisted or even company-grade officers. Caswell was about as close as they got, all her schooling being civilian, and all of it contaminated with woke apologetics that only rephrased the problems without actually addressing them in a meaningful fashion.

She hated to think her presence had thrown off the transition. The Bykos had done a detailed scan by their standards, and she'd even made notes about some of it.

She caught a snippet of conversation between Armand Devereaux and Letitia Oyo and decided to listen more closely. It would be rude to do so without acknowledging, so she pushed out of the chair and walked that way.

As she approached, Devereaux said, "Whatever you want to tell us and can."

Oyo shrugged in response, and then nodded to Amalie.

She said, "I guess it's not been too bad. Argarak didn't like black people, especially girls. Never touched me. I mean, I would have, to help the guys, but he only looked at Frenchy. I also kinda hinted I was with Jake Uhiara at first. I told the LT if we just pretended we had mates in the group, it would be fine. But then he was worried about fraternization with us. And then it was fraternize with them to make things cool. His brain really wasn't working." She looked exasperated and put upon.

Devereaux said, "Yeah, we handled things differently."

The woman added, "But you really do need a family here. Breotah was decent enough, and was quite pleased with my skin."

Amalie got close enough to participate and asked, "Mate?"

Oyo admitted, "Yes, but all he knew was hunting, and I'm an MP. We didn't have a way to explain my role other than warrior, but here warriors are also hunters."

Amalie replied, "Makes sense." The cultural gulf was uncrossable, really. The locals didn't even comprehend a wheel.

"He was decent and appreciative, but we've got nothing in common."

Devereaux said, "I don't know if you wanted kids—"

She shook her head, "Not here, no."

He finished, "—but it's easier at our end that you don't."

Oyo almost smirked. "Yeah, I gave a lot of strategic blowjobs, which are very popular here. But it was reaching the point where they were strongly urging me to bring forth youth."

"Ah. Well, I'm glad this worked in your favor."

Amalie said, "I've made a note to go to the deployment prep cadre, and to the SERE schools, noting ways to avoid getting intimate with locals even under pressure. Other than with Inuit, Sami, or Yupik tribes, of course."

Devereaux looked puzzled and asked, "Why not them?"

She explained, "It's not uncommon to provide a woman to guests to avoid freezing to death. Though there are still acceptable ways to avoid sex."

He replied, "Ah. Makes sense."

Oyo asked, "So once we get back, what do we do about training and promotions and stuff?"

"You pick up where you left off. Remember, it hasn't been five years back home."

"I remember," she said. "But I've gotten rusty on a bunch of things."

"You can get refresher training, and you'll be paid a bonus and such. General McClare takes good care of us, and his assistant will carry on when he retires."

"Awesome. Can we have music in camp?"

Doc replied, "You mean a group dance? Yeah, we did that. We have a pretty good library."

"Damn. Orange juice, coffee, ice cream, R&B. I'm feeling a whole lot better already." She stretched and smiled.

Amalie asked, "Did you hunt?"

"Not really," she shrugged. "A few runs. You have to hand-carry everything back. That's more of a male thing. They were teaching me things like scraping hides and draining guts for rope and sausage. Disgusting work."

Amalie remembered seeing demos on the reservation, and handling some recent kills in field studies. "Hell, yeah, it is."

"I was trying to learn flint and bone working. That's also usually a male thing. And that's when they kept telling me I should have a baby. I'd given up and actually tried, but didn't catch."

Amalie hinted, "There's various reasons that might be."

Oyo shrugged. "Cool either way. I want kids, but not out here."

"Any other skills?"

"I did teach them some new ways to braid ropes and hair. The women liked me well enough once they knew I wasn't a threat, so there's that. But I was pretty alone out here."

Devereaux replied, "I know what that's like. I was literally the only black person in the world. And same in Bykostan. They're... evasive, but they have Asians, Euros like them"—he indicated the Guardians—"and some Pacific-looking types, but I never once saw anyone African."

Oyo said, "Some of our guys were a bit dickish, too. Partly me being black—and to Izzy as well—but also because I was basically on patrol to check local females. Some of them were treating me as a leech. Once here, it was worse."

Amalie had studied anthropology for a reason. "I can guess which ones."

Oyo sighed. "Yeah. Burnham was good, though. Honestly, I wish he'd been in charge. I don't know if he could have done much, but he kept order."

Devereaux agreed, "He does seem to have a decent grasp. He also had to defer to the officer for most matters. Given the circumstances, it's hard to blame anyone."

Actually, he seemed pretty pissed at Cole, but it was diplomatic not to say so.

"It's all good now, if we get home," she said. Though that seemed like a diplomatic comment, also.

Dalton came by. He had a sandwich as a snack. "How's it going?"

Devereaux replied, "Hey, Rich. Mostly social stuff. We distracted Dr. Raven from something."

Amalie grinned. "While I love haplogroup tracing, it's not the most exciting process to read fine charts and sequences."

Dalton asked, "What do you have?"

She gestured at the screen. "Pretty solid evidence for a Yeniseian MRCA for Amerind populations and contemporary Siberians, which we were sure of, but this hammers it down. The split was about twenty KYA, though interbreeding continued and will do so for a while. There are three immigration waves to North America, and what I'm finding here is the major link between the continents. There were others before and after, but this is the one that ties almost all American groups to the Asian lineages."

"Twenty thousand years," Dalton said, looking awkward.

Amalie sighed. "Yes, I know about your religious background. I didn't make all that data up for fun," she explained, waving at the screen. "It's as solidly scientific as gravity. We're just refining details."

"Sorry," he said. "I didn't mean to denigrate your work."

"No harm," she said, and didn't mean it. How could the man still be a fucking Creationist nutjob when he was literally standing in the Upper Paleolithic?

At least it had created enough distraction for Oyo to slip away.

CHAPTER 18

Sunday morning was a bit brisk, but clear. Sun burned off the dew. Rich Dalton was up with the sun without any prompting. Everyone else was already about. Arnet and Sheridan had breakfast ready.

Spencer ordered, "Listen up! Commander's briefing will take place while you get breakfast and seats, so keep quiet. No formal formation at this time."

Elliott took over. "Thank you, Sergeant Spencer. Today is a semi-down day. We'll be doing some camp cleanup, some administration, and some details. Stick around after eating and we'll assign those."

Rich stood up, and said, "It is Sunday. I'll be holding a nondenominational worship service down by the rock near the north fence."

Caswell prompted him. "When?"

He replied, "As soon as breakfast and the commander's assignments are done."

Elliott said, "Start that now. Chores can wait a few minutes. They're on the roster here." He indicated a very normal-looking rollup board, hanging from the awning post.

Rich grabbed his ruck and strolled down to the rock, and people straggled in over a couple of minutes. Caswell came along. The commander nodded from over near the command area. He was listening in as best he could.

"Doctors?" he called up to the scientists.

"I'm good," Sheridan replied.

Raven's response was pure ice. "No. Thank you."

He just replied, "Very well," and turned back to the group.

He opened with, "Would anyone like a Bible?"

Oyo said, "I would."

Hamilton nodded. "Please. Mine was destroyed."

SSG Burnham agreed, "I'll borrow it, certainly."

"These are exact copies of mine," he held his up. "It kept me, and most of my element, comforted and supported while we were lost. I hope some of the wear and tear and warmth of it will help you, even if only as reminders of the wear and tear we've all been through here."

He had a decent gathering, including Caswell and the captain. Doc was busy. Oglesby had never been very religious. Sergeant Spencer hung around at the outer edge. He was a hard atheist, but very supportive of his people. All the recoverees were present. Some were certainly religious. The rest were probably here to grasp at familiarity of their home. That was a perfect opportunity to offer them the spirit of Christ.

He started with Psalm 50:15. "'And call upon me in the day of trouble: I will deliver thee, and thou shalt glorify me.'

"Like you, we were lost in time. Though our stay was only two years. Looking back, that seems so short, though at the time it certainly felt like an entire life. The uncertainty was tough on some of us.

"But I had faith that God would provide for us one way or another. If we were to stay, He would support us. If we were to return, He would arrange it. He did so for us, and He has brought us to find you and bring you home.

"I give thanks to Him for the experience. As rough as it was, I learned much about myself. I formed strong bonds with people I hadn't known, and learned much about them, and by extension, all of my fellow men and women.

"We should seek the positives from any experience, to learn and grow, and glory in conquering the adversity, with God's help, if we will let Him. I find I am stronger now against any challenge, calm and secure, and I pray that all of you will find renewed strength from this experience."

He wrapped up in few sentences, and led a prayer. He was

pleased to see that most of them did look a bit lighter and more cheerful.

The little girl was attentive with her mother, and seemed to grasp this was important. He had orders not to proselytize, but he'd encourage her participation if she stuck around.

Rich felt refreshed and calmed, and he'd helped others with their spiritual needs. Ministering to others was one of the greatest things he was privileged to do, and he thanked the Lord for the opportunity to spread His peace to those in need.

So it was very important that he walk back up the hill to that tent.

It was opaqued, but he assumed it was one way, and not silenced.

To it, he said, "Sergeant Lozano, it's Sunday. Would you like to pray or read scripture?"

"Fuck off."

Not a promising start, but he simply replied, "I'll leave you alone, then. May God bless you."

"Wait..." Lozano hesitated and sounded almost afraid.

"Yes?"

The man admitted, "I would like to talk to someone. Someone else, I mean. Not my group."

Rich offered, "I'm here. Let's talk."

"Look, I have a good thing here, you know."

He nodded. "I heard you'd adapted well."

Lozano let out a short laugh. "'Adapted.' It's the first place I ever felt welcome."

"Oh?"

"That's all. Maybe more later."

"I will sit here for a few minutes."

"Nah, I'm done."

"That's fine."

He sat patiently. The Lord had made it clear this man needed help. He'd be as nonjudgmental as he could and wait for God to enlighten them both.

The sun burned off the rest of the dew, and the woods below glowed green with yellow tinges of impending fall. The ground was chill, but his clothing was warm, and the pully cap kept his ears covered. He watched his breath mist.

Eventually Lozano said, "You're really just going to sit there, aren't you?"

"I have no pressing duties until later. It's a beautiful day. I can relax anywhere."

"I'm as middle class as they come," the young soldier admitted.

"So am I. Nothing wrong with that."

"Yeah, but I hated it."

Rich wasn't sure where this was going. "I see."

"Here I'm someone. A respected hunter."

That was an opening. "Well, good. We did well by each having a valuable skill. Mine also was hunting. Do you go for those ugly antelope? Related to the saiga?" He hadn't seen any around here so far, but maybe...

"The ugly nose? Yes."

This was a good start. Rich said, "Yeah, those. A bit tough, but a good flavor."

"You have to slow roast with hot coals and nibble as you go."

He nodded. "We did a bunch of things. We penned some goats, too, but they kept getting out."

"The goats are tasty. Young ones taste better. As they all do."

"We got some milk and cream on occasion, too."

"I do like having milk again. Even if it's fake."

"It's chemically real. The Bykos have amazing ice cream."

"Eh. I can manage."

"Sure. That's important."

Rich sat for another thirty minutes, plucking at grass, flicking at bugs, examining some tiny pebbles with neat grain. Lozano said nothing else.

The man was obviously done for now, so Rich said, "Have a blessed day, Christopher. If you need anything, let me know."

"Later."

Well, that wasn't much. But something.

He could follow up with Uhiara, who was glad to go home, eager to see his wife, and needed reassurance that God would not punish him for cheating when there was no expectation of return. He was a good man and, like Rich, his faith had kept him strong.

"Jake!" he called. "How are you doing?"

"Rich, thank you for the service!"

They could split firewood and speak of faith.

✧　　✧　　✧

Since they had to account for as much property as possible before leaving the area, there was no reason not to continue debriefing at the same time. Much of that fell to Martin Spencer.

After that, he had to explain where the Guardians came in, and their society. That was less contentious.

"They have the ultimate sci-fi party world, but you won't get to see much of it. You can guess from their field rations, though, what it's going to be like. Top-quality food and booze. The women are amazing, and yes, most of the men are chiseled like these guys. You can't see most of the technology, you just ask and there it is. The important thing from a personal and professional standpoint is that there's no privacy. At all. Anywhere. They have AIs monitoring everything from the conference room to the shower. They won't say anything and won't intrude, even if you're rubbing one out. But they're there, and everything is recorded. So absolutely nothing of a military nature is discussed without being in the common area and after consulting with the captain or myself. And don't do anything stupid because we'll find out."

They looked serious. Keisuke asked, "So it's *1984*?"

That was a valid comparison. "Yes and no. Literally everything is monitored for safety, but they have very strong privacy mores. A bit like Japan. They ignore anything that they're not invited to know about, ask politely, and only review records for emergencies, or research under certain circumstances and with certain permissions. It takes getting used to."

He concluded with, "So there's going to be more in-depth debriefing, and we'll try to give you some more useful info before we transit to their time. We also have to try to account for literally every piece and scrap of US gear to minimize problems with the timeline. Plan on daily PT followed by daily paperwork."

A couple of them responded, "Hooah."

"I'll let Dr. Raven give you some nerd updates."

She smiled and stepped forward. He left her to it.

CHAPTER 19

Each day, Sean supervised debriefing. The first round with Doc had been to heal minor matters and kill parasites. Each of the displacees now had a full physical, which was quicker with Arnet's gadgets—about an hour versus several. This also apparently included data for temporal transition. Then, Doc needed their impression of their history, with Captain Elliott requiring specific markers. After that, Doctors Sheridan and Raven had a series of tests and questions on diseases and vectors. He had to get all their military background and operational actions. Cryder wanted information for the Bykos. It would take a week to fully debrief them, while the Guardians flew drones looking for contaminating artifacts, read over the reports, and asked some specific questions about movement patterns and the natives.

Kita ran around, watching people. It was clear she was trying very hard to grasp what all these things and goings-on were. She was popular as a mascot, and adored by Caswell, Raven, and Spencer.

Sergeant Spencer took statements on chain of events. At least with Byko gear it could be done verbally and auto-transcribed. Caswell was chaperone for the females, Dalton for the males. They all had approximately the same story, and it was rough to hear them. The loneliness, panic, terror, disgust all came through. The relief at contact, and yes, Noirot sounded cold and distraught about being offered up as trade goods. She needed to be told she was heroic for doing so, but how to phrase it?

He was given summary reports. Cavities. Scars. Infections healed. Local taskings the troops had. Keeping Lieutenant Cole in the loop, both as informant and subordinate. Gradually explaining to the man how badly he'd fucked up and that it must never be mentioned outside the designated circle.

Sean said, "I'm probably not even referencing it in my written AAR. We'll verbally inform the counselors. They'll need to deal with it."

Cole asked, "They don't report back?"

"They all have religious degrees and thus privileged communication. We're lucky to have General McClare. He takes very good care of us."

Cole said, "My three concerns are Noirot and her kid, Lozano and his...interests, and I'm not sure about Munoz."

"'Interests'?"

"He likes his girls barely pubescent."

"...Oh."

Well, that explained a couple of things, and made others that much more complicated.

Sean replied, "We also need to consider your official status as commander and the unofficial debrief. Nothing here will affect your promotions, but it's certainly going to color your actions, and how the informed command recommend you."

He nodded. "Sir, I realize I fucked this six ways from nothing, and my first reaction to anyone would be, 'let's see you do better,' but obviously you did. I'll take whatever's coming to me, but I want to make sure my troops are taken care of first. They're not at fault for anything."

The man was near tears again.

Sean replied, "That's a very professional answer. I agree with your concerns and we'll do everything we can. I also want to make sure you're treated fairly, because as you note, there's nothing that could have prepared you for this. Our tech experts will talk to some other people and hopefully eventually there will be more training on how to deal with strange cultures. I got lucky with Sergeant Spencer and Sergeant Alexander, who were both skilled reenactors with SERE training. Sergeant Barker had a lot of primitive skills. Caswell is trained in sociology and wild food. I can't say I wouldn't have wound up in your shoes, but it wasn't impossible. We made a point of setting our own camp, and two years in we were about to start settling down with the natives.

"At the same time," he noted, "you did get stuck in this rut and even without blame, you're going to have this as your first command experience."

The guy nodded seriously. "Yeah. Sir."

"So we'll deal with your people and recovery, and keep talking about this among ourselves, without saying a word to anyone back home until we decide what they need to know."

"Roger that, Captain."

While that went on, the Bykos' primary concern was recovery of twenty-first-century artifacts. Drones went out over all the identified areas the troops had been in.

Cryder's recon gear was top notch. After noon, at the CQ, he reported, "We have more lurkers."

"Oh?" Sean prompted.

"About five hundred meters that way." The man indicated roughly northwest.

Sean whistled. That was pretty dense terrain.

"How's their progress?"

Looking at his screens, Cryder said, "They're not advancing. Maintaining a small camp."

"Ah. Have you looked for an OP?"

"'OP'?" the man asked.

"An observation post."

"Ah. Stand by."

The zone imagery shifted around, changing both direction and orientation. It was dizzying even to watch.

Cryder informed him, "Yes, there they are, three of them. They're watching from that outcropping, one hundred three meters at seventy-two centimarks."

"Seventy-two hundredths of a circle, hold on, that's about two-sixty-two degrees, so just past due west."

"Yes."

Sean scanned with his eyes, focused on several features, then saw faint motion. "Ah, there. I bet they have some sort of noisemaker, and they're waiting for us to go outside the wire."

Cryder nodded. "That seems logical."

"Argarak is a smart bastard. We've taken his people and

valuables. He knows he can't beat our fence. He's going to wait for opportunity. I expect they will rotate out and have dried meat and such."

"It's clever, but not clever enough."

Sean asked, "I expect you have a way to stun them from here?"

The man agreed, "Stun or kill. I'd far prefer to continue nonlethal force for several reasons, but I'm considering it may not effect."

"Right. It's okay for apprehensions, but it doesn't dissuade dedicated attackers as they know they can come back."

Cryder said, "We'll need to relocate, but our vehicles leave a trace, and I suspect they could follow our steps, too."

Sean noticed the man's English was very precise, yet chopped. Versus his native dialect that crammed entire paragraphs into a few words.

He considered the information and replied, "I would bet money on it."

Cryder offered, "Sufficient distance may convince them pursuit isn't feasible, and we're not a threat."

Sean noted, "We still need to get those other items, though."

"We've an alternative, though it means using some power and more force."

"Go ahead," he prompted.

"You're aware our active concealment is near invisible to the unaided eye."

"Yes."

Cryder elaborated, "We have two sets on hand, and enough replacement parts to improvise a third. Three troops can advance unseen and recover what they can."

That was possible, but... "If they get IDed, they will probably get dogpiled."

"We have a stronger defensive weapon. Remote neural stimulation."

"Ah. We have one that induces heat sensations."

"This is simply pain. A lot of pain. It causes damage to the brain after only a few seconds."

"Oh." He understood. "It has to be intermittent. Okay."

"Its range is limited, and recuperation time is much faster than from stun, if the individual has a high pain tolerance, which their environment suggests. It'll discomfort a person entirely and near instantly, and... gives them opportunity to retreat."

"How can they retreat if they're not sure where you are?"

The man gave a wry smile. "Exactly. This isn't at all ideal. But, if infiltration is successful, it won't be needed until we're well inside the village. Problem comes if someone is inside a habitation. They'll have no cue to evacuate, but may flee when they feel a presence inside."

Sean said, "It would work handily with six troops."

"Precisely. We can take three."

"We may still have to stun some."

"Yes. But, they will not be able to see us, making distance weapons far less viable for them. They won't be able to easily approach."

Sean said, "Obviously, one of you must go. One of my troops, whomever is best up close, which is probably Sergeant Dalton. One of our scientists. Raven again? She's performed well."

"Let's find out." He pulled out his phone.

Dalton's response was, "I'm in if you need me, sir. Tell me what I need to do."

Raven said, "Given the circumstances, it might be best to send Sheridan. I'm better at forensic matters, but that's not a critical concern for this mission. I'm probably a bit stronger, but she's stable on her ankles and I'm not."

"Very well. Dr. Sheridan?"

Sheridan came over from the science awning.

"Yes, Captain?"

He explained the operation.

She nodded. "I can do that. It's true I'll be sturdier. I'm a bit apprehensive about potential violence. I don't have any training for it."

"Sergeant Dalton will be tasked with providing force. Arnet will direct and act as reconnaissance."

"Okay. When are we doing this?"

"Probably tomorrow, early."

He texted Oglesby. FIND OUT FROM SHUG WHEN THE HUNTERS AND GATHERERS ARE LIKELY TO BE OUT WORKING.

Oglesby's response was, HAMILTON MAY KNOW BETTER.

I WANT TO KEEP THIS WITHIN OUR GROUP.

AH, ROGER, STAND BY, SIR.

Shortly, Oglesby came over in person.

"Shug says as soon as they can see, they will probably be

getting a bite, then going out to work for what I gather is about two hours."

"Okay, so we want to be in place BMNT, and proceed from there."

"'BMNT'?" Cryder asked.

"Begin Mean Nautical Twilight. Basically as soon as we can see."

The man obviously considered the etymology of the term.

"Yes. Also, culturally, historically, and linguistically, that's a beautiful phrase."

"I'm sure it is, two hundred, five hundred years from our time?"

"In a future with different terms and a changed language, yes." There was a definite hint of a smile on his face.

Damn.

"Okay, I'll write a quick fragorder for my two people." God, even here, again, in the Stone Age, much of his time was spent doing administrative crap.

"I'll send Arnet to discuss other details and demonstrate the gear."

He said, "Seems like it's a good thing we allowed time for recon, recovery, and transit."

"It's never as simple as the plan."

"Never has been." They definitely agreed on that.

He sighed. If it had been possible to zero in better and hit the exact tick, they could have recovered these people within days.

"Hey, Cryder, why didn't your scientists send a probe, like they did for you, and zero from there?"

"They already had our transition to zero from, and they still only got within about a year."

"Ah. Makes sense." Well, shit.

If this wasn't successful enough, he might have to discuss the odds of any remaining artifacts being found, versus the possibility of another trip later to suppress them, versus hoping for the best.

He pulled up a chair and a screen, here where pretty much all command and control took place. The one thing that remained true was there was no private office in an element of this size. No doubt the Bykos had field buildings for bigger events, but they'd done well with two vehicles.

He'd just sat down to notate activities and write the frago for this, when SSG Burnham came over.

"Sir, sorry to interrupt, I've got a question from our team."

"Go ahead."

"Can we take a walk?"

"The two of us? Sure, what's up?" He got to his feet.

"No, I mean our team, take a walk." The man was trying to sound casual.

"Outside the wards?" He asked in clarification.

"Yes."

"For what purpose?"

"Exercise."

"I really don't think that's a good idea."

"Why not? We know the area well enough. We'll be safe."

"That's not the concern." He realized several of the others were not far away.

Burnham asked, "Captain, are you stating you don't trust us?"

He glanced carefully around. Dalton, Caswell, and Spencer had strolled up and looked ready to respond in a moment. Arnet gave him a sidewise glance and the barest nod of acknowledgment.

"I'm stating my orders are to see you returned home. I can't risk anyone getting displaced again, or lost. Our schedule is much tighter than it sounds."

It was entirely obvious they understood their status was "detained recoverees."

They clustered a bit more, but it didn't seem threatening, yet.

With a few glances, they changed tacks.

Maldonado asked, "What about our families here?"

"Does anyone else have any offspring?"

"No."

"Then unfortunately we are not authorized to relocate them. Offspring are relevant due to genetic footprint. Local involvement is not a concern the Army or the Bykos are prepared to deal with. The return mechanism can handle us, you, and a limited number of offspring."

Maldonado continued, "But we don't have the 'terp anymore, so you could fit one more."

"That's Kita, and others are not within my orders, nor Shuff Cryder's. I'm sorry."

"Can't we at least have a chance to properly say goodbye?"

"We don't consider that feasible under the already hostile circumstances."

Munoz said, "It wouldn't have been hostile if you hadn't just started zapping people and dragging them off."

"Soldier, we are not having a discussion on this. There are orders from two governments, two chains of command, and they match. The circumstances are what they are. I cannot, and will not, approve a variance at this point. If circumstances make it feasible, I will let you know. If one of the villagers approaches peacefully, that discussion can take place, and any relatives you've met here can visit here under controlled circumstances."

They glanced around at one another.

"They can come here?"

"In small groups, for limited amounts of time, yes." He realized they'd probably gotten what they actually wanted this way, and why didn't they just fucking ask?

"Can we communicate with them about this?"

He really didn't like even this much, but it was going to be tough to wrangle them, after five years.

He said, "It's possible we can do audio through a drone. I will discuss with Shuff Cryder."

Burnham replied, "Thank you, sir. By the way, which one of you ranks the other?"

"As with the Romans we met, there's no exact translation. His title roughly translates as 'chief,' but it's more like 'station commander' than chief warrant officer. He's approximately my rank, and we're working in parallel, not one under the other."

Burnham noted, "So you're the sole decision maker."

"For matters pertaining to US personnel, yes. No one else can give you orders, but it's a good idea to take any of their suggestions under strong advisement." That was a valid concern, and he was glad to see it codified.

The man nodded. "Fair enough. Thank you, sir."

And why had they sent the NCO to ask that question, not the officer? He wondered where LT Cole was. They should have gone through him. Either they didn't trust their own commander, or he'd already nixed it and they were trying to go over his head. Given the previous conversation, he was betting on the latter. They'd need to be reminded how things worked. The local way of doing things was no more. It was the Army way, as screwed up as that often was.

They needed to do more interviews shortly, but he had to be there personally to get the best nonverbal reading of things.

He walked over and got close enough to his counterpart to minimize volume.

"Cryder, is it possible to communicate with that element via drone?"

It appeared the man had overheard. "It is. I'd prefer our element monitor requests, and that they be done as a recording."

"Exactly."

The big man shrugged and stared. "Though how willing Argarak will be to let others visit after we've absconded with people...I mean, I have doubts about it."

"He may want hostages in return. But, that would let us get a couple more people into place in the village temporarily."

"Yes. We can only do it once, though, and that ends any future compromise with them."

"I wish these people had thought to bring those when we said, 'all-issue gear.' It didn't occur to me they'd think of an emergency trade as binding."

Spencer asked, "None of the gear was restricted though, right? Not weapons, not technical gear."

"Right. So they probably thought of that as expendable."

"Okay, if we can make this work, we'll see if they can trade for the trinkets, and we should still have tried for that before using force."

Cryder said, "Possibly, but I suspect force will be needed."

"What can we offer them?"

"Delicious food. A good supply of salt or alcohol."

"Yes, salt and booze. Both excellent commodities and expendable. Sweets in the form of fruit?"

"I think we have a container of dates."

"Perfect. Also, this means I don't have to write another order just yet."

"I understand."

"Let me do this, then." He wrote out an outline, then had to ask about printing.

"Sheet copy?" Cryder confirmed. "Yes, limited per day. Tap here, tap there."

"Got it, thanks."

Being able to just tap his own computer screen without any add-ons was neat, though it reminded him the Byko network had access to everything they had on device or spoke near one.

He printed the page and called, "Sergeant Burnham! Lieutenant Cole!"

They came over quickly enough without sprinting.

"Sir?" "Yes, Captain?"

"Okay, we'll record a request and send it to the hunters observing us. I'll allow three guests at a time, not to exceed twenty-four hours, and everyone must understand it's goodbye. I don't want to have to detain anyone else the way we've detained Lozano, but if there are issues, we must."

"Is private time included?"

"Yes, couples may have private time. We're also going to offer to trade some choice items for the few remaining issue items. I'll write it up, you offer it, and we'll relay it back on each exchange, too. Which of you has better local language skills?"

Burnham said, "We're both about the same. I seem to have a better accent."

"Okay, here's the summary," Sean said, and handed over a printed sheet they could mark up.

INTRODUCTION: Note you are speaking via a magic device.

It is necessary for us to return home to our people, now that the spirits have seen fit to allow it. While we will miss you all, we must leave, it is the will of our spirits.

They and our chiefs have agreed that we can visit briefly with you before we depart. Three at a time can visit our camp for one day and night at a time.

Before we leave, (those of us with wives) would like to spend a bit more time with them. We will always appreciate the hospitality and grace you showed us, and miss you much.

If Argarak (or other) wishes, we can discuss this at the fence (Wall?) of our camp.

Our spirits guarantee the safety and accuracy of this message.

"We'll have you record that and relay it."

Burnham looked at it. "I understand the summary," he said. "I'll need to adapt it slightly."

Sean agreed, "Go right ahead. Any reasonable phrasing that makes those points is acceptable."

"I'll work on it for a few minutes. Thank you, sir."

"You're welcome."

Dr. Sheridan came back over.

She was surprisingly quiet and discreet as she asked, "Captain, do I understand their local mates will be coming in?" She seemed tense.

"Some of them, possibly. Is that a problem?"

"Not at all. It makes gathering DNA samples that much easier. If I can find any excuse to swab them, I can have all the data we need as a cross section of those."

He understood her tension now. It was eagerness, not concern.

"Oh, good. I love things that make my task easier."

"I'll find an excuse. The specimen tape is basically just that. As long as I make contact, I'm good."

"Make it some sort of blessing or greeting."

"Exactly."

Sheridan was a lot friendlier overall than Raven, and nominally in charge, but it seemed to him that Raven should be the senior scientist. She certainly appeared to have a broader skill set and knowledge. Possibly it had to do with assignment date, or papers submitted, or some other political issue? Or just being friendlier. She certainly enjoyed watching fit young men exercise. Raven acted as if they didn't exist. Personal reasons? Or just disregard?

He checked with Cryder.

"How is the local recon element?"

"They've not moved the slightest since this morning. I'm impressed."

"Okay. Hopefully they'll be receptive to the message. Why them and not directly?"

"Partly to follow their chain of command. Partly to make it clear we know where they are, but not clear that we know where he is. If need be, we can escalate. When we eventually do reach our limits, we can bluff for more."

"Solid reasoning."

Burnham came back a bit later.

"I'm ready to record, sir," he said.

Arnet brought over a tiny mic that wasn't attached to anything. Burnham looked at it, shrugged, and started talking.

The language sounded almost Russian, almost French, almost Pashto in its intonation and delivery. Was this possibly one of those ancestor languages to the entire continent? Cool, if so, and now they had more recorded samples.

"That should be it."

Sean replied, "Okay, we'll transmit that to the drone shortly." Then added, "We'll let you know on response," when it appeared the man wanted to hang around.

As soon as Burnham left, he texted Oglesby to bring Shug with him.

When they came over, he ordered, "Please listen to this and tell me what it says."

Oglesby showed Shug how to listen to Byko audio, simply by letting the device know you were ready. It arranged projection to the listener's ears all by itself. He apparently asked Shug to repeat back what he heard. Oglesby listened also, and said, "It's roughly what you wrote. Nothing deceitful."

"Excellent, thank you. Let's send."

Rich Dalton decided to approach Lozano again.

"Hey, Christopher," he announced, as he neared the tent.

The response was a grunt.

"I was thinking about differences between us."

Nothing.

Rich said, "So you've done well here. I managed to keep calm and faithful, but I can't say I was happy with the actual event. Only with my relationship with God."

Lozano grunted.

"But you actually managed to be happy."

"Yeah, I scored four women here."

That really wasn't that impressive. Though for some it might be.

"Good. Was it enjoyable for all of you? Or was this all at once?"

"No, one at a time. Well, two of them once. Holy fuck, that was hot. It was like her visiting friend from another camp, and she got invited into our house, so . . . anyway."

"I can see how that would be amazing." Also rather sinful, but he couldn't say he'd turn it down. Flesh and human instincts were the cause of sin, after all.

"They start younger than we do."

"Yeah, we noticed that on our trip. It was something we were very careful with."

"I like them young."

"It happens."

"No, I really like them young. The oldest was seventeen, near as we can tell. The youngest was thirteen."

Yeah, that. "It won't be a problem back home. No one needs to know, and this isn't our culture."

"If I fuck a thirteen-year-old back home, my ass is getting raped in jail."

Oh.

"So, you've become accustomed to young girls."

"Accustomed? You could say that. I haven't even looked at the older ones. Even when Frenchy was putting out. All I could think was that if she was ten years younger and a lot tighter, she'd be alright."

That was disturbing. But . . . "They age faster here. In their twenties, they're old."

"It's not that."

"Well, you should at least see what the future women look like. And they may be able to help you with this problem."

"Who says it's a problem? They're fucking amazing. Or amazing fucking." He laughed.

Rich swallowed hard. Lozano needed more help than he could offer. He was afraid if they took the man back he would start preying on young girls. It was definitely a taste he had acquired, and he seemed to really like it.

A more disturbing thought: Hopefully he'd acquired it here, not before he left.

He'd have to ask Caswell or Raven. He wasn't sure how.

"Our law is clear, but doesn't apply here. As far as culture, yeah, you know how ours feels. The scientists tell me it's within normal range for people, which is why it happens, and why we have the laws we do. As a Christian, I guess I understand that everyone has their own path. It's not up to me to judge you. That's between you and God. I'll admit I'm uncomfortable with the idea."

Uncomfortable? Hell, he was revolted.

"But if you want to talk, I'm here."

"There isn't much to talk about," Lozano replied, and stared at him through the mesh. "If I fuck those chicks back home, I become a prison bitch. I'm not interested in being 'cured' or 'made better.' I like what I am. I like it here."

"I think liking the girls is a big part of why you like it here."

"Yeah, so?"

"God has a challenge for everyone. For Sergeant Spencer, it was fear of everyone else magicking home while he was in the latrine. Caswell was deathly afraid of all males—"

"She was right."

"Some at least, yes. One of our others had health issues that were breaking her apart. Memory loss, cognitive damage, physiological stuff. People die slowly of cancer. Others are abused or orphaned or abandoned. I struggle trying to understand people who aren't like me, and to help them find God if they're willing. You have traits society won't endorse."

"If God cared I wouldn't be this way."

"It's very human to think so. God may want you to face this, and yourself."

"Yeah? How do I do that, smartass?"

"I don't know. I wish I did. The answers always come from within."

"You sound like a fucking mystic on a mountain."

"Well, we're sort of on a mountain, and enlightenment is obviously needed."

Lozano laughed at that.

"You're stubborn and devoted, Dalton, I'll give you that. If all this hasn't shaken your faith, nothing ever will. Dumbass."

"It's been shaken. Hard. God sent me a message through the least likely channel, so I knew it was real."

"Yeah?"

"Sergeant Spencer's a dedicated atheist. He told me I had to hang onto my faith."

"That's kinda the first sergeant's job."

"Context matters."

"Yup. And thirteen-year-olds are fine in this context."

"All I can do is pray for you."

Lozano's voice had a mocking tone. "For me to give up my sins?"

Nice try, he thought. "Nope. For you to find whatever answer you need."

"Unlock me and I'll walk down the hill. Problem solved."

"Whatever answer fits the available circumstances."

"Yeah, always a catch. Did you get what you needed from this discussion?"

"For now, yes. Have a good day, Christopher."

"Yeah, whatever."

Had he gotten what he needed? If he needed to be disgusted with humanity, certain particular elements of humanity, science, and the world in general, yes.

He'd have his own discussion with the Lord about all that.

Dr. Raven was at the CQ and apparently saw his expression. "What's up?" she asked.

He pointed with a twist of his head. "The man's a f...damned pedo. He likes the teenage girls."

She almost shrugged. "Some are attracted to the first blush. Within evolutionary constraints it's acceptable. Older is safer for reproduction, but it's within the mean and evolutionary process doesn't care about safety in the short term. As society has evolved it's become unacceptable, but that's a much faster change than the base instincts. Then, we have a spectrum of ephebophiles who regret it and seek help, and others who are sociopaths who hide the desire and use children as objects. Though we have to question how much of that sociopathy is native to their personalities or developed due to personal or societal shame."

Rich didn't like that as he processed it. "Are you're saying it's okay?"

She glared at him. "Oh, fuck no. I'm just explaining where it came from. In this time frame, murdering people for food is also a thing. In ours, it's no longer acceptable. Exposing infants is considered okay. As I said, societal and social evolution is much faster than physiological."

He said, "That's more an argument for us being created than for any evolution."

She just shook her head and replied, "I have no idea how to respond to that. You're so far off you're not even wrong."

"Maybe, but I know *that's* wrong." He pointed with his head again.

"So do I. Believe me."

CHAPTER 20

Jenny Caswell was on the one hand bored, and on the other nervous about the shuffling around and low-grade conflict attempting to recover artifacts. If she'd been in charge, there'd be no discussion of conjugal visits and a quick relocation to the evac point, then if anything else was needed, return from there.

She conceded, though, that Elliott's plan would work, and would make certain technical aspects easier to handle. Then, there was relocating Shug, and it wasn't clear which direction he needed to go, nor how far.

In the meantime, the interactions made her curious about some science matters.

She watched Sheridan and Raven under their awning doing what was clearly fieldwork, with a lot of samples from the troops, the recoverees, local flora and fauna. She hadn't considered how many possible things could be sampled, but it made sense that everything that evolved slightly, especially fast-mutating things like bacteria, and edible plants. She waited until they took a short break.

Sheridan was usually friendlier, but Raven was closer and seemed amiable enough. She approached.

"Dr. Raven, you said something about compatibility."

"I did? Oh, that." The woman leaned back and adjusted her gloves. They had fingers that folded aside for typing, that she pulled back over for warmth. It was a chilly day, sitting still in the wind, even with partial cover.

She asked, "Did you mean these people are not biologically compatible with us?"

"That seems to be the case. First, most of our people are Rh positive. They're also largely A and AB types. The locals are Rh negative, a huge problem for the females, and mostly B type, a partial problem. Then there's literally dozens of other relevant factors, and I gather a slight difference in ovum implantation. It's a wonder Kita survived. We suspect the 'strong periods' Oyo experienced were in fact early miscarriages. She also apparently has a bicornuate uterus. She's lucky she didn't die of what's basically an ectopic."

"On the one hand, that's terrible. On the other, not having kids simplifies things."

"For the extraction, yes. It just complicated my professional career exceedingly."

"I'm sorry."

She smiled with a slight shake of her head. "Don't be. That means knowledge and more research."

"Ah." Though that meant she'd acquired knowledge relevant to her field, but couldn't share the source back home.

"It's fascinating."

Jenny asked, "Is your personal background part of where your interest in genetic groups came from?"

"How do you mean?"

"You mentioned the reservation."

Raven glanced up, and replied, "Oh. I was born on the rez, but raised entirely white."

"Which nation?"

"Cherokee reservation, but I'm Natchez."

"Ah. I recall you shared space?"

The woman replied, "If you mean we have no land of our own, yes."

She hadn't meant to hit a touchy subject. "I'm sorry."

Raven shrugged. "No language, either. Natchez has no native speakers, only a half dozen second language speakers."

"So you used Cherokee."

"I suppose I might have if I lived on the rez long enough. I'm told I used it early on. I don't know a word of either, now. Nothing about them. Cherokee is agglutinative, hard to learn, and almost extinct, too."

"One of those colonial aggressions that people aren't even aware of."

The woman wrinkled her brow. "Eh? It's human typical."

"It is for nonwhite populations, yes."

"'Nonwhite'? Ask the Irish, Welsh, and Scots about the English. Ask the Sami about the Finns and Swedes. Or the Bretons and Normans about the French. Populations displace, repress, enslave, absorb, and eliminate one another with dreary regularity. I apparently have an Irish ancestor, but I don't know anything about him, either. My genetic profile says there's African in here, too."

She pointed, and Jenny realized Raven was indicating her face. Yes, just barely. Her features overall were dark-skinned and high-cheeked, but her lips were slightly full, her nose just a little flat, and her eyes a bit round.

"Then there's what the Lakota did to the Pawnee and Omaha, and the Azteca to everyone around them. No one has a corner on violence. Once I tried to draw a map, based on a hundred subjects and their analyses. It turned into a tangled ball of yarn very quickly, complicated by the fact that Amerind profiles are almost nonexistent."

Jenny didn't catch that. "How's that?"

Raven said, "If you get a commercial genetic test, they are largely based on an incomplete set of too few subjects with no purebloods. They don't even show Natchez, Choctaw, Seminole, or a bunch of others. Nor most of the West and Northern populations."

"Geez."

The scientist shrugged. "All we can do is keep trying to reconstruct it. We've done amazingly well with the little data available."

Jenny changed tack. "What do you know about the locals?"

"Not much yet, until I get the samples back home for better testing. It's very likely, though, that they do share a common ancestor with the groups presently crossing Beringia. Which we knew, but this refines it slightly. I just hope someday I can publicize that finding, if we can come up with a way to justify how we found it."

"Is that possible?"

Raven leaned back and explained, "One of the 'finds' a couple of years ago was the hide your team brought back. We claimed the hairs had been found frozen in the Himalayas. Which isn't local enough for solid science, but is good enough for a close approximation, which is all anyone would ever see."

"I could learn a lot from you. I wish I had better skills in STEM."

"Not everyone does."

"I couldn't get past chemistry and physics. I managed trig but struggle too much with calculus."

Raven nodded. "Yes, calc and organic chem are essential for this sort of work."

"I tried."

Raven glanced from the screen and noted, "Few men and fewer women can. It's a brain-mapping issue."

Jenny bristled. Sheesh. "There's no reason women can't do as well as men."

Raven shook her head. "There absolutely is. The same reason men are better, on average, at spatial relations."

"That should just be environment."

"It sort of is. You notice here the local hunters have the entire area mentally mapped, are very good at throwing spears to point of aim, and can sit doing nothing, silently, for hours. Conversely, the women browse for edibles while chattering to keep contact with one another and children, or while in camp. They're evolving that brain mapping as we speak, and have been for millennia."

This highly educated, brilliant scientist was a strong, self-assured woman, and had just kicked Jenny's own education to the curb and stomped on it. A woman with how many STEM degrees didn't think women could handle it?

Raven continued, "Then, even in this field, I constantly have to make it clear I'm one of the guys, don't hold back on language, or the men get resentful of me in their territory. And there's often a grabby jerk. So a lot of women get into the field and then get out."

"Right. That's a lot of it."

"That keeps some women out of it, but it doesn't change the parameters."

"I guess not."

At least she knew why there weren't more cross-bred children. And that Raven was a very weird sort of feminist. But then, she'd completely dismissed the repression her ancestors suffered. Culturally, they didn't exist, and Raven wasn't really bothered. Or was it just a coping mechanism?

If Dr. Raven of several advanced degrees was that blasé, what were the odds of ever educating the general public?

Midmorning, a lone hunter came to the wards and called for attention. At a nod from Elliott, Dan Oglesby went over with Shug and Hamilton.

He was starting to get a bit of a handle on the language, but he let the native and the second handle the discussion, while he provided transliteration to the captain.

Hamilton said, "Argarak wants exchange. If three are here, he wants three back. Especially the dark woman and the red... Caswell."

Elliott said, "Well, he can want all he wants. I'll send the three I choose. Make it politely clear that our spirit guides absolutely do not allow our females to be shared, and will send lightning bolts and death if they try."

"I'm not sure how to phrase that."

Dan said, "Just tell him directly that while we wish good terms and will send a party in response, they will be to guarantee safety, and absolutely cannot interact. They are sworn to others back home, which is true, and our spirits will punish violators."

"I'll try."

To Elliott, Dan said, "You may have to send a larger, better-equipped party."

"Like we did with the Romans, yes."

Hamilton said, "He's not buying it."

Elliott looked at Dan with a look that told him to continue. Shrugging, he said, "Tell him the only people who would suffer are his women who were mated, who won't be able to say goodbye. We'll manage either way. Offer another jug of liquor."

There was more back and forth.

"He says he'll have to talk to Argarak and get back to us."

"Then he should do so. Give him a nice piece of steak to eat on the way. Thank him for his efforts on everyone's behalf."

The emissary was pleased with the meat and said so with thanks. He left, and the Americans went back to the HQ.

Dan got to see a very tense discussion on the matter.

Elliott said, "This is the first go-round of the deal. Argarak wants you ladies as trade goods. I was very clear up front that will not happen." He shook his head and made a cutting motion with his hand. "He was told you're both spoken for, and our spirits will punish transgression."

Sheridan replied, "Thank you."

"However, I would like to send one of the scientists to finish their samples and ensure the goods are accounted for. I'd also like to send Sergeant Caswell as backup. If I send one more, I'm not sure two troops and a civilian can handle it if it gets bad. If I send too many, it looks like a raid."

Cryder said, "If Arnet goes separately, behind our camouflage screen, then he and another can provide support if needed."

"So, combine what we discussed earlier. I like it. That means four combat effectives plus one more set of eyes."

Raven said, "If I go, I can take Spencer's Glock. They might not recognize that as being like the other weapons."

"Good. But I was thinking of sending Sheridan, since it's not who he wants—"

"'She,'" Caswell put in.

"Grammar. I'm sorry. Since she's not who he wants. Also, she wasn't in the last raid."

Sheridan said, "I can do it."

Caswell asked, "What are my rules of engagement, sir?" There was a slight prickle in her voice.

"The minimum necessary, but I want our rules enforced. They do not touch our women in any nonprofessional fashion."

The woman seemed relieved. "Thank you."

"Oglesby," Elliott said as he faced Dan. "You're going since you can translate a little."

"So can the translation gadget. Dalton's much better in a fight."

"Yes, so Dalton will be going with Arnet as backup. And if I can, I'm slipping Doc in with you."

"That only leaves you, Spencer, and Cryder here. And Dr. Raven."

"We'll be fine. This all depends on them agreeing."

A shout sounded. The envoy had returned. Dan hurried back with Shug, Hamilton, and Elliott.

Hamilton said, "He agrees to an exchange on those terms. He doesn't want any magic devices brought. Clothing only."

"Is he guaranteeing their safety on whatever they use as an oath?"

"That's the tone he used. I haven't known him to lie."

"Okay, we can start this evening if he has people ready. I'll send an escort with each female, unarmed, but with a bag of their own supplies. He can inspect."

"That seems agreeable."

"Then we'll wait for the three mates and their escort."

"You'll have to sleep on the ground and eat their food," Elliott advised.

Dan shrugged. That was easy for him for twenty-four hours. "Hooah, sir."

Caswell looked a bit tense.

"I'd much rather be armed," she said.

"He only ruled out magic weapons."

Caswell said, "True. I wonder if Spencer has another big knife I can carry."

"If not, I'm sure Arnet can fab one."

Raven added, "I always carry a machete in my gear, for clearing brush, and romantic interludes."

She did have a sense of humor, after all. It just didn't surface often.

Sheridan said, "I better load up on ibu. I'm going to ache badly tomorrow."

"Gather what you need to."

"Well, delousing powder, when we get back."

"Easy," Arnet assured her.

Shortly, the exchange party floated up the hill. Three women, obviously made up for presentation. All young. One very, very young. As they got closer, it was clear they had their hair dressed and tied up in buns atop their heads, not behind. They wore makeup of a sort, dark streaks out from their eyes, and reddish around their lips. How long had that been a thing?

They were also wearing garb that obviously came off fast. One of them looked a lot like a dark-haired Wilma Flintstone, complete with toggles on the white dress. The fur wraps completed the look.

Jenny was tense as all hell. The exchange was scary enough. Going without weapons terrified her. She had her utility knife and a larger one from SFC Spencer, almost a machete. That was something. And he kept it sharp.

Dr. Sheridan had a big dagger from somewhere, very pretty.

The blade looked sturdy enough. Oglesby had a machete, and she wasn't as comfortable with him as she could be. He'd thought he was flirting that one time, and she wasn't interested.

Two hunters waited with the three local wives. They stood patiently.

Oglesby said, "I guess we step out first. Sergeant Caswell?"

She was nominally in charge, though Oglesby would have to translate and Sheridan wasn't really in chain of command, but attached.

"Let's do it," she agreed, trying not to stutter.

She led the way through the fence.

The three women took that as a cue to enter.

That third one...

Sheridan asked, "God, what is she, thirteen?"

Jenny said, "Maybe. They age faster than we do. Lozano did say he liked them young."

Sheridan commented, "That's not uncommon in a primitive society, but decidedly creepy among ours."

"Yeah." No wonder he was more comfortable here, if that was his fetish. Yuck.

The hunters split, one leading, one following. As the element walked away with them, Jenny went completely cold and emotionless. The deal was no one would touch her.

She didn't trust that deal.

At the very least, she expected Argarak was going to figure the three of them were more valuable to the captain than the three wives of his newcomers were to him, and try to push a hard bargain.

At worst, he'd already expressed a fascination with her.

It's the red hair, she thought. *I really should dye it dark brown for this. I'll check with Arnet.*

Breedable women were valuable to these societies. Exotic-looking women—older ones with Alexander's busty figure on the last trip, unusual ones with red hair, different skin, or full figures—had societal and status value. Though apparently Argarak had a nice racist streak and didn't like black women. But that worked out better for Oyo, so take the bad with the good.

She tried to get her brain onto paying attention to the route and movement.

"I hope those two guys are behind us," she said softly to Oglesby.

Sheridan said, "We also have a drone." She started to point, suddenly jerked her arm back, apparently realizing what she was doing. She ran it through the side of her hair. Good recovery.

They trudged the six kilometers down and around to the village. Argarak was at his throne, so to speak. It was the same spot in front of the fire he'd been at last time. It was interesting that textiles of processed fibers were starting to appear, as both fishing nets and clothing.

Oglesby struggled through a greeting, apparently comprehensible. Jenny recognized about five words, badly mutilated from their previous trip. This language was related but not the same as that one, and both would be utterly gone soon, long before any root of modern languages came about.

It turned into a back-and-forth, with Oglesby being insistent on something, then more so. He stepped closer to her.

She heard him mutter, "Play along."

He wrapped an arm around her and she forced herself not to tense up, understanding the ploy. Sheridan shuffled in and reached around both of them. He kissed her, but it was the corner of her mouth only, and the edge of Sheridan's at the same time. From not far away it was obviously an intimate gesture, and might even appear explicit.

There was finally some sort of acquiescence, and one of the senior women stepped forward.

Oglesby said, "Okay, I told him we were mates. He wanted the two of you in one lodge, and me in with the single men. That wasn't going to happen."

"Thank you," she said. Yeah, that's where she figured it would start. And would it end with some late-night visitors?

They were led to a guest lodge, barely big enough for them to sleep, with a log for sitting on inside at the rear. It was already dusky outside, dim inside.

He continued, "I want us to rotate on watch all night. Dr. Sheridan, can you do that?"

Apparently he'd forgotten who was nominally in charge, too, but it did make sense.

Jenny said, "I'll set watch for us. Make sure they have food for us, and try to make it stuff we'll eat."

"Hooah. I'll do that while you get settled in."

Sheridan asked, "Are they going to expect us to be noisy love bunnies like they did the lieutenant?"

"It's one night, I'm not even pretending to play along." That idiot Cole had established an entirely bad precedent.

A faint buzzing sounded.

"That's the drone," Sheridan said. "At least one. I gather there's something smaller and unmentioned along."

"I hope so. Do we know where our escort is? If they are?"

Arnet's voice sounded quietly from the bottom edge of the woven wall, away from the door.

"We are nearby, in observation. Everything will be kept as agreed and low key until the guests leave the fence. If we're able to grab anything then, we will. Otherwise, there will likely be two more visits in rotation."

Jenny muttered, "I'm afraid to ask how much of our private activity is observed."

Arnet-via-drone said, "Only what is necessary for security concerns, and of that, I only see what the system can't interpret or deems needs a human in the loop."

"Thanks, I think." On the one hand, it didn't really bother her to take a leak around other soldiers. On the other, video was a different issue.

Argarak's word was apparently good. A woman brought food to them on platters made of split, carved wood. Other than that, no one interfered, but Jenny did notice more guards than previously, including one behind and one in front of the hut.

The food was okay. Meat with a little salt, some sort of edible tuber with some herbs, and some green leafy stuff that didn't taste like much of anything. They had some iron rations in their packs, including something like a superdense sugar cookie and nut bars.

Latrine breaks involved all three of them trudging to the edge of the clearing where the designated area was, avoiding recent fecal drops, carefully not watching one another while making it look as if they were not-not watching one another, because modesty wasn't a thing here, then hiking back.

The Byko sleeping mats, thin as they were, worked very well even on the packed earth floor of the hut. It wasn't bad, just boring. She had nothing to read, little to occupy her time. Sheridan was educated, but it was easy to see why Raven didn't care for her. She was nattering on about some *Doctor Who* episode and someone else's fanfic about it.

Sheridan took a break with, "I just wonder what kind of stories these people will have from it all."

Jenny replied, "Ideally, none. They shouldn't be aware of anything other than some strangers visited with strange stuff they couldn't describe."

"Right, but there's so much of that in history."

Jenny agreed, "Lots of cultures have mythology or fiction. The early ones weren't aware they were asking 'what if,' but that's what they were doing. Like that *Doctor Who* episode."

"*Doctor*... oh, no, *Blake's Seven*. Though there was a *Red Dwarf* time travel arc. It's actually relevant to—"

"I've seen it," Jenny said. "I'm not really up to talking about it now, though."

"Sure. I wish we did have video or books or something. Heck, I could be crunching numbers on our findings."

"Can Raven take some of the slack while you're here?"

The woman admitted, "Oh, easily. In fact, this should be a one-person job, but it is a valid idea to have another for backup and POV, and just so the science section isn't a single attached woman. There's nothing she's doing that I can't do, and we've had to rerun a couple of experiments."

"She mentioned. How did those come out?"

"The same way, but I thought we needed better documentation of process."

More likely you didn't understand it. Though I shouldn't be critical. I wouldn't grasp it, either. Jenny didn't like a lot of Raven's ideas, but at least they were coherent arguments.

Oglesby was mostly silent. He and she did not get along well, though she wasn't afraid of him this time. She probably shouldn't have been last time, but he was never good at reading people's signals.

They took a latrine break at 2230, using thin visors of Byko night vision rather than artificial light.

It was stuffy and cold in the hut, even with the walls made of woven twigs. The night lasted forever, but the bag was warm enough. The air outside was brisk, but the bag included a light mesh that ensured oxygen and CO_2 transfer, while retaining warmth.

Morning came, and they were given a roasted fish. It was a river trout or similar that had been in leaves in clay in the coals all night. It needed salt, and she had some, and then it was quite tasty. Moist without being wet, and hot. That felt good in the chilly air.

It was near 1000 when the guests from up the hill returned. Oglesby made their courtesies as Jenny covered him, and Sheridan stuffed the sleeping bags into their compact containers. Then they walked.

About a kilometer up the path, the air shimmered for a second and Arnet appeared in front of them, walking. She meeped and kept moving. She looked back and Dalton was there. The two closed in.

"Damn," Dalton said. He was wet with sweat. "So, you hide yourself entirely, even electronically, and it gets hot, fast. I was leaning against a tree all night, with a motion sensor to hide me when anything big enough came along."

"It has a sensitivity setting," Arnet said with apparent mirth.

"Yeah, I'm not gamer enough to figure it out."

"You did the crect thing to avoid overheating."

"I guess I can get more practice later."

"Since we have to do this twice more, yes."

Jenny really hoped they were swapping off. Two more days of this would be more arduous than a ruck march, all of it mental.

Sheridan said, "We didn't get to actually look or trade for anything we needed to recover."

Rich Dalton was wired and tired from that all night op. He wondered if Doc might have something to help. The fatigue was there to stay, but the overall ache was awful, and he wasn't young enough to pretend otherwise.

He checked in with SFC Spencer, who said, "Sure, go see Doc." He turned to the other vehicle and its awning, where Doc and Arnet were discussing something.

"Doc, minor issue?"

"What is it?"

He explained, and Arnet said, "If you don't mind, I have something for it."

"I don't mind. Doc?"

"Go right ahead. I've got ibu, some topicals, and Flexeril."

Arnet nodded and offered, "If you take this, you'll feel better at once."

The man flipped a tiny vial out, and Rich took it. He knew to pinch the top to open it, and drank, knowing whatever it was would taste decent. This one was pineapple.

At once he did start feeling better. The aches were fading, the discomfort from the gear, the abrasions that the sweat stung itched less. Even the fatigue burned away and clarity returned.

"Dang. That's good stuff. What is it?"

"General operational enhancer we use in the field. I can only administer one dose every five days for no more than forty days. For a second dose in five days I'd need consent from Cryder. For three, it would have to be life or death humping out of a bad zone."

"The one should be fine. Thanks. That's amazing."

"You're welcome. Expect to be very hungry in an hour, and to sleep heavily tonight. You should go to bed an hour early as well."

Doc said, "I'll clear that with the captain. Take it as scrip."

"Hooah, Doc. And thanks again, Arnet."

"Noprob."

Sergeant Spencer came up to check something, and nodded as he entered the overhang.

Looking over at the detention tent, he asked, "Lozano had his...woman come in?"

Doc said, "Girl. Yes. And she obviously adores him."

Raven said, "That's not terribly surprising under the circumstances. Outsider, effective hunter. Apparently better hung than the local males."

"Woah, TMI."

She was grinning as she said, "That's from verifiable reports and my own observations. You guys probably all have about an inch on them."

"Well, there are all kinds of jokes there."

"Hanging there," Doc grinned and emphasized dramatically. "Dangling and waiting. Pendulous. Standing by proudly. Stiff at attention."

He laughed at that. "Yeah, seriously though. She was willing?"

Spencer said, "Very. He made her come alright. Loudly. Fucking disturbing to hear a girl that young panting and screaming."

"Good," he said, and added, "I mean, I'm glad you don't approve."

The man looked really disturbed. "My daughter's older than that and I wouldn't want to hear it."

He asked, "Are we doing it again?"

"The captain is hoping the exchange establishes our status and disinterest in Argarak's people."

"I hope so, too."

Spencer said, "I almost wonder if we'd be better off leaving them here and calling them dead. They're at least as fucked up as someone coming out of decades in jail."

Rich noted, "Or a long hostage situation. We can't leave them." As screwed up as they were, they had to go home. Not just professionally, but morally.

Spencer agreed, "I know. There are good reasons we can't. But they're never going to recover. Hell, I'm still twitchy."

Raven said, "They'll need therapy for a long time. We'll have compiled notes for the mental health staff."

Martin was at the gate point when another pair of women and a man arrived with their escorts, just in time for dinner. They were agog at the vehicles, amazed at the tents, and leery of the wards and future weapons. They greatly appreciated the crab and turkey synthesis that Cryder served. Around unmannered mouthfuls, the women jabbered away with Uhiara and Burnham, though the two had made it clear they weren't going to be intimate with their now former mates. Oyo's partner was actually rather handsome, with styled hair and beard, great muscle definition. Some of the beard and buff subcultures would have been all over him.

Elliott said, "So that wraps this up." Hamilton and Keisuke didn't have mates. They lacked the status. That partly explained why they were eager to get home.

Noirot replied, "I don't have anyone right now." Her expression was partly wistful, partly relieved, and partly frustrated, probably at losing her status as a goodwill ambassador.

He wanted to cheer her up and keep her focused on family. "Well, you'll have plenty of time with Kita, and we'll try to keep things entertaining and friendly."

The girl heard her name, smiled at everyone, and hugged her mother some more. She really was a cute thing.

Oyo said, "I can give Breotah a proper thank-you, I guess."

Martin said, "Oh? I hadn't heard you mention him."

She shrugged. "I did in my debrief. I guess it'll be the right thing to say goodbye, but I was mostly hooked up because you have to have a mate, and none of the others were anyone I'd want to be with. I'll make it good for him, though. He's been kind. He even asks about home."

"What have you told him?"

With an ironic smile, she said, "Well, the languages are a barrier, and I can't explain most things other than magic. Magic pictures. Magic sleds to travel on. Things like that."

Caswell arrived and said, "That's harmless enough. At worst they become myths, and mutate into even less fathomable tales that mean nothing."

He looked at her again.

"You changed your hair." It was now a medium brown color, and just like that she was far less remarkable, though of course, he had years of interaction with her as a redhead.

"Yes, Sergeant. The red was getting too much attention. I'll finish this trip as a brunette. Arnet had a wash he says will last a week, and I can just do it in the shower."

"I can see that. The locals always pay attention to you."

"That doesn't even begin to describe how uncomfortable it is, but I think you get the idea."

"Absolutely. The color is within regs and we're under special circumstances anyway. No issue. I was just surprised."

"I cleared it with the captain already," she said, with a bit of snap in her voice.

"Sorry. I was trying to be reassuring."

"No offense taken," she said, sounding a bit less irritated.

Keisuke commented, "It's probably a good thing we didn't actually interact with the other group."

"Other group?" Wait, this was interesting, probably important.

The soldier said, "Yeah, later than this group, not Stone Age."

To verify, Martin asked, "Another displaced group?"

The man nodded. "We think so. They were wearing cloth and had swords."

That was rather important information to have.

Overhearing, Elliott asked, "Where?"

"West of here." He pointed.

Martin quickly asked, "What type of swords?"

"I dunno. Swords."

He raised an open hand and tried not to sound annoyed.

This was easy for him, but obviously not for others. He asked, "Rapier hilts? Cross guards? Small guards?"

"About that long." Keisuke indicated a bit less than three feet with spread hands. "Oh, and shields."

Sighing, Martin asked, "What shape?"

"Round."

"Iron or bronze swords? Sorry, I need details."

"Steel, I guess. White metal, shiny."

Martin said, "Dark Ages or Middle Ages, probably."

Caswell asked, "You don't interact with them?"

He shrugged. "We both tried a bit. We didn't get their language and they didn't get ours. They didn't know any local words last time we crossed paths. We just sort of wave at each other."

Martin said, "That's going to be tough."

Elliott asked, "Can you speak to them?"

Shaking his head, he said, "Not much. I learned enough Icelandic to read the Sagas, but I never learned to pronounce it, and I forgot most. I list my skill level as 'survival skills only.' Most of those are modern words. They won't be the same as Old Norse, and if they're some other Germanic tribe, I won't know more than a handful of written words, if they have anyone literate. I do have a copy of the Ogham alphabet. If it's Old English, I might do slightly better. If it's Rus or something else, no dice. And then they might be proto Finno-Ugric, Samoyedic, Hungarian, or something else and I'll have no fucking clue."

"You could have just said, 'No.'"

He shrugged slowly with a faint grin. "Well, it's not a complete no, and I'll try, but we have to meet them first." He turned to Keisuke. "How far west?"

"Dunno. Less than twenty miles, for certain. Probably less than fifteen."

Elliott said, "We will definitely have to take that up ASAP, after the grave recovery."

CHAPTER 21

Based on Cole's input, Sean Elliott was leading an element to take care of the grave of Akhtar Malik, the element's deceased interpreter. He had Cole along. Cryder was well behind where he could shoot anyone. Dr. Sheridan was along for samples and such.

He was glad of the soft rain, even if it was cold. It damped down noise and traces.

They were dangerously close to the village here. Argarak had shown no signs of slacking off. There were probably two factors at play. First, he had to show he was strong in the face of a threat. Second, none of his warriors had suffered any long-term harm in these engagements, so there was no need for him to stop. There was every reason for him to continue, and every reason for the Americans and Bykos to only use stun. It was a game they played. Still, those spears could kill, and the armor the soldiers wore didn't cover everything all the time.

The graves had markings, if you knew what to look for.

Cole pointed at a slightly sunken area with a crescent of rocks above it.

"He's buried here. And so is their son. He died of a fever about a year ago."

"I'm very sorry to hear that." The poor Afghan really had a shitty life. Raised in a post-war zone, then a war zone, then displaced in time with no way to comprehend it, and now dead.

Cole asked, "Are the buried corpses a problem? I can't think why, but I gather you're worried. Would they be apparent?"

Under her dripping Gore-Tex hood, Sheridan said, "Very. Wrong bone structure, wrong wear and age patterns, possible dental work. DNA mismatch. Archeologically and anthropologically, we have to make those go away."

"Ah," Sean said. "I guess I was aware of that, but it's not something in mind for me."

Sheridan said, "That's why I'm here."

Sean nodded. "Okay, then let's dispose of them."

Cryder asked, "Do you have rituals we need to observe?" He was now only a few feet back, but still scanning around, and had one of his mini-drones orbiting, leaving a cut through the droplets.

Sean Elliott, Captain, US Army said, "I'm going to make a decision here that must be kept secret."

"Go ahead."

Sheridan put in, "Obviously, we can't take the bodies to our time. I'd love to, and look at them in my lab, but I know you don't want us to, and they'd be found by others. There's no way I could keep the research secret."

Sean said, "If we can't have them, and they can't stay here, then we either need to take them quietly for your purposes, or find a way to destroy them in place."

Cryder seemed relieved. "I'm actually glad you're practical about it. I wasn't sure how Sergeant Dalton would act."

"I think he'd agree, but he shouldn't know, or the others. And Lieutenant, you can't mention this."

He looked concerned. "What do I say if asked?"

"Tell them we marked the grave for later recovery with specialized equipment."

Cryder said, "I'm marking it now, actually."

Cole asked, "How will you make it match?"

Cryder held up a vial. "I've an enzyme formulation that can ensure rapid decomposition of any remaining tissue. Then a small drone that can disrupt soil. Substantive traces will be gone. Chemical traces will be minimal."

Sheridan agreed, "That sounds properly effective."

Sean said, "You have my clearance to proceed, if you need it."

"I can do it by drone."

Five minutes later, the drone was on location, lowering to

the ground and rotating slowly. Everything seemed clear nearby as it landed.

At Cryder's control, the drone extended a probe into the ground. He got a reading he liked, nodded, and retracted it.

"Material sample," he said.

Next, the drone hovered and drained the fluid over the ground. That looked rather obscene. A small container came from somewhere else aboard and dropped a device that looked a hell of a lot like a sci-fi movie creepy crawly. It was about two inches long with claws all around an open maw. It drilled its way into the soil in about a minute, then there was nothing. As far as the liquid . . .

There wasn't any real activity to be seen.

"That's it. We can check it tomorrow."

"What about the device?"

"It'll recover when I call, and they're easy to destroy with fire or other oxidation processes. Onetime use."

"Cool. On the one hand, I'm glad you have it. On the other, it's a bit disturbing. How many do you have?"

"Enough for each of us, all of them, and presumed offspring."

That also was disturbing, that it was so matter of fact.

Still, that item was accounted for. Sean would write it up, and that was one less item to be concerned with for either the US or Bykos.

Kate walked across to the lab awning, munching a bagel with cream cheese and ham. The field rations were very good here, and it tasted fresh. She wasn't sure if this had been packaged, reconstituted, or converted, but it was good.

There was a stack of samples to run basics on—personnel samples of various bodily exams, some dirt, some clothing, especially footgear. Disgusting, but informative. She finished the sandwich in two bites to get that out of the way before work.

Raven was already processing something, with charts on screen.

Kate paused for a moment, then said, "That isn't the same screen as yesterday."

Raven replied, "I needed different processing, so I adapted it."

"Did you cha—"

She stopped as the woman glared at her.

Right. Don't be overheard. On the other hand, how were the

Bykos going to miss the fact that the twenty-first-century woman had cracked and reprogrammed some of their software? They might regard it as hostile.

Kate thought furiously if she should order it to stop, or look aside. She certainly was not going to mention it to the Bykos, either way.

They were trying for as much information as possible. If Raven could get it this way, great. There was a risk in anything. If she was good enough to crack their software, she might be good enough to hide it, though that seemed awfully smug and pretentious.

Instead she said, "Is it working better for you now?"

"It is so far."

"Good. We'll process a lot of data this way. I hope our hosts will be happy as well."

Shug came over with some specimen jars, and pointed at the southwest corner.

"From there," he said.

Raven replied, "Thank you very much, Shug. Now I need the same thing from down at the bottom ward." She pointed.

He nodded and took more containers. He walked off with them.

Kate confirmed, "You've got him running sample errands?"

"Yes, he wants to help and he's detail oriented, although he has no idea what I'm doing here."

That was actually a plus. The kid was illiterate and couldn't blow cover.

She acknowledged with, "I'm glad he's able to help and feel useful."

While they handled samples and data, she kept a random eye on the goings-on.

The visiting local girls seemed nice enough, polite enough. Was that best behavior as guests, or impressed by magic equipment and weapons? That might be something to follow up on. She made a note.

Arnet and Sergeant Caswell fed them, and there was the usual after-meal booze, and then a bit of music. Oglesby came over with more food and drink for them.

He said, "We're giving them some space."

Kate said, "Good," at exactly the same moment as Raven. She was amused. Raven didn't appear to notice. She was actually working both screens at once, samples on the right, some sort of Byko program in their screwy alphabet on the left.

She checked her own sample processes. They were going as planned.

There was nothing else to test at present. The Byko gear took a lot of the fussy detail and chemistry out of it. They didn't even have to wait for results. Bang, there they were. The genotyping was fascinating, and one theory on occupation of the New World just got a big boost, while two others were pretty much out of the running. Unfortunately, there was no way to release that yet.

As to the technical matter Raven was covering, there was no way to even discuss that it existed. The woman was impressive, but damn, she was arrogant. That extra PhD was probably cause and effect of that.

Kate walked to the kitchen and grabbed a drink, then wandered down to the fire and awning, which by default was the village green, local pub, gathering spot, living room, etc.

To her nonmilitary eye, it was still apparent who the displacees were. Their body language was different. In some ways, more casual, but also more alert and attuned to the surroundings. They were clearly tracking animals, wind, other noises. She could hear something like a dog or coyote. Was that domestic or wild?

She took a seat, took a sip of her rum and Coke, and listened to the minimal conversation. There were updates on stuff back home, on the Byko equipment, on what was going on in this time elsewhere in the world.

Most of them seemed ready to return, and trying to acclimate as best they could for now. She really wasn't sure about Munoz. He seemed like the type who, if he didn't think there was a good lawsuit coming, might just decide to stay. Then there was Lozano and his . . . kink. That brought up bad memories for her. She still hadn't talked to him and planned to avoid doing so.

It was a fascinating study in sociology and motivational psychology, though. She'd make notes and offer them for the researchers and therapists. It was amazing how much data could come from such a short study, given the richness of the material.

Sean texted his people and the Bykos, then restrained himself until after the visiting women went to their tents in the dark. They seemed very disappointed their chosen mates weren't sleeping with them.

Everyone in his unit gathered by the first vehicle, the de facto HQ, and Cryder fingered his controls.

"The audio is one way in now."

So was airflow, apparently. There was a bit of heat from one of the vehicles, and it was much nicer than the near-freezing damp outside. That and hot coffee made it much less unpleasant.

He opened the discussion with, "So, it appears there's another displaced group nearby. Sergeant Spencer thinks they sound Medieval. We need to figure out how to handle this."

Spencer said, "Dark Ages versus Medieval. It matters."

"Hell yeah, it does," Raven agreed.

Cryder raised a hand enough for attention and said, "Can't take them on this return. The process is coded for us, your displacees, and a very limited number of others. We hadn't anticipated offspring, nor another element."

Sean said, "That makes sense. So, that's another trip for someone."

Arnet said, "We need as much info as possible first, from drones, cameras, persop, anything tha cn make transition estimates more accurate."

"So we have to be in this general area until then."

Cryder agreed. "Correct. Also, we have to recover items in the cave. Get Shug to his people. Then proceed to departure point and wait."

Oglesby said, "It seemed so easy in the planning stages."

Sean smirked. "Yeah. Feel for me. I have to make all the calls, then justify them when we get back. There is no higher authority."

Dalton noted, "I'm amazed the Army didn't force you out and a colonel in."

Sean replied, "I almost wish they had."

Spencer commented, "I'm glad they didn't. He'd have decision-making authority, and probably a complete lack of any subtlety. Or else he'd be so oversensitive we'd have daily EEO briefs."

He knew that too well. "You're probably right."

"I hope you avoid all those pitfalls if you stay in, sir."

"I'll do my best. A certain amount of flexibility is necessary to do so, however. It's not as if you can refuse some of those orders."

He continued, "The second issue is that we're not going to have less interaction with the local group. We have to recover more material, and you're all aware of the emotional bonds that have to be broken."

It was Jenny Caswell who said, "We really should relocate as fast as possible. For their emotional well-being. The drawn-out interaction is almost a taunt, and doesn't allow proper coping."

Spencer said, "Right. Except we have to get those other artifacts. That's the quandary. The easiest way to avoid conflict is just hump to the departure point now. However, we have to research this other group as best we can. Cryder says we can't take them with us. Mass amounts."

Dalton opined, "Then we should aggressively seek those artifacts. Minimal force, but whatever we have to use that's non-lethal. Then unass."

Sean felt tired.

"This was supposed to be search and rescue, not low intensity conflict and cultural strife."

Spencer said, "No plan ever survives contact with the enemy."

He had to grin. "There wasn't supposed to be an enemy."

Spencer grinned back. "Nope. So the universe provided one, just to fuck with us."

"We still have to get Shug home, too. We've also got to find artifacts, dispose of remains, relocate the boy, move to departure point, and avoid major conflict in the process."

"Once the guests leave, we need to appear to vacate the area. They'll probably still follow, but we'll at least slow them down with distance, and give the right impression."

Arnet suddenly put in, "I have interesting news."

"Oh?"

"One of the recon drones found some of the expended cartridges. They're small enough it's able to recover them with onboard equipment."

"Excellent. How many?"

"Seven so far. I'll have it perform a pattern in that area, looking for others."

"And, of course, we'll need to sneak back for any remaining artifacts we can find."

"I wish we could assume that because nothing happened forward, they were never found."

Cryder shrugged. "That seems logical to me, but the scientists don't want to take a risk."

Sheridan nodded. "I agree. Fewer variables is almost always better, unless one is doing a scalar compara... Anyway, yes, do try to get them."

"Moving will also keep them busy with the process."

Dalton sat up suddenly.

"How about a compromise?" he put in.

Sean asked, "What do you mean?"

"Moving keeps them busy. We relocate partway. That means they're packing, moving, unpacking, pitching bivouac, and occupied. It puts us farther away from Argarak and his goons, which extends their logistical train. It also makes us appear less of a threat. As long as we have the vehicles and are within a couple of hours, we can get things accomplished."

That was a very workable idea.

"Cryder?" Sean asked.

"Gives us a measurable radius for operations. I can do a terrain recon now and see what there is."

"Please do. Sergeant Dalton, thanks, that was an excellent suggestion."

"You're welcome, sir. Glad I could contribute."

"As soon as Cryder and I agree on a location, we'll prep to move, and I assume we can move after breakfast tomorrow. Be advised."

There was a volley of "Hooah, sir." The awning opened enough to be public, but kept the draft out. Some dispersed to the fire, others to bed. Sean took his coffee to the fire and sat watching flickering flames hissing against raindrops.

Shortly, Cryder waved from the orderly room, and Sean strode up the hill.

"What do you have?"

Cryder had a map, an aerial photo, and a corrected and enhanced overhead view.

"This location is thirteen kilometers away, has a running water source, timber for fire and as windbreak, around a sufficiently clear hummock and meadow to allow easy encamping."

Sean looked it over. It easily fit all those requirements.

"That seems perfect."

The man grinned. "No, but for our current requirements, it's excellent." He obviously understood the rhetoric, and was just being a smart-ass.

Sean ignored it and said, "Let's plan to move after breakfast."

Dan Oglesby dug into the movement. He was basically excess at this point, with reliable local translators available. Shug remained with him, as usual. The breakfast dishes were stowed, the kitchen folded into the back of Roller Two. He helped Arnet fold and stow the awning. The latrine would be near last, after ensuring everyone had a chance to use it.

It was cold but clear, frost burning off, and exercise was welcome.

Arnet instructed, "Press there while I close the cover . . . that's it. Can you assist Dalton with the wards?"

"Hooah," he replied, and jogged over. Shug followed him.

"Hey, dude."

Dalton replied, "Yo. Want to carry them over as I pull them?" The man grabbed the one nearest, heaved, and it erupted from the ground with some grassy clods of Earth. He banged it off and handed it to Dan.

Once he and Shug each had a half dozen in their arms like firewood, they trotted them up to the vehicles and Arnet stowed them. In short order, the camp was struck, folded, stowed, and they were ready to roll. All their gear was aboard. They didn't even need CamelBaks for the hike. Though Caswell and Dalton were armed, in addition to the vehicles' onboard weaponry.

There was no way for them all to fit on the vehicles, but the captain ordered rotations at each rest break, with Dr. Raven and Kita to ride all the way. Lozano got to ride in back outside, cuffed and with a stun collar. His expression was still a sociopathic challenge. He didn't care what they thought.

It was awesome to watch the little girl climb in with her mother, so nervously. Since the vehicles were near silent, she only noticed activity when it started moving. She clenched and gripped hard, pinching her mother's elbow, but settled down shortly. She climbed atop Noirot's lap to watch the landscape move by, and seemed delighted at the amazing pace of fifteen miles per hour. After all, they didn't even have draft animals here. No one had even put dog teams on a sled for winter, yet.

He wondered why the troops hadn't suggested that, but the terrain wasn't really viable. Those travois things might work, but he didn't know anything about them.

Shug was happy to walk, delighted to ride, and pleased to be grasping more English. The kid would make a great recruit. Eager to work, worked until told to stop, tried hard to understand, and assumed leadership had a plan, even if he didn't know what it was. Almost the Army's ideal. Of course, once he learned a bit more, he'd get jaded. Though Elliott was a far better commander than most.

Dan thought about himself. He wanted to figure out what else he could do, since translation was pretty well covered by Hamilton, who was quite reliable, and Shug, who was a good parallel while around. They'd probably need Dan to keep cross-checking the others, and listen in on any recorded convos for intel. In the meantime, he was a general support NCO for everyone.

When Dr. Raven got in next to him, he asked, "How is the research, ma'am?"

She replied, "It's going well, though much of the analysis will have to wait for either a Byko lab or ours." She shifted in the seat and winced as she found a spot for her ankle.

"Man, their lab would be great, if they allow it."

She squinted and replied, "Yes, and no. When I write it up I need to explain the processes used, and that isn't possible with theirs. Also, they've said there's certain data they won't allow. But it's political rather than technical. If I can get the samples or the findings at least to our labs, I can study it to the best of our ability and go from there."

She had her tablet out and was doing something with complicated symbols he couldn't comprehend.

He replied, "I see. Theirs would be better, but yours is more supportable."

She glanced up and said, "That's a good way to describe it. How similar is this language to the one from your previous trip?"

"Well, it's interesting. It's obviously been a long time, and the dialect change probably would give some insight."

"Oh?" she paused and stared. "Can you describe?"

He thought about that. "Well, complicated terms are different—for things like hunting, material preparation, dealing with the spirits. Simple terms, like food, water, lodge, are recognizable even with some drift."

She nodded, and winced as they rolled over a hummock. "That makes sense, based on the little I know. Can you write up a comparison with the terms you've encountered? Even a few hundred would be useful to paleolinguists. They might match to some early known languages, or they can use it to study separation, which would help with gauging population spread."

He asked, "I thought you did that with genetic markers."

She nodded. "We do, but also with linguistics, artistic styles, technical industries. It's all relevant."

Twisting his head, he replied, "Honestly, it would be hard. These aren't written languages and they use a bunch of tones and sounds that we don't have in any modern Eurasian language."

"Yes, you'd have to create or define symbols for the sounds."

He pointed out, "That's basically creating a new alphabet."

She smiled. "Uh-huh, that's what Sequoyah did to create the Cherokee written language, though it's a syllabary."

She was definitely suggesting he put the effort in.

"I guess I'll do what I can," he said, not sure he really wanted to, as interesting as it would be, but damn, he'd be writing a fricking book. "In the meantime we can find some way for me to record."

"We've been recording Shug and anything the recoverees put in that language since we found them."

"Oh, well that helps. But they're more fluent and might be better suited."

She noted, "They learned it, but I don't think any of them have an extant knowledge of ethnology and linguistics."

"Mine's only a self-taught level, and what DLI taught me. But I am interested in studying more."

"I can absolutely suggest certain agencies fund your study in exchange for your findings."

"Sure, but how do we possibly explain how this happened?"

She shook her head and replied in detail. "We don't. What we do is extrapolate and see what we find in the known languages, apply that, and see what sort of drift we get. That would be compared back to what you have, and then used to retroactively define some findings. You'd be listed as an analyst and proposer and we'd make up some reason you were interested. Which I dislike, but under the circumstances is necessary. I just hate any dishonesty in the process. It always gets used to justify more."

His name on a professional paper, actual professional training in linguistics, and possibly several years work analyzing his own notes.

Well, hell. "Bring it on then, ma'am."

"Awesome," she said with a cheerful grin. "I'll get you set up to record and write. And I'm not opposed to offering suggestions, but you need to make it your work because you have the knowledge."

"Hooah, as we say."

✧   ✧   ✧

As they walked alongside the rolling vehicles, Armand Devereaux talked to Keisuke and Maldonado.

He was straightforward, but kept his tone casual.

"How are you gentlemen adapting?"

Keisuke replied with enthusiasm and no hesitation. "Ready to go, sir! I'm a bit tense, because it doesn't feel real, like I'll wake up back here."

"Yes," he agreed. "We were like that after we got notification."

"How did you get that, sir?"

Armand remembered it clearly. "Cryder and Arnet rolled around camp, left tracks, then approached in daylight completely invisible, but with a PA system. That was a shock. We met up, they came into our camp, set up their gear, which wasn't quite as nice as the full kit here, but still good. We were all getting along and slowly building diplomacy with the locals. I even had a couple of dates. Then one morning, there was this sort of bang-pop, and there was a dayglo box with some sort of transponder and notes. They'd found us. There were directions to the evac point, and then we had to get the Neolithic types, the Romans, and the East Indians all to come along. That took some diplomacy and juggling. It was two years for us, a bit less for some of the others. We sat there waiting and then wap!, we were in the Cog...Bykos' time."

"Neat. I'm going to be nervous, but I'm waiting for it."

He said, "Excellent. We'll have some more admin crap to deal with, that will help with the time."

Maldonado asked, "How long have you been a doctor?"

"I'm actually doing civilian residency now," he replied. "Which is a bunch of bullshit, because I did reconstructive and lifesaving surgery here using available tools and the remains of my field kit. I hate being the new guy, when I'm not."

"I can see that, sir."

"What about you, Maldonado?"

The man shrugged. "I guess I've come around. First it was, 'Yay, home.' Then it was, 'More Army bullshit I'm gonna hate, and I hate it already. Those fuckers owe me.' But, yeah, I want to go home. I don't suppose there's some way to credit this time against my current enlistment and just get the fuck out?"

Armand replied, "Actually, I'm sure you can. I don't think the general will have a problem at all signing that."

Maldonado raised his eyebrows and seemed a bit mollified. "No shit? Well, good. So, five more weeks here, about the same in Bykoland or whatever, and then for the Army?"

"Probably about the same, yeah."

"That'll leave me needing a job and lodging, but I'll have leave pay."

"You'll get some bonus and back pay, too. They should be able to work something out."

"Well, cool. I wish I'd known that before I was an asshole. Sorry."

He grinned. "You could have asked." He was about the same age as Maldonado, but felt old and wise in comparison.

"It never occurred to me to ask the Army for anything."

Yeah, he had a point there.

Keisuke said, "I'm going to consider that, too. I definitely want to go home, no question. But if I can get out as well, that's even sweeter. No, this wasn't the Army's fault, but it wouldn't happen if I wasn't here. So, fuck 'em."

Armand noted, "We're not sure it doesn't affect civilians. We haven't seen any displaced from our time. But the Gadorth—Neolithic—and whichever group you say is west of here aren't really military. The Romans were. The small group of, I guess, sixteenth-century Moghuls were, but there were ten of them that I know of. So half and half on military versus civilian. Though I guess the earlier ones were still hunting bands. And this other group..."

He thought for a few minutes.

"You know, I'll need to ask Cryder about this."

The Byko electronics must have informed the man of the comments, because the vehicle moved out of line, alongside, and Cryder leaned out the window frame.

Cryder said, "It seems to favor remote groups who tend to be hunting parties or military. We haven't seen displacement from heavily inhabited areas yet, and we'd prefer not to, for obvious reasons."

"Yeah, that could be a disaster of leaks or deaths or both."

"Definitely both."

Kate Sheridan was glad to ride most of the way. She knew Raven was, too. Rough country hiking—and what was rougher than completely untamed wilderness?—was definitely for the young and fit.

Though really, most of it was riding, with the troops not aboard clinging onto the vehicle shell with its conveniently placed loops and steps. They only dismounted over really shaky terrain.

It was quickly apparent that Cryder could monitor all the conversations. She reminded herself to never talk about their other research where he or the vehicles were within reasonable range. And just how sensitive were they? She tried to calculate audio wave propagation vs. distance vs. air density, and realized she'd need to sit down to do it. But it should be possible to calculate safe distances for whispers, conversation, shouts, and apply a safety margin. There were things they had to discuss occasionally. Also, some could be masked as other conversation.

The seats in the vehicle even fit her large frame. Well, they adapted, contouring her hips and shoulders and providing a neck rest. She could easily nap like this, but wanted to stay awake. The windows were almost a dome and allowed an excellent view, and the terrain was really pretty for not having been shaped by humans. The trees had a chaotic, fractal beauty. The erosion was unique. Not having a road ahead gave it a surreal alienness. And it all smelled so clean, earthy, and fresh. The outside temperature felt only slightly cool with the vehicle and her clothes. But it was present.

Arnet was the one who first said, "This is it. We're now twelve kilometers from the village. There's a small stream we can draw from." He pointed. "Sufficient terrain to reduce wind. Good field of view. Plenty of sun."

That latter was becoming important as the season cooled.

Cryder said, "It fits my parameters. Captain Elliott?"

The Army officer agreed. "It works for me."

The new camp went up quickly, wards first, and everyone understood the multiple reasons why. She helped carry them from the truck to the soldiers setting them. At least it wasn't just "We don't trust the lost contingent." There were threats human and animal, and it was good to have a defined border.

The troops shook their bivvies out and set them in a ring around the fire, and she followed. Sergeant Spencer took charge and requested the officers to be nearest the vehicles and on each side, Byko and American. He then directed himself and Dalton at the far point just outside where the vehicles posted. He put all five females on one arc between them, with Noirot closest to himself. Sergeant Caswell was next to her, then Raven, then Kate, then Oyo. Dalton's side had all the recovered males. Lieutenant Cole was directly adjoining Elliott.

She approved. That should keep things under reasonable control. This was a pretty effective Army unit, and it meshed well with her and the Byko. They weren't really "locals" but they were certainly "allies." She'd been on some recovery support where no one talked to anyone and the Army had sticks up their ass.

Unheard by the rest, Sean Elliott asked Arnet, "Can you automate a stunner to respond to that arc if there's an issue?"

"I can. I will, after confirm with Cryder. I assume he'll agree."

"Perfect."

That left one matter. He walked over and talked to the prisoner.

"Sergeant Lozano, you have to retain that collar. But if you will agree to come along with the program, even under protest, you can have a tent with the rest of us."

"With respect, sir," he said with little, "I'm actually kinda cool off by myself."

"If you insist. I hope that wasn't an attempt at reverse psychology."

"Nope. I would actually prefer to keep my separation from you fucks."

Fair enough. The man could have that. "Suit yourself. Arnet, Oglesby, can you erect the jail over there?"

Arnet grinned broadly and said, "With extra wards."

Ultimately, though, the man was going to be a problem. And until he was passed off to higher authority, he was Sean Elliott's problem.

All of them were going to be problems. Pissed off, worn out, disgruntled, reproduced, psychologically damaged. Why couldn't the Bykos have gotten them in within two years?

Shug found it all confusing. They moved camp a good day's hike away. The shape of the camp changed. People moved. Other than that, he couldn't grasp a reason for it. They weren't chasing game like the nomads to the north. They hadn't moved that far.

This was a good place if the weather stayed nice. They had a clear view, a nearby woodline again, along a stream, and the ground was even enough for a camp. He helped carry wards

and shelters—"tents"—and cleared rocks and debris. He stomped
down a couple of anthills. Arnet ran one of the tools across the
ground to the stream and they had water, and another back for
waste. The wards went up. The ground was cleared of grass by
a tool with a fast whirling thong.

The tools were amazing. He could often tell which were
American and which were Byko. The American tools were usually
less complicated and single purpose. Byko tools were just magic,
even if they said they weren't.

Once his tent was set up, he washed his hands at the waste
area and stood ready to help with dinner.

As they lined up, he greeted those he could.

"Hello, Amalie," he said, feeling honored that a shaman that
even the captain and Dan held in respect granted him her bare
name.

"Hello, Shug. We'll be doing more samples tomorrow, if you
can help."

He grasped that. They used special bits of dirt, grass, and
rock for their learning, and the long lines of signs they drew
were an entire tribal memory of knowledge. She had even shown
him their exact location on a picture that shrank to show what
she said was the entire people world. That was done with something else, but their work was important to all people, and he
was pleased to help with gathering. She said that certain special
shamans would have his name remembered as helping, even it
was in a small way. He worked hard to remain humble, because
he didn't even know how to explain that, since he barely understood it, and what would it mean to anyone? But these very wise
people trusted him, and he would do all he could to make them
pleased with his effort.

"I will," he said. "Dinner smells good."

She replied, "Yeah, it's some sort of chikken. That's a bird
that doesn't fly. It has a big breast and lots of meat."

That sounded good. He'd had chikken before they came back
here. He wondered . . .

"Is it here? Or some bird like it?"

"I don't think so," she said. "It comes from far south and
changed a lot over many families."

That was sad, but he'd enjoy it while he was here. Hopefully
he could get back to his village soon.

CHAPTER 22

Rich Dalton found the move okay. It was good to get a bit of exercise, and see some of the landscape. One thing he always hated was how little of an area he got to see while deployed. One couldn't get a sense of the area, or of God's work, from a narrow strip of patrol and a firebase.

The camp went up easily enough. The weather was coolish but decent and he still loved how fresh the air was with every breath. Invigorating.

For dinner they had chicken with a choice of some sort of curry, something like a sweet hot barbecue, or a peppery lemon dusting. He had a little of each. The curry was green and incendiary, but had a savory undertone. He enjoyed the conflicting sensations. The barbecue was very good, with a flavor he couldn't quite identify underneath. The lemon pepper as a powder rather than sauce was interesting. The chicken strips had a crisp outside and fluffy, tender meat inside. Certainly processed, but very good.

He got around it in a hurry, and was sitting back when Keisuke asked, "Sergeant Dalton?"

He responded, "Yes, what's up?"

"So what was it like for you guys for two years?"

Damn, did that trigger memories.

"Well, when we arrived we completely spaced out for three days. We just froze. I prayed. Doc kept inventorying stuff. We were spooked by every animal noise. I prayed. I don't really remember much else."

The man nodded. "Yeah, that sounds familiar."

"The LT, now the captain, moved us downhill to the river. There was dispute over that, I think. We were still hoping to get radio signal."

Keisuke shook his head. "We never did."

"Nor did we. We figured out we could reach each other and nothing else."

Keisuke shrugged. "We only had the one."

"Man, that sucks. We could talk between MRAPs. That clued us in."

He looked wistful. "Trucks would have been nice."

Rich went on. "We had to ground-guide them the whole way down. Then we bivvied, and a single native found us, and then we went to greet them. The Urushu. Friendly folks.

"We were still totally confused, and terrified. I hung onto my faith in God, but not much else, I admit. It was rocky. We talked to the natives—Urushu, then. And we moved upstream from them to a nice little creek on a rise. The captain had us build a palisade. I thought he was nuts, or just trying to keep us busy, you know? But then some group from about this time, from all the way over near what's now England, was also displaced. There were a couple of hundred of them. They moved in on the Urushu, and eventually we had a fight to try to displace them. And we had predators. So it turned out okay. We were actually turning into a trading village. Which was good, because we didn't have much to hunt with.

"We lucked out because Staff Sergeant Barker with us knew flint knapping and such. He got a tepee up right away, until we built other stuff. Caswell is very good with wild vegetables and plants and even found us berries and nuts for dessert. We had Staff Sergeant Alexander, and she was able to get a primitive network up for the phones, log and monitor everything, act as CQ, and she could spin and weave. SFC Spencer knows blacksmithing, and I gave him a rash of crap about it, but in spring the next year he started smelting iron. That was awesome. Barker built a sweat lodge that doubled as a smokehouse for meat, which made it easier than using the tepee fire. We kept burning our eyes out on smoke until then.

"Winter was nasty. We rotated on watch, which sucked since there was mostly nothing. And it was freaking cold.

"After the winter it got easier. We built a second tepee and used that for compacted snow so we had ice all year. We graveled things. I never actually expected Sergeant Spencer would get his forge going, but he did, and made us a lot of tools—shovels, axes, picks. We built a log cabin for each pair of us. Except then the other group displaced, the Gadorth, wanted a fight. Then we had Roman legionaries show up, and they wanted a fight. The palisade saved our asses.

"They had ten East Indian musketeers that Sergeant Spencer figured were from the 1600s. They didn't have enough numbers or tech, so they were basically specialists for the Romans. It was hilarious when they tried to impress us with their boomsticks. They fired one volley. Sergeant Caswell took down two goats at a hundred meters and rattled off a burst on auto. That pretty much shut them up.

"The Romans are tough bastards, though. Seriously. They tried twice to take us down, and then when we wanted to talk to them, they were pretty bent on being top dogs. They enslaved the remaining Urushu, and the Gadorth, which was kinda poetic, but I wouldn't wish that on anyone.

"So once things settled down, we were a trading village, and Doc was doing a lot of medical support for everyone.

"We built the smokehouse and sweat lodge. We even managed to smoke some bacon and make some wine, between our two awesome NCOs. Trinidad, Navy intel type with us, knew how to dig wells, from the PI. We had a screened latrine. Solar charging of phones and such at the trucks, which were our HQ and gunnery platforms—had to use that with the Gadorth. The phones were only good for a hundred meters or so, but that helped on watch, especially when it was cold.

"Then the Guardians showed up, and you've seen what their vehicles can do." He waved at the two trucks. "They had one, they'd been living in it, but suddenly we had hot showers and a better latrine, liquor, better food, some chemicals for working. Sergeant Spencer and Alexander got the meds they needed, and we got a lot of salt for curing stuff.

"So, with the Guardians and some extra tools, they helped build a hot tub, using the heater on their truck. That became a pilgrimage point for locals, and we basically got all our meat brought to us."

Keisuke looked sad, and pissed.

"Are you okay?"

"No."

"Need anything?"

"I guess I didn't actually want to know how shitty we had it by comparison."

He'd been so busy reminiscing...

"I'm very sorry," he said. "I can't tell the story to anyone else, and I didn't think about how our events were different."

"Yeah. We're here eating bugs and half-rotten meat, sleeping on sticks, and you talk about bacon, log cabins, and a fucking hot tub."

"I really am sorry."

Dammit, why had he done that? He'd let himself get distracted, and he was proud of their accomplishments, and that wasn't what these guys needed to hear.

Honestly, without the whole team, it was likely he'd be in this same spot now.

Sergeant Spencer put in, "Hell, we even got to change our underwear. Of course, I had to change with Doc, and Dalton had to change with Oglesby..."

That got everyone laughing, and the mood lightened again.

Spencer was good at that. He appreciated it.

Uhiara asked, "Say, Mr. Arnet, does Coca-Cola still exist? Obviously you have the recipe or something close."

Arnet replied, "I know of the brand and beverage. Our organizational approach differs from yours. But if you ask for Coca-Cola at one of the parties or venues, you'll be served."

"Well, that's good. Other brands of stuff, too?"

"Probably. I don't know which ones no longer exist." He grinned. "But certainly a great many do."

Rich took the change in conversation as an opportunity to bow out and take dishes for cleaning.

Sean Elliott enjoyed the clean air, currently very cool but very fresh with just enough breeze to move it. It was quite pleasant weatherwise. With the after-dinner cocktails serving social and medical destressing functions, and with a bit more distance from the local village, it seemed a good time to follow up further.

He asked the group at large, "You mentioned your other gear was secure, but not at this . . . your last location. A cave, you said?"

Keisuke said, "Oh, the LT stacked all the weapons in a cave, way back, over a ledge. Said he hoped they'd be found in the future. He buried a couple of the rucks with a flat rock he carved a message into. Lots of, 'Don't send us on this mission.'"

"Why didn't I think of that?" Elliot mused aloud.

Spencer said, "Because you're smart enough to realize it wouldn't work that way, sir. But now we have to retrieve those."

Munoz asked, "Why? If they don't matter, what's the harm?"

Spencer replied, "Because they could still get found, which wouldn't change being lost, because if it did you wouldn't be here, but could screw something else up."

Cryder said, "This is a third-order effect we'd considered. It'll have to be dealt with."

LT Cole said, "I still don't get it."

"I don't, really," Cryder said. "But the boffos tell me it's important."

Sean asked, "Okay, can you show us on an aerial where that cave is?"

Cole half winced. "Maybe. It's upriver a bit, uphill next to a bluff."

"How far is that?"

"From here? It was . . . most of a day from the village."

"Call it twenty-five klicks?"

"Probably. We were pretty used to humping by then. It wasn't hard. I didn't keep a pace count. Sorry."

Of course he didn't.

"Klicks? Kilometers?" Arnet asked.

"Yes. So, that makes it how far from here?"

"I can probably show you on a map."

"Okay. Cryder, can you bring one up?"

The tall man replied, "Yes I can."

It took him less than a minute to lay down his equivalent of a laptop, pull out a paper-thin screen the size of a posterboard, and have an aerial shot from their previous location up.

"The village is here. We were here. We are now here." He indicated by pointing.

Cole looked at the image, reached out, and traced along the river. He paused his finger at a bend with a bluff.

"About here. I can show you."

Cryder said, "I can send a drone and get closer images to make sure."

Sean nodded. "Okay, we'll add that to our priorities and deal with it. What exactly is stowed there?"

Cole recited slowly, obviously counting as he went. "Eleven rucks, helmets, and IOTVs. Ten weapons. One radio. Three GPS units. Eight cell phones. Six NODs. We kept the CamelBaks, clothes, sleeping bags, and woobies."

Cryder asked, "Why that cave?"

"Sir, it was a combination of that being a sacred site to them, and them needing us to separate from the old ways, basically, and me hoping that something would be discovered that led to us."

Cryder's drones had accounted for 547 empty 5.56mm cases in three locations, including nine from the village. That was far from the starting loadout of 300 for each Soldier.

"They're still sweeping that last place," he noted. "They'll likely find more, but the rate is slowing significantly. I presume there are others. If we find the locations, we'll get more."

Sean said, "I asked and interviewed at length, but they were both highly stressed and had no map reference. Even with these as markers, they have no idea where they might have gone next." That was as diplomatic as he could phrase it.

Cryder shrugged. "That's fair."

He seemed to mean it. Sean had no idea how badly the two Bykos had freaked out on finding they were lost, or if they had. But it was certainly reasonable for people under sudden stress of that level to do so.

"Lieutenant Cole," he said, "can you organize a sweep for firewood, debris, and general organization inside the perimeter? Your people, and any of mine who aren't otherwise occupied."

"Yes, sir," the man replied. On the one hand it was makework and everyone knew it. On the other hand, it did need to be done, and the troops needed to accept that Cole was still an officer. Then, Sean had to plan this recovery op, with input from Cole, so needed *him* to think of himself as an officer.

Cryder was still scanning images, and said, "I've aerial photos for Shug to look at, assuming he can comprend them. We'll find his location so we can re-home him."

"Good, let's try it." He turned and called, "SHUG!"

The boy came up from fire tending. He did well at maintaining fuel, cover, other prep work and perimeter patrol. He was probably bored as hell. He wore leggings under his tunic, and shoes a bit like moccasins, but did use a Byko-fabricated Gore-Tex jacket. A unique mix of garb.

Oglesby came along.

Sean explained, "These are pictures of the river from above, and from hilltop angles. Can you tell where your home is?"

Oglesby relayed it, and Shug looked confused, then curious, then reasonably informed.

"He'll try."

At least the boy was familiar with the concept of pictures, and could recognize things in them.

Cryder handed him a printout from a high altitude. Just how far could those little drones go?

Shug turned the image around from several angles, settled on one he liked, from the north. It took him a few minutes of tracing, but eventually he indicated several bends in the river.

Oglesby said, "He thinks it's one of those."

"Okay, can he describe the area? Outcroppings, hills."

There was back and forth.

"He says the one upstream of where he should be should have tall, bare rocks. It sounds like a fault that turned vertical."

"Hold on." Cryder scanned through the recording, narrowed down with finger motions, then turned his finger to rotate view.

"Is this it?"

Shug squinted and shook his head.

"Well, then we have to go downstream quite a bit." He did more scanning, following, rotating.

"This one?"

Shug got excited. He pointed and talked at length.

Oglesby grinned. "He's telling me all about it, but yes, that's it."

"Okay. I don't have images past that one, but I will tomorrow. Tell him we almost have it."

They knew where the lost element had hidden its modern gear. They knew where to take Shug. Things were shaping up well. Those done, they could try to recover a bit more brass and, apparently, not worry if they didn't get it. Then back to Bykostan and then home. Though there was also this possible other historical element they needed to know about. They were running out of days fast.

✧   ✧   ✧

The next day started with PT, sick call, and more summaries of the displacees' experiences. Those narratives would have to be vetted here for anything best kept unsaid. That included anything from smoking pot to sex with locals other than in the context of being married, species of game hunted, and various injuries and losses of equipment. In short, their reports were going to be fabricated bullshit for the bureaucrats, with certain facts furnished to the counselors, and other data that Doctors Sheridan and Raven would hide for their own purposes.

Martin Spencer and the captain were going to have to coordinate all that. In the meantime, he collared Burnham again.

"Sergeant Burnham, it's cocktail hour again."

"Absolutely, Martin. I wish this ritual would catch on in the Army."

Martin chuckled. "It was a thing around World War Two, I hear. I like it."

"Do they have plain old beer here?"

"I don't see why not. Let's ask." He raised his voice. "Arnet!"

The man stuck his head out from the CQ awning.

"I am here."

"Is it possible the kitchen can dispense something like beer?"

"Easily. Already programmed for my preference, but I can open it up for other types. Give me a mo."

Martin could see Arnet's hands swiping over the tablet he used to control everything.

When done, the man said, "You can mix anything you want, no matter how disgusting now. Or just plain old beer."

"Thanks. Much appreciated."

"Noprob."

He looked at the screen on the foldout surface, and used the touch keyboard the Bykos had helpfully set up.

He requested ALE, LOW HOP, HIGH MALT, BROWN, and waited to see.

It filled a cup, he grabbed it and took a sip.

"That's a respectable nut brown," he said. "And perfectly cool, without being iced."

Burnham tossed his head to one side. "Fucking amazing. Let me see if it can do a lager."

Apparently it could. Burnham typed, it filled, he sipped and nodded.

He said, "Well, this just makes the day perfect so far."

Martin replied, "Heh. Wait until I brief you."

He'd rehearsed a summary of how to AAR to please the system—what heroics to promote, what issues to keep zipped about, how to phrase interactions. He ran down the list as Burnham paid attention. The man seemed to be much mentally healthier than he had been, and better than most of the others.

Martin summarized and concluded with, "You absolutely can't mention anything that will get the EPA, EEO, or any other agency or group writing papers and issuing citations."

Burnham replied, "But if I'm following what you're saying, basically nothing happened. We met the locals and sat around eating venison for the duration."

He replied, "Venison is probably safe. Don't admit to hunting aurochs, any of the predators, any migratory birds. The fish are okay. You absolutely haven't killed any lions, tigers, bears, or antlered anything other than local deer."

Burnham stared. "I can't believe that's an issue."

"Our own debriefer very diplomatically told us not to mention anything about aurochs, specifically, since they're extinct."

Wrinkling his brow the same way Dalton had when he'd been debriefed, Burnham said, "Yeah, but long before we came about. In our time, I mean."

He nodded. "I know. Don't expect rational behavior from the government."

"I'll do it," the other NCO agreed, swigging more beer. "I believe you. But holy shit, man."

He nodded. "I know. Also, nothing happened to Noirot except she married a local."

The man looked properly pissed.

"Martin...I don't want to burn the LT for being in over his head, but she should not have to hide what happened."

He tried to be reassuring. "The counselors will know about it. Dr. Fairley, who I talk to, is very good, and knows all the stuff that never went on paper. The general treats us right. The bureaucrats get told what they need to file reports."

Burnham looked a bit less antagonistic. "Okay, I guess. For that matter, how do these bureaucrats not blab everything in their reports?"

"We were officially lost with a local tribe for six months with comms down and awaiting proper negotiations and safe passage back. Yours will probably be a month or so."

"But it's been five years..." He left it hang. He looked much older than thirty, and had a deer in the headlights expression.

"I know. The Bykos will reduce the aging a lot. You'll be very fit and not worse for it."

He nodded. "Got it. But I can't pretend things are normal."

Martin grimaced. "Yeah, I know. We're all doing what we can. Want another drink?"

The man sighed. "I shouldn't, but yes, please. More of that mango juice with rum."

"Cheers."

By dinner, Cryder had more overhead images of the river valley. Sean Elliott called Shug over to look at them. The young man took the sheets, turned them around, held them while turning himself in relation to the terrain, and then shouted out excitedly.

"That's it," Oglesby said. It wasn't really necessary. Shug was obviously pointing at something he recognized.

"He says his village is up that bluff, under the trees, partly visible in that clearing."

Cryder raised his eyebrows and said, "So it is. I hadn't seen that detail yet, but that's definitely a structure."

They knew where to take Shug.

Sean said, "That's tomorrow's mission, then." He raised his voice. *"My element!"*

They all appeared in short order.

"We know where to take Shug and that's tomorrow's op. I'll write it up."

Sergeant Spencer looked at the indicated point and said, "It's on the other side of the river."

Cryder said, "The vehicle can cross it. The current is slow enough and the depth isn't great. Means limited rations here when we take the kitchen vehicle. Will precook some stuff."

Spencer said, "Okay, then."

Sean took them at their word. Those little Hummer-size vehicles had insane capabilities by his standards.

He referred to his screen. "I'm sending Sergeant Spencer in command. Oyo to translate. Oglesby as escort for Shug and cross-check on translations. Caswell for cultural input as well. Dr. Raven for science stuff."

"'Science stuff,'" she repeated with a giggle.

"And anthropological stuff," he added. "Take Shug home, take gifts, be as diplomatic as possible and hopefully there's no action. Make nice, say goodbye from all of us, come back. Oyo will not be armed."

"It seems like a tidy element," Spencer agreed.

"Hopefully. We'll be here prepping to recover the abandoned gear. After that, we move to extraction point. We should be there for a few days, just getting it to look neat when we slag it."

Martin noted, "Aircraft would make this a lot easier."

"They would," Cryder agreed. "Two people can't support an aircraft and ground. Need at least five."

Spencer grinned. Sean remembered he'd been a flight engineer. "That's better than we'd do."

"Also, landing facilities will be a problem. We use these as support for ground, as you may notice." Cryder indicated the trucks and awnings.

"I have, and they're excellent for it."

"It does shorten the hike."

Spencer said, "We couldn't move our vehicles. Fuel was too limited. Had we been forced to stay, I could eventually have made alcohol fuel, but I have no idea how well it would have worked, or how long it would have lasted."

It was nice to hear the guy from the far future say, "You did impressively well with what you had."

Sean noted, "If I'd had an entire company, or at least a good-sized platoon, it would have been ten times easier. Anyway, rations, gear, weapons, and move out early so you've got the whole day for travel. Ideally you're back in three days or less. I've allotted a week, just in case."

Spencer replied, "Good planning, but if it takes more than four days, the festivities have gone from diplomatic to party, or from diplomatic to bad."

"Yes, but you can call for backup if you need to."

Raising his eyebrows, "I will do my best to avoid that necessity. Also, sir, that leaves you with four here, including Cryder and Dr. Sheridan."

"Yes, but there's more facilities here. I want you to have

enough muscle if you need it, and good translation options. It also shows that Shug is well regarded."

Sheridan said, "That is important. I may not be along, but I concur with the idea. Though of course, I'm a technical specialist, I can't judge the operational aspects."

Sean asked, "Cryder?"

"With Arnet driving and operating, you've an excellent setup for support. Leaves us a bit light, but external threats should be well controlled and your element here is in better emotional state."

Spencer seemed comfortable. He said, "Hooah. Oglesby, tell Shug this is it, and he can say goodbye to everyone in the morning."

"Yes, Sergeant."

Daniel Oglesby was up early, crawled out of his tent to drain and shower, and Shug was already awake.

"I greet you, Shug."

"I greet you, Dan."

"What would you like to eat?"

"The warm rice and bacon." The boy grinned. "I will miss those."

"Yeah, those are good." Dan dialed for rice pudding with a side of bacon for Shug, and then got bacon, eggs, and hash browns for himself. Hot sauce for the eggs, ketchup for the hash browns, and a cup of coffee with another of orange juice.

Others woke up and wandered over, got food and went to sit. It was gray dusk, cool, the air still and barely damp. The birds were active and loud.

Sergeant Spencer came over, squinty-eyed and looking frazzled. He dispensed two cups of coffee, chugging the first as the second poured, then keyed for ham with biscuits and gravy.

"God," he groused as he sat near them. "Slept like crap. It's theoretically reveille in ten minutes, but I think everyone is up." He started shoveling in the SOS with the ham in reserve.

Lieutenant Cole came over right then and said, "Just about. Sergeant Burnham is going to wake anyone left at oh six hundred."

"Thanks, sir. Saves me the trouble."

"Not a problem, Sergeant Spencer. You've done right by us. Thank you."

All three of the primary element's women came over together.

Dr. Sheridan said, "Shug, we made this for you." She held up one item as Caswell and Dr. Raven held the others.

It was a buckskin shirt, breechcloth, and leggings, with fringes and some beads, and a pair of sturdy moccasins.

He looked wide-eyed. He put down his plate and spoon, and stood up.

"Tank you!"

"You can shower and change before we go."

It took him a moment to parse that, but he nodded.

"Doctr Raben, please will you shape hair?" He indicated his head.

Dan asked him, "Do you want her to style it?" just as Raven asked the same in English.

He got the details and relayed, "He wants it pulled up with a hawk feather and some beads."

She nodded and smiled. "Yes, I can do that."

Everyone else got on with early morning routine, as Shug showered and changed, grabbed his spirit bag, spear, and knife, and came back to the CQ area.

He sat in a chair while Raven pulled his hair back, ran a comb through it, clipped it up with a stick tied with what looked like horsehair, and stuck in the feather and beads.

"How is that?" she asked, holding up a phone shot from behind.

The boy grinned.

"I look good!" he said.

The sun was up and burning off the early haze. The entire contingent lined up ready to see Shug off.

He hadn't been with them long, nor able to interact fully, but he was certainly part of the element. It was clear he was attached to them, too.

LT Cole shook his hand and said in English, "Your support has been helpful. For my people and my nation, thank you very much." He then translated into the native language to get the details correct.

Cryder echoed that with, "We have learned from you. We wish you well."

It went down the line. Dr. Sheridan hugged him.

"We'll miss you, but your people need you. Be well."

Then she handed him a bundle and said, "Shug, we'd like you to have this coat as a gift from our people." She shook it out.

It was coarse linen, quilted with what Dan assumed was fur or wool, trimmed with fur and embroidered with minimalist landscapes in line of thread. She'd done that by hand. Three rows of hills at the top led to fields in the middle, with boulders and a couple of happy little trees. To the bottom and foreground were visible stalks.

Shug teared up.

"Is vera beautful," he said in workable English. "Thank you much."

"Thank you for being a most interesting, honorable, and worthy guest," she replied.

With his coat, gifts, and small personal effects, they loaded into the vehicle and prepared to roll out.

CHAPTER 23

Jenny was impressed by how well these vehicles handled extreme terrain. Rocks, furrows, stumps, it just rolled over or around. Nor was the ride excessively harsh.

"Any idea how the suspension works, Sergeant Spencer?" she asked, hoping for a lay answer.

From the front, he said, "Very little. It appears to be hydraulic with a long range of flexibility. Other than that I can't say."

"And I wouldn't understand. But I was curious."

"I can't guess and Arnet won't say."

Arnet, driving, shrugged. "I can't explain the details anyway."

Spencer said, "It's very tempting to try to stay here—I mean, in their time—to learn it all."

"Yeah, but we'd leave our entire world behind, and families."

He nodded with tight lips. "I'd definitely miss my kids. I'm not ready for that step yet."

He didn't mention missing his wife, she noticed. She would make a point of never bringing her up unless he did.

From the back, Oyo commented, "This is so much easier than walking. We walked patrol, but rode to location and back. And since we got here, it's just been a slog every single day."

Jenny said, "We did all our construction, hunting, everything on foot. Our vehicles were parked once we found a site."

At the river, they stopped, and Arnet used what were obviously binoculars, while standing atop and scanning. He got back in and they rolled downstream a bit farther, twisting over rocks and riverbank.

They stopped again, he sprung easily up to the roof and scanned. Pointing, he said, "We'll cross right there."

"It's pretty wide here," Oglesby said. "And there's a herd of aurochs."

"Yes, that means it's shallow."

"Oh, right."

Back in again and they rolled over the silty, muddy bank, down into the shallows, and across. The animals snorted and mooed and ran out of the way. One bull tried to charge and bounced off. Arnet seemed to shift controls into some equivalent of off-road low gear.

Most of the trip was an easy roll. They hit a deep spot, and the motor note changed as the wheels or whatever spun for traction, finally finding it, bumping them onto a gravel bar. Then they splashed more, revved through another channel, and across more rivulets and rock.

"Lots of glacial runoff," Arnet commented.

"It's still like that," Spencer said with a nod.

"Also in our time."

That was a minor point, but she made note of it. They weren't too far in the future.

Near the far bank, there was one deep section where the motor howled, the truck bobbed downriver and spun forty-five degrees before the drive train caught something and rolled them up again. Shug laughed loudly, enjoying the ride without any concern.

"On the way back I'll remember to vault that at speed," Arnet said casually, as Jenny tried to calm her pounding pulse.

"Impressive," Dr. Raven said. "That's a lot of torque well applied."

Spencer loudly proclaimed, "I have got to get me one of these!"

"For rural Missouri?" Doc asked.

"And Arkansas, yes."

The vehicle was quite smooth over mixed terrain up to about twenty miles per hour. At faster speeds the ride got a bit bumpy, but not as bad as a HMMWV, and nothing like an MRAP.

By midday they were only a few kilometers east of the bend where Shug said his village was.

"Here we get out," Arnet announced. He popped hatches on

all sides, and the vehicle turned into an awning while they pulled out rucks and weapons and loaded up. Jenny had her regular M4, a patrol pack with CamelBak and two MREs, uniform change and supplies. The Byko fabric uniforms and hat meant no body armor or helmet was needed, which was a huge plus. Even the Army female-cut armor was a boob-squashing beetle case that made movement awkward and slow. This fabric would stop everything that would and more, and was basically a shirt. She wore an older-style vest with her magazine pouches, knife and IFAK.

Oyo was not armed. Dr. Raven was, and seemed familiar enough with an M4, so Jenny didn't presume to ask. The older woman raised it, checked chamber and safety, checked magazines on her vest, and slung the rifle. Doc had a Byko weapon. Sergeant Spencer had his uber-AR rifle in a caliber big enough to stop charging buffalo. Oglesby had an M4. Shug had his spear. They should be able to handle any local predator and small groups of hostiles.

Arnet told Oglesby, "Have Shug lead."

Oglesby relayed the message, Shug nodded, and took point. He strode easily across the landscape, leading them downstream and slowly away from the bank, and up.

It didn't take long to reach the bend, long and wide as it was.

Dr. Raven pointed and said, "This is a relatively recent meander, which is why it's still cutting into the bank. Depending on runoff and seasonal floods, this might only last a decade or a bit less."

"Interesting," Jenny acknowledged. She watched Raven pause and squat to take a sample of dirt in a tube that she marked as she walked, then slid into a pouch on her belt.

Sergeant Spencer said, "It's good terrain. It won't erode too rapidly, but they might wind up on an island if there's too much activity. An ice dam or heavy seasonal melt upstream."

"This bluff will all erode long before our time," Raven agreed. "Probably within a century or two."

There were obvious paths worn into the bank. Most were narrow and rutted from years of feet treading them down. Some were wider, where bedrock allowed. The growth had been trimmed by people with tools to make a clear passage. The tools changed over time, but the effect was the same: making nature fit human needs.

Ahead, Shug started calling. It was obviously a greeting.

Someone called back, a querying tone in their voice.

He shouted again, arms up and outspread.

A man appeared and came toward them, spear over his shoulder, but gripped short enough to swing into action. They were all in the open, and not threatening, so he seemed comfortable enough, but not easy prey.

He stopped about fifty meters out, and called a greeting.

Shug shouted back.

The contact looked confused, jogged in a bit closer, called again.

Shug replied with a nod and grin.

The man raised his spear. Then he lowered it. He closed the distance further, and stared. He looked back and forth at all of them.

Then he looked back at their escort and said, "*Shug sok repa?*"

Shug replied, "*Aka!*" loudly.

Then the two were hugging and laughing.

The exchange was obviously, "Where have you been? You haven't aged. It's been a long time."

Shug's reply was clearly, "I've been away, the gods took me somewhere else, to these people's land, and they finally found a way to bring me home."

"It's good to see you. Everyone will be excited."

"Let's go!"

The other man, named Gol, led the way, walking sideways to jabber at Shug as they went. The Americans followed.

At least it seemed safe enough so far. Hopefully this tribe didn't have any sexual demands for visiting dignitaries.

As they topped a slight rise, Gol started shouting. Then he grabbed Shug by the wrist and ran.

They had to sprint to close the gap, and Caswell tried to keep visual on the rest, and on Dr. Raven, trudging along as best she could on short legs with a bad ankle.

Fortunately, the village was right there. Wood and hide huts protruded from the embankment. She could swear that muddy slide was actually used as a slide by the kids when weather allowed. There were ropes and timbers marking walkways and handholds. Farther up it flattened out. This was the low suburb, apparently. Knapping and hide processing took place here, the messy activities.

They caught up as locals gathered around. They were a mix of shocked and thrilled. There were shouts and hugs. Some started dancing and singing.

Between Oglesby, Oyo, and Arnet's device, they had a pretty good translation of various goings-on.

Oyo was nearest Jenny and Raven and said, "His father is out hunting, will be back later and thrilled to see him. That's his mother and siblings hugging him. Friends over there, and the umma."

Oglesby monitored Shug. "He's explaining again about the gods and his trip. He's calling us friends who found him."

Arnet simply nodded. He appeared to be listening for any words that might indicate a threat.

Along those lines, Spencer had that .338 caliber rifle of his ready for anything large. Arnet and Doc had their space guns ready, as did she and then Raven, but it all seemed fine.

It was some time before the elation died down, and Oyo had to translate that time ran differently in other parts of the world, which wasn't at all true and would probably lead to some interesting myths, though Jenny wasn't sure if this was the root of stories like that, or if they already existed, or just developed independently.

It probably didn't matter.

A girl brought smoked meat and handed out strips all around. Maybe not girl. Probably an adult here, possibly sixteen or so. She seemed mannerly and aware of her role.

The umma came over to talk.

Oyo took the translation.

"He's very happy, and thanks us for bringing Shug back. They thought him dragged off by a leopard."

Spencer said, "He is most welcome, and we're very glad we could help, sorry it wasn't sooner. It took time to come back here, and the gods twisted the seasons around. We don't know why."

Oyo nodded and translated. She still seemed thrilled to be back in American company and eager to return.

"He wants us to eat and smoke and . . . visit."

"We will be happy to eat. Some of us smoke, but some spirits deny that as a sign of purity. If I get the other, all of us are mated or are forsworn while traveling, but we are very grateful for the hospitality, and wish to offer some gifts as well, since we couldn't make this sooner."

Jenny understood the exogamic drives here, but it would be nice if literally every encounter didn't have "wanna fuck?" involved.

No, she didn't. But the Americans did have magic spear points and pot. Magic points that would work until the magic was gone, then go away.

Spencer took over the presentation. The arrow points really were colorful, symmetrical, beautifully shaped, and valuable trade goods for these societies. The pot was, she understood, stronger than the local weed. He brought out a bag of drilled stone beads. Then he brought out a half dozen larger blades with antler hilts, with pouches for sheaths to hold accessories as well.

The village was very happy with these guests, and were still chattering and delighted at Shug's return. Good. Hopefully this time everything went smoothly.

The umma, Gora, apparently, was effusive. He also had a headdress, and pulled feathers and what appeared to be bear teeth out of it. He presented them with one of each. Jenny accepted gratefully, and asked, "May I put it in my hair?"

Oyo translated, "He says of course you may. He also has another gift and wants us to come with him."

Spencer said, "Sure. Caswell, come along, and Oyo. Oglesby, stay with Dr. Raven." He stood and indicated.

"Hooah." She stuck the feather through her hair band. It was probably from a large hawk or some kind of eagle.

Arnet fell into line, casually tossing something into the weeds that was probably one of his listening bugs.

The umma and his assistant led the way, apparently trusting the strangers. That was a good thing. No one had questioned women on the walk. Even better.

Into the woods and uphill they went, then along a path to a tiny clearing.

Inside the clearing was a small island of growth.

The copse was nothing but saplings, growing very straight. They'd been pruned by stripping twigs so there was only a lush crown, which was also topped to hinder main growth. The trunks below were about two inches thick at the base including bark, and split into limbs about eight feet up. They were perfectly bred spear hafts.

Oyo translated, "He says these are their magic-and-something spear trees. He wants us each to select one for ourselves."

Spencer said, "That's a pretty fucking special gift in context."

Caswell asked, "Yeah. Do we accept?"

The NCO nodded. "Absolutely. Ask him if we can do the favor of cutting them for ourselves, and the honor of cutting a fresh one for him?"

The umma was pleased with these strangers.

Spencer whipped out his folding saw, selected three saplings that looked particularly straight overall, and started sawing right at the base. If he did this cleanly, the roots should coppice and regrow within a couple of years. Good job.

The chief was very excited about the saw, pointing and gesticulating. It was very obvious he wanted one.

Spencer looked at Oyo and said, "Tell him sorry, it's a gift from our gods and we can't share. But we have more gifts at dinner."

She translated, the chief seemed to accept it, and was very pleased with how smoothly the haft was cut at root and limb. He was courteous.

The trip back felt quicker, downhill to a known point. In the upper village, the senior women and some men had dinner cooking over and in the fire.

The Americans were bade sit on benches made of split logs under a woven awning. There was what might have been an invocation, then the meal was served.

The roast venison, it seemed like, was well salted; the tubers were okay once soaked in animal juice. There were small fish, roasted whole. It was all served on a scraped out split wood platter, with long slivers of twig as skewers. For dessert, the baked apples were edible if tart, though Jenny did have to use a skewer to carefully scrape out some baked bugs that had been caught unaware as their home was put in the coals. She politely declined the roasted locusts and grubs, pointing to indicate what she had was plenty.

It was amazing how she'd gone from vegetarian bordering on vegan, to anything edible. Rough conditions did that to a person.

The place was very hospitable, and it seemed Shug was required to greet everyone, sample their food, accept blessings. They were definitely close knit.

As eating concluded, Sergeant Spencer said, "It's time for another gift."

Oyo translated.

"We bring some of our fermented drink, some made very strong by careful boiling and freezing with the right prayers and magic. Please share, and thank you for your hospitality, and raising Shug to be a fine young man who has helped us recover our lost people here in your part of the world."

He raised three containers of beverages, stunning ceramic jugs that would also go away in due time. The locals were very impressed with the workmanship, judging from the oohs and aahs.

He raised one jug to his lips and passed it to the umma, then the other. The first was wine, and it was received with grins and enthusiasm.

The second was rum.

The umma took a sip and clenched up at first. As in the previous encounter, he exclaimed in shock and probably thought it was poison, until the alcohol hit him. He took another careful sip, then a bigger one.

Laughing heartily, he passed it along.

Oyo, next to Jenny, said, "He says it's magically strong and to be careful."

"Good," she agreed.

She took a polite pull off each when offered, and passed them back around.

Dinner was followed by dancing and singing, though the singing was more akin to animal noises, drones, and hums, accompanied by several hollow percussion instruments—gourds, bones and sticks, plus flutelike bones that were a bit out of tune, but recognizable. Several dancers wore capes of animal teeth that rustled and clattered in rhythm, while someone else did rhythmic breathing that was almost throat singing. It echoed among the huts and trees and cliff face, in a weird resonance that was hypnotic.

One man plucked a bow to generate tones, stretching it across his toes to change frequency. Another ran a bone down his while rubbing the strings.

"Damn, that's almost a diddly stick," Oglesby commented.

Jenny grasped what he meant. She'd never heard the term. "Oh, is that what those things are called? Yeah, it is."

The dancers swayed rhythmically, stepping and stomping and waving batons and hides. It wasn't quite pantomime storytelling, but it was more than just simple steps. She listened to the raspy buzz of bows and the hollow call of the bone flutes. "They use the same scale we do," she thought out loud.

"Pentatonic A," Oglesby identified.

"That's a common scale, right?"

He nodded. "Very common, standard for blues."

"And they had flutes in that scale this far back?"

Spencer said, "Possibly thirty-five-K years. I'm not surprised by them here, but it is awesome to hear them. I recorded some on my phone. Hopefully we can keep it."

"I did, too," Raven said. "Beginning to end. Also some of the language for the intonations. I'm having nerdgasms here."

After a couple of hours, the performers chugged water from wooden jugs and gourds, sat back sweating, and wrapped in blankets of felted fur, or hide, breath misting.

Sergeant Spencer stood, and said, "We have one last gift for Shug, who has been a gracious guest, a help in translating with others, and a wise voice about local matters we don't know. Shug, this is for you." Oyo rattled it off in their language.

He brought out the gift, and Jenny raised her eyebrows. That was neat. It was a sizeable stone blade, probably six inches long and leaf shaped, attached to a long haft with very pretty wrapping and knotting, almost like Japanese sword grips. The wood was carved and burned in patterns, and there was a leather sheath with a shoulder strap. Shug tried it on, and it hung just below his ribs, in easy reach but not where it would snag easily.

The boy handled it with respect and awe.

"Thank you, Martin," he managed in decent English.

"Thank you, Shug. Use this with our thanks and blessings. You should show them your cape."

He nodded, grabbed his roll, opened it, and donned the fabric cloak.

There were appropriate oohs and aahs. They knew handwork had gone into it.

"We will leave in the morning. You are a fine people and we appreciate your presence. Your entertainers are wonderful."

Oyo translated again. She was competent with the local culture, but seemed happy to be heading home. If only the rest were like her.

They rotated on watch for the night, but there didn't seem any particular need. During her midnight to 0200 shift, Jenny sat across from the lone fire tender and patrolled the inner circle of the village, huddled in the Byko-made jacket. It was thin as a PT jacket and warm as a parka. It wasn't yet that cold here, but low forties without activity got chilly fast. Inside the jacket, though, was quite comfortable. The local man was dressed in a pullover hoodie of what looked like goat hide. It was probably quite warm. Under that he had leggings and ankle boots. She nodded at him opposite from time to time, and he nodded back with a smile. They had only a half dozen garbled words in common, so it really wasn't worth trying to talk. Anyway, she needed to be alert and not possibly distracted by someone who would be the obvious decoy for trouble.

But there wasn't any.

They were served a porridge for breakfast that seemed to be flavored with grubs and a half-developed egg. She managed a spoonful to be polite, nodded, and passed it on. No one seemed eager to try it. Doc and Spencer muscled it down, Arnet was utterly emotionless, indicating it was just business, and Raven made an awful face.

Shug was dressed in something more formal, a pullover in sueded, smoked leather with a few bits of antler and shell attached. He was with his parents and siblings, from a baby of perhaps two up to adults who may have been younger than he but were now older, physiologically. The relationship was obvious, though the eldest might have had a different father.

He insisted on hugging each of the party, then making a clap in front of them. She recalled the Urushu shaman had jumped and clapped above a person's head as a protective invocation.

She hugged him, and he seemed so young and lost again, even as he was home. She clapped and nodded back at him.

Very carefully, he said, "I will miss you, Zhenny."

"I will miss you, Shug. I know you will grow and learn, become wise, and be of great benefit to your family and village."

Oyo helped translate that.

"Yes," he agreed. "Thank you."

Dr. Raven said, "Our researchers—call them shamans for translation—are very pleased with what he has told us of his people. We will keep his name in our stories."

When that was translated, there was a ripple through the crowd. That had definitely raised his status from "lost boy" to "worthy adventurer."

With those finished, there were waves, and they started the trudge back to the hidden vehicle.

Right then, Arnet cupped his ear, said something fast and complicated, turned and told them, "We're needed back at camp. Run."

She moved to double-time with the rest, then hung back to ensure Dr. Raven would make it. The heavy woman ran at a trudge, wincing every time her bad ankle bent.

Jenny offered, "I don't know what I can do to help." She wanted to do something, but...

Raven replied through gritted teeth, "There's nothing you can do, but thanks. I'll make it."

Her pace was decent. It was obviously taking a toll on her.

In five minutes of rough cross-country running, they were at the vehicle, and Arnet didn't take any niceties with terrain. The vehicle bounded across hummocks and between trees, careening over rocks, and making very respectable speed. Whatever suspension it had smoothed things a bit, but the impacts were jarring and hard.

CHAPTER 24

Rich Dalton woke up drooling. On the half-frozen ground. In the weeds.

It wasn't drool, it was stinky, greasy, lumpy vomit.

Another heave caught him, but it was just acid, rasping the back of his throat.

He got to hands and knees, feeling very nauseous and disoriented.

The crap?

Cryder arrived at a run, slapped a patch on his neck.

"Poison," he explained. "In the food."

Munoz had poisoned them.

"I was worried about him spitting in it or not washing his hands."

"He's gone, along with Lozano."

"Fuck, I thought Munoz was all in to get home and try to sue."

He looked around. Captain Elliott was functional. He was on his knees, talking to Cryder who squatted in front of him, nodding. Dr. Sheridan staggered over with a bottle with some sort of fluid. She said something and offered it, and the two leaders took a swig each. She headed his way.

Sheridan stood in front of him. "Best we can come up with on a guess," she said. "This should counter the poison somewhat and clear your guts."

He nodded, accepted the bottle, took a gulp, and it was orange-flavored goo.

It was soothing as it went down.

Cole stumbled over from where he'd collapsed. There was used food on his face, down his uniform, and on his right hand.

Rubbing his neck with the other hand, he said, "Lozano probably reminded him about young pussy and no need for Army discipline. He was always a mouthy fucker."

Rich commented, "Yeah, well, let's get them."

Elliott said, "Without accusing anyone of anything, it's even more impossible for any of the displacees to be trusted at this point. We don't have time for long discussions, chases, whatever. I've asked Cryder to tighten the wards. If you try to leave, you will be stunned. If that happens, you get an invisible fence collar. After that, detention tent. I'm sorry, and I know it shouldn't be necessary, but I can't take any risks with the safety of the rest."

"I understand," Cole replied. "At the same time, that's going to be even worse for morale."

"You're going home—starting home at least—in four weeks. *That's* your morale. I wish I could offer more. It's going to be a long road to recovery."

"Yes, sir."

Cryder held up a tablet and said, "Got them. Only option is hard stun, await for Arnet, then we can retrieve."

Rich asked, "Why not retrieve now?" His voice was still gravelly.

"Can't leave the camp insecure. Can't entrust a vehicle to non-Bykos without escort."

"I see." The caste system put the displacees at the bottom, but the other Americans weren't much higher.

Cole's smirk was one he wanted to punch, if he wasn't an officer. Then he reconsidered. The man at least understood there was more than one hierarchy here, and it wasn't personal.

He didn't want to ask how much more fucked up things were going to get, because he knew they probably would.

In the meantime, Captain Elliott ordered, "Everyone shower and clean up, see Doc for a quick check, stay near the firepit for accountability. Dalton, you and I stand armed guard and swap off with Arnet if a shower seems feasible. Dr. Sheridan, can you assist?"

Rich replied, "Hooah, sir." It was good to have a decisive officer giving intelligent orders. He jogged over to Cryder, took the lump the man handed him, and transformed it into the heavy stun setting. He and Elliott stood across from each other, well outside the firepit, watching each other and the recoverees, now detainees.

Sheridan held a weapon and split the circle in three, giving them better coverage.

"Keisuke, you're first, then by rank. Clean up quick and get back."

"Yes, sir." The man nodded and ran.

Cryder was armed with something larger and heavier than before, and obvious armor with a helmet now. He took up position as well. He was talking into his helmet, presumably to Arnet. Though it could be programming for the system.

When the man paused, he asked, "Cryder, can you explain what happened?" He wasn't sure it was a good time, but figured the Byko would evade the question if need be.

Cryder replied, "Munoz put something toxic in the food. Don't know if it's some native plant, if he found a way to program the dispenser, or took something from the science station."

Sheridan said, "We don't have anything on hand that would do that. But . . . we did get the dispenser adapted to take our requests for food."

Cryder's helmeted head shifted, as if he were cocking it to one side and nodding.

"I see. If it wasn't given a hard limit, it's quite flexible. I'll fix that."

Yeah, Rich remembered that. Apparently, the kitchen wasn't limited to just edible stuff.

Cole offered, "He was pretty good with laptops back on post way back. Cleaning out malware, updates, whatever. It wouldn't surprise me if he learned how to pull a file."

Cryder said, "Not a file. I can think of several ways to do it that wouldn't trigger any warnings. Fixing that now." He swiped at his tablet. "You'll be limited to video and audio, and will have no access for material selection. You'll need to request your meal options. I've set some standards for after hours so you'll have limited variety."

Cole replied, "That's decent of you, and I apologize for these circumstances."

Cryder replied, "Your comprehension and acceptance are appreciated."

Yeah. Still, this was messed up. They were supposed to recover these troops, and you'd think they'd be grateful.

Then Rich realized most of them were, and they each had their own struggle with life or God or both.

Cryder suddenly spoke into his communicator, and there was the sound of brush being smashed, faint and distant, but growing quickly. In a few moments the vehicle appeared, doing a very good off-road run. It slowed, cruised to the wards, and rolled in.

The occupants unassed in a hurry. Spencer had his .338. The rest had Byko weapons. They were loose and ready.

At once, Arnet asked, "Where are they?"

Cryder replied, "Still tracking. Approx two four five marks, six kilometers. They made good time."

They were using modern English. Interesting. They were sharing the info.

Arnet ran to the other vehicle, ducked down, stood up, and he was an armored giant, too.

"I'm connected to system."

Cryder said, "I'll lead the retrieval. I'd like to take Sergeant Dalton and Lieutenant Devereaux for combat and medical support."

Elliott said, "I agree and concur."

Cryder nodded and pointed. "Thank you. Soldiers, let's board."

Rich took shotgun, Doc got in back. He still felt queasy, but water stayed down and he could jog a little.

Cryder's helmet sectioned itself back almost like Iron Man's. That movie would never be the same after this. Rich wondered what other capabilities it had.

The bumpy ride over lumpy terrain almost spilled more of his lunch. He sipped water and watched a fixed point ahead. Apparently these vehicles had plenty of speed off-road, if you didn't care what the ride felt like. He estimated they were doing fifty. At least it was a short ride, barely three minutes. The differences between foot marches and vehicles were stark.

"We hold here," Cryder announced. "They're closer than a kilometer."

They weren't any farther than six kilometers from the base. If the men were smart, they'd have moved a lot farther, a lot faster. They obviously underestimated the Bykos' tech abilities.

Cryder scanned an aerial view and marked on a screen. It was a route that kept terrain between the two men and the vehicle. They shouldn't see anything, and as long as Cryder drove carefully, not hear anything, either.

With the vehicle max camouflaged, it wasn't hard to get closer to the two escapees. Cryder took it slowly and followed terrain, to minimize brush noise. The engine was effectively silent. Munoz and Lozano apparently thought themselves safe for now, two ridges away, in a tree-ringed hollow. Cryder's drone, or perhaps a directional mic, brought the audio in.

They were using the native language.

Rich exclaimed, "Crap, get Hamilton and Oglesby on the net."

Cryder said, "That's my intention."

It took under a minute for him to contact Arnet, get the two, and get them listening.

Hamilton said, "It's mostly idle chitchat about fucking women and how the hunting looks. They plan to head north from there to the river, then turn back east . . . they're not sure about whether to go around the sword group's camp, or quietly nearby. Lozano thinks he can make a sneak."

Cryder looked over and said, "The drones have too limited payload capacity for recovery, but can be used to stun, or to drop small charges to herd them a bit."

Since he was being asked, Rich said, "The former sounds better. I suspect they'd just dodge any fire and sprint."

Doc agreed. "I concur. Seems minimally forceful, from what I know of your stunners.

"Can you just get in there and zap them? We can heave them aboard easily enough."

"That seems optimal, unless there's anything else you need."

Doc shook his head.

Rich said, "No. I don't think they're going to reveal any treasure or anything."

"Okay, down it goes."

Seconds later, both men slumped into the terrain.

"Let's move." He reached for the door release.

Cryder raised a hand and said, "I can get closer." He gunned the engine, however it was powered, and the vehicle lunged silently across the slope.

Even with its futuristic suspension, it was a rough ride, jolting them into the air and slamming them back down. Rich was glad the roof was open. He understood the hoods on the Byko uniforms served as helmets, and possibly the cap he wore did, but it would still be hell on the back and neck. It was bad enough as it was, his spine grinding into his tailbone, into the seat, then up and almost weightless for a moment, which sickened his abused stomach, then dropped it back down into his guts.

Just before Rich heaved again, Cryder pulled up about twenty meters from the two unconscious soldiers.

"Hell, that makes it a lot easier." He meant the end of the maneuver, not the closeness to the scene.

"You're welcome."

Doc said, "We'll get them. Do you have restraints?"

"Yes."

Shortly, both men were trussed with futuristic cable ties, elastic enough to maintain blood circulation in the bound wrists and ankles, tight enough to hinder movement. Those were hooked to padeyes that extruded from the inside surface.

Doc examined them, seemed satisfied, and said, "Okay, back we go. I'm also wondering if we need to collar them all."

Cryder replied with a shift of his head, "It might be a good idea, but I leave the social ramifications to you."

Rich agreed, "Yeah, there is that. Definitely for these two. Possibly for anyone else if they mouth off at all."

"I have the gear if you need it."

Doc thumbed his chest. "I'll suggest it to the captain."

"I'll support you, sir," Rich agreed.

Martin Spencer shouted, "Listen up! Formation, right now!"

Yeah, this wasn't going to be fun.

His own element was prompt. Most of the recoverees were reasonably fast. He noted Maldonado lagged last. It might be coincidence, but there was little trust left. The two scientists stood back, present but not in the military formation. The two prisoners were inside their awning.

He turned and saluted Elliott, and said, "Element present and ready for your comments, sir."

Elliott saluted back with, "Thank you, First Sergeant." He raised his voice. "Post."

Cole marched forward and stood in front of his element as Burnham stood behind. Elliott took position behind their short squad.

Elliott started in directly.

"Company, at ease. We all know what happened and approximately how. The system has now been secured so that can't happen again. That also means menu choices are limited. You'll have to wait for anything you want that's not handy, and you will not wake our Byko element because you're hungry for ice cream. Clear?"

There was a chorus of "Hooah."

"Additionally, and I hate that it comes to this, the recovered element is getting fitted with what are basically invisible fence collars."

There were grumbles and outraged exclamations.

"At ease!" Martin reminded them.

Elliott resumed. "You'll need permission to go anywhere or you get zapped. It's a bullshit idea, but that's where we are. We're taking you home, and you will have to deal with it. My orders are to return you alive and as fit as possible, and that's what happens until I pass you on to other authority. Got it?"

"Hooah." It didn't sound enthusiastic, just an acknowledgment.

"Thank you. Lieutenant Cole, please have your element line up over here when we break. Element, attention! Fall out."

They definitely grumbled, and Cole did the right thing by stepping up first, followed by Burnham. They all acted as if these were a combination of dog collars, fetish slave collars, and actual slave collars, and that's pretty much what they were.

Noirot looked concerned, and directly said, "I can't handle anything tight around my throat."

Arnet replied, "It will be loose and comfortable, you just won't be able to remove it."

"Thank you." She sounded relieved. The collar was a stiff loop of cable that wouldn't fit past the jaw, and merged back into itself when fastened. It was a plain hoop of dark olive that looked like plastic. Kita mumbled something, and Noirot shook her head. Martin gathered she wanted one, too.

No, kid, you really don't.

Uhiara looked pissed to the point of being murderous, but his laserlike glare was directed toward the two prisoners detained in side-by-side awnings. He knew what had led to this.

Cryder personally walked over to the two-cell prison.

He held up the collars and said, "I can put these on you, or using slang I heard from Sergeant Spencer, I can beat you like a left-handed, redheaded stepchild, and put these on you. Which will it be?"

The man was wearing his uniform pants and a T-shirt, and was ripped. He was 6'6" and probably 280 pounds, in a physique that looked like a recruiting poster.

Both nodded evenly without evident fear or anger, but they were compliant. Cryder opened the awnings in turn, snapped the rings around their necks, and closed back up.

Martin was glad to see they accepted this reality.

Cryder raised his voice. "Everyone pay attention for a moment, please."

He waited a few seconds as people raised their heads, turned, or otherwise took note.

He then touched a control on his tablet and both prisoners dropped to the ground, shaking as if electrocuted, and making "Ahaaahaahaaa!" noises. The jolt stopped, they cautiously rolled to their knees, then back up. Now they looked pissed.

He spoke clearly to everyone. "That's two on the scale from one to ten. Ten will put you in the box for organ failure. Not going to debate any instructions. I'll just start zizzing people. Understood?"

There was a chorus of hooahs.

"Also, your phones are now limited to chain of command and entertainment, no talking to each other."

Martin realized a demo had been necessary, though he wondered if that was a bit harsh. On the other hand, Munoz had poisoned him, and both deserted. A little zap was probably the low end of what a court-martial equivalent might do.

He just hoped no one fucked up to where they all had to be collared.

He'd reiterate to everyone that the Byko were gracious hosts but had no room for bullshit and no sentimentality at all. They were perfectly willing to kill to accomplish their goals. They'd even discussed it in council.

CHAPTER 25

Amalie Raven made a discovery when she started work for the day that pissed her off pretty thoroughly. Those two fuckwits had caused the Byko to tighten up their system, and the access she had was gone. She didn't dare ask about it, and hoped they hadn't identified her leak. She didn't want to answer questions and sure as fuck wasn't going to wear a slave collar. Someone would be bleeding out before that happened. That meant she really couldn't try to access the system again. Some of the troops could play dumb and get away with it. Some of them wouldn't even need to pretend. However, Cryder knew her background and skill set and would assume intent on her part.

On the plus side, neither of the Russian mountains, as she thought of them, had said anything about it. She also remembered a good portion of what she'd processed and discovered from their net. She ran through, committing it to memory and pondering if she should write any of it down in her own coded shorthand.

On the negative side, her ankles didn't like the cold, yesterday's sprint, or the impending weather change. Then, migraine about to start. She actually felt like a shaman, predicting a weather change without any tech needed. It was probably a warm front, by 5°F or so.

Right then, Cryder came over.

"Doctor Raven, I need to talk to you," he said. Damn, that baritone and accent.

"Yes?" she replied, trying not to panic.

"You're reasonably well read in tribal matters generally."

She felt a bit less tense and said, "Yes, paleoanthropology is one of my minors and I've worked in multiple cultures."

"Come along while we recover the abandoned gear? It's in a cave they believe is sacred. I've no background for it."

That let her relax the rest of the way.

"I can offer what I know on-site or by drone. Right now, my ankles are killing me and my head is about to explode as the weather front moves in."

"Will Arnet's treatment enable you?"

"Yes," she agreed.

"Good. Please see him. I welcome your input. Thank you."

He left, just as Sheridan came from the food truck with a rolled-up waffle. The woman had no impulse control and starch was going to kill her. They were apparently really good waffles. Amalie hadn't tried one. She didn't need to trigger crack-like cravings for stuff she couldn't have.

She said, "I'm going on their recovery operation today. Can you manage without help?"

Sheridan said, "On my stuff, yes. I can probably get someone to help pass samples back and forth. On your specialty processes, they'll have to wait. I'll be busy."

That was actually perfect. She didn't want her putative boss screwing around with the real data.

"That's fine. If I'm a bit behind, I'll just work into the night. We'll be back from this thing when we're done."

"Good luck."

"Thanks."

She walked stiffly and gingerly up to the CQ. Arnet was lounging under the awning, stood up as she approached, and asked, "Sick call?"

She replied, "Ankles troubling from yesterday's thing. Headache from weather. General offput from not being comfortable. Whatsisname said to see you."

Arnet replied, "You appear to have mild aphasia."

"Yeah." She nodded. "Storm hurt brain." It was hitting her badly.

The man turned to his concoctions and long seconds later handed her a tube.

She drank it down, and felt ice-cold clarity seep back into her neurons. Then her fatigue retreated in a warm mist that felt like waking from a refreshing nap. Her calves stopped aching, and her ankles at least felt half as swollen, if not actually healthy.

"Thank you," she said in relief. "That was a pretty bad hit. I'm estimating pressure drop at about a thousand pascals."

The man glanced at his screen, raised his eyebrows, and said, "Close estimate. It's dropped one zero five three in the last hour."

"Yeah. When does the storm hit?"

"It looks like we'll avoid it, just overcast and dark."

"Good. Do you think I'm fit to function? And thank you very much." She was always embarrassed at how stupid she sounded when her brain fogged up. She also rarely realized it until it was on her.

He said, "You should be fine. The medication isn't just palliative. It does some reconstruction. Though obviously there are limits in the field. If our medics can do more before you return, it will help longer term."

"Why didn't they before we transitioned here?"

"Did you ask?"

Oof. "No. It didn't occur to me."

"Apologies," he offered with a slight nod, not quite a bow. "Our cultural privacy is not to ask or offer unless the subject is raised first."

"I can see that," she agreed. "Please consider the subject raised, and I welcome any help possible."

"Roj. I'll make a note for our debrief."

"I greatly appreciate it. Thanks again."

With that, and feeling mostly fit as a fat thirty-five-year-old with bad ankles could, she walked down to her tent to grab gear.

Cryder was leading the recovery, along with Captain Elliott and Sergeant Spencer. Having the two seniors along and the senior NCO seemed unusual. She was along for "science stuff," as they put it, which was quaint, but she appreciated that they realized the relevance. Oglesby was along as support and to cross-check translations. Hamilton apparently knew where everything was and rounded out the group. He wasn't armed, and he still had his collar.

The two officers ran down a checklist of weapons, food, water. The clothing everyone wore should be proof against natural damage and anything made of stone or bone. The Byko tech and process greatly abbreviated premovement prep. In minutes, they were aboard the vehicle and rolling straight through the wards.

They drove west and slightly north, roughly paralleling the river, largely back the way they'd come a few days before. She kept an eye out, but nothing looked familiar. If they were only a few hundred meters off, she wouldn't recognize anything. This was all fresh territory.

Cryder drove hard and fast, too. The seats were well cushioned against bounce, and the undercarriage, whatever it was, had some flex. It took only a couple of hours to reach a section upstream where rolling terrain turned to bluffs.

Spencer exclaimed, "Holy crap, this area looks familiar."

Cryder replied, "If you're thinking of the bluffs from the last displacement, it's similar, but nearly one hundred kilometers distant."

"Erosion only takes so many forms, I guess."

"I think so. Specialist Hamilton, is this correct?"

The man nodded. "I think so, sir. It looks like where we stopped to camp and do some sort of stoner prayer."

"'Stoner prayer'?"

"We called them Stoners until we joined up, and there was some sort of fasting and praying before we went in the cave."

"I see. We should proceed, then."

They popped the doors and debarked, Amalie feeling reasonably fit, but she'd reserve judgment until they finished hiking up to a cave. In the vehicle the temperature had been perfect. Outside it was cold but clear, and the sun felt good. Cryder locked it by remote, like any twenty-first-century car, and it shimmered and faded into the growth, still visible as an outline, but disrupted.

With everyone carrying backpacks, mostly armed, and ready to move, Cryder said, "Lead the way."

Hamilton hesitated.

"I only really saw it from a distance, four years ago. It's up that way for certain."

Cryder nodded. "That's fine, take lead."

Hamilton shrugged and started walking.

Spencer said, "Sir, I recommend a bit of spacing. Not combat distance but, say, three meters or so in case the terrain has issues."

Elliott chuckled. "I was just about to give that order. But I appreciate the support."

"Sorry, sir."

"That's the spacing, everyone got it?"

"Hooah." She joined in because it was convenient, and to avoid standing out. It was ingrained habit from that recovery in Afghanistan, where she'd been one of a half dozen civilians stuffed into uniforms and trying hard to avoid looking important enough for enemy sharpshooters. At least here she didn't need body armor and a helmet.

They slogged uphill fast, and she was quickly winded trying to keep up, as the terrain progressed from scrub slope to rocky crags with grass and brush protruding. It was too narrow for the vehicle, though it would certainly handle the climb on a broader track. As they got farther upslope and upriver, there was more green and brush, and she had to be careful of her ankles at every step. The cool air became pleasant as she sweated.

Sergeant Spencer dropped back and paced her.

"You doing okay, ma'am?" he asked.

"I have shorter legs than you giraffes," she half joked.

He replied at once, "True. Want me to slow the pace?"

She thought and said, "I do, but I don't want to hinder anything we're doing."

"We can slack it off a little," he said. Raising his voice, "Hey, short legs in back. Ease the pace, Hamilton."

"Hooah, Sergeant!" the man called back, and did slow somewhat.

"Thanks, that helps," she said in relief. It was still a brisk pace and an ankle-breaker of a hike, but she could breathe and wasn't experiencing stabbing pains yet.

He told her, "We've traveled about three kilometers while climbing about two hundred meters, on very rough terrain. That's a stiff hike for anyone not in regular mountain training."

It wasn't long before they bunched up. Hamilton was at least breathing a bit hard. The rest were panting a bit, except Cryder, who didn't seem at all stressed.

"I think that's it," Hamilton pointed. "Right direction at least."

There was definitely a cave up there, in a long, descending crack that widened.

The bushes moved, and suddenly there were people out front who looked concerned about them approaching.

✧   ✧   ✧

"Well, shit," Sean Elliott muttered. "I guess we need to try some diplomacy."

Cryder said, "I prefer diplomacy, but I'm not willing to wait long."

"Yeah, so what do we tell them? Hamilton?"

The man stepped over.

"I'm not really sure, sir," he admitted. "It's a sacred cave and they do other things here. I'm not sure how our tribe got access. We didn't speak the language much at the time, and I didn't ask since."

Sean asked, "If we radio Lieutenant Cole, will he know?"

"Maybe, but I don't think so."

"Well, let's do it. Spencer, keep an eye on that pair up there."

"Four of them now, sir."

"Noted."

Cryder spoke into his tablet, for want of a better word. It controlled everything, and Sean wondered what would happen if he lost it, though it was attached to the man's uniform with a lanyard that was probably stronger than an anchor chain, despite being the thickness of a USB cable.

"Call Arnet. Cryder request Lieutenant Cole."

Arnet responded immediately with, "Stand by, Shuff."

Moments later, Sean heard, "This is Lieutenant Cole."

He said, "We're at the cave. There's a native contingent here. What information do you have on access and permissions?"

"Uh...ask, I guess. It was empty when we got there but we had to do some praying and stuff. That's probably the way in. It's like a church for them. Voices quiet, listen to the usher, very holy."

"We'll attempt that, thank you."

Cryder looked at Sean, who looked back with a shrug. He turned and ordered, "Hamilton, please call up to them and tell them we need to enter. What is the best way for us to do so?"

"Yes, sir. I guess I just ask."

The man turned to talk, and Sean muttered softly, "Oglesby, check him."

"I always do, sir," the man replied.

Hamilton waved, called, and asked. It was pretty obvious the response was a negative, complete with curt voices, knife hands, and headshakes.

He turned back.

"Sir, they say they don't know who we are and the spirits won't allow us in. We must leave at once. There's some sort of ritual in a few days and they're keeping the cave holy from animals and they definitely won't allow people in."

Cryder asked, "Think there's any way to negotiate?"

"No, sir. They're pretty serious."

"Okay."

Cryder unslung his weapon, raised it as it morphed, and swept it across the cave mouth. There was a faint buzzing with a high-pitched wail. All four sentries fell over, and something dropped out of an overhanging tree branch.

Dr. Raven spoke quietly and urgently.

"I understand you have to juggle speed with diplomacy, but I don't think this is going to help any of the latter."

Cryder apparently heard her and replied, "My scientists would say same, but no time to socialize. Follow me quickly. Stun anyone you see."

"How long are they out?" she asked.

Cryder spoke over his shoulder as he ascended the bluff.

"Twelve hours, max safe load for healthy males."

Good enough. Sean followed along, pointing at Hamilton to stay with him, Oglesby to accompany Dr. Raven, and Spencer to cover the rear. There were strewn rocks, random weeds, protruding tree roots. They did make great handholds for climbing, when they were solidly mounted. They also were a trip hazard and some dislodged. He found that out when he grabbed a protrusion and the rock ripped loose and rolled behind him.

"Rock!" he announced as it bounced downhill.

He waited for his climbing buddy. "What's your take, Hamilton?" he asked as he trod over downed greens.

"Uh, honestly, sir?"

"Always, please."

"Yeah, it's gonna piss them off. The tribes do talk, and we're already a thing they talk about. They're going to hear about this and zapping Argarak. We won't be welcome here again."

"Hopefully in a few days that will never be a problem again."

"If it all works, yes, sir. I'm eager to get home, but I don't want to screw things up here if we don't have to."

Ahead, Cryder bounced lightly up the incline like a two-legged mountain goat, and reached the shallow scree slope in front of the cave. There were marks hammered on the inward curves of the rocks that seemed to be some sort of notice or tribal designation.

The man scanned the sentries with a wave of a wand, seemed satisfied they were out cold, and started dragging them where their heads were slightly elevated. Sean moved to help, then followed as Cryder led the way in. A strip on the front of the man's shirt lit the way ahead of him. He also had those NVG that looked like shades. His gear had everything.

Sean lit his own chest light and followed, directing Hamilton ahead of him, ensured Raven and Oglesby were close behind, and trusted Spencer to bring up the rear.

His shirt didn't light up, but he had a perfectly good head-light on a band that he slipped around his forehead. Behind him were other lights.

It was evenly cool in here, though actually warmer than outside, fifties rather than forties. It was definitely damper and with a smell of moss and mold. Water dripped and he could see a few trickles.

Cryder asked, "Which way?"

Hamilton replied, "Um, sorry, sir, but I didn't get to come in. I know it wasn't far in."

Spencer said, "I knew we should have brought Cole."

Cryder was blunt. "Cole is incompetent and I don't trust him. I've the rough map he drew for me. We'll work with that."

The cave led quickly down over worn sedimentary rock, and tumbled rubble. Behind, Oglesby assisted Dr. Raven literally step by step, walking ahead and letting her lean on his shoulders for support. For the rest it was just rough terrain with reasonable step distances for the most part. Some rocks were jagged, others tumbled to coarse roundness, and a few near the watercourses smoothed by limestone deposition.

At the bottom of the crusted slope, with shadows reflecting and dodging everywhere, each of them looking like the shadow of a rising hostile, was a shallow trickle of stream. Then they were climbing back up.

This deeper section of the cave was smoother, and seemed to be from a different geological form. He turned and saw the small bright slash of the entrance, and Dr. Raven getting her feet under her at last. He asked her.

Through panted breath, she said, "It's not my field, but I'd speculate this is old erosion from glacial runoff, and it was exposed by that stream, which seems to be seasonal from uphill. We crossed a small brook outside, which is probably this. The scree outside and inside suggests some sort of tremor made the opening. If they were around to witness it, or just found it one day where it hadn't been, that would definitely make it a special site, along with how we know primitive peoples liked caves for many reasons."

"That makes a lot of sense, thanks," he replied.

Ahead and slightly up the V-shaped incline, Cryder said, "I have it."

Martin Spencer loved caves. Kentucky had a lot of them. He hated being alone, or last in line. His back itched constantly, psychosomatic. He was angry about it, but knew it was a thing for him.

Cole could have picked an easier place to abandon gear, Martin thought. He wasn't sure why it had to be this secret cave. For that matter, the man could have buried or burned stuff or just tossed it into deep water.

The cave was dark, echoey, the shadows nightmarishly creepy. He didn't like any of this, but it was the assigned task. He clenched up and trod along, reaching to caress the rifle over his shoulder and check the safety by touch.

Worst of all, Cryder was the real backup, and he was all the way up front. Raven could shoot, but he had no idea how she reacted under stress. Oglesby and the captain were okay. Hamilton wasn't armed.

But there was nothing here, it was just a cave.

That the locals had guards to keep animals out of.

Ahead, the ceiling lowered, the floor leveled out, and Cryder held up a hand.

"Here."

Martin hurried to catch up with the rest.

Cryder held up ... a butterfly? Martin guessed it was a drone, though whether mechanical or biological or both he couldn't guess.

It flew too directly to be natural, so one way or another it was engineered. He assumed, though, that it had a random setting for concealment. There literally was no way to ever be private in their world. He shuddered. The servant programs furnished the only privacy possible, but even they had data, which meant someone could hack it. Either they had absolutely bulletproof ID and coding, or just didn't care about embarrassing things people might have done.

"I see rifles, racks, and other gear," Cryder said.

"Racks?"

"That you carry gear in."

"Ah. Backpacks. Or rucksacks. Rucks."

"Thank you. Those. We'll switch tools," he said, as the butterfly landed on his hand to be inserted back into a pocket.

He started making gestures in the air, which was still disconcerting, and shortly there came a low noise of rotors. Martin turned and looked at the device silhouetted in the flashlight.

It looked like a typical quadcopter, and why shouldn't it?

When he turned back, Cryder had donned a lens over his glasses, and obviously had an image from the drone. He steered it with a finger point, over, sideways, down out of sight. Shortly it came back up, rotors buzzing hard for lift, with a rifle, and Martin reached out to snag it. He checked it was clear, placed it down with the bolt locked open, and turned to get the next.

After the third rifle, a ruck came up. Then another. Then another rifle.

In a few minutes there were ten rucks, eight M4s, one with an M320, an M249, nine NVGs, ten helmets, ten sets of IOTV plates—pretty much the entire gear the element had—and eight cell phones.

Cryder said, "We'll destroy the phones. The other gear will be cleansed, or technically duplicated to avoid contamination or debris."

Martin said, "Got it. Captain, need help?"

Elliott was checking all the ruck compartments for anything.

"Please. What's your plan, Cryder?"

"We'll extract what data there is. How long would these be active before failing?"

Dr. Raven said, "Uh, no more than a week. Less if they panicked and were trying to call."

Hamilton said, "Yeah, mine was dead in two days."

Cryder nodded. "We'll get the data, then destroy them. They already effectively did so."

Elliott replied, "True. Rucks are expendable and easily accounted for. What other gear? NVG and rifles are Army property. If we are able to return them, we should. If not, they can be destroyed or go to your time for a museum or such."

Cryder said, "We'll take them and see what capacity we have for the jump."

That seemed to make Elliott feel better. He said, "Okay, I'll secure them—bolts out and locked."

Martin understood it. Handing the gear over ended the matter for the Army. Accounting for them missing would take paperwork.

They stuffed and wrapped the gear into rucks. It was going to be heavy and would have to be staged outside. Bringing it in must have taken a party. They consolidated to six bundles that a fit man could carry, as long as someone helped him balance up the slope and back down.

Cryder watched, seemed satisfied, and said, "Let's see what else they left. He said they marked the cave."

Martin didn't want any more cave time, but they did have to follow up. He took a breath, shook off the nerves, and followed. The floor was more even here, terraced with layers of limestone. The ceiling came down lower, though, and there were lots of stalactites.

Dr. Raven said, "We really shouldn't touch them because skin oils actually hinder growth and affect cave development. On the other hand, are these even going to be here in ten thousand years? And damn, it's so weird to say that."

"I know what you mean," he agreed, glad to have someone to talk to.

Ahead, Elliott said, "Yeah, there's the gouging. Name, rank, date of disappearance. Off it goes."

Cryder ran some sort of scan and imaging, possibly for record, possibly to ensure he didn't find other markings. He raised the power tool, placed it against the rock face and started it up.

It was surprisingly quiet, more like a hand vacuum than a drill or grinder. It threw dust and chips out the side, and in a couple of minutes, the wall was recontoured and didn't show any signs of chiseling. Impressive.

He inspected his work and said, "We should check farther back to be sure."

Elliott said, "He said only one mark, but good idea."

Cryder pointed. "Yes, there is another. It's the same content."

Hamilton offered, "He may honestly have forgotten that."

"Possibly, since it's the same info." His tool buzzed, and the markings came off to bare rock. Even if that lasted another 10,000 years, it would look as if it were done now, which it was.

Modern lighting made it much easier to walk the cave than it would have been for locals. At the same time, the sharp spotlights threw garish, macabre shadows off the features. Martin had never liked that. Woods shadows were okay. Cave shadows disturbed him. But he liked caves. Well, those with guided tours.

Raven said, "There are obvious signs of movement back here. Scuffs on the walls, some on the rocks and protrusions."

"I see," he agreed. Though they were visible, they hadn't been obvious to him. They were now. Step by careful step they moved over and around the lumpy floor. Water had flowed through here at some point, eroding and washing the surface. The ceiling dropped until it was barely five feet high and everyone had to scrunch, even the short woman scientist.

Farther back they found other markings, certainly not done by a modern person. It was cave art.

Martin was surprised. "That's surprisingly colorful."

Elliott asked, "Are cave paintings this early? I thought they were later."

Raven said, "Yes, well established in this time frame, not this location. We know about the ones in France and such, much older than this. So it's reasonable there's some here."

Martin said, "But what is that?" He looked at the painting and his blood froze. He didn't like caves anyway. When he saw a painting that showed stick figures abandoning weapons as they ran from . . .

Elliott said, "It almost looks like a giant, winged squid."

Her face screwed up, Raven said, "I . . . don't like that."

"Yeah, me neither," Martin agreed. He was going to have nightmares, even if he didn't sleep.

Hamilton reached out as if to touch it, stopped, and asked, "How would they know about squid this far inland? Crayfish, maybe?"

Elliott said, "Crayfish don't have tentacles. Actually, I don't think they're animals. I think they're tornadoes. That's a weather god."

Martin thought, Yes, let's call it that. If they didn't know what a giant, winged squid might be...and he hoped to God they were right, because the alternative...

"I want to get out of this cave, right the fuck now."

Hamilton turned and asked, "Yeah? Scared?" He seemed pleased to finally have something over on the recovery team.

Raven said, "We really should. There's a risk of contaminating the inks. Note the location so the Byko experts can find it. And I still hate those fuckers for shutting us out of most of this. Sorry, Cryder."

"I understand your frustration," he replied.

Elliott said, "Okay, but let me get some photos."

Raven sounded stern. "Captain, believe me when I say if we don't get out right the fuck now, you are going to have a problem with me. This is not something we should be messing with."

Elliott shrugged and turned. "Okay. I want you to explain this later, though. I may choose to come back."

The expression on his face said he really had no idea what Martin and Raven were talking about.

I hope I'm crazy, and it's just silly coincidence, Martin thought.

But Raven had seen it, too.

At the gear pile, Cryder unslung his backpack, and pulled out a frame that unfolded like one of the mesh grocery carts. It had no wheels yet. It looked far too spidery thin to support the gear, but he was able to lash three rucks of gear to it with futuristic bungees. Two held helmets, phones, and other small gear, as well as a set of armor plates each. The third, the rest of the armor.

That left two rifles each to go over shoulders, with the M249 strapped atop the dolly, and some random NVGs and pouches. That dolly was a nice piece of equipment.

Two rifles plus his own was a tangled bitch, though, that kept jabbing him in the ribs. He tried different positions, but either they stuck out the sides and caught on rock, or stuck in him.

When Cryder pulled, the cart suddenly stepped forward, the legs articulated and moving.

That could have been neat, but it was disturbing as fuck with the nightmarish cave art. It stepped along, the legs forming geometric shapes as they followed the terrain. One briefly was a rolling swastika, and didn't *that* just make this a horror movie? He was going to ask Arnet about some tranquilizers.

They scrambled carefully back down the widening passage,

Martin moving in front of Oglesby and damn the marching order. He felt better when he could see the slash of daylight above. It was overcast now.

They heaved and pulled and clambered up the loose slope, dislodging rocks and catching on the sides. Oglesby was stronger than he looked, helping heave the cart up the slope until it was too steep to continue. They lugged the gear, and had to dismount it for the final climb. Martin felt tickles and prickles and jolted at every faint sound.

The walking dolly was impressive, but even it struggled over terrain. Outside in bright, welcome daylight, even with rolling gray clouds, Martin felt much relieved, and helped strap gear back to the cart.

Outside it was misty and chill, droplets barely visible under a steel-gray sky that had scudded toward them.

The guards from earlier were still out cold as the unit started back down toward the vehicle. That was reassuring, but what was their shift cycle and when would they be checked?

Cryder led the way as they slipped and kicked down the slope. Some of the growth was slippery as it crushed and oozed. Dirt shifted. It was harder than climbing since grabbing for support was more difficult. Raven was favoring her ankle a bit more.

Cryder twitched and looked around urgently.

Elliott asked, "What is it?"

"A large party approaching. Twenty or more."

"From where?"

"Upriver, along the bank."

Hamilton noted, "That's a big hunting party. We usually only had six."

Cryder tilted his head. "If so. Drone out."

He tossed the small device to launch it, and it buzzed away.

Hindered by extra gear and steep terrain, complicated by cold, misty drizzle, they carefully kept going down the slope. Around a huge boulder, slipping in the mud draining past it. All their boots and pants were a frigid, filthy mess. Over the distorted root mass of a tree that leaned at a crazy angle. Carefully over a huge, half-rotted, moss-covered downed trunk. Then through weeds they had to clutch in fistfuls for stability.

Cryder muttered something that was obviously a curse, turned and showed a screen.

Elliott glanced at it, and said, "Those look hostile."

He shifted to let Martin see it.

The element was mostly larger men, wearing hide as outerwear, carrying thrusting spears and the blocking sticks they used as shields. Most also had clubs.

"They do."

Elliott firmly ordered, "Keep moving. We'll shoot if we need to. I have an idea."

He moved in front and led the way upslope diagonally to make distance toward the bend. It was unfamiliar and rougher terrain, with a couple of significant drops. It was shorter, but involved more climbing interspersed with the dips.

Martin heard noise, and reported from the rear, "They're gaining. Not as quickly as they were, but still closing. Five hundred meters."

CHAPTER 26

Dan Oglesby wasn't worried about the outcome of any battle. The Byko ray guns and an AR-10 would definitely stop anything the Paleos wanted to do. At the same time, he knew they should avoid doing that. Time constraints and wish to contact as little as possible made any relations very difficult. Time constraints and lack of relations made dealing with the locals nearly impossible.

He and Spencer each had a side of Dr. Raven, who was wincing as she stumped along, making decent time given her shape and height. But unless they could get to a run, they weren't going to outpace the party behind them, who were moving at a fast lope.

Then they started what was obviously a loud, angry battle cry.

Spencer reported, "Under three hundred meters."

Raven said, "We're not going to make the vehicle. We'll have to fight."

Cryder replied, "Understood, but I want to get as close as we can, and have open terrain."

They jogged carefully over even ground, slowed and stepped where it was slick, rocky, or full of roots.

Elliott announced, "Slope ahead, straight down to the vehicle."

Spencer said, "They're about a hundred meters, in arrow range and almost in spear range, don't wait much longer."

To punctuate that, a couple of shafts dropped and stuck in the ground.

Cryder slapped the handle on the dolly, and it continued

straight ahead, carefully choosing where to put its wiry legs. He turned, raised his weapon, and it emitted an audible *zzap.*

Then he shot twice more.

The charging party dove for cover. That gave time to get onto the grassy slope and make better time.

The Paleos paused, apparently checked that their casualties were still breathing, then formed back up and resumed their pursuit.

Dr. Raven growled as she forced her ankle straight and adjusted her gait to keep moving. He had to respect her endurance. She was pretty fit under the surface fat. He remembered her hefting gear in camp. She'd done well.

Right then another volley of shafts arrived. One hit his back and bounced off, feeling like someone poking with a stick.

It was good to know the arrows couldn't penetrate the clothing. Their heads and faces were still exposed, though, and even if the armor could handle clubbing, once they were on the ground they were far more exposed to any kind of attack—stabs to the face, smashings, even fire.

The hostiles were getting close.

He quipped, "Think we can bribe them?"

Dr. Raven replied, "Probably only with a sacrifice."

"That was my guess, too, dammit."

Spencer said, "They've been after us for half the distance to the truck. I expect they're going to chase us the whole way."

Raven spoke through gritted teeth. "This is as fast as I can move. My ankle is tearing."

Cryder shook his head. "We could've fixed that in our time."

She replied softly and sadly, "I know . . . and at the time I didn't think to ask. I'm sorry."

"We will when we return. For now, you lead and make best speed. We'll follow."

She muttered, "It would be easier if we weren't hauling all this crap."

"If needs be, I can slag it all."

The captain said, "If we can take it, we should. Unless you have enough imagery to completely fake them."

"It's not just that."

"Okay, keep stunning, we'll keep humping."

Cryder zapped another, but the rest went to ground fast this time. They were quick learners. Elliott took a shot, too.

The pursuit was numerous. Elliott was reasonably accurate, but if you winged a man with a stun weapon, he literally walked it off and kept coming. Near misses didn't do anything at all. Energy cracked softly, like potent static charges, but moving shooter to moving target meant the hit probability was low. Nor could Spencer help, even if he was probably a better shot. He had no talent at all with the Byko weapons.

Elliott bagged one, who tumbled into the dirt. One of the rear guard ran up to him, checked him briefly, and shouted what was clearly "He's just sleeping!"

The other pursuers had been lagging behind. Hearing this, they renewed their pace.

Spencer said, "They run like Kenyans. Barefoot, all day."

Dan noted, "And are lighter over obstacles."

Martin Spencer said, "Apparently they're aware of the limitations of nonlethal force."

Elliott made eye contact. "Are you asking for permission for lethal force?"

"Sir, I am. I think a bit of hydrostatic shock will change their attitudes. And I've got thin cannelure soft points in this. It's messier and louder than the ray guns." He waved the AR-10 for emphasis.

"Yeah. As few as possible. We want them to stop."

"Hooah!"

Martin turned, unslung his rifle, lined up the sights on that one near a tree, just coming out of cover and moving at a sprint.

"Tough shit, dude," he muttered, and squeezed the trigger.

The rifle cracked loudly, even with the suppressor, but remained very stable, in case he needed a follow-up shot.

The bullet hit the man center mass, tearing through his hide, him, and out the back. He bent over on himself. There was a visible moment when his consciousness left his lifeless body, and the corpse sprawled teeth-first into the growth, his head flopping loosely as blood and matter gouted out his back.

The others definitely slowed their pace, stared and considered as they reached him, but then they continued forward, still whooping and shouting.

Martin carefully lined the sights up on a second one, raised them and considered if he could get a head shot in, and did so.

The man's skull split and shattered like a melon. The corpse flopped in and piled up, shoulders to the ground, ass in the air, then fell over sideways.

The rest of the pursuit stopped.

It not only stopped, they all dove for hard cover with creditable alacrity. In two seconds they were all invisible.

"Let's move while we can, sir," he suggested. "They may decide to continue."

"Yup, leg it."

They ran at Raven's best pace for another minute.

Cryder advised, "The vehicle is just ahead."

It suddenly unmasked and was visible, the hatches and doors all swinging open. And wasn't that perfectly normal civilian feature very useful on a military truck.

Cryder tossed his load into the back, made a "gimme" motion with his hands, and took everyone else's gear as they came up. Raven was in obvious agony, favoring one leg, wincing and with wet eyelashes, which weren't from the mist. She handed over her share and near collapsed.

Cryder put a hand under her arm, steadied her easily and got her into the rear seat.

The captain started unslinging rifles from people and tossing them in the back. Martin came up last, jumpy and keeping an eye out for sneaky hostiles. He shoved in next to Raven.

The vehicle moved slowly at first, since they were still in scrub. That was relative, though. Every bump threw them at the roof.

"We can get clear for certain," he said. "But the track we're leaving is easy to follow. They might."

"If they do, we'll respond," Cryder assured him. He handed back a vial. "Raven, drink this."

She gasped for breath and chugged the potion.

"Thanks," she mumbled as she finished. She drew in more air, and seemed to have some idea of recovery breathing from martial arts. He figured she'd be fine in a bit.

He asked, "So it's a sacred cave. How the hell did they get let in to deposit their weapons?"

Raven said, "Possibly as gifts to the spirits, possibly disposing of contamination to the purity of society. Those are common elements in these situations. I'm more concerned about the angry pursuit."

He was concerned about the nature of the sacred cave. It wasn't a cheerful place.

Elliott asked, "Cryder, can you mass-stun an area?"

The man replied, "Takes a lot of energy. Think of the volume of space being treated."

"Yeah, right."

He continued, "Then, unfocused, it's a weaker effect, so inverted square of that."

"So no, not an option."

He shook his head. "Not feasibly, not with this." He held up his weapon.

Elliott said, "The problem is, we're slow enough they can follow. They're doing interrupted sprints."

"Do you want to shoot more of them?"

Elliott shook his head. "I'd prefer not, since it didn't work. Obviously we violated the spirits badly. I wouldn't be surprised if that was the home of the gods."

"Given that cave art..." Raven hinted.

Martin said, "Yeah, let's just not pursue that thought. Cryder, can you move faster?"

"On this terrain, I'm doing as well as possible. Once we're out of the trees, I can speed up."

"Right." He had to drive around the trees. The pursuers had to do less dodging on foot, and could follow the vehicle's wipe through the undergrowth.

He reached the meadow they'd traversed on the way in, and gunned the power plant. It was like riding a paint shaker. Then it was like off-roading on sand dunes. Then it almost leveled out. They were briefly doing near 80 KM/H, 50 MPH when Martin checked the display.

A couple of klicks later they slowed for more woods.

Hamilton finally spoke again.

"They will probably follow. I expect they can see us, or have sent runners to high points to watch."

Martin said, "They are absolutely going to follow us. Last time, we got along with all the locals and none of the displacees. This time, we've pissed off all the locals except Shug's." Though given the quickness necessary for their mission, he didn't see a nonviolent outcome.

It sucked having such a high-tech vehicle that was limited by terrain features.

Cryder said, "Should've brought heavier weapon."

Elliott asked, "It's not aboard?"

"Di'n't anticip fer a cave."

Oglesby told him, "Your accent is slipping."

"I had no expectation to need it. Once we saw they had guards on-site, I should have figured."

They had a really good lead, and had broken contact, but he was sure they'd follow.

"Got a plan?"

"Yes, one I really didn't want to use." He pointed as they entered thicker trees.

Arnet stood atop a platform raised from the second vehicle. He manned what was obviously the equivalent of a pintle-mounted weapon.

Cryder rapid-fired something in what didn't even sound like their mangled English, but did sound like a cross between German and Russian.

Arnet started shooting, and there were loud slapping sounds. The targets were hundreds of meters away, and barely visible in the terrain.

The weapon seemed to shoot force-field spheres. Wherever they struck, debris erupted and blew. The lead pursuer dodged the first round. The second one hit him like a giant invisible medicine ball and tossed him ten feet.

The mass scattered, but still pursued. They definitely hadn't liked the reception, but they were determined. Tossing them around wasn't having enough of an effect.

A moment later, though, one of them shouted in pain, though nothing was visible.

Ah. Arnet has switched to that neurological weapon.

"They definitely think that's the work of gods or wizards."

"I am both," Arnet called down, and laughed heartily. "They left."

Cryder looked around, grinning. "We'll need to reinforce the wards."

Eyebrows raised, Elliott asked, "Who's in charge back at camp?"

"Lieutenant Devereaux."

Doc? With only a couple of backups?

Elliott said, "I trust him, but is that enough?"

"Arnet armed Dalton, and took precautions."

"Okay."

When they got back to camp, it became apparent what those

precautions were. All the recoverees were inside a second set of wards, looking variously pissed off and depressed.

Man, this was just getting suckier by the minute.

They made it back in good time. Once the camp was within view he started looking. Nothing was on fire, nor anyone trussed or dead.

"Looks okay so far, sir," he commented.

Elliott agreed. "Doc can handle command."

"I have no doubt about Doc," he said. "Eight on four, though, could be a problem."

From the rear, Oglesby said, "It looks good."

Sean Elliott wasn't really sure how to address this, but Cryder did arrange for steak dinners from the cargo supply, along with some good reconstituted potatoes, gravy, and something that seemed like broccoli but almost flowery. There was additional rum, too, and some sort of mousse for dessert. It helped a little, but the troops were definitely looking like they had second thoughts, and little Kita gave them stares that indicated she understood there was tension and hostility.

He made notes in his phone, ate dinner in between, and then consulted with the others. He called formation for his own element up at the CQ.

First thing, "Doc, well done, and thanks."

The man grinned a yard of teeth. "You're welcome, sir, but it was easy enough. Wards, and Dalton was armed."

"I'll thank him later, and also privately. It's not something to rub their faces in. How were they?"

"No trouble, between wards, collars, and eight of them being able to follow orders."

"Good. Sucks about the collars, but they've been a handful."

Sergeant Spencer said, "Being fair, they've acclimated here and are struggling. It's almost like making fresh recruits fit in again. Especially given what we know of how these early peoples had much more laid-back societies."

"I know." He nodded. "I want to be fair, but they also have to comply."

Caswell said, "They're going to take time. I'm having trouble imagining how fucked up they are, even knowing how we were."

Damn. She didn't swear often. She was serious.

"Dr. Raven, Arnet says he can treat your ankles."

"Yes, sir. I'm going to see him before dinner."

"Now is fine if you wish. This next bit is military oriented."

"Thanks," she said, and stumped over to the reparked vehicles, with their awning roughly placed.

He continued, "With this done, I think we can now see about following up with this other element. As much information as we can get, but especially date, location, and exact numbers."

Cryder said, "They'll have to understand we'll make another trip for them."

"What's your accuracy going to be? Five years? Six months?"

"With established parameters and transference presence, I understand it will be within weeks at worst."

"Then, given the hostile attitudes here—not that I blame them at this point—we need to locate these others and unass to the departure point."

Cryder noted, "We have thirty days, three of them movement. I'd like two days to fully set our position for extraction. That leaves twenty-five days of filling in time."

"It seems like plenty, but something will eat into it."

He made a few notes on his tablet phone, looked up, and addressed his three seniors and Dr. Sheridan.

"What's our presentation for this other displaced element? Sergeant Spencer?"

"Assuming they're Germanic, firm, polite, armed, with some sort of small gift to offer, and up front that we can take them home."

Cryder asked, "Armed for show or defense? That is, do we want to appear to be armed by their manner? Or just in case?"

"Some of each is ideal. The captain should have a sword. It doesn't need to be functional, but it should be dressy enough to show he's a man of means. Any metal we can wear will show status—iron, gold, silver, bronze."

"It'll be real. Do you have a style?"

"Yeah, it's on my stick."

Oglesby asked, "What about language? Old English? Old German?"

"I have a partial gloss from throughout that time frame—again, assuming that's what they are, sight unseen. It would be Germanic, but might be Old Norse or a predecessor, Old

Germanic, proto-English, and I have no idea how to pronounce these, just a gloss."

Oglesby said, "Show me what you have and I'll do my best."

"Will do."

Sean asked, "Do we take women?"

"I would not take women." Spencer said, then explained, "They will very much want to talk man-to-man. Women's status in several of those is unique. They're above women in a lot of contemporary cultures, but they are still women, and have a parallel structure, not equal."

Caswell said, "There's that one very documented find of a female with a military burial."

"Yeah. One."

She said, "No, I'm agreeing with you. There's one. Which means there may be others, but we've only found a single one."

"Right. That's the significance."

Next question. "Okay. Do we need armor?"

Spencer replied, "Not really. Most of them wore quilted gambesons, possibly some leather or chain sections to reinforce it—and I mean chain, like the stuff we drag vehicles with, not mail. Mail would be very rare, and not at all expected or necessary. If they were traders or raiders, they're traveling light."

"Got it. Bows? Spears?"

The NCO nodded. "They probably do. We can take the same if you like, but I'm thinking status, and if there's any kind of violence we show them god weapons, since we have the means."

"Got it. Any further details?"

"We march when close, keep good formation order. That will indicate we're professional warriors. We'll have good gear as well. They'll recognize our status, and then we can treat as equals."

"Noted. Anything else we can do about language?"

Cryder said, "Our system can recognize words and phrases with time. That means we have to have them talking, and we must have referents."

"Alright. Will we have drones?"

The man smiled. "Of course."

Sean considered and ordered, "The party will be myself, Sergeant Spencer, Doc in case we need him, Sergeant Oglesby, and Sergeant Dalton. Remaining here, Sergeant Caswell will be in charge of the camp. Which Guardians are coming?"

"I will," Arnet said. "Cryder will maintain our presence."

"Got it. The scientists remain here. I will impress on Lieutenant Cole that until he's properly reintegrated, Caswell is in charge, but he is, of course, in charge of his element for work details, PT, and such."

Spencer asked, "Are we planning to stun or kill if we have to?"

Arnet said, "Stun."

Sean said, "Right. You better do that. I'm not sure if we can go beyond just shoot with your weapons, if stressed."

"I can't," Spencer said with a frown. "But if I need to shoot, Eugene here will make them notice." He slapped the AR-10 on the rack next to him.

"If it gets to that, sure. Okay, I'll write it up for our records."

Rich Dalton checked his gear over for the morning. It was cold but clear now, and would be freezing by morning. His tent was sealed with the heater on low, and that was an amazing bit of kit. Everything was in order, but he was always meticulous about it. He'd seen too many junior enlisted scramble for something they forgot at the last minute. It was unprofessional, and even worse in a leader.

The steak for dinner was tender and quite good. The vegetables were reconstituted and he could just barely taste the difference, now that he knew what to taste for.

The dinner conversation was muted, and more and more, the two elements were distinct. Having slave collars installed couldn't help. As he was one of the troops who recovered the deserters, they weren't ever going to be on good terms. All the discussion with Lozano was probably a loss. Even the ones who didn't like him obviously felt a rift between groups.

After dinner, he took a walk around to gauge people's morale states. Sergeant Spencer was a bit shaky again, but no worse than he often was previously. The captain was obviously flustered from recovering the gear that was now stowed in the second vehicle. Oglesby seemed okay. Dr. Raven had that focus that said she was very bothered and hiding. She also looked irritated.

He approached slowly, in full view.

When she leaned back from her screen and faced his way, he spoke.

"Dr. Raven, how are you doing?"

She twisted her neck. "Still buried in work. Though my ankles are a bit better."

"I'm glad Arnet can help you. They did wonders for one of our troops."

The woman nodded and replied, "Sergeant Alexander. I've read her file. We have a couple of related issues, but mine are better managed with my background. Still, I'm going to take their offer."

"Excellent. How are you and Dr. Sheridan doing with the data?" The other scientist was still down at the fireplace, talking to Caswell about some game or other.

She shrugged. "It is what it is. It's going slow. I'd almost work faster alone." She turned back and resumed typing.

There was a definite undertone of dislike there.

Rich said, "I guess I got the wrong impression. I kinda thought you two were friends."

She turned and gave him a look of pure disgust.

"No. I can just barely work with her professionally. I don't like her. She's not my type intellectually. Nor are most people, period."

"Intellectually?"

"She's stupid."

Wha? He wondered where that came from, and his thought vocalized, "...She's a PhD."

Raven scowled and said, "Brighter than average, but still stupid. I've been rerunning experiments to suit her when I know the answer is right."

"I just...you're both...I mean, highly educated."

She stopped typing and stared at him. "Education doesn't make you smart. If you learn the correct things, index, and use them, they can make a smart person more effective. It doesn't matter how much education you give a rock."

"She's smarter than a rock."

She shook her head. "Not much, by my scale." She faced the screen again, though was still talking as she typed.

Raven didn't at all sound like she was boasting. She was stating a casual fact.

"How do you measure it?"

With a shrug, and while typing data, she replied, "Oh, I'm sure she's borderline gifted or a bit more on a baselined IQ test, but as I said, what you do with the information determines how effective you are. She can't be decisive, blathers on about feminist dialectic and TV, and even in her own field she's not familiar with several major experiments."

"And you?"

She paused and looked at him. She did have very pretty eyes, and they bored right through him. "Dude, I break IQ tests. They don't go that high. The only reason I have a boyfriend at all is because he's about as smart, and knows how to be rational as well."

He realized she'd been typing a technical paper while holding a completely separate conversation. Holy crap.

"Geniuses aren't rational?"

"People excel at finding ways to convince themselves their prejudices are true. Consider you and these genetic markers."

"I'm just trying to stick with my faith."

"And on this matter, and anything else to do with science, your faith isn't even wrong. It's just not relevant. You're theoretically very smart, but you can't drop your mystical beliefs even when facts are stacked up in front of you."

He didn't want to argue, but she was wrong. "That's not how faith works."

"No, but it is how science, reason, and reality work. Speaking of which..."

"Sorry. I'll let you work."

She said, "Look, we're on the same side, okay? Just don't expect me to ever like religion, ever be comfortable with it, or even acknowledge it."

He asked, "Do you have a picture of your boyfriend?"

"Why?"

"Just curious."

Sighing, she pulled out her phone, swiped and held it up. It was a professional portrait shot.

The man shown was older than she, probably mid-fifties. Fit, though, with a military bearing, clean-cut hair, and strongly handsome. He'd damned near make a recruiting poster if he was younger. He had muscular arms around a gorgeous, dark-haired little girl. Their daughter, he guessed.

She said, "You expected a fat nerd, didn't you?"

Damn, she could read him like a book.

He evaded that question.

"Cute kid."

She smiled. "Thank you. Keri is my entire world. I won't be able to have another. Medical issues. I always hate being away."

He switched subjects back. "How did you meet?"

"He was in the Army, intel. Then he went to school and worked for the Navy on propulsion. Now he consults and reviews documents for publication. We met online when I was just starting college. Mutual friends. I gave him links and info on some biology aspects of the machine applications he was looking at."

"How long have you been together?"

"We started getting together at conferences, but we didn't live together until after his wife died. Cancer."

"Sorry to hear that," he said automatically. "Wait, you got together, but . . ."

"She knew. We were friends."

Broken moral compass. Brilliant, but separated from the rules that made society work.

Her voice cut through. "I didn't ask for your approval, and you shouldn't presume to voice it."

Again. She did it again.

"As long as he likes you as much as you do him," he said, diplomatically.

"He does," she replied. "And my tongue."

Whaa?

For just a moment, her eyes smoldered and she smiled.

He realized she was completely toying with him. He'd irritated her, and she was getting back by making him uncomfortable.

He wondered for a moment, but he was pretty sure she was being entirely truthful.

She was terrifyingly smart. And fat or not, she was strong even by male standards.

Holy Father, you keep giving me lessons to learn from, and I'm trying. But if it pleases you, can you slow them down just a little so I can try to keep up?

CHAPTER 27

The recovery element set off to meet the Germanics. All six of them fit into the vehicle with a bit of working.

Sean was pleased with his sword. It certainly looked lethal, and had bronze and faux garnet inlay, with a scabbard that looked like leather shaped over carved wood. He wouldn't mind a real one at some point. It was classy looking. It was most certainly the mark of a warrior, and much more so than the parade swords officers dressed up with these days. This thing looked as if it would actually cleave bone.

Sergeant Spencer also had a sword, slightly less elaborate, as did Arnet. The men all had knives or machetes showing that were obviously weapons. Doc also carried a wooden club, almost a mace. With the Byko fabric armor, they should be well protected apart from their faces, and they did have eyepro.

From the driver's seat, Arnet said, "As before, there's significant terrain interruption and the last part will be on foot."

Dalton commented, "I gather this thing can't blow through the trees."

"Easily," Arnet assured him. "That will be obvious and threatening, though."

"Oh."

"How far?" Sean asked.

"Appears to be about twenty kilometers. That's probably outside their hunting radius, as well."

"That would be ideal. You said they had some agriculture, though?"

"They appear to raise rice, and some sort of grain. A small patch, but likely enough for their needs. They also have fish traps and seem to hunt."

Spencer said, "All well within their tech."

The vehicle rolled over the terrain. While smoother than a US military vehicle would have been, the suspension couldn't flatten out actual hummocks and slopes. It wasn't a jolting ride, but it was certainly a shifting ride.

It took only a few minutes to reach the edge of the woods, and stop among some scrub.

Arnet opened the doors and hatch.

"Dismount," Sean ordered.

Once everyone was out, the vehicle closed back up, turned shimmery and largely disappeared, then reappeared looking like a gray rock outcropping. Nice trick.

Two buzzing tones announced the hummingbird-size drones Arnet had to accompany them, and they lifted until they were barely visible and barely audible, circling like insects.

Arnet had a helmet that appeared metal, which obviously included sensors and displays. He looped his sword over his shoulder by its baldric, and Sean followed suit.

Arnet stepped forward and said, "This way."

Sean ordered, "Sergeant Spencer, you may load and please sling your weapon for now. Everyone else keep a relaxed hold on your weapon." He'd gone without. He'd let someone else shoot on his behalf if need be, though he certainly wished for something. He'd gotten used to being armed all the time.

"Sergeant Dalton, rear guard, please. Five-meter spacing."

"Hooah, sir."

They spread out and moved forward. Arnet pointed at what appeared to be a game path and they moved onto it. At this point they were all experienced, and strode quietly through the growth, ducking limbs or carefully moving them aside as needed.

It was only twenty minutes before the woods thinned slightly. They thinned because they'd been harvested. Every tree under about a six-inch diameter was a stump, and much growth was trod down. They were obviously close.

From behind him, Sergeant Spencer said, "Now is the time to start talking, sir, so we're travelers, not attackers."

"I understand," he said at a normal level. He raised it slightly and turned over his shoulder. "How's it look back there, Dalton?"

"Fine, sir. I think I smell smoke."

"Good call." Yes, that was definitely campfire smoke.

Almost at once there were voices ahead.

They turned into shouts, and what were obviously orders. There were rustling and camp noises. Dogs. Everyone had dogs now.

Spencer hurried forward and asked, "Sir, if I may?"

"Go ahead."

"Thank you." He raised his voice and shouted, "*Hallo! Laager! Stadt! Borg!*"

Someone shouted back "*Allo!*" and something unintelligible. It could be German, if German was also Swedish, very fluid, and had too many vowels.

They all kept moving. In a few steps, Sean could see rising smoke, and then the tops of log buildings. That was familiar.

"Formation and march," he said. "Route step until we're in view, then patrol march."

They trudged through growth, and onto a well-worn path that was obviously a route to the fort. It even had brush and gravel filling in dips and holes to even it out.

"They maintain this area," he noted.

Shortly, they emerged into a clearing. He wasn't sure how much was natural and how much cleared woods. It was big enough, though. Several acres.

This was definitely a defended position. The palisade wasn't as tall as the one he'd built, but it had a ditch like his as well. It also had an abatis outside. He realized that would have helped the defensibility. He'd thought too modern.

Over there was a goat pen, very much like the one they'd had. Some antelope and deer were in it, too, apparently lamed to stop them vaulting the fence. There were several horses, not modern, but not feral primitive either. They were domesticated.

Ahead was a welcoming party that looked as if it could become a war band very quickly.

The element facing them was twenty men in two offset ranks. The men did have swords, shields, spears. Most were in tunics, a couple in padded armor.

Then he did see some fence on high ground farther in. They were building out, it seemed.

"Almost a motte-and-bailey defense," Spencer said. "And they definitely look and sound European."

That was neat, but he wanted to deal with diplomacy before the details. Hopefully this group would be more amenable than the Paleos.

"Cool. Can we manage to talk to them?"

"We'll try. Oglesby, with me."

Spencer stepped slowly forward, hands held open.

"Allo."

One of the opposite nodded, opened hands, and agreed, "Allo."

Spencer indicated Sean with a nod and a noticeable but not excessive bow.

"We speak for Captain Sean Elliott. We also were lost, but we have a way home."

Reading from his tablet, Oglesby slowly enunciated something a bit more complex in something German sounding.

Sean watched the leader and the men behind him. They seemed alert, though not aggressive.

It appeared Oglesby was able to make himself understood, in an interrupted, piecemeal fashion. It didn't take long to get to firm handshakes and smiles, and the contingent visibly relaxed.

Spencer turned and said, "No obvious hostilities, sir."

That was good.

"Stand down, but stand ready," he said in a conversational voice. The troops relaxed into parade rest and let themselves shift about a bit.

Shortly, the chief seemed surprised.

Oglesby repeated whatever he'd said, and the man's eyes got wide. He held hands up to heaven and invoked something.

Spencer asked, "Sir, can you come forward? We seem to be at that point."

"Of course," he replied and stepped off.

He strode forward, slowed as he closed, and stopped two paces behind Spencer and Oglesby.

Spencer turned again, bowed fractionally, and said, "Captain Sean, this is Wulf, who I think best is considered a band leader."

"Handshakes?" he asked.

"Yes."

Sean nodded, stepped another step forward as Wulf did, and offered his hand. The man's skin was coarse, warm, and his grip very firm, but not with intent to hurt, just to be solid. He returned it.

"It is good to meet you," he said with a nod and smile. They locked eyes. Wulf appeared intelligent, confident, determined. He was an equal.

Wulf was about his height, very blond, tanned, with blue eyes and a lot of beard. It was well groomed, as was his long-ish hair. The helmet he wore looked to be a metal frame with leather inset into it. His shield was well worn, and his sword not as clean or elaborate as Sean's, but maintained. He wore quilted fabric, natural colored under the stains with some repaired tears, leather boots, and what appeared to be skin pants. He'd probably had those made to replace worn-out fabric.

"We are explaining that there is a way home, but it will be difficult."

"I understand. Should Arnet join us?"

Spencer said, "Yes. Arnet, if it pleases you to join us," and nodded fractionally that way. "Also, men, please come within five paces and stop."

"The men" at this point were Dalton and Doc. Dalton said, "If I may, sir?" to Doc, who nodded.

Dalton continued, "Element, by my command, attention, forward, march." The two strode evenly across the ground, stopped where indicated, and Dalton ordered, "Element, halt. Parade, rest."

Well done. It should be obvious they were an orderly military unit, and friendly, but capable.

Wulf turned and dismissed his men, who shouldered arms and marched back inside their village. He indicated for the Americans to follow.

Sean asked, "Sergeant Spencer?"

"Sir, I get no bad vibes at all. He's more than happy to meet with someone who has something useful for him, and he obviously can't steal it. We've made an offer in his favor. I think it's all good."

"Fair enough, but everyone remain alert, watch your positions and cover, and be ready just in case."

"We're ready, sir," Dalton assured him.

"Then let's go in. Be alert but polite."

"As always. Well, as always before this trip."

Inside the ditch and abatis was the earthen rampart and palisade about five feet tall, then another ditch that was soggy and wet from runoff. A planked, removable bridge crossed that. Then there was another palisade, very much like the one the Americans had built last time, though rounder and less regular.

Inside was a small village of mixed Paleos and Germanics. At least three of the women seemed native to the Germans. Those also had spears and were keeping the other women and a few children both corralled and protected, by their demeanor.

Central to the village was a longhouse, several smaller houses, and obvious workshops, including a blacksmith's shop and a pole lathe.

Sean muttered, "Damn, Martin, you were spot on."

"It's three-thousand-year-old tech, sir. The basics are well described."

"Yeah, but you knew about it. Our recoverees didn't. Even with it right here."

"It can be hard to motivate, sir."

Hewn wooden benches and chairs awaited them under an awning of stitched leather. One of the local women stood ready, in a Dark Ages dress of undyed wool, with a wooden pitcher.

They all sat, Wulf at the head nearest what was probably his lodge, with his presumed wife—from his culture—standing there directing servants. He had a man on either side, probably advisors, in the first seat on each side.

Sean chose to sit next to one of them, facing the entrance to the camp. Arnet sat across. Oglesby was next to Sean, Spencer next to him. Doc sat with Arnet, and Dalton sat at the end where he could watch their host. That left four spots for others, who were apparently men of status. The dogs were on leashes and were tossed occasional scraps. That kept them quiet.

The servants delivered wooden platters with what was a sort of bread, baked from what might be a predecessor of modern wheat, and crackers that were obviously rice and acorn flour. All were gritty and dense. There was roast meat, probably aurochs, and some gray salt. The men were given wooden cups. Sean, Arnet, and Spencer were provided auroch horns, carved with figures and filled with a beverage from a ceramic jug that was recognizable in design.

Spencer said, "Probably mead or beer."

A moment later, Wulf raised his horn and made what was obviously a toast.

Sean followed, and sipped carefully while their host chugged.

Sweet, tart, definitely alcoholic. There was a slimy aftertaste he really didn't like, but it was drinkable, barely.

"Mead," Spencer said. "Fermented from honey, though it seems more beerlike than wine. Also, breaking bread and alcohol is significant. They're trying to be diplomatic, not hostile."

That was good news. "That's a first this time. Let's try to get a discussion going."

Arnet's device had picked up a couple of words and started translating out loud. That shocked them, and Oglesby tried to explain it was good magic.

"I think I managed to get 'clean' across, and that it's to help talk between groups."

"Good."

Oglesby said, "This is definitely some form of proto-Germanic or proto-Scandinavian as Sergeant Spencer guessed. Some of the words are passingly familiar."

"Good. Analyze later, though, please." It would be fascinating, but he wanted this to go as quickly as possible.

"Of course. Wulf asked how our gods brought us here. Should I tell him our wizards did?"

Sean thought and said, "Arnet's wizards did, to find our lost element. They're very powerful."

"Got it."

There was back and forth, and the man seemed surprised and impressed, to a point. A handful of words came through. "Shrieker" was one of them.

Spencer replied, "He doesn't think highly of our lost element, apparently. They got in with the savages instead of building like men."

"I see. I guess I need to explain that they are not our warriors, only . . . what?"

Spencer said, "Some peasants and serfs. They're not trained to fight or build, only for menial work."

"That's really not fair, but I guess if it makes this go smoothly . . ."

Spencer nodded. "It will. Say we were honor bound to bring them home, as sworn to us, and the wizards are helping, but at a price."

"Hooah." Oglesby got to it, picking words carefully.

Wulf seemed to accept that with a gruff nod. He spoke back.

"He says we're to be respected for being honorable to our peasants. He also appreciates the offer of magic to return. How do we proceed and what will it cost him?"

Arnet said, "We're fixing a problem caused by others, and it's beneficial to all that he return where he is needed, so we do not need pay. Additionally, we may have a small gift from the defeated wizard who caused it. Is that okay?"

Spencer said, "It is. Add that small gifts to seal the agreement are certainly welcome, as is his generosity, but he also is a man of honor and we take the compliment as payment."

"Whew." Oglesby tilted his head and commenced to translating. The machine went along, and was slightly different.

Oglesby said, "I think the machine has it now. I'll just check it as we go. Anyway, he's pleased with that, and says basically that he appreciates working with fellow professionals after so long trying to talk to the savages, though I gather he was trying to make them serfs or underlings."

Spencer grinned. "I guarantee he was. Do you blame him?"

Sean considered. "No, we were more diplomatic, but that was the long-term plan. We had the advantage of comprehending the scenario."

"Correct."

With both parties showing peaceful strength, both with the goal of returning home, the discussion proceeded with more beer and food, and smiles and laughter.

Wulf asked, "Where is this strange land we are in? We went downriver and saw nothing beyond more savages. After fifteen days we came back."

Spencer scrolled down his phone screen, and said, "Tell him we're east of Derbent and the land of the Bulgars...but a long way. That river ends in a sea, and across that sea is a desert, and across that desert another sea before he'd reach that land. There are no people, and monsters that would take an army." To Sean he said, "I don't want the man thinking that a slightly longer boat voyage would get him to a Rus trading post. If he's late enough to know who the Rus were."

Wulf replied, "I don't know of those places. They must be east of Anastasios's lands."

"Oh, yes," Spencer replied with a nod, then turned and

elaborated. "Apparently, they don't have any solid trade connections down that way. Early German."

Spencer looked at Sean and said, "They have rather sophisticated swords for that early. Not what I expected."

"Possibly you were wrong about this era?"

Spencer wrinkled his brow. He seemed a bit perturbed. "Possibly everything we know is slightly wrong. We've got few documents and a handful of artifacts to deduce from. There's a lot wrong."

"Like what?"

"If they're Merovingian they should be Christian and speaking Latin. They know a bit of Latin, and they know about Christ, but not in much detail. They're still very pagan, but it's not quite Germanic paganism. Nor is it a mix that would place them in the northeast fringe, near the Saxons. I can't identify his group or nation. They're obviously somewhere in that range, and he claims 715 AD by Roman figuring. Which leads to all the questions I have above. Early German but not what they should be."

"Are you going to record it all for the experts?"

"I already have," he said with a tilt of the phone in his hand. "Video, audio, comments."

The twenty-three Germans, who called themselves "Nordwandlaz," had been here for three years. There were four couples and fifteen men who arrived single. There were six mixed kids and two who'd come along. They'd done quite a bit of building. A small number had local wives, and there were a couple of camp prostitutes who seemed glad enough to exchange favors for the advanced facilities and expectation of marrying off eventually.

With the machine translating on its own for the most part, Wulf said, "I don't want to deal with the scrian . . . screechers."

Spencer said, "I think that's similar to what the Norse called the natives in the Americas. Skrælings. Shriekers."

Arnet said, "He doesn't have to deal with them, but our camp is near theirs and he'll need to come there. He can bring an entourage. I reserve the right to limit how many actually enter camp at any time, and also, Cryder will have input on that."

Oglesby said, "I'll see what we can do." He turned back to Wulf and the machine.

It wasn't an angry discussion, but it was a diplomatic one— who had what authority, what was a reasonable meeting place and terms. Was there shelter?

Arnet agreed shelter for them would not be a problem, and said, "We have an awning we can erect with sides against wind. With a fire, it will be comfortable at night."

Sean said, "That's my thought. Impress them step by step so there's always some new trick. It keeps them interested, aware they're subordinate, and hopefully impressed enough to take instruction."

"You're well versed for a savage," Arnet replied with a grin.

Sean wasn't sure he was joking.

He offered, "Well, they can follow us now, establish a route of their choosing, or they can go to the native village and then proceed from there, though you can let him know we're not thrilled with the natives either, but have them under control."

Oglesby translated and said, "They'd like to send five men now. He wonders how we control even savages, given their numbers."

"Tell him we were only as forceful as needed to make the chief understand."

Spencer added, "But, if they cause any grief, we're capable of wiping them out." He turned to Sean. "These are professional warriors, sir. It has to be kept in terms of strength."

"I trust your judgment."

More back and forth, and more mead. It was sweet and alcoholic, but whatever they'd aged it in, probably a salt-cured skin, gave it a tang that was vile. He managed to sip, take the occasional guzzle when they did.

Really, they'd managed as well as his element, since they were used to field conditions like that, and didn't need modern utilities.

Finally, Oglesby said, "Okay, five of them will come with us now, then will return and report back. He understands the time frame for our departure. We haven't discussed other details."

Arnet said, "Make sure he understands it'll require a separate magical trip. We only had plans for one."

Oglesby agreed, "Right."

Sean tried to count the locals present. They'd have to bring any children. The wives were possible, depending on the Byko rules. Everything else would have to be slagged.

"Then please let us thank him and get on our way, with whomever he wants to send. Spencer, I want you and Dalton behind them, just in case."

"Understood, sir."

Sean rose, extended his hand again, and this time Wulf clasped his elbow with the other hand. He returned it. It seemed to indicate a closer relationship. The man certainly seemed cheered at the prospect of returning home.

Five of the Germans were ready with packs and bedrolls. They also bowed fractionally in respect, and Oglesby translated marching orders.

"That's it," he said. "Lead the way, sir."

Sean nodded, turned, and started walking. Arnet fell in next to him. Oglesby and Doc made a second rank, then the cluster of Germans, with Dalton and Spencer bringing up the rear with firepower.

They moved briskly through the woods, and Oglesby was kept busy trying to translate small talk about the route, how they traveled, and other relevant queries. He wore down fast from the additional effort. Fortunately it wasn't a long hike, though mostly uphill through heavy brush.

Arnet unscreened the truck before they reached it. At the vehicle, there was another discussion, of how it was a wagon without horses, moved by magic, and they would need to hold on. Dalton climbed up and showed them where to place their feet. They tried not to look nervous, stood where shown, then held onto the rack.

Arnet started slowly, creeping over the terrain. As the men adapted to being passengers, he increased speed. It probably helped that the vehicle was near silent. A diesel engine would likely have made them more twitchy.

Very quickly they were enjoying it.

Oglesby translated one's comment as, "Like riding a horse, but smoother."

The man laughed deeply in baritone.

CHAPTER 28

Jenny Caswell felt very alert. Here she was, an E-5, in nominal charge of a US contingent with attached assets in the Stone Age. This wasn't something Airman Leadership School covered. She had Cryder to back her up, which was a plus. She knew him well enough, and he'd have no issue using force competently and responsibly. Dr. Raven wasn't physically fit, but was certainly intellectual. Dr. Sheridan a bit less so, and it irked her to admit the most feminist member of the element was a hindrance.

She sat in the CQ area where she had a good view and ready access to weapons and support from Cryder. Lieutenant Cole had his people reviewing some Army doctrine, and handling firewood, trimming, and cleaning details.

Right then, Sheridan walked up and grabbed a drink from the kitchen gear.

"How is it going, Sergeant?" she asked.

"As well as it can be," Jenny replied. "How's the research?"

"Taking a short break from fresh stuff and double-checking some of the extant projects. Amalie does a good job, but it's my name on the documents so I want to make sure it's correct."

"That makes sense," she agreed. It did. Raven took it personally, but possibly it was just bureaucracy.

Sheridan stepped a bit closer and spoke a little more softly. "I'm surprised they put you in charge, not Cole, him ranking, and male being a bit of it."

That was notable, and part of her tension. Technically he could take charge, even though Captain Elliott had specifically given her the task. Maybe. Status mattered. He could argue the point, though.

She would have to explain at length. "Unit differentiation. We're a tasked unit, they're a recovered unit. Until he's officially cleared by our command his status is similar to a recovered POW. It would have to be an emergency before he could do so."

"Right." Sheridan nodded. "Also, what mental state are they in after all this? I'm just giddy as hell at being here. It's a dream, no matter how real it is. I'm looking at completely raw wilderness and geeking out. They don't find it as fun, though."

"No, they don't. We didn't either. It's so much more relaxed this time," she admitted.

Sheridan sounded disappointed as she said, "I wanted to see more of the future. There were quite a few female researchers and personalities, but what about their leadership? It's a very technical, egalitarian, post-scarcity society. How do gender roles break down?"

Jenny noted, "They've been quiet about that. I think the captain said the council was predominantly men but had a large number of women by our standards. A third, maybe?"

Sheridan rolled her lip and said, "Not true equality, then."

Jenny shrugged. "I don't know. That was one specific council for that matter. How they do the rest of it, there's no telling."

Sheridan said, "Yeah, I'd love to see."

"They probably will never let us see that much, from what I understand of your discussions with them."

"No, likely not." The big woman placed her cup in the wash rack and said, "Back to work. Have a good day."

"You too, Kate."

She watched the recoverees work on a running track, leveling the ground with Cryder's power shovel, and then adding gravel. It did keep them busy, and it was at least slightly useful. It served as light exercise. On the whole, a good plan on Cole's part.

She didn't want to get involved if she was the only one of her unit present. But she needed to appear occupied so they didn't get jealous.

The ground around the CQ needed some attention, so she went to Roller Two, acquired the multitool, and thought hard about trimming grass. It shifted and formed into something not dissimilar from a grass whip that buzzed with power. She walked around the trucks and awning area, holding it a couple of inches off the grass, and it trimmed every blade and leaf. Much easier than a weed whacker. She'd found out previously it didn't even hurt if it hit flesh.

That done, she went into the CQ and noted current activity, weather, and personnel. She was able to check the Roller One system on minerals and water level, which wasn't necessary, but she needed something to do, too. There was a running weather forecast from the drones, and that said it was going to be a cool evening, into the thirties Fahrenheit. It was that time of year.

Cryder strode up, nodded and went to his console. He sat, waved the screen open, then sprung back up immediately.

"Hostiles," he said.

She asked, "Where?" as she got up fast herself.

"From the east. Possibly related to the gear recovery."

Jenny saw them. They were almost to the wards, some with bundles of spears, others with quivers of arrows and heavy-looking bows.

"How did they get so close?"

"They carry very little that trigger a sensor. Didn't ping until close enough for bio readings."

Right then, an arrow dropped inside the wards.

"You said you can block overhead?"

"I can, but that disperses power from the sides. Prefer full strength against impacts, and let them get stunned."

"Meantime we have incoming indirect fire," she complained, shaking her head. She grabbed a weapon off the rack.

Turning, she shouted to the recoverees, and ordered, "Get in the tents!"

Cole called back, "What? Say again?"

"Shelter in your tents, now!"

"Sergeant, I know you're ranking for your element, but this calls for—"

She thought about the stun setting, recognized the shift, raised and shot. Cole dropped cold. That kind of bullshit was exactly why she wanted them in the tents, separated, unable to coordinate.

"Get in your goddamned tents. They're spearproof. Uhiara, Burnham, stuff him into his or drag him in with you. *Move!*"

They did as they were told. Kita was hiding in the corner of CQ, waiting for her mother. Crap.

She waved with her hand. "Come with me, Kita. *Shooshi*," she said in the closest she could manage. Hopefully a simple word hadn't changed much.

Kita ran over and clutched her thigh. She scooped up the girl, who clung as she edged toward the tents.

"Noirot! Come get your daughter!"

"Right here! Thanks, Sergeant!"

"Hooah." She sprinted back up the slope that suddenly felt a lot steeper than it had. An arrow thumped against her uniform and fell away. It stung slightly, but hadn't penetrated the reinforced fabric.

"Cryder, what do you need?"

"I'll illum point targets. How's your accuracy?"

"Expert by our ratings."

"Well good."

"What do we know about their weapons and tactics?" she asked.

"Only what we've seen," he admitted.

"Okay, let me ask." She turned and raised her voice. "*Hamilton!* CQ now!"

Cryder said, "I tightcast to his tent. He heard directly."

"Thanks."

The man came jogging quickly up the hill. He'd been half out and watching. In fact, all of them were out gawking, near but not in their tents.

Growling, she snapped, "Get inside! You can watch on video if you can figure out how."

Cryder jumped to Roller Two and pulled at gear in the rear shell.

Hamilton arrived. She looked down at him, pointed under the awning.

"You'll be safe from most fire there. What can you tell me about weapons and tactics, fast?"

She glanced up to see how many archers and spearmen were at work.

They had babies strapped to their backs.

"*What the fuck is this?*" she shouted. "*Are you fucking kidding me?*"

Hamilton called up, "They do it when defending the village.

It wasn't entirely clear, but what I figured out was that it means the babies are protected by a warrior's spirit. They talked about how the crying baby drove them to greater urgency, because they wanted their sons to live. They also said it would build courage in the boys by exposing them to fighting young and strengthen their spirits."

Below in CQ Amalie Raven muttered, "I have to write this down. There's a paper in this, but no one will believe it."

Jenny checked the weapon was still set to stun. She understood killing was a more effective tactic, but she didn't like it in the first place, and absolutely not babies.

"I'm becoming a firm believer in social evolution," she muttered. That guy up front with the impressive limed Mohawk was in range. She raised the weapon and stunned him cold, just as he heaved a spear. He wasn't carrying a kid, thank God.

They moved fast. They were probably experienced at dodging spears and arrows. This was a line-of-sight weapon. She wasn't sure if it was light speed or less, but it was fast enough they'd have no time to react. They never held still, though. They were in constant motion, shooting and hurling as they moved. She lined up on one with spiky dreads, led him, and shot, but he shifted as she fired and avoided the blast. He shouted to the others, and she glimpsed his spear dropping enough in front of her not to be a concern.

They were now hurling all their fire at her, apparently figuring to saturate and overwhelm, then pick a second target. The volley rained in, and she ass-bumped off the vehicle to the ground, under the awning. Behind her, stone tips chipped and clattered on the truck roof, and a few thumped into the fabric overhead.

What was Cryder doing? He was still atop, with his hood deployed, and arrows impacting and dropping from his uniform. Whatever he was setting up was a weapon on a mount, and it appeared he was done. He jumped clear as it pivoted, pointed, and started doing instantaneous air defense. Incoming projectiles disappeared in cracks of lightning and trails of smoke, almost like in a cartoon.

That done, he pulled a face shield out of his collar, grabbed his weapon from the bench, and walked toward the wards. They were strong enough nothing came in directly, though a mass of men were able to deflect it a couple of feet so far.

That stopped mattering as he raised it, morphed it to stun setting, and slapped something on his communicator. He started shooting, and the wards flickered.

Right, he couldn't shoot out through, so he had them synched to drop as he fired, and close again immediately.

Jenny finally understood the term "mowing them down." Cryder laid them unconscious in a swath. She hoped it was light enough the kids weren't harmed. Some men ran for cover, but there wasn't anything significant nearby. The hollows and other terrain features they'd used to approach didn't offer as much protection going out, with a tall man, impervious to their weapons, striding after them.

His voice sounded through the truck.

"I need two volunteers, recommend Dr. Sheridan and Specialist Hamilton."

"Understood," she replied, raised her voice, and shouted, "Hamilton, go out and do what Shuff Cryder directs. Dr. Sheridan, please assist if you can." She thought and added, "Dr. Raven, I need you here."

She'd forgotten Hamilton was right there. He replied, "Hooah," and headed out at a run. Sheridan jogged and trudged at a decent speed for her build, and God, Jenny hoped she never bulked up like that. A good reason to exercise and skip dessert.

Raven was a bit behind, and her ankles were a valid excuse for her build. She also had better muscle tone than her counterpart. The woman still winced as she arrived.

Jenny handed her the other weapon.

"Help me keep this group covered until Cryder is back in."

"Can do. Does he still have the shock collars activated?"

"I assume so, but we've got a lot going on and only two of us at present."

"Yes," the scientist agreed. Still, she dragged a chair over to where she could keep a clear view of the camp while sitting.

Conversationally, Jenny offered, "We learned last time that you never have enough people when shit hits the fan."

The older woman smiled.

"That's true everywhere," she agreed.

There was movement. It was Maldonado.

"No one said to leave your tent," she told him, while waggling the weapon. Was he going to be a problem?

No, he crawled back in, and she felt a bit less tense. She was not the right person to do diplomacy, and Cryder obviously wasn't, but possibly next time they should have someone trained in negotiation. This was a ball of suck.

Hamilton came back, followed by Sheridan and then Cryder, all of them carrying armloads of spears and bows. The wards hummed as they reengaged, and the camp was secure again, for now.

"On the one hand I'm glad you've disarmed them," she acknowledged. "On the other hand, they need those for hunting, too."

Cryder sounded almost reasonable as he replied, "Then they can negosh and we'll explain our position. Or they can do without. Things clear here?"

"They are. Can we let them out now?" She waved at the recoverees.

"Yes. That was a good move. Thank you."

Jenny replied, "You're welcome. Are the kids okay?"

"Yeah, light stun. Force is fine, nonlethal preferred. That's our default go-to."

She thought it, but Raven said it first.

"That explains a lot. You're used to reasonable people, and if they're not, stun and explain later. The Paleos lack any context for status or parity of forces, and don't respond to force that isn't harmful or lethal."

"I can always switch to a pain charge next time. Maybe I should."

Raven winced. "For the adults, probably. But the kids..."

"If they want to learn to be warriors, this is part of it," he replied. She couldn't tell if he was being sarcastic or coldly serious.

Jenny did feel much more secure with Cryder back inside. She remembered that she needed to release the other troops.

"All clear, resume normal duties!" she announced.

The recoveree element came out of their tents, and immediately wanted to examine the weapons.

She quickly ordered, "One bow, that one, and one spear, that one. I'm sure you've seen others."

Lieutenant Cole said, "Yes, but this is a different clan with different styles."

Dr. Sheridan said, "Not that much different. Possibly some stylistic marking variations."

Cryder reported, "Sergeant Caswell, the recon team is fifteen minutes imminent."

"Thanks for the update," she said very calmly. Inside, a massive load lifted and she thought, *Thank God*.

She did feel she'd acquitted herself well, though. Now she had to write it up.

Sean Elliott asked Arnet to report their position.

The man replied, "I am. Fifteen minutes your time, close enough."

He replied, "Excellent, thanks."

"There was an attack. It has been dealt with and everything is controlled."

"...Thanks." Okay, that wasn't reassuring.

Shortly they were in view of the camp, then approaching, then through the wards.

Something had happened here. There was a pile of weapons. Confiscated? Arrows littered the CQ. Everything seemed under control, but he wanted to check with Cryder and Caswell ASAP, without appearing to be concerned.

The Germans dismounted eagerly, and recognized the camp for what it was. They seemed aware the wards were both markers and defense. They stood close enough to support one another without getting tangled up. Definitely professional warriors.

Sean announced, "Welcome to our camp. Sergeant Spencer will show you around."

Spencer made a minimal salute to indicate deference, and opened his hands in welcome.

"Oglesby, you and the machine help me translate. These wagons are our... meeting area. Lieutenant Devereaux and Gajin Arnet are our medics. They will see you any morning if you are sick, or any time you are injured. This enclosure is the latrine..."

Sean watched as he made a slow, measured walk to the CQ.

After a tour of facilities and perimeter, Spencer led them to a square popup Cryder had erected.

"You may rest here as you wish. We serve meals three times a day, and there are snacks as needed. The captain and Shuff Cryder will discuss details of our return. Welcome again."

In the meantime, Sean arrived at the CQ.

Caswell stood from a terminal and nodded as he arrived.

"Sir, I'm composing an AAR now. Approximately three hours ago, the camp was attacked by a large force of men with spears and bows. It appears to be in response to the cave recovery. The wards secure the perimeter well, but are less effective overhead. I ordered the recoverees to shelter in the tents for both safety and to keep them separated and controlled. I had to stun Lieutenant Cole to get compliance when he attempted to assume field command. Shuff Cryder and I defended the perimeter, and he erected a point defense. After doing so, he mass-stunned the area, and took Specialist Hamilton and Dr. Sheridan outside the perimeter to secure their weapons." She pointed to a pile. "There is the potential to use those to negotiate with the locals to leave us alone in exchange for return. Dr. Raven and I kept the inside secured. There were no complications from the recoverees once they understood the instructions. Specialist Hamilton was helpful in an advisory role before assisting in securing weapons."

He raised his eyebrows. That was succinct, complete, and she sounded pretty sure of herself, possibly only a bit twitchy after what was apparently a huge wave of attackers.

"Well done," he assured her. "I'll look at the AAR when it's complete."

"Thank you, sir," she agreed, and resumed her seat.

Knowing all that, he took a quick patrol of the perimeter. Sergeant Spencer had the Germans tented and bedded with additional mattress material and quilts that Arnet must have provided. They seemed quite pleased.

The recoverees were mostly under control. Cole was really not measuring up. The man had his orders and should understand his status. Burnham and a couple of the enlisted were really stand-up troops under the circumstances. Cole, Lozano, and Munoz not so much.

The attacking force was apparently waking up, finding themselves bereft of weapons, and very concerned. He strode up that way as Hamilton and Oglesby chattered through the wards to the attackers.

Cryder stood back. As Sean approached, he waved a finger.

Sean walked over and asked, "Yes?"

"Can you play subordinate and awed? I have an idea."

That was a bit uncomfortable. He actually was subordinate to the larger man with the higher tech and the only way home.

"Probably. What do you have in mind?"

"Act as if you're begging me to save them."

Good cop, bad cop, he thought. "Sergeant Spencer is probably a better actor, but okay."

They approached together, and Cryder made the same suggestion to Hamilton and Oglesby. Oglesby immediately backed up while waving his hands.

"Please, sir! Let them go."

Cryder grabbed his weapon and let it hang.

"What did they say so far?"

Hamilton also ducked back.

"They say we violated the cave, but they hadn't realized we were so powerful."

"That's a good start. Tell them we had to talk to the gods and that was a good place."

Hamilton nodded vigorously, turned and translated.

Outside the wards, the apparent leader glanced nervously at Cryder and replied very evenly.

Hamilton turned and said, "Sir, he says they didn't know, but if they had they would certainly have made you welcome."

Sean offered, "Why would we care if they made us welcome? They have nothing we need. You can lead up to giving them their trash back if they agree to never return here."

Cryder nodded. "Very workable. Hamilton, tell them that first part."

Again the vigorous nod and a hand wave, as Cryder fiddled with the weapon.

The soldier told them where things stood.

The Paleo looked sad and hurt, and replied at length.

Hamilton turned, "He says he's humbly sorry for insulting you. He appreciates your mercy in not killing them all. I told him you could do so easily."

"Good, give him the rest. Weapons back, never return."

"Yes, sir." The man turned and spoke.

The opposite replied, and Hamilton gave it as, "He says they are most thankful for your mercy, and offer any prayers or votives you wish, if anything of theirs is good enough not to offend a warrior so powerful."

Sean said, "That's better. We don't need anything, but if they take the time to hunt us two fresh yearlings, it will prove they're earnest. I say give them their stuff back, and if they don't show up, who cares, and if they do, we know they were honest as well as intimidated."

Cryder said, "I like it. I'll talk for a moment to make it sound as if I'm considering it. Can you offer a polite bow? Then we'll throw the stuff over the wards. Gently, but without any real respect for their toys."

Sean bowed, and replied, "Good plan."

Shortly they were tossing the bows and spears in high arcs, flat rather than point first. The natives caught them and quickly redistributed, calling names and handing them around, with obvious "That one's mine" to several pieces. Then the quivers and spare arrows followed.

Cryder said, "Captain Elliott and I will return to the vehicles now. Please scavenge the loose arrows and tell them how lucky they are."

"Hooah."

As they walked, Cryder smiled at Sean and said, "Now I have to figure what to serve for dinner."

Arnet called, "Already done, Shuff, with Dr. Sheridan helping. Rabbits as what she calls 'pot pie.' Stew in shell with cheese."

"Sounds good."

Caswell said, "I took it upon myself to order a few more log sections as seats, sir." She pointed where sheared sections were supported by wedges around the fire, offering plenty of room.

"Thanks again, Sergeant," he replied. She'd really shaped up. Last time she'd been an effective if nervous and angsty enlisted. She was doing well as an NCO this time, and far more self-assured and much less annoying. Either maturity or wisdom or both.

Sean said, "I want the guests to eat first."

"Roger that," Oglesby replied, took his tablet, and spoke into it. "Attention visiting warriors. We are serving dinner. Please join us and be welcome."

They came over quickly but without rushing, probably to be polite but not appear needy. He waved them forward to be served by Caswell and Dalton.

He also wanted them first so he could keep an eye on them, and he didn't want to lower the status of the recoverees below that of Dark Age barbarians. That would be cruel.

It was clear enough for everyone to gather around the fire and sit on logs. The Germans approved of the food and said so.

Oglesby said, "Sir, they're asking about ale or beer."

He replied, "I don't know. Sergeant Spencer? Arnet?"

Spencer said, "Typical for their cultures. I don't know if a rum mix will work. Is beer okay?"

Arnet replied, "I locked most choices out but they're available." He rose and went to the kitchen kit. He waved and keyed and shortly there were mugs. Right after that he started filling them.

"Someone else can carry it down," he said as he came back and resumed his seat.

Apparently inferring the comment, two of the Germans ran up, grabbed six mugs each, returned, and repeated.

The mug was plain plastic, brownish with some color striations, and was full of a cool beverage that did taste like a dark beer, without being too bitter.

Spencer smacked lips and said, "Perfect. Hops were not really a thing, but herbs were."

Apparently the men agreed. They raised mugs and toasted, and dug into the pies, bread, and beer.

They were also very pleased with berries and cream for dessert.

All in all it was a busy day.

Sean had Oglesby translate as he briefed.

"We'll talk to them about plans tomorrow. We'll need to finish our move shortly. For tonight I'd like people to hang out around the fire and talk a bit, since our guests have no idea how the technology works. Singing, talking in small groups, at least socialize in their presence so they're not neglected. I'll authorize an extra two drinks each. Sergeant Spencer, your judgment on how much they drink."

Spencer nodded. "That seems reasonable, sir. We can explain it's a field limit on transport."

"Good. Normal watch for the evening. Dismissed."

CHAPTER 29

The next morning, Armand Devereaux sat at CQ for sick call, then joined for PT after it started. He could see the Germans gathering for breakfast. They were quite pleased with the pork options and eggs. A couple asked for porridge. Toast went over well.

They watched the morning PT with interest. They clearly understood this was military drill. They also seemed to grasp that one element was subordinate to the other. Hell, go ahead and say "inferior." The recoverees were very much supplicants and while they'd survived, they hadn't done so with much dignity or skill. It was fair to say his element was top notch, but even with that as an outlier, these guys had failed hard. The Germans could tell who was who.

It took them a while to figure out the females. Caswell's duties made her a camp follower, but they probably couldn't figure out her military status, and the uniform didn't help since everyone was in the same clothing. It had been explained that the scientists were scribes and wise women, and they seemed to get that. He saw two of them talking, pointing and nodding. He followed the gestures and indications and they'd apparently figured out the Bykos were their own senior element. They knew the captain and SFC Spencer were senior for the Americans. As medic, Armand had a high status. As obvious charge of support, Caswell had some status, but he couldn't tell how they interpreted it. Dalton was armed on perimeter, obviously a trusted armsman. The scientists they'd been told about, and the rest were the peasants they'd been described. He watched more gesturing as they noticed that none of the recoverees had any visible weapons, not even knives, while the others all had big field knives and obvious items of status.

It was fascinating to see how their background colored their own interpretation, and that he could see it from their interactions.

When Sergeant Spencer came up to refill his CamelBak, Armand asked him.

"How do you think the Germanics are interpreting this? Caswell seems to confuse them."

Spencer filled the bladder, capped it, sat down and leaned back.

"Women warriors aren't totally unknown in their mythos, but she hasn't done anything relevant in their sight. They assume we're warriors based on presentation, and they definitely interpret the other element as serfs. They're not sure about the Bykos, but can tell they're peers to the captain. They accept that the scientists are doing something for the gods and don't need or want details. It's women's magic, and men stay out of it."

"That was pretty much my take."

"Yeah. It's going to be interesting to see how they react. The captain wants to talk to them about recovery as soon as daily schedule is set. They're well impressed with the food so far."

"Hell, so am I. They must be amazed."

"Likely. Hopefully getting them set and home is an easy add-on. I need to go, Doc."

"No problem, thanks for the insight."

There was a bleep from the system, and Arnet said, "It's the locals returning with the game we asked for."

Spencer was suddenly alert. He grabbed his phone and quickly tapped something.

Shortly, Caswell walked up.

"Sergeant?"

"You get the game from them, inspect it, remind them to stay away, and dismiss them. Status show for the Germans."

"Ah, got it." She nodded and strode deliberately toward the wards. "Hamilton, I need your assistance, please."

The private ran to follow.

The men arrived with two good-looking, bled and gutted carcasses. He assumed the thoracic organs were still inside. Those were choice cuts to these people.

Caswell took her time inspecting them, and made comments, translated through Hamilton. After a few minutes, she nodded, made a gesture that was almost a blessing, and pointed the way they'd come. They showed obvious subservience as they turned and left.

She called, "Keisuke, please help Hamilton move the meat to the kitchen."

"Hooah!" he replied, and ran up. She let them do the carrying as she led the way.

Spencer said, "Excellent."

Armand replied, "Establishes status for her?"

"Yes, she's at least a senior householder. They should give her some respect. I have no idea if we need it, but it's there."

"And we get venison for dinner."

Sean Elliott sat down with the Germans, Cryder, Spencer, and Oglesby.

He began, "Please use whatever honorific is appropriate, and adjust as needed. Spencer will advise and offer holds if needed, but I want to be as open as possible. Everyone please do your best."

Spencer raised a forefinger, and said, "Want me to start then, sir? You two are senior and should be . . . well, senior."

Cryder almost laughed. "Go ahead," he agreed.

"Sure," Sean echoed.

Spencer nodded. "Greetings, men. We're going to cover some details of returning home, though the finer points will be up to the wizards, who aren't here. We will depart with our serfs. You may have noticed they are less favored, and struggle a lot."

Whew. That was harsh, but it wasn't entirely inaccurate, and it did establish position and probably a noble obligation.

There were nods and comments to the affirmative.

He continued, "We will move from here to a departure point chosen as a bridge through the heavens. Everything will go with us. We will then return with our carts and tools, to return you with us, to the wizards' castle, and then to your home. There are limits on what you can take with you."

There was discussion, intermittently translated by the machine, until the leader spoke.

"I am Gurm. When can this take place, and what strictures do the wizards have?"

Spencer looked at Cryder and said, "I believe this is your call, sir."

Cryder nodded. "It'll be several weeks. I'll ask the wizards as soon as we return, but there is always preparation time. They must gather energies and sacrifices, and then confer with the signs of the gods on when and where. You can all bring personal items, and a limited amount of things you've acquired. Some family will be able to come along, but not all retainers. Many of the locals will need to stay."

Sean thought that quite a good presentation that should be clear.

Gurm asked, "Can we send a message or offering to your wizards?"

Cryder replied, "We can relay any message. Offerings aren't necessary. Our council of kings has instructed them to fix the mistake."

"Wulf would like to have a time and place."

"If I had one I would tell you. I can't speak for the wizards or the kings."

"Will you swear a blood oath?"

Cryder looked over at Spencer.

Spencer said, "Probably he means a slice of the hand, some dripped blood, and probably the captain, too."

Nodding, Cryder turned back. "If it is a fair...not harmful oath, I can. Captain Elliott, are you also agreeable to an oath with these men?"

Here we are, he thought. He spoke carefully for the translator.

"They are honorable men and I will gladly swear an oath with them."

Gurm nodded, pulled out a small, pointed knife, and made a slice near the heel of his hand. Blood welled and dripped at once. The man gave no indication it was at all uncomfortable.

Sean clenched his teeth and tried not to show it. He drew his Cold Steel that actually saw little use. Following Gurm's lead he made a small cut on the edge of his palm that burned and stung and dripped.

He saw Cryder had already done so.

The three of them basically high-fived, and that stung more. Blood smeared, and that was a bit disturbing, having someone else's blood mix in. It was far more personal than just being splashed. He understood why such oaths carried power.

Arnet arrived with clean white cloths to bind the cuts, and noted, "Medicated, will heal quickly. His will take slightly longer but faster than natural."

"Thank you," he replied in relief as he carefully wrapped the fabric around his hand and felt the stinging throb dull to a tense ache.

Cryder suggested, "We can return you to your camp tomorrow. There is a marker for us to use to locate you when we return. This evening, please join us for a feast and revel."

Gurm agreed, "That's very hospitable."

The evening was fun. Roast venison with herbs and salt. Mashed potatoes from the pantry. Some local greens and more herbs. Gravy. Beer, wine, and flavored rum. String, horn, and wind music from archive, and Sergeant Spencer had some band called Skáld on his memory stick. They sounded very Viking, and the Germans were quite enthusiastic, once they got over the shock of the musicians being elsewhere.

When they were told they could keep the quilted blankets, they were even more appreciative. They bedded down in a well-intoxicated haze and snored. Arnet adjusted something and the walls of the shelter became soundproof.

It was a chill night, foggy, damp, and then sharp. It was late October and felt like it.

Sean alternated socializing with writing up the day's summary. His hand had already healed, which was impressive and appreciated. Primitive rituals he could do without.

Kate Sheridan watched as the Germans boarded the vehicle and headed back to their village. It was early, with the sun burning through the fog, but hot breakfast was almost instant, so she grabbed coffee and sausage and warmed up at the fire. As field conditions went, it was quite decent. The toilet was still cold, but with a draft of warm air to make it a bit less challenging to go. The hot food and fire helped. The wards were a nice touch. She saw signs of a bear that had ambled by late.

The Nordwandlaz were a nice bonus on their genetic analysis. Certainly there were burial finds with occasional DNA, but living beings left complete codes. Of course, no one here had managed to place exactly where they were from. Hopefully that could be deciphered, rather than having to guess.

Others rose, cleaned up, got food. It was less organized than the Army seemed to prefer, but the resources made it work. Amalie came up blinking, grabbed a double coffee with a huge amount of cream and a bacon stick.

"Morning."

"Morning," she agreed. "Ready for the move?"

"Supposed to be the final one. Not ready, but let's get it done."

"Yeah. The troops aren't doing PT this morning."

"While everyone else was partying, I took care of processing more samples."

"I'm sorry. I should have helped." The older woman never seemed to take breaks.

"Don't be. I hate company. I was much better over there. I heard the music and laughter. That's enough for me."

"Okay. You might want to see someone about that, though."

"Or I might not." Amalie's tone was very cold and hard.

"Well, if it works for you, then that's fine," she said hastily, trying to cover the gaffe.

Down at the fire, Captain Elliott was doing his morning briefing.

"Striking camp will again start with personal gear, then tents, then group gear. The wards will be last, and Arnet and Caswell will handle our detainees. Once the wards are down, those collars are all we have. If you run, it's going to hurt. Not that I think anyone else will; you want to go home. But that's the rule. The faster we do this, the faster we can be comfortable at our final point, which can get boring at the end, though this time we have entertainment at least."

Cryder added, "I've set safety at ten meters outside the ward radius. Generous, I think. Outside that, you get a beep, a tingle, a zap, and unconscious, about that fast."

Elliott resumed. "That all said, everyone has a few more minutes for breakfast, then start with personal gear. Report that to Sergeant Caswell. Sergeant Spencer is handling the perimeter. Arnet is in charge of the CQ. Scientists, can you hear me up there?"

"Yes, sir!" Kate called back.

"Anything you need?"

"We should be able to pack it all down alone."

"Roger that. I show 0823. By 0845 teardown should be in progress. Any sick call, see Doc ASAP."

Kate and Amalie finished eating and downed their coffees with a couple of gulps, then folded down the laptop-equivalents and stowed test strips and vials. The Bykos had really good tech to share. She was still pretty pissed at the control of their findings.

"I hope we can keep enough data to matter," she commented. "I'd hate for the work to be wasted."

Raven muttered, "Memorizing everything I can. Also pics. I suggest not mentioning it."

She gave a single nod of assent and didn't reply. Her counterpart did have an amazing memory, though the details of genotyping were pretty complex.

There weren't any issues and it happened quickly. By 0930 the camp was struck, and she offered help hauling the ward posts back to Roller One. The graveled running track went away with some device that threw gravel almost like a lawnmower would, and roughed up the soil. That made sense. Plowed terrain untended would blend quickly. A compacted mass of gravel could last thousands of years under the right circumstances.

By then, Arnet had assembled some sort of trailer.

"It has seats and a folding overhead. It's not very comfortable, but better than walking."

It was obvious who was riding in that.

By 1000 everyone was loaded up, she in Roller One with Caswell, Oglesby, and the captain in back, Dalton and Cryder up front.

The Byko warned, "This will be an all-day trip and we might need ground recon for water features."

"Trouble crossing?" Dalton asked.

The man shook his head. "None at all for the vehicle, but it might be overly steep, scary, and painful for occupants."

"Ah, so pick good slopes?"

"If and when needed. I see two streams on the map and some depressions that might be."

"Roger that."

This was always the frustrating part. She was the least qualified person at this point, despite a PhD. She could handle a firearm at an amateur, occasional trip to the range level. She didn't know enough to recon for a vehicle crossing, nor anything about winches or anything if they needed them. She was strictly a passenger along for a bumpy, cramped, uncomfortable ride.

At that, this was far roomier than a HMMWV, but she wasn't small, and it was still tight quarters. Younger and leaner people had it much easier.

She never liked helmets or even hard hats, but even with the smoothing action of the vehicle's track system, it was a chaotic ride, and her helmet bumped the overhead repeatedly. They were crossing terrain. The river was far north from here, but all the runoff from these hills fed it. She wondered how it changed with glaciation, and what the millennia of wind, rain, and winters would do to it. It would be fascinating to mount a long-term camera and take an image a day.

They jolted into and out of a deep rut, almost a gully, which was followed by a rock.

"Cryder, technical question," she asked.

"Go," he prompted.

"Have you heard of what we called terrastar wheels? Three wheels rotating around a planetary hub."

"Yes. Those lack springs and bars. They work okay as water paddles, roll in and out of low-terrain dips well, especially at speed. At slow speed or deeper obstacles, they require considerably large pneumo tires or a hydraul mechanism to level the ride."

"Ah, so not as good?"

He shrugged. "Better than some axled wheels. Almost as good as some of your tracks. Not as effective as the be...system we have here."

He'd almost named it. Belt? Bed? Bearing? She guessed the name would give something away, but he wouldn't answer now, so she didn't ask.

"Okay. I've seen them and built models but never ridden on them."

He tilted his head over his shoulder again. "This is as smooth as it gets."

Captain Elliott said, "I've seen those, and I'd love to try them out sometime. They were used on an artillery piece."

"Huh. I saw them in a movie and in schematics."

"I get what he says about unsprung weight and suspension, though," Elliott noted.

"Yeah, that's something I look at from time to time."

Elliott was a civil engineer, not mechanical, but neither was she. They talked about gear ratios and cog angles for a bit. It was fun.

She asked, "What are you thinking about, Dan?"

Oglesby shook himself alert, and replied, "Dr. Raven suggested I write up the linguistic separation for her to refer to someone."

"Oh, yes, that. What do you think?"

"I can do it," he said. "I have no idea how it will be adapted for anything in our era."

"Neither do I," she admitted, "But our research group has been really good about getting information out."

She realized she shouldn't tell them any more, and certainly not around Cryder.

Luckily, Caswell interrupted. "Excuse me, but I'm watching the trailer... it's struggling."

Elliott looked back. "Yeah, that's a rough ride, and maybe some bruises. I think Noirot and Kita are okay. The others are getting a shaking."

An hour later, Kate realized Cryder wasn't kidding about the ride. With Dalton guiding, thigh deep in a narrow stream, the vehicle dropped into the course at a combination pitch down thirty degrees and left roll forty. The nose jammed into the far bank and wouldn't lift, until something protruded and cut enough earth for it to clear. The near-silent motor hummed and buzzed with power as the drive forced the nose to scoop through the earth and rise. Dalton scrambled ahead and to one side, shouting and pointing.

"Nose is jammed! Oh, shit. Okay, you're clear. Left is about four inches out, right almost in contact. Whoa! Whoa! Mud jammed everywhere. Okay, you're... flat, plane, whatever to the ground. Nose is above the terrain line. Clear!"

The vehicle slammed up and ahead, rolled forward almost plane, and stopped. Dalton ran back to check the other truck.

Roller Two rose up behind them, with just enough room past the gully for the passenger trailer. Cryder bumped forward a bit more to give them some space.

Dalton opened the door.

"Is there a tarp or something you want me to sit on?" he asked. He was soaked and caked.

Cryder pointed back. "Use the hose to clean off, and the air blast to dry. We can wait a couple of minutes."

"Hooah." The man stepped back, shrugged and pulled off boots, socks, and pants. He pressure-washed everything and blew them with hot air. Not for the first time she admired his nice calves. He definitely walked a lot and did some lifting. He dressed quickly and got back in.

They stopped for lunch, eating in and around the vehicles. It was decidedly chill now. Dalton had to be really glad to be warm and dry.

Because she was concerned, Kate made a quick check of the recoverees. They seemed mostly calm despite riding down those ravines in an open trailer, and still pissed off at being caged. Noirot clutched her daughter, who definitely wasn't happy with the trip.

Raven nodded and had nothing to say. She understood some of that was OPSEC, but the woman had always been remote, asocial, and detached.

She returned to Roller One and accepted a ration packet that opened easily. There was a tube of something that claimed to be chicken noodle soup, which heated itself on opening and was pretty good, even sucked through a straw.

While munching onion crackers and some sort of meat-cheese spread, she noted, "No flying cars for this, eh?"

Cryder replied, "Possible, but obviously uses more energy. Larger footprint for payload. Makes slow ground approach impossible. Nothing here is far enough to justify one."

"You don't want to take a loop around and check out the geography?"

"I might." He grinned. "This way I'm not tempted. The boffos want us to minimize interaction and engagement."

"I get that," she replied. "It would be fascinating."

"They may set a mission for that," he said. "This isn't it."

"Pity." She really would like to see more.

"Going to have to roll faster where terrain allows. I want to avoid a bivouac en route."

"Yeah, why do that if we don't have to?"

"Finish eating and we'll drive."

Cryder wasn't kidding. They had to be hitting 50 MPH on the flats. His control panel had a terrain monitor like some video games, but it only gave approximations. They slammed across a few dips and hummocks, and she was near nauseous when they slowed to cross another stream, this one thankfully shallow and not too wide.

Dalton commented, "Huh, about like the one we based near last time. Including a damp, seasonal feeder."

"We're a long way from there, but it's typical for the terrain," Cryder explained.

"Yeah, just interesting to see and brings back memories."

"That plateau up there is our destination," the man said as he pointed.

"Good. It's getting dark fast."

It still took another half hour to reach, with terrain obstacles including jutting rock outcroppings and copses of scrub.

As they circled around one, Dalton asked, "Can this thing drive over or through those?"

Cryder almost squinted and said, "If it were urgent enough I could slam through, but we'd ride over the downed trunks. I could push through a thin spot and force some space with a bit more time. Otherwise I'd cut through with fire or explosive."

"How much time would that save?"

"It'd be slower. Going around is much easier generally."

"Okay. I just wondered because this thing is on par with some of our armored vehicles."

"They have a mass advantage, and possibly a frame advantage depending on incidence of angle and mass-impact vector."

Kate understood that at least. This was physics.

"What about armor?"

Cryder laughed. "You've nothing close to this. And this is what you'd call a truck. Equivalent to your patrol armored cars."

"Damn," Dalton muttered, clearly impressed.

Arnet announced, "Stopped."

Martin Spencer unassed, and stretched upright. God, that ached. It was early dusk, fading quickly. He looked forward, and got a nod from Captain Elliott.

"Listen up!" he ordered. "Wards up first. Tents second. We'll take care of details in the morning. Wards are Dalton, myself, Uhiara, Oglesby and Dr. Sheridan. Sergeant Caswell is in charge of tents, she'll pick her team. Hamilton, Oyo, please assist Cryder with the vehicles and latrine. Captain, Cryder, any additions or comments?"

Elliott called, "Doc is available for any travel discomfort, once Arnet is free from setup. Get done fast and I'll authorize a holiday fire and some rum."

Several troops sounded off with, "Hooah!"

Rough setup was done quickly. His team didn't waste time, and everyone was sweating in short order from hauling wards, spiking them in, and folding the feet into place. The grass was knee deep and full of brush, stalks, weeds, and other scrub.

The wards were powered up, the latrine dug in, and the tents arrayed in an arc. Caswell had someone do a rough cut with the trimmer so they didn't have to pitch atop plant stalks. The mounted gun atop Roller Two was live, and he assumed the captain had them on rotation tonight at least. The prison tent went up and the two least trustworthy went into it.

It was dark, but smartlights from the vehicles followed everyone, buzzing little helpers that tracked eye movement and illuminated whatever one was working on. He also had the chest-mounted light in the Byko field harness. All in all, it took a half hour to do what would take several hours with a larger cooperative element.

Both the scientists needed painkillers for joints. Someone snarked about "fat chicks," but he knew what age did. None of them were old, but certainly late thirties was older than mid-twenties. A couple of the recoverees had been shaken about riding as cargo. There were some bruises and scrapes. Burnham had a pretty good welt on his left tricep.

"Additional order!" he shouted. "Everyone who was in the trailer, see Doc for a check-over. ASAP."

Arnet assisted Doc. Cryder took over on housekeeping and opened up the kitchen. There was bread, several types of spreads—meat, cheese, peanut butter, some vegetable stuff that had the texture of relish but tasted fresh, not pickled—and condiments. Next to that, the beverage dispenser had field rum, a sports drink, and water. Caswell stationed herself there.

She pointed at the dispensers. "One drink per person, but it's a double. There's grape juice for Kita."

The little girl grinned at her name, happy again to be in a camp and with food and people. Children had simple needs and concerns. She chugged grape juice and got straight into a peanut butter sandwich. She reminded Martin of his own daughter at that age.

The captain and Sergeant Burnham had a fire going, with a loose rock circle denoting the pit. A handful of cushions and boxes from the vehicles, and some rocks, provided enough things to sit on. As field conditions went, once again it was pretty damned good.

There was enthusiastic talk around the fire.

Dalton informed the recoverees on process. "We'll be here getting bored, getting tense, then *bang*! We're in Bykostan. Fr—"

Keisuke asked, "It's called Bykostan?"

"Yeah, Central Asia, future from us. All high tech, a research facility in the wilderness. They have a place for us to stay, eat, get debriefed. From there we'll be going home."

"But you have to come back for those German guys."

Arnet said, "We do, you don't. It'll be fine. You won't notice that aspect. Then we send you all home, following our council's guidance."

"Finally. It's been a long fucking time."

Arnet added, "Remember it hasn't been long there. It's been a few months subjective. We should have you back within days of when we transitioned."

Oyo twisted her head and said, "That's going to take some adjustment."

Martin offered, "It will, but you'll have lots of support. We have counselors, contacts, benefits, paid consults, and we all have private communications with each other. You can set that up among yourselves."

A faint, cold mist started descending. The tiny drops stung and tickled, then coalesced into an icy glaze on skin and clothing. The Byko fabric uniforms were great, and he was dry underneath, but his neck and hands chilled and dripped.

"Everyone may as well lights out," he suggested. "Tomorrow we start turning this into a comfortable place to stay for the remainder."

"Why bother?" a male voiced asked. He wasn't sure who.

"So we have something to do. We'll hunt, have fires, music, movies, and generally stay active until the last countdown. Any comments, sir?"

Captain Elliott had been over talking to Cryder. He turned and said, "Oh six hundred wakeup. Breakfast, sick call, PT, and then camp improvement as Sergeant Spencer mentioned. It'll all go away before we leave anyway."

With that, people did start crawling into tents. Enough light leaked from seams that he could tell they were watching some combination of movies, games, or porn. As long as they woke up ready to work, that wasn't his problem.

Martin once again exercised the privilege of rank for first watch shift. Staying up late suited him. Getting up early less so. A two-hour chunk in the middle of the night was somewhere below taking a dump in a porta-potty in Alaska at -45°F.

He sat atop Roller Two at the turret, which could be controlled from inside, but he wanted a view of the camp. There was a near invisible folding screen that covered him from the drizzle. Arnet sat below at a monitor station.

"How late are you up?" he asked.

Arnet replied, "Caswell replaces me in an hour, then Dalton replaces you. Staggered shifts."

"Cool," he nodded. "Think it'll be an easy transition home? Given they were five years on this one?"

"They should be," the man said with a nod. "They wanted to ensure they were well past the other element's arrival. In our case and all other cases, subsequent transitions are very accurate. Cryder got back to you within a day of their target tick."

"Oh, good." That was reassuring.

Nothing of significance happened. Some wildlife wandered by including a hyena. People woke up to drain excess beer. The rain tapered off. When Dalton crawled out and came over, he told the man exactly that.

"Quiet is good, Sergeant," Dalton agreed. "Sleep well."

"Thanks. Hope it stays quiet."

He'd thought he was still awake, but once he was horizontal in his bag he was warm, drowsy, and quickly asleep.

CHAPTER 30

Rich Dalton felt reasonably rested despite late guard duty. He did have a second cup of coffee, and damn, the Bykos had good field coffee. With some sausage and biscuits, he was in good shape for PT before drawing a ray gun for hunting detail.

The captain had said, "Get us something tasty we can roast old style."

With Oglesby along, he found a bush overlooking the trees and hunkered down into a comfortable position for shooting. Then he did the man thing of "nothing." He let his mind go blank. Next to him, Oglesby was as motionless, staring.

Shortly, the other man tapped his leg and pointed very carefully.

Near the woodline to the west foraging for food was a young, tender-looking deer. Hunting became so much easier with a Byko blaster. Rich slowly raised the weapon, and the animal tensed slightly, but at this range he was certainly out of arrowshot. The stag had no reason to believe he was at risk yet.

Rich pointed the gun and squeezed. There was a *thump*, a rush of air, and the deer fell over, dead.

It really wasn't sporting. But, it was a good way to feed people.

Next to him, Oglesby said, "Nice shot!"

"Thanks. Let's bundle it."

If they were quick, they wouldn't even need to gut it here.

He unrolled the sled, as they called it, that was more slippery than snot on ice, and made it easy to drag the corpse across the terrain. They were only about a kilometer from camp.

Ten minutes later they reached the wards. Nothing looked dangerous, but the camp was upgraded.

Rich entered the perimeter and paused. They'd barely been gone an hour.

The wards were wider, covering more area. Everything inside was mowed to lawn level. Brush was trimmed and stacked as kindling. Several scrub trees had apparently been sacrificed to make a pile of firewood. All the rocks were around the fireplace, or part of a cairn in one corner. Tents had been relocated into the previous layout. A tethered balloon and orbiting drone watched from above. The CQ was as it had been, with a trench from the shower running downhill to a sump covered with more rocks.

That pole with a hose appeared to be some sort of well or siphon, probably to ensure they had enough water. The vehicles and awning collected runoff and dew, but that composed a limited supply.

Okay, the Bykos had erected another enclosure. That's what had changed. He dollied the carcass over to Roller Two, for Raven and Arnet to prep, and paused again.

"What's going on in the new tent?" he asked.

Arnet replied, "Hot tub," as he bent over the deer and flicked a knife blade out from his combination tool.

Rich was taken aback. "You have a hot tub?"

Arnet was busy bleeding the deer, but said, "Yes, packed in the vehicle, but it takes a couple of days to process up and down, so I didn't want to pitch it until we were confirmed in a location."

Rich complained, "You let us struggle for weeks building ours, piece by piece."

"It kept everyone occupied and focused," Arnet pointed out.

"Yeah, but—"

"And you had a sense of accomplishment when finished." The man sounded so reasonable.

Dr. Raven started pulling out entrails and cutting them free. "Granted, but dammit..."

"Also, we didn't have one in the vehicle. I added the necessary struts on this mission."

Son of a... "You're a... prankster, Arnet."

The man didn't look up, but replied, "I believe you meant to say 'asshole.'"

Raven giggled.

"I meant it, but I try not to say it. It's crass."

"We were on a field exercise then and only had limited kit aboard."

"Wait, so your limited exercise kit includes a shower, mineral fabricator for booze, and porn?"

The tall man stood at last, and replied, "Yes. Are you bothered?"

"No, more like jealous."

"Sanitation and recreation are critical to maintaining peak operating health."

"Yeah, but our logistics can't support that yet."

"Anyway, the tub is open if you want to shower and get in."

"Shorts or naked?"

"No one is wearing clothes I know of, and none are needed."

He rather preferred something over his junk, but once in the water, no one would see, and he didn't want to be That Guy. He dropped gear in his tent and walked back to the rec tent in shorts. He opened the flap to find it was a vestibule, and stepped through the second door. Inside it was lit, with an inflated and framed tub with a stepladder, and an area for sitting and dressing.

The tub was big enough for five at a time, but the other half of the tent had a floor, seats, and warm air. This had to be using some power. He sat on the bench next to Spencer, and waited.

Spencer said, "We're doing ten-minute rotations. And damn, this feels good as you get old. A hot shower is amazing. This is like being Caesar."

"Yeah, I remember last time, the shock and thrill. I actually haven't been in one since."

Doc called, "Time!" and thumbed the current occupants out.

At the tub, he focused on the women. Caswell was actually quite shapely, and better than last time. He did prefer women who shaved and trimmed. Oyo was very hot, long and leggy and lean. Noirot was in good shape with some stretch marks but had less figure. On the bench, Sheridan was flat-out unattractive in the face, and ugly in the body. He didn't want to be judgmental, but she didn't fit his type.

The men were just men, and he'd have been fine showering naked. That was typical for the field. It was having women along as well that complicated things. Had it been all women, that would have been fine, too. The mix felt inappropriate.

The recoverees seemed both thrilled with the tub, and very, very jealous. Five years they'd been here, from their point of view, and they had been fully native the entire time.

Captain Elliott said, "One week to go. Routine schedules all around, relax time after dinner, and we'll shortly be in the Bykos' time."

"I'll be thrilled to see it," Maldonado said.

"You will," Sergeant Spencer assured him. "Though culturally it's a shock. They don't have to wait for anything. The coffee is served before you even finish asking, for example. If you want a steak, it might take ten minutes, but sometimes only three."

"And the architecture," Sheridan offered from the bench. "It's weird. Not even free-form. They don't look like buildings, just blobs and angles, all pure art. But inside they're total sci-fi."

Ten minutes was enough for now. He felt very refreshed, his skin tingly. The tub had some combination of salts and minerals to keep it clean and invigorating. It really was therapeutic.

What Sean Elliott thought of as the upper management tended to hang out in the CQ. He had to be here to log absolutely everything for the Byko leadership and the Army. Cryder did his with a combination of video feed, voice, and text with finger swipes. Arnet monitored drones and operations. Doc was here because all the clinic equipment was here. Sergeant Spencer liked having a good view of the troops to keep an eye on them. Sergeant Caswell did a great job of tuning recipes to suit twenty-first-century Americans. The Byko choices were strongly flavored and weird. Both Arnet and Cryder agreed they could tolerate her recipe choices.

At present, Dr. Raven was skinning out the deer and removing certain parts. They had a rotisserie to mount the main carcass on. She explained as she cut.

"It's a fresh kill, but it's had a couple of hours above fifty degrees, which should be okay for aging. We need a lot of salt in the cavity, with crushed herbs, and we'll tie it closed. Then that pepper and sesame paste can go on the outside with more salt."

Caswell said, "That's a lot of salt."

Raven shook her head. "Not per mass it's not. There's forty pounds of muscle meat here, plus the organs."

Sean asked, "Are we going to use those?"

"Not the brains. I don't think there's prions here, but who wants to find out, or start a trend? I have a sample to look at later. I can make a pie or stew with roast meat, veggies, kidneys, and liver if anyone wants it. I can tolerate liver and onions, but I won't ever ask for it. I tried both in London. Once. Heart and tongue are okay, but not impressive."

Caswell said, "Yeah, we wound up using everything. Liver went into sausage in sparing amounts. It's strong."

Spencer offered, "I'm told impala liver and scrambled eggs is popular with big-game hunters. No thanks."

With his approval, four of the recoverees spent the morning digging a shallow pit and prepping the pile of firewood for roasting coals. Spencer took his machete and with surprisingly few cuts turned two limbs into rests. The spit had a larger end with flats cut on it that enabled steady resting with each partial rotation. This accomplished the twin goals of a good meal and keeping troops occupied. They had a week to go. Still, that was all that was left.

He turned to Cryder. "We've got a week until departure. How did six weeks get used up that fast?"

"That's part of why we had that window. Estimating between longest safe operation time and longest search time."

"Yeah, I guess it's a good thing you did. We'd hate to have run out of time on the Germans, and could easily have needed more time with Shug or the cave."

Cryder said, "I set the wards to work both ways. No one can exit without my key. If no one tries, we won't hear anything about this. If they do, they'll be stunned, and we'll know who to watch."

"I understand. I'll make sure we stay inside. It's roomy enough for a walk."

Cryder sounded deadly serious as he elaborated, "We can't leave anyone behind, or risk leaving others who are trying to recover them."

"Definitely. I'll have them bust ass making the camp neat, then see if we can watch movies or other entertainment for the remainder."

"Last hunting trip tomorrow," the man warned in conclusion.

"Understood."

It was a small cantonment, and six days and a wakeup to go. He still wasn't used to the wards, with no physical barricade against threats. He understood it was adjustable for outside, anything from invisible to opaque to making the camp invisible. His brain wanted a fence, palisade, abatis, trench and earthwork, something.

They had an area right about thirty meters across. A quick calculation showed it at just about a quarter of an acre. That was all the bivouac space they had, and nowhere else to go.

Oglesby went out with Arnet on Roller Two to drag back a substantial dead tree. They all chopped it up for firewood using machetes and axes, which killed a good chunk of a day, and counted as exercise.

That night was venison stew with ground and chunked meat, reconstituted potatoes, carrots and peas, and huge chunks of crusty bread. Off to the side, Dr. Raven ate venison plain with a slice of something not-bread that Arnet had made from coconut flour.

She looked pleased, and said, "I need the recipe for this. It's almost like real bread."

The man smiled. "Glad you enjoy it. Yes, that's an easy recipe and we can share it."

"Thank you!"

It was pleasant enough to big-screen a movie outside, so they sat and sprawled and watched *Iron Man*. The response was enthusiastic.

The next day was full of baked goods including cookies, and an evening dance party. There was as much recreation as work, but they had to keep everyone focused on something.

Two days out, departure countdown started seriously. Much of the gear was cleaned, prepped, and put away. The hot tub and tent came down. The wards were reduced in perimeter to bring things in closer. Cryder marked a spot on the ground and a radius around it.

"That's where we'll transition from," he explained.

Sean remembered last time had been similar, but he wanted to make sure. "What is the circular error probable on that?"

The man grinned his usual grin. It was reassuring, not smug, but always carried a hint of condescension.

"As last time, I've gone small and they go large. It'll be fine."

Sean felt he needed to justify that. "Good. Just nervous."

Cryder admitted, "I am, too, but we've done this before."

✧   ✧   ✧

The morning of departure day, everyone lined up for what should be the last field breakfast. Rich Dalton offered a brief prayer, and others joined him.

"Holy Father, we thank you for our friends and technology that enable this recovery, even if their misuse caused it. We've all learned and grown, and forged strong friendships and trust. We appreciate Your support and wisdom in this sequence of events, and look forward to our return to our friends' world, before returning to our own. Amen."

As he finished, Captain Elliott announced, "I'll brief while you serve and eat. After this, tents come down, vehicles get packed. We'll mark a latrine area with a screen. We'll have water on the vehicles. Everything buttons up, and we stand in the redeployment area. There's margin of error, so we hope it's on time, but it may be a bit early or a lot later. All we can do is wait for it to happen. Wards will come down, so we'll have sentries against wildlife. Fireplace has to be dismantled. Stand by for instructions. We're going home."

There was a definite wave of elation through everyone, notably Uhiara, Keisuke, Hamilton, and Burnham.

A gust of cold wind blew leaves from trees. Temperatures were dropping fast now. They hadn't had the color change he was used to back home. A hint of color, brown, and down.

Within an hour everything was stowed, lashed, or crated. Arnet was atop Roller Two with the mounted weapon, and something else with a large bore.

"Bring me the fireplace rocks," he ordered.

Rich had a guess, but he watched as troops eagerly grabbed the still-warm stones and brought them over.

At a gesture, he tossed them up to Arnet, who did something with the large bore tube, and then *THOONK!*, launched one across the landscape to cheers from the soldiers. He followed that with another. In a couple of minutes, they were all scattered distant. That was a hoot. A giant air cannon.

Cryder ran one of his tools over the ashes and scorched ground and churned it up. It didn't seem that a single fireplace would be much of an issue, even if it survived thousands of years. As last time, though, the Guardians erased all traces. It was just their OPSEC.

With that done, Cryder waved everyone inside the transfer

point. Lozano and Munoz were in Byko restraints that seemed to be cuffs and shackles magnetically bound to a guide bot on the ground in front of him. They looked pissed. They'd struggled once or twice, and seemed to accept it was impossible to escape. Kita was on a leash her mother held, and didn't seem bothered.

Rich hoped the future would offer what the past and present couldn't. He wanted Lozano to find a way out of his sins by himself, not be forced to comply. Though if that's what it took to stop him from going after tween girls, then force was certainly a valid option. Judgment was the Lord's, but it was reasonable to assist in the Earthly elements of some of it.

They had a time tick in twenty-seven minutes.

CHAPTER 31

Martin Spencer was tense. Three minutes to go. No apparent threats. No one making a break for it, people on watch. Just wait for the recall, like last time.

Two minutes. He watched time tick down, second by agonizing second.

One minute. This was it, they hoped. Unless something went wrong.

10, 9, 8, 7 . . . 6 . . . . . . 5 . . . . 4 . . . . 3 . . . . 2 . . . . 1 . . .

Nothing.

No need to panic. It could be wrong by few seconds, minutes, or hell, even days. They got us back last time. They'll do it this time.

"Shit, they're late," Oglesby said.

Cryder calmly replied, "There's a window. That was the soonest we could expect connection. Remain calm and wait."

Martin echoed the sentiment. "Don't alarm anyone. Remember last time it was a significant span."

Lozano had to open his yap and ask, "So, a minute? A week?"

Cryder said, "I expect it within a few minutes. Refinement has improved, but every jump is different, and, of course, you're all new elements for them to calculate around."

Lozano asked, "Can they see us?" He looked around, perhaps for a drone.

"They can read the signatures we emit, but only for a moment before transition."

"So you don't know how long then."

BANG!

They dropped about two inches to the floor, along with a layer of grass and dirt.

"About now," Cryder said, deadpan and flat.

The Byko hangar was becoming a familiar, welcome sight. Researcher Larilee Zep was there to greet them.

"Soldiers! Welcome. Will you all please come with me?"

The other element followed nervously, glancing around. Martin remembered that tension from their first trip. He and Elliott brought up the rear.

Behind them a squad of what were obviously Guardians filled in, in tactical uniforms with batons.

They followed markers into a hall like the one his unit used. As they entered, all the collars and restraints fell off. Lozano and Munoz rubbed at their wrists. All of them rubbed at their necks, looking surprised.

Martin explained, "There's nowhere to go. But this is a very nice waiting area."

"Cell," Munoz replied.

"If you like. Though part of the restriction is for your safety. This place is part science lab, part desolate wilderness. Anyway, House, please introduce yourself."

The entity replied, "Greetings, soldiers. I am the patron for this facility. I can address you all individually. I provide food, beverages, entertainment, furniture, light or dark for activities or sleeping. You can ask for anything, and if it's within our rules you can have it, pursuant to your own guidelines."

It only took a few minutes to explain House and the holding room to them. They didn't have the immediate trouble with food and beverage that Martin had had. The acclimation before the jump had helped.

Martin asked, "House, can we get a lollipop for Kita, please? Shug's dialect is close for her, she doesn't speak English well yet."

A fruit lollipop of some kind, in generous size, appeared on the servace. Martin called her. "Kita! *Shooshi.*" He handed it to her and she was delighted.

The unit seemed more impressed by the House patron than their element had been. They were giddy about the food choices, but House knew what to expect and kept the portions small.

Oyo loudly exclaimed, "Oh my God! Flush toilets and tiled showers! First!"

Elliott grinned and ordered, "As you were. Showers in a few minutes."

He turned and addressed Cole.

"I will try to check in at least daily. You should maintain a schedule of meals, PT, and sleep. There are no assigned duties at present, but you might want to conduct whatever regular training you have. Most of our manuals are on file with House. Video is possible, often reconstructed but usable."

The LT looked a mix of relieved, overwhelmed, and still ashamed. Maybe Dalton should talk to him about that last.

The man replied, "Yes, sir, I got it. It's . . . odd. One moment in the Stone Age, then you arrive, now we're here."

"I'm always impressed by this place. Just make sure they remember they're soldiers." *And you, too, pal* was unsaid but implied.

"Will do. Thanks, Captain."

Martin noted the squad of enforcers had slowly moved into the background and away. He expected the doors here wouldn't open to the recoverees unless they were escorted.

Elliott finished with, "We'll be nearby and House can call me as needed. Hopefully, you can acclimate, rest, and handle routine alone for a couple of days."

He turned. "Sergeant Spencer, please lead the way to our quarters."

"Yes, sir."

It actually did feel a bit like a home, rather than just a barracks. "House, I need a guide, please."

In under a minute they were in their own dome, less restrictive than their charges, but he was now aware again that there were restrictions. But why not? It wasn't their home and they were visiting allies. There were always controls on those.

He just noticed it more.

Sean Elliott was glad to be here. The retrieval had gone nearly perfectly, though that delay had been a bit nerve-wracking. They'd accounted for everyone, recovered all except one, returned Shug to his people, recovered all the gear possible.

They'd also identified another element.

He already had the lengthy narrative of events from his point of view, and input from his soldiers. He had trouble reading the technical reports from the two scientists, but he'd skimmed them and noted the details he could.

He assumed there'd be a lengthy debriefing, as the local experts went over all the reports for everything. This was an entire scientific village, after all.

House had a beer waiting for him on the table. He took a refreshing slug, noted the others also had beverages, and turned to their human hosts. Larilee Zep was present, as were two other scientists he recognized from their previous visit.

"Good day," he greeted. "I recall you, but I'm afraid I've forgotten your names. Please forgive me."

"That's okay," said the male. "I am Ed Ruj." He wore a bit more clothing than last time, shorts and a pouch, with platform shoes. His hair was again styled, this time into steps like a flowerpot.

Behind Sean, Spencer muttered, "Are we not men? We are Devo."

He tried not to snicker.

The woman introduced herself. "I am Gella Xing." She wore a very elegant tunic in layers of blue. She was darker than most here, with obvious East Asian ancestry.

Sean replied, "Thank you, and it's good to meet you again, researchers."

"It should be an easier interface this time," Ruj noted.

Sean offered, "I hope so."

Before he could raise the matter, Researcher Zep asked, "There's another displaced element?"

"Yes, ma'am," Sean said, defaulting to his forms of address. "Sergeants Spencer and Oglesby are under the impression they're Germanic or Old Norse, based on what language hints and equipment they had."

She nodded. "Understood. What documentation do you have?"

"I have a report, and I believe Shuff Cryder does, also. We have video and audio."

Her smile seemed genuine and interested. "Excellent. We will review those."

Larilee was apparently in charge now, at least as far as liaison and interface.

She told him, "There will be official notice soon, but for now, commendations on an optimally run mission."

"Thank you."

"Please relax for the rest of the day. We will schedule interviews and summaries for tomorrow. We will copy all your data and return the originals."

Her statement was neither request nor order. It was just a fact. He knew better than to attempt to argue. Though it wasn't his report he was worried about. What had the scientists discovered, and how much of that was of concern to Byko OPSEC?

She turned, and continued. "Sergeant Spencer, an aspect of your previous report is still of interest in this community."

"Oh?"

"Would you consent to demonstrating iron ore reduction?"

Spencer paused for a moment, then nodded.

He said, "I'm agreeable. I need several people to help and it's a process that will take at least two days, and several hours over both."

"You may ask anyone of your people you wish, and we will certainly have volunteers if you can instruct them."

"Okay, then. When?"

"Shorter is better, as we will need to address the other element."

"Okay. Day after tomorrow to start the charcoal, the day after that, and possibly the one after that. Then we'll need to do the iron reduction after I get some ore."

"That is workable. We can record for those otherwise engaged. There will be several observers, though."

"That's great."

Sean offered, "I'd like to help. Last time I mostly watched while you and the young bucks did the heavy lifting."

"Certainly, sir, and thanks."

The Byko wasted no time debriefing. Sean Elliott could still taste the breakfast waffles when he was ushered into the circular theater they used for these meetings. He recalled how he felt last time, like a bug on a microscope plate.

He was a bit less nervous this time. He wasn't the subject of the discussion, nor was he sitting in the middle.

He was informed that the recovered element was getting med

checks, including scar removal, tooth repair, everything to make them healthy and fit as they had been, and a bit better. That was definitely one benefit of this.

Someone told him, "The lengthy disconnect was unfortunate, and probably complicated by your additional personnel. We'd tried for a span between six months and eighteen months after."

He didn't like the implication that was the fault of he or the US. The Byko had never been forthcoming, and this was all their tech. For that matter, the root error was theirs.

His own pages and images scrolled across the wall, each one for only a few seconds, with a translation into their text next to it. That also was sort-of English, the letters simplified and overlapping so entire words looked like diphthongs. It would take a short amount of time to fit in here linguistically. Though he suspected Spencer or Oglesby would have it down in a week.

While he was beginning to grasp their dialect, they were talking very quickly, over one another, and there were certainly technical, cultural, and colloquial terms he wasn't getting. He understood a handful of words here and there, and all he could decipher was that it was about a return trip for the other displaced element. Which he knew.

He did wonder why the displacees seemed to cluster. Though it was only two groups this time, not four, and Shug had been a lone individual. So maybe not. There could be a lot of factors. He doubted calculus and diff eq would get him anywhere close to comprehending the math involved.

While he tried to sort out the overlapping voices of this council, Larilee Zep's cut through directly to him.

"The summary is we need to go back and retrieve them, of course. Are you and your people available?"

He'd expected that might be the case.

He replied, "So who do we send back this time? I would prefer to have all of us, for backup and cohesion."

"That's what we would prefer. We have your signal, aura, definition—there is no exact word—programmed. Transitioning you all is easier in that regard. Also, the fewer transfers the better. It would be ideal to send you all either there, then back. Or just send you all home. Splitting the element into multiple tracks is undesirable, and you have some experience."

"And the civilian scientists aren't an issue?"

"Possibly, but removing them now would be a different issue."

"Well, that simplifies that discussion, then. Though our two attached experts do get a vote. I'll check with the soldiers. I can't really order them. I can't really let them vote, either."

"I comprehend."

How was he going to raise this?

Their council was more like a mob or a party, with people walking about, talking into the air, their voices shifted wherever needed by the patrons. Several attendees appeared to be holograms or similar presentations, not present.

Suddenly Zep was in front of him.

"There is one matter we will need to address in person, for courtesy." It was immediately a lot quieter. Some sort of silencing screen was in use.

"Yes?" he asked.

"Crossbred offspring can't return to your time frame. They must remain here for the time being." Her statement was direct and factual, but she sounded embarrassed.

He understood what they meant, but not the details. "How long a time?"

"Until she is old enough to decide certain matters."

"Adulthood, then?" he asked.

Zep elaborated. "She can't reproduce in your time frame. She must be old enough to agree to sterilization, or to remain here permanently. I'm sorry."

That wasn't totally unexpected.

"I would guess that once raised here, she'll be uninterested in our time."

"Probably," Zep agreed. "Though the choice exists and is hers."

"And her mother?"

"She may return, or remain."

"I can guess what she'll choose."

"Likewise," the woman agreed. "We don't always have choices in these matters. The pretense must be acknowledged."

He understood the concern. That didn't make it easier to tell a young woman her life was fucked up and she wasn't going home. Unless she actually wanted to abandon her kid, in which case she was already fucked up.

"That's going to be a tough discussion. Can I give them a day to get settled in?"

"Or two," she agreed.

Goddamn, he needed a drink.

Back at their quarters he announced, "I have some issues to take care of tomorrow, and we need to ensure we return all the gear and get it signed for...yes, Doc?"

The doctor said, "Sir, Sergeant Spencer and I took care of that. House confirmed return of everything we were carrying, and our twenty-first-century stuff is here ready when we are."

Good, though he'd hoped it might take a little bit of time. There was so little work to do here it was a problem.

"They're organizing a trip to recover the Germans. They prefer to send the entire unit to eliminate a few variables, I gather. I told them I couldn't order any soldiers on a second excursion, and I'd have to check with our attached contractors."

"We're in," Raven said.

"Yup," Sheridan echoed with a nod. It was apparently her turn to pet the cat, and she seemed very interested in his development. She had a hair sample, and was getting images and measurements while he was in her lap.

All the soldiers offered a "Hooah" or a nod. Everyone was in. He was pleased, and had expected it, but it was still good to see that level of confidence.

He simply said, "Excellent, thanks. We'll need to help the Byko with further debriefing of our other element. I have some items personally on that list. If everyone is ready tonight, I'm authorizing recreation. Don't exceed a BAC of point zero eight, that includes me. House, can you monitor that?"

"One of our network can, yes."

"Thanks. Return by oh one hundred, reveille oh seven hundred. Sign out with House as previously. Oh, and Dr. Raven, they'll fix your ankle tomorrow."

"In what way?"

"I gather some sort of surgery, internal cybernetic stuff, and such. They said you'd be fine by lunch."

"Yes, but will I be able to lift a car?"

"Your ankle might, but I suspect your wrists will break."

She giggled. "I always hated the physics of shows like that."

"Good luck, ma'am."

"Thank you, Captain." She turned, looking a bit nervous.

More softly, he said, "House, I'd like a quiet place for a drink, possibly with low background music or landscapes. If any of our people or our assigned staff wish to find me, they can."

"Certainly, Sean. Please follow the guide to the Overlook."

Amalie Raven wanted away from Sheridan, and didn't want to deal with any of the low-level twits. That left Sergeant Spencer, Doc, or the captain. The captain seemed pretty reserved. She assumed he wanted to be left alone.

Spencer had some personal issues and she didn't want to be involved.

"Armand," she called. He turned and faced her.

"Yes, Dr. Raven?"

She tried to smile. "Amalie. I want to have someone with me while I go nerding about. Would you join me?"

"Sure," he agreed. He didn't sound enthused. He rarely did. He seemed agreeable, though.

"Thanks, one moment. House, screen please."

The air shimmered and opaqued. "Can I have one of those western mountain tunics in deep greens, please? And blue jeans."

"At once."

In moments a servace rose up with jeans that actually fit her hips and a tunic that concealed them. She'd never look slim, but she felt much more presentable.

She pulled them on, then asked, "I'd like comfortable footwear that looks like what we call cowboy boots."

Those arrived moments later, in green and brown leather.

"Thank you," she acknowledged. "Done."

She stuffed her feet into the boots as the air cleared, and yes, they felt very flexible.

Armand had changed into a high-necked shirt with flaring shoulders.

"Very sci-fi," she grinned.

He smiled. "Yeah, I was copying one of the old hip-hop artists I followed as a kid."

"It works well here. Shall we start at the Mad Lab and work out?"

"Sure," he agreed. "House, guide please."

The light pinged on the floor, pulsing and waiting for them.

She felt short next to Devereaux. The local men were taller

up to another six inches. It wasn't intimidating per se, but it was uncomfortable.

As they walked, he asked, "How's your research? I helped briefly and then got tied up with Army stuff."

"It's a pile of data still to process, and we'll still be doing some of that here while you do Army stuff. Of course, they already pulled some of my files." She didn't say she had a hidden backup, written notes, and a near photographic memory.

He smiled. "I'm not sure which I'd dislike more."

"I enjoy my work," she said. "I keep hoping they'll relax some of the medical standards and I can get on a mission to Mars."

"That would be cool," he agreed. "One-way trip, though. Would your boyfriend go with you?"

"No, that would be an issue, but he would support me anyway. And I'd go anyway, once my daughter is grown. It's Mars. I can't really explain it beyond that." He really would. She loved him, and missed him. If only he could be here. But Mars...

"I get it," Devereaux said with a nod.

They crossed the walkway, now edge illuminated. The stairs were as wide and long as before, then the cursor led them along a mezzanine.

There was a different club, HEISENBERG's, with a front display of a maze of rolling balls clattering around on tracks.

"A Rube Goldberg machine!" she exclaimed.

"Like the cartoons?" Devereaux asked.

"Exactly."

The balls rolled, bounced, pinged keys, arced across gaps, and the track went all the way around the room.

"That's neat." It was something that hadn't changed in concept since their time. She followed it along part of one wall, realized it could take all night to track, and headed for the bar.

She was instantly jealous of the woman serving. Tall, dark, busty, tight waist, oval hips, long legs, with a shifting black gown that showed most of her off as she moved. Her hair was in long streams that stayed separate, but unbraided.

As they reached the bar proper, the woman smiled. "Oh, Americans! I hope my accent is okay."

Devereaux said, "It's very good."

It was. There was a definite accent, part Asian, part German, maybe? It wasn't Arabic.

"Thank you. What can I mix?"

Amalie carefully said, "I need a cider, or a perry. Dry and without additives."

"Sure! We have a late-autumn tart apple cider with a hint of effervescench. Is that how you say it?"

"Effervescence. Thanks, I'll try it."

The woman turned, waved a control, pulled a tap over a glass, and turned back with a beautiful cut-crystal tumbler.

She took a taste, and it was perfect. One of those was plenty.

"Very nice, thank you," she complimented.

"You're welcome. And you, sir?"

Devereaux smiled that huge white-toothed grin. "I'm a simple man. Lager, cold."

"At once."

In moments he had his.

She suggested, "Let's find a table near the wall."

"Right there," he pointed.

"Good."

It was a tall table with high-backed seats. It gave them a view while being out of the way. It appeared some sort of performance was going to happen soon.

A man walking by stopped suddenly, stared for a second, and then continued walking slowly.

House spoke in her ears. "A scientist would like an introduction to you. May I acknowledge you and invite him?"

"Oh, please," she agreed. Scientists here were much more her crowd. She might enjoy more temporal liaison work. And, she could not worry about her ankle they were going to carve up.

The passerby changed direction, came back, and said, "Thank you for accepting. I believe you're one of the American life scientists? Or both?"

"I am Amalie Raven, a paleobiologist," she agreed.

Devereaux said, "I'm a physician. Armand Devereaux."

They shook hands briefly. She gathered it wasn't common for them, and being done as a courtesy.

"Wolgem Kam. I'm a forensic climatologist."

That sounded way too cool.

Out loud, she said, "Oh, that's fascinating. Can we discuss any of it?"

He agreed, "Some. If you tell me what you know, I can more

easily tell the limits." He had a tall drink in a black, obsidian-looking tumbler.

She pulled at files in her mind. "Where to start? We are, or were, in a glacial interstadial. There are at least four solar cycles at play. The geological factors include tectonic. Critical atmospheric elements are water vapor, methane, and CO_2. Multiple processes are not well understood and are outside my expertise, but I read up on them."

"Okay, that establishes quite some baseline. Certainly the solar cycles are critical. I think I can safely admit we've resolved much of the pollutant issue."

"Oh? Fossil fuels do seem out of fashion here."

He smiled. "They are, though that wasn't the primary factor. I am plotting curves of change based on incomplete historical data."

"Are you able to use empirical data? Core samples or tree growth?"

He nodded. "Yes, though there's less of that than we'd like, and less accurate than we want."

"Ah. Were our measurements off by a lot?"

He seemed very irritated.

"You could say that. All the data we have from the mid-1980s until...a later time are completely untrustworthy."

"That bad?"

"Worse. Your climate scientists were so desperate to prove their points that they threw out data, changed archives without notation, recycled used data, even fabricated some. It's not all, or even most, but so much of it is contaminated, none of it is trustworthy. We're having to go through archive by archive, reconstructing to determine if the base figures are relevant. And, of course, almost all the models were completely wrong. There are multiple factors you don't know about. But rather than say, 'We don't know yet,' they felt compelled to force the data to fit.

"So with that problem—which was ephemeral, and should have been understood so by anyone with a grasp of the history of science—out of the way, we're trying to engage in long-term trend lines. As we go back through records, though, they get less and less reliable, then they get less and less accurate. Then, as you say, we're stuck using secondary attributes, but the eras with the least reliable and confident data also have the least of that evidence to work from. So there's a massive gap of incongruity we can't confidently assign."

She admitted, "I knew we had some falsifications, and even a couple of trials. I didn't think it was that bad."

He took a pull at his drink. "It's worse. Your entire era until... later is only usable in part, and questionable even then. One of our teams just cleared another paper. It was an excellent treatise, and even acceptable as a first-order estimate in its predictions. Except it was based on entirely fabricated data from the outside source."

Amalie blushed. She knew about the NASA archive that had retconned data, and had no extant copies of the originals. That was apparently an endemic matter.

"Can you tell me what you do know about the future trends?"

"Possibly. Our current research is attempting to confirm when the next glaciation is supposed to commence. Then, we need to determine if we should permit it with either relocations or oases, or if we should counter it. There are philosophical, climatological, and societal matters involved."

"I can understand that," she agreed. "We have an estimate of five thousand to fifty thousand years for onset of glaciation."

"That is a correct approximation. Ours is revised and narrowed somewhat."

She asked, "Is any of the temporal displacement helping with data?"

"Only as... bitshots?"

"Snapshots," she offered.

"Yes. They're narrow, instantaneous grabs that we can insert into matrices, when we have them. As much as we urge people and outfits not to attempt temporal translations, we ask that they furnish any and all data if they do. It's a complicated matter since some are hoping to sell the data, or use it as justification."

Devereaux laughed.

"There's always someone angling for a buck," he said.

Kam turned and said, "I deduce the phrase. Yes. Whether financial or positional."

"Researcher Kam," she said to get his attention back. "I will furnish whatever data I have from known, trusted sources, and if we return I will attempt to bring... well, as many summaries of every science I can acquire and load. I gather some are actually missing."

He raised his eyebrows. "Thank you. Yes, a lot of data has been a combination of misplaced, lost, unarchived, misattributed, became apocryphal, and unsourced. Obviously, your future, our past, has had incidents. That's all sciences, not just mine."

"I'm fascinated that you have a culture focused on science and research."

He said, "Not entirely. We have a substantial development sector."

Devereaux asked, "Who does all the menial work?"

The man sipped his drink and replied, "Machines mostly. The patrons control a lot of that via . . . I don't know what I can say. Their machine aspects. Apparently that's acceptable."

"So what about people who aren't brilliant enough to do research or fabrication?" Armand was digging, she realized.

"There are people who focus on arts, handwork, support. They sometimes operate in groups with direction. You're meeting a very elite here, if I can put it in those terms."

She noticed he hadn't really answered the question. Did they have eugenics here? Controlled gene selection for reproduction? Almost everyone she'd met was high end of the curve by her contemporary standards, but unless there had been drastic changes in genetics, some sort of radical cleansing, or it was a lot further in the future than all her studies showed, a tend toward the mean should lead to people of normal or subnormal intellect who needed either simpler work or caretakers. He'd hinted at that, but what did they do?

More important, why did they all need to hide it? Especially from what they'd regard as simpler people?

She glanced at Devereaux and his fractional nod indicated he had the same question.

Kam said, "We can talk more later, and you can always page me. Looks like entertainment is about to start."

"Have you all learned our dialect?" she asked.

"Oh! That." He seemed surprised. "It's not terribly hard. English is functionally the same, we just slur and abbreviate a lot. Think about the difference between your common daily texts and say . . . .those of your early colonial era. Those who were literate practiced it. As it became more common, it became more mundane and simplistic."

"That makes sense." At least that was a straight answer, and one she understood.

She added, "I've been watching our Internet do that for twenty-five years, and evidence suggests it started before that."

They were interrupted by sweeping chimes, resonances, and notes. The entertainment was music played on something like a theremin but with much more tonality.

"Well, that's cool," she said aloud.

She sipped her drink and tried to discern the shapes of those waveforms.

Rich Dalton was outside Heisenberg's at a bar served through a window. It was quieter out here than inside, and less intense. He'd gotten used to the quiet.

He was watching passersby. Most wore what he'd consider street clothes, though there was even less distinction between male and female here. Some, though, were dressed up and he couldn't tell the difference between evening wear, costume, or cultural. He recalled Zep had worn feathers when they first met last time. Had she come from some event with no time to change? Or didn't think it was an issue? Or wanted to gauge their response?

An amazing looking brunette strode by apparently nude, but groin and nipples blurred by some visual effect. Another woman had blue skin with a brushed texture, and her male partner green with scales. Then a guy in a perfectly normal kilt, one in pants, a chick in a tunic and shorts. They were all over.

He saw Alakri Mommed approaching. The man fairly glowed.

"Mommed!" he shouted. "You look very pleased."

"I am most pleased, Rich!" the man replied. "Today I have achieved jihad!"

What? Was that still a thing, as secular as this guy was?

"Um . . . what's that?"

He gestured to the table and Mommed sat down.

"It means a struggle, a fight against a chosen enemy. Thank you for the seat."

That was a sudden revelation and he wasn't sure about sharing. What happened?

He said, "I know what it means. But I thought you said that wasn't a thing anymore?"

Mommed shook his head. "I did not fight a person. This goes back many years. When I was six my mother died of thalamic glioma. It is a very rare, vicious cancer that attacks the thalamus. Once within the tissue, it is almost impossible to fight, even with very fine nanoneurotracer inhibitor biophages. They destroy the cancer, but damage nearby neurons to the point where the thalamus is unrecoverable, and death follows. It doesn't destroy the cortex, the reasoning part of the brain. It destroys the autonomic nervous system. Occasionally, there is sufficient substance to allow an implant to take over the base functions and life of a sort is possible with proper support. In her case...it did not help. She showed symptoms, and was dead within days."

"I am very sorry for your loss," he said.

The man looked focused and intent as he said, "I swore before God I would *find* a way to eliminate it at the genetic level, to drive it into extinction."

"Very good." That was. Had he?

The man nodded reflexively and continued. "Thank you. Today, both patients treated with my mitochondrial therapy tested clean, and a reconstructive nano was able to align new, healthy neurons their existing tissue has exploited. They are fully, permanently cured with no side effects."

The man grinned, spread his arm, and announced, "Sergeant Rich, I have destroyed a disease!"

Again the man glowed as only a true believer can.

Damn. Just, damn. And why couldn't that be a thing in his own time? What could a million fanatics do with years of study and determination, with money and facilities? How many diseases, how much poverty could be eliminated, and how much great art and science could be created?

"That is absolutely amazing," he said, and realized he had damp eyes.

"It is not entirely my work. I organized a team, but I feel validated that my determination and direction was a key part that made it possible."

There was one thing Rich could offer in the physical realm. "Will you join me in a drink?"

"I will absolutely join you. May I see if they have a good rum punch?"

"Please!"

He turned to the bar, and the server approached.

Alakri asked, "Can you show me options for rum, please?"

"And me." Rum was very much a thing here, it seemed.

"Yes."

A screen appeared in the air, and he chose ingredients, keeping the booze on the light side, keeping the pineapple down as it was very sweet here, adding a touch more lime.

"That should do it," he said.

"At once," the bartender agreed. He flipped glasses and bottles even more elaborately than show bartenders back home, and furnished two glasses on delicately folded cloth napkins.

Rich raised one and toasted, "To your success, Mommed, and to your faith in God for it."

"And to you, Rich, a valued friend, and your faith."

The drink was just about right, even improvised from guesses. Mommed took a sip, then a full chug.

He said, "Very tasty and refreshing. I'll remember this."

"I'm glad you like it."

"I do. And now I have to find another challenge, something else to focus my efforts on. I've spent forty-three years fighting this fight. Now it is complete."

They sat for a moment, and Rich pondered that.

"Mommed, two things come to mind."

"Go ahead."

"You could mentor others into their own work and accomplishments. Or find another child who has lost a parent, and take up their cause for them."

The man raised his eyebrows and smiled. "That is an excellent idea, Rich. I like that very much. I will start on that tomorrow."

"You might rest for a few days to let your spirit relax and be sure of your direction."

Shaking his head, the man replied, "No, you are correct. God clearly made this discussion happen, that I might find a new direction. We still have disease and death, and the survivors are still hurt by it. I will find a case tomorrow, of a child who has been orphaned, and I will begin anew."

"Well, good." Damn. That was truly inspiring. God had made this conversation happen, that Mommed might find a new cause, and Rich could learn from it.

Rich would have to consider how the closest person here to his moral and theological position was a Muslim.

But it just showed that God was everywhere, if people would only listen.

And how could he deliver that message in a way people would hear?

CHAPTER 32

Sean Elliott didn't have a superior authority to discuss with here. He was the final word, and he was only a captain. Much as Cole's career was going to be affected, negatively, by circumstances beyond his control and his responses to them, Sean's was hinging on decisions here.

He planned to ask Spencer, and possibly Caswell, for input. Hell, even Doc and perhaps Dr. Sheridan. The decisions were his, though.

He sat at a single table and chair produced on the spot for him, on a rooftop balcony. It was a medium-size building, and he could see a skyline of wilderness and other structures, walkways, gardens, people on foot, and occasional vehicles. Over there appeared to be the massive block containing the facilities his people were housed in. It was an amorphous anthracite lump, as if a kid made a brick from modeling clay. The sun was still barely tinging the horizon. He suspected some sort of dome or field, because it should be cooler and it wasn't, but the air was very fresh. There was no one else around him.

The lost element's interpreter had died here. Reporting that wasn't a huge problem for him, no matter how much it sucked for the family. Report, let the Army handle it.

Cole's failures, which they were, no matter the circumstances, were something to write up and pass on. If asked, he'd note that he'd managed better under similar circumstances.

Burnham should have stepped up more, but he was enlisted and subordinate to his officer. Officially everything else was consensual, so he couldn't really be blamed and shouldn't be. And he'd managed to keep the respect of the other troops.

The two detainees. Not his problem, but he'd have to report on their activities. The general would decide if additional discipline came into play. His best recommendation was to grant them discharges immediately, so they weren't an Army problem. At the same time, they needed support and counseling. Though the Bykos could quite probably erase memories or manipulate thoughts to reduce the issues. The questions there were: What would the Bykos think of that professionally, politically, socially, ethically? What did Captain Sean Elliott think of it? And what would the US Army think of it? As nonpracticing as he was, what would God think of messing with a man's mind to change his personality?

If he didn't raise the question to the Bykos or mention their skills to the Army, that avoided all that, but still left one man very socially and mentally sick, and another in distress if not outright anger. It wouldn't be his problem on paper, but could he respect himself with that outcome? The problems were theirs to deal with, as others had, but the triggering events weren't, and he had options. It was all ugly.

Then... Denise Noirot. A very broken but overall decent young woman—with a child. The child couldn't go to their time. Noirot probably, hopefully, wanted to stay with her daughter. They could probably be happy here at first, but they'd basically be pets and lab rats. The child might grow up trained in everything this society offered, but Noirot, while not stupid, wasn't the type to grasp any of the advanced sciences. What could she do for a living here?

He had no real control of that. It wasn't his issue, but she was one of his troops and he had a moral obligation as commander.

The second part was explaining her back home as a casualty, when she actually wasn't. The lie didn't bother him in context. Everything about this time frame was deniable and denied. What about her family, though? Or her thoughts of them? "Sorry, we went back to the wilds of A-stan to find this missing element and, well, she was dead." Any story told like that would suck. She'd been through more than most, and she was getting punished for Cole's failure, as well as the Bykos' fuckup.

He was definitely going to lay the latter at their feet and demand... something.

This wasn't a set of decisions a mere captain should have to make. Nor, really, anyone should have to.

He was startled by House's voice. "Captain, you are needed at the facility."

"Crap, what now?"

"Disciplinary questions require your input. Should I brief, or will you return?"

"If there's no violence, let me go back."

An illuminated platform appeared in front of him. He stepped aboard, and a saddle rose up. In a moment, he was rolling... floating... something, back toward the facility, and fast.

It was barely three minutes before the scooter had him along the walkways, through the tunnel and gate, around the perimeter and in front of the detention area. He leaned forward and up, stepped off the transport, and through the arch.

Cole was right inside, and offered a salute, which he returned.

"Thank you for coming, Captain. I needed additional support."

"Very well, what's up?"

Cole explained, "I called because you are the senior officer. It has been detailed to Sergeant Munoz that he can comply with our regulations and my reasonable orders for schedule, or he will be fed only the nutrient biscuits the system can provide. I've ordered lights out, he's refusing."

"That seems fine. You just needed my confirmation?"

"No, sir, the caretaker required you to be present and confirm for him. It?"

"Ah. House, that is a reasonable order for our people, and I endorse it. In fact," he continued, being sure to be heard, "I endorse any discipline that maintains nutrition and fitness, including curtailment of all entertainment, and liquid nutrition only. If they want to sit sixteen hours a day, staring at a blank wall, drinking glop, in preference to complying with our procedures, they may do so. Kill the lights when the ranking member asks."

"I understand, Captain. I have confirmed with our leadership, who endorsed similar limits as safe and enforceable if necessary."

"Perfect. Listen up. You lot want to go home. We want to take you home. I realize it's been a rough five years, but you're here now. We can talk reasonably, offer support, limited local counseling, and very good accommodations. Comply with the process, we'll get you home and arrange all the benefits we can. Otherwise, you can sit in individual detention. That's all.

"If you do have any concerns you can't address, and need a shoulder, advice, comfort, we'll do our best. But that's contingent on you making a credible effort. Capisce?"

Several voices responded, "Hooah." They didn't sound thrilled. He said so.

"I'll expect more enthusiasm later. Now, if you can go along with things until dinner tomorrow, I'll make sure you get equivalent recreation and downtime after that." He wasn't sure what that might entail at this point, but good liquor was probably part of it.

On the one hand, he was very sympathetic to how fucked up things had been for them. On the other, they were back in civilization and needed to readapt.

And how rough was it going to be in their own time? With at least one of them threatening to scream to the media? Even if they weren't believed, it would be a scene.

This hadn't resolved any of his concerns.

He stepped back out.

"House, please take me where I was. I need another hour alone to destress, and back to our lodging."

"Confirmed."

The sky was beautifully clear here, almost as much as the Paleolithic. He saw a streak of a meteor. Just a line that crossed the sky and faded.

An hour later, no closer to answers, House announced, "Sean, you wanted a time notification."

"Thanks. House. Guide back, please."

He did sleep with mild help from House, and woke up feeling physically better.

He started to load down on breakfast, then realized he didn't need to. He was in the habit of "post field, grab something good," but they'd had plenty of decent food. He switched to bacon, good scrambled eggs, and coffee.

He let everyone eat, then called formation in formation. He liked being relaxed, but the military did these things for a reason and they should be upheld.

"At ease," he ordered. "I have some follow-up with the other unit, and I need to discuss with a couple of you first. I assume once I'm done with that, everyone here can handle their own PT, collate notes and summaries, and remain available for follow-up?"

There was a collective "Hooah."

"Good. We still have work to do. Then this follow-up."

Spencer came to attention and raised his hand.

"Sergeant Spencer, go ahead."

"Sir, I need to start prepping for that demo they want me to do, and I need some other hands."

That was handy. "Excellent. Proceed with that, anyone who is free will assist, and I'll help as much as I can once I handle this."

"Yes, sir."

"I need to consult with Spencer, Caswell, Doc, and Dr. Sheridan if you're free."

"I am."

"Company, Attention! Fall out."

His selected advisors came over. He bade everyone sit and get beverages.

"Here's my biggest issue for now," he introduced. "Noirot's daughter has to remain here."

Caswell exclaimed, "Oh, no!"

"Yeah." He summarized the issue. Daughter to remain to avoid reproducing in either past or their present. Noirot probably to remain with her.

"First question, Dr. Sheridan: Does that seem reasonable within your scientific background?"

The large woman made a face, and sat quietly. He let her think in silence. It was a solid two minutes before she replied.

"There's a notable genetic difference between the Paleos and us. Any trace would show an abnormally high Central Asian parental haplogroup. There's no significant genetic risk, and if there were problems, the fetus would likely not survive to term. From a scientific risk, *if* I were someone who had some reason to examine her genome, even a commercial DNA test, I would notice the aberration.

"Of course, they may know something specific, or just have a generalized risk assessment, against allowing the possibility. Without knowing their threat matrix or anything about time travel, I can't even guess on that. What did they say?"

He shook his head. "They didn't offer and I didn't ask. If

they say no, I'm not sure the details matter. So it's some sort of caution on their part?"

Sheridan held up her open hands. "That seems the case from presentation. They took all our data on return. As in, our files were updated with what they wanted us to have, and we'll have to beg for the other data."

"Okay, accepting that, I have to break the news to her. Then, we will have to be prepared to offer a cover story. I'm not sure we can tell leadership without an issue."

Spencer said, "These kids are all blabbermouths. Keeping it from the public will be hard enough. From command? They'll know everything about it in loud whines five minutes after we return."

"Yeah, I was hoping that wasn't the case."

Caswell cautiously said, "Sir...there's no really good way to present it. But if you can get Noirot a tour here, since they plan to keep her, she may warm up to the idea quickly. We could take her with us, then they can give her a guided tour. I can summarize my concerns for their counselors. We tell the general when we get back. They manage the cover story."

Doc nodded. "I'm not a psychiatrist but that seems valid. Let her become amazed with this place. Ask her what she thinks of staying. Follow from there."

Sean sighed in relief. "I guess part of me is glad I don't have to do it today. I honestly hadn't thought about the positives beyond, 'this place is neat.' But it really is, isn't it?"

Sheridan said, "I wouldn't mind staying if they'd let me work and keep my findings."

"I can see that and I understand your frustrations. Okay, let's do this. Caswell, can you come with me to collect her?"

"I can."

"House, can you page Researcher Zep and run the conversation we just had past her?"

"I will."

"Also, why wasn't she already here or raising these matters?"

"I don't have any information on that."

Sheridan cocked an eyebrow. "I almost wonder if they wanted to see how we handled it internally first."

He shrugged. "Being fair, part of it is up to us. They don't want to step on our cultural toes."

Zep appeared at the doorway.

"May I approach?" she asked.

"Please."

"Thank you. I heard your summary and it is approved. After you help her acclimate, we can show her additional features. It may not actually be necessary to demand she stay. She may ask."

He was irritated. "I wish you could have said that up front."

She said, "As you discussed, we wanted to give you as much room as possible in your own milieu." She could be friendly, but she was also a scientist at work, and they had a structure of regulations as much as he did.

"Thanks, I think. Okay, let's get started. Everyone else help Sergeant Spencer prep."

He rose, and led Caswell and Zep to the adjoining facility.

As they entered, Burnham shouted, "Attention!"

Good, the man had his military discipline in place. So did most of the element. It took a couple of seconds, but eight of them did stand to attention. He ignored Lozano and Munoz.

Sean at once said, "Thank you, at ease. Does anyone have anything needing my attention at this moment?"

There were some glances but no hands or questions.

"Good. Lieutenant Cole, you've had breakfast and PT?"

"We have, and inspected our gear and stowed it over there." He pointed to a stack.

"Good." The man was doing much better in a safer environment.

Sean began with, "We need to discuss some particular items with Sergeant Noirot. We'll be following up on some items individually. There will be some scheduled recreation later that includes a local bar. I recommend following up with our current events. House, can you give them a feed of whatever you have between their time ticks, I guess? Alternate our info and entertainment, get them up to speed."

House replied, "Records are incomplete, but I'll create a list of what we have."

"Thank you. Lieutenant, with your permission, we need Sergeant Noirot and her daughter."

"Go ahead, sir. Thanks for asking."

"Thank you. Noirot! Please come along with your daughter."

"Yes, sir!" she acknowledged. Her daughter was watching

kaleidoscope images on the wall and clapping. They stopped, she took the girl by the hand, and came over. The girl was wearing a calico dress that tied at the shoulders and was belted, with shorts underneath and sandals. Those seemed to be the easiest footwear for her.

Caswell said, "That's adorable."

"It is."

"Yes, sir?" Noirot asked as she approached.

"You're first for a tour and some background. Ms. Zep, is there a transport option like last night?"

"Yes," the woman agreed. "This way."

Outside the hall, a sled waited. It looked like a sled, just no animals. They stepped in, took seats, and off it went, with Kita clutching her mother's arm before relaxing. She was getting used to the idea of movable people containers.

He could now see the rough outline inside, of what he'd seen outside. This was a substantial block of buildings.

"I hadn't realized how big it was," Noirot said.

"Honestly, neither had I," he admitted.

Caswell added, "It's gotten bigger, I think. I wonder how they construct things."

"Probably printed from the inside," he suggested.

They drove past several large items of equipment, and the transfer pad. Then there was a more normal-looking section that could almost be offices.

Suddenly they were outside. Sunlight, gardens, fountains, walkways on the ground and in the air, people traveling in conveyances and on foot.

"Wowww!" she said in awe, while her daughter just stared. The kid was obviously trying to figure it all out, and obviously processing it.

"Yeah, it's neat."

"This is cool."

That didn't begin to cover it. Everything looked like a presentation garden. He saw a couple of apparent workers, and several small machines handling weeding and edging.

Zep led them down a path that led around a building, and there was a playground. It was recognizable at once. There were things to climb on, rock on, swing on. They were more sophisticated, and of materials he couldn't identify, but it was functionally the same.

Noirot burst out, "Oh, thanks! This is great!"

They dismounted, and the woman had to hold her daughter as the girl clutched her legs for a couple of minutes, unsure how to react. There were other children playing, in randomly shifting groups, but Kita was a complete outsider.

Finally, she tried a slide and laughed, a swing and giggled, and climbed better than the local kids up a maze of ropes, bars, hoops, and rods. She didn't speak any language in common, but they were all playing. Noirot led the girl around and assisted, and seemed as delighted as a young mother could be.

Caswell said, "Note the adults. Those are caretakers but not parents."

"You can tell?"

"Presentation, yes."

Zep said, "Some are parents to others, some are facility staff, some are individually contracted. Any of them will step in as needed."

Sean said, "Huh, that's how it used to be in the US, before everyone became lawsuit happy and afraid of perverts."

Caswell asked, "What are the neck bands all the kids are wearing? Like shoulder pads?"

"Emergency helmets. If they fall those deploy."

"How far does a kid have to fall for that to be a problem?"

"Any head injuries are bad."

"Yeah, but helmets even to run around and play?" It wasn't really a helmet, but the effect was the same.

Zep said, "It only takes one bad fall. Once they're steady on their feet, those are removed."

It seemed ridiculously overprotective, given their medical knowledge, but apparently they were that cautious. It wasn't his business.

There were microdrones around, watching everything, and on the far side was a Guardian in the fluorescent uniform they wore on patrol here.

From there, they took the child for old-fashioned cotton candy. Nothing like sugar to dial a kid up. Then a ride around the buildings and a walk through the huge loaf shape where the bars were. It was sort of like a high-tech mall. Some of the other facilities were stores or outfitters.

Really, Sean could be back doing other things, but he rationalized it as familiarization, and really, he needed a bit of downtime to help focus things. Yeah, familiarization . . .

Kids were a handful, and he was a career military officer, but he was probably going to be married at some point...

He recalled playing with his younger brother, but only two years separated them. This was a different perspective.

Finally, though, he announced, "I need to attend to other things. Sergeant Caswell, are you good with this duty?"

"Absolutely, sir."

"Good. We'll meet back at dinnertime. This evening we take them out."

"Yup. Hooah, sir." She saluted, he returned it, and he left.

No one had mentioned their uniforms, though he was sure every adult knew who they were.

Armand Devereaux enjoyed spaghetti for dinner, and a pile of fresh strawberries after. Having everything served actually made it easier to eat healthy.

It was a late dinner, and past 1900 when they were done. He headed for the bathroom, because it was much more elaborate than a latrine, and let it shower him clean. Though "clean" here was relative after field conditions.

He asked for jeans, white shoes, a blue turtleneck and a white jacket. Anything street style would be meaningless here, and he really only wore stuff like that in clubs that catered to it. This was a more upscale, suburban, arty crowd.

He emerged and looked around, and holy crap, was Caswell wearing a dress? Green, shoulders, knee length. And her hair was red again. Damn, she had a good figure. Earrings, too, he noticed. Even Dr. Sheridan was in some sort of dress that didn't look like a sack on her. Raven wore something definitely tribal and long in blue with glyphs, with short sleeves, over slacks. She had a silver hairpiece woven through a long braid. She seemed giddy.

"Armand, look!" she said, and did a deep squat. Then she hopped. "My ankle bends!"

"Excellent," he agreed. He wondered if the bad ankle had hindered exercise, leading to some of her weight.

"And they say I should have a permanent improvement in migraine symptoms and metabolism."

Honestly, she had amazing breasts and a round ass. She had extra weight around front he didn't care for, but she wasn't huge, and she did have striking features. Those dark eyes...

The guys were in various mixes of pants, tight shirts if they could get away with it, collars, and coats.

Captain Elliott, in similar dress to him, said, "Okay, people, let's do this. I let them dress as they wish. Let's pick them up and take them. Cryder and Arnet will be around...here they come, in fact."

The two tall men strode over, and holy crap, Arnet was wearing platforms. He was almost 6'9" like that. He wore tight pants, his abs showing and chest covered. And yeah...his cheeks were on display. Jesus. Armand had seen other outfits like that here, but seeing it up close on someone he knew was different.

Cryder wore what was almost a dress uniform, with shoulder flares and tucked boots.

Elliott continued with, "Good to see you again, and thanks for coming. I'm told there's backup?"

Cryder grinned. "Well, there's us. In three seconds we can have other Guardians on-site, and there will be some mingling. Several of the researchers will be around to observe, and to step in if they see an issue. Ready?"

"Yes, let's get them."

Next door, the other element was dressed up more twenty-first-century club. Kita was occupied, apparently with a professional caretaker who was showing her board games and Legos.

"Ah, Danish caltrops," Spencer quipped.

Armand lost it for a second and everyone looked at him.

Elliott asked, "Everyone ready? This is informal, just follow us. Lozano, Munoz, good of you to join us."

Lozano shrugged. "Yeah, well a bar sounds good, and there's nowhere to go from here at present."

Munoz sort of half smiled, looking almost ashamed.

They followed a guide light out, down the perimeter of the building, up and across a walkway with the sun starting to dip into clouds that glowed like an oil painting.

Elliott spoke as he led. "We haven't seen a lot, only a couple of establishments and this amazing view. You'll be pleased, though. I asked for music and dancers and they agreed. Otherwise, there's no telling what the entertainment is."

They entered the commercial building and the long stairs that were almost a ramp, down one floor and right.

The captain continued, "Anyway, along this way, this is the

Mad Laboratory." It had a different façade again, looking like old cut stone. He pointed to the sign that almost looked like English, with what almost looked like Russian underneath, and what might have been some derivation of Chinese on one side.

Through the door, and Armand saw Zep, Twine, Ruj, Researcher Xing he knew from their last trip, and two others he recognized but didn't know. Twine was in what was almost a leotard with slack legs, as hot as she always was. And there was the brunette babe Spencer had been hanging out with.

Damn, the women love me, he thought. He'd never seen another black person, or anyone with any African ancestry. They were all Eurasians of some type. He always had women wanting to talk. He now saw Uhiara get the same attention, and Oyo get it from the men.

Much as he liked hot chicks wanting to dance, and that amazing woman Alani he'd slept with the night before they went back, he needed to keep track of his patients. He was trying to find a polite fiction for the patron when Alexian Twine slid up next to him and placed an arm on his.

"Can I assist?" she asked with a melting smile.

"Yeah, keep me from having to deal with anyone else."

She grinned. "I'm flattered." Quickly, she added, "No, that's fine, I understand your concern."

Good.

The music was sensual, with a lot of modulation, a steady tempo, and a good beat with plenty of subsonics. There were elements of Indian, Arabic, Continental, and Russian. It was absolutely dancing music, and he did some, as far as he could dance, which wasn't much. Twine was very fluid and even sexier. Caswell, damn. Once she felt safe, she could move. She even let two of the local men touch her and actually dance, sinuous and slinky and looking very happy. Good. She'd been almost a basket case their first trip. It was reassuring to see her comfortable.

Oyo was managing as well, and it looked as if she might want to sneak off for some private time with one or two of her dancers.

He held up a hand to Alexian, stopped. "House, can I talk to the captain?"

"Hey, Doc, I'm here."

"What rules do we have on them hooking up?"

"If House can ensure their safety and avoiding more children, midnight curfew remains, and I may extend it slightly per circumstances."

"House, can you let everyone know?"

"How should I phrase it?"

"Tell them they can leave the area as long as they let you know, and must return by midnight."

"I will do so."

Granted his experience was a singular, but getting laid in the future, by people who knew what they were doing, might help shake them loose from the past a bit more.

In fact, most of them seemed to be connecting, almost as if those were either paid professionals, or volunteers who'd had a chance to check them over first. Even Lozano...

"...House, how old is that girl with Lozano?"

"She is an adult professional by both our standards, if that is your inquiry."

"Yes, thanks." Adult by his standards, so at least eighteen. She looked thirteen. How had that son of a bitch arranged that already? But at least she was an adult.

Security turned out not to be an issue.

As usual, Dalton was watching from the side, and both Raven and Sheridan became spectators after a few rounds on the floor.

Still, it appeared everyone who wanted to was able to connect with someone. Cole and Burnham did not, but appeared to be in officer and NCO mode. Burnham was also married. Uhiara limited himself to dancing without touching. Of their own people, he didn't see Oglesby...or Caswell. Well, good for her.

By ten, everyone had either gone somewhere else, or was gathered as leadership, watching the dance floor and enjoying some serious groove.

"Good plan, sir. Drinks and dental work."

Elliott laughed. "I like that phrase. Still, it seems they're enjoying the best we can arrange."

Armand wondered what better could be arranged either for money or as a favor for having been lost. There were probably professionals here with serious skills.

They edged toward the door and started to make their way back.

Cryder clapped their shoulders. "Thanks for inviting us. Fun to see and to be comped."

"Comped?" he asked.

Alexian said, "This was covered on the research facility budget."

Cryder returned, "Indeed, and appreciated. Actually have to get back to prime and child, though." He nodded and left.

Damn. Married with a kid? No reason why not, but he'd never mentioned it once in . . . months.

It made sense. Privacy was a construct so you held what you had.

Alexian brushed Armand's arm. "Hopefully we can catch up tomorrow after the demo and not be corralling people."

"Sure," he agreed.

"Have a good evening."

He could think of ways it could be better, but he had officer crap to do.

CHAPTER 33

Martin Spencer looked around at the crowd. They had folding chairs, but many stood. Tiny recording drones hovered all over. He had an audience of a couple of hundred. As always among these people, he felt like a midget.

The amphitheater was a perfectly manicured bowl on the bank of a perfectly cut stream, which had grass to the bank and occasional gravel, and appeared to have its assigned place and how dare it disrupt the plants.

The weather was clear and bright. He'd never seen skies this deep a blue before. He figured part of it was geography, part of it a massive cleanup of the pollution of his era. It was actually too bright for what he had planned, but he'd make it work.

"Greetings. I'm Sergeant First Class Martin Alan Spencer of the US Army, but I'm here right now as an experimental archeologist. I assume you've all read a summary of our circumstances. We were short on resources and had only limited hand tools for fabrication, so I used the knowledge I had to make an iron reduction furnace and forge. It worked. After I got back, I did more reading and visited with some experts, so I have a better refined method, which I think is reasonably close to the historical way of doing it, in several parts of the world, including this area."

He took a drink of water from a future equivalent of a CamelBak, and got to work.

"We made charcoal already, which was a two-day-long process.

It's going to take a bit longer to do this, and I'm actually making it quick and dirty for the demonstration. A slower, more refined process would make it more reliable. This is just a demonstration of technique."

Everyone had agreed to assist, and it was still going to be a three-day process, he hoped. The area had been carefully prepared with all the "natural" things he needed—a flowing stream, some shade, a flat rock, lots of large river cobbles. They'd built crude shovels from wood and had ore and other items ready.

"First, we have to build the furnace. This is clay from the riverbank. This is horse manure. Regular straw also works, but can cut up your hands. It's actually easier to use processed hay, through an animal."

There were some mutters, some *ews*, some snickers, but mostly fascinated interest and conversation about how that would work. Most of these people were science oriented, after all.

Onto a real animal hide from one of the food growing labs, he used a flat split of wood to shovel manure and clay. He mixed it with another thinner split of wood, until it was evenly mixed.

He saw Maralina, but really didn't want to acknowledge her in public, and certainly didn't feel socially acceptable covered in dung and clay.

"This was also used as a building material you may see referenced as 'wattle and daub.' Wattle was woven twigs. This is the daub. Here, though, we make it into thick ropes and coil it up as a chimney. Rule one is, never touch your face during this process."

There were laughs at that.

It took a couple hours to build the furnace, everyone mixing dung and clay, coiling up the tower. He made it about four feet tall, with an internal diameter just over a foot. He explained as he went, about the vent in the bottom to let the charge out, and any slag. The tuyere where the air went in, made from the same material around a large animal bone. He rinsed off in the stream several times, wondering exactly how close this was to the historical Amu Darya river that was now so much a part of his life. Periodically they drank water and grabbed a sealed bite of food on a skewer that didn't require fingers on the food.

"Okay, we have the raw furnace. Doc and Dalton are now going to work on two different types of bellows, with Amalie and ... Sean helping. Kate and I are going to cure the inside. Jenny is going to work on cracking charcoal."

Caswell had a flat split of limb as an anvil, a mallet made from a tapered smaller branch. Along with her knife, she commenced splitting and cracking charcoaled sticks into pea-sized lumps. She was black with dust within seconds.

Doc and Dalton used two whole goat hides, open at the neck, to create bags with one-way valves. Two other more recognizable bellows were made of split planks, leather, and carved wooden muzzles.

He and Kate started a small fire inside the furnace, then began feeding sticks in steadily.

"You'll see a couple of small cracks. I'm going to squeeze more mud in as mortar on those. We're using the inside fire to harden the material into a concrete. It would be better to have more air-drying first. Again, this is just a demonstration."

People had come and gone as this went on, but the drones hovered around. He learned to quickly ignore them. He did note the buzzing things never entered a private area, though they were all over everywhere outside and in the public atria.

He had ore, the bellows looked ready, there was plenty of charcoal—everyone had chipped in to help Jenny as soon as they finished the other tasks. They had a pile of charcoal.

"Okay, we'll pick up tomorrow at oh seven hundred in our reckoning. It will be a long day."

He needed a shower, and a beer.

Armand stepped into the shower and doused off, before asking for thick gel to scrub with. Ironworking was as filthy here as it had been in the past. Talk about getting down and dirty.

He was actually off duty for the rest of the day. The Byko had better medical care than he could provide if anyone got hurt, and all his Army gear was inventoried. He had nothing practical to do until they went back for the Germanics.

House announced, "Armand, you have a contact request from Alexian Twine."

"Sure," he agreed. What did she want?

"Armand, I gather you're free for the rest of the day?"

"Yeah, what's up?"

"I'd like to socialize."

"Of course. Where should we meet?"

"We can meet at Heisenberg's and go from there."

"Sounds good. I'll head that way now. House, I probably don't actually need a marker, but please give me one anyway."

It wasn't as if he couldn't find the place by now.

Twine was standing in the entrance when he arrived. It was now a double-width doorway, arched and with a fake portcullis. Part of why this place never got boring was the perpetual changing.

She was wearing something skintight that faded away instead of having defined edges. Under that were flat sandals and over it a cape that flowed out from her cleavage over her shoulders, and holy crap, did she have a rack. He'd always known that, but damn, now he could see it.

"Afternoon," he offered.

"Good to see you," she returned with a smile. She approached, hand on his arm, and then kiss on his cheek. He'd seen that here. It was a personal greeting. He tried to return it without hesitating, and felt a bit awkward.

She asked, "Shall we get a drink to go and I can show you more of the village?"

"Sure," he agreed. They turned to the bar near the door, and he ordered a beer. She rapid-fired something that seemed to include "Wodka" and "Limo." Whatever she was served seemed to match.

He wondered if this place ever closed. It wasn't busy at present, but there were several people drinking and one man singing in the corner, with a deep baritone supported by music from somewhere.

She tilted her head to indicate direction. "This way."

They took ramps, slideways, and broad stairs until they were at the top of the building. It had a transparent guard that he stood well back from, especially as there was a bit of a breeze.

"That will take some getting used to," he said.

"That's okay," she said, leaning on the rail and bending over, and goddamn, what an ass. She shifted balance on her left foot and he exhaled.

"It's a really great view," she said, sounding relaxed and happy.

"Very much so," he agreed. Both the scenery and the scenery.

From there, they went down one level and across a walkway to another building. This was an asymmetric pyramid, leaning back against itself, in what looked like black marble. Once inside, there was a lot of gold décor, and he was pretty sure it was real gold.

The club there had a sign that clearly read SARCOPHAGUS, and lots of marble in colors other than black, with green and yellow veins running through it. There was music and dancing, and the crowd seemed a bit younger. Possibly college age for here?

She confirmed that when she said, "The interns like this. Though I'm older and still come here at times."

The barmaid, if that was an acceptable term, was topless, in a white Egyptian girdle and with a headdress. Nice curves. She served him an "Anubis" that was dark, sweet, and had a bit of licorice. He took a second sip to be sure.

"Interesting, but not really my taste," he told her.

"What flavor would you prefer?" she asked via translator. She didn't speak American English.

"Coconut or pineapple, maybe. I know it doesn't match the presentation."

"I can fix that," she nodded, poured in something else. He took a taste, and the licorice was gone entirely, replaced by a tropical mix with coconut and pineapple.

"Awesome, thanks," he agreed.

Alexian took him through the building, hand on his shoulder, then his arm, then his hand.

"The marble is from south of here, the black stone, east."

"All by air?" he asked. "No roads."

"Yes, we use whatever transport is available, often air or sea."

"How far is the sea?"

"We're in the middle of Asia, not far from where you were. The Aral Sea has been re-flooded, and there are canals from the Caspian to the Black Sea, but that's still not close to here."

That was interesting. He'd have to look at a map to refresh his memory of how those all connected.

She asked, "Can I take you to dinner later?"

"Sure," he agreed. Anything she wanted to do was fine with him. "When?"

"We have a couple of hours until then. Want a snack?"

"Just a small sandwich or something."

She gestured, he followed, they stopped at a stand in the corridor, more of a plaza, that had sandwiches of a sort, almost as if the bread had been baked around the fillings, and perhaps it had been. Ham, cheese, cucumber, mustard, tomato, and something like lettuce but not as bitter. It was half the size he was used to, but quite filling, and he used the rest of his cocktail to wash it down.

They were still walking past shops and offices, and it was fascinating that everyone walked here even when instant transport was available. They liked seeing one another and getting fresh air. Several people waved at Twine, and a couple greeted her. There was a short interlude where he felt out of place while she and a man jabbered away in what sounded like a dialect of Russian about some project or other. They waved and he moved on.

"Come on," she said and led him through a door. They emerged in sunlight and she said, "We'll get transport here."

More than the flying carpets or the sled he'd seen so far, this was more of a trike. She swiped the controls and it started driving.

"I'd like to show you my place. It's at the south edge of the village."

"Sure." Yes, he'd love to see local lodging, especially hers, and damn, was he having thoughts.

She was holding his hand and leaning against his shoulder, and that seemed a very solid hint, so he faced her, and she smiled, and their lips met...

She was an amazing kisser. His pulse hammered, he heard it rush and thunder inside his head, and he broke out in a sweat.

They separated and he said, "Thank you, that was amazing."

"It's a treat for me, too," she said. "I've been managing a project for months with little downtime."

They pulled up at a broad block of what could be European condos, with gardens in between. There was so much open space here, no one needed much personal yard.

There was an elevator, silent, covered, and quick, to a fourth floor. The walkway was perfectly flat paved to a door, apparently hers.

Once she opened it, he whistled.

It hit him in bits. Open floor plan, tiled, couches, geometric artwork, cool grays. Kitchen corner. Dining table. She led the way in and he followed.

It had to be a function of her height, but those hips were gloriously full without being saggy. She had great tone all over. She was amazing to look at, and phenomenal to talk to.

"I'm going to change, if that's okay."

"Of course," he agreed. He could look at the layout of this place.

"Want to help me choose an outfit?"

"Yes," he replied. He was all out of clever remarks.

She waggled her head, walked toward the wall that opened for the private area, and as they stepped through she started peeling the leotard down.

Oh, shit.

In three seconds she was naked, and spectacular.

"Do you want to scrub my skin? I put a salve on earlier. It should be working now."

"What type of salve?"

"It inhibits the skin. It's getting inflamed, and you can treat it." She smiled.

That was an odd fetish, but seemed harmless enough.

"Sure," he agreed.

She turned back around.

He was momentarily taken aback. Her shoulders were covered in pimples and zits, with red, angry pinpoints of other irritated pores.

She stepped to the bed, lay down, and pointed.

"That's an acetyl treatment that cleans and tightens, and there's a scrubber."

That was certainly an invitation to touch her.

He sat next to her, grabbed the textured cloth, and splashed some of the cleaner on it. Yeah, that was a distillate. A strong one. He rubbed carefully across her left shoulder, was rewarded by several of the welts breaking and oozing. She hissed slightly from the sting.

"Is there something less strong? That won't hurt?"

"Oh, it's fine," she said, and he could see a grin on the side of her face.

Very well.

He finally noticed the bed looked completely normal, because form followed function, but the mattress was hard to describe. Firm, yielding, padded, cool, supportive even while he sprawled. The frame was wood with a nice grain.

He rubbed in increasing pressure and motion, using the astringent as needed. It took a couple of minutes to rub the bumps smooth, and the gel cleaned out some clogged pores as well. He worked down a line of them near her spine, to a cluster above her buttocks.

"Do you like my skin, Armand?" she asked.

"Yes. Very much," he replied. Those shoulders were gorgeous cream over healthy muscles, and her back was bare to the swell of her ass. Her butt was large but beautifully shaped and proportional to her legs. That was just perfect. He liked fit women. He also liked a round ass. It was hard to find both, but her height required a certain amount of pelvis and glute, and there it all was.

Damn.

He worked out another eruption. On the one hand, it was fascinating to see so much of her skin up close. It was certainly intimate. The fetish didn't really bother him. He guessed it was a bit like bubble wrap for some people. But then, it was like being on duty.

That was the problem.

"This really isn't working for me," he said.

"I'm sorry. Unpleasant?"

"No, it feels like I'm being professional. I can't get personal when I'm on task."

"Ah. I see. Well, let me wipe a counteragent on this, and we'll wait a bit. If that's okay?"

"Sure," he said.

"In fact, shall we bathe?"

That seemed like a very good idea.

She led him to her bathroom, and rattled off, "Temp norm, fade ep fyv fyv, mist all, face clear, thnks."

The water started, and he could tell it was already hot, no waiting. The shower had a shallow bowl under it, with raised walls except on the entry side. The air was warm, the water contained, and there was no need for a curtain.

Well, the only thing to do was get naked and join her, and damn.

He felt a bit awkward pulling off his pants, and realized he should have already. She turned away, either conveniently or intentionally, and asked for something, which was a bottle. She splashed that over her shoulders and back.

"Armand, if you rub that all the way down, my skin will clear up in a few minutes."

"Sure." He flipped off his briefs and stepped in behind her.

He couldn't help brushing against her, and she didn't object. He felt her flesh, and warm water, and was ready for anything she might propose.

Her skin did clean up quickly. It wasn't surprising that their tech was adapted to sex. That was a human standard. Once her skin was smooth again, she pulled her hair back over her shoulders and let it hang.

"Would you like to help me wash it?"

"Of course!" he said. "Shampoo?"

She pointed to a recess in the wall. It was empty, but at a guess, he put his hand in and was rewarded with a palmful of another gel.

He started at her scalp and worked it down her tresses, fingers running through the soapy lines of it, while she leaned against the wall.

He was trying to decide if he could fuck her right here, but she turned under the spray to rinse out her hair, leaning her head back, and he got another fantastic view of her amazing tits.

Shortly the two of them were blown dry, warm, and clean, and the mist disappeared. She stepped out and coaxed him with a nod of her head.

It was surreal. On the one hand, it was part of the rush to get a girl's clothes off. However, one who just peeled and said, "Shall we?" was a different kind of rush.

The wall shifted and they were back in her bedroom. Though seeing it from this angle, it seemed more like a hotel room. That wall was for viewing. There were few things in sight. Was it a rec room for romance?

It also had a bar. She grabbed a bottle personally, rather than through the devices, poured two glasses, and handed him one.

He took it, and sat in a chair across from the one that appeared for her. The patrons were unobtrusive, but always present.

He felt a bit uncomfortable. He hadn't sat around naked with others just making small talk. She and he had started intimately, now just sat romantically, sort of, and he was throbbingly aroused, but they were sitting and drinking.

She looked totally relaxed, and stunning.

The wine was good, too. He'd never been a wine drinker, but this was very nice without being either too sweet or too "dry," which for him always tasted sour. It was certainly grape, lightly sweet, and with a bit of a kick.

She asked him, "What do you like of what you've seen here?"

He paused for a moment, ran through all of it, and replied, "The architecture is just wild. It doesn't fit any of the rules I expect. People are great, but different. Friendly, almost all cheerful, innocent in a lot of ways, but so massively overexperienced in others. And...well, you're fantastic, dressed or not. I think every guy in our element had the hots for you."

She grinned, eyes aglow as they bored into him.

"That certainly pleases me," she said in lush tones.

Her mouth was on his, and he didn't recall her moving. It was another mind-blowing kiss, her tongue active without being intrusive. His brain thudded, he felt a buzz, and his body temperature and pulse rocketed. Her hands caressed and he tried to reciprocate, gently but attentively.

He wanted to go down on her, or get her lips on him, or something, but the touching turned to face-to-face to snug heat of being inside her. She was tall enough he probably wouldn't go too deep, which meant in moments he was buried to the hilt, driving into her, feeling her flesh and her legs and her nipples on his chest . . .

It was delicious. She writhed, arched, convulsed. Her PC muscles were like a vise, and she could use them to hold and draw him in. Transcendental fucking, and then her eyes locked with his. It was intimate and almost intimidating to look into her as he and she ground and thrust. He found a rhythm that worked and gave him good control, because he was fucking a woman hotter than any supermodel back home, who was a real person with real intellect, and that was the most exciting combination he'd never dreamed of.

She reciprocated, meeting his driving thrusts, wrapping her long legs around his, and mashing his lips for another full kiss.

Then her body convulsed, her eyes rolled back, and he could watch her conscious brain shut down.

That did it. He felt his own muscles flex, tauten, and then a hot flood from him into her.

He would have felt bad about it being over so quickly, if she wasn't still clenching around him, and panting.

They lay entwined for a while, skin cooling in the air, sweat still sheened between them. They kissed now and then, and he ran fingers and lips over her skin.

Eventually she coaxed him to roll off, and they cleaned up with a conveniently provided towel.

He felt uncomfortable again, at the presence of the patron, and tried to put that in context. They were servants, but he wasn't sure how much personality was there. Was it automaton? AI? Actual humanlike intelligence? He didn't ask because he really didn't want to know.

Into his musing, she said, "We have time before dinner or other obligations."

"Sounds good," he agreed. What did she have in mind?

"What about wrestling?"

To clarify, he asked, "Us? For fun?"

"And play. Yes."

"Sure!" he said, a moment before she sprang at him.

Damn, she was strong for a woman. He pried his arms from her grip and it wound up in a tangle on the floor-bed. He rubbed against her naked body. Breasts and ass against him, cock and chest against her. He shifted carefully a few times to make sure they didn't pinch each other in bad places.

She squirmed and twisted and he wound up pinning her arms behind. She whipped her head and her hair slapped across his face. He twisted to dislodge it, and she did it again.

Pinning her right arm carefully, and grabbing her left, he freed up his left hand to clutch her hair and give it a yank.

She moaned.

Hmm.

He pulled again, and she writhed a bit, then uncoiled like a spring and broke his grip. He clutched and twisted and pushed, and got her face down across a cushion. He pushed her right arm up and secured a half nelson on her left.

"Well," she said. "That leaves you with a couple of options."

He realized he was breathing hard, very erect, and his shaft was laying on the crack of her ass.

Oh, damn.

She said, "Servs, slick, please."

The tray next to him lifted up to reveal what was obviously a bottle of lube.

"Here, Alexi," the house mechanism said.

There it was again. He was suddenly less aroused. He wanted to ask what the service mech saw, but of course, it saw everything, everywhere. Privacy here was a construct.

He thought, *Armand, you're seconds and inches away from drilling the hottest woman you've ever met. Ignore the robot butler. Just keep a good hold, and retrieve that bottle.*

Ten minutes later, he was struggling again, because she orgasmed even harder than she wrestled. And damn, did she scream. And he'd never had a woman orgasm *that* way before.

It was an eye-opening experience. Among other openings.

That wasn't a bad thing at all.

He collapsed across her, spent and sheened with sweat. Of the odd dozen women he'd been with, she was undoubtedly the most amazing in bed. And utterly uninhibited. Once in, all in, so to speak.

"Let's just rest here for a bit," she said.

"Agreed," he replied. Yes, he was quite happy to lie here, and admire and fondle those fantastic tits, run his hand over her ass, and admire the artistry of her shape, the tone of her muscle and skin, and the fact she was brilliant as well.

He felt her breath on his wrist, warm and gentle.

She asked, "Would it be rude of me to ask when you'll be rested enough for another round?"

"No. That's fine." Totally fine. He'd need a couple of hours, though. "I am hungry. Can we get that dinner?"

"Good idea. There's a place here that hand cooks. I haven't been in a while."

"Shall we clean up and get dressed?"

Rolling to her feet, she replied, "Yes. May I offer a suggestion and an outfit?"

"I'll consider it," he agreed.

They did clean up briefly in the shower. Between fluids and sweat, it was obvious what they'd been doing. When he stepped out, she had an outfit waiting on a hook.

Softly and slowly, he muttered, "Damn."

It was whiter than any outfit he'd ever seen. It was reminiscent of something from the Napoleonic Era, with a long coat, a ruffled shirt, a sash, and low boots.

"I like it a lot," he said, finding the system had included fresh briefs. He dressed, piece by piece, and of course it fit him perfectly.

Once done, he looked in the provided mirror, and was impressed. The cut made his physique even more angular, and the white contrasted against his skin to make it almost a monochrome effect. He noticed the three visible buttons on the shirt were black opal or something similar. They were all the contrast the outfit needed, with his skin tone outside.

Alexian's gown was black, and seemed to be all crushed ribbons. It wrapped around her neck and both shoulders, draped her breasts, then back around and over her hips, before arcing down and across her thighs. It bunched over her right hip and hung below her left knee.

"Amazing," he said.

"Thank you. You fill that outfit perfectly," she replied.

They contrasted and complemented each other. They only had a short time together, so he was eager to enjoy it to the fullest. She took his arm and the servant said, "Follow."

The illuminated cursor moved ahead at a pace that encouraged him to stride stately and proudly, so he did.

People dressed in as much variety here as back home. The two of them were definitely among the flashier, and quite a few passersby nodded or acknowledged them, and three times people asked them to pause for photos. That was still a thing. People didn't change in the fundamental ways.

They took a slideway through the center of town, sitting behind a windbreak. It was a clear, bright late afternoon and from the angle of the sun it felt like October. The buildings were stunning. Some were geometric and clean, very sci-fi. Delicate towers with balls on them or rings around them. The one that was almost a pyramid. Another had three spokes from a central hub. Four others were blobs that didn't have a term for their shape, but long and ovoid. One tower was blazing turquoise with black accents. The three-lobed one was white. One of the blobs was a reflective charcoal gray with orange streaks.

They reached a roundabout and turned toward that one. It grew and he stared as they plunged into the side, which was well lit, but gradually dimmed to a comfortable indirect interior lighting.

It was fascinating how labs, offices, shops, and restaurants all intermixed, and apparently periodically relocated. Each was a little neighborhood, though the building with the Mad Lab and Heisenberg's was what passed as the commercial center.

The restaurant appeared to be constructed of brick, inside the atrium. The smells were amazing, and Armand was sure real hardwood charcoal was in use, as well as cast-iron griddles. Herbs, spices, smoke, and meat scents drifted out. It was signed in their sort-of Latin alphabet, and he puzzled out it was The Roaster.

He almost felt at home here. The seats were straight-backed hewn and smoothed wood with leather, the table tiled inside a wooden frame. The light fixture looked like electric lights pretending to be oil lamps.

"Very twentieth century," he commented.

"Thank you, I tried." She almost beamed.

"Your work?" he asked.

"I told them what décor we'd like. They can do it for any of your people."

"What does that cost?"

"It's on your account, and I have a certain amount of courtesy here with my position."

"I see," he said. "Well, thank you." She thought well enough of him, and it was neat to be treated to the date rather than paying.

They took chairs, and he could puzzle out the menu. His eyes noted "honey sage fire-roasted chicken," and he could smell something similar on the grill in the middle.

The server was a machine, rolling on wheels and not anthropomorphic. Human service for that probably cost a lost extra. It announced in English, "Please order anything you like at any time."

"I think I'll have water to drink, the mixed salad with pickles, and then the honey sage chicken, please."

"I have your order. How do you want your chicken cooked?"

"Honey sage," he repeated.

The machine confirmed, "I understood. But how well cooked do you wish the meat?"

"Uh...cooked. Fully white. It's chicken."

It queried, "Well done, then?"

"Not burned, but all the way through. Isn't that how you do chicken?"

Alexian said, "Most people like it warm and pink, some just cool."

He was suddenly not comfortable and very disturbed. "Good God, no. That's dangerous."

"I just would have figured...didn't they have proper infection control in your time?"

"Pork was getting better, but chicken? Ugh."

"Well, if you like it well done, I guess, but I look at it and sigh. It's so damned overcooked. All the flavor is gone."

She turned to the machine and rattled off something. They spoke English, but slurred and softened, and there was definitely some Slavic intonation sneaking into it. He wondered how many actual working languages existed.

It couldn't hurt to ask, so he did.

"I can discuss some of that," she agreed. "English is a primary, but as you know, softened in inflection and simplified for nontechnical subjects. It's a technical language, which is why everyone here speaks it to some degree. Mandarin and Hindi are common using languages, but less so in science and engineering, but common in business. Then there's what we call 'home languages' that people speak for cultural integrity. There are lots, but Russian, Spanish, French, German still remain, and others."

"What about Swahili? Yoruba? Shona?" he asked, naming three major African languages.

"They exist," she agreed with a nod. "Though we're in the middle of Asia, so they're almost never heard here."

Okay. He wasn't sure how much evasion was there. The lack of anyone African was concerning, and the interest everyone took in him as some sort of exotic creature had its own disturbing vibe. It didn't sound as if Africa was significant here.

"What about the Americas?"

"They're still here." She smiled. "They're development oriented rather than research, and North America, as it was in your time, is a massive food producer, even more than before. South America has a lot of ranching and nature preserve—the rainforest. The Pacific forests are less prevalent."

"Population issues?"

"Among others, yes, but we shouldn't discuss that much, and here's food."

The machine laid out their plates. His steamed and was redolent with smoke and spices, with the tang of the honey cutting through. Wonderful. The rice alongside looked like American wild rice, with large grains that crunched. The salad was on the side, with beets and onions and other pickled items on a huge leaf of lettuce.

"This is good!" he allowed between bites, then slowed down out of politeness.

"It is. Would you try a bite?"

She held up a fork with a bit of pinkish chicken on it.

Armand couldn't imagine raw chicken unless he were three weeks starved. He looked at the offered sliver and shook his head.

"Oh, well. Do enjoy it."

"I am," he said. "Very tender, almost too juicy. Very plump. It's a huge piece."

They talked and ate, and avoided any more discussion of the culture. He got the definite impression population was down, and that somewhere was an underclass. Not everyone could have advanced degrees and do research or technical development. And Central Asia had a huge European presence, some domestic presence, little from the east, and nothing from anywhere else.

They finished eating, and he wondered about a dessert but couldn't. He was stuffed, and it was fantastic, and he didn't want to be overfull. Anyway, he could order any food later and it would be there.

They rose and walked, holding hands and touching, then boarded the vehicle and returned.

He asked about the patrons. "That was a bit disconcerting, in the middle of sex," he admitted.

She replied, "Yes, the patrons are with us from the moment we're born. They can reassure us for a few moments while a parent responds. They remind us on schoolwork and tasks. Mine is my best friend."

"On the one hand I think it's awesome. On the other, it's disturbing."

They dismounted and took the invisible elevator up to her apartment again.

She noted, "Did you notice we use different forms of address for them?"

"How so?"

"If I call for 'service' it means I only need service. If I say 'companion,' then I'm asking for interaction."

Different personae for different functions. "I get it."

He did. He wasn't sure he could tolerate even his best friend hanging out that much, but if he grew up that way, he'd likely insist on it.

It was neat having doors that knew you were coming, and closed at once.

"So let me get you out of that," she said with a predatory grin.

She did. And he got her dress out of the way. Her mound was slick and lush and nicely textured. Her lips on him were warm and firm, and she apparently had no gag reflex.

Given they'd already had sex twice, it should have taken him longer to come, but the cascade of new sensations and her stunning looks had him convulsing in minutes.

Armand wondered if there'd be some sort of ambassadorial staff to the Bykos, and if he could be attached.

That was entirely apart from banging the superhot chick.

CHAPTER 34

The second day of iron reduction was long, as it had been the first time Martin had done it, and every time, in fact. He had a better-refined technique now, but it was still going to be slow.

There was still a substantial crowd, and about as many drones flitting about. Maralina was here again.

"We've ashed out the curing fire," he said. "Now we start the charcoal fire. There's a small pile at the bottom, right where the air can reach it."

He had enough practice that this part was easy. He pulled out a prepared stick and sockets, started sawing until he had charred dust, leaned onto it until he saw smoke, tapped the ember into tinder, blew gently, and got a flame. He lowered it quickly into the charge and pulled his hand back. There was conversation, some applause and enthusiasm about his fire by friction. It took him less than a minute. He'd seen Bob do it in under thirty seconds.

Dalton knew what to do, and started gently working his bellows. Smoke increased, Martin glanced in, and saw a nice, glowing ball in the middle of the charcoal.

"Pump it," he said.

Dalton and Doc pumped the traditional bellows, the Captain and Raven lifted and pushed on the goatskin flap bellows. All four fed air into a manifold made of another goat hide, weighted with a rock to keep the pressure going.

A roar of heated air shimmered above the chimney, and with

a nod to Sheridan, he started shoveling charcoal in with a thick section of bark. She followed his lead.

"Now we need to get it hot enough fast enough," he explained. "The entire furnace will have to be heated sufficiently to contain the charge. Jenny is going to pass around a container with the ore. You should each take a small sample with the cups provided, and hang onto it. The ore came from downriver, and is red ochre."

He'd made sure to get extra ore for this, though he'd used modern ... futuristic ... tools to get it all. Scooping dirt didn't need any explanation.

He went back to shoveling charcoal until the chimney was full.

"This basket contains about fifteen minutes of fuel," he said. "If it takes longer, we need to keep pumping until the fire reaches that temperature and consumption rate. Once we're at that speed, we'll start with ore and fuel mixed."

Jenny came back with the bucket and he said, "The ore you have is Fe_2O_3, mixed with clay, silt, and whatever else is in the ground there. Take a taste and hold it," he said, grabbing one of the small plastic cups and tipping a half spoonful into his mouth.

"Go on," he prompted, with it on his tongue.

First a couple, then more, and finally with some shrugs, everyone, took a small taste.

A moment later someone asked, "Whar we tastn?"

He said, "There's a slippery texture. That's clay. You can spit that out carefully." He did so. "Now there's a gritty texture. That's sand and loam. Carefully put that aside or spit it." He spat that, too. "What's left is the actual ore with the metallic taste. It seems to be about half, which is a very good ratio. Now I'm going to ask Dr. Twine what the actual test showed." He spat out the rest.

From the front row, she called, "The test sample indicated fifty-four percent ore content."

Not bad, he thought, pleased with himself.

"That will yield about ten percent mass in raw iron," he said. "We have about one hundred kilograms. We'll wind up with about ten kilograms of iron bloom."

Raven raised her hand, he nodded and said, "Jenny, take over on bellows four, please."

They swapped without missing a pump. Raven stretched her arms and back and came over to rest. Then Oglesby swapped out for Sheridan.

A few minutes later, forty-five after they'd started, he looked at the furnace level, judged it good, and said, "Okay, we have enough heat. Now we start with ore and fuel."

He dumped in about a cup of ore, and Sheridan followed it with a bucket of fuel, a scoop at a time. The pumping continued, and the charge level visibly dropped as one watched. When it was down a couple of inches, he poured in another cup of ore.

"This is going to take a while," he said. "I'd like some volunteers to swap off on the bellows."

There were quite a few, and three men and a woman came up eagerly.

"Watch what they're doing, talk if you need to, fill in when you can."

Someone asked, "Do you have an expected time frame?"

"About ten hours," he said. To their raised eyebrows, he replied, "Yeah. It's going to get hot, tiresome, and dirty." He punctuated that by adding another bucket of charcoal.

The Bykos could pump, though. They were very fit in comparison to early twenty-first-century America. He expected people to tire after fifteen minutes or so. That came and went, and the same ones were still pumping, while he added fuel and ore. They didn't seem tired at all.

"You can slow slightly," he advised. "Also, it's fine to swap off in short rotations so everyone can try. One at a time, not all four at once."

He let everyone break for food and water, and it was weird to have a drone-lifted shade that followed the arc of the sun to keep them cooler. It was also rather neat, though.

Observers left, others came. There was definite interest.

Maralina was still here, with her own drones and a tablet of some kind. She was obviously in professional capacity, guiding the flyers around, tapping and speaking notes, apparently pulling up info in front of her to edit.

About noon, he pulled out the ceramic plug at the side using a stick and peered in through a polarized screen.

"They'd have looked through slitted fingers or slitted goggles," he said, "and done this mostly at night."

He continued, "We have a good puddle of slag underneath, with a bloom of iron floating on it. I'm recording here, and the inside sensors will get whatever you told them to get." There were a few chuckles. He carefully replaced the plug, wobbling the stick until he got the plug lined up, then using another stick to push it in place.

An hour later he said, "We have too much slag in the bottom. You see how the fire is choking and sputtering. The air inlet is getting clogged. I'm going to pull the bottom plug and let some slag out."

Of course it was burning hot, and he wasn't sure how this was handled historically. Possibly multiple ceramic plugs? That was his guess. He had three. He used the stick and pulled the one. It came loose, followed by a flow of hot glass. He gave it a few seconds to puddle and flow like lava, then shoved the second plug in. He rolled the first one aside to cool.

The fire was definitely responding better.

He ate a sandwich in bites between work and comments. They made damned good bread here. The filling was ham, cheese, mustard, veggies, mayo. Gourmet sub, delivered by robot servant. The same machine brought fruit-flavored water and something like Gatorade all day, along with occasional cookies and bites of sausage.

He drained slag again about 3 PM. About 7 PM, the last bucket of fuel and cup of ore went in. He had some ore left over, but the charcoal was done. This was it.

"Just a few moments now," he said. "Dalton, Captain, get ready."

They donned leather aprons and hand wrappings, oversized mittens.

"Originally I did this what I thought was a Japanese way," he said. "It's too specialized for what we're doing here. This is more accurate for early reduction and most of the world."

He deemed the fuel to be getting low enough, and grabbed the breaker. It was a sapling with a root bulb and a large protruding root.

"Fire in the hole!" he announced, and swung. The clay cracked, and he kept swinging.

The side collapsed, a huge river of molten silicate gushed out across the ground. He beat, pulled and got the entire side open.

He took two more large branching sticks, rolled out the matted, thready ball of yellow iron bloom, which cooled to orange as he teased it. Carefully, as he'd practiced, he got it on both sides, lifted the spongy mass onto the flat rock, and held it. Smoke erupted from the contact areas. Those damned drones zoomed in again.

Dalton and Elliott ran up and bashed it with large, smooth river rocks. It got less spongy, more compact, and more cohesive. He rolled it a bit, they hit it again. He rolled it...and it fell and thumped on the ground. The grass under it blackened and flared.

"That's fine," he said. "That's a bloom of iron. From here, it can be chiseled with rocks, hammered with rocks, and eventually made into products."

There was a wave of applause and cheers.

Someone asked, "Would bronze tools already exist?"

"Yes," he agreed. "But, bronze will contaminate the iron. If you're hammering down a piece, that's fine. If you're trying to do any welding or casting, that will ruin it before you start. I don't know if that was done, or if it was done this way. The technology is obviously correct, and the furnace is provably known. Other than that, I'm speculating, as were the people I learned from."

The spectators came forward for closer looks at the remains of the furnace, the still shimmering-hot ball of iron, and the cooling, glassy puddle of slag.

They were impressed.

He was impressed.

From the glow in Maralina's eyes, she was very impressed.

"Thank you all," he said. "I can do an after action Q and A later, if you like, but I really need to cool down and clean up."

There was more applause as he corralled up the others and urged them ahead.

"Let's get clean," he said.

He walked through the crowd, and took the waiting bus back toward "the dome," as they called it, even though it wasn't that shape outside. He climbed out of the vehicle in sunlight and walked in.

It was always jarring. One moment he was outside in fresh air under sun and puffy clouds, and a moment later he was inside the dome, almost as if it expanded to cover him. Maybe it did.

He turned down the perimeter track, into the lodging area, and into the Army's space.

It was divided into almost private rooms now, which were open to the dayroom area unless closed for sleeping or privacy. The recoverees were on one side of the divider, the main element on the other. The latrine/shower/spa was to one side, and he cleaned up quickly, getting back into uniform.

In the common room, Sergeant Burnham was watching a screen that showed the post reduction process.

He turned to Martin and said, "So that's how you did it."

"Eh?"

"We watched the iron smelting. That's how you did it."

"Approximately. I did it mostly from concept the first time."

"Yeah. We had no idea."

"We got lucky. I barely got it right." They seemed tense.

"When do we get home?"

"We have to go recover that other element. I'm not sure on the time frame here for doing that, versus our subjective time." He noted they were all going to die younger than they would have, by the calendar. Or maybe not. The Byko medicine might prolong their lives.

On that subject... "How are your teeth and other healing doing?"

"They're fine. And we're really grateful. But we want to go home."

"I know. We're working on it for us, too. You should take this up with the captain."

Caswell came out of the bathroom, hair clean and still barely damp.

She said, "Remember our debriefing took weeks. Yours will, too."

Burnham sounded depressed and disgruntled. She could see their point of view. They hadn't managed to maintain much of anything modern, gone full native, and not enjoyed it. It was a coping mechanism, not a proper adaptation. Her element's arrival and stories made it clear they'd done better in comparison. Watching Martin make iron, and knowing about weaving, herding, even the hot tub, was grinding their face into the ground. The Byko society was a sci-fi utopia in comparison to that, even if it really wasn't. They wanted to get home and forget the whole thing.

It was going to continue to be hard to interact with them. They'd had entirely different experiences.

"Why can't we do it here?"

The captain arrived and said, "It's not the Army way. You know how that is. We've been doing some of it. I'm also coordinating going back for the Germans, apparently in four days, and there's some other complications."

He let the captain handle it while he headed for the bathroom.

Martin tossed his clothes to the floor, knowing the system would take care of them.

"House, I need a lukewarm rinse, then increasingly hot for muscle relaxation."

"I can do that. Alternate hot and cold would work better."

"I'm sure it would. I prefer it my way."

"Understood."

"Can I get some power washing for my hands?"

"At once."

"Thanks. Also, is there some sort of lotion for them?"

"To effect repair of the skin wear? Yes."

"Please."

"Do you wish any release?"

"No, thanks. It's not a comfortable subject especially with you presenting as male."

"I can easily adopt a female persona."

"No. That would be worse."

"I understand. One of your party had a discussion with a local about it. You think of me as a servant and support. To them, we're a friend or alter conscience."

"I can see how that would change things. However, for us, it's a very private matter."

"Understood. How is the water temperature?"

"Slightly hotter is just right. Then I'd like to cool it down just a little. I want to soak quietly for about five minutes and then dry. Dim lighting."

"I will do so."

He let his brain drift and followed the sensations of the water pouring over him, watching it swirl away through invisible drains. He was relaxed, it was dim, quiet, and he was alone, or as alone as he could be, while safely within reach of others. That was a dichotomy he dealt with a lot. And how much was related to having a wife who was present but not responsive?

Though he'd felt that way before their issues, too.

Was that why they'd gotten along well when they did? Both constantly traveling?

The water slowed and ended, the air temperature rose as humidity dropped, and in seconds he was dry, much like in Iraq, only without sand.

Cleaned up, he felt much better. There was nothing romantic about primitive life. It was filthy, even if one understood and made the attempt to stay clean. He'd never gotten this dirty in aircraft or vehicle engines. Even in field repairs in the mud. This had only been a demo and it was that filthy. It reminded him what he—what they all had dealt with, and the poor bastards of this element. They might not recover properly from that. God knew he still had nightmares.

Tomorrow with Dalton's help he was going to forge out some rough tools. That was an easy demo, especially in comparison. Tonight, he was free, and they had their established curfew.

"Can I get some contemporary slacks and one of those Mandarin-collar shirts? Navy blue for the pants . . . no, white, and make the shirt blue."

"At once. Pockets?"

"I don't really need them here, do I? But I'm used to pockets, so yes, hip and front."

"They will arrive in two minutes. Do you need shoes?"

"Anything comfortable and stylish is fine. Those should probably be white, too."

The outfit arrived with fresh socks and underwear. He dressed and straightened up.

There really wasn't a need for CQ, but it was good to keep in practice. He told House, "For record, I'm going to the Mad Laboratory. I can be reached through you as needed, and will be back by oh two hundred."

"Noted, Martin. Do you need a tracker?"

"Just warn me if I get anywhere I shouldn't."

"Understood."

At this point, their element came and went. There was a scheduled conference with some of the local experts on the trip for the second element. They did PT every morning and checked in via the patron. Otherwise, it was R&R. Though in addition to his demo they were about to load for the second recovery. He'd enjoy it while he could.

The walkways offered a beautiful view, once you acclimated to the fact that the edges were safe. Really, they were wide enough it wasn't an issue unless you deliberately reached the edge, but those wards were strong enough to keep anyone in.

He wandered a building north, and found it closed. He took

an outside balcony around, then headed east. That building was open, mostly vacant, but had a couple of late-night restaurants. People noticed he was shorter than average, but didn't pick him out as anything special. Euros, Caucasians, and North Asians blended in easily here. South and East Asians were notable. Doc was obvious to everyone. The two scientists were visible from their overweight builds, and Raven for her obvious Amerind features.

Among the locals, one man stood out in an angular outfit of fluorescent orange and green. He carried a baton, a small pack marked with what was obviously the future version of the Red Cross, and wore a fitted cap that was probably armor. Even by local standards, he was fit and broad. Martin felt like a kid as the guy passed. He had to be 6′8″ and built like a wrestler. He was a Guardian, or some local cop, on duty. As they passed each other, the man nodded and half saluted. He obviously recognized the American.

He suspected everyone would pick up on them being outsiders in close proximity, though. None of his era had the fitness and tone of these. Their diet and exercise worked brilliantly.

The walkway south had very subtle lights coruscating in geometric art crossing and winding along it. He watched that for a few minutes. He noticed a male youth and a woman had sat down to enjoy the view from the other end, so he followed suit. She nodded, he nodded back, the kid nodded. They said nothing and followed the lights.

He realized the pattern never quite repeated. It was a slow electronic kaleidoscope. He stood and made his way south, past the other two watchers. He entered the building through one of those invisible curtains, and descended the ramp into the atrium.

Here was the Mad Lab. The façade had changed, as had the light color, and, of course, they could change things in minutes here. He wondered if that's why there wasn't really a cohesive style. If trends came and went in mere minutes as whims took people, then do what you want and don't worry about perceptions. Everything old would be new again anyway.

He recognized some of the crowd from previous nights, and a couple seemed passingly familiar from his lecture. There was no live entertainment yet, but a light show swirled behind the stage area.

There was Maralina. She smiled vividly and approached.

Her tunic was a dark fall rust-orange, waisted and belted with a colorful, braided sash. She had complementary trim at the neck that framed her face perfectly, and other trim down the seams. Her boots looked like steppe riding boots, though they flexed more than historical ones. The comb in her hair sparkled with stars, and her earrings also looked like something he'd seen in Northern Asia. It had to be a deliberate look on her part.

"Martin!" she exclaimed, flowed up to him, and embraced him. He felt a kiss on each cheek, and she stepped back while his brain processed.

She smiled with a glint and said, "Your presentation was fascinating. Seeing it done in all the detail is far more informative than historical mentions."

"Thank you," he said sincerely. "It was a lot of work. Far more efficient than my first attempt, though."

"Oh? That's mentioned in your documentation but not at length." She spoke as she gestured at a couch, and took a seat. He joined her. The volume of the crowd retreated slightly, just enough to let them talk quietly.

"Ah. Well, I didn't use fine charcoal, just lumps. I added limestone as a flux, which is necessary in a large furnace but not in these. I had two bellows and no manifold, then I shattered the hot bloom in water to get different carbon contents. It worked, but I probably got half the yield I did from this."

"That would be significant with that many labor hours."

"Very."

"Still, it was incredibly informative and fascinating. I love the sophistication many early cultures had, that were forgotten as the technical skills were. They had as much specialized and research knowledge as we, just organized differently."

"That's it exactly."

"Preliterate cultures make my work much harder, but so fascinating. Can I try one of your drinks?" she asked.

The sudden shift took a moment to process.

"Yes. Service, please."

One of the tables glided over to his side and asked, "Order, please?"

"If you can simulate Elijah Craig bourbon, please do."

"I have a flavor profile from . . ." Followed by silence, then, "It is the best approximation I have."

"We'll try it. Neat, please."

"Do I infer you wish it straight and unmixed?"

"Correct."

"Stand by, please."

The surface delivered two glasses, each with a good double shot of something that looked right. He took them and handed one to her.

"Guide me," she asked.

"First, you nose it," he said, waving it carefully and smelling the wafting vapors. That was a close approximation at least. She did the same.

She closed her eyes in concentration, then smiled. "Strong, yet sweet and woody."

"Yes. Then just a sip on the tongue, roll it back and it should almost vaporize on the way."

"Oh my. Mmmmm. Strong, yet not harsh. That is fascinating, and more complex in profile than I would have expected."

He said, "I enjoy it a lot. The Scottish even age their whisky in used bourbon barrels to capture some of the flavor."

"I had heard that. But that didn't happen until after bourbon barrels were regularly available."

"Right. I don't know much before that."

"It was far less refined. The bourbon was an advance in flavor and chemistry."

"Well, that makes me proud to hear, being from Kentucky."

She laughed lightly as he smiled.

"It does go well after the long hours today. I took note of the chemical transformation through my monitors."

"Oh? What did you see?"

She said, "Given the low temperature, your process was surprisingly efficient as far as conversion, though not quick. The completely subjective feeding and heating was far more effective than I expected."

"Thanks. That's good to know."

She actually understood quite a bit of basic metallurgy, at least as much as he did. She had a fascination with the Napoleonic and Regency eras that he didn't know much detail about. Shakespeare was still popular, with many interpretations out there. She had a fascination with the Battle of Kulikovo, which he knew of. The Rus duchies that would become the Russian Empire, versus the Golden Horde.

"I've seen some of the spears," he said. "Well forged. Strong tenon and clean welded sockets."

"Oh, yes. There was a significant find of *this is restricted* that... argh. Sorry. I guess we should stick to more mundane matters. I am very pleased with all the data you brought back this time."

"Do you handle all of it?"

She said, "I am in charge of the historical contextual aspects only. Of course I have to be aware of the med, bio, climate, and other matters, but documentation such as that cave art is my focus."

"Yeah, that cave art. It was very reminiscent of something several of us found disturbing."

"It is probably coincidence, though there is some question as to the chemistry of the paint."

"Oh?"

"Some of it appears to incorporate human blood."

Oh, fuck. Once again his pulse hammered and he really wasn't sure about a return trip.

She continued, "However, it's not conclusive that the blood matches the local phenotype, or any nearby in that era. It's possible it's out of context, either a lost element or a prank."

"I really hope it's a prank," he replied. Really, really. But, *displaced element*? That...

There was a momentary interruption of a man walking up.

"'Scuse," he said to Martin with a smile, turned to Maralina, and bent down to kiss her.

That was a sexy kiss. This man wasn't just a friend. Her shoulders rose and her chest heaved.

They broke, she muttered something with a smile, and then raised her voice.

"Sergeant First Class Martin Spencer, this is my prime, Diagnostician Karpos Rune."

This was slightly awkward, as fascinated as he was by the man's wife.

"Pleased to meet you, sir," he said, standing and extending his hand.

Karpos shook hands firmly. He was shorter for this group, only about 6'3", so slightly less intimidating.

"Also you. I saw someyr presentation. Well good." The man seemed friendly enough and not put upon.

Also of note. He wasn't part of the project involving the Americans and his dialect was less accurate.

"Thank you very much. It's a knowledge I'm glad I had when we first were lost."

"No doubt. Iron bettern stone."

He turned back to Maralina.

"Busy talk?"

"Fascnatng. Also sosh."

"Props?"

She shrugged. "Lsee. Have fun?"

"Yup, Elsati over." He pointed at a tall, very blond woman. "Buzz her, tell later?"

"Yum. Go do." She grinned and her eyebrows flared.

"Love you."

"And you."

Martin processed that in a hurry. It seemed so casual, but there were obvious nuances, rules, and implications in that exchange. Certainly "prime" implied "second," and she'd mentioned it before. It just seemed so straightforward for them. Except, by having designations of prime and second, there were obvious rules of engagement.

Fuck, he had trouble with one relationship.

She turned back to him and said, "I do admire your willingness to get dirty for your work. It takes a lot to get some of our researches into the wild, much less into such very savage conditions."

"It's not fun, but necessary," he said. "I appreciate your improved plumbing for cleanup afterward, though."

"Yes," she agreed. "Oh, I also have a couple of sensual shower programs. One is somewhat inspired by the Roman bathhouses, and one by the Finns of just before your era. Changing temperatures, water chemistries, olive oil for the Romans, and wood and perfume scents. I added in a localized pulse frequency for the hip-level spray. It's very popular with women, but men report favorably, too."

He tensed for a moment.

"That's perfectly logical and very impressive," he said, and laughed. Damn. How did that fit into his rules?

"Thank you. I don't know if such things existed in your era."

"At a very simple level, I've heard of people using running water or flexible shower heads for stimulation."

"Interesting. Personal pleasure is as important to people as food, warmth, and shelter. Even above companionship or sleep for many. Your own documentation from the recent trip adds to that."

Oh, he knew that. Two years with no one to touch had been emotionally deadening.

Then after he returned, a year with almost no companionship had been even worse. He'd lost a lot of sleep.

It was very clear she was interested in him. Enough to send her prime off to see his apparent second. That was a strong hint, because the gaze between her and Karpos smoldered.

"I do have to retire soon," he said. "We're still planning the second excursion."

"Of course!" she said, almost too quickly. "I'm fascinated on what we might learn from that group."

"So am I, if they're who they appear to be."

She said, "If you do find yourself available to socialize, my schedule is variable. As I don't directly interact with most of my subjects, and am paid on results, not time."

Martin said, "Maralina, I'm very interested but my relationship is in . . . transition, let's say."

"I understand yours are often informally locked, or formally coded for life, though that can be cancelled through official action."

"That's mostly right, yes. My wife—my prime, as you'd say,— and I expected this to be a lifetime commitment. Apparently it's not. But I'm stuck between wanting to do my damnedest to save it, and realizing that's hopeless, and needing her, and needing someone, and wanting to be alone, and terrified of loneliness."

She gave him a very understanding and compassionate smile as she said, "That sounds remarkably human. Friends of mine have had similar issues with their partnerships."

Whew. She got it.

"So, bluntly, you're amazingly hot and I'm very interested, but I don't know if it's a step I can take."

He knew he was doing the right thing, because he was going to regret not nailing her forever. And as it was, Allison could never hear a word of it, and there wasn't really anyone else he could discuss it with. Gina would let him talk about how hot Maralina was, and not be bothered by it. She knew quite a bit about his intimate life already. That was part of what Allison was pissed about. But he couldn't share those details with a man, and Allison both didn't want to hear it, and couldn't be allowed to know some of it. He'd have to create a private account she couldn't access, and he shouldn't have to do that...

"I do hope to meet again soon, though, Martin. In whatever circumstances you have."

"Thank you." He stood, she stood.

This time, she offered a hand, he took it to his cheek. It was warm, supple, and very, very human. Before he realized, she pressed against him in a hug, held him firmly with her hips and breasts pressing him, and kissed both cheeks again. He tried to reciprocate.

Even her ears and hair were sexy, and she had some scent that wasn't perfume but was very clean and warm.

"I'll try," he said, smiling and stepping back.

"Have a good evening," she replied with a tilt of her head and a smile.

He was drunk and dizzy, and it wasn't just the bourbon.

The air outside was cool and a bit foggy. He could enjoy it to its fullest with the transparent shield overhead. It gave him time to think.

Dan Oglesby felt like an afterthought. Once they had native translators, and Shug returned to his people, his usefulness as a translator and interpreter had gone away. He was just labor pool, in a unit with the most ridiculously high-tech support equipment possible. The last three weeks had been him offering, "Here I am," and hoping for some kind of task.

The Bykos had debriefed him on the German language. He couldn't offer much. They did have his notes, and some machine translation. That was it.

He'd given himself a new task, as liaison between the recoverees and the Bykos. The soldiers were getting limited rec time, and the captain had agreed for him to be along, keep eyes on them, and call House or Guardians as needed. The latter hadn't been necessary yet, but the patron did a lot of interceding between people.

Uhiara was very popular with the ladies. House recommended, and he'd approved, limiting them in number and contact. It was fine if the man hooked up, but he recalled Uhiara was married and devoted, and didn't need excess temptation. So far he'd been a gentleman.

Hamilton was having fun dancing and drinking, and didn't seem likely to score.

Keisuke was actually talking to a woman who looked Japanese, though taller than he by several inches. Apparently he spoke Japanese, and they were discussing the language changes, much like English had warped and softened.

Maldonado was trying to hit on women and only being moderately successful.

The two scumbags weren't here, and only were let out with a discreet Guardian presence. It wasn't as if they could run far, but why give them any opportunity?

This was still pretty laid-back work, but he told himself it was important to monitor their activity and apparent mental state.

They all looked very self-conscious and he could see elation and sadness in them. Five years of savagery and filth, because there was nothing "noble" about it. This was a relief, but it was also a taunt. They'd have to leave it behind. Neither would have been relevant or known if some asshole in this time hadn't fucked up, and created a system for other people to fuck up. He imagined this was like the nuclear tests of the 1950s, or the rocket launches. Everyone wanted to get their hand in, give it a try, and see what they could do.

From his unit, Sergeant Spencer was talking to that amazing Eurasian babe. He'd seen her at the iron furnace demo, and they seemed to be talking about something technical, but he was pretty sure the woman was interested in Spencer. She paid close attention.

Captain Elliott walked through, nodded, walked behind Spencer, smiled, and waved as he left. Commander's random recon.

Caswell sat back in a corner with Dalton, and they seemed to be doing the same thing he was—monitoring the recoverees.

Well, shit. Apparently they were all pretty redundant.

Tomorrow he got to talk to the linguists again and help plot the evolution of the languages. They knew he had, and would, take that information back to the twenty-first century, and so far weren't attempting to stop it. So that was good.

Dan walked through the Lab, avoiding the loosely defined dance area that changed as tables and chairs came and went, and approached the bar.

"Good evening," the server greeted. She was a very attractive female, nude to the waist but looking aesthetic rather than sexy. Long dark hair rolled back in a pinned bun, makeup subtle but carrying down her face to her collarbones, and wearing some equivalent of spandex over slim but well-shaped hips, that blended away and came back as tabi boots.

He paid attention to her face, and damn, those eyes could pin you in place.

"I'd like a wheat beer with a hint of citrus. Do you know what I mean?"

"We've Belgian ales or Hefeweizen that fit that."

"Can you recommend one? Based on my previous choices?" He guessed they had that on file.

She blinked, and appeared to be reading a one-way screen in front of her.

"I think so," she agreed, turned around, swiped and waved, filled a stein-shaped glass under the tap, and turned back around.

She gave a professional smile as she offered it with, "Please tell me if this works."

He took it, sipped it, and it was really good. Refreshing, lightly alcoholic, and cold. How much of these were actually brewed, and how much was fabricated from blends with alcohol added? He didn't care. It was what he wanted.

"Thanks very much." He nodded and stepped back. She half bowed and turned and damn, aesthetics aside that was an amazing ass.

As he sought the others he asked, "House, please tip her twenty percent for the service. She hit it exactly."

"I have directed so."

"Thanks."

He approached the other two. Caswell waved to a seat. Good.

He slid in and sat down. Dalton was in his usual sleeved shirt and slacks. Caswell was in a short-sleeve blouse, and pants with cuffed ankles. That was interesting.

He held up his glass. "Last one before bed. Only one, actually."

Dalton asked, "Are you watching our charges, too?"

"Yeah, not much else I can do."

Caswell said, "Everyone loves automation until their job goes away."

Dalton shrugged. "Most of them stopped bothering with worship as soon as we got here. I'm not surprised, it's typical. But it is disheartening."

Caswell finished her drink with a swig.

"Rich, I'll still show up. You have uplifting sermons. I've always appreciated them."

"Thanks, Jenny." The man seemed more cheerful.

She stood. "I'll see you back there. I've had enough weird lighting and random almost-English background convo."

"Later," he replied. Turning back to Dalton, he offered, "I'll try to attend. We all did appreciate it, and it's good for bonding."

"No worries, my man. I'm more concerned with them. They had it rough and need God, especially in these fleshpots."

"Uhiara is doing a great job of being faithful to his wife. So is Burnham."

"Yeah, those aren't two I'm worried about."

"Ah."

"Yeah, the ones who need help, or the Word, the most often won't seek it. If they do, they're often below rock bottom. Sooner is better."

"You sound like Caswell talking about counseling."

"What do you think we were talking about, dude?" the man said with a broad grin.

"Valid," he returned. "I'll finish this and go crash."

"Later, my man. I'll be a few minutes behind."

He placed the finished stein down, offered a fist bump, and turned to head for their dorm.

Martin Spencer walked back into their quarters and rubbed at his eyes. He was going to be tense and frustrated, and he wasn't sure about being alone, but he didn't want to pretend to be sociable. He did need some coffee, late as it was, and maybe another shot of bourbon. Once stressed, it took him a couple of hours to unwind before sleeping.

Caswell was in the common area, sprawled on the couch with one foot up and watching a shifting seascape on the wall. She was munching carrots and celery with dip. Both scientists were reading over their notes and making additional notes. They were certainly dedicated. The board they used to track location said the captain was asleep, as was Dalton. Oglesby was just returning with the authorized recoverees. Doc was "accounted for," and good luck to him.

He went to sit down with his bourbon and coffee at the central area.

Caswell looked up from her food.

"So who was the chick you were talking to, Sergeant Spencer? If it's okay to ask."

"Oktabro Maralina. She's a temporal archivist, has read all our reports."

"Cool. That sounds interesting. I thought I saw her at your demo."

"Yes. She was interesting to talk to. House interrupted her twice. I guess she got out of the proper era."

"It's disconcerting having all that oversight. I hate having to pretend I'm in private."

"Yeah. I was nervous enough talking to her, without people listening in."

He was about to say *Sorry, House*, and realized it wouldn't be fair to that entity to invoke it into the conversation. House was listening, but the pretense was important.

"I imagine," Caswell said. "And damn, is she hot."

"I noticed," he said diplomatically.

The cat jumped up and Caswell started petting him.

She looked back and said, "Oh, you definitely did. You didn't even see the captain walk right behind her."

That caught him. "I didn't?"

She half snickered. "Yeah, but who'd blame you? Even by standards here, wowza."

Was this a feminist telling him this? She'd definitely changed. Or possibly just been tense during their displacement due to fear? Heck, she was a year older in the time frame when young adults matured fast.

He was talking to a lot of single women this trip, dammit.

"She's apparently married but also available for a second partner."

Nodding, she replied, "That's something I saw, too. I even saw one couple swap off in mid-dance. They were doing a little more than just dancing."

"Oh? Did I miss that, too?"

She said, "It didn't go past kissing, but they were very lusty kisses."

"Hmm."

"I presume you're monogamous."

"Yeah," he sighed.

"That doesn't sound comfortable."

Well, shit, he had to talk to someone, though Caswell was effectively an uptight younger sister.

"So . . ." he said with a slow sigh. "You know Gina and I were interested in each other."

"I guess that's the term for it," she agreed. Right. She'd obviously taken the nude photo Gina had sent him from inside the women's cabin. He wasn't sure if Caswell knew more than that, but she knew enough.

"We've had some very frank, but nonsexual, discussions since we got back."

"I assume we all have."

"Yeah. These never crossed any lines, but there was more than once I had to pull myself back."

"I understand."

"Allison, my wife, found the window, and started reading."

Caswell looked alarmed. "She didn't find anything about the trip, did she?"

"Everything about the trip just referred to it as 'the trip.' We've been very careful to never say more than that. And 'our hosts,' 'the other people' and 'the Italian element.'"

"Very good." She smirked. "It makes sense the history nerds would find an easy way around."

"Thanks. Yeah. But Ally read a very frank, monthlong exchange I had with a woman I was deployed and detained with. She gathered we weren't detained quite as prisoners, and had plenty of chance to interact."

"Yeah. That doesn't sound easy."

"She blew up. Assumes we were bunking together, even after I pointed out both females had their own quarters segregated from the rest, and that I was in a cabin with Doc."

"I see."

"I have no idea what to do."

"What do you think you can do?"

He shrugged. "I do feel guilty, because Gina and I did have a couple of conversations that . . ."

"I know they existed. She never gave details."

"Right. Well, we weren't expecting to go home. And we were never in contact physically. It all stopped entirely once we were away from there. Even when we were here."

"You're both very honorable people," Caswell said. "I realized when we got back how totally professional you were, and that you were keeping an eye on me for safety. I thought you had designs. I realize that was wrong. Uh...I'm sorry."

He blushed hard.

"I got one nude shot of you once. You were bathing. I was where I had a view. I took the shot."

"I see," she said again. She sounded flat and unemotional this time, and he knew that was bad.

He quickly said, "I deleted it two days later. When Oglesby was acting a bit pushy."

"Even he was being persuasive, not aggressive, but it was intimidating. And thank you."

"I'm glad you're not pissed."

She shrugged. "Human nature is what it is. People make mistakes. In our case, most of us held up very well."

She added, "You know Gina was on watch when Oglesby got blown, yes? By that Urushu girl, out in the field."

He laughed. "Hah! I think everyone knew that."

"Yeah, she had it on NVG and gave a commentary that was hilarious."

"Oh, shit," he said.

"So how are you handling it at home?" she asked.

"As well as I can," he said. "She stopped sleeping with me. Says she has to 'reconsider' our status, and perhaps she can eventually trust me. My counselor offered some relationship exercises."

"Like?"

"Careful hugging and kissing at the door when one of us gets home."

"How's that working?"

He grimaced. "Day one, she threw a hand up between us. No hugging."

"What a bitch." Caswell looked pissed.

"Eh? She wasn't ready for it."

"That's why you have those exercises. Look, that's what I studied. You know I've almost finished my degree, right?"

"Yeah."

"I was deployed with you in the tensest situation possible. I saw how afraid you were of separation. You talked about her a lot. You know what I was afraid of. We both pulled through. I know how honorable and professional you are. How long have you been married?"

"Almost twenty years."

"So she should trust you at least as much as I do. If she doesn't, and there's no previous issues you're not telling me about..."

"No, never. We even used to talk about it when I met someone fascinating. But I don't think I ever dare mention Maralina to her, even though it's been two short, chance meetings."

Caswell paused a moment, then said, "It seems to me she has made her choice not to trust you. I don't think there's anything you can do to fix that. It takes you both to make it work, but only one to ruin it, and she's done so."

"I don't know..."

"I only have your POV, but I have no reason to believe you're inaccurate. If she's not even trying, I...I'm sorry." She seemed genuinely sad for him.

"Yeah, so am I. I love her. I want it to work. It was great to be home, and then it wasn't. Then it just went downhill. I remember counseling younger soldiers about this type of stuff. Then after twenty fucking years, it happens to me."

"She should know better. I met her back in November, remember? Before everyone split in different directions."

"Yeah. What was your impression?"

"Not favorable. Leave it at that."

"Oh?"

Caswell sighed again. "She kept making snide comments about you while you were out of hearing. She was acting like you were a disabled vet and needed a caretaker."

"I never heard any of that."

"That says something."

"Well, all this is why I left early. Maralina hits all my buttons for a hot chick, and has a brain, and was obviously interested. Seconds longer and I'd have been asking about a private spot on the roof."

"She'd have said yes. It was obvious."

"I'm sure she would have."

"I'm a woman. She would have."

"So I did the right thing, then."

She didn't respond. She shifted her eyes toward her water glass and paid attention to it.

"Did I?" he asked.

She replied, "You made the choice you had to with your conscience."

"I guess I can't ask you to make it for me. Especially as we're in the same unit."

"It wouldn't be mine to make anyway. I'm happy to listen. I owe you the favor."

"What would you say if I'd gone off with her?"

She barely shrugged, and her expression was neutral. "You didn't, so it's not an issue."

"That's not an answer. I need to know." He knew, though. She was younger than he, but the paleolithic trip had aged and wisened them all. First Gina, now Caswell were very carefully not telling him to pack it and leave. But it was obvious what they thought. And while Gina might have romantic interests affecting her judgment, Caswell was a cross between younger sister and subordinate soldier. She had no skin in his game.

She responded with, "I wouldn't have said anything. It's not my place to judge the actions of someone I'm not responsible to or for. And nothing that happens on this trip is for any kind of outside consumption. Nor is it one of those things our handlers need to know about. Remember how they kept probing about what animals and people we killed?"

"Yeah, they wanted Doc to rat out the captain for those mercy killings."

She nodded around a carrot. "I think they guessed, yes. None of us are ever going to tell them. There's a lot of things that are just for us."

He sighed.

"I'm very tempted for next time. And I don't know if I should feel guilty about that or not."

"That's your call to make...Martin. I can't make it for you. But I'd say Allison decided the marriage is over. Nothing you do here will fix that."

"That doesn't make it easier."

"I know," she said. "For what it's worth, the rabid feminist is saying you don't owe her anything."

Fuck. That really didn't make it easier.

"I need to pretend to sleep," he said, rubbing his eyes. "I have to get up early to answer history questions for the Bykos. Thanks for the talk. Though I'm no closer to an answer."

CHAPTER 35

Sean Elliott had an early meeting with Researcher Zep, Cryder, and a Eurasian gentleman identified as Controller Shan regarding the next transition. It was a conference room that looked high tech, but not dissimilar. Other than the melting door they all had here.

Shan shook hands, and started with, "I'mno great wiv oler Englsh. Dy get m sayn?"

It took Sean a second, but, "Yes, I understand you. May I ask you to speak slowly?"

"Wellgood," the man agreed. "Cernt sked fer transit in two days. Extnt mass n persons. Kwip list fru Shuff Cryder. Any adds?"

"I think everything we need is already on his list. Correct?"

Cryder replied, "Everything you already requested is accounted for."

Shan nodded. "Optim. Akchel count for return. Crect?"

He showed a display in the air that listed the known persons, the number of others, and the offspring.

"That matches what I noted, yes."

"We'll approx mass essimate. Dration's twenny-one days. Retro point nearby, min complications."

He looked at Cryder, who replied, "Short and simple, we hope. They're favorable, get them organized, move, jump."

Zep spoke. "The complication is bringing any offspring, but not local mates, which you report are all female."

"Yes, best we could tell. The only Germanic women with them were already wives."

She nodded. "You'll have to separate them before the return."

He whistled. "That's going to lead to violence."

"Possibly. If necessary, you can use force, and you have protection against most of their weapons."

"What if they don't agree?"

Cryder raised an eyebrow and didn't quite smile, but that expression wasn't mirth. "Then we bag and drag."

"That could get awkward."

Zep looked very, very serious as she advised, "If they can't be made to come along, they have to be eliminated from the time frame."

Sean felt a hard lump.

"I don't think my orders cover that, and I'm morally not okay with it."

Cryder gripped his wrist, and it seemed supportive.

"My job if we must."

That wasn't necessarily reassuring.

"How do you feel about that?"

The man shook his head. "Not at all good. Going to avoid that as much as we can."

Sean let a held breath out. "Agreed. Thank you."

"Might mean a lot of pig wrestling."

"I'll let Dalton know. He'll be good for that."

"Yes, and also have Arnet."

Zep put in, "As much as possible, we want them all alive and unhurt. But they can't stay in that time. Including the offspring."

Sean felt tense and a bit nauseous. This was awful.

"I'll do everything we can."

Shan nodded. "Glad to have yr help. 'Scuse, must go." He stood from the table and left.

Zep continued, "This is why we've tried to stop the 'experiments' and random jumps. Every one of these hurts the people caught in the . . . ripples is your term, and it fits. Recovery is going to be awkward, dangerous, expensive, and potentially deadly."

"No way to stop it?"

"It's a technology. There's no way to stop someone using it, any more than one can stop people fabricating weapons or building their own astro sensors. Though more of the latter would be better. It does seem to be improving with refinement, but there are still going to be discontinuities and . . . deformities to time, is probably the best term."

"Yeah, I get it. It's an ongoing thing in human history. Develop a tech, screw things up, fine-tune it, hopefully in time."

"Exactly. You might want to discreetly inform your people. That's your decision of course. Shuff Cryder has some gear to assist in restraint, but that means you'll need more people to stand alert."

"Yes, so I'm glad it's a shorter time frame."

She nodded. "That was part of the consideration. But that schedule is fixed, so you must be persuasive quickly."

"I understand," he said soberly. Christ.

"We can summarize for your unit now. I won't mention the mandate."

"Thanks. I'll need time to break that to them, and hopefully we won't need to."

"You have excellent leadership ability, even by our standards," she allowed.

It didn't come across as condescending, but he understood his society was considered less sophisticated than theirs. *Gee, thanks.*

"Okay, let's do that, and let them prep personal gear. I almost wish we had more stuff to do. We do PT, and that's about it at present. There's none of our usual Army stuff to do."

Cryder said, "If you had more time, you could do some of our training. It's all graduated in pace."

"You know, if you have a confidence course or such, that would be neat."

He replied, "We do, but no free time."

"I should have asked four days ago. I'm pleased you could configure this fast at least."

Zep said, "They've been working hard to do so. They really are progressing the tech."

"Okay, let's tell them everything except that last detail." He stood.

His people took it seriously but without significant reaction.

Dalton commented, "If we need to wrestle, these guys are strong. We'll want to hit them low and have Arnet stun them."

Caswell's contribution was, "I'm trying to think of a way to propose it so they accept it as a demand from the gods, but I've got nothing so far."

He simply said, "We'll play it by ear." He didn't shrug. A good leader didn't present like that.

Spencer noted, "They are probably going to insist on bringing loot and any acquired women. And they have children."

Sean said, "Is there some way to differentiate the people during transition? Once we have them here, it stops being a problem what they think."

Zep said, "That may eventually be possible, but is not at this time."

"So we may need to be . . . persuasive."

"Yes."

"Can we detain that many?"

"We will first try to be persuasive. If need be, we can make offers of benefits."

"We should take something impressive to show them, then."

"Such as?"

"Valuables. Images and video of things and people. Quality weapons. Stuff they can handle here."

"Will that work?"

"Some, at least. Their culture is used to movement and trade."

"Okay. If that doesn't work, we can stun and detain a certain number. We'll take equipment to secure them, but that then means we have act as both internal and external security for a large number, and provide all their needs."

"Is there a backup plan?"

"Their acquisitions come here. We'll either send them back or keep them here."

"I see."

Zep shrugged. "It's not ideal, but we can make it work."

"You will only have twenty-one days. That is the best window we can arrange."

"As we know where and who, that should be doable."

"It should. You've been very capable at this, especially given your background."

That was a bit insulting, though it probably wasn't intended that way. They'd been given a mission and time frame, and accomplished it. That's what one did. Nothing about it was too extreme—find an element, bring them back.

Two days later, they were ready to transit again. His troops had had plenty of social time and he was quite sure the single ones all got laid, which was a plus. The Army officially wanted monks who sat in cells between operations. In reality, soldiers who got to drink, have sex, and occasionally get in a recreational fight performed much better in the field.

They had an escort of experts as they rolled to the platform, hauling their personal gear. Ms. Zep was along and he raised a subject he'd wondered about.

"I have no idea if you can answer this, or if you will if you can. I noticed a relationship between displacements."

"Oh?"

"The mammoths were from prior to the time frame we were in, and fairly local. Then we have the Gadorth, from Western Europe, and about eight thousand years before our time. The Romans were two thousand years and from northern Italy. The Indians were four hundred years and just down the road. We were from our time, and barely half that distance. It looks like there's a mathematical relationship of longer time, shorter distance."

She admitted, "It does, and I know that's been studied. I am not informed if it's considered relevant, and if so has been graded, or if it's pure coincidence. Note the elements this time have a different set of time to distance, and Shug came forward to your time. I really don't know. Only that all the details have been logged and are being studied."

"This element had a casualty, and a child. How does this get fixed? How do deaths back then, and deaths out of place, and people missing, not screw up the time stream?"

"How's your knowledge of temporal calculus?"

"Uh . . . none?"

She shook her head with a faint smile. "Then I can't explain it to you, even if that was my field. I'm mostly a social scientist, so I don't have much math past the tensors and unified calcs I did in school. But be reassured, none of these events pose a risk. The Temporality is fairly robust and can withstand being knocked about. The problem becomes if too many of them go on for too long."

"What happens then?"

"There's a risk of our world pinching off from the rest of what we think of as reality."

"And going away? Lost?"

"Well, we'd still have history, and future, but it would be

disconnected from yours. Of course, if you were here when it happened..."

"So there aren't multiple time streams?"

She said, "I'm told they are possibly infinite, but there's only one that matters to us."

"Got it."

"Think of it as pollution. A little isn't really noticed outside its immediate area. Get enough of it, though, and it affects the entire system."

"Our little was noticed by us."

"Yes, it's not an exact comparison. But your incident didn't have any major effects. You were found once we identified the wave that displaced you, which was caused by something else entirely."

"Can you say what that was?"

"Even if I knew, I couldn't. I was brought in after we determined Arnet and Cryder had gone where they did, that several other bubbles had gone over the same crest, and that there was a good chance of human habitation where all those went."

"Why do these waves seem to pick groups of people instead of empty dirt? Or are those only the ones we notice?"

"I wish I knew. Our temporal scientists won't discuss it at all."

That was probably for the best, he thought.

She did say, "We should be able to get you closer both physically and temporarily."

"I've never heard that word in that context, but it fits and is fantastic."

She smiled at last. "I see. It is correct, though."

"Indeed. We're ready."

They gathered on the now familiar launch pad and awaited the transferen—

BANG!

CHAPTER 36

BANG!

After the transition, Sean and his element were standing in a chewed-up circle of dirt inside a snowscape.

"It appears to be winter," Oglesby said needlessly. It was goddamned cold. The wind bit, the driven snow stung, and skin burned.

Everyone dove for the vehicles as the Guardians opened the clamshells. Sean wriggled into the gauze-thin outer garment, and felt warmth returning quickly. He was thankful again the Byko had damned good field gear.

"This was bound to happen eventually," he said.

Cryder pointed some instrument at the leaden, drooping clouds, and said, "Time's about seventeen hundred local. Estimating late February. We're within near five kay of their location."

"What year, though?"

"I don't have that yet," he admitted. "I will need stars."

Sean said, "Meanwhile—" as Arnet said, "We should pitch camp."

The bivvy tents unrolled just as easily. Arnet directed everyone to face them inward in an arc, and Sean took over on that. Meanwhile, Cryder drove his vehicle around with an attachment that turfed up a berm, sort of like a massive plow. Just how much torque and horsepower did those trucks have? The wards

473

were placed in a tight circle, set high to diffuse the wind. The vehicles were parked on the windward side, and dropped curtains underneath to cut the blast. The shower and latrine were set up, and Arnet ran what was apparently a handheld ditch witch to create a drain channel.

An awning inflated over the small camp, with a central hole for ventilation or smoke. A windbreak deployed on a third of the arc. It was a combination Roman castra with a Mongolian yurt.

With all that and a small space heater, it was quite comfortable, and Sean was even able to unzip partway. It was probably about 30°F inside the perimeter. He checked his phone. Yes. 28°F.

Cryder tossed down something and struck a flame. Whatever it was was a source of fuel, and they had a small fire. It added little to the physical heat, but a lot of emotional warmth. Fire was home, and had been for humans for how many thousands of years?

He asked SFC Spencer.

Spencer replied, "As far as I recall, definitely a hundred-K years, possibly a million, some evidence as far back as two point three but it's inconclusive. Arnet, Cryder, any insight?"

Cryder said, "Your information is within range of our own estimates."

"Is it? Or is your information within my range and more refined?"

Cryder smiled, shrugged, and said nothing.

Sean said, "So fire's an intrinsic part of our soul."

Dr. Raven put in, "What you have to remember is that fire, shelter, and sharpened sticks and rocks predate us as a species. We inherited those. We are genetically toolmakers and fire builders."

"Hmm. I hadn't considered that."

She asked, "What's your first instinct if something doesn't move that should?"

"Hit it with a...damn, you're right."

She actually grinned. "Yup. Not even a conscious thought. Grab a rock and hit it. Grab a stick and pry it. Grab a rock, sharpen a stick, and poke it. Concepts beyond most animals are innate to us. We've certainly had fire long enough to predate Homo Sapiens and behavioral modernity."

Dalton looked a bit uncomfortable, but less so than he had in previous conversations.

Spencer said, "Well, we're comfortable for tonight, which is impending. Do we try to sleep when we just woke up? Hardball through until tomorrow?"

"Watch a movie?" Doc asked.

Sean replied, "Cryder, my plan is work a bit late, sleep a bit short but long enough, and get to attempting contact in daylight. What do you think?"

"That seems reasonable. I hope to have stars to compare by then. I'll know exactly."

Doc asked, "You have that good of a reverse star atlas?"

"Yes."

Doc said, "I have something like that, but it's all estimates, not exact enough for that range."

"We have all those estimates, plus additional observation window. Ours is more accurate, and we're obviously revising as we do these trips."

"I wish I'd had that."

"You did remarkably well. When we arrived and discussed it, I was quite impressed."

"Can you share that atlas? It seems benign enough."

He shook his head. "Sorry. I'd offer more with monitoring and let the symwork clip if it needed. Here I'm reluctant to discuss anything technical."

"Fair enough, but dammit."

Food was ready in short order, and since they'd restocked, it had fresh fruit and vegetables, and a very savory dish of meat with onions, with a side of pickled salad.

"Lamb?" Doc asked, and Dr. Raven replied, "Mutton." It was obvious she was not a fan.

Chunks of meat that were apparently mutton. Potatoes. Carrots. A savory broth. Buttered bread to dip in it. It was an appropriate meal for the environment, though pot roast would have suited him better. Mutton was just okay.

That aside, the campsite was very comfortable, and an engineering marvel. It had taken minutes only to berm, revet, cover, and pitch. He wondered what else field equipment like this was used for. You didn't need defensive wards for rescue operations. Certainly they were a useful safety feature, but they'd been thrown in place here as a deliberate step of the construction, obviously rehearsed. Nor did you need a berm for animals. A berm was for stopping armed intruders. The ability to do both indicated the anticipation to fight in a rural environment that favored these tools. It wouldn't work in a paved MOUT environment. It probably had some provision, though.

He didn't think it was a good idea to ask.

They sat around the fire for a bit. He called final formation and let people head for their tents to watch video or whatever. Most of them stuck around sipping a warm cider-like beverage as the fire's fuel pellet burned.

Overhead, the blowing snow eased off. There were occasional gaps in the clouds, but he had no idea how many referents were needed to isolate their location.

He crawled into his tent and activated the video. He pulled up the original *Star Wars* and watched the familiar classic, dozing occasionally because it was dark and he had nothing else to do.

After it scrolled away, with that amazing closing theme, he crawled back out of his bag, pulled on boots, and headed for the latrine. It was chill outside now, but workably warm enough. His phone said it was 44°F. The enclosure worked.

Cryder sat in the reestablished CQ, though it had additional windscreens now, and another space heater. Well, expecting to go back soon, they could afford to use more energy. The vehicles had a decades-long power source.

The man had his one-way viewscreen up and was typing and swiping in the air to write or code whatever he was working on.

Sean waited for a momentary break and asked, "Did you get any starlight?"

Cryder nodded. "Just barely, a few minutes, but enough. We're four months later than our last visit."

Oof. "Better late than early, but that's a fair piece. I hope they're not too unhappy."

"Assuming they're still there, though it seemed a workable location."

"Only about five kilometers, you say?"

"Yes. I did some overhead recon. We can drive to within a kilometer."

"How should our advance be?"

"Everyone, armed. We'll secure the camp, drive in, walk in, discuss. That way we have backup. I'll have Arnet in solid position with the heavy stunner."

"That's a sound approach. I like it."

He crawled back to bed for a few hours. He woke again when Arnet buzzed at the crack of twilight.

Some things didn't change with time, though it might be partly the military. Breakfast offered hot beverages, biscuits and gravy, hot oatmeal, and hot sausage with scrambled eggs.

He forced some of each down, to ensure he had energy, though he wasn't hungry at the moment.

That done, everyone armed up and loaded up. The sun was just making a glow behind the still-present clouds, which were now a heavy gray.

The camp self-secured. They rolled out, and the wards remained active. Nothing other than a few birds could get in.

The vehicles did leave a visible trail in snow.

Behind him, Spencer noted, "That's what I saw the first night they approached us. Suddenly there were those broad tracks, not animal, probably machine, but nothing had been on thermal, IR, or visual."

Arnet said, "We were as discreet as we could manage."

"Oh, it's fine. But it was disturbing as hell at the time."

It was impressive how the onboard nav system even found paths between trees, rocks, and other features. On screen, he could even see roots and rocks highlighted. Their route meandered and rambled a bit, but inexorably moved toward their destination. In thirty minutes, they were much closer.

"This is a good location," Cryder announced, and the vehicle powered down.

The captain dismounted, Martin Spencer and the rest followed his lead. He moved back a bit, and watched as the vehicles vanished. There was a faint shimmer and fade as the screen neutralized. Up close, about three feet away, there was just barely a demarcation visible.

Cryder said, "Let's go. Please lead us the way you did."

Right. It was Arnet along last time.

Elliott said, "I want buddy pairs, three-meter spacing. I'm not aware of imminent risks, but if anything tries to flank we can envelop. Oglesby with me. Spencer with Cryder. Caswell with Dr. Raven. Doc with Dr. Sheridan. Arnet with Dalton."

"Lead on, boss."

The gear was warm, but the snow was still a hindrance. It varied from a dusting to knee-deep drifts, depending on how it blew through the woods and collapsed from the limbs above. The ground under was well frozen. The leaves and twigs crunched loudly, but they wanted to be found, so he didn't worry about it.

The dogs alerted first, echoing in the cold air. They marched within two hundred meters of the clearing when a voice shouted out, obviously asking who was there.

"Hellooo!" Martin called back. Carefully enunciating he added, "We are the Americans from last year." They might not understand it, but it should at least sound like a modern language.

There was a response, and it sounded like the same dialect as last time, fluid, definitely Germanic, but with undertones of what sounded like Latin or French or Scandinavian.

They came into view of each other. The sentry was atop a platform about man height, giving him a better view but without excessive issues getting up or down. He called behind him, and there was more loud conversation.

Someone familiar peeked over the palisade.

"That's Wulf," Oglesby confirmed.

"Well, good."

The gate slid open, and Wulf appeared with a handful of picked men.

He wasn't hostile, but certainly not friendly. It took a bit of effort with Spencer, Oglesby, and the translation device to get discussions going.

"You took a long time," the man groused.

Martin offered, "Traveling can be very difficult. But we are here now."

Wulf bid them enter the village, and had mead and biscuits brought out. This time, the local children were visible. That was interesting. A quick count showed the same twenty-three German adults, two children, and six mixed kids.

"Who are your others?"

"Shuff Torand Cryder is the band leader from the wizard's world. His wizards are the ones fixing the problem. The women are wise advisors and manage our meals. Those two speak to the gods." He hoped that was good presentation.

Wulf faced the women and offered a nod of his head, and an outspread arm of welcome. All three returned the nod, and

Raven did it over cupped hands, as some sort of gesture he might take as beneficial.

Wulf noticed and replied, "Thank her for me, I appreciate the blessing."

Elliott turned to them. "He says thanks, so I guess it worked."

"You're welcome," Raven replied. She seemed quite serious about a ritual he was pretty sure she didn't give a crap about. Good.

Wulf asked, "When do we travel home?"

"Twenty days. We must meet the Bykos at a shaman spot, a revered place for them. The proper prayers to their gods will make the travel happen to their land, and they can easily send you from there to your home."

"Yet it took you all season." He didn't sound doubtful, but he did sound concerned about the issues. He munched a biscuit and chugged some mead.

The captain continued, "The travel itself was brief. They had trouble reaching the right location."

"How do we approach this?"

Cryder said, "We must all walk to the location. It's about four days' travel. We will depart from there."

"That seems easy enough. Why wasn't this done before?"

"We had to know you were missing, locate you, travel here. We only were able to do the first two because we were looking for the other group."

Wulf nodded once, curtly. "Fair enough. How much space is there for goods?"

Cryder said, "You can take any personal goods you can bring. However, the gods will not allow people from this place to travel to your place."

Wulf shook his head dismissively. "That is unacceptable. We have taken wives, they must come with us."

"It's unfortunately impossible."

Wulf waved that aside.

"I'll sacrifice to the All Father and it will be fine."

Martin said, "Cut translation. I'd say this isn't the time or place to argue with him."

The captain nodded and tried a distraction.

"The Bykos have many fine items. Look at this sword," he said as he drew his.

The man paused, looked, then took the weapon to examine. He

held it up carefully to sight along the blades and flats, breathed onto it to see the layered pattern.

"It is very fine work," he admitted. "Among the best I've seen." He hefted it some more, obviously pleased with its balance. Martin didn't blame him. You picked that sword up and wanted to start gutting Saxons.

You've never seen anything close to this quality, Martin thought.

He said, "Their wizards can do metal work of this quality."

Cryder took over. "We've only a few days to be in place for the wizards. You can bring what you need, but it will have to be portable. None of the tools and shelters are necessary."

"There's valuable iron in many tools," Wulf pointed out.

"Yes, of course bring those. They are important." They had to be relocated or destroyed anyway.

Wulf nodded, turned, and started shouting orders, interspersed with gestures.

After a few moments, he turned back. "You have sufficient food for us?"

Cryder said, "As last time, as I'm sure your armsmen can tell you, our supplies and preparation are up to the task."

"How far must we walk?"

"The first is only about three thousand paces. The elderly and needy can have transport some of the way, on our carts. We can come back in two days."

"That's generous of you. Two of the women are near birthing, and Adan is spry for his age, but our eldest."

"It will be an honor to let your elders ride. I hope we can hear their stories and learn some of their wisdom."

This was getting easier. Really, all the cultures wanted the same courtesy, exchange, respect. Details varied. Against that were the time constraints. Building a relationship was something he'd seen in A-stan. It took time they didn't have here.

"Let us know when everyone is ready to move."

"It will be soon. I am unhappy with the shortage of horses. We came with four. We have only seven."

"Do bring them of course. And the dogs."

"Excellent."

Yeah, until we leave your women behind. This is going to suck.

Cryder said, "We'll return then."

❖   ❖   ❖

They walked and drove back to the camp. Once inside the wards, Cryder immediately gave orders in a calm, clear voice that said he was used to being obeyed.

"I need the wards moved out ten meters, with a bias to include that stream." He pointed. "Arnet will follow with the trencher. I have additional screening and tent panels here. I need three people to assist."

Sean ordered, "Dalton, Oglesby, Caswell, please assist with the wards. Spencer, myself, Doctors Sheridan and Raven will help with the tent."

The tent was sectional, but very lightweight and hard to control in even a breeze. Though once one corner was fastened, the rest went together much more easily. It was a modified lean-to with a peak and partial slope on the open side. Sean recognized the overall style as something the Germans would be familiar with.

Then a folding awning/side panel attached to the sloped peak and it was a proper wedge tent, about 15'x30' and a good 18' tall at the peak. The wards were apparently done, and Dalton came over with a pile of folding mattresses and blankets that would keep everyone warm. The lightweight fleece would probably be recognized as a high-status fabric, above that of the wool they were used to.

Oglesby hauled in a wagonload of wood, already cut and split with the Byko tools.

In short order it was an impressive camp, and everyone was hot, worn, and grimy.

Two days later, they went back to the Nordwandlaz.

It took a couple of hours, some of it standing around, some of it sending Oglesby and Dalton, then Caswell and Sheridan, to assist in packing and moving. He watched Sheridan swipe a few test strips and drop them into marked bags for later analysis.

Gear was distributed among all the men and some of the women. They packed as much food as they were able, and there was no reason to prevent that. They'd be more comfortable with their food and it reduced the drain on resources. It all went into baskets and haversacks, looped over shoulders, and some of it onto a sledge to be dragged, including the jugs of mead. The horses were mostly being led, two dragging the sledge, two others hauling a small wagon. Sean gathered the complete lack of roads limited the usefulness of tall wooden wheels. The dogs were harnessed to travel alongside, and how many of them were mixed between some sort of German hound and the archaic breed?

Wulf announced, "We are ready. I wish there was time for a sacrifice. It would make for better omens."

Cryder offered, "I can bring a live yearling to sacrifice later, according to the gods' wishes."

That got a smile and a friendlier nod. "Excellent, sir. Thank you."

They started tromping and dragging back through the woods.

Cryder apparently unscreened the vehicles from a distance. Both were visible as they approached.

He and Arnet reached down and deployed the running boards at side and rear, and popped up what appeared to be a bench like a golf cart's.

"Your elders will sit here, out of the wind. The young and the women may hold here." He indicated the rails above the running boards. He gestured, and Martin assisted in pulling out the trailer. It unfolded as a wire cage that was much stronger than it looked. He snapped the corners open and gave a thumbs-up.

Cryder indicated the side.

"Your goods go here. More may ride in here. I'd suggest children and mothers. The rest walk between the carts."

It was near another hour before everyone was coordinated. With modern drill the Army might have done it a bit faster, but with administrative delays, it was probably pretty close. That these people were used to the cold was an interesting factor. It didn't cause them haste, but it didn't bother them, either.

Several stared suspiciously as the vehicles moved without draft animals, but the near silence appeared to satisfy them it was some sort of constrained magic.

The Germans sang a low tonal march as they moved. Sean looked around and Sheridan held her phone up, indicating she was recording it.

It was only about an hour to the site, and the Byko clothing was very effective even against biting wind and stinging snow.

Arnet explained the shower and toilet, and Cryder had one of the domes up.

"No hot tub," he said, "But we do have a sweat lodge they might appreciate."

"Excellent," Martin agreed. They probably would.

Oglesby and Raven were setting low extruded benches on log sections around the fire. Caswell had something delicious ready to serve.

"What do we have, Jenny?" he called.

"Venison stew with carrots, celery, potatoes, peas. Thick bread and butter to dip in it. A cheese pie I'm told they might like. Berries and cream for dessert."

"Damn, that sounds good."

"Along with hot cider, ale, mead, and plenty of clear water."

"You remain amazing, thank you."

Arnet was actually busy programming the fabricator. Whatever he was doing took detailed input, and he was even sketching on a physical tablet. He muttered occasionally, made faces, and looked like any contemporary artist with a problem. He pulled at his chin, rubbed the back of his head, and nodded. Then he switched back to fingers in the air and on a touchpad, and whatever he was working on commenced function.

The entire crew lined up gratefully for dinner. There were a half dozen children and Martin was surprised it wasn't more. Must be more of that incompatibility. They were mindful, much more so than contemporary kids, and thrilled with the camp.

"Captain, can I suggest a tour of the wards and such for the kids? And some sort of light show and music? Poppy with a good beat and some illumination?"

"Good idea. I'll talk to Cryder and maybe Caswell about it."

Everyone piled into the food, quaffed drinks, and toasted both their hosts and the unseen wizards.

"It will be great to be home!" Wulf cheered, and the others concurred with raised cups.

Dalton slid alongside Martin and the captain.

"I have an idea that might help," he said.

"Yes?"

"Ask the ones with local wives if they're married back home and how they plan to explain it."

Elliott nodded and raised his eyebrows. "Possibly. What do you think?"

Martin shifted his neck. "I'm not sure," he said.

"Oh?"

"Some of the younger ones may still have been single, or single again, wives dead in childbirth. Some might bring them back as mistresses, de facto second wives." And dammit, he didn't want to delve into that subject. "I suppose it's worth asking discreetly when you get a chance."

"I'll see what I can do."

Sean Elliott thought the idea had potential. Any they could persuade gently they wouldn't have to use force on. This ray gun diplomacy was easy to use, but easy to cause trouble with. So far it had meant displays of force and anger, with no real subservience or agreement.

Then the idea fell completely apart.

Cryder stood in the middle with a bundle of cords. He held up one of the amulets Arnet had fabricated, and spoke.

"These are magic medallions from our shaman. The symbols hold the power of the travel spot. You must wear these." He walked slowly, methodically, and almost ritually around the circle, handed them out one at a time, and ensured each man wore one.

"I would suggest you also pray to your Allfather for success. He knows of this magic, of course, and will bless it."

Wulf noted, "We will need a sacrifice. You mentioned a good yearling, and some of our mead will draw his favor."

"I will find the yearling."

"It might even require a human sacrifice. A strong warrior's spirit."

That was disturbing.

Cryder responded completely seriously and calmly, "That shouldn't be necessary. There are many gods at work here, all wanting the return to go well."

The conversation continued, and by the end the Nordwandlaz seemed satisfied. Cryder returned and sat at his desk under the awning. The young kids all swarmed into a game of tag. The cold didn't bother them, and it was quite nice here. They were attractive kids, with mixed features and coffee-colored skin.

Sean walked up, and asked, "Did you just equip them all with restraint collars?"

Cryder replied completely flat, "I did."

Trying very hard not to bust a gut laughing, he replied, "Man, they're gonna be pissed."

Again, the reticence. "That's acceptable."

Sean had to admit the presentation had been brilliant. Nor would it matter if others asked for collars, too. He assumed the Bykos could easily set the controls to exclude or include whomever they wished.

"How far from here to departure point?"

"Only eight kilometers this time."

About five miles.

"Easy for the fit, and you have space for the young and the old."

"Yes, we'll move in a day or so."

"When are you going to separate them?"

"Haven't decided yet. Soon has advantages in moving fewer people. Waiting means less discussion. Either way we'll have to subjugate them. Any input?"

"Let's wait a day and see."

"We can do that. We'll need to move after that."

CHAPTER 37

Jenny Caswell had a task. Morning formation was done. The weather had cleared up and warmed a bit, into the forties. She had Dr. Raven with her, one of the native wives, Uka, and one of the Germanic women, Lils. They were trying to dig up some herbs and greens to go with the feast. The machine could replicate most seasonings, but it would add to the ritual of the event to use real greens.

She'd gotten pretty good at this during their time in the Paleolithic. Uka was amazing, though. She was wiry and fit and looked perfectly average in a woolen dress. Lils was experienced and cheerful, a curvy woman of about twenty-five. Dr. Raven was partly along for support, partly for professional interest and specimen gathering, but did recognize a couple of plants. They had one weapon, Jenny and Raven had machetes and knives, and the two "primitive" women, which seemed rude, but she wasn't sure how else to put it, had little utility knives that could cut plants and not much else. There was a huge contrast in armament and attitude between them.

"Oh, that's cumin," Raven announced at the edge of the trees, amid rotting snow.

Uka agreed in broken German, "*Es yuotz.*" Jenny's phone translated it as "Very good."

Lils found some tree fungus under a log.

Shortly they had a mix of green herbs and mushrooms.

They walked back to the camp, with a bagful of seasoning and garnish for the intended meat.

Cryder was true to his word, and brought in three yearling bucks of some sort of deer. Far prettier than the ugly saiga and relatives, these were something that looked a lot like Bambi. Two were dead, one was trussed. Along with that were a dozen fat fish.

"How did you get fish that size?" Jenny asked. "The stream can't have anything like that."

"Sent a drone down to the river," he replied.

"Three deer?"

"Two to eat, one stunned for sacrifice." He prodded it with his boot. "Which we can eat if they choose. Didn't ask."

"Nice hunting," she commented.

"Line-of-sight weapon and drones to flush them." He pointed at the two devices settling back into Roller Two.

There was a sizeable fire for roasting, and she and the other women got to work cutting, shredding, pressing, chopping. Lils was amazed by modern kitchen knives.

"*Scarf,*" she noted, holding a knife up. *Sharp.*

"Very," Jenny agreed.

Shortly they had an entire table of native herbs ready, with wild garlic and onions, and some coarse ground salt.

"Did you find them under the snow?" Oglesby asked.

"Some are pretty durable. They're wilted and brown, but still edible as seasoning. It should work out, though."

He asked, "Are you going to take charge of that?"

She replied, "I can. They expect a female cook, and of course I know how."

"How much does that bother you?"

Jenny shrugged. "That's normal for their culture. As long as they respect my boundaries, and it helps the process, it's not an issue. But I will not make you a sandwich."

"That's fair," he agreed. "I probably have more experience anyway."

"Nice try," she snickered.

Rich Dalton watched as the group elder took charge of the sacrifice, stringing up the live deer by its hind legs, over a pole Arnet erected. He had some sort of bundle of leaves from a tree, a knife, a headdress with horns, and a bowl.

He was really uncomfortable with this pagan ritual, but understood that the word of Christ had not yet reached their lands. He prayed silently that they find the Holy Spirit soon, and stood as far back as was polite.

The deer alternated between struggles and holding still, and obviously understood it was in grave distress. Its chest heaved, though the position might have something to do with that. It flailed with its hooves and Rich almost hoped it clobbered the dude. But, this had to go well to assuage some of their concerns.

The man intoned, and chanted, and called, arms raised. Then he slashed the beast's throat. It squealed, snorted, and sprayed blood from the wound, and then wriggled less and less as it bled out, with muscle tremors continuing.

In the meantime, its blood gushed into the slush, and the bowl. He figured he knew what that was for, and he was correct. The first hot flood spurted into the wooden hollow, and the man took a drink, then turned to offer it to Wulf, Cryder, and the captain. It steamed in the cool air.

Damn, the captain had to eat all kinds of crap on these missions. More so than the rest of them. He took it stoically, though, raising the proffered bowl and at least pretending to take a mouthful, and it was certainly a sip.

The Germans seemed happy with the result, their shaman raised his hands and shouted again, with "Wotan" being almost audible in the invocation.

Then the man sliced the belly, yanked out the guts hot and steaming, and fairly expertly cut the liver out.

It was very clear he expected to cook and eat it, and at least cooking was part of the process.

The horses seemed unbothered and continued munching grass. Apparently, they knew they were safe.

Shortly everyone was gathered around the roast venison and herbs and weeds, and the sacrifice was being hacked into gobbets and skewered over the fire. The dozen dogs got lots of leftover guts, organ meats, and bones to chew.

Rich walked forward, found Sergeant Spencer, and asked him.

"What is all this for, and why do they eat it after sacrificing it? They didn't burn or expose it, just ritually killed it."

Spencer said, "We don't have a lot of records from that time, and rituals varied greatly between groups. I also haven't read up on them. You remember I had trouble placing them at all. So I really don't know, other than it was a sacrifice, and the blood and liver probably indicate strength and life for the transition."

"It's amazing how much all these cultures had similarities before modern times."

"Yes, and it all got incorporated into early religions, then into the Church, and then evolved into modern evocations that don't require actual sacrifice, but keep the base concepts. A bit like your friend Mommed, who's less Muslim than you are by his time."

Rich was slightly disturbed by that, but it was true. "Yeah, I supposed God is adjusting His message as we move forward. You know, that gives me hope that eventually we all become worthy."

"As a member of the Loyal Opposition, I'm glad to help," Spencer offered with a grin.

Rich snorted back.

"I very much appreciate that God can give me messages from those who believe differently."

Spencer nodded. "If he exists, that's exactly how he should do it."

"Indeed. The message is universal. Thanks again, Sergeant Spencer."

"You're quite welcome."

In the shadow of a pagan sacrifice, he'd reaffirmed his beliefs, and the support of his friends.

And the meat smelled really good.

After noshing down meat, veggies, bread, a mug of the ale that was quite tasty, he sat back and watched as six of the Germans started up with drums, wind instruments, and a flute. Like the ancients, they were carved horn and bone. And the music was quickly repetitive and the dancers started swaying, almost in a trance.

Well, shoot, if the twenty-first century had a genre called "Trance," and the Bykos had something similar, and Paleolithics and the Dark Ages, that seemed to be pretty much a human universal.

Men and women strutted around the fire, banging sticks, blowing horns, painted in deer blood. Some moved back and chanted in slow tones. Dr. Sheridan carefully moved in with them, as did Oglesby. It appeared they wanted to experience it for a bit. After a few minutes, they stepped back out.

He could use a second drink, but he'd seen enough primitive dancing he didn't need more, though the scientists were recording it all. He eased back from the circle and headed up to the kitchen.

On second thought, a ginger ale would be good. The one beer was enough.

Captain Elliott and the Bykos were up here. Sergeant Spencer appeared to be the command presence by the fire.

He drew his drink and stepped under the awning.

Elliott greeted him, "Good evening, Rich."

"Evening, Captain," he replied. "Are we good to move, then?"

"Yes, whenever they're up and about in the morning, or oh nine hundred if they're not. We're going to relocate to departure point and see about separating them."

Rich flared his eyebrows. "That's going to be awkward." He took a cold, refreshing chug, even though it was a chill night.

Cryder had a thin smile as he said, "For them, possibly."

"Is there anything I can do to help make it easier?"

The captain shook his head. "No, but we are going to try to get support from Shug's people."

"Oh?"

Elliott explained, "Separated women will need support and a place to go. We never did figure out if they were captives, diplomatic trades, purchases, or volunteers. And they're going to be heartbroken missing their kids."

"Yeah, that part is awful. I try not to think about it."

"Offer all the prayers you can. That's all there is. I wonder how many myths of demons who steal babies are about to start."

That brought him up short. He'd encountered some of those. "Oh, damn."

Elliott nodded and replied, "Anyway, we move first, get backup, then split everyone up before we move. They're going to hate us, but it has to be done."

Cryder put in, "Unfortunate, but as with any casualties, we have to proceed with the rest of the mission."

"I just wish the mothers could come along. Separating them is hard."

Dr. Raven had just arrived. She stepped into the light and said, "Keep in mind they expect to birth a child about every three years, and lose about half of them."

She was getting coffee and selecting additives. Migraine?

"Sure, but dead is not the same as abducted. One has closure."
She looked sad herself.

"It's tragic," she agreed. "All of this has been."

"I guess I'll pray," Rich said. He couldn't think of anything else.

"It can't hurt," the second hard-core atheist told him.

The next morning was gray, biting cold, and gusty, but there wasn't any snowfall. Porridge and hot sausage were encouraged for breakfast. Armand Devereaux chose sausage, scrambled eggs, and a couple of steaming cups of coffee. With everyone fed, dressed, and ready to move, they struck camp. Wards, tents, covers came down, were stowed, and everyone formed up.

The movement started with the Nordwandlaz traveling behind Roller Two on foot and in their wagon, as Arnet used Roller One to rip down and flatten out the berm, disperse the remains of the fire, and clear a couple of other things. Then the clan mounted the running boards and jump seats on both vehicles, and others sat in the trailer. It was a bit tight, but everyone was able to take transport.

It took less than an hour to reach the evac point, and another hour to cordon it off. It was another plateau at mid-hill, but this one had a number of trees across it.

Cryder announced, "We will stay here eighteen days until recovery. There will be limited hunting parties and wood gathering for fifteen days. Then we will secure the perimeter and remain inside until departure. Does everyone understand?"

The machines translated, and there was some back-and-forth, but everyone understood it.

While Armand helped with the wards going up, Arnet shouted a warning and started blasting trees.

Each one got shot with some sort of explosive that blew the base apart. He knocked them all down—there were seventeen—and then unlimbered a boom with a chain saw and sectioned two of them up.

As Armand placed his last ward of the stack, Arnet sprayed some sort of chemical.

"They're firewood now," he announced. "Burn away!"

With the camp cordoned, the man continued with a future version of a stump grinder, shaving the roots to ground level.

After that it was time to set the rest of the camp.

Armand had to admit, the Germanics were pretty damned good builders. They dug, and cut logs and had small leantos up within the day. They were about the size of large doghouses, but sod foundations, log pillars and layers, and thatched roofs yielded very warm structures. The captain even loaned them the two basic axes on hand, which they quickly learned to love, with the contoured handles and better steel of the twenty-first century.

"Your smiths are blessed by the gods," Artis pronounced.

Spencer told him, "They are, and they have huge, lever-powered hammers to ease the forging."

"I look forward to seeing it."

Arnet fabricated more timbers and threw together a jungle gym with swings for the German children. They were on it at once. Armand watched them immediately play King of the Castle, and swing around in a game of follow the leader.

So that took them down to fifteen days. The Germanics had huts, the Americans had tents. Armand held sick call every day and dealt with calluses, blisters, sprains, and strains. There were fewer of those than he expected after three days of building. These men were tough. One of the women came up and shyly explained her symptoms. It sounded like endometriosis, and he asked Arnet for assistance.

"I've something that can deal short term. Long term means no kids."

She was very nervous about the machine translation, and kept staring at the speaker. She agreed to short-term relief, being about a year.

Armand half frowned and shook his head.

"I wish she understood how the return is working."

Arnet shrugged. "Still better off n she was."

"Yeah. Let's do it."

He called Dr. Sheridan as a chaperone to hold her hand and keep her calm. Then they had to explain to her husband that the relief would be temporary, but there would be no kids in the interim, either. He shrugged and nodded and agreed.

"It is good she not hurt."

"Okay, then."

Arnet raised a screen, Armand assisted. A probe went into her vagina, the screen showed cervical passage and uterine entry, and some medication dispersed from the end.

Her eyes went wide and she seemed relieved almost at once, relaxing and stretching.

They removed the probe, she straightened her dress, and she was simultaneously shy and excited at the same time.

Armand felt like an ass for how they were going to separate everyone shortly. He was only too glad to get back to an infected blister on the heel of a man's hand, from axe use. He debrided and cleaned, Arnet sprayed it with what might as well be a healing potion, and then applied a bandage, while the man's friends made masturbation jokes. Some things were universal.

CHAPTER 38

Daniel Oglesby was watching a firewood-splitting contest while snow blew around in swirls outside the wards. The Germans loved the Americans' axes for their ergonomics, sharpness, and durability. They were working on single-swing splits of smaller limb logs, and generating a nice pile of firewood in the process. One of the dogs played catch with chopped limbs, and dropped them into the pile.

His phone buzzed. He pulled it and glanced down at the screen. It was the captain.

"Yes, sir?" he answered.

"CQ."

"Yes, sir." He stepped back from the festivities and walked to the center.

"Here, sir," he reported as he arrived.

"Dan, you and Sergeant Spencer are going with Cryder. Plan to translate."

Well, good, that was actual use of his skills.

"What am I translating?"

Spencer said, "We're going to ask Shug's people if they can take the separated women."

He nodded at once, but replied with a caution. "I can do that, but, sir, they're likely to be unhappy with how we're treating people. I'm sure they've heard of our other activities."

Elliott nodded. "Probably. That's why I'm sending Sergeant

Spencer as well. I need Dalton and Doc here to back me up with Arnet if anything happens. The three of you should be able to hold your own and disengage at least, and then we try a Plan B. Ideally, though, we get the locals to take the women back in, and either adopt them or re-home them with their previous tribes."

"Hooah."

Cryder said, "Like to leave in thirty. Fabbing more gifts."

"Hooah again," he agreed, and went to grab some supplies and knock down his tent.

Shortly the three of them were moving in Roller Two.

Cryder told them, "First we 'limnate their village."

Dan remembered that, and being surprised by it. "Ah, like last time."

"Yes. Faster, hang on." The man gunned the drive and the vehicle bounded across the landscape.

Dan paid attention to the trees as they drove to the village. The route was shifting, turning, bouncing even with the Byko vehicle. If he didn't keep eyes out the window, he was going to get sick.

This was the opposite direction from their previous trip, and the terrain was thicker and more overgrown. Progress started out smoothly, then lagged.

The vehicle slowed as they reached a point where the trees were too thick to proceed. Cryder studied his charts and scanners, apparently seeking a detour. Not finding one, he fingered the screen and glowing markers indicated trees just ahead. He grabbed the joystick for the weapon control and announced, "'Fire in the hole,' I think you say."

Two shots flashed, two trees erupted near their bases and slowly bent over, creaking and splintering and toppling. They'd been hit near flush with the ground, and despite the protruding slivers, seemed passable. In fact, they were as Cryder drove over them, the vehicle rising, bending, and shifting as it rolled over the shattered trunks and stumps.

Then he had to squirm the truck between other trees, and Dan swore the vehicle actually bent as it did.

It was a matter of minutes before they pulled up next to what had been the Germans' palisaded village.

He said, "I'm actually surprised no one else has moved in yet."

"They would," Cryder replied. "Might maintain it. It must go."

"Yeah, I can see that." He was slowly feeling better. Damn, what a ride.

Martin Spencer asked, "Can we take a look around real quick?"

"Yes. Interest?"

"I want pics of some things."

"Noted. I can get some too."

They dismounted, and walked in alert across slushy, mucky ground. It hadn't been maintained in several days, and the straw and twigs outside had been trod down by departure. Inside there was a corduroy walkway of staked limbs. That made things easier.

Martin wanted pictures of all the industrial operations. That was a small charcoal furnace. In the next building was the smithy, and he grabbed a sample of slag in a plastic bag. Cryder let a drone circle, getting multiple spectra. He hoped that gave good info and that it could be shared at least privately.

In a half hour he had good views of a loom, hand spindles that looked exactly as he expected, pole lathe, vise bench hewn of wood, several bloomery furnace remains on a built-up rise, leather tanning tanks, an outhouse with barrel that stank until his eyes watered but was similar to military first-deployment builds he'd seen, a smokehouse, a sauna, and the cooper's shack for making the wheels.

Oglesby said, "Damn, you and Gina really did know your shit. Those tools look the same."

"Pretty much. Concept leads to form, which follows function."

Cryder ran his image drone around everywhere and it took samples as well.

"Need anything else?" he asked.

Martin shook his head. "We have data, all their stuff, the rest can go but I wish I could keep some of it."

As they trudged back to the truck, Cryder smiled. "You guys built better."

He continued, "My sensors are clear, too. I'll start at the left and work over, then." Cryder sat down in the seat, touched his control panel, and the weapon array rose behind the cabin. A few more fingertaps, and tiny rockets HISHed from their launchers. They impacted about ten seconds apart, shattering the palisade timbers, exploding cabins, turning everything into splintered debris. Each one sent a pressure wave slapping the vehicle, throwing dirt and leaves, and blasting the undergrowth in perfect atmospheric rings. Within a couple of minutes, the entire...borg was probably correct...was nothing but firewood.

Cryder's second weapon lobbed fireballs. They were probably rocket lifted, but were certainly oily, liquid incendiaries. He was faster on the trigger with those, and their overpressure waves were smaller, though the heat was palpable through the open window.

"Should do it." Cryder nodded in satisfaction. "River'll change course, the ash'll be dispersed, no evidence should remain."

Spencer agreed, "Seems likely. You surprised us the first time you did that."

"Wasn't sure how anyone would react, and wanted it done quickly."

"It was fine. We weren't coming back."

Cryder noted, "Yet here you are."

Dan returned, "Yup. So are you."

The man grinned. "Agreed. Like a curse."

Cryder steered the vehicle north and across the river. He had two drones out, and the onboard sensors, building a map on a dash screen, almost like playing some computer game. The man sought shallows as far as possible, but the truck was capable of deeper water, and crossed a section briefly.

Cryder looked at his screens. "Bank steep. Need to roll downstream a bit to rise."

The banks were steep, and rocky, but shortly widened again to broad pebbled beaches and muddy shallows. The man took the truck up and inland, then resumed maneuvering through trees.

"There we go," he suddenly announced, and turned.

The drones had bagged a doe. He hopped out, ran a blade down the belly, zipped out the guts, and used a loop to tie it to the fender padeyes. He was done in five minutes.

It was amazing how little distance they'd actually covered, and how close together all these groups really were. Twenty miles made a difference when it all had to be walked.

It was midafternoon with broken clouds, and above freezing, when they reached the area near Shug's village.

Cryder announced, "Got good return route plotted. Can go faster."

In back, Oglesby softly said, "Please not too much faster. This is disorienting."

"Will try," the man agreed.

Martin felt a little shaken himself. It was a very smooth vehicle to ride until the terrain wasn't.

They climbed out, Cryder camouflaged it, and they started east and north toward more low bluff. Cryder wrapped a plastic sheet over the deer and shouldered it without issue. There were already signs of people—trodden paths, marks on trees, low areas around what must be fruit bushes.

They strode along, while Cryder had audio playing from his gear, of some sort of future pop music. It was loud enough to announce their presence, not too loud for comfort, but it sounded weird. Martin had heard pop from all over Arabia and the Middle East, Africa, and Europe. He'd heard several evenings' worth at the Byko village. He could sort of pick out some Afghan and Euro roots to this, but it was not similar.

Dogs started barking. It was amazing how fast they'd spread as a domestication. Almost everyone had them.

Shortly a voice called an interrogative. He nudged Oglesby to reply.

Oglesby called back, and in a couple of minutes they were greeting hunters who at least knew of their background from the last meeting. Cryder showed them the deer and they were quite pleased. It was a good opening gift.

Oglesby talked as they walked, and translated in between.

"They say Shug is hunting north, but the party is due back today, very soon."

Martin raised his eyebrows. "Good. That could have been an awkward delay."

He could pick out some words as similar to the some words he'd learned of the group millennia earlier than this, but it was like comparing English to old low German, which he had a great example for. And doing so with no background for the language. Oglesby and the machine would do a much better job translating.

Dan Oglesby was glad to be out of the heaving vehicle, and ecstatic to have actual work again. He'd practiced this language enough to be proficient, and was compiling that data Dr. Raven had suggested.

The locals greeted them, and he was at work at once.

The umma came forward and spoke in a very straightforward

manner they used before switching to methods used for diplomacy or negotiation.

"I greet you. What do you need?"

"I greet you, Umma, on behalf of my myself and our leaders. Sergeant Spencer you have met. Shuff Cryder is new, but his professional hunter was here last time. We bring a deer as a gift."

He paused. "What do I tell him we need? How far can we go?"

Spencer said, "Tell him as friends of Shug, we hope he can provide a favor for us, and we can furnish him with gifts in exchange. Cryder, can you produce a hundred kilos of salt? And a bunch of basic bifaces that match this era?"

"Yes."

Dan ignored the latter part, translated the first part.

It was right then Shug shouted, running across the village, slowing to a walk, and arriving. He was wearing a parka against the chill, and long leggings with boots. With a fur hat, he almost looked like a tall predatory animal. He was covered in dust, mud, and bits of animal. He'd definitely been hunting.

"Friends!" he called. "I greet you!"

"Shug, we greet you."

"You have returned! It is great to see you all. You must come and be welcome."

"We like that, but have only little time. We are hoping you and your people can do great favor. And we can visit briefly."

The umma smiled indulgently at the young man, indicated with a flattened hand for him to wait, and turned back to Dan.

It took a half hour to explain.

After some background and simplified summary, the man paraphrased, "So you must leave the women here, while the men travelers and children must return with you to the Byko lands."

"That's it."

"We can do that. It be very hard on the women to see their children go. They don't go to the spirit world, or grow up. They leave the world entirely."

"Sadly so. If there were an easier way to do it, we would. This is the only way, according to our shamans, and the spirits."

"You mentioned gifts?"

"Yes, we have them at our camp."

He paused and turned back. "Can we provide them baskets or a sled or something?"

Cryder looked at Spencer. "You know this matter best."

Spencer twisted his lip, stepped back, and went into the pantomime he used when "talking to the spirits." He raised his arms, turned, then turned back.

"Tell them we can provide leather bags to carry the gifts of salt and good bifaces. I've seen travois here, so we can make one of those for them. We should also provide some good twisted rope of any local fiber. If you can reduce pine pitch, a volume of that. Is that possible?"

Cryder agreed, "Yes."

Dan struggled over salt, but they understood it as a dirt that dried things and made food taste better. They understood spearpoints, rope, and pitch, and containers.

The umma said, "Yes, this is a generous agreement. When and where do this?"

Cryder apparently had that planned for. He handed over a map drawn on light leather. It had the river, the village upriver the recoverees came from, the Germanics' camp, and their departure point.

"The other strangers' village was destroyed after they left, as the spirits ordered," he noted.

He turned and asked, "Cryder, how fast do we want them there?"

"Three to five days. Will have to leave again at once. We can furnish food."

"Hooah." He turned back.

"Can you get there in three to five days? And we have food for the return trip."

The umma called over a couple of advisors and jabbered away. Dan caught about half the conversation, but it seemed to be a discussion of how.

"Yes, we can do that. We are pleased to ___ with you again."

Dan didn't get that word, but it seemed to be about friendly exchange.

"Thank you. We will go back now and see you in three to five days."

Sergeant Spencer handed him a jug of rum, a bag of weed, and a small bag of arrowheads. Apparently, the Bykos had plenty of quality pot available for things like this.

He took them and handed them over and tried to look solemn

and friendly. The umma took them and smiled back, then offered a big hug to each of them.

He then gestured, and Shug stepped forward to do the same.

Dan said, "You are a good friend, Shug. I'm glad we could see you again."

"I am still grateful for my return. I hope one day I can travel to the Byko lands."

"We do, too."

He did hope so. It was very unlikely it would ever happen, though.

"We will see you in a few days."

"I will walk with you to the veecul."

"Sure, if you wish. We would enjoy your company."

The young man accompanied them back along the raised bank.

"We speared a young buck antelope, and I hit three hare with my throwing stick."

"You deserve your name, then, Stalker of Hare."

The young man grinned. "Yes, but a buck ___ feeds more."

Dan thought the word was for one of the ibex species.

"Well done on that, too."

"Thank you. How are your lost friends?" he asked.

Dan said, "They're in the Byko part of the world, getting healed and cleaned, before we go back to our part, where our elders will help them fit back in."

"Will Kate and Ama-lee help?"

"They are so far, but we have other shamans who specialize in helping people with recovering. So do the Bykos."

"I hope they will be well. I am doing good hunting, and Ama-lee gave me status when she said I was helpful to you. Can you thank her again?"

"If you're coming to help pick up the women, she'll be there."

"Oh, good." The young man seemed excited.

They reached the vehicle, and Cryder revealed it.

Shug startled, then smiled. "Your magic is always a surprise."

They all hugged again. "I will see you soon, Dan, Martin, and Cryder. Travel safely."

"We will. Good hunting to you, Shug."

They climbed in and Dan made the decision to ask, "Cryder, do you have anything for nausea in here?"

The man popped a compartment, reached in, pulled out a tube, and squeezed a single pill into Dan's hand.

"Thanks," he said, and popped it. It was chewable, as most of the Byko oral meds were.

"Driving," the man announced, and apparently took the medication as justification to dial up the speed across the terrain. They left a roostertail across the river, threw mud up the south bank, and bounded through the trees.

Dan was glad of the medication, and it seemed to work. He wasn't sick, only terrified, as they raced between trees and over obstacles, down into gullies and then launching back up and out, with airtime. Apparently, the onboard system remembered the route, and between that and semiautonomous controls, could find its own way. It was less than an hour, with the sky getting dusky, when they pulled into view of the camp and rolled in.

They were last in line for dinner, but there was plenty. He grabbed pasta with sauce and garlic bread. That was the special Modern Only service. The Germans seemed quite happy with stewed or roast meat every night, and porridge and bread with cheese during the day, plus some fruit and veggies around the edges.

He chugged a liter of water and added some of the Byko equivalent of Gatorade. That and sitting on a chair let him relax from the ride enough to have a warm cider. It was still damned cold here in February.

CHAPTER 39

Sean Elliott was anxious. It was half a day into the third day. Their backup was supposed to arrive, but it could take another day and a half. The sooner they split things, the better he'd feel.

Everyone was discreetly near a weapon. The scientists had melding weapons sitting at their table. Cryder and Arnet stayed near the vehicles with the additional support weapons. Spencer had his AR-10.

Far away near the trees, though, that looked like movement, which resolved as multiple figures. Hopefully that was the expected party. If not, the weapons would be needed ASAP.

Arnet flicked a mini-drone into the air, swiped his finger across his controls, and it zipped out of sight, up and toward the approaching party.

He brought up zoom shots, and yes, that was who they were expecting, and there was Shug. It was nine men, no dogs.

"Ready trade goods?" he asked.

Sean indicated so with a point. There was a pile of baskets, tunics woven of the local cloth, pot, liquor, rope, bags of the fake flint tips, and how were those affecting the local economy, where knappers were a meaningful and valued member of the tribe? They'd have a reduced workload for months.

During fabrication he'd asked Arnet about the fake points. "How do you do that?"

Arnet's reply was, "Our system programs a matrix that has an asymptotic decay rate."

Sean realized he'd basically said, "It's magic" in slightly technical terms, without explaining it.

Within the hour, the group was at the wards.

Shug was along, wearing the coat they'd gifted him with. He grinned at Sean, and impressed his tribe by saying, "Hi, friends. Come can in?"

Sean replied firmly, "Welcome, Shug, and umma, and friends." He repeated it in a phrase he'd asked Oglesby for, and memorized. He added the "and umma" from what he remembered, and apparently was close enough.

It was interesting that the chief had come along. Probably he wanted to be able to bargain or instruct.

Once inside the wards, he invited the party over to the CQ.

Through Oglesby, Sean greeted the umma, whom he'd not met until now. The man was tall, buff, had a full head of thick hair hanging to his shoulders, and seemed very composed.

"It's good to meet you at last. I'm the co-commander of this mission. Does that translate?"

Oglesby replied, "I can make it work." He chattered something, and at least this dialect had less of the clicks and glottals they'd encountered in the past before this. Parts of it almost sounded like a recognizable language.

They exchanged formalities, and he pointed to the pile. "There is a good basket and sack for each of you. The pouches contain our best bifaces, and we hope they meet your approval." They should. They were produced to be at the peak of human visual symmetry, just random enough not to look machine fabricated. "They also have some strong cord, some treated tinder." Which was nitrated to smolder and burn very fast. "As well as ochre, and some very pretty polished stones." Arnet had fabricated azurite, malachite, garnet, smoky quartz, and something else. They were striking. "Here is a package of the communing leaf, for you to distribute per your customs." He handed over a large pouch with a lot of weed in it. "Also two containers of the very strong beer," which was what they called the rum last time, apparently. "This is a coil of our best rope," from bark from local trees. "I added some spear shafts we spent a long time straightening." There were a dozen, quarter split from a log, and then turned round.

It was all quality goods for this era, and amazingly cheap

for his own, much less the Bykos. But it would serve as a good diplomatic gesture.

Cryder said, "Lastly, here is travel food." He held up sticks of dried meat and fruit, and slabs of what were basically an enriched sugar cookie. "This will sustain you."

Oglesby looked pretty wrung out after explaining it all and trying to get the courteous nuance into it.

The umma expressed his gratitude with claps, and asked back, "May we drink to our good meeting and your good departure?"

"Sure," Sean agreed. "Everyone gather around."

They walked to the firepit, and dragged a jug of mead and one of rum.

He announced, "We will share in friendship before we depart." He took a chug and passed the mead, which was better than last time, but not by much, and then the rum, which was really good, which he passed the other direction.

Himself, Cryder, the umma, Shug in a high status spot for this, Spencer, Wulf, Sheridan, Raven, Oglesby, Dalton, Caswell, then on to the Germans.

It was going well, until one of the tribesmen said something, and one of the women exclaimed.

Oglesby muttered, "Aw, shit. He just said they were taking the women."

"Fuck."

Cryder and Arnet leapt out of the circle, were atop a vehicle as Shug tried to hush the man, and the women started jabbering.

The women were suddenly penned by force fields.

Wulf turned around looking murderous, and bellowed a war cry as he charged at Sean, with Gurm right behind.

They fell down and plowed in, out cold. Sean could just hear the ZIZZ from Arnet's weapon. Spencer lowered his carbine. He'd been ready to shoot to defend his commander, no questions asked.

The dogs went berserk, straight into defense-and-attack mode, and Arnet stunned them all.

Wulf's wife ran to his prone form, shouting. She tugged for his sword and rose, ready herself to do battle. She apparently had some familiarity with weapons, too. Arnet zapped her. Lils was right behind, and thought better of it, stopped.

By now everyone was armed. Caswell was keeping the Paleo

women and men separated. He was puzzled for a second, then got it. All the groups needed to stay apart until it was under control.

The women's force field slowly coalesced until they were one group. The Germans were all penned individually, along with shrieking children. Several drones circled overhead, apparently taking charge of that. Cryder was ready on the support cannon to mass stun. Arnet focusing on point targets.

Sean called, "Oglesby, tell the women they need to go back to their people."

He translated.

They shouted and cried. Then the men started shouting.

"The spirits demand this. It's unfortunate but necessary."

Wulf and his henchman were just waking up. That delayed things momentarily, but didn't calm anyone down. They shouted among themselves, pointing to one another and the Americans and Cryder. One fingered his collar and went into a long diatribe.

It was surprising how quickly the Germanics figured out the collars were the cause, and again tugged at them, desperate to remove them.

The two stunned leaders twitched and moaned, then rolled to all fours, and rose unsteadily.

With a hard eye, Wulf faced Cryder and stated, "You are an oathbreaker." It was obvious he'd be demanding a duel if he could.

Cryder replied, "I never promised your request. I said we'd discuss it later. This is the discussion. You will comply. That is the discussion. Now we are done."

The separated women hunkered together behind their force field. The children tried to run to them, crying and calling out.

God, it was heartbreaking.

Sean turned to the umma. "As soon as you are ready, we can release them to your care."

The man had a shocked and appalled expression, and replied through Oglesby.

"He says, 'We will keep our words. It seems yours are questionable.'"

Shug, in English, said, "You much hurt everyone."

He felt compelled to reply, but he couldn't explain.

"I apologize for the necessity of our actions. The gods tell us what we must do and time is short."

The former was a lie. But he couldn't explain the necessities.

The umma said, "We are ready, then."

Cryder tossed a coil. "Here's more rope to secure them."

"Jesus," Sean muttered.

They literally collared the women with rope, and how old was that symbol of control and slavery?

Shug helped round them up, looking back in something bordering on contempt. Whatever goodwill they'd had with him was gone.

Once the ropes were well tied, all the Byko shock collars they wore popped free and fell.

Cryder spoke, "We do wish you well, and good health and long lives. It's unfortunate it must be this way. We will leave soon, and not bother you again."

Once rounded up and kitted out with pack baskets and satchels, the party made to depart. Shug came over and made a point of hugging Amalie, Caswell, and Sheridan, and no one else. Not even Oglesby.

Sean felt like crap.

As the group trudged off, the children's wails rose to a crescendo.

Sean felt worse.

"They hate us. The village hates us. The Germans hate us. The people in charge of the cave would probably try to kill us all over again. This has not been a good trip for diplomacy."

Cryder actually seemed to show some emotion.

"I agree. No casualties of us, though. Minimal outside. Best we could manage."

It didn't seem like enough. "I really wish you could have taken the mothers."

The man finally broke into a scowl. "Didn't like that order myself, friend. Want a hit of something to forget it?" He pointed at the box that held the medical kit.

"No. Let's just get the fuck out of here."

He turned, and he was facing Caswell, Raven, Sheridan, and Dalton.

Caswell said, "Sir, I want to do what I can to keep the children occupied."

Raven told him, "I'm a parent. I need to do something for them."

Sheridan shrugged. "I'm not, but damn, please."

Dalton said, "I can even avoid talking about Christ, but these people need some comfort. I'll talk to the men."

Sean turned back to Cryder.

"Can stun from remote if we must. Your ruling."

Sean sighed. "If you can."

As he expected, everyone shied away from the Americans. No one tried for hostages, though. Apparently either that wasn't in their code, or they realized it was a waste.

Wulf waved for attention, and he approached.

"How may I help you, Wulf?"

"Several of us have changed our minds and will stay," he stated.

Sean sighed.

"The gods will not allow that, nor their wizards." He thought fast, and before Wulf could object, added, "Our worlds, our cultures, can't mix now. It was a horrible mistake, and undoing it is awful, but it must be done."

The man looked angry, but his response was measured.

"Will we be able to talk to the wizards about this?"

"Possibly. You can talk to their leaders. I don't think it will change anything, but you will have the opportunity."

"What do we do for food and shelter now?"

"You have cabins, we've got firewood, food will be provided. We will magically move to their world in ten days. You should all comfort your children. Our wise ones can talk to you if you wish."

"There is nothing for you to say that we will hear," the man replied. That sounded like an insult.

That evening, the Americans sat around eating silently. The Bykos sat in Roller One. The Germanics gathered around a fire near their huts, speaking in low, angry tones.

Dalton finally commented, "I'm not sure they'll ever get over it, and I feel like crap."

Sean sat still, but replied, "I think everyone does. We go back in ten days, so there's that."

Spencer said, "I hope those collars stay working."

Right then, Cryder came over from the CQ.

He waited for them to all pay attention, and said, "For the remainder, I want two on watch at all times. Can you schedule that?"

"We can," Sean agreed. "It's a good idea, too."

Dalton asked, "How are they doing over there?"

Cryder replied, "Telling stories to the kids. Women dishing up the extra pudding I made for them. Looks like they'll all bed down in a couple of cabins with the women."

Raven's voice cracked. "I hope it helps. Poor kids. No way to grasp it."

Oglesby's comment was, "This wasn't going to be fun to start with. Now it's a disaster."

They resumed silence and finished eating.

It was ten days of boredom and mistrust until they were ready for transition. The atmosphere was chilly physically and socially. The day before movement was spent clearing camp, reducing footprint, and warding everything into the proper radius. Trash was gathered and recycled, wood products burned. Another tent was erected, the Germans moved into it, and their cabins dismantled to burn. They seemed to understand their presence here was being erased. The horses and dogs were penned in with them, at one end of the oval they occupied. The horses were very restless with nowhere to run. Arnet fabricated extra-long leashes and collars that let them graze wider and walk.

Dalton and Arnet did the demolition, with two of the Germans helping, under watch and looking bored, but in need of exercise. Both were buff and fit. They did well enough, though Dalton impressed them with his strength, and they were awed by Arnet, who picked up entire logs by himself and carried them to the edge of camp.

Once done, Roller Two deployed a scraper blade and shoved them all into a pile. Once it was parked, Cryder lit it up from Roller One, and the timber burned hotter and faster than it should, with occasional bursts.

"Extra oxygen?" Sean asked after one of the flare-ups.

"Liquid ozone."

"Damn. Impressive."

By night it was a large bed of coals. Arnet staged a small turbine fan to blast that into yellow-hot plasma. Then he used Roller Two to disperse the remains across the landscape.

"That's it," he announced with a faint shrug.

All long-term evidence of displacees should be gone.

The final morning broke clear and warmer, over 50°F, and the radius was reduced even more.

Cryder shouted for attention.

"Today is it. We go to our place, then send others home. That will take time. We leave here any time in the next several hours. Stand by and wait."

Sean watched his troops wasting time on their phones, obviously avoiding any thinking, while Dr. Sheridan and Dalton stood guard with Cryder.

He was contemplating that when

BANG!

✦⟶ CHAPTER 40 ⟵✦

BANG!

Once again, they materialized a couple of inches above the ground for safety, and dropped with a layer of cold muck underfoot.

Martin Spencer exhaled in relief. They'd done it. Hopefully they could wrap up shortly and get home.

Inside the hangar, the Germanics looked around quickly, assessing threat, preparing to react. Slowly, they decided it was safe enough to trust their escorts, though only not to be slaughtered. They were unlikely to trust anything they were shown or told.

All the Bykos present wore pants and lab coats.

Larilee Zep was in attendance, and apparently had studied Old German to a workable degree.

She spoke in that language, and immediately her voice came from the House persona, in English.

"Welcome to our village, Wulf and people of Wulf. You are welcome, and I will take you to lodging and food."

They seemed inclined to accept this offer, though he suspected that she being an attractive female had something to do with it. Or maybe not. He wasn't sure what their standards were. Still, they followed, along with the Americans and two Guardians, and he noticed other Guardians surreptitiously following around the perimeter, and watching discreetly. They all had batons he assumed were stun devices as well. He expected any trouble would result in a slumber party.

Several handlers approached the horses and led them away, while others coaxed the dogs with meat. He expected some sort of field was lulling them, too.

The Nordwandlaz's facility looked like the inside of a huge lodge, with fireplaces at each end, wooden benches, sleeping berths along the walls, and another hearth in the middle with cooking utensils. Next to it was a large table he knew concealed the serving surface.

Zep waved in welcome and said, "You will rest here, and our doctors will check you. You will have food and fire—"

Wulf cut in with, "When can we talk to your wizards?"

She smiled and continued, "—and you will be able to talk to our council. They will address your concerns as best we can arrange."

The man glanced around and seemed quite aware of who the warriors were, and that they were all taller and fit. Wulf still had his sword—that had been a gesture that he was a captive equal, not an inferior or defeated. It wasn't going to help him here.

He nodded, waved a "come on" to his people, and headed for a bench.

Well, that had gone better than Martin expected.

Their own quarters were familiar and comfortable after all these trips.

Elliott announced, "Formation, please."

They lined up, and he addressed them.

"At ease. We're back, I'm calling this a down day because I don't know how long we have and we need to unwind before we wrap up. It's been another three weeks, and a rough set. We'll pick up here at oh nine hundred. Usual rules apply. Dismissed."

That was generous and much needed.

Martin stretched and turned, and Doc was there.

"Do you think we're done?"

"On the one hand, I hope so. On the other, there's so much to learn here, and it's fucking amazing."

Amalie Raven came over. "It is. But I doubt they'll let us stay."

"You're right of course. It's still awesome to have seen what we have."

✦   ✦   ✦

Sean Elliott sighed. The Byko desks were very comfortable, and they'd fabricated a touchpad keyboard that worked better than the one on his laptop. He assumed they were logging everything he entered, in addition to everything anyone said. There was just no way around it here.

Paperwork, paperwork, and more paperwork. He had the full AAR for the Bykos and the general. He had the sanitized AAR for the Army to use officially. He was finishing a file on every recovered soldier, with notes, on what to look out for and deal with. He wasn't sure it would be possible to keep them all quiet, but all he could do was furnish the best information possible. At least this time they wouldn't have to prove where they'd gone. Command knew about the matter. How long before there were leaks there, also? It was pretty much impossible to keep this secret. That it wasn't all over the tabloids already was a miracle.

The big three individual concerns were Noirot and her child, Lozano and his issues, and Munoz, who might actually try to get attention and sue. The rest could probably be debriefed and manage in some fashion, as he and his element had.

He was still writing when the troops straggled back from rec. It appeared several had a good time. Being single here would be amazing, but he had both duties and a relationship to manage. Command had obligations.

He wasn't sure if it was complete enough, but it was as complete as he was going to get it. He sat back, rubbed his eyes, accounted for all his people, and sprawled on his bed.

The next morning he let Doc handle formation while he spoke through House.

"Can you tell Researcher Zep I have completed files for their review?"

The entity responded, "One moment."

Seconds later, Zep's voice came through. "Thank you very much, Captain. May I extract the files now?"

"Yes."

"Done. Do you have a scheduled formation with the other element?"

"I should, but I don't."

"Can you meet me there shortly?"

He looked over. The minimal formation was concluded, everyone was doing PT under Doc's direction. After that it would be routine chores, video training, and attempting to find more info on their hosts, an ongoing, unreferenced task.

"Yes," he agreed. "I'm free now."

"Please bring Sergeant Caswell if she's free. I can be there at once. Off."

He took that as "out," and asked, "House, it's right next door, yes?"

"Yes, I'll have the doorway marked for you."

He called, "Doc, I apologize for interrupting your formation." The man replied, "Go ahead, sir?"

"Caswell, we're needed next door, if you're available."

"Yes, sir!" she replied at once, added to Doc, "Sir, may I fall out?"

"You may."

Formalities, but important. She stepped back, came over, and asked, "What is it, sir?"

"We're meeting Zep. She didn't say why."

"Hooah."

Zep arrived at the doorway as they did, dressed in the usual slacks and coat that were almost uniform here.

Something he'd wondered for a long time caused him to ask, "Ms. Zep, the first time we met, was the unusual dress of your contingent on purpose to gauge our response?"

She smiled. "Yes." Then she added, "You did fine, it wasn't a test. You've seen how people dress casually around here."

"Or undress, yes."

"Exactly. Shall we go in? You have a query."

"Yes," he prompted.

They entered, and he noted with approval the troops were in PT uniform, and appeared to be cleaning up from a morning session. They were still very fit by US Army standards, from five years of manual labor. So they had that going for them. They glanced his way, and SSG Burnham shouted, "AttenSHUN!"

He waited just long enough to ensure they did come to attention, then ordered, "At ease and carry on."

He looked at Zep. "What do we need?"

She indicated with her hand, as Noirot approached.

"Captain, may I speak with you?"

"Absolutely, Sergeant, what is it?"

She spoke in a rush. "There are complicating factors. I'm really not sure I can explain Kita back home. I'd have to claim she was adopted, or lost, but she's obviously my daughter, and you say we'll be back within a month or so of when we left?"

"If they do things well, yes."

"I can't leave her here alone, sir." The woman was sobbing.

"Have you discussed this with anyone?"

She wiped her face and nodded. "I asked Lieutenant Cole, and then I talked to Ms Zep, who talked to some of their people. She said they can arrange for me to stay, but it has to be cleared by the Army and cleared by you."

Well, that made a bunch of his fretting pointless.

Still, he needed to be sure she made the right decision.

"Do you think you'll be happy here? Did they tell you what you can do or how you'll live?"

She looked quite a bit more cheerful as she blurted out words. "I can be a child minder for now. They have training classes for it, everything from first aid to psychology and even a theory of play. I'll have to learn their dialect and one of the other languages, but I'm sure I can do it. They said anything else would require additional education, but they're willing to help if I can. And Kita would grow up with the best they have to offer. Rural Louisiana isn't bad, but there's so much more here."

He gave that a second, and it actually sounded like an honest deal.

"I have final authority here," he told her. "But I have to explain back home. Your daughter is a complication either way, but I think having you stay is easier administratively than bringing her. I was never considering separating the two of you." And he was still really glad that she hadn't decided to do that. Or that she already had children back home. He hadn't even thought about that but, oh, shit, that would have been a nightmare.

She asked, looking hopeful, "So you're okay with it, sir?"

He said, "There's no good solution for me, but I think that's easiest for the Army, and best for you and for Kita."

She welled up tears again as she muttered, "Thank you, sir."

He made a point. "The one thing to keep in mind is we have to close the incident. You'll be reported dead. There's no secret messages home, no coming back later."

She nodded and looked very serious.

"I'll miss my family, but Kita is the most important thing in the world to me."

"It's a hard position you're in, and I'm very sorry they weren't able to get us to you sooner."

The woman nodded earnestly. "It's not your fault, sir."

"No, but it's the mess I have to clean up. When do you want to officially transfer?"

She looked confused for just a moment. "You mean out of here to wherever? Uh, when's convenient?"

"If you're staying here, then there's nothing further required from you in a duty status."

She was wide-eyed. "Oh. Wow. I mean, discharge from the Army usually takes a while."

"It does," he agreed. "But you're being declared dead." He didn't want to cut her off, but he wanted to make sure she grasped that.

She nodded. "Can I say goodbye to everyone? And see you off again?"

He nodded. "You're welcome to visit as a guest, but I'd recommend limiting it. You're doing a one-way trip to here."

She nodded again. "Yes, they made that clear to me as well. I hate that I'll never see anyone, but it was always a risk outside the wire. When we got lost it felt like we'd been abandoned by the world. Even by God. We felt we were dead. And we were slowly moving on in a shitty excuse of an afterlife. Then you showed up. It feels like I've been given my life back, and I can give my daughter a universe we never dreamed of."

"That sounds like a good position to move forward from," he said. "I recommend you grab the little personal stuff you have and say goodbye. We can plan to see you again before we leave."

"Thank you, sir, and thanks for tolerating my . . . issues."

He was glad of that closure, and reassured her, "Sergeant, you did a hell of a job under extreme circumstances, a lot more than you should have had to, and it's a shame no one will know how heroic you were for your unit. Can Ms. Zep take you where you need to go?"

The researcher raised her voice and said, "I can."

"Excellent. The general gets my report of what happened, but after that, the official story is you were a casualty somehow. They'll work out details. Get your daughter and have an amazing life."

He was almost tearing up himself. Poor woman. And lucky at the same time, but what a choice.

She stood and turned. "Kita! Come here, girl. *Shoosa eki.*"

The girl ran over and took her hand.

Caswell walked over and handed Noirot a bag. "That's your stuff," she said, and gave Noirot a quick hug. She knelt down and hugged and booped Kita. "Be good."

Everyone insisted on hugging them and smiling at the little girl. Even her future was complicated, but certainly a lot more comfortable and longer than it would have been.

Carefully, he gave her a hug himself, and the girl who was barely the size of his leg. They were so small, but surprisingly durable.

Then he said, "Sergeant Denise Noirot, there's no SOP for this, but in front of witnesses, you are released from the US Army and into the care of the Byko people. Good luck and best wishes."

She was crying now.

"Thank you, sir."

She scooped up her daughter. The girl seemed unsure between her mother's tears and the hugs and safety.

She asked, "Which way do we go?"

Zep smiled and pointed. "This way to transport." She accompanied them out.

In a moment they were through the visible doorway and gone.

It wasn't a good ending. But it was a new beginning. Leaving their world, but embracing the future and all it offered, even beyond the glimpse they'd had.

His musing was interrupted with, "Excuse me, sir."

It was Lozano, at attention, and actually being polite.

Oh, Christ.

"Yes, Sergeant?"

The man was direct. "You could just leave me here and fix another problem."

He was as blunt. "Sorry. Request denied."

"Frenchy got to stay."

"She has complicating circumstances best resolved that way." He held up his hand against the man's protest. "Your complications are your own. I'm sure, though, that the Byko can adjust your outlook without hurting your memory."

The man shook his head and actually didn't smirk for once. "No thanks. I'm fine the way I am."

"That's why you spend the duration locked up."

Lozano's shrug came across as a challenge. "Yeah, whatever, Captain. I tried to give you an easy way out."

"It's easy for me to take you back. How you handle it is your problem."

"Thanks for nothing, sir." The man turned and walked off without waiting for dismissal.

Sean shrugged. It was shortly not to be his problem.

He spoke to Cole. "Lieutenant, we'll catch up shortly on some matters before we rotate home."

"Yes, sir. Do you need anything regarding Lozano?"

He shook his head. "No, he'll be someone else's issue soon enough. He doesn't get any more liberty, though."

"Roger that. We're wrapping up, then?"

"As soon as they can cut us loose, we're ready. Keep them under control."

"Yes, sir."

He nodded, looked up, and called, "House, we're going back."

"Yes, Sean, this way."

He was glad the mission was nearly over. It was still gut wrenching.

Armand Devereaux realized he liked these people less and less. They might have reasons for their assholishness toward recoverees, but they didn't seem to do much about it. Sure, everyone was getting their health updated, teeth fixed, and to be physiologically as sound as when they were lost, to cover them. Lozano was not the only one who needed serious therapy. As for the Germans, entire families had been ripped apart. What was going to come of that he wasn't sure.

Even Lex was a puzzle. Did she find him interesting as more than a novelty, being from the past, and black? That was certainly part of it, and he didn't like it.

He sipped a beer while thinking. The sex was amazing, but did he want that kind of involvement?

He wandered over to Dr. Raven and asked her.

He kept his voice low around others, realizing House would hear no matter what.

"Do you have any idea yet how races are set here?"

She shook her head. "That wasn't something I was tasked with, and I haven't paid much attention, other than the baseline samples of our two escorts." While she spoke she scribbled on a scrap of paper, and raised her hand just enough for him to read.

Wait for home.

Then she crumpled it.

"Dated the Germans yet?" he asked.

"Late 600s, early 700s, if I'm correct. They claimed 715 AD. There were lots of fragmented groups."

"Spencer can't place them to a group, though."

"No, but we have no idea what our hosts found. They may have exact info. Or better than ours at least."

"Yeah, ripping those kids from their mothers sucked. If I have nightmares, what's it like for them?" Hell, he'd hate being separated from his mother now. As a kid...fuck.

She shrugged. "It happened enough to our ancestors. No need for us to feel guilty. Byko machinations, not ours."

"True, but still." Neither of them knew more than driblets about their ancestry. His family was from Antigua, but how had they got there from Africa? As for her culture, it barely existed as a footnote.

Shug was right, though. These were not nice people or good friends.

That evening Zep was back. She appeared in the doorway.

The captain greeted her. "May we help you, ma'am?"

"I have a briefing for all of you, if I may."

Elliott called "Sure. *Listen up!* Gather 'round for a briefing from Dr. Zep."

Armand stood up and paid attention.

Once everyone was nearby, she spoke.

"First, your information is complete, and the council is considering your mission final. We can send you home as fast as we can prepare and calculate. Late tomorrow."

There was a ripple of excitement over that. It would be good to be done.

She turned, "Assuming you don't need anything more from us, Captain."

Elliott replied, "As long as our recoverees are fit, I have what I need. I'll need some restraints for a couple of them, as discussed."

She nodded. "Yes, that's on the file."

She continued, "The next item is to ask if you can return for another mission."

Armand replied first. "Who's missing?"

She said, "One of ours has taken a considerable amount of resources, traveled back, and is a risk for temporal stability."

Spencer asked, "Why us? Don't you have people?"

She almost seemed to sigh.

"It's complicated. As explained, the physics team tells us it's easier to transition people already on file, in a manner of talking. The baselines are more consistent. Then, you've actually been effective. Apparently there've been other attempts at fixing displacements and those didn't work optimally. Also, you've demonstrated a level of personal trust that matters, especially in this issue. They were a bit disappointed in the changes in personnel since last time, but would like to continue the process."

Armand asked, "So are we going home or staying here?"

She smiled and replied, "Home first, then back here. We certainly care about your personal well-being."

Do they really? he wondered, given some of their other activity.

She added, "We need an answer before you leave, but it doesn't have to be now."

Elliott twisted his head. "Good, because we need to discuss that. So basically, you've got an established pipeline to us, precise measurements of our auras—for want of a better term—and it's easier to control our movement than others. And you say we're reliable."

"Yes."

"Aren't you afraid of what we might learn here?"

"You, no. Your scientists, yes, and they will not be returning here again. I hope that's not offensive."

Raven said, "If I do, it will be to stay."

Zep faced her and gave a single nod. She said, "That is a possible discussion, but not one I can have."

Armand said, "I have a question about Noirot. We're declaring her dead. It's pretty final. She's staying here. Can you think of any way to send her home later? Once you've learned enough to stabilize things." Was it possible?

The woman wrinkled her brow and replied, "We may be able to eventually. If she wishes, and once her daughter is grown. We can possibly arrange an insertion with enough assets to reestablish her. Possibly. If Kita elects to be sterilized they can go back, but would they want to? After having been raised here?"

"So they're casualties who get a beautiful prison and can never go home."

"Unfortunately so. If we could have avoided this we would have. As it stands, our knowledge and control are getting better, but the incidents are becoming more common. The technology is out there and too many people are experimenting."

"Even utopia has its issues."

"I can see how you would say that. Yes."

Dr. Raven said, "Like all the people who chiseled bits off Stonehenge for 'study,' while complaining about those doing it for souvenirs. None of them actually were studying, they were just lying to themselves."

Zep nodded. "I wasn't aware of that detail, but I know the site you speak of and that would be an accurate parallel."

Raven asked, "What about us? We've learned quite a bit."

"You have, but you wouldn't be believed, you don't know enough technical details to affect anything—we made sure of that—and displacing that many of you would be difficult to explain."

Armand noted, "You thought about it." This was a terrifying society.

"We had to consider all possible actions and outcomes."

"I know. That's what scares me every time."

He really wasn't sure about banging Lex again.

Dan Oglesby waited for the captain to brief them. He wasn't sure about doing this again.

Elliott echoed his thoughts.

"On the one hand," the captain started, "it's a nice gesture to help our hosts who've helped us. On the other hand, they caused most of these issues, and our cultures aren't entirely compatible."

That was putting it mildly.

It was Doc who noted, "It might also reach a point where they engage in that brain-wiping or exiling they keep in reserve for problems."

Dalton said, "We haven't had those problems yet, though, and ours have been pretty significant. Heck, even Lozano is going back without further comment, as is Munoz."

Elliott stated, "This is a poll of us, which I will take under advisement and relay to General McClare, who will let us know if the Army allows it. And obviously, no one is obligated, though it's not impossible the Army may change that."

Caswell said, "There's only four of us the Army or Air Force can give orders to. If they need the whole contingent, that puts a kibosh on it."

"There is that. They're not letting the scientists back, but do you have any input?"

The two women shook heads.

Sheridan said, "Nothing relevant. It's neat to study here, and we might expand our baseline surveys, but..." She bit her lip, obviously not wanting to continue the comment.

Raven replied, "I can't advise you. I have the wrong background."

Elliott nodded. "So who's in if we get called again?"

Dalton's hand was first up, alongside Elliott's. Caswell was a moment behind. Dan shrugged and threw in. He'd support his people. Spencer was slow and it was obvious he wasn't enthused. Doc was last and it felt like he was doing so only for them.

The captain half shrugged. "The summary is we're not thrilled with the idea, but agreeable, depending on circumstances. I'll relay that. Also, they really should be offering something as a bonus for special duty work."

There was that. Dan didn't want to be a contractor, but the money appealed, and basically, that's exactly what they were.

"Okay," the captain finalized. "Fall in."

Dan did so, though these formations were notional with two officers and a senior NCO.

"Last night here. Everyone back by midnight. You can drink but stay sober, unless they can fix it before you sleep. No hangovers. Tomorrow we go home. Oh seven hundred wakeup, and get everything ready to roll. Dismissed."

Rich Dalton took one last round at the Mad Lab, watching people pass by outside, and as they entered and left. There was an enthusiastic energy he'd never seen elsewhere.

He recognized Alakri Mommed, who waved, sped up pace, and arrived in moments.

"Sergeant Rich! Good luck and safe travels, and congratulations on your mission accomplishments."

"Thank you, Mommed. How is your work?"

"I have narrowed the field to three diseases, though two are related. My understudies are eager for the challenge, and we hope to begin focus work, soon."

"That is excellent. May I offer you a prayer?"

"Absolutely!"

He bowed his head and let the words choose themselves. "May the Good Lord bless and support your endeavors, with His wisdom and beneficence, leading to a speedy accomplishment, saving the lives of your patients, and may you all grow and learn from it."

Alakri replied, "May the God of Abraham, Jesu, and the Prophet hear your words and bless our work. I thank you, my friend."

They shared another drink, and watched the soldiers visit, say goodbyes, and return. It didn't appear anyone was fraternizing tonight. They wrapped up and headed back.

"I have to leave soon, Mommed."

"Of course. If you return, though, I hope we will meet again."

"Absolutely. Be well and goodbye." They shook hands warmly.

Everyone bedded down, the preps being much easier this time. Their personal gear was ready to go. He lay back and watched an aurora light show from the far north as he dozed off, warm and as comfortable as he'd ever been in the Army.

The next morning was straightforward. Up, shower, fresh breakfast, gather gear, assemble in formation, prepare to move out. They sat around with their bags playing hurry up and wait. Once out of the quarters they joined the other element.

The recoverees were accompanied by Guardians, and Lozano and Munoz were in futuristic handcuffs. Apparently, they weren't trusted here, either.

It was a loose route step, not a march, but they moved in a semblance of formation back around the hangar to the familiar location. They did have a farewell escort.

Sergeant Spencer got a very intimate hug from that gorgeous Eurasian woman. Doc got one from Ms. Twine, and there was a mix of interest and awkwardness there he wasn't going to pry into. Her assistant had Cal, and everyone from the first mission had to skritch the fellow. He was a fine example of a cat, and apparently very popular here.

Noirot and Kita arrived, Noirot in a local coverall with pockets, and Kita in yellow dress with scarf. She seemed to like that style. Noirot insisted on hugging everyone. She even hugged the two prisoners who couldn't hug back. He heard her say, "Lozano, dude, you can do this. You have my thoughts."

He tried to shrug it off, but muttered, "Goddammit, Frenchy... Fuck it all, I'll try."

"I know you will."

She hugged Hamilton. "Thank you, my friend."

"Good luck, girl."

Zep said, "We hope to see you again in a few weeks. Good luck, and thanks for all your efforts. We've arranged for a bonus to be transferred with you." She handed over a small case. It was obviously very heavy.

The captain nodded and accepted it. Rich stared at it and looked at the captain.

Elliott leaned close and whispered, "Five ounces of gold for each of us. Easiest way for them to transfer funds."

"Wow." He wasn't sure exactly how much that was these days, but it was several grand.

"What about them?" he asked, indicating the recoverees.

"Also for them. How that gets transferred is something I have to work out."

Zep announced, "It's time."

They stood on the platform. He was on one side of Lozano, Spencer was on the other side, and he realized how large Spencer actually was by comparison—height, chest, arms. Also, his rifle was loaded.

Doc and Caswell flanked Munoz. All the other recoverees were in front, with the scientists at the rear.

Zep said, "It will only be a few moments. You have the contact module that can transport through. If it's agreeable that you return, I look forward to seeing you again. If not, it has been a pleasure to work with you. Good luck and live well."

There was a chorus in return. "You too, Doc." "Thanks, ma'am." "Good luck with the temporal matters." "We enjoyed the hospitality." "Later." "Best wishes." There were even some thank-yous muttered from the other element.

She stepped outside the marked safety radius, holding the cat's leash. Farther back at their screened control booth, the techs made adjustments, waved hands over controls, and—

CHAPTER 41

BANG!

This was the hangar they had departed from, at least. They were back in A-stan. Rich Dalton felt relief. *It worked.*

There was a sleepy-eyed MP on watch inside, or rather, he had been sleepy-eyed. He startled suddenly, sat up from his chair, almost juggled his weapon, and came to attention.

He held up a hand to indicate they should wait, and keyed the radio mic on his armor.

"Control, this is Depot. They're here, over."

A crackly voice replied, "Is that what we heard? Over."

"Yes, sir. They're all here, over."

"Roger that, stand by, over."

Elliott ordered, "Everyone stand fast."

They did, buzzing and almost muttering.

Only a couple of minutes later, the general, the colonel, and a handful of staff arrived, along with a squad of MPs.

The general loudly announced, "Welcome back, soldiers."

"What date is it?"

"You've been gone fifty-four hours. It looks as though you were successful and they brought you back promptly."

That was a relief.

Elliott saluted, "Sir. Mission accomplished with some variances. Shug returned to his people. Our element recovered with one casualty and one remaining behind. I'll detail in debrief."

McClare nodded and frowned. "Excellent. I do want to know about that."

He turned and faced the recoverees.

"Gentlemen, ladies, welcome home. There's a necessary debrief, as I'm sure you're aware. We will get you all home as quickly as possible. Please follow the MPs to quarters. We'll have rations, recreation, and hot showers at once."

Even Lozano looked sober and damp-eyed.

"We're actually home," he said.

Rich replied, "We are. Good luck, Christopher."

The man nodded as he followed the MPs. The squad leader pointed and raised an eyebrow. "Cuffs?"

Spencer told him, "They can come off now. We had to make sure he complied."

"Got it. Watch out for him?"

"Probably not on post, but we'll have supplemental info."

"Understood."

Dr. Raven shoved to the front of their team.

"General, I need a voice recorder and a big notebook right this second. I have some of the info you wanted."

"Yes, ma'am." He turned. "Captain, give her your notebook, and set your phone up to record, at once. This is critical intel."

"Er, yes, sir," the woman replied, fumbling her phone out of a pocket and handing over a ruled book and pen.

Raven took the chair the MP had sat in, dragged another over, and furiously started scribbling.

Colonel Findlay took over. "We have your billets waiting, and no trust issues this time," he said. Rich chuckled. It had been intense trying to prove they'd been separated in the past and future. This time, it was understood.

In ten minutes he was in a room shared with Oglesby, his gear on a bunk, and getting comfortable in a chair for a few moments.

"Damn, what a trip."

Oglesby said, "We did the best we could."

Rich agreed. "We did. Not perfect, but I can't think of anything better. I still feel like crap about how we treated the kids, and Shug, though."

Oglesby stretched in his chair and nodded. "It sucks, but the Bykos didn't leave time for niceties."

"Yeah, they're mostly pretty blunt SOBs."

"How's Lozano?"

He thought about it and said, "I really don't know. I hope he can adapt back to our world. They're going through an easier debrief than we did, since they don't need to explain where they were. On the other hand, they're going to have a hell of a time fitting in."

"Also Munoz."

Rich nodded. "Yeah, they're going to be trouble. It's in the captain's AAR, with details. I did what I could. Elliott made a note to even monitor their morale calls home."

"You were amazing, Rich."

He was always embarrassed when someone thanked him for doing what he would do anyway. "Thanks. And Dan, I know you felt out in the cold a few times, but when you contributed, it was critical. Well done and thanks."

The man smiled. "I do appreciate it. Yeah, once we had local language experts and computer translation...but I did have to double-check."

Two hours later they were in a private chow hall with food delivered. It was Army contractor standard, not bad, though nowhere near the Byko version. They were spoiled.

Dr. Raven still had a headset on, and was dictating apparently as things occurred to her, and between bites of roast beef.

She was speaking to Caswell. "—I've got three projects at least from this, regarding haplogroups and mDNA, which Kate's team will expand on at length. I've got three variants of rhinovirus and what may be the MRCA of the Coronavirus family. Yet none of us got sick with the unfamiliar viruses. So that's a project—oh, wait." She adjusted the headset mic and tapped the phone. "Translation took a notable fraction of a second, though breakthrough proper was near instantaneous. There is atmospheric displacement, but I noted no ozone content. More to follow." She turned back. "Yeah, it's going to be like this. I'm doing everything from memory other than the basic disease stuff. They wouldn't let us bring some of the haplogroup files. They kept all that. I can guess why."

Rich asked, "So what is your actual field?"

Raven almost smiled as she said, "That's the question no one asked. I do have a doctorate in the field. My bachelor's was endocrine biology, my master's paleobiology. My first PhD is paleoepidemiology. It was both interest and preparation."

Everyone had gathered around.

Spencer asked, "For?"

The woman glanced upward. "For going to Mars. My second PhD is plasma physics, but I also took classes in neurological interfaces for electronics."

Oglesby burst out, "Jesus. How old are you again?"

She replied, "Thirty-five. I had my BS at nineteen, MS at twenty-one, doctorate at twenty-three, the second one at twenty-five."

She really wasn't kidding about breaking IQ tests, apparently.

"How did they bring you into this?"

She grinned with deep, enticing eyes. "Who do you think was studying your displacement? You brought biological samples back—those quilted hides—and that device that self-destructed. We're studying what we can of those, Sergeant Alexander's photos, and every little bit of anything we can scrape up."

"Who's 'we'?"

"The research element assigned to your event."

"What and where is that? How many?"

She shook her head. "I am not at liberty to discuss such questions. I can say that Kate is one of the other biologists."

Sheridan giggled, then looked a bit put upon. "I was doing real work, and was in charge, and then I get told she's going to try to crack their technology."

Elliott commented, "So they really screwed up in letting you along."

She shrugged. "Maybe. I do have data and observations. What we can do with it remains to be seen. And then I have the ethical concern on if I should actually develop anything that might interrupt the issues they're already having."

"The US Government will be mighty pissed if you have a conscience."

Her expression was half disgusted, half amused. "And what will they do? Fire me? They need me." She shook her head. "I don't need them. I can be on SpaceX ground crew, or heading a radiation oncology section by Monday next week. Though I do find this fascinating. But I can't be bullied."

Elliott said, "Well, good luck to you, Amalie. And thanks very much for all your support before."

"You're welcome. It was an awesome thrill to come along."

Rich added, "Yes, ma'am. It was very educational, and you were great support under fire and with the natives."

She smiled. "I do appreciate it. I wish I could come on the return trip. You are going, right?"

They all looked at Elliott. "That's up to the general, but he understands the matter. In the meantime, we rotate out day after tomorrow."

Caswell looked surprised. "Damn, that's quick. Awesome. Now I get to go back and deal with an assault charge."

Rich gaped. "Do wha?"

She blushed. "Some mouthy asshole in a club opened his yap and was really, really crude, and I smashed his beer pitcher into his face."

"I will happily be a character reference," he offered.

Spencer loudly said, "Yup, she's a character."

They all laughed for a moment.

Elliott cut in with, "The incident is resolved. I spoke to the general, he spoke to some people. They were told to make it go away, no questions asked, and Counselor Fairley sent a letter covering you as a PTSD issue, which it is and is more than fair."

She did look relieved. "Thank you, sir."

He spread his hands. "It all points out how long recovery is, and how rough a road it's going to be for our charges. We're still dealing with it and will be. They'll never be the same."

Armand Devereaux asked, "Amalie, the issue you wouldn't talk about in front of the Bykos. There was some sort of genetic effect that killed all the Africans, wasn't there?"

She sighed, put her head in her hand, then looked up. "It wasn't all Africans, but most above a certain fraction. It was genotype linked to melanin production. It might have been an attempt to eliminate skin cancer. It wiped out entire haplogroups, as best I can tell from the samples we got. That's one of the things they've been trying to hide."

He sat in shock as she continued. "And they do have African DNA. Some of them. It's thinly spread, but present. It's blatantly obvious, though, that there are few if any actual black people there, because not only didn't we see any—and we should have, given the genetic mixing I find—but the way every chick in sight homed in on you."

He had to ask. "Genocide?"

"It could be. I'm very sorry."

He really wanted it not to be true. "What? How?"

She shook her head. "I don't know more than that, but it appears to be about six generations back from the Bykos. Some sort of massive population bottleneck. None of the Asian or European genotypes seem affected. There's spillage into Arabian lines, but a lot of them have African influx. Anyone more than one-eighth sub-Saharan seems to have either become sterile or died. That would include me if I were alive at the time."

Armand felt cold. There were always a handful of racists, and a few of them were ignorant assholes. But this suggested pure evil. His gene line was doomed.

"Could it have been accidental?" he asked hoping.

She shrugged. "It could. It might have been an attempt to fix a genetically linked disease—sickle cell anemia, for example— that had some deleterious side effect. It could have been some random mutation, but that's incredibly unlikely. As thorough as it appears to have been, I'm betting on deliberate action. I don't know if it's worse if it's negligence or maliciousness. Armand, I'm very, very sorry."

"Yeah, me too." There wasn't more to say than that.

Black people weren't allowed in paradise.

He really wasn't sure he wanted to be involved with any of them, either, knowing that.

Dalton asked, "So how far in the future are they?" He said it a bit too loud, obviously trying to steer away from a bad subject.

Sheridan said, "I can tell you approximately when we were, based on mDNA generations."

Dalton asked, "When?"

She giggled. "You don't believe in that stuff, remember?"

"Why wouldn't I?"

"This is the same science I used to check the locals to the present time, as confirmation. It's reliable. But it doesn't agree with your Bible."

"Okay. I'm listening."

She said, "You can never mention this around Bykos. You understand this?"

He agreed. "Yes. As secret as everything else."

Sheridan nodded.

"It was an easy enough calculation. Absolute minimum one hundred fifty years, maximum five hundred years, probable median two hundred and twenty-five. Ish."

Dalton looked shocked. "That's all?"

Armand said, "I checked their stars. Calculating forward, it wasn't very different from our astrography."

Oglesby said, "The linguistic drift is present but not great. I was figuring less than a thousand years, more than a couple of hundred."

Sheridan said, "Their technology isn't that much beyond us. We can at least recognize it. The Neoliths couldn't. You said the paleoliths didn't. The Romans recognized your vehicles as vehicles. We recognize most of the tech the Bykos have as achievable."

"Yeah."

Raven said, "They also seem to be from a technological center point."

"Oh?" he prompted.

"At least one development of agriculture was invented not far from where they are. So was the spoked wheel, as far as we know. Cities and iron working aren't terribly far. They seem to have invented time travel. It makes me think of the SF stories where certain locations are pivotal to the universe."

"Hmm. It does sound if they're from somewhere in the same geographic region."

"Armand . . . Doc, nailed that down at once. So did I. He looked at the stars and calculated back."

"Oh."

"Right. Not long after our own time. I looked at DNA, and their naming conventions give it away. Bykostan is obviously named after the Baikonur Cosmodrome."

"Russia?"

She said, "Kazakhstan, but they lease it to the Russians in our time. It's obviously still a science and tech headquarters."

Armand commented, "It was dangerous of them to let you come along."

"Yes, which is why we will never mention it. They have to know we'll guess some of it."

"I understand," he said. There were far too many events and discussions here way above his level. He'd just say nothing.

And question how much support he should give such a society.

EPILOGUE

Martin Spencer decided it was certainly a far less stressful return than their last one. The flight was long and grueling, but no worries about reception. The plane landed, taxied, they debarked with the other troops. They cleared Customs with barely a pause, the agents glancing at their orders and saying, "Welcome home, troops," and waving them all through.

They gathered together, and Caswell said, "And in a month we come back and do this again. I really don't get why they keep wanting to use us, if temporal jumps are such an issue."

Sheridan repeated what they'd been told. "They said the factors of the individuals were easier to account for than distance through time."

"Sure, I get that. But use their own people they trust?"

"Unless they don't want to risk them? Dunno, they use Cryder and Arnet, but no one else."

"Yeah, it could be some political or cultural thing. And they can be whirling assholes."

Raven looked wistful. "I do wonder what it takes to stay in their location," she said. He understood she meant *their time.*

"I wonder if we dare ask, or if they'll suggest it."

Caswell pointed. "Our domestic flights are pending." She turned. "Good luck to you, Dr. Raven. I learned a lot. Thank you." She hugged the scientist hard and quick, then turned to Martin.

"And you take care, Sergeant Spencer. Ping me if you need to talk."

He might actually take her up on that. She was part younger sister, part detached counselor, and he knew he could trust her absolutely. She had a better grasp of his background than Dr. Fairley. "I will. Thanks for all you've done for everyone."

They shook hands all around, shouldered bags, and he headed for his flight as they did for theirs.

And apparently it wasn't their last trip.

⊹ END ⊹